Escape to Gold Mountain

= Goam Soon
= Gam Saan

CBC – Canadian Born Chinese
ABC – American Born Chinese

Tony Mucciatelli
11-10-2012

ESCAPE to GOLD MOUNTAIN

A Graphic History of the Chinese in North America

DAVID H.T. WONG

Gold mountain
was anywhere in the U.S.
but particularly San Francisco

For Tony...
Thank you &
Best Wishes!
David

ARSENAL PULP PRESS Vancouver

ESCAPE TO GOLD MOUNTAIN

ARSENAL PULP PRESS
Suite 101 – 211 East Georgia St.
Vancouver, BC V6A 1Z6
Canada
arsenalpulp.com

The publisher gratefully acknowledges the support of the Canada Council for the Arts and the British Columbia Arts Council for its publishing program, and the Government of Canada (through the Canada Book Fund) and the Government of British Columbia (through the Book Publishing Tax Credit Program) for its publishing activities.

Cover illustration by David H.T. Wong
Book design by Gerilee McBride
Editing by Susan Safyan

Printed and bound in Canada

Library and Archives Canada Cataloguing in Publication:

Wong, David H. T., 1959-
Escape to gold mountain : a graphic history of the Chinese in North America / David H.T. Wong.

Includes bibliographical references.
Also issued in electronic format.
ISBN 978-1-55152-476-4

1. Chinese--Canada--History--Comic books, strips, etc. 2. Chinese--Canada--History--Juvenile literature. 3. Chinese--United States--History--Comic books, strips, etc. 4. Chinese--United States--History--Juvenile literature. 5. Graphic novels. I. Title.

FC106.C5W65 2012   j971'.0049510222   C2012-905205-1

"Knowledge is not knowledge, unless it is shared."

My grandma's favorite saying

"David! Stop drawing on the walls! When you grow up, you had better still not be drawing cartoons!"

My grandma's second favorite saying

Special dedication:

- to my loving parents, **Wendy** and **Bing** (1933 – 1999)
- to my dear friend **Ed Wickberg** (1927 – 2008)
- to my maternal and paternal **grandparents**, who loved storytelling

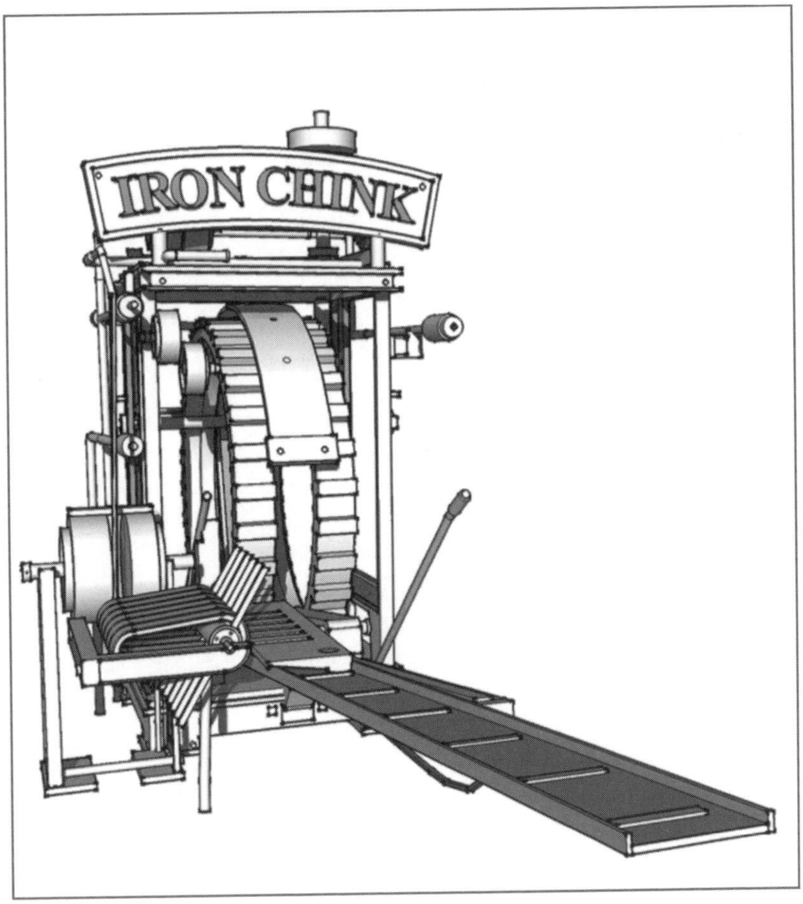
IRON CHINK

CONTENTS

PREFACE

This graphic novel is dedicated to those early Chinese men and women who came across the Pacific and helped build our nations —America and Canada.

Initially, this book was going to explore the history of the Chinese in Canada, but it soon became apparent that sharing only part of the story gave an incomplete picture of the Chinese experience in Gam Saan (Gold Mountain).

And racism knows no boundaries.

The early Chinese did not differentiate between Canada and the United States. They traveled to where they believed there were opportunities and had kin, and to where they were allowed in. The new continent was one; it was Gam Saan, the strange new land.

Our pioneering ancestors were subjected to incredibly harsh discrimination and unspeakable atrocities from ordinary folks and from legislated racism. Institutional racism included the Chinese Exclusion Act of 1882 (US), the Head Tax (Canada, 1885 –1923), and the Chinese Immigration Act of 1923 (Canada). These laws effectively shut the Chinese out of Gam Saan for decades.

The result of this institutionalized racism on generations of separated families was great hardship and a Chinese community of predominantly aging men in North America.

Written words are important. I wish to add to the written word using my drawings. I hope this presentation of knowledge in a cartoon format will add to our learning experience.

This is the story of one Chinese family, the Wongs, in Gam Saan. It depicts the world our early forebears experienced. I hope this story will help spark an interest in learning about the struggles of one group of people who helped build our new world.

Although a fictional story, Escape to Gold Mountain is based on facts, on my own family's experiences, and was inspired by the many elders and friends I've been fortunate to meet along my journey of discovery.

I hope you will enjoy reading this book as much as I enjoyed creating it.

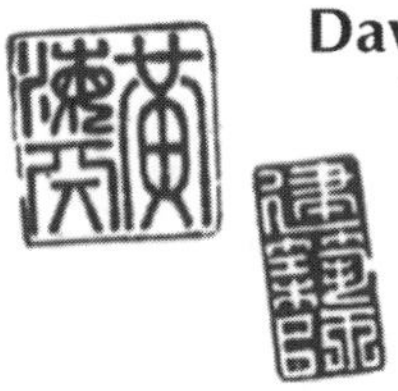

David H. T. Wong
Vancouver, BC
2012

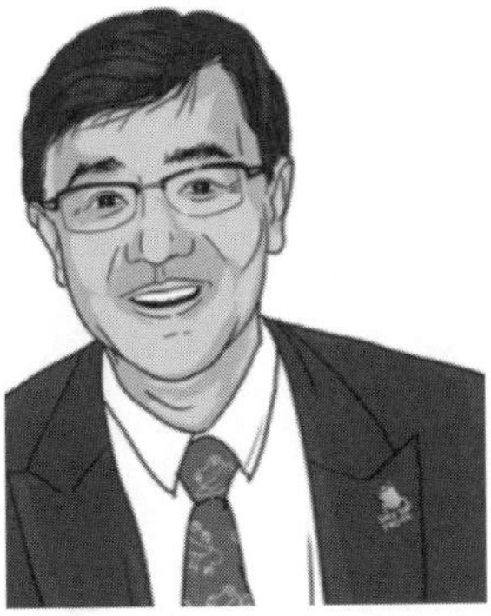

INTRODUCTIONS

Imogene L. Lim, PhD

BAM! POWW!! ZAP! KA-BOOOM!!! KLUGNK! The format of the graphic novel is familiar to many as the comic book writ large. Where else do you find word balloons containing dialogue all written in cap letters, as well as onomatopoeia followed by triple exclamation points for punctuation? The classic story follows a hero who is pitted against adversity, endures privations, does battle, and finally overcomes hardships.

Escape to Gold Mountain has all of these elements. It covers the 150-plus years of the history of the Chinese in North America. During the gold-rush days of the mid-1800s, western North America, in particular, was known to the Chinese as Gam Saan or Gold Mountain. When traveling to Gam Saan, the Chinese made no distinction specifically between Canada and the United States. As a history and as a graphic novel, this book is unique in providing parallel stories of the Chinese in both countries.

Imogene L. Lim, PhD
Professor, Vancouver Island University
Founding Board Member, Chinese
Canadian Historical Society of BC

If your family was part of the first wave of Chinese immigration, the story in this book is yours, too. It is also personalized by being told through one family over five generations. Imagine your great-great-great grandfather arriving in Gam Saan and facing adversity solely for being Chinese, while today you have the full rights of citizenship. Escape to Gold Mountain takes you from the nineteenth century into the twenty-first, giving voice and face to various characters, from politicians to the common man and woman, placing their lives in the context of the time that began with restrictive legislation.

The histories of the Chinese in the US and Canada are similar yet different, affected by their respective government's policies on immigration and the resultant legislation. In the United States, Chinese were excluded in 1882. Rather than outright exclusion, Canada created barriers to discourage Chinese immigration. When the US Exclusion Act came into force, Chinese labor was still needed to build the Canadian Pacific Railway, if it was to be completed on schedule. One of British Columbia's stipulations for joining Confederation was the promise of being linked by rail to the rest of the country. This nation-building task

was completed in 1885—the same year that Canada implemented a head tax of $50 on Chinese immigrants and which increased to $500 in 1903; the Chinese were the only immigrant group who paid such a fee or tax. In 1923 Canada passed its own Chinese Exclusion Act.

These various acts affected Chinese abroad and those already here. At $500, the cost of immigration to Canada in 1903 was prohibitive; the amount was equivalent to two years' wages or the price of a house lot in Vancouver. The result was a community primarily of men. Those who could afford to bring wives and have families were relatively few in number. In many cases, families were separated, with wife and child(ren) in China and husband in Gam Saan. During the period of exclusion, 1923–47, fewer than fifty Chinese immigrated to Canada.

Even if born in Canada, Chinese were not citizens of the Dominion of Canada until 1947. Section 18 of the Chinese Exclusion Act of 1923 required anyone "of Chinese origin or descent in Canada, irrespective of allegiance or citizenship" to register with the Chief Controller of Chinese Immigration within twelve months of the Act to obtain a certificate. Without it, the individual could be fined $500 and/or be jailed for a year. My mother, born in Vancouver, BC, held registration certificate #18620 (dated June 20, 1924), while my father, born in Cumberland, BC, was #6278 (dated March 17, 1924); they were six- and five-years old, respectively. On each certificate was written: "This certificate does not establish legal status in Canada."

In effect, legislation was based on racist policies enacted by federal, provincial, and municipal governments. The titles of two books on early Asian immigration say it all: **White Canada Forever** (Ward, 1978) and **A White Man's Province** (Roy, 1989). After surviving the dangers of building the railway, especially through the Fraser Canyon where the death toll from accidents and harsh conditions was high, Chinese were restricted in what they could do and where they could live.

Many today are probably unaware that historic Chinatowns were, in part, an outcome of government policies. Viewed as undesirable immigrants, Chinese were allowed to live in certain areas, often marginal; this may not be so apparent in the twenty-first century city. As well, some of these Chinatowns "disappeared" from the physical landscape and were remembered only by former residents and descendants (as in Nanaimo or New Westminster, BC). Others were not even towns within towns but separate locations.

For example, my father's birth certificate reads "Place of Birth: Chinatown, near Cumberland, BC." Only in 2002 did that Chinatown become part of the town of Cumberland. Today we view historic Chinatowns as places to visit to have an "authentic" Chinese meal, experience other aspects of Chinese culture (such as a Lunar New Year's Parade), and perhaps to learn something about Chinese Canadian/American history.

In the US, the repeal of the Chinese Exclusion Act occurred in 1943, while in Canada it occurred in 1947. If Canada had not signed the UN Charter of Human Rights, this event may have been delayed. Although Canada followed the early policies of the United States regarding the Chinese, it also led by being the first nation (in 2006) to offer an official apology for its anti-Chinese policies,

including reparations. The US Senate passed a similar resolution in 2011, though without compensation, followed by the House of Representatives on June 2012.

The graphic novel is a way to make such history accessible to people who might find the subject "dry," or who don't like reading or find it difficult. Escape to Gold Mountain offers perhaps the perfect vehicle to reach that wider audience, for "a picture is worth a thousand words." Until school curricula include Chinese Canadian/American history as part of a larger discussion on national history, this book bridges that knowledge gap.

This format also allows the reader to visualize individuals as just plain folks—they are your relatives, your neighbors—not people to be suspicious of or feared. There are no caricatures of the slant-eyed, buck-toothed, or conical-hatted individuals that have been frequently used to stereotype Asians; in Wong's drawings, we see real people. For those more familiar with Chinese Canadian/American history, notable individuals are readily recognizable (e.g., Douglas Jung, Jean Lumb, Wong Foon Sien, Wing Luke, and Judy Chu).

These individuals are heroes and role models who have worked at gaining social justice for their communities. Those who endured and fought the good fight may not be the masked or caped superheroes in the comics, but they were (and still are) the ones who pushed against barriers to make a better life for their descendants and ultimately for all citizens of Canada and the United States. **Escape to Gold Mountain** acknowledges their contributions to the larger society, for they are the heroes upon whose shoulders we stand.

Bettie Luke

When issues of Chinese immigration, hardships, and discrimination surface in the content of **Escape to Gold Mountain**, they strike echoes in my heart because they reflect the stories of my family and other Chinese community families I knew while growing up in Seattle, Washington. During World War II, while my oldest brother, Wing Luke, was in the Army fighting for the United States, our family was evicted from our hand-laundry business when the landlady tripled the rent.

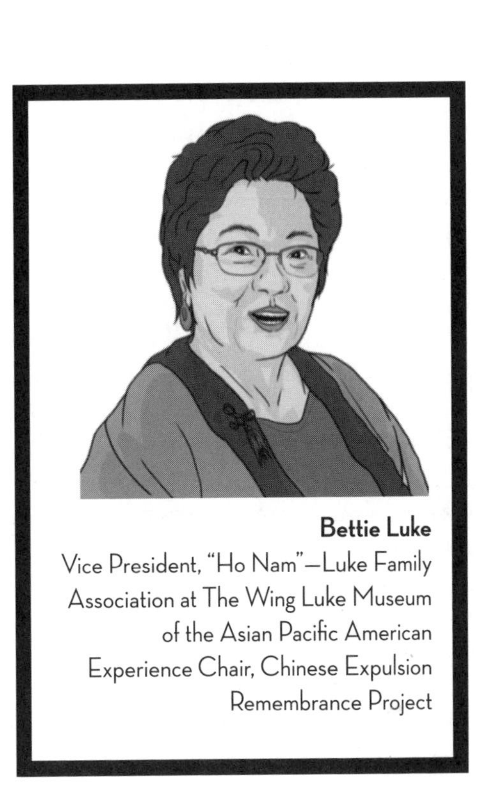

Bettie Luke
Vice President, "Ho Nam"—Luke Family Association at The Wing Luke Museum of the Asian Pacific American Experience Chair, Chinese Expulsion Remembrance Project

During the same time that Canada imposed a Head Tax on Chinese immigrants, towns throughout the US randomly imposed taxes on the Chinese under a ridiculous range of conditions: taxes on dwellings, on miners, and on laundries and other businesses. Sometimes taxes were collected more than once. An informal "tax collection" existed in my home town until the 1960s; whispered stories told of policemen collecting "protection money" from Chinatown businesses.

The US Chinese Exclusion Laws had an impact on our lives for decades. I never knew what it was like to grow up with grandparents or other relatives. When I first learned about the Chinese being driven out of Seattle in 1886, I asked my father if he knew anything about that event. He told me that an uncle was present but was spared expulsion because he was the Mayor's houseboy—a prime example of the power of politics and the politics of power.

In the twentieth century, in a very different example of politics and power, my brother Wing Luke was the first person of Asian ancestry to be elected to public office in the Pacific Northwest. Despite smear campaigns implying he was a Communist, Wing won the election for Seattle City Council by the largest margin in the history of the city. He was actively involved in changes to open housing, fishing rights, and historic and cultural preservation.

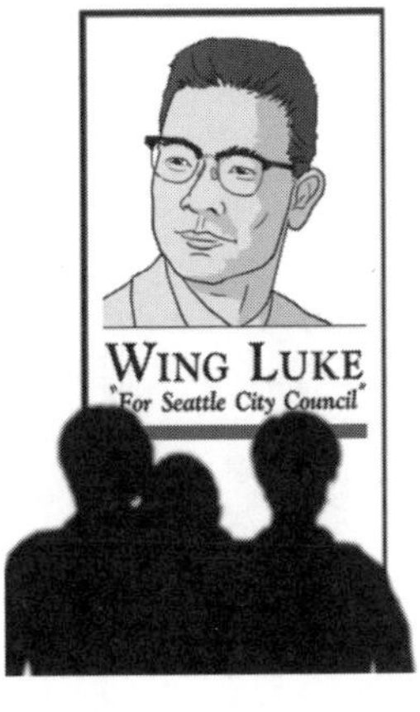
WING LUKE
"For Seattle City Council"

David H.T. Wong's **Escape to Gold Mountain** is a seminal example of how the power of images can convey oftforgotten events more deeply than words alone. The reader is immediately engaged—visually, cognitively, and emotionally—captivated by a deep and long-lasting impression.

As an artist and multicultural education trainer for thirty-five years, I believe this book to be an exceptionally effective example of conveying stories that may be considered sensitive and painful, but need to be told. The use of line drawings is deceptively simple—graphic depictions of characters and stories that disarm the reader, reduce resistance, and open minds to important information. Ultimately, the reader is pulled in, making this book an effective teaching tool for all ages.

It is not easy to emerge with a healthy Asian-Pacific-American identity when subjected to many decades of racism. Hopefully, "long-time" immigrants can now recognize that their necessary "survival mode" deprived them of rights they deserved and can now stand up for. Likewise, younger generations will learn about the price paid by the "long-timers" and acknowledge those whose shoulders they stand on.

In February 2011, I organized a rally and march to recognize the 125th anniversary of the Chinese being driven out of Seattle in 1886. Since Chinese were rounded up and taken to the docks to be shipped out to San Francisco, the Chinese Expulsion Remembrance Project (CERP) organized a reverse march: gathering at the docks, we marched into Chinatown as a statement that "We Are Here to Stay!"

More recently, on June 22, 2012, I took part in the Chinese Remembering conference in Idaho, which focused on possibly the worst crime against Chinese in the US: the massacre of thirty-four Chinese miners on the Snake River in 1887. The place is now called Chinese Massacre Cove. I organized the dedication ceremony of a granite monument inscribed in three languages—English, Nez Perce, and Chinese. It represented a gesture of healing.

That the organizers of this event were almost all non-Chinese is a tribute to the fact that, across cultural boundaries, they did not see this horrific crime as a "Chinese problem" but an American problem, which needed to be publicly addressed with justice and healing.

Escape to Gold Mountain carries the same message.

Dr Connie C. So

Despite profound contributions to the Americas for more than 150 years, the story of the Chinese in the United States and Canada remains mostly unacknowledged. David H.T. Wong's graphic novel, **Escape to Gold Mountain**, stunningly documents the historical prejudice, discrimination, and hostilities faced by Chinese Americans and Chinese Canadians. While focusing on the Wong family's epic journey from Southern China to North America, the author skillfully recounts a larger story about the Chinese people in the Americas.

My family emigrated from Hong Kong to the United States in 1969, when I was four years old. We left to rejoin my mother's family, already in the United States. Since the mid-nineteenth century—after the Opium Wars, drought, and famine in Toisan/Taishan, and the occupation of the country by foreigners—my maternal ancestors had sought opportunities in "Gold Mountain," the name given to the United States. But America was not a welcoming land of gold; instead, Chinese immigrants were often greeted by prejudice, outrageous taxes, and physical violence.

Dr Connie C. So
Senior Lecturer, American Ethnic Studies,
University of Washington,
Seattle, Washington

Overcoming the hostilities, many Chinese immigrants, like the Wong family profiled in this novel, adapted and made the new country home. Growing up, I heard many family stories about my Toisanese/Taishanese great-great-great maternal grandfather, a gold prospector in California; my great-great maternal grandfather, a translator at Angel Island detention center; my maternal great-grandfather, a labor contractor and the founder of the Woo Family Association in Seattle; and my maternal grandfather, a member of the US military police. While there was overt discrimination, there were still more economic opportunities and a greater possibility for a more promising future for their children in the United States.

Like many others, my mother's family was separated by wars and immigration laws. It was not until after the 1945 War Brides Act that my maternal grandmother (and other Chinese women) could finally join their husbands in the US. After changes to the Immigration Law of 1965, my mother could finally join her family. I grew up in the predominantly Asian-American neighborhood of Beacon Hill in Seattle, Washington, where the consequences of

this historical separation of families was widely felt. Yet, during my entire secondary-school education, the stories of Chinese Americans and other Asian and Pacific Island Americans, were noticeably absent.

Using historical documents, excerpts from interviews with elderly residents, and finely detailed illustrations, Wong captures the pain, frustration, and courage of early Chinese pioneers and their contemporaries and makes it understandable for readers of many age groups. This was information I actively sought as a young student. The result of Wong's efforts is a moving portrait of a heroic people collectively resisting oppression, adapting to an unfriendly land, and ultimately transforming it into a home for their descendants.

Thank you, David, for writing our collective story.

CHINGLISH

Chinese phrases and words used in this graphic novel reflect the terms and expressions that best represent the dialect of the first wave of Chinese to North America. These peoples hailed from the four counties (Sze Yap) of the southern Chinese province of Kwangtung (Guangdong) – Hoy Ping, Sun Wui, Toisan, and Yen Ping counties. Names and places in this story reflect this historic context. The following words were originally used by our pioneers, with today's "spelling" form in parentheses – (i.e., Mandarin Pinyin writing equivalent).

Canton	(Guangzhou)	廣州
Kwangtung	(Guangdong)	廣東
Ching	(Qing)	清
Hong Kong	(Xianggang)	香港
Peking	(Beijing)	北京
Hoy Ping	(Kaiping)	開平
Toisan	(Taishan)	台山

In addition, the original Chinese terms used by Gold Mountain pioneers will be employed. Here is a summary of some original Chinese phonetic descriptions, followed by their literal English translations, and the actual name used today:

Hum Sui Fahw	' Saltwater city '	Vancouver
Dai Fahw	' Big city '	San Francisco
Yee Fahw	' Second city '	Sacramento (or) New Westminster
Tong Saan	' Tong Mountain '	China
Gam Saan	' Gold Mountain '	North America
Tan Heung San	' Fragrant Sandlewood Mountain'	Hawai'i
Mei Gok	' Beautiful country '	America

Some place names used were the same in America and in Canada. For example, "Yee Fahw" (second city) was used to identify a smaller city or community in relation to the main city (e.g., Sacramento to San Francisco, New Westminster to Vancouver).

The prefix "Ah" before a name is a common southern Chinese colloquialism when addressing a person. So someone with the surname Lee would be addressed by the Cantonese as "Ah Lee" and Mr Smith as "Ah Smith"; it could also be added to a first name, so Brad would be addressed as "Ah Brad" and Susan as "Ah Susan."

Because Chinese words are phonetically anglicized here, the English "phonetic" spelling will undoubtedly be met with variations. An example is the Chinese word for Gold Mountain 金山. It has been written in English in various forms, including Gam San, Gham Sun, Gum Saan, Gim Tsun, Gaam Shan, Ghum Shun, and so on. This graphic novel uses Gam Saan, which appears to be the most commonly used version.

TIMELINE

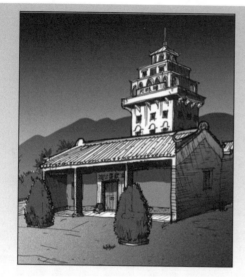

GAM SAAN

GOLD RUSH

CENTRAL
PACIFIC
RAILROAD

CHINESE
EXPULSION

CHINA

FIRST OPIUM WAR

WHITE LOTUS REBELLION

SECOND OPIUM WAR

FIRST SINO-JAPANESE WAR

TAIPING REBELLION

... 1750	1800	1850

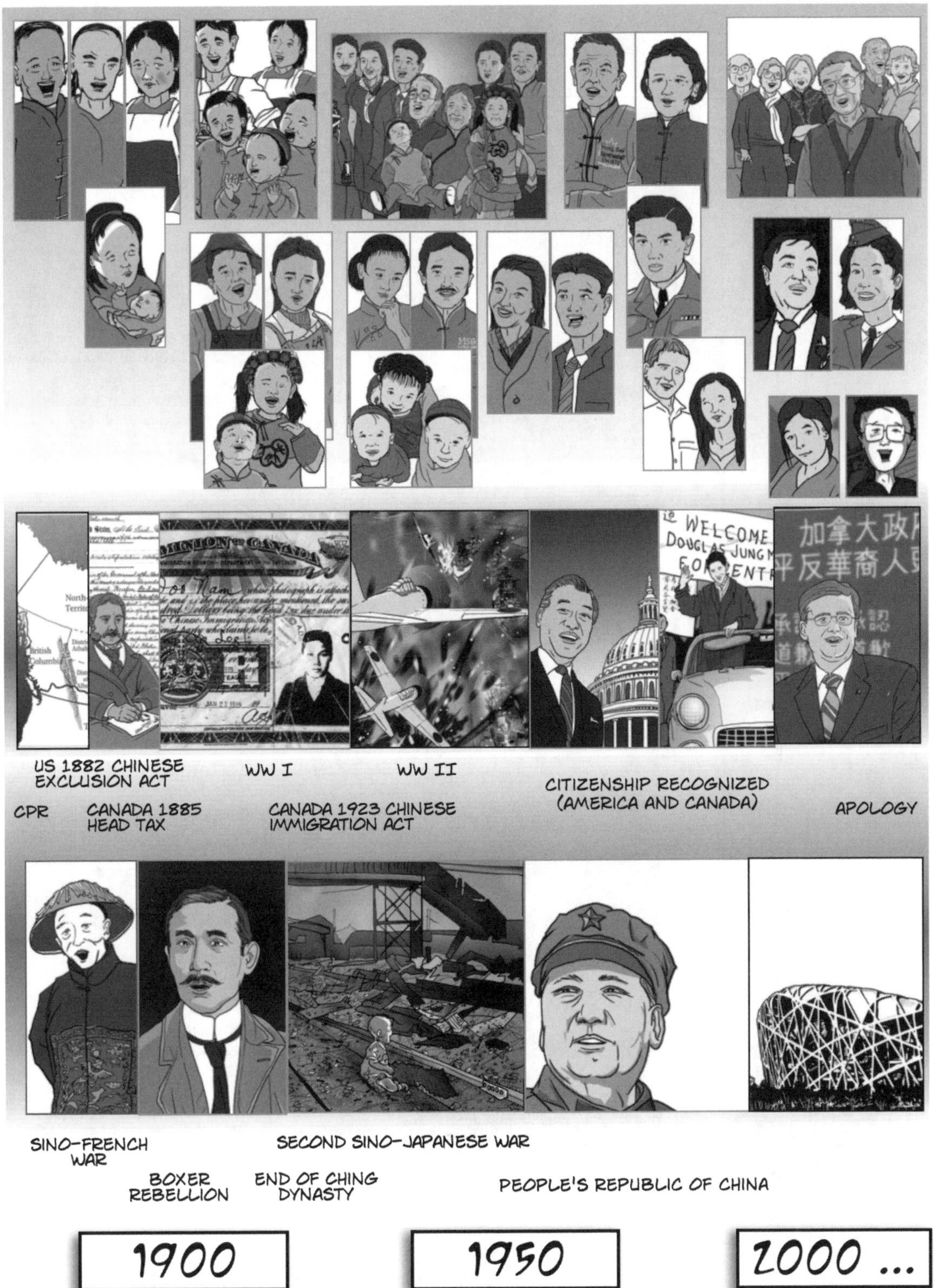
US 1882 CHINESE EXCLUSION ACT
WW I
WW II
CITIZENSHIP RECOGNIZED (AMERICA AND CANADA)
CPR
CANADA 1885 HEAD TAX
CANADA 1923 CHINESE IMMIGRATION ACT
APOLOGY
SINO-FRENCH WAR
SECOND SINO-JAPANESE WAR
BOXER REBELLION
END OF CHING DYNASTY
PEOPLE'S REPUBLIC OF CHINA
1900
1950
2000 ...

TRAVEL MAP

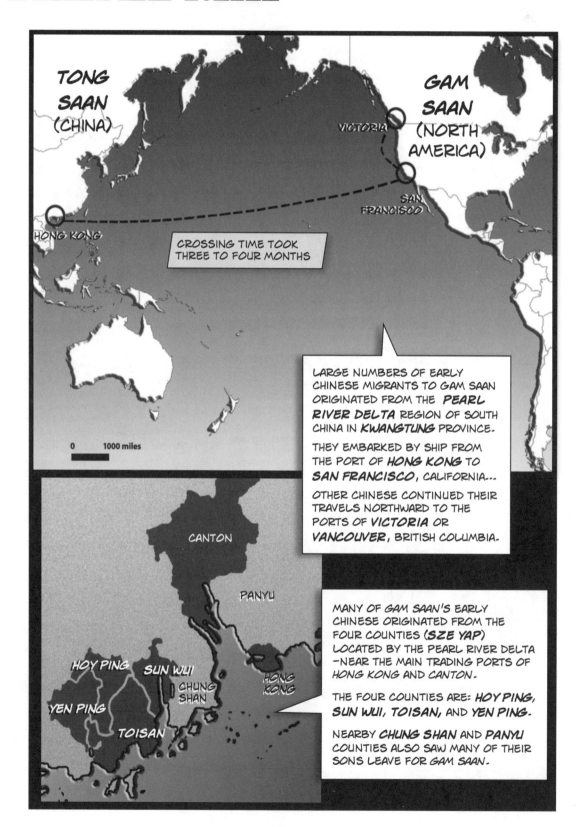

TONG SAAN (CHINA)

GAM SAAN (NORTH AMERICA)

VICTORIA

SAN FRANCISCO

HONG KONG

CROSSING TIME TOOK THREE TO FOUR MONTHS

0   1000 miles

LARGE NUMBERS OF EARLY CHINESE MIGRANTS TO GAM SAAN ORIGINATED FROM THE *PEARL RIVER DELTA* REGION OF SOUTH CHINA IN *KWANGTUNG* PROVINCE.

THEY EMBARKED BY SHIP FROM THE PORT OF *HONG KONG* TO *SAN FRANCISCO*, CALIFORNIA...

OTHER CHINESE CONTINUED THEIR TRAVELS NORTHWARD TO THE PORTS OF *VICTORIA* OR *VANCOUVER*, BRITISH COLUMBIA.

CANTON

PANYU

HOY PING   SUN WUI

CHUNG SHAN

HONG KONG

YEN PING

TOISAN

MANY OF GAM SAAN'S EARLY CHINESE ORIGINATED FROM THE FOUR COUNTIES (*SZE YAP*) LOCATED BY THE PEARL RIVER DELTA —NEAR THE MAIN TRADING PORTS OF HONG KONG AND CANTON.

THE FOUR COUNTIES ARE: *HOY PING*, *SUN WUI*, *TOISAN*, AND *YEN PING*.

NEARBY *CHUNG SHAN* AND *PANYU* COUNTIES ALSO SAW MANY OF THEIR SONS LEAVE FOR GAM SAAN.

PROLOGUE

THROUGHOUT THE AGES, THE CHINESE HAVE WRITTEN OF A LAND CALLED *FUSANG*. IN THE *7TH* CENTURY, FUSANG WAS SAID TO BE *20,000 LI** EAST OF *CHINA*, KNOWN AS THE *MIDDLE KINGDOM*

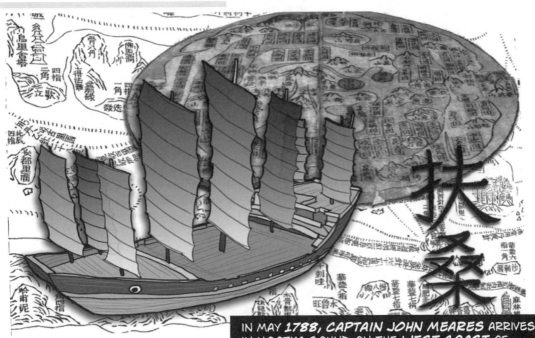

ON AUGUST 9, *1785*, THE SHIP *PALLAS*, SKIPPERED BY *JOHN O'DONNELL*, ARRIVES IN *BALTIMORE*, MARYLAND. ON BOARD WERE *3* CHINESE SEAMEN, *ASHING*, *ACHUN*, AND *ACEUN*. IT IS THE FIRST RECORDED INSTANCE OF ASIANS ON THE EAST COAST OF AMERICA.

IN MAY *1788, CAPTAIN JOHN MEARES* ARRIVES IN NOOTKA SOUND ON THE *WEST COAST* OF VANCOUVER ISLAND WITH *50* TO *70* CHINESE MEN TO HELP MAINTAIN AND SHELTER HIS SHIPS WHILE TRADING FURS...

MEARE'S CHINESE CREW IS SAID TO HAVE CONSTRUCTED THE *FIRST NON-INDIGENOUS* SAILING VESSEL IN THE PACIFIC NORTH WEST

* *LI* = CHINESE MEASUREMENT OF LENGTH; EQUIVALENT TO APPROXIMATELY HALF A KM (0.3 MILE)

OUR STORY BEGINS *200* YEARS LATER...

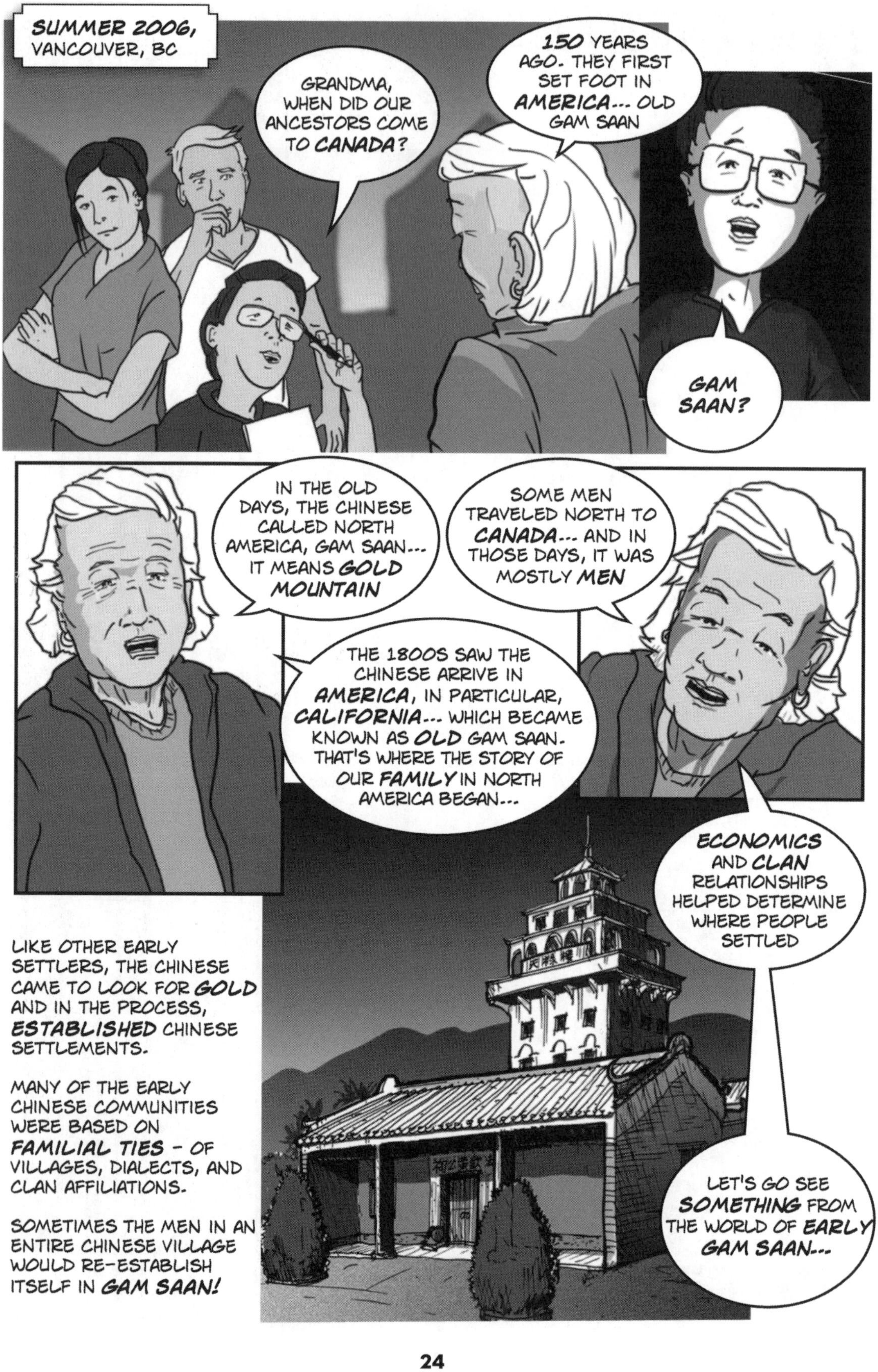
SUMMER 2006, VANCOUVER, BC
GRANDMA, WHEN DID OUR ANCESTORS COME TO CANADA?
150 YEARS AGO. THEY FIRST SET FOOT IN AMERICA... OLD GAM SAAN
GAM SAAN?
IN THE OLD DAYS, THE CHINESE CALLED NORTH AMERICA, GAM SAAN... IT MEANS GOLD MOUNTAIN
SOME MEN TRAVELED NORTH TO CANADA... AND IN THOSE DAYS, IT WAS MOSTLY MEN
THE 1800S SAW THE CHINESE ARRIVE IN AMERICA, IN PARTICULAR, CALIFORNIA... WHICH BECAME KNOWN AS OLD GAM SAAN. THAT'S WHERE THE STORY OF OUR FAMILY IN NORTH AMERICA BEGAN...
ECONOMICS AND CLAN RELATIONSHIPS HELPED DETERMINE WHERE PEOPLE SETTLED
LIKE OTHER EARLY SETTLERS, THE CHINESE CAME TO LOOK FOR GOLD AND IN THE PROCESS, ESTABLISHED CHINESE SETTLEMENTS.
MANY OF THE EARLY CHINESE COMMUNITIES WERE BASED ON FAMILIAL TIES - OF VILLAGES, DIALECTS, AND CLAN AFFILIATIONS.
SOMETIMES THE MEN IN AN ENTIRE CHINESE VILLAGE WOULD RE-ESTABLISH ITSELF IN GAM SAAN!
LET'S GO SEE SOMETHING FROM THE WORLD OF EARLY GAM SAAN...

ESCAPE to GOLD MOUNTAIN

CHAPTER 1 The Iron Chink

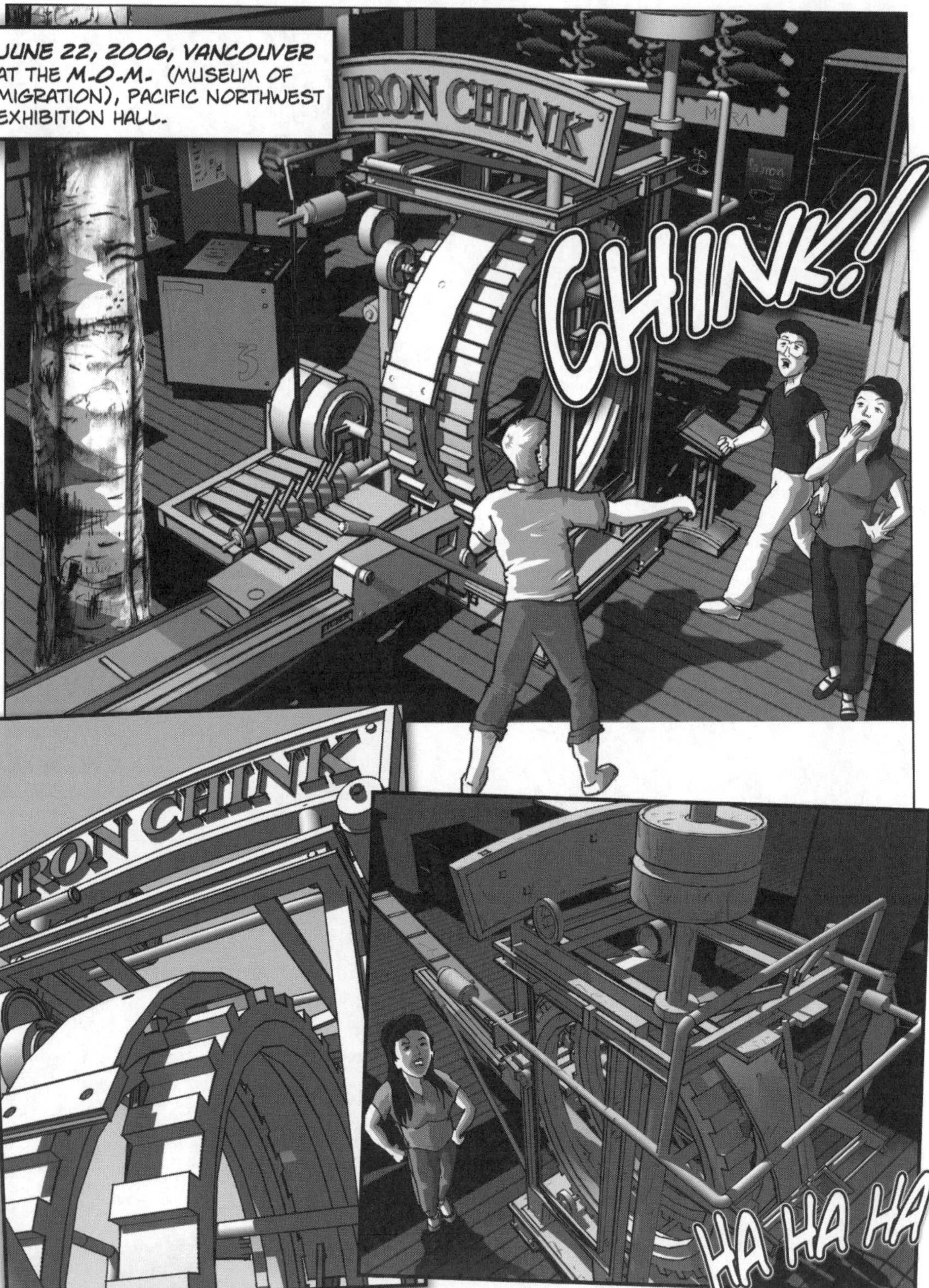
JUNE 22, 2006, VANCOUVER AT THE M.O.M. (MUSEUM OF MIGRATION), PACIFIC NORTHWEST EXHIBITION HALL.
IRON CHINK
CHINK!
IRON CHINK
HA HA HA

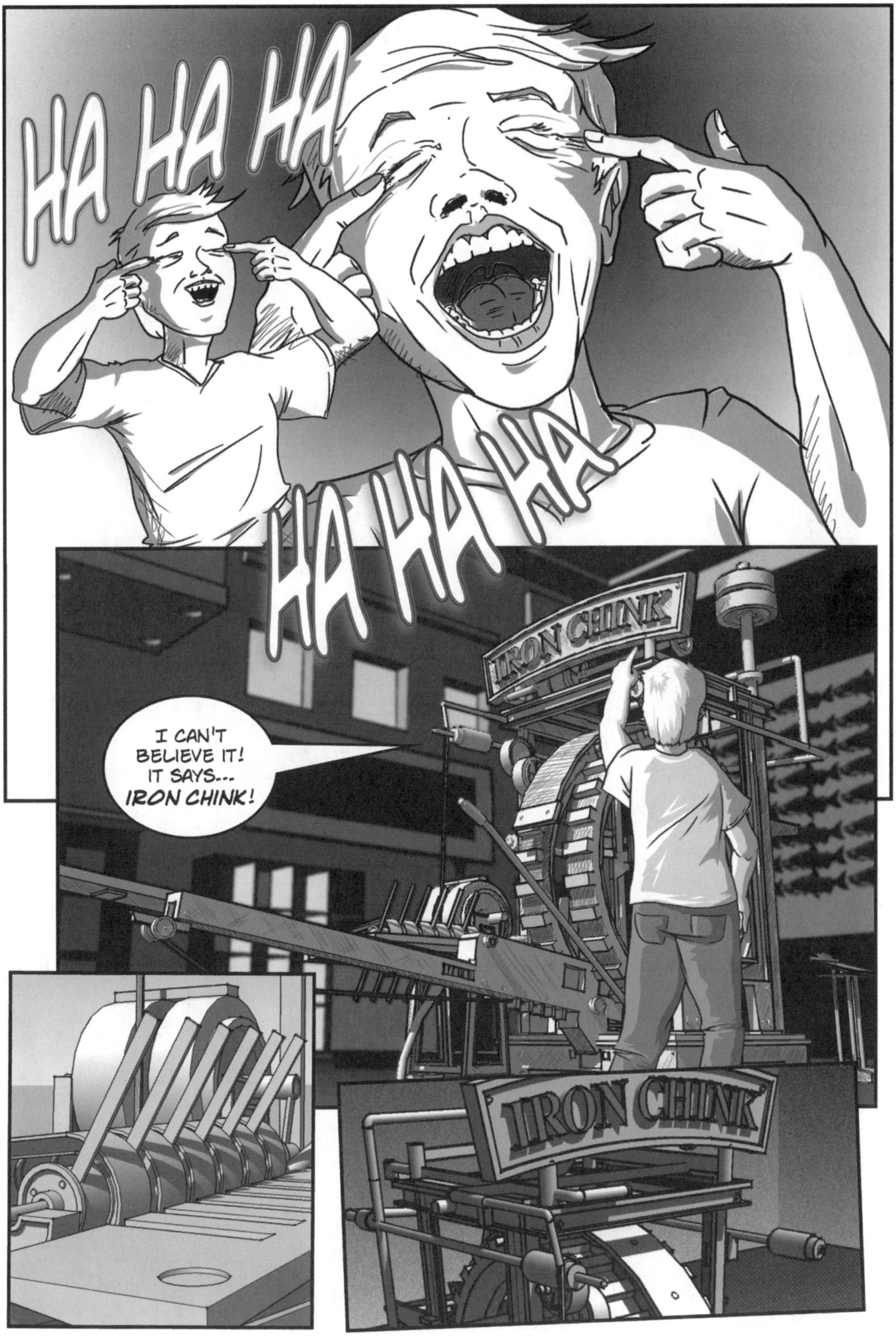
HA HA HA
HA HA HA
IRON CHINK
I CAN'T BELIEVE IT! IT SAYS... IRON CHINK!
IRON CHINK

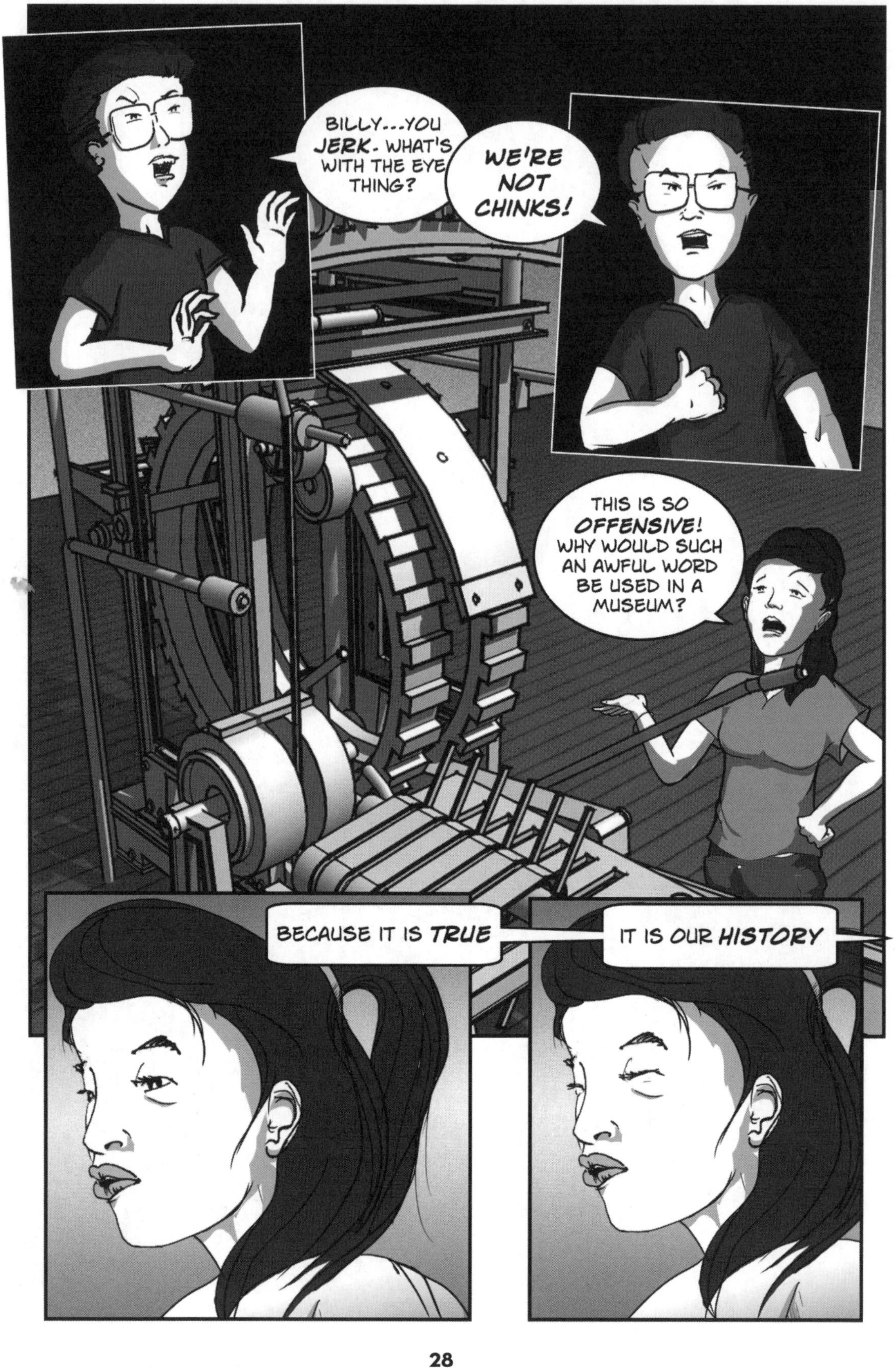
BILLY...YOU JERK. WHAT'S WITH THE EYE THING?
WE'RE NOT CHINKS!
THIS IS SO OFFENSIVE! WHY WOULD SUCH AN AWFUL WORD BE USED IN A MUSEUM?
BECAUSE IT IS TRUE
IT IS OUR HISTORY

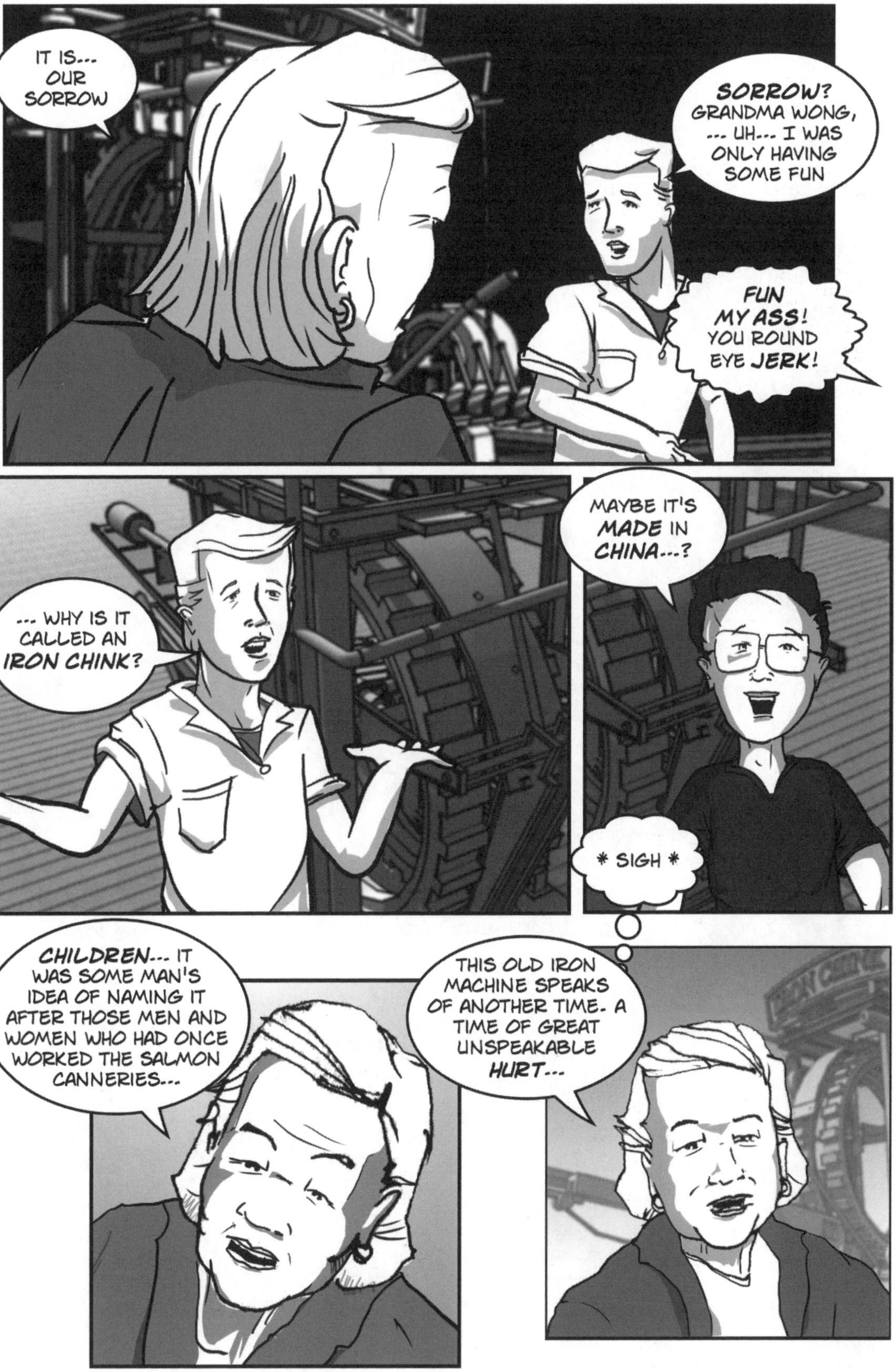
IT IS... OUR SORROW
SORROW? GRANDMA WONG, ... UH... I WAS ONLY HAVING SOME FUN
FUN MY ASS! YOU ROUND EYE JERK!
... WHY IS IT CALLED AN IRON CHINK?
MAYBE IT'S MADE IN CHINA...?
* SIGH *
CHILDREN... IT WAS SOME MAN'S IDEA OF NAMING IT AFTER THOSE MEN AND WOMEN WHO HAD ONCE WORKED THE SALMON CANNERIES...
THIS OLD IRON MACHINE SPEAKS OF ANOTHER TIME. A TIME OF GREAT UNSPEAKABLE HURT...

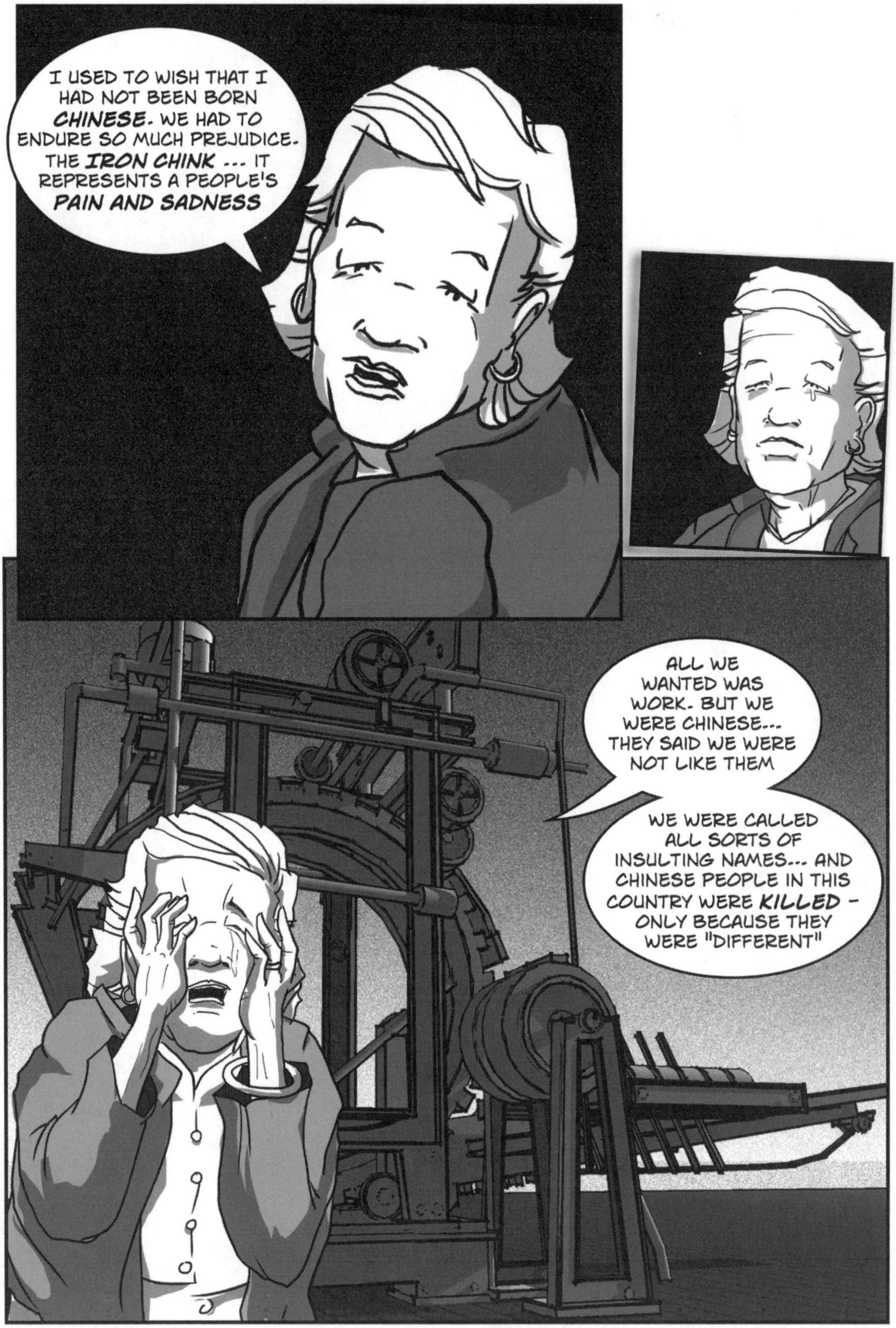
I USED TO WISH THAT I HAD NOT BEEN BORN CHINESE. WE HAD TO ENDURE SO MUCH PREJUDICE. THE IRON CHINK ... IT REPRESENTS A PEOPLE'S PAIN AND SADNESS
ALL WE WANTED WAS WORK. BUT WE WERE CHINESE... THEY SAID WE WERE NOT LIKE THEM
WE WERE CALLED ALL SORTS OF INSULTING NAMES... AND CHINESE PEOPLE IN THIS COUNTRY WERE KILLED - ONLY BECAUSE THEY WERE "DIFFERENT"

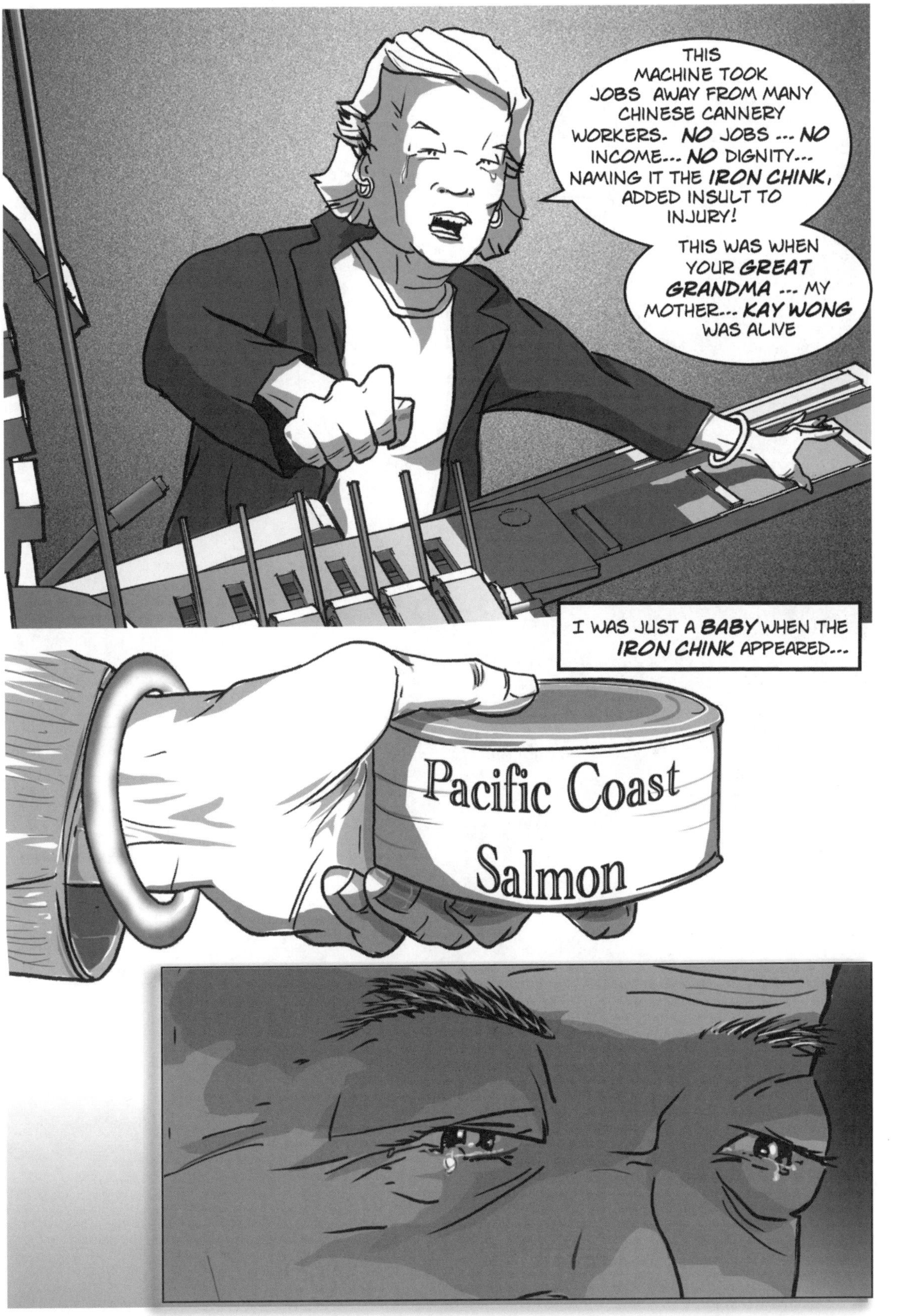
THIS MACHINE TOOK JOBS AWAY FROM MANY CHINESE CANNERY WORKERS. NO JOBS ... NO INCOME... NO DIGNITY... NAMING IT THE IRON CHINK, ADDED INSULT TO INJURY!
THIS WAS WHEN YOUR GREAT GRANDMA ... MY MOTHER... KAY WONG WAS ALIVE
I WAS JUST A BABY WHEN THE IRON CHINK APPEARED...
Pacific Coast Salmon

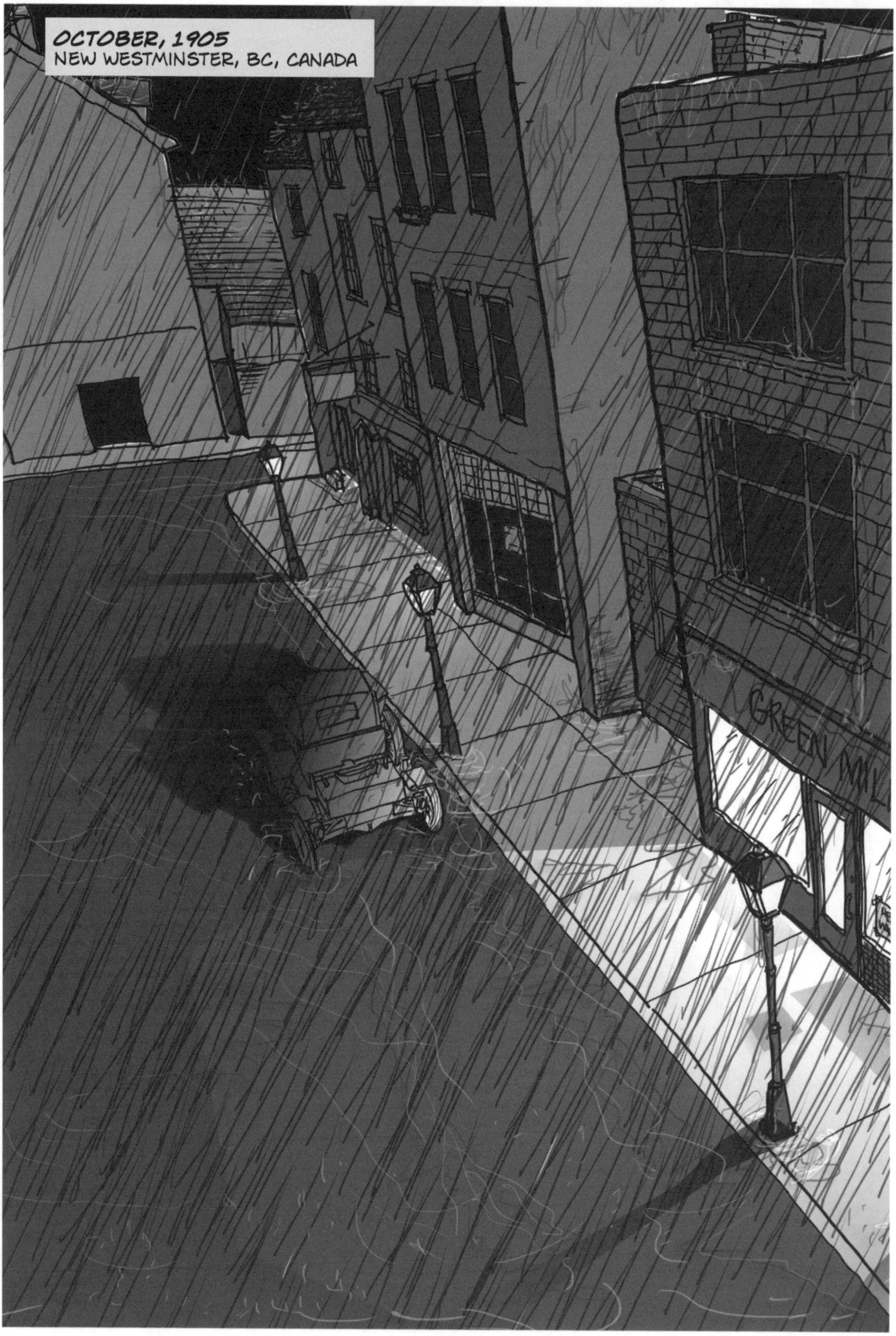
OCTOBER, 1905
NEW WESTMINSTER, BC, CANADA

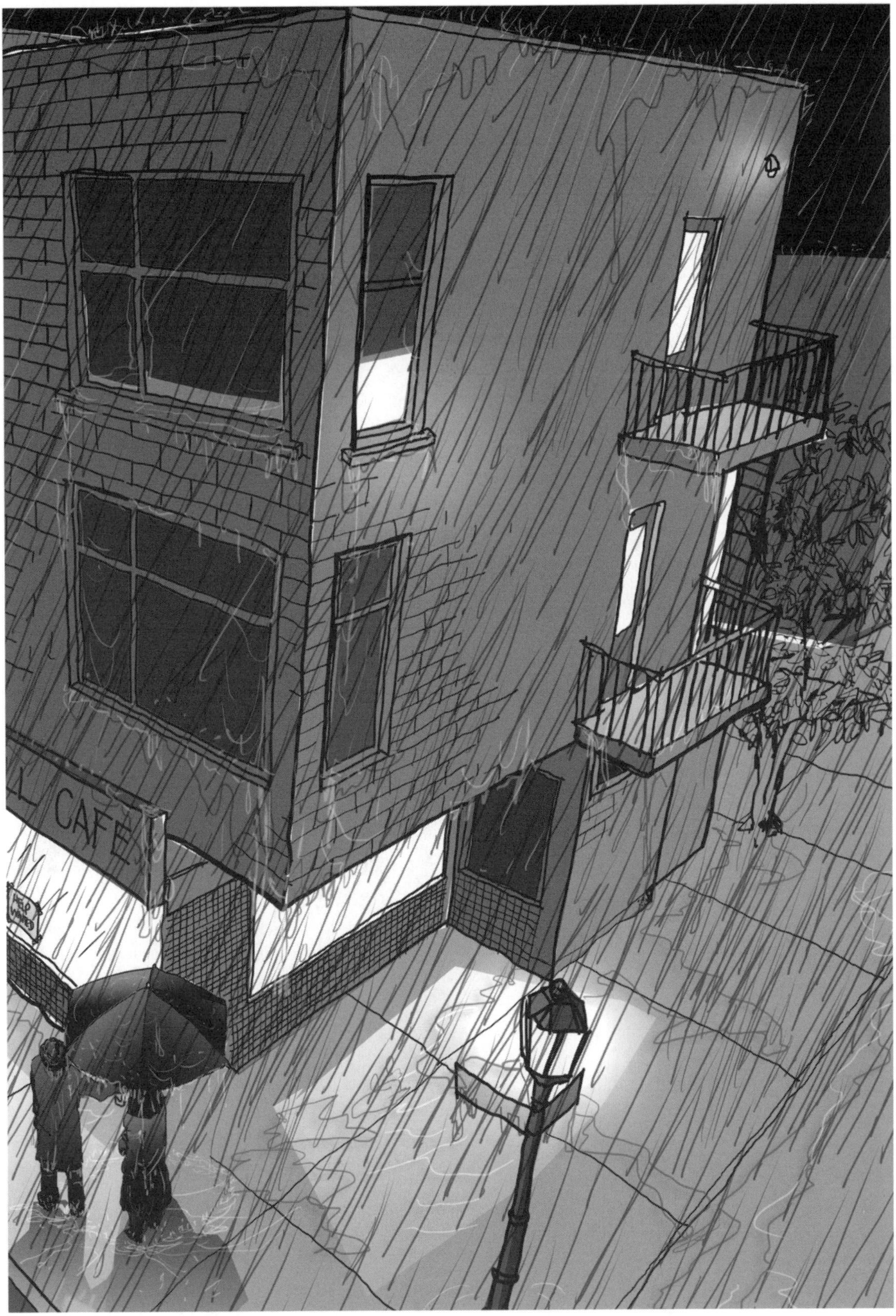
CAFE
HELP WANTED

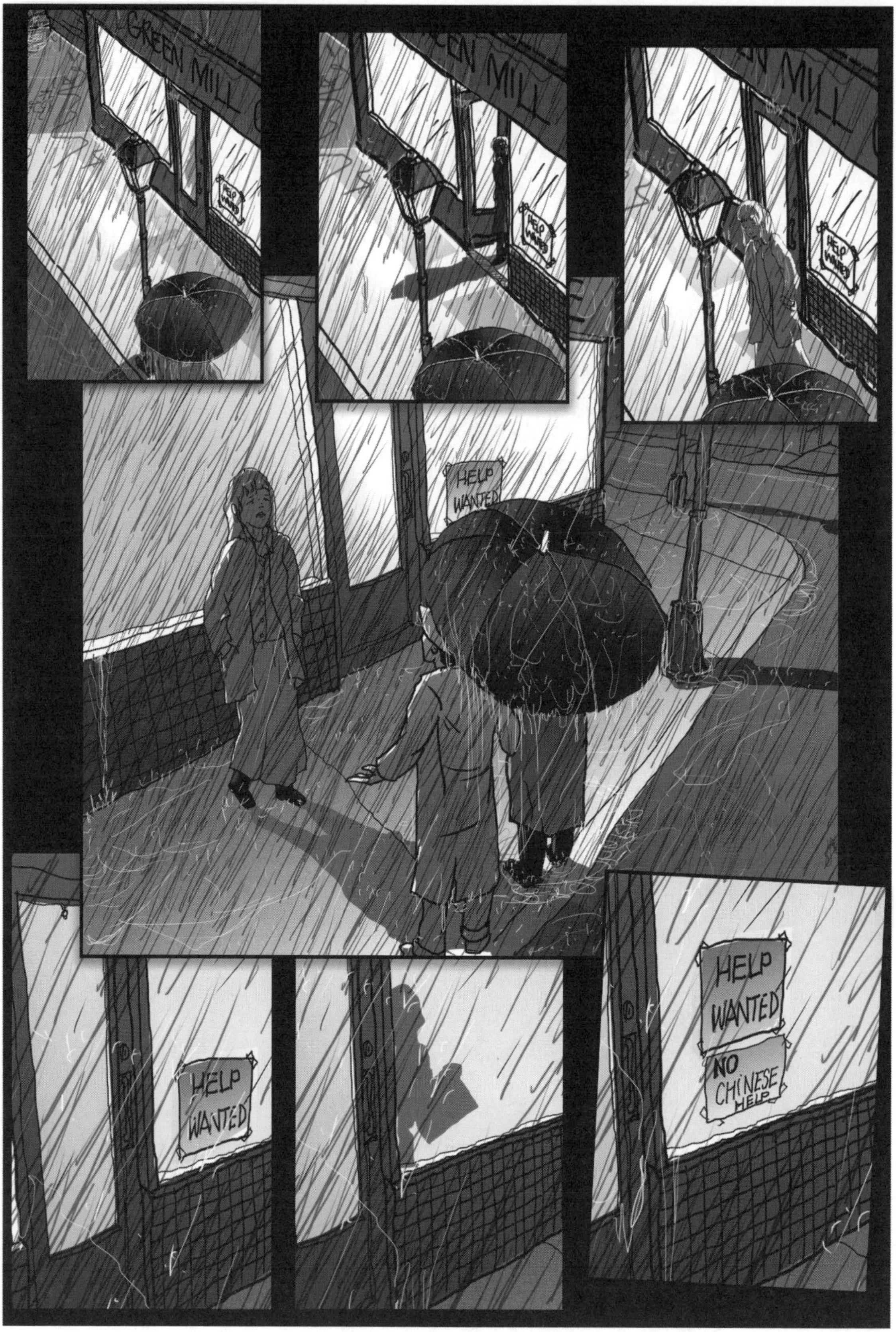
GREEN MILL
HELP WANTED
HELP WANTED
HELP WANTED
HELP WANTED
NO CHINESE HELP

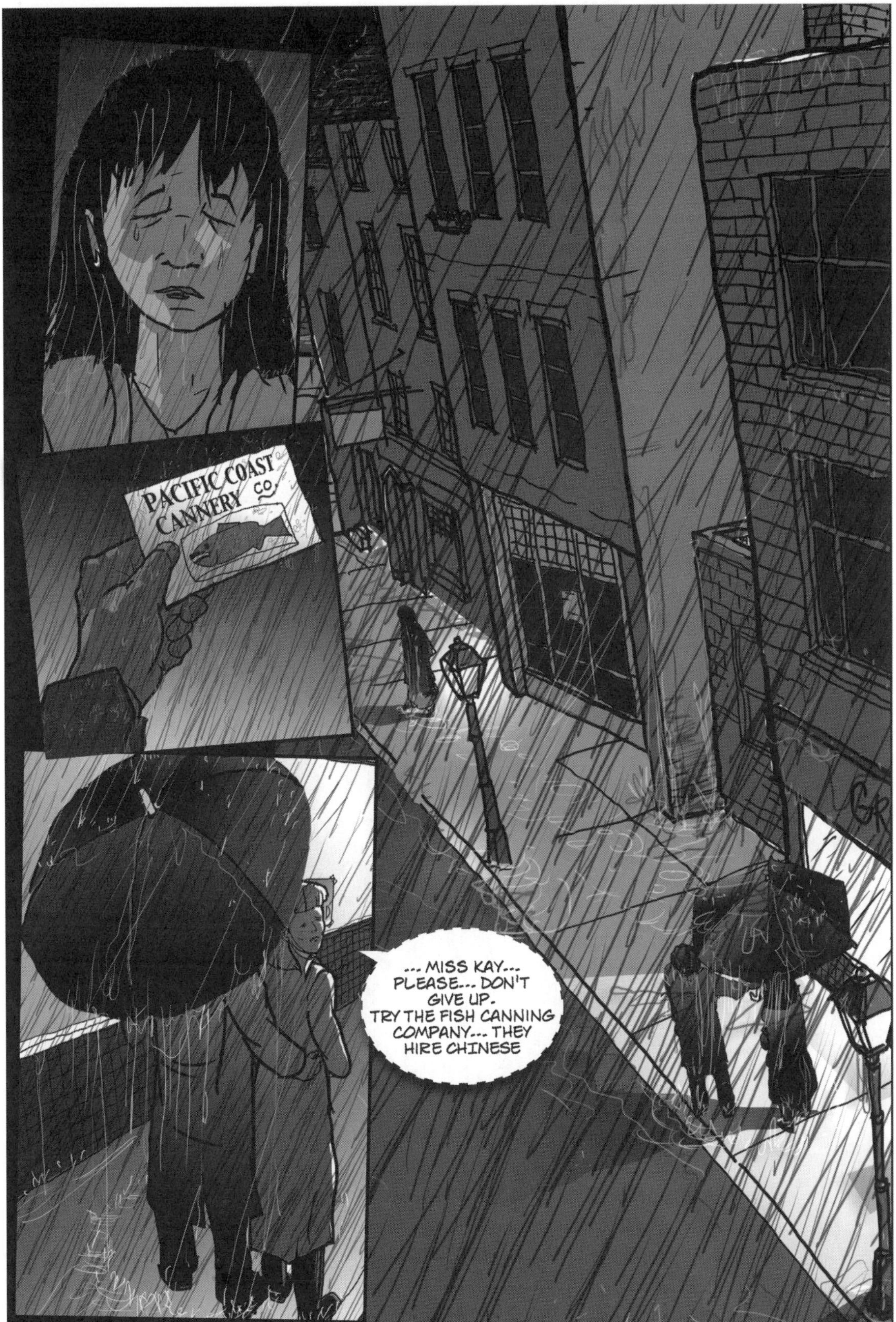
PACIFIC COAST CANNERY CO
...MISS KAY... PLEASE... DON'T GIVE UP. TRY THE FISH CANNING COMPANY... THEY HIRE CHINESE

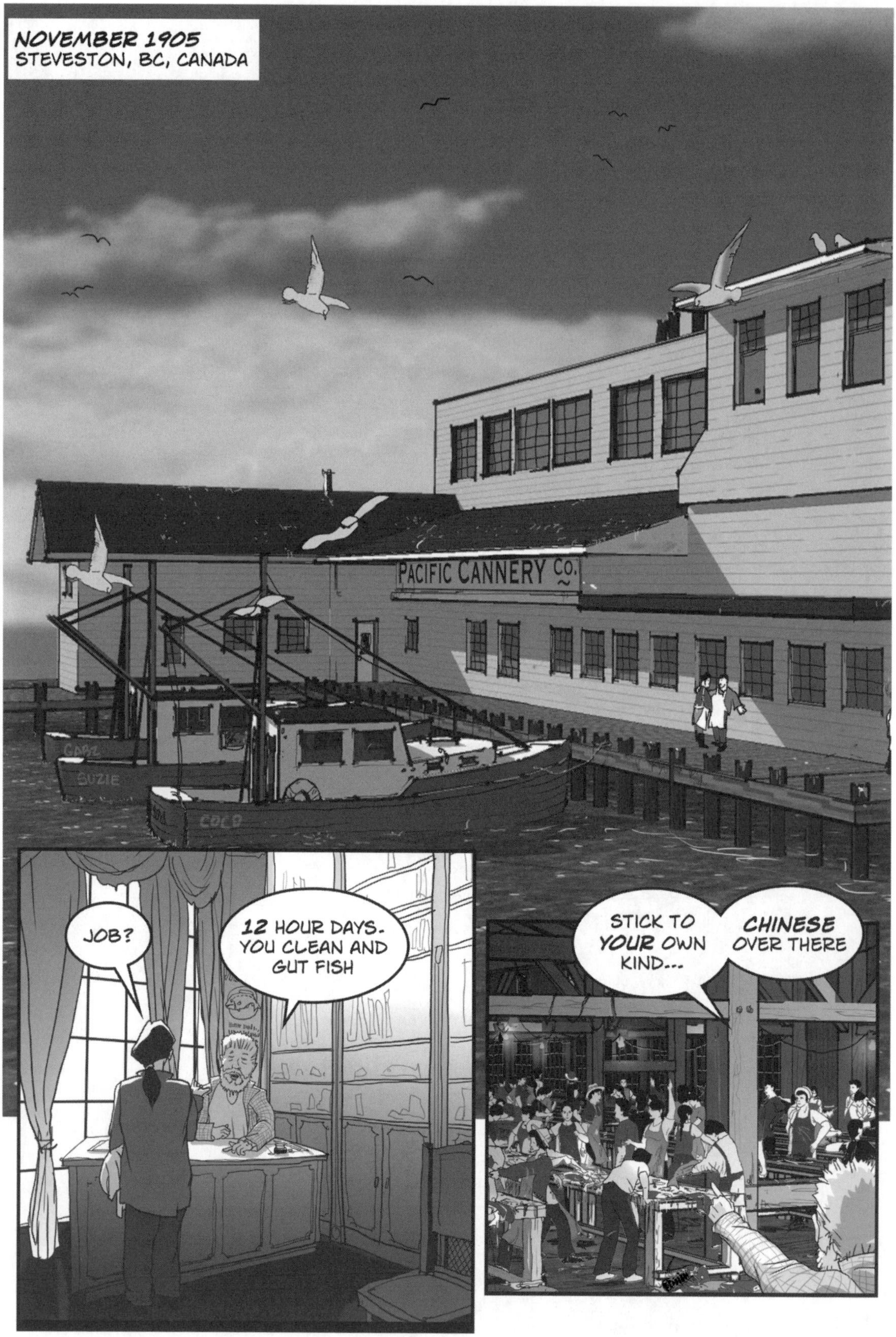
NOVEMBER 1905
STEVESTON, BC, CANADA
PACIFIC CANNERY CO.
SUZIE
JOB?
12 HOUR DAYS. YOU CLEAN AND GUT FISH
STICK TO *YOUR* OWN KIND...
CHINESE OVER THERE

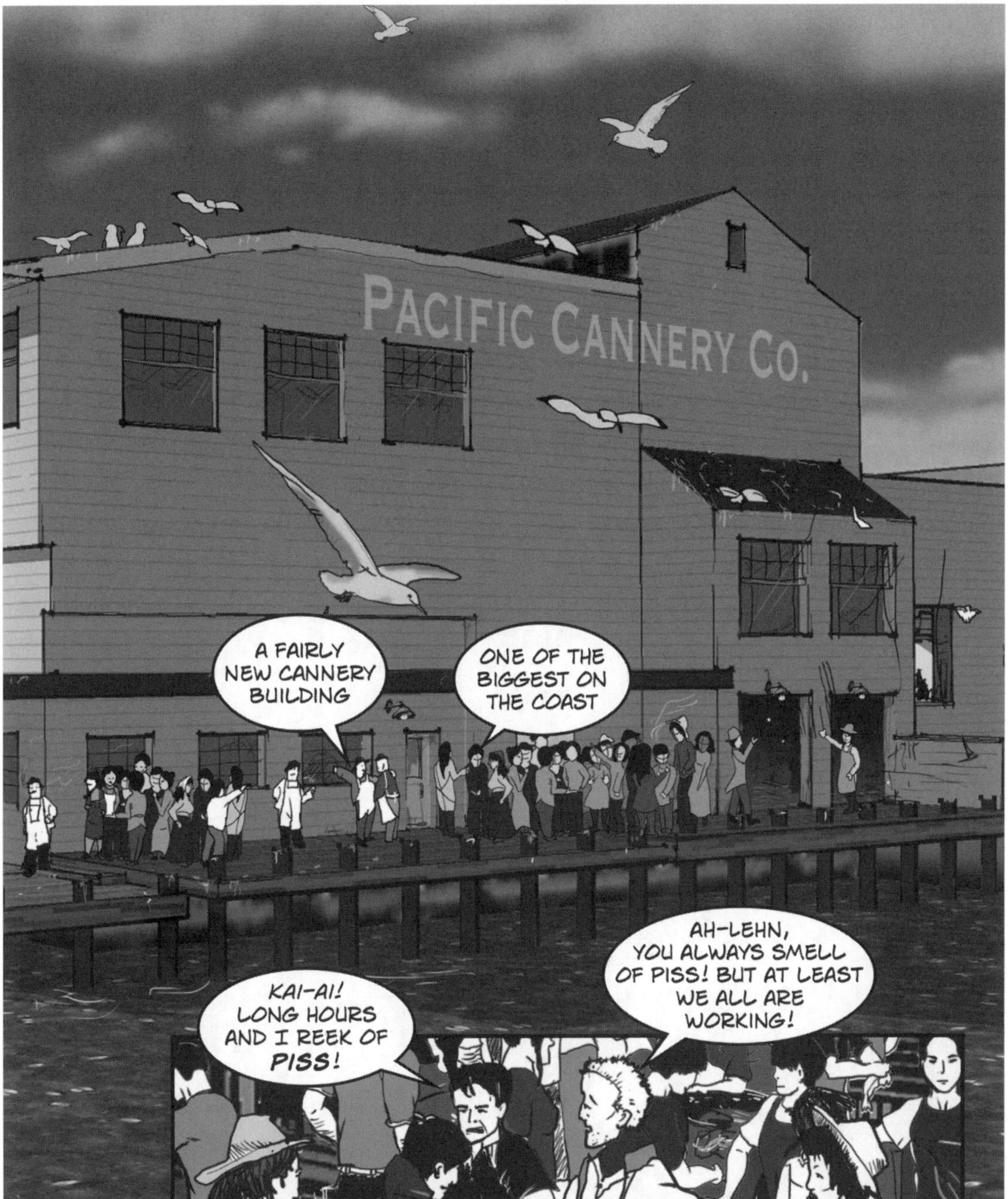
PACIFIC CANNERY CO.
A FAIRLY NEW CANNERY BUILDING
ONE OF THE BIGGEST ON THE COAST

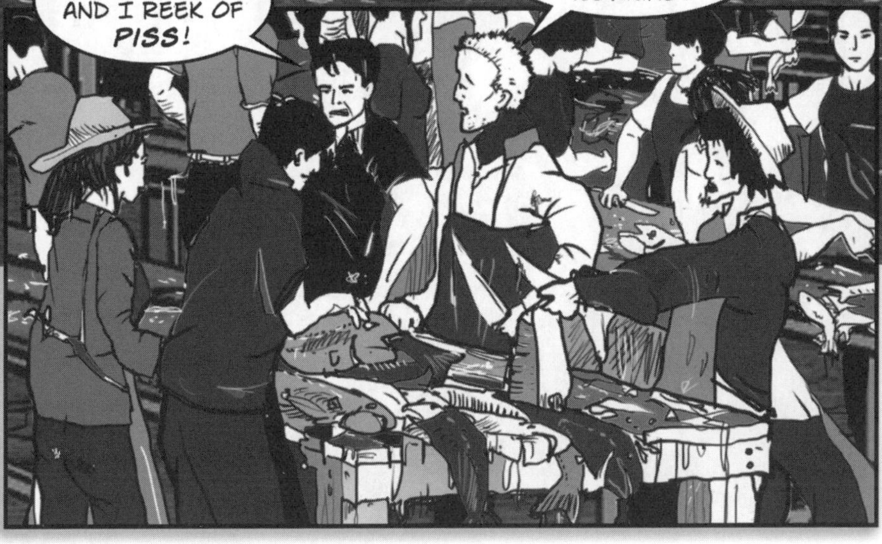
KAI-AI! LONG HOURS AND I REEK OF PISS!
AH-LEHN, YOU ALWAYS SMELL OF PISS! BUT AT LEAST WE ALL ARE WORKING!

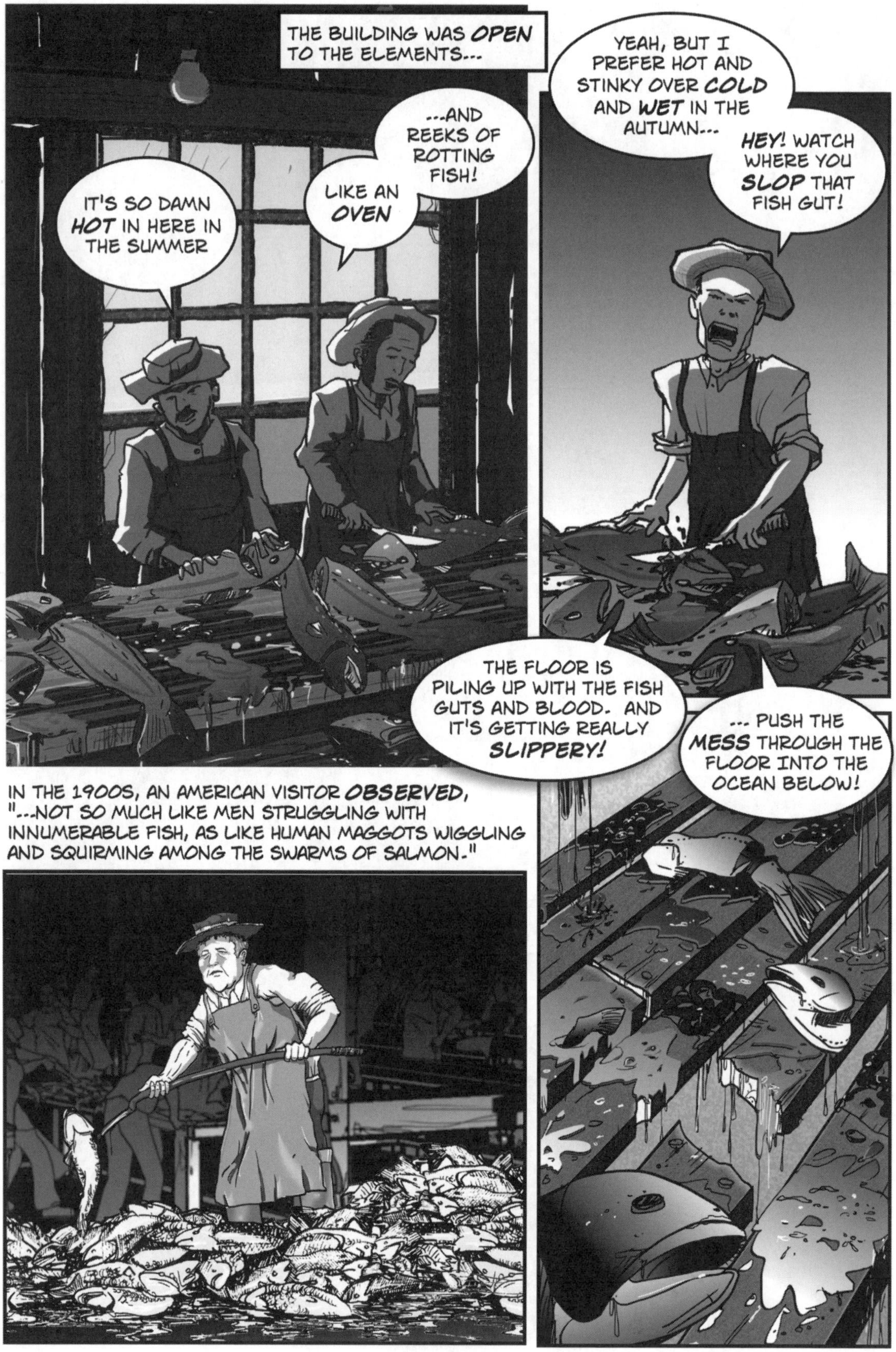
THE BUILDING WAS OPEN TO THE ELEMENTS...
IT'S SO DAMN HOT IN HERE IN THE SUMMER
LIKE AN OVEN
...AND REEKS OF ROTTING FISH!
YEAH, BUT I PREFER HOT AND STINKY OVER COLD AND WET IN THE AUTUMN...
HEY! WATCH WHERE YOU SLOP THAT FISH GUT!
THE FLOOR IS PILING UP WITH THE FISH GUTS AND BLOOD. AND IT'S GETTING REALLY SLIPPERY!
... PUSH THE MESS THROUGH THE FLOOR INTO THE OCEAN BELOW!
IN THE 1900S, AN AMERICAN VISITOR OBSERVED, "...NOT SO MUCH LIKE MEN STRUGGLING WITH INNUMERABLE FISH, AS LIKE HUMAN MAGGOTS WIGGLING AND SQUIRMING AMONG THE SWARMS OF SALMON."

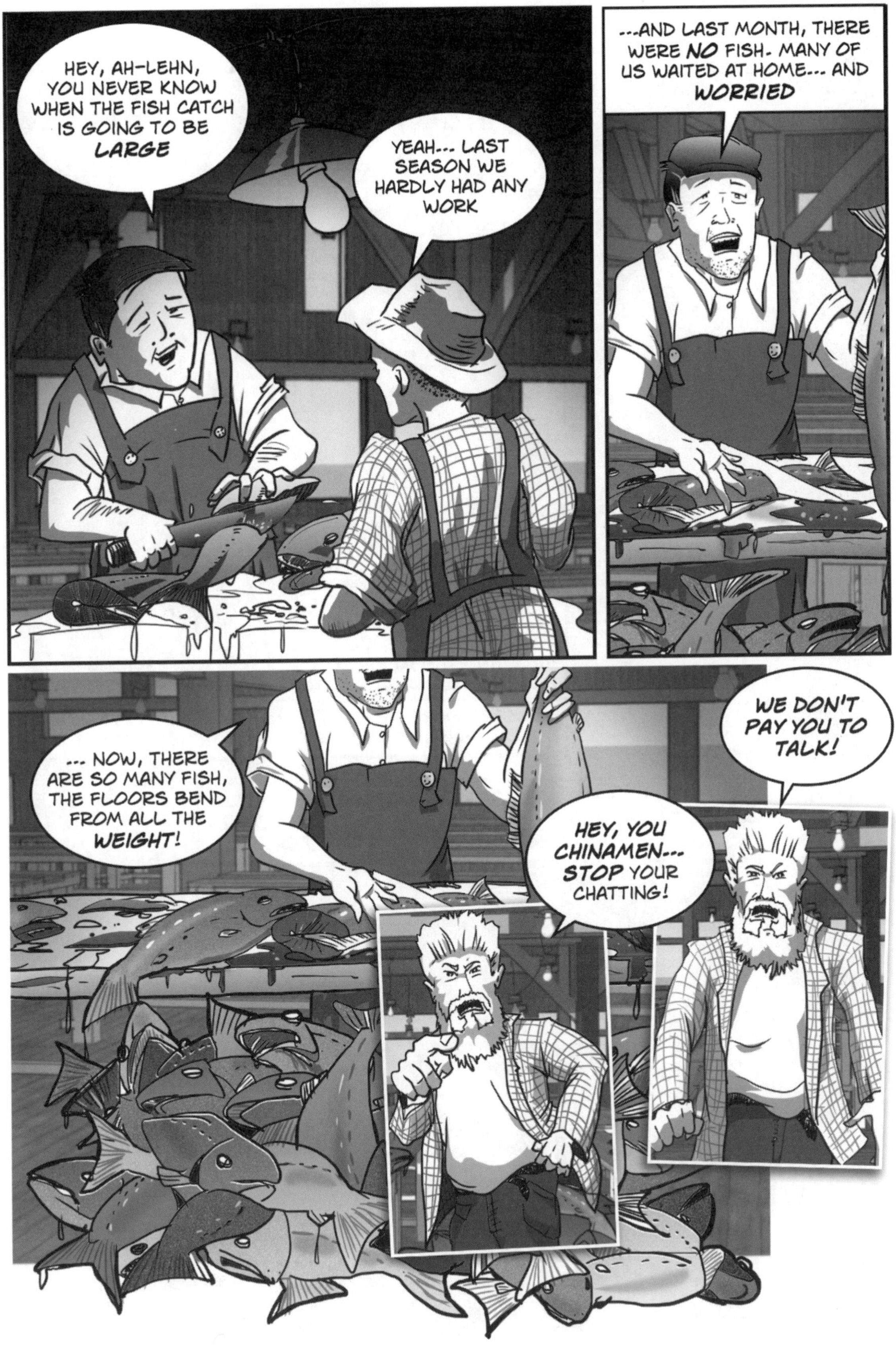
HEY, AH-LEHN, YOU NEVER KNOW WHEN THE FISH CATCH IS GOING TO BE **LARGE**
YEAH... LAST SEASON WE HARDLY HAD ANY WORK
...AND LAST MONTH, THERE WERE **NO** FISH. MANY OF US WAITED AT HOME... AND **WORRIED**
... NOW, THERE ARE SO MANY FISH, THE FLOORS BEND FROM ALL THE **WEIGHT!**
HEY, YOU CHINAMEN... STOP YOUR CHATTING!
WE DON'T PAY YOU TO TALK!

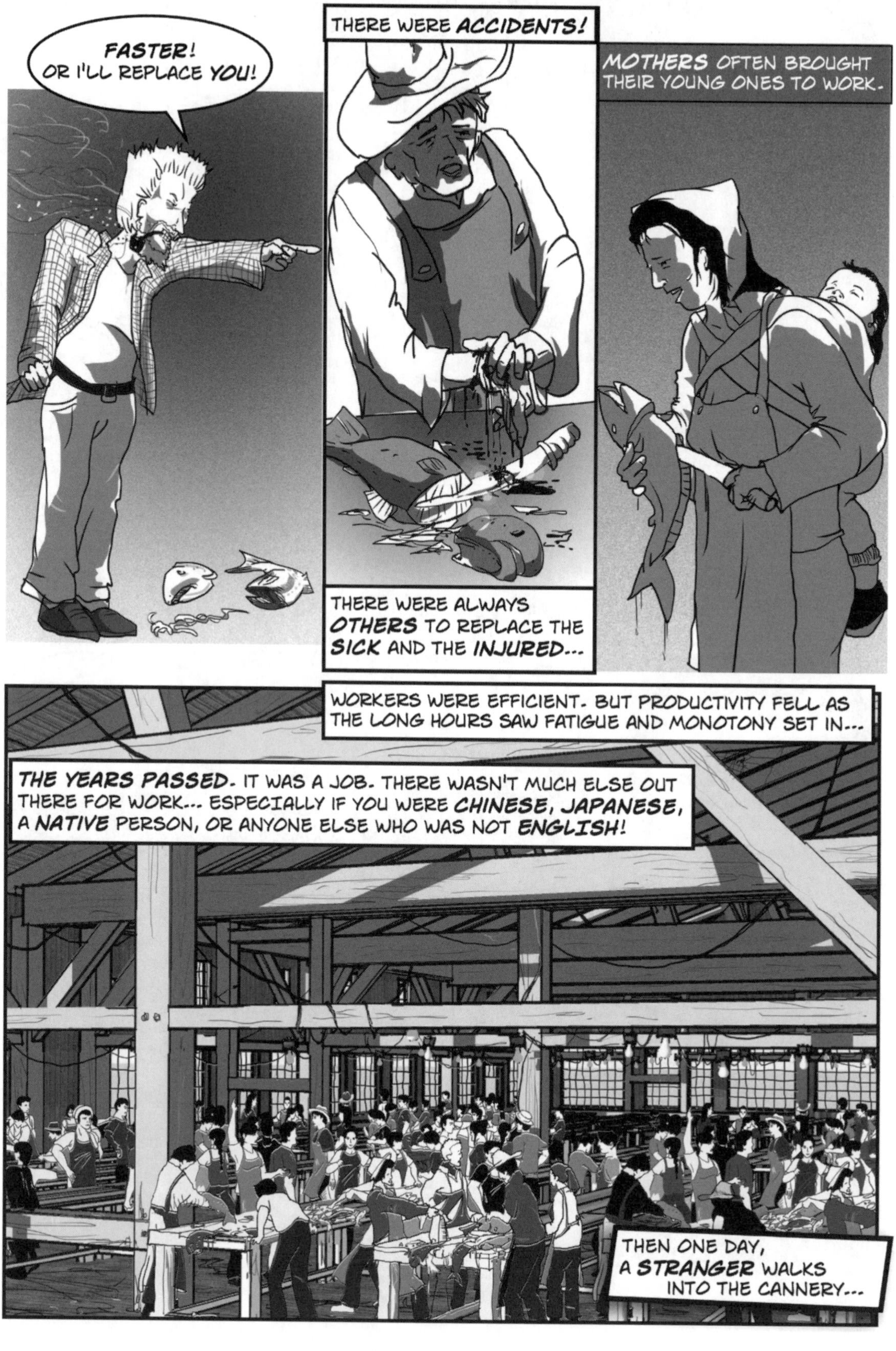
FASTER!
OR I'LL REPLACE YOU!
THERE WERE ACCIDENTS!
THERE WERE ALWAYS OTHERS TO REPLACE THE SICK AND THE INJURED...
MOTHERS OFTEN BROUGHT THEIR YOUNG ONES TO WORK.
WORKERS WERE EFFICIENT. BUT PRODUCTIVITY FELL AS THE LONG HOURS SAW FATIGUE AND MONOTONY SET IN...
THE YEARS PASSED. IT WAS A JOB. THERE WASN'T MUCH ELSE OUT THERE FOR WORK... ESPECIALLY IF YOU WERE CHINESE, JAPANESE, A NATIVE PERSON, OR ANYONE ELSE WHO WAS NOT ENGLISH!
THEN ONE DAY, A STRANGER WALKS INTO THE CANNERY...

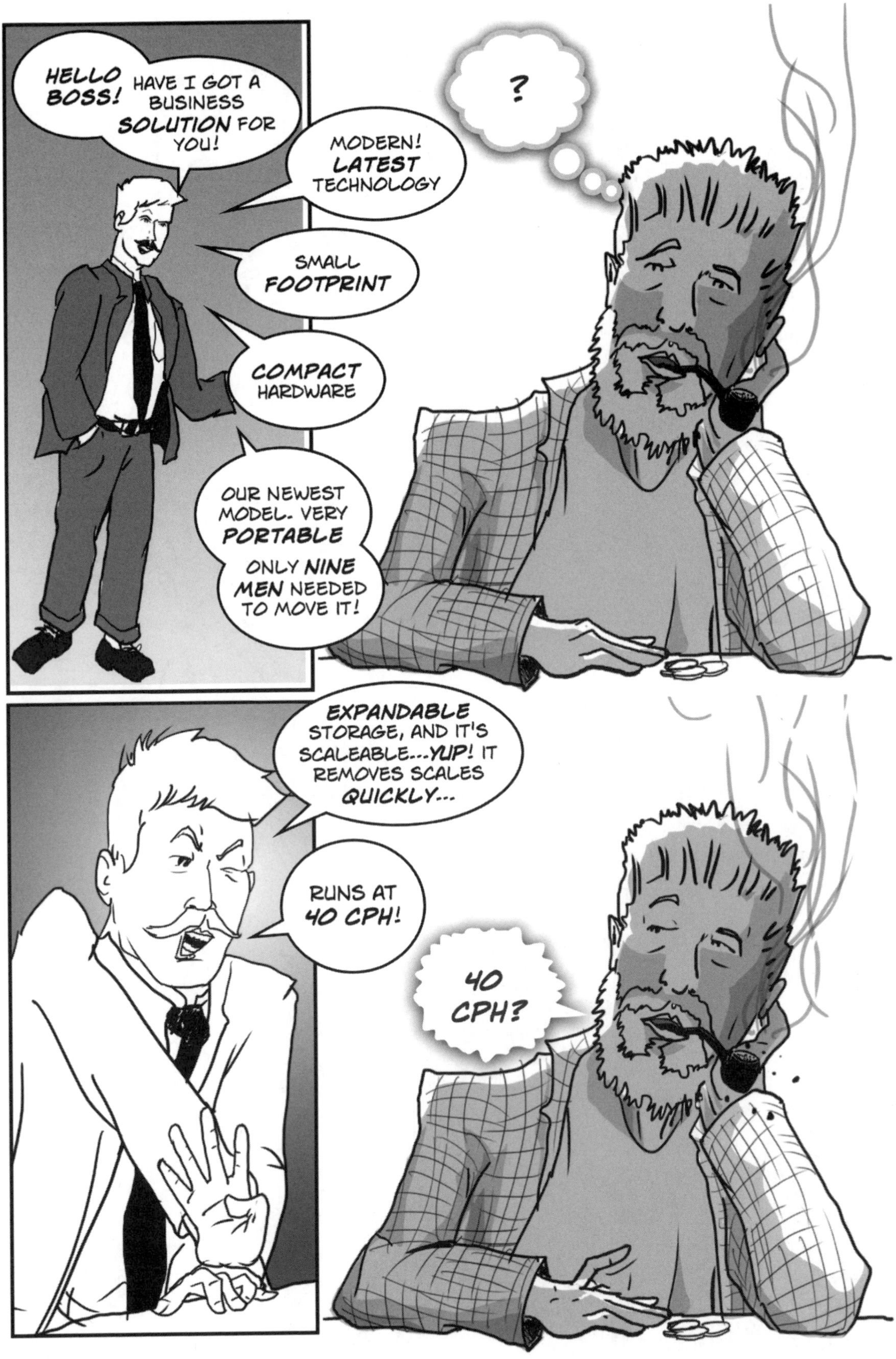
HELLO BOSS! HAVE I GOT A BUSINESS SOLUTION FOR YOU!
?
MODERN! LATEST TECHNOLOGY
SMALL FOOTPRINT
COMPACT HARDWARE
OUR NEWEST MODEL- VERY PORTABLE
ONLY NINE MEN NEEDED TO MOVE IT!
EXPANDABLE STORAGE, AND IT'S SCALEABLE...YUP! IT REMOVES SCALES QUICKLY...
RUNS AT 40 CPH!
40 CPH?

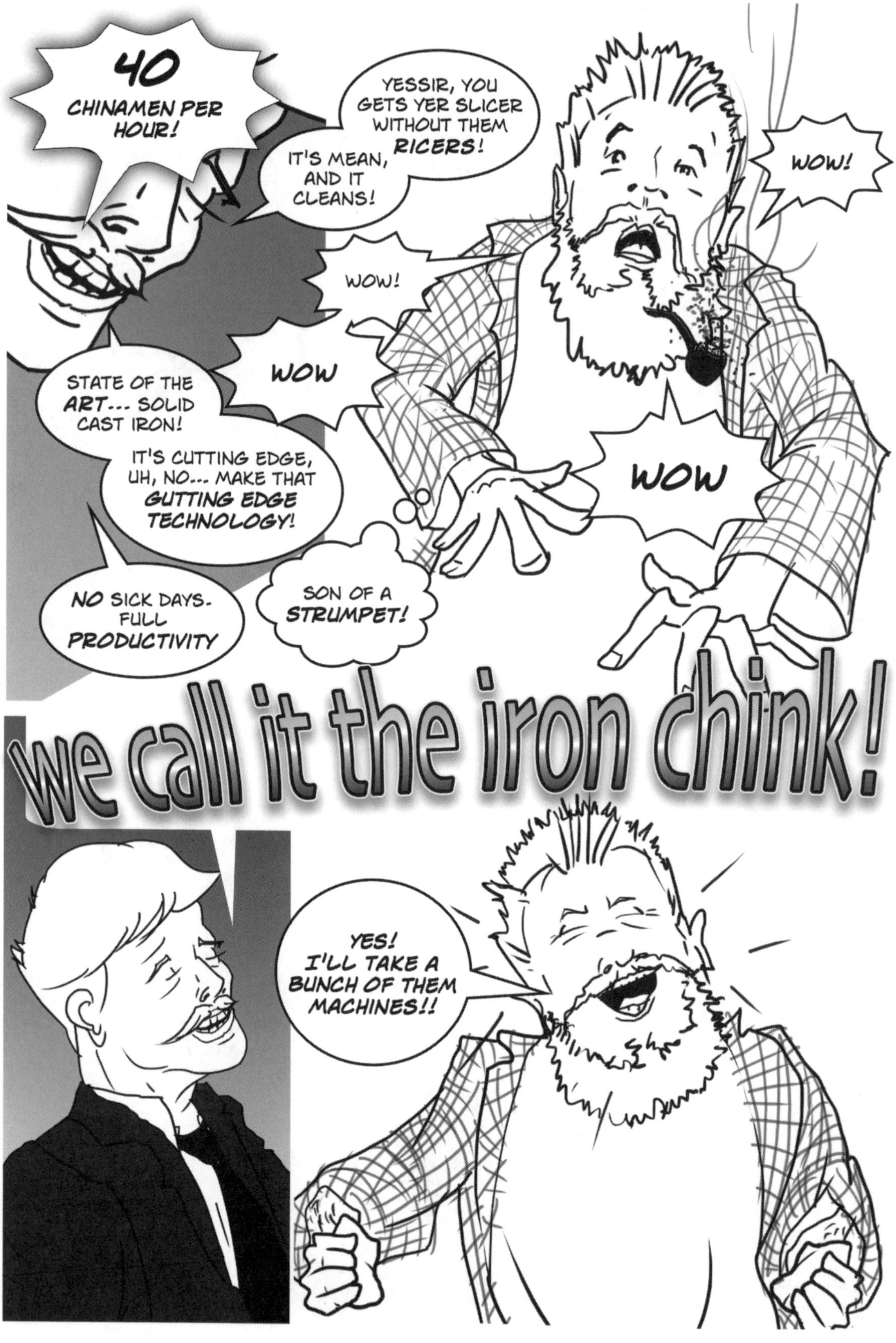
40 CHINAMEN PER HOUR!
YESSIR, YOU GETS YER SLICER WITHOUT THEM RICERS!
IT'S MEAN, AND IT CLEANS!
WOW!
WOW!
WOW
STATE OF THE ART... SOLID CAST IRON!
IT'S CUTTING EDGE, UH, NO... MAKE THAT GUTTING EDGE TECHNOLOGY!
WOW
NO SICK DAYS- FULL PRODUCTIVITY
SON OF A STRUMPET!
we call it the iron chink!
YES! I'LL TAKE A BUNCH OF THEM MACHINES!!

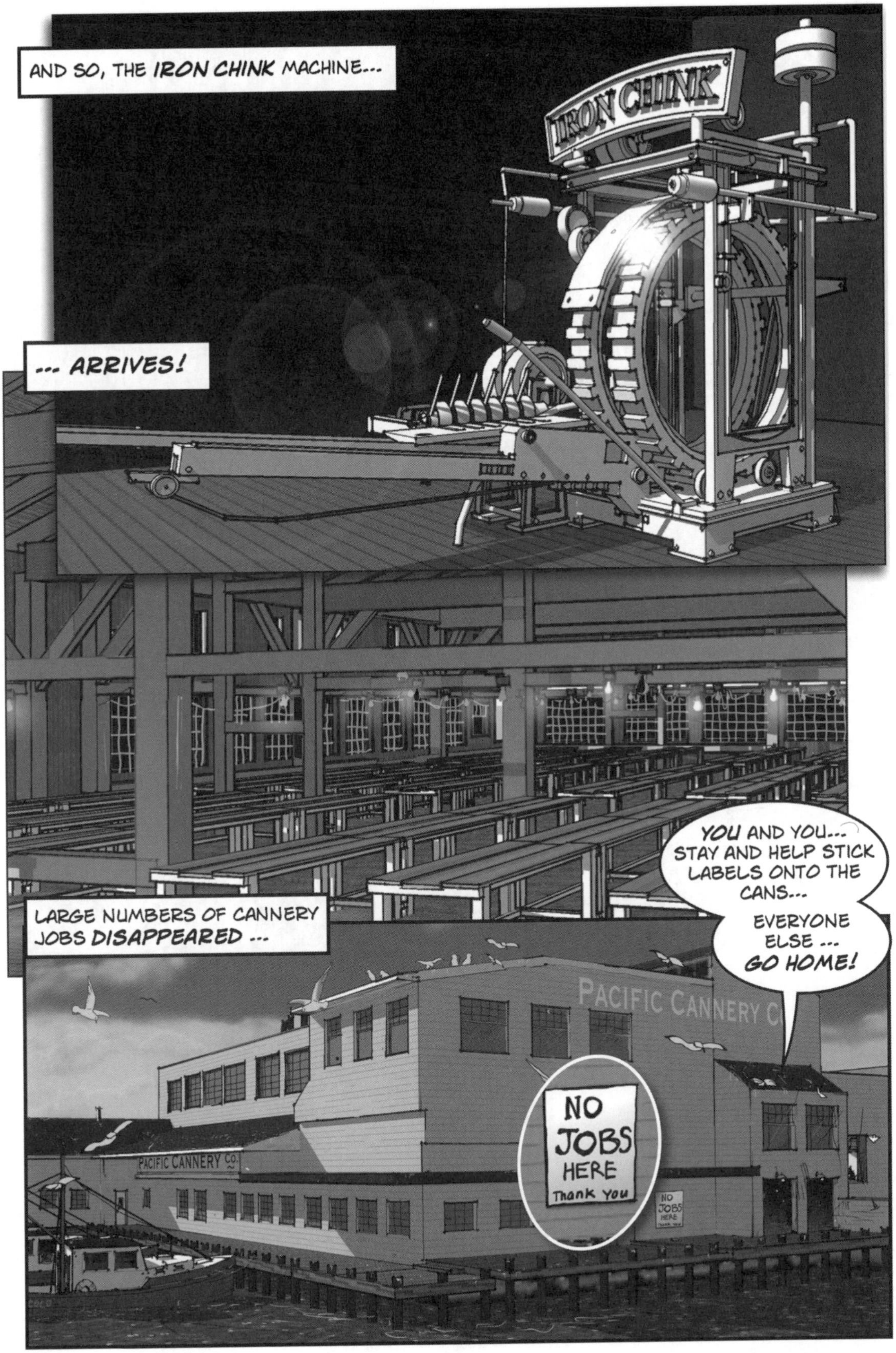
AND SO, THE IRON CHINK MACHINE...
IRON CHINK
... ARRIVES!
YOU AND YOU... STAY AND HELP STICK LABELS ONTO THE CANS...
EVERYONE ELSE ... GO HOME!
LARGE NUMBERS OF CANNERY JOBS DISAPPEARED ...
PACIFIC CANNERY CO.
PACIFIC CANNERY CO.
NO JOBS HERE Thank You

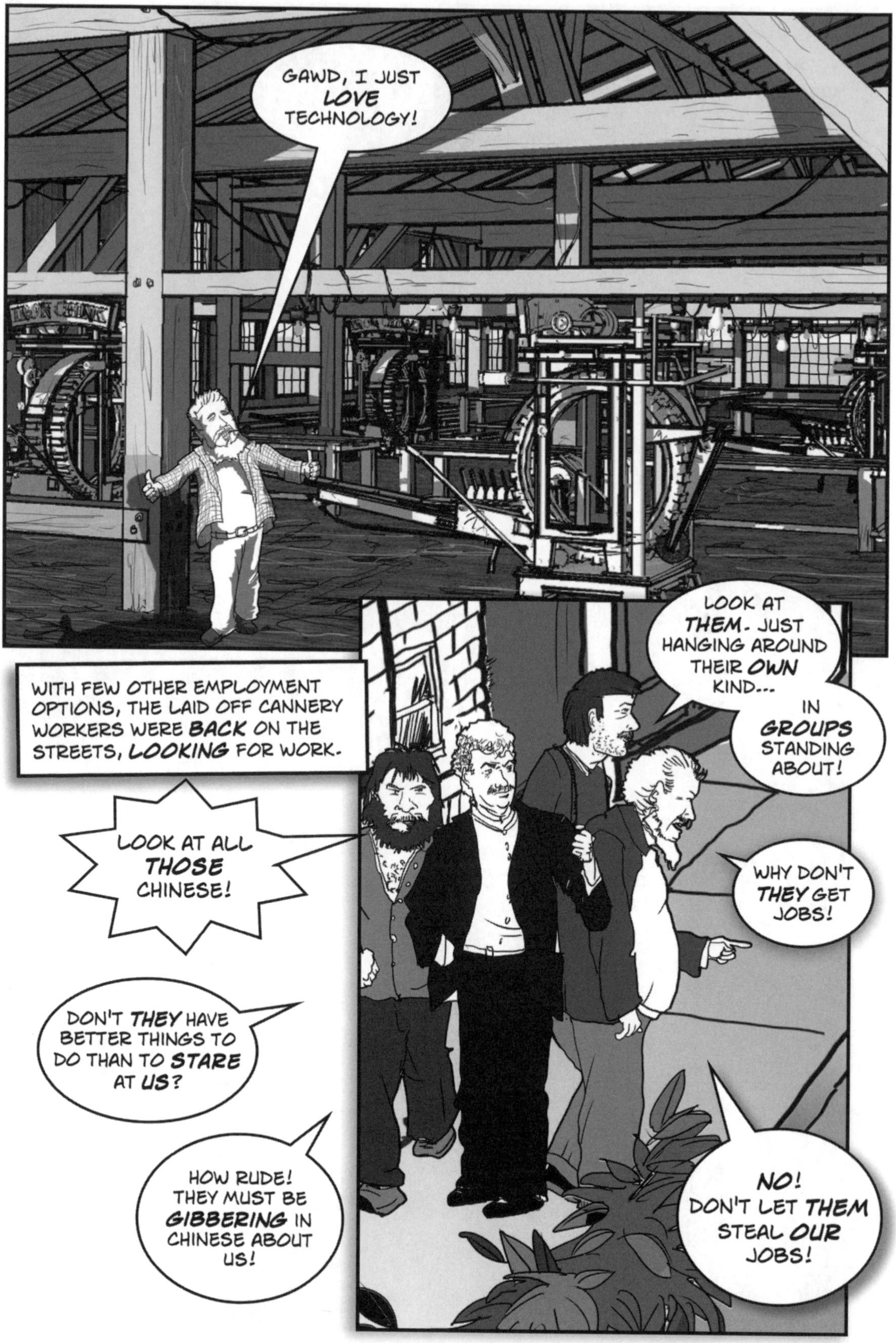
GAWD, I JUST LOVE TECHNOLOGY!
WITH FEW OTHER EMPLOYMENT OPTIONS, THE LAID OFF CANNERY WORKERS WERE BACK ON THE STREETS, LOOKING FOR WORK.
LOOK AT ALL THOSE CHINESE!
LOOK AT THEM. JUST HANGING AROUND THEIR OWN KIND...
IN GROUPS STANDING ABOUT!
WHY DON'T THEY GET JOBS!
DON'T THEY HAVE BETTER THINGS TO DO THAN TO STARE AT US?
HOW RUDE! THEY MUST BE GIBBERING IN CHINESE ABOUT US!
NO! DON'T LET THEM STEAL OUR JOBS!

CHAPTER 2 China, The Sick Man of Asia

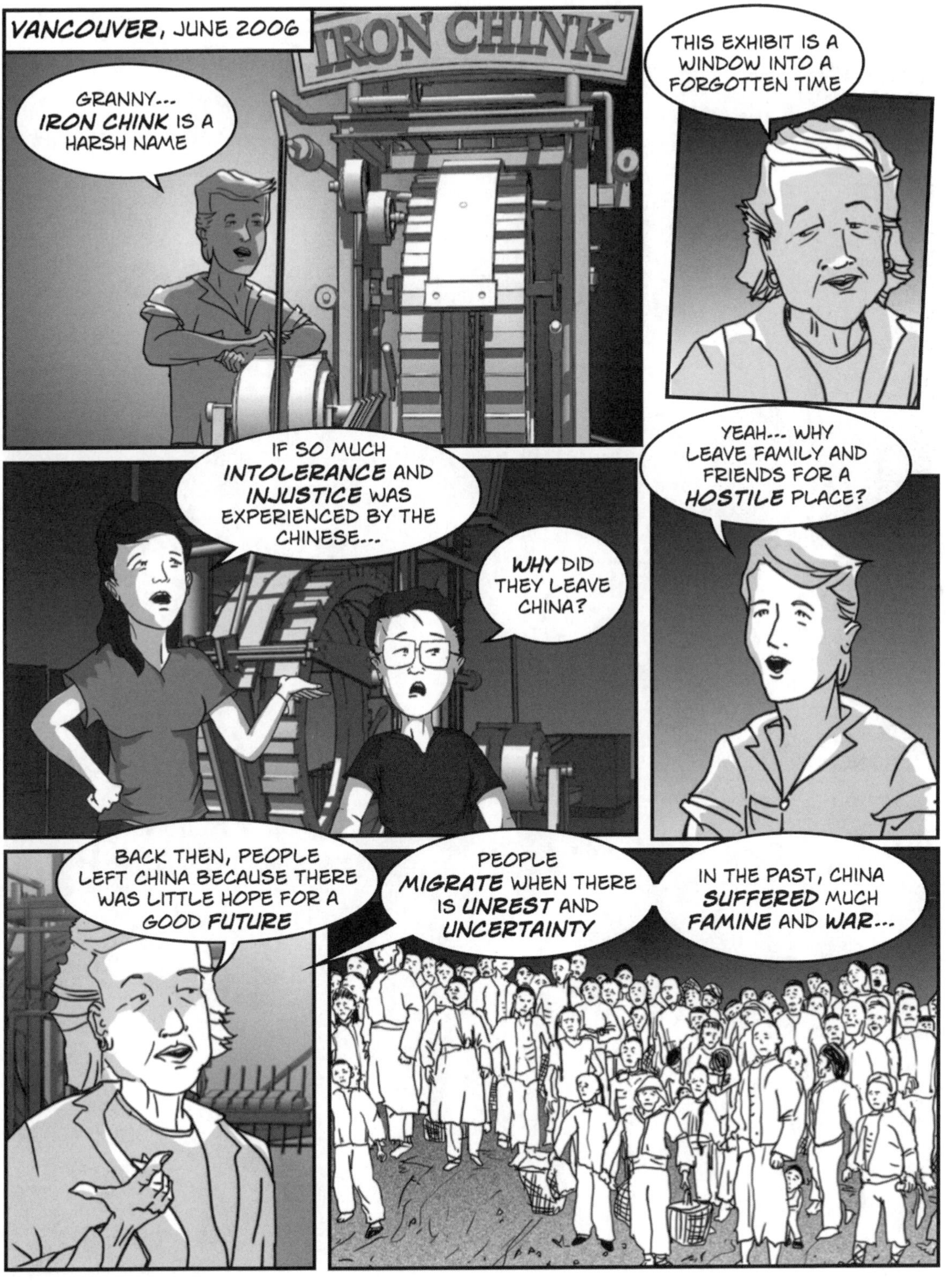

VANCOUVER, JUNE 2006
IRON CHINK
GRANNY... IRON CHINK IS A HARSH NAME
THIS EXHIBIT IS A WINDOW INTO A FORGOTTEN TIME
IF SO MUCH INTOLERANCE AND INJUSTICE WAS EXPERIENCED BY THE CHINESE...
WHY DID THEY LEAVE CHINA?
YEAH... WHY LEAVE FAMILY AND FRIENDS FOR A HOSTILE PLACE?
BACK THEN, PEOPLE LEFT CHINA BECAUSE THERE WAS LITTLE HOPE FOR A GOOD FUTURE
PEOPLE MIGRATE WHEN THERE IS UNREST AND UNCERTAINTY
IN THE PAST, CHINA SUFFERED MUCH FAMINE AND WAR...

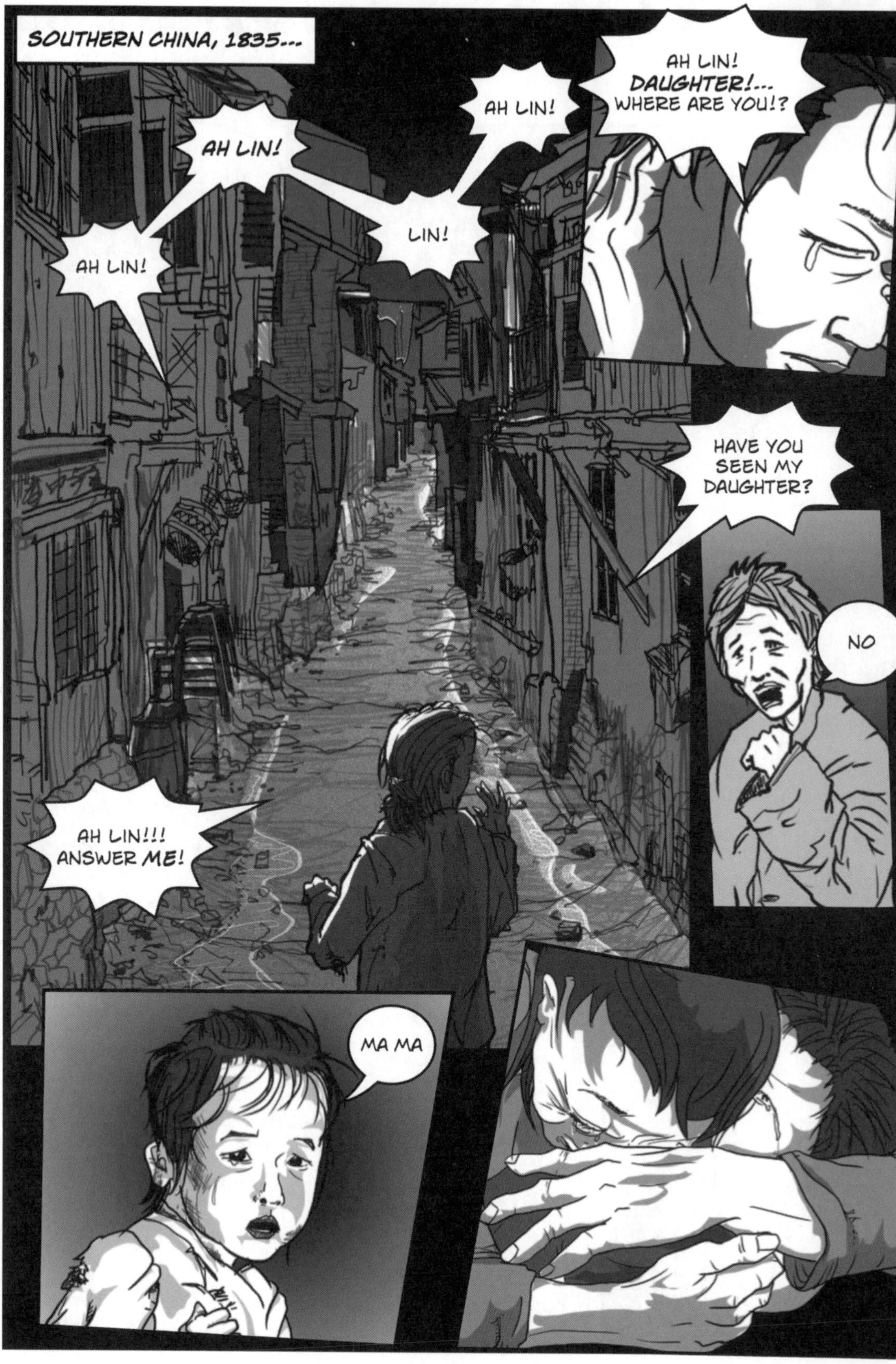
SOUTHERN CHINA, 1835...
AH LIN!
AH LIN!
LIN!
AH LIN!
AH LIN! DAUGHTER!... WHERE ARE YOU!?
HAVE YOU SEEN MY DAUGHTER?
NO
AH LIN!!! ANSWER ME!
MA MA

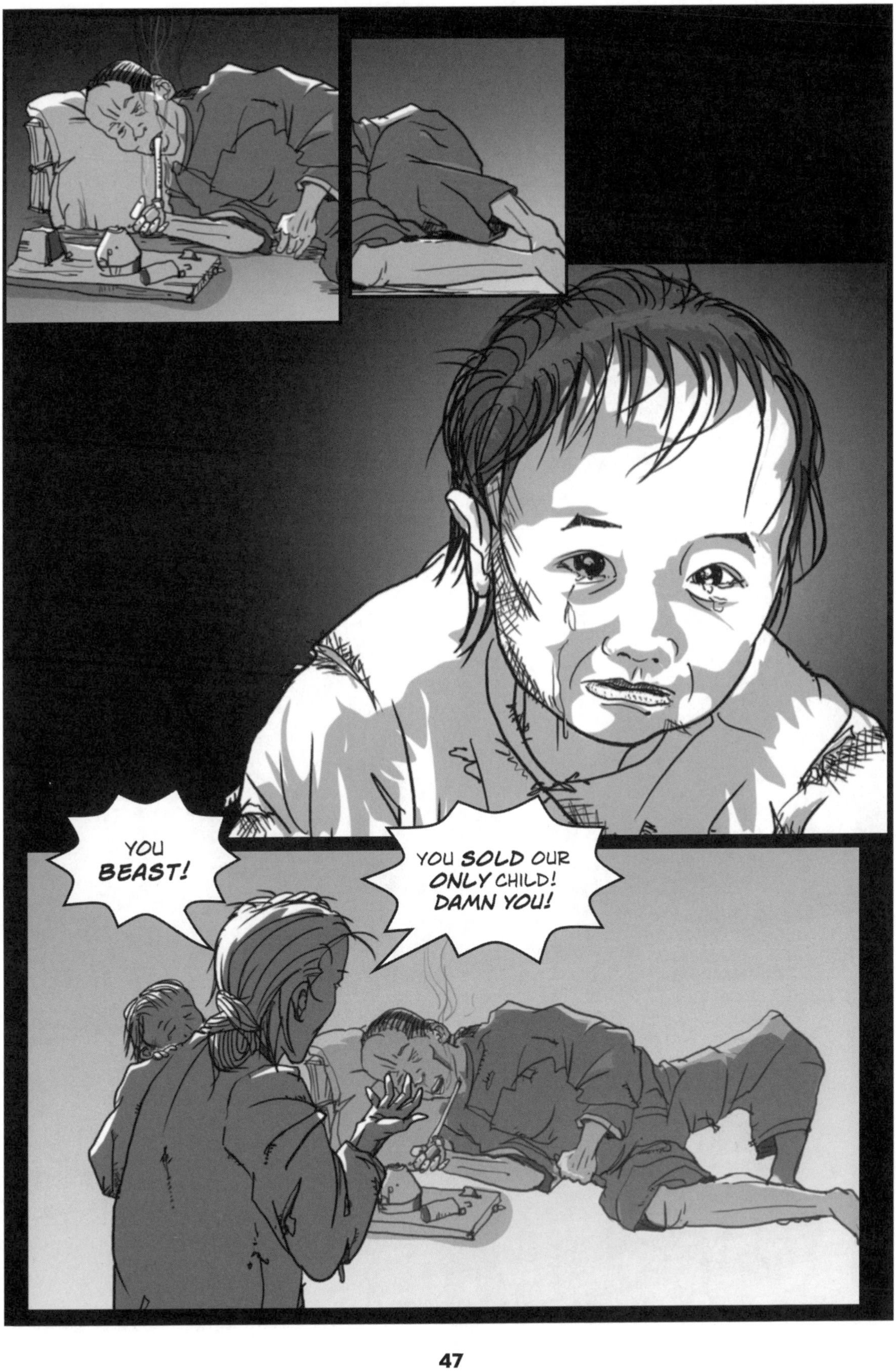
YOU BEAST!
YOU SOLD OUR ONLY CHILD! DAMN YOU!

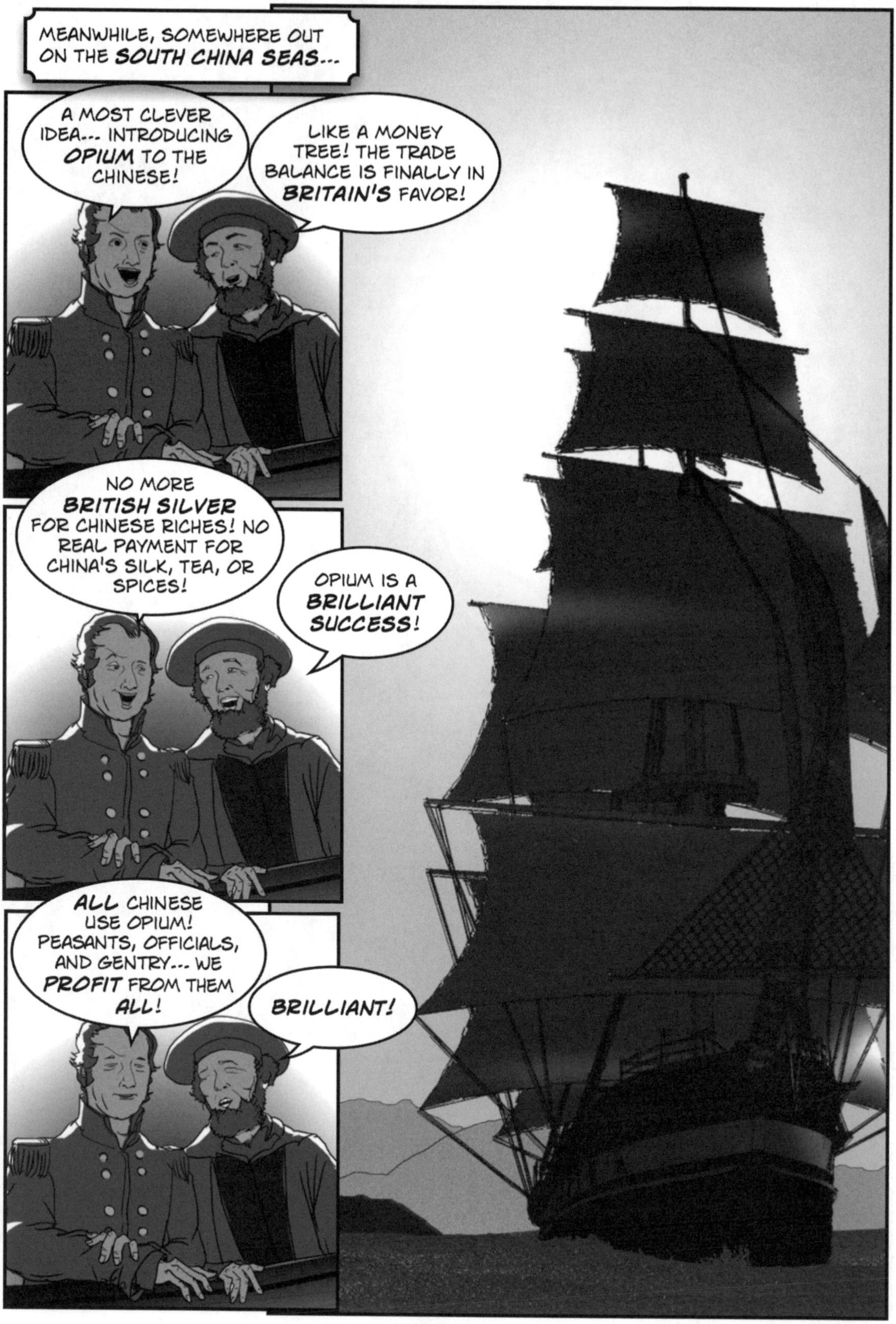
MEANWHILE, SOMEWHERE OUT ON THE SOUTH CHINA SEAS...
A MOST CLEVER IDEA... INTRODUCING OPIUM TO THE CHINESE!
LIKE A MONEY TREE! THE TRADE BALANCE IS FINALLY IN BRITAIN'S FAVOR!
NO MORE BRITISH SILVER FOR CHINESE RICHES! NO REAL PAYMENT FOR CHINA'S SILK, TEA, OR SPICES!
OPIUM IS A BRILLIANT SUCCESS!
ALL CHINESE USE OPIUM! PEASANTS, OFFICIALS, AND GENTRY... WE PROFIT FROM THEM ALL!
BRILLIANT!

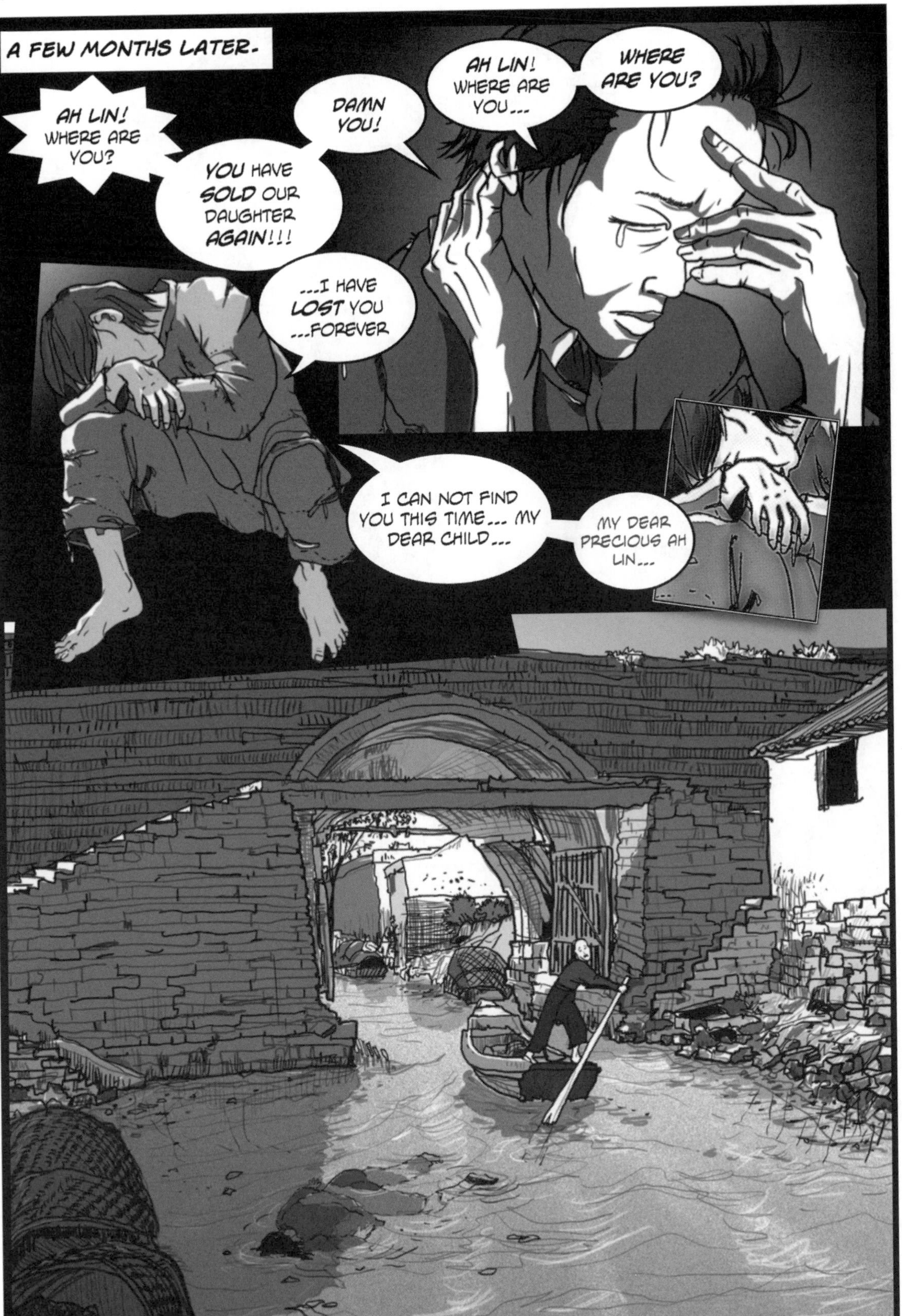
A FEW MONTHS LATER.
AH LIN! WHERE ARE YOU?
YOU HAVE SOLD OUR DAUGHTER AGAIN!!!
DAMN YOU!
AH LIN! WHERE ARE YOU...
WHERE ARE YOU?
...I HAVE LOST YOU ...FOREVER
I CAN NOT FIND YOU THIS TIME... MY DEAR CHILD...
MY DEAR PRECIOUS AH LIN...

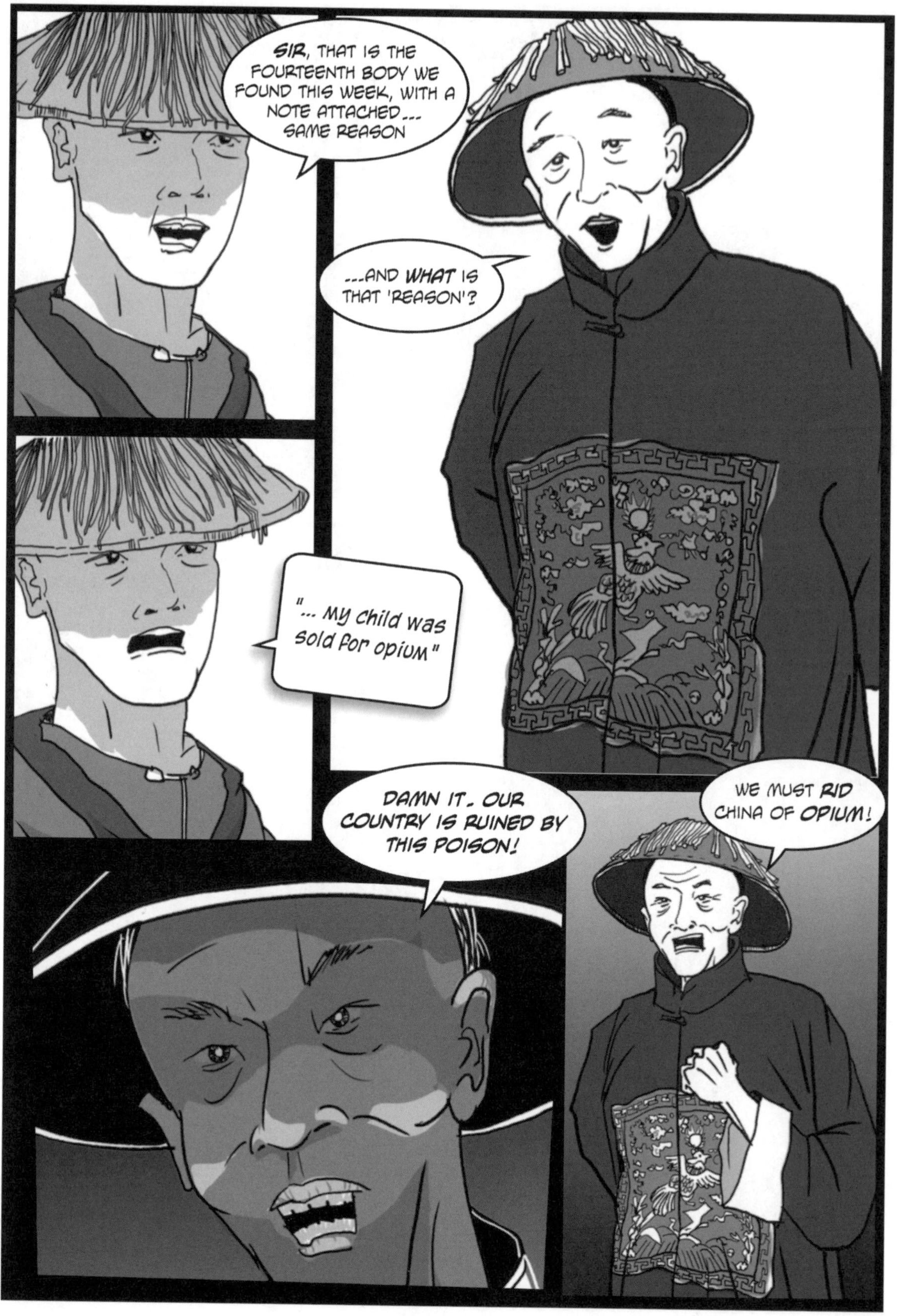
SIR, THAT IS THE FOURTEENTH BODY WE FOUND THIS WEEK, WITH A NOTE ATTACHED... SAME REASON
...AND WHAT IS THAT 'REASON'?
"... my child was sold for opium"
DAMN IT. OUR COUNTRY IS RUINED BY THIS POISON!
WE MUST RID CHINA OF OPIUM!

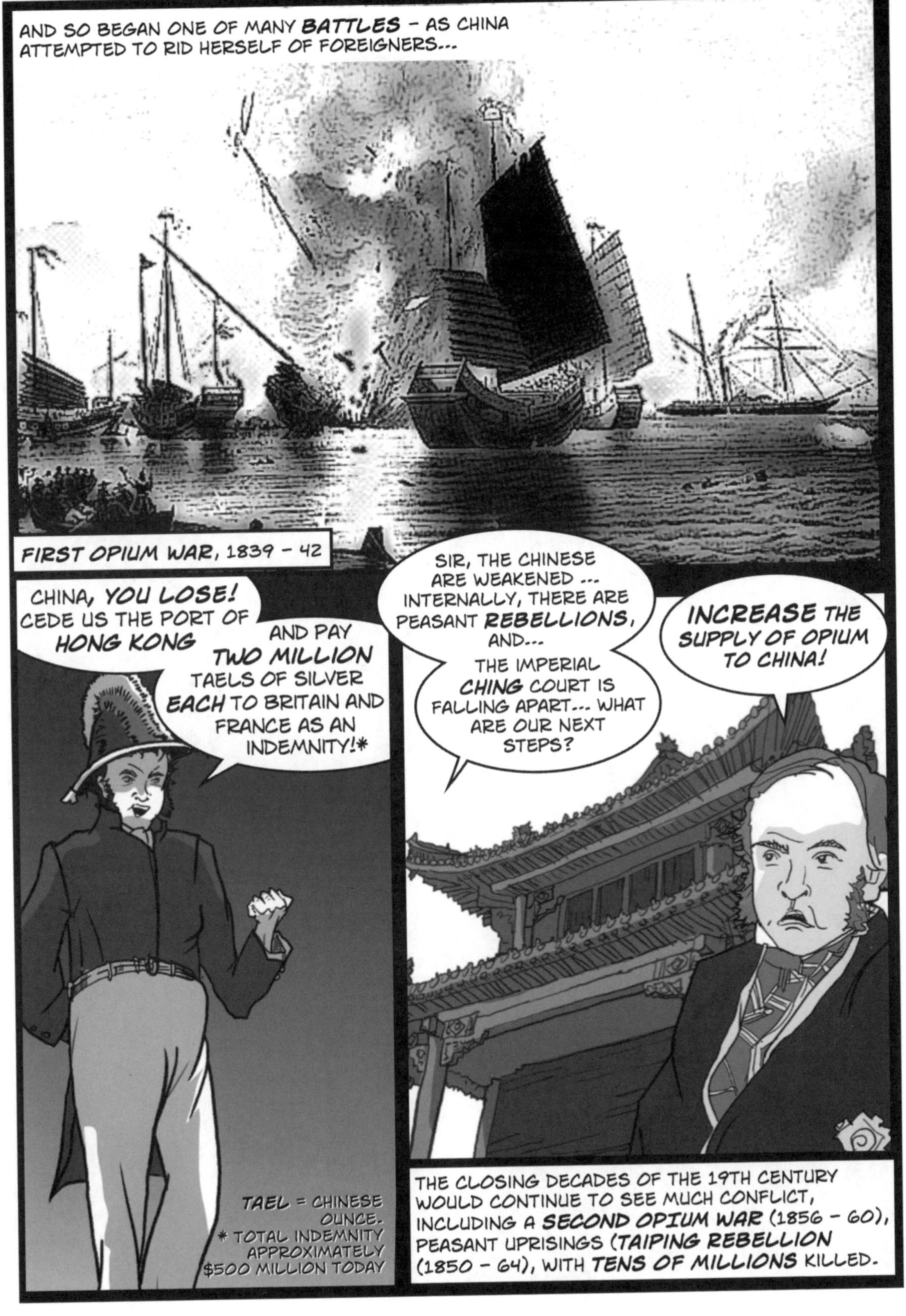
AND SO BEGAN ONE OF MANY BATTLES – AS CHINA ATTEMPTED TO RID HERSELF OF FOREIGNERS...
FIRST OPIUM WAR, 1839 – 42
CHINA, YOU LOSE! CEDE US THE PORT OF HONG KONG
AND PAY TWO MILLION TAELS OF SILVER EACH TO BRITAIN AND FRANCE AS AN INDEMNITY!*
TAEL = CHINESE OUNCE.
* TOTAL INDEMNITY APPROXIMATELY $500 MILLION TODAY
SIR, THE CHINESE ARE WEAKENED ... INTERNALLY, THERE ARE PEASANT REBELLIONS, AND...
THE IMPERIAL CHING COURT IS FALLING APART... WHAT ARE OUR NEXT STEPS?
INCREASE THE SUPPLY OF OPIUM TO CHINA!
THE CLOSING DECADES OF THE 19TH CENTURY WOULD CONTINUE TO SEE MUCH CONFLICT, INCLUDING A SECOND OPIUM WAR (1856 – 60), PEASANT UPRISINGS (TAIPING REBELLION (1850 – 64), WITH TENS OF MILLIONS KILLED.

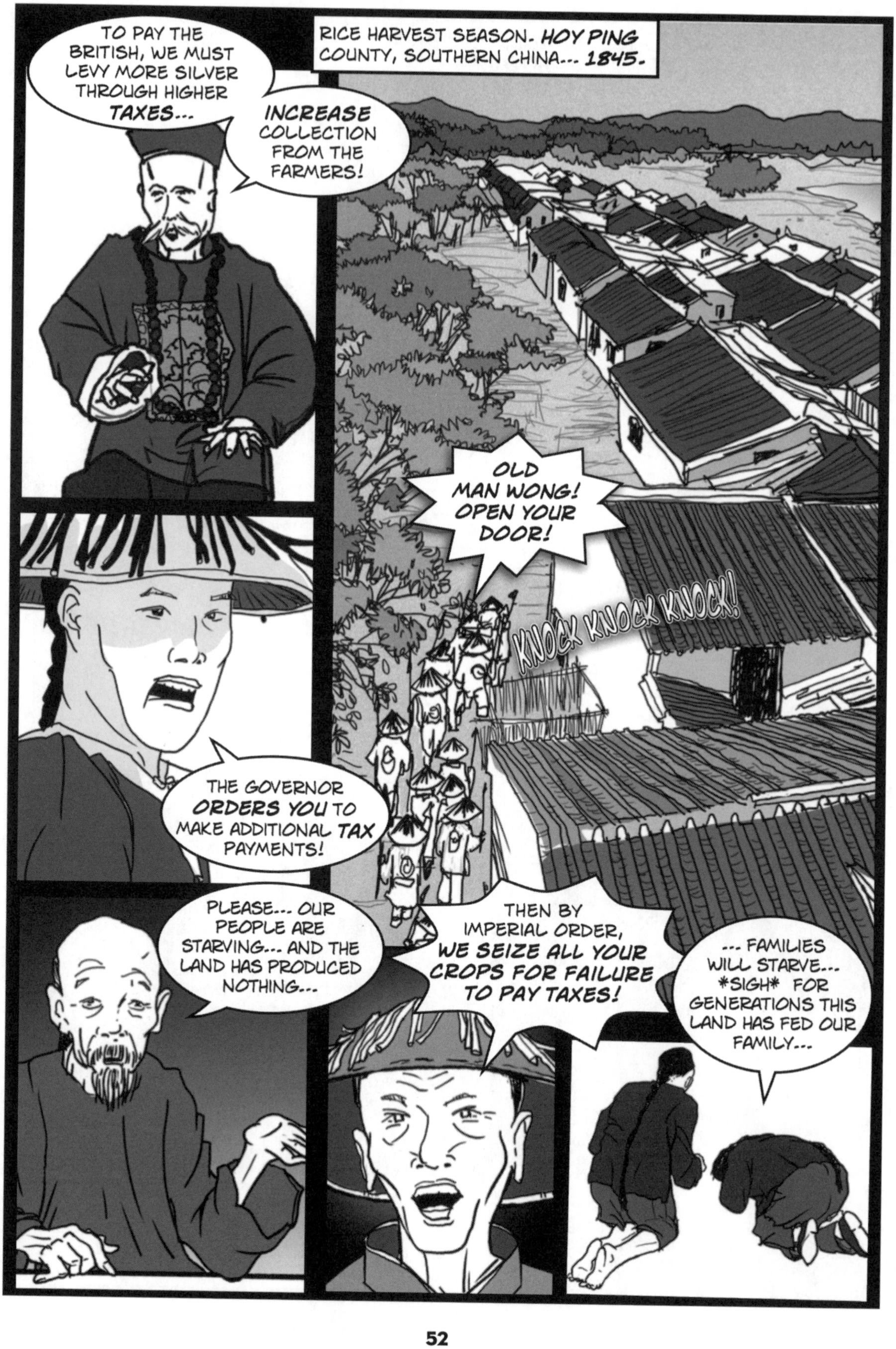
TO PAY THE BRITISH, WE MUST LEVY MORE SILVER THROUGH HIGHER TAXES...
INCREASE COLLECTION FROM THE FARMERS!
RICE HARVEST SEASON. HOY PING COUNTY, SOUTHERN CHINA... 1845.
OLD MAN WONG! OPEN YOUR DOOR!
KNOCK KNOCK KNOCK!
THE GOVERNOR ORDERS YOU TO MAKE ADDITIONAL TAX PAYMENTS!
PLEASE... OUR PEOPLE ARE STARVING... AND THE LAND HAS PRODUCED NOTHING...
THEN BY IMPERIAL ORDER, WE SEIZE ALL YOUR CROPS FOR FAILURE TO PAY TAXES!
... FAMILIES WILL STARVE... *SIGH* FOR GENERATIONS THIS LAND HAS FED OUR FAMILY...

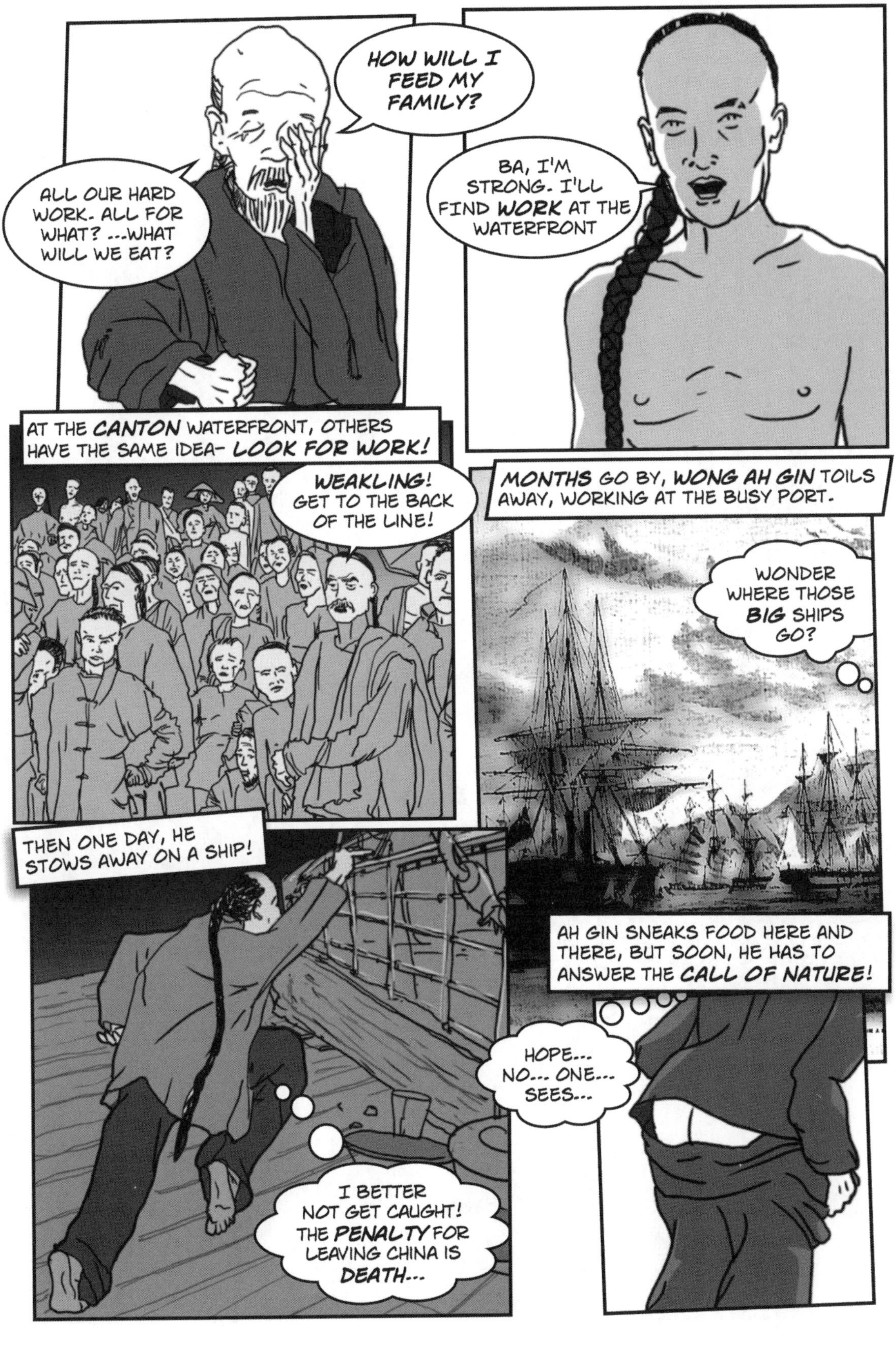
HOW WILL I FEED MY FAMILY?
ALL OUR HARD WORK- ALL FOR WHAT? ---WHAT WILL WE EAT?
BA, I'M STRONG. I'LL FIND WORK AT THE WATERFRONT
AT THE CANTON WATERFRONT, OTHERS HAVE THE SAME IDEA- LOOK FOR WORK!
WEAKLING! GET TO THE BACK OF THE LINE!
MONTHS GO BY, WONG AH GIN TOILS AWAY, WORKING AT THE BUSY PORT.
WONDER WHERE THOSE BIG SHIPS GO?
THEN ONE DAY, HE STOWS AWAY ON A SHIP!
I BETTER NOT GET CAUGHT! THE PENALTY FOR LEAVING CHINA IS DEATH...
AH GIN SNEAKS FOOD HERE AND THERE, BUT SOON, HE HAS TO ANSWER THE CALL OF NATURE!
HOPE... NO... ONE... SEES...

CHAPTER 3 Escape to Gold Mountain

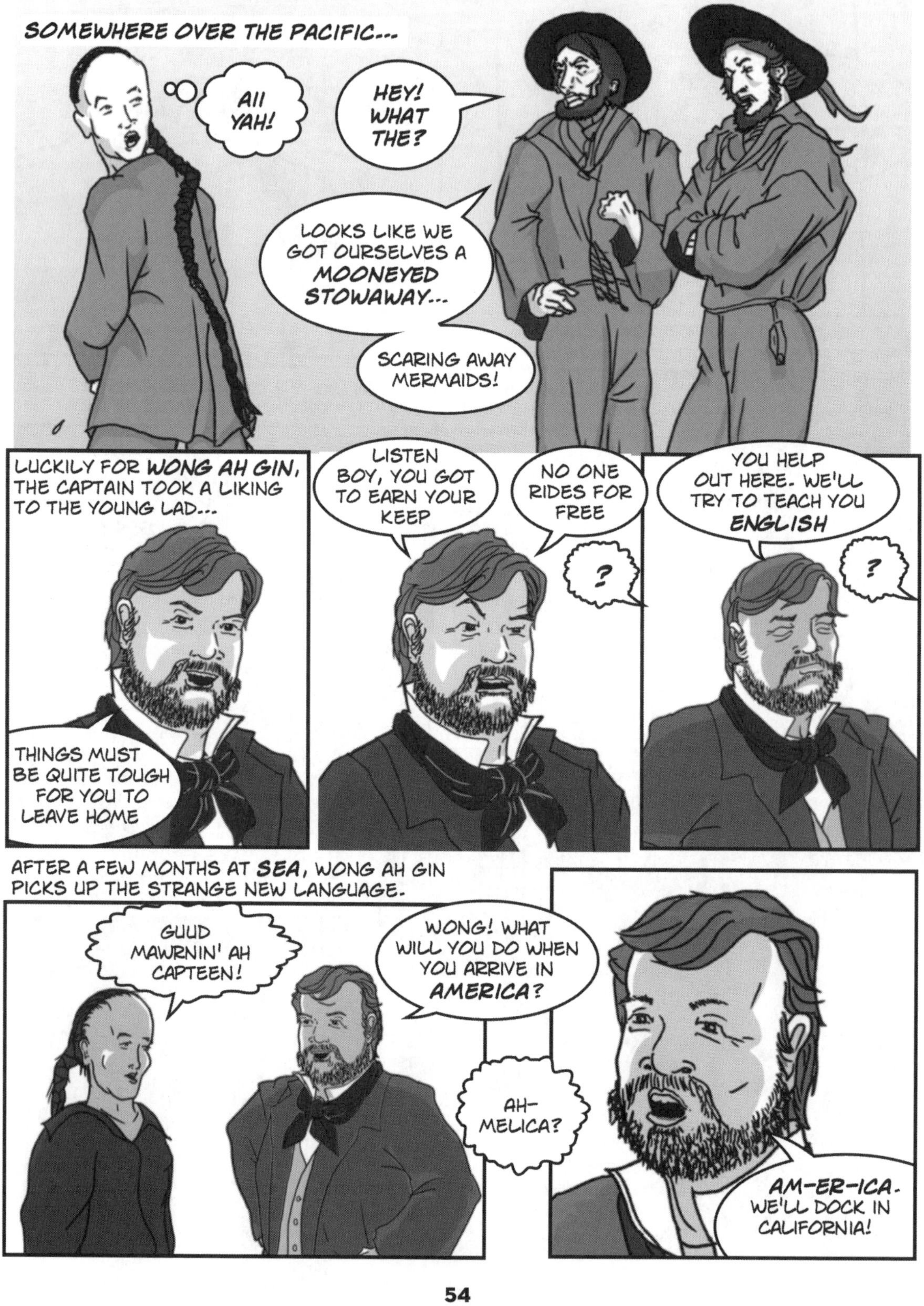
SOMEWHERE OVER THE PACIFIC...
AII YAH!
HEY! WHAT THE?
LOOKS LIKE WE GOT OURSELVES A MOONEYED STOWAWAY...
SCARING AWAY MERMAIDS!
LUCKILY FOR WONG AH GIN, THE CAPTAIN TOOK A LIKING TO THE YOUNG LAD...
THINGS MUST BE QUITE TOUGH FOR YOU TO LEAVE HOME
LISTEN BOY, YOU GOT TO EARN YOUR KEEP
NO ONE RIDES FOR FREE
?
YOU HELP OUT HERE. WE'LL TRY TO TEACH YOU ENGLISH
?
AFTER A FEW MONTHS AT SEA, WONG AH GIN PICKS UP THE STRANGE NEW LANGUAGE.
GUUD MAWRNIN' AH CAPTEEN!
WONG! WHAT WILL YOU DO WHEN YOU ARRIVE IN AMERICA?
AH-MELICA?
AM-ER-ICA. WE'LL DOCK IN CALIFORNIA!

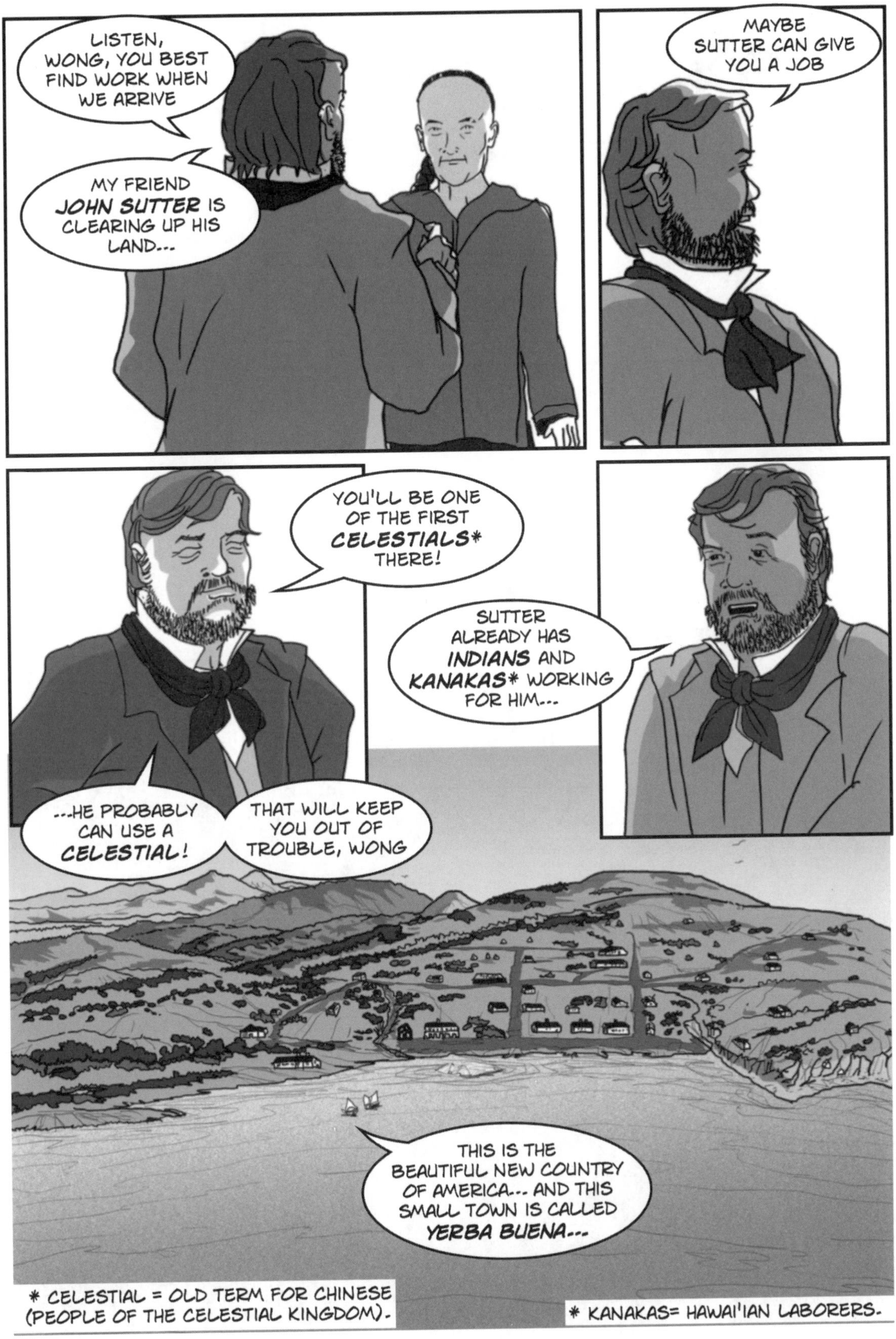
LISTEN, WONG, YOU BEST FIND WORK WHEN WE ARRIVE
MY FRIEND JOHN SUTTER IS CLEARING UP HIS LAND...
MAYBE SUTTER CAN GIVE YOU A JOB
YOU'LL BE ONE OF THE FIRST CELESTIALS* THERE!
SUTTER ALREADY HAS INDIANS AND KANAKAS* WORKING FOR HIM...
...HE PROBABLY CAN USE A CELESTIAL!
THAT WILL KEEP YOU OUT OF TROUBLE, WONG
THIS IS THE BEAUTIFUL NEW COUNTRY OF AMERICA... AND THIS SMALL TOWN IS CALLED YERBA BUENA...

* CELESTIAL = OLD TERM FOR CHINESE (PEOPLE OF THE CELESTIAL KINGDOM).

* KANAKAS= HAWAI'IAN LABORERS.

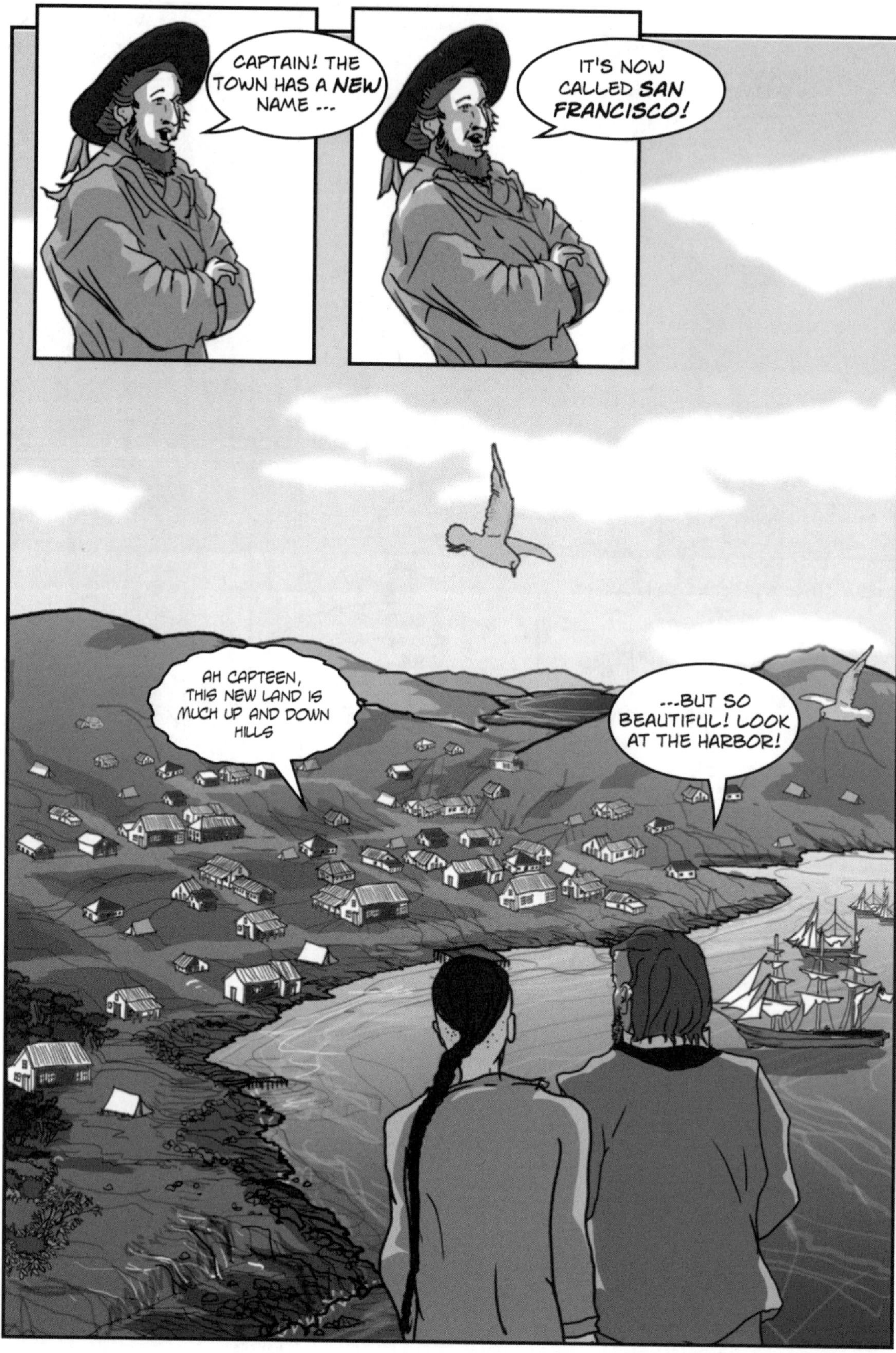
CAPTAIN! THE TOWN HAS A NEW NAME ---
IT'S NOW CALLED SAN FRANCISCO!
AH CAPTEEN, THIS NEW LAND IS MUCH UP AND DOWN HILLS
---BUT SO BEAUTIFUL! LOOK AT THE HARBOR!

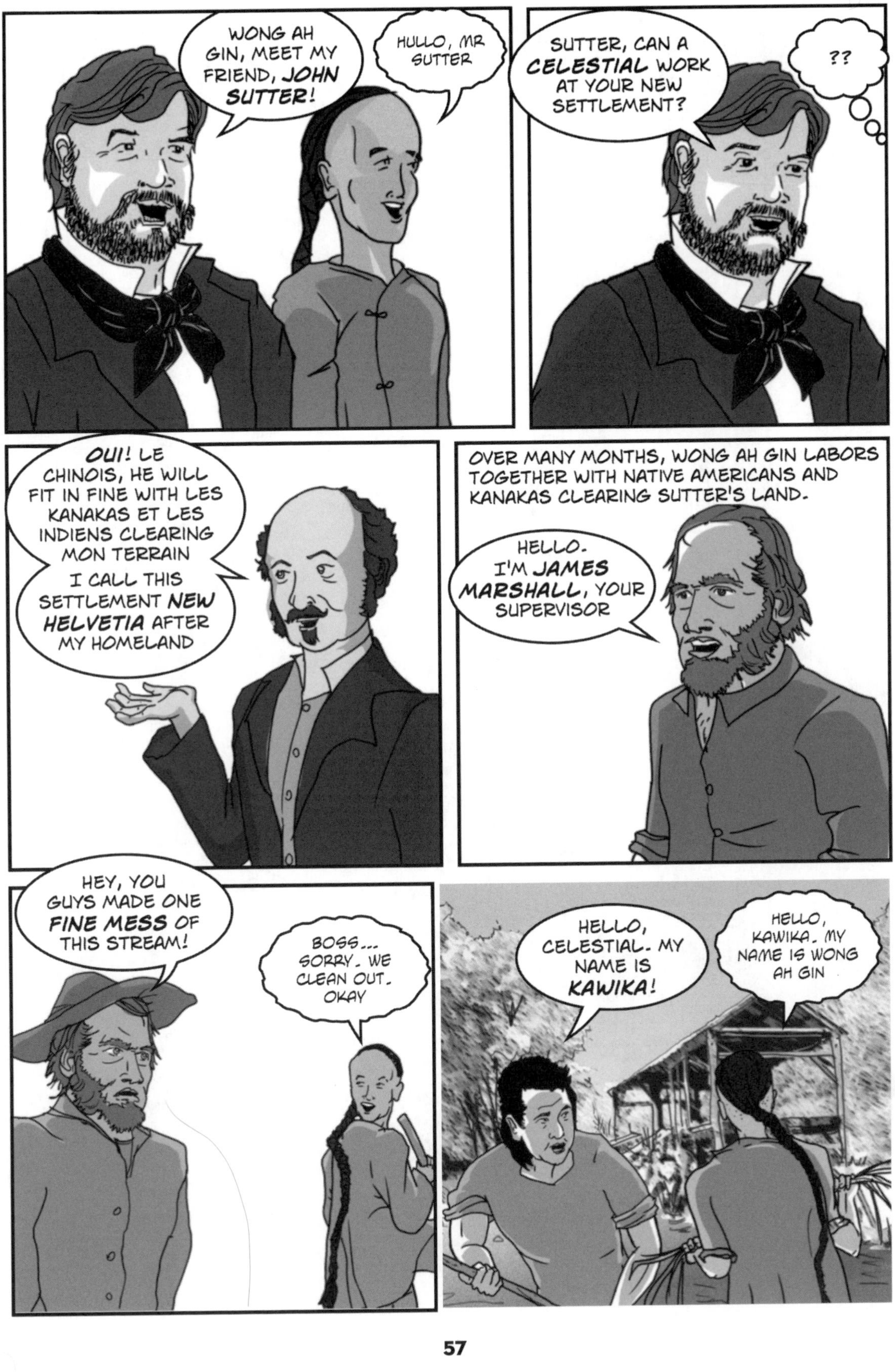
WONG AH GIN, MEET MY FRIEND, JOHN SUTTER!
HULLO, MR SUTTER
SUTTER, CAN A CELESTIAL WORK AT YOUR NEW SETTLEMENT?
??
OUI! LE CHINOIS, HE WILL FIT IN FINE WITH LES KANAKAS ET LES INDIENS CLEARING MON TERRAIN
I CALL THIS SETTLEMENT NEW HELVETIA AFTER MY HOMELAND
OVER MANY MONTHS, WONG AH GIN LABORS TOGETHER WITH NATIVE AMERICANS AND KANAKAS CLEARING SUTTER'S LAND.
HELLO. I'M JAMES MARSHALL, YOUR SUPERVISOR
HEY, YOU GUYS MADE ONE FINE MESS OF THIS STREAM!
BOSS... SORRY. WE CLEAN OUT. OKAY
HELLO, CELESTIAL. MY NAME IS KAWIKA!
HELLO, KAWIKA. MY NAME IS WONG AH GIN

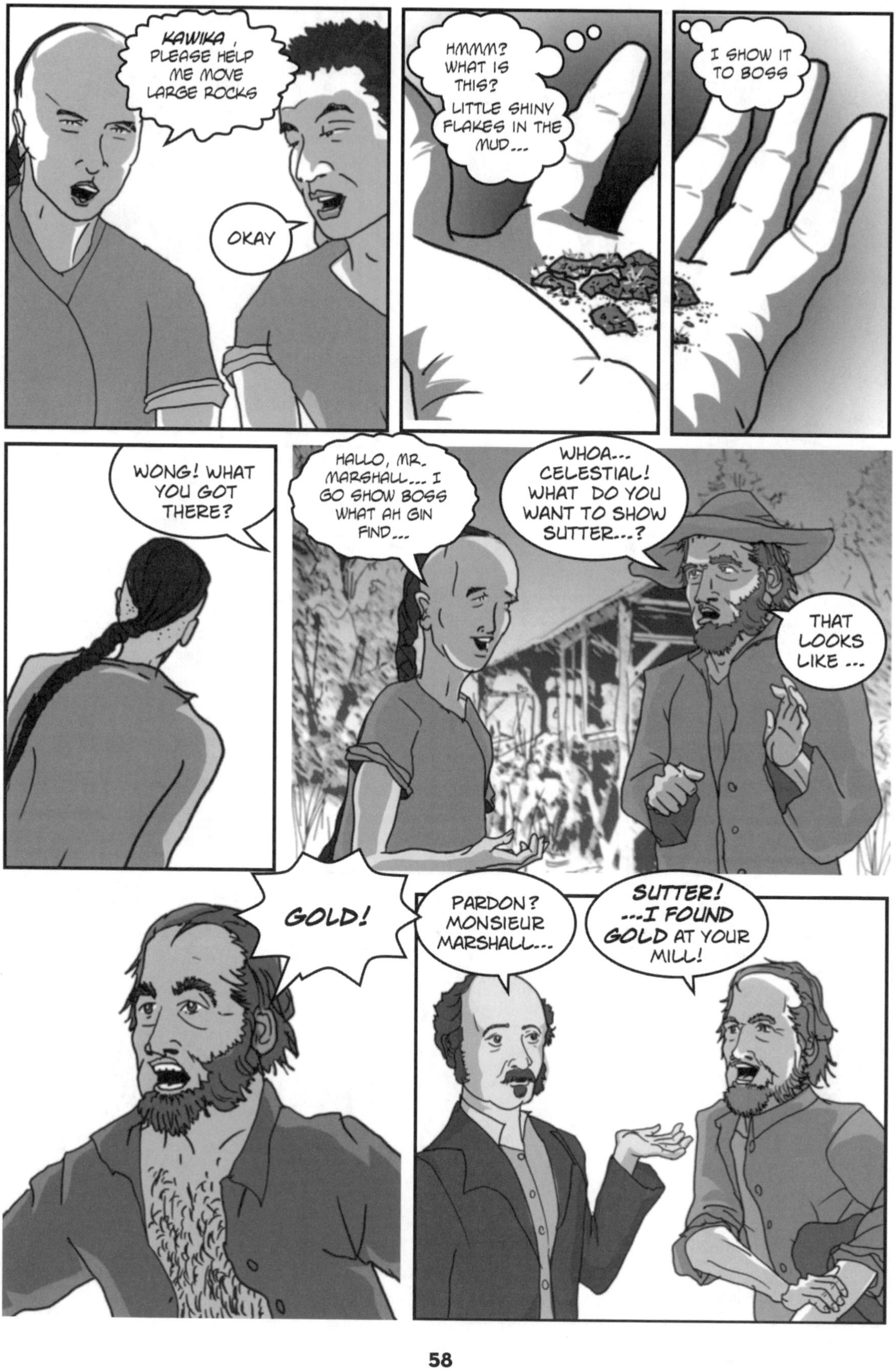
KAWIKA, PLEASE HELP ME MOVE LARGE ROCKS
OKAY
HMMM? WHAT IS THIS?
LITTLE SHINY FLAKES IN THE MUD...
I SHOW IT TO BOSS
WONG! WHAT YOU GOT THERE?
HALLO, MR. MARSHALL... I GO SHOW BOSS WHAT AH GIN FIND...
WHOA... CELESTIAL! WHAT DO YOU WANT TO SHOW SUTTER...?
THAT LOOKS LIKE ...
GOLD!
PARDON? MONSIEUR MARSHALL...
SUTTER! ...I FOUND GOLD AT YOUR MILL!

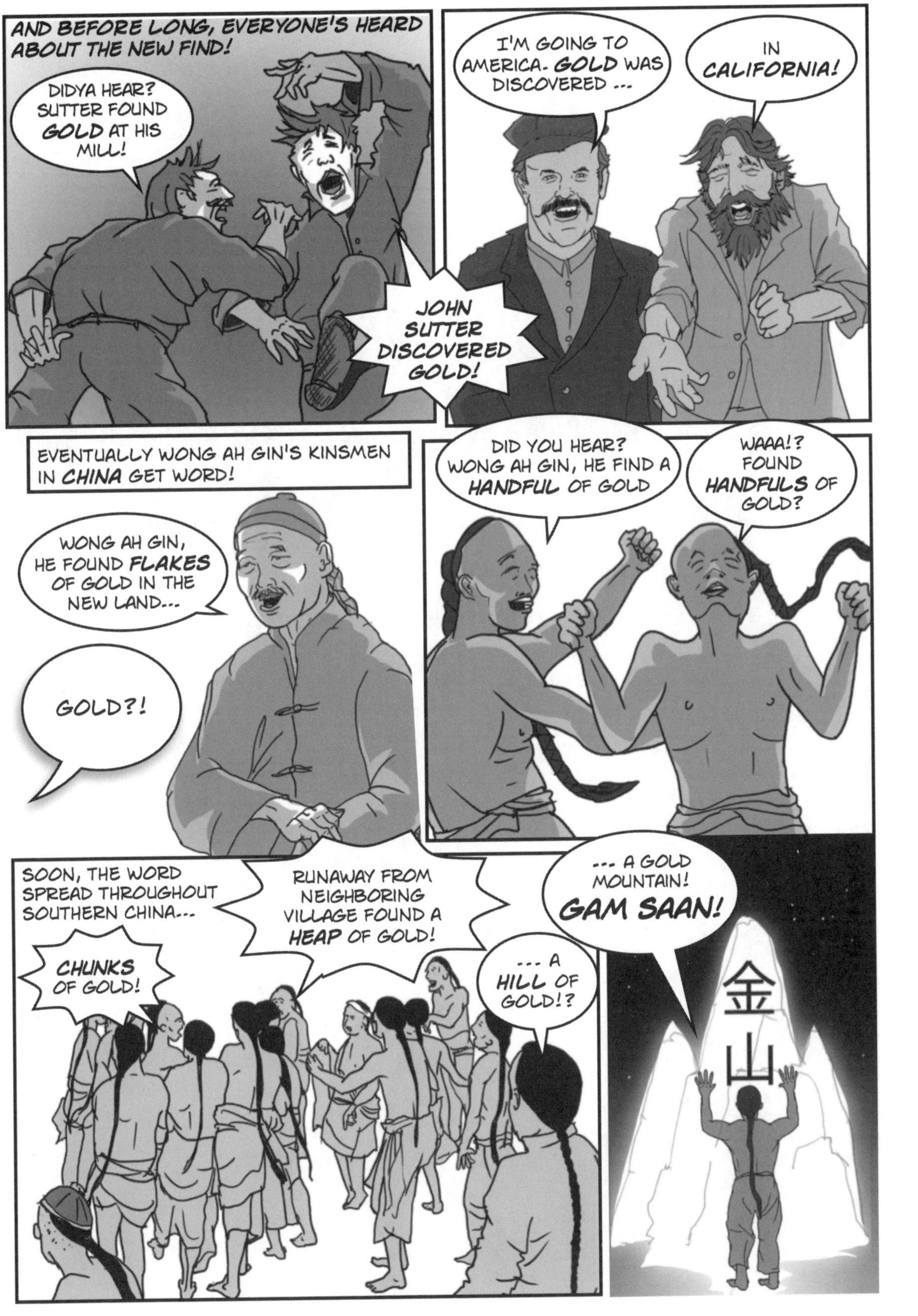
AND BEFORE LONG, EVERYONE'S HEARD ABOUT THE NEW FIND!
DIDYA HEAR? SUTTER FOUND GOLD AT HIS MILL!
JOHN SUTTER DISCOVERED GOLD!
I'M GOING TO AMERICA. GOLD WAS DISCOVERED ...
IN CALIFORNIA!
EVENTUALLY WONG AH GIN'S KINSMEN IN CHINA GET WORD!
WONG AH GIN, HE FOUND FLAKES OF GOLD IN THE NEW LAND...
GOLD?!
DID YOU HEAR? WONG AH GIN, HE FIND A HANDFUL OF GOLD
WAAA!? FOUND HANDFULS OF GOLD?
SOON, THE WORD SPREAD THROUGHOUT SOUTHERN CHINA...
RUNAWAY FROM NEIGHBORING VILLAGE FOUND A HEAP OF GOLD!
CHUNKS OF GOLD!
... A HILL OF GOLD!?
... A GOLD MOUNTAIN! GAM SAAN!
金
山

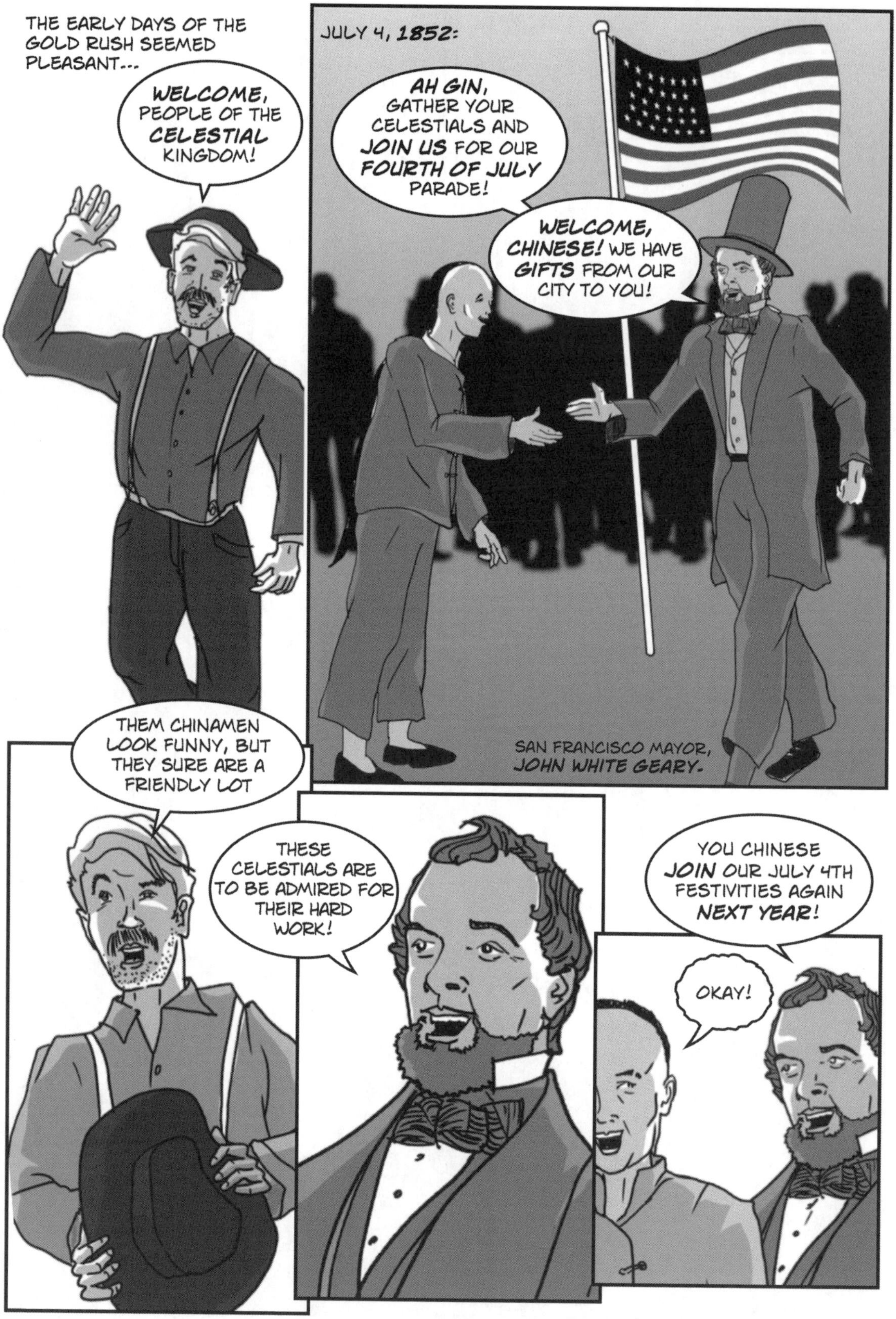
THE EARLY DAYS OF THE GOLD RUSH SEEMED PLEASANT...
WELCOME, PEOPLE OF THE CELESTIAL KINGDOM!
JULY 4, 1852:
AH GIN, GATHER YOUR CELESTIALS AND JOIN US FOR OUR FOURTH OF JULY PARADE!
WELCOME, CHINESE! WE HAVE GIFTS FROM OUR CITY TO YOU!
SAN FRANCISCO MAYOR, JOHN WHITE GEARY.
THEM CHINAMEN LOOK FUNNY, BUT THEY SURE ARE A FRIENDLY LOT
THESE CELESTIALS ARE TO BE ADMIRED FOR THEIR HARD WORK!
YOU CHINESE JOIN OUR JULY 4TH FESTIVITIES AGAIN NEXT YEAR!
OKAY!

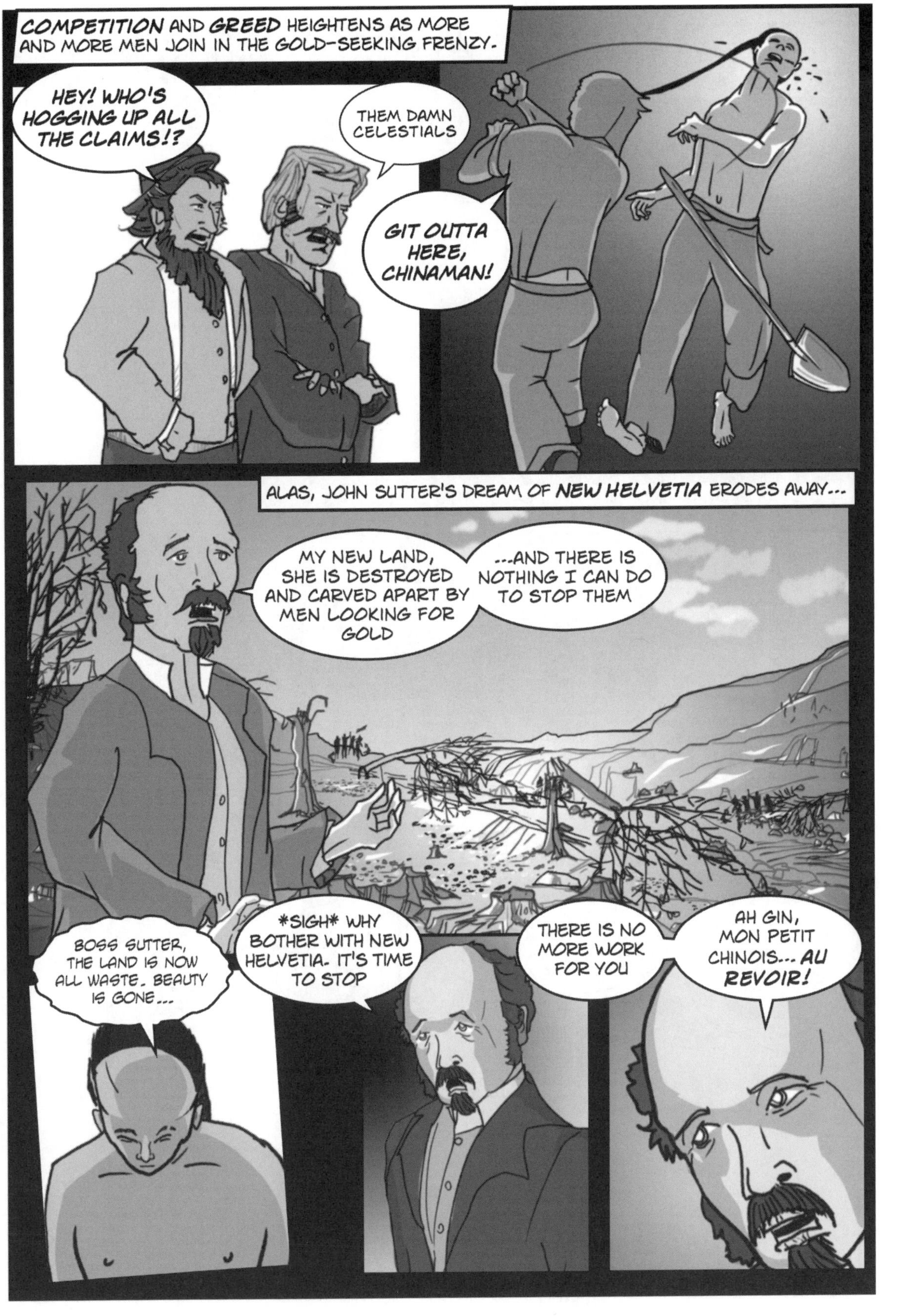
COMPETITION AND GREED HEIGHTENS AS MORE AND MORE MEN JOIN IN THE GOLD-SEEKING FRENZY.
HEY! WHO'S HOGGING UP ALL THE CLAIMS!?
THEM DAMN CELESTIALS
GIT OUTTA HERE, CHINAMAN!
ALAS, JOHN SUTTER'S DREAM OF NEW HELVETIA ERODES AWAY...
MY NEW LAND, SHE IS DESTROYED AND CARVED APART BY MEN LOOKING FOR GOLD
...AND THERE IS NOTHING I CAN DO TO STOP THEM
BOSS SUTTER, THE LAND IS NOW ALL WASTE. BEAUTY IS GONE...
SIGH WHY BOTHER WITH NEW HELVETIA. IT'S TIME TO STOP
THERE IS NO MORE WORK FOR YOU
AH GIN, MON PETIT CHINOIS... AU REVOIR!

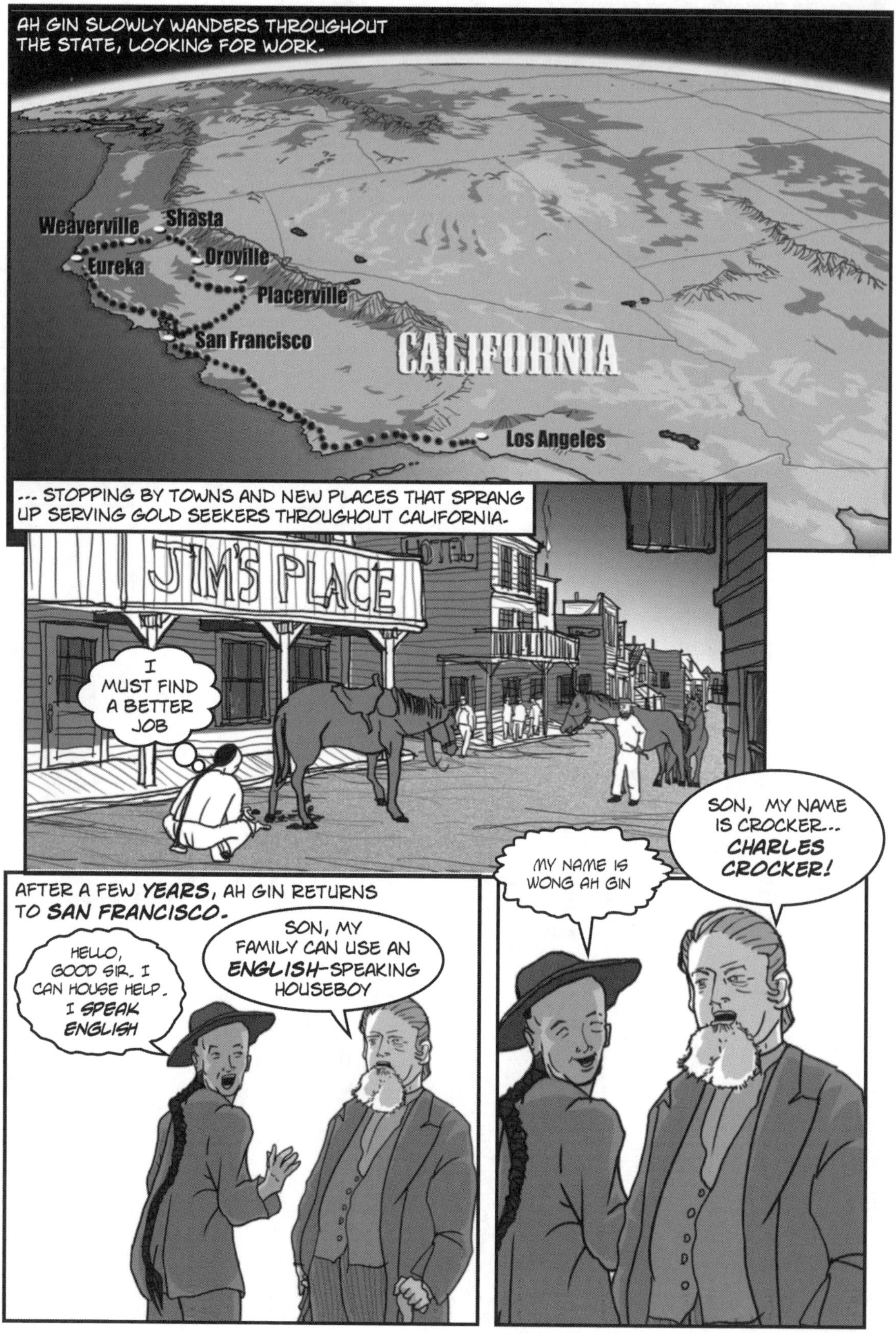
AH GIN SLOWLY WANDERS THROUGHOUT THE STATE, LOOKING FOR WORK.
Weaverville
Shasta
Eureka
Oroville
Placerville
San Francisco
CALIFORNIA
Los Angeles
... STOPPING BY TOWNS AND NEW PLACES THAT SPRANG UP SERVING GOLD SEEKERS THROUGHOUT CALIFORNIA.
JIM'S PLACE
HOTEL
I MUST FIND A BETTER JOB
AFTER A FEW YEARS, AH GIN RETURNS TO SAN FRANCISCO.
HELLO, GOOD SIR. I CAN HOUSE HELP. I SPEAK ENGLISH
SON, MY FAMILY CAN USE AN ENGLISH-SPEAKING HOUSEBOY
MY NAME IS WONG AH GIN
SON, MY NAME IS CROCKER... CHARLES CROCKER!

CHAPTER 4 Crocker's Iron Road

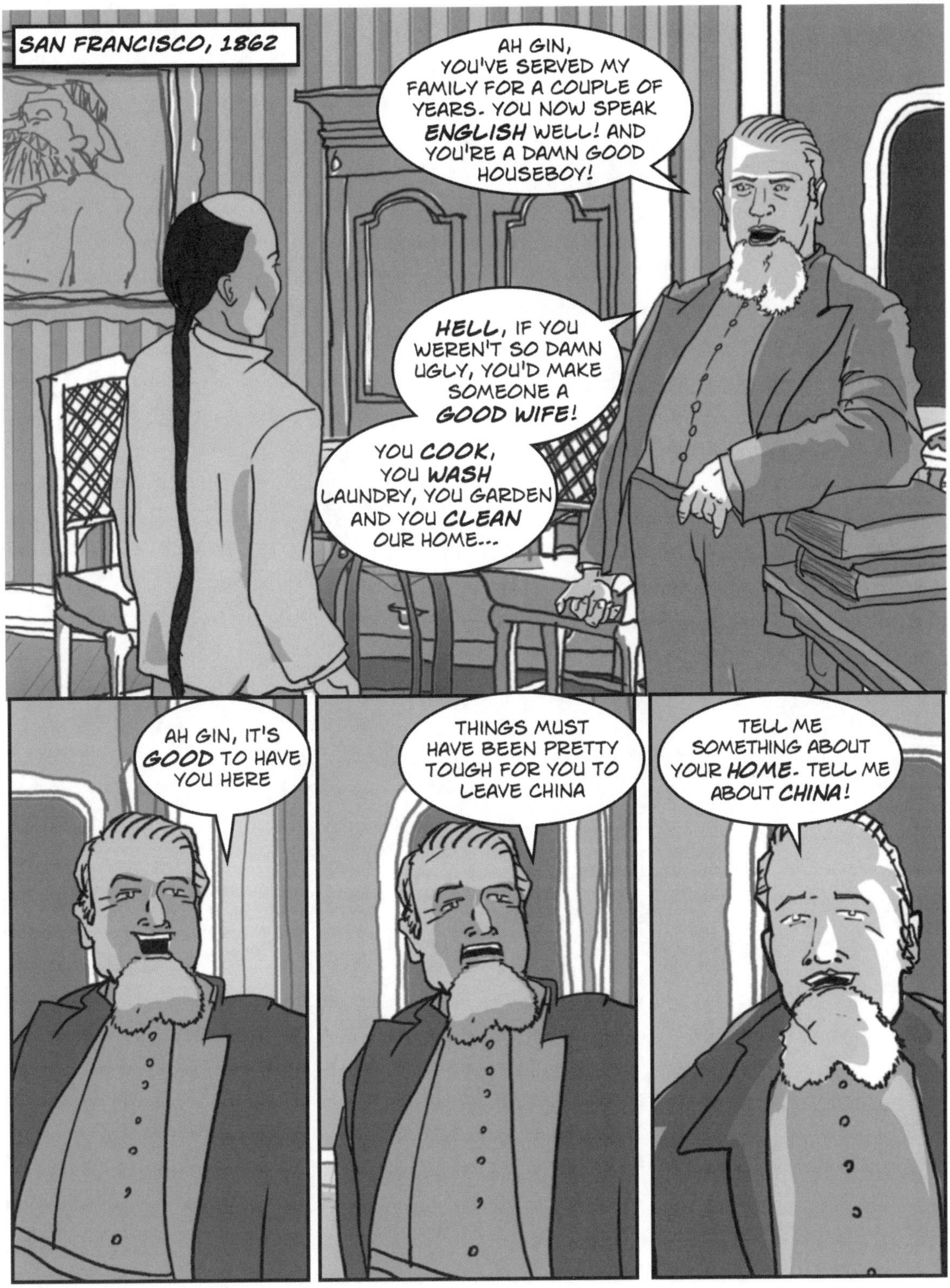
SAN FRANCISCO, 1862
AH GIN, YOU'VE SERVED MY FAMILY FOR A COUPLE OF YEARS. YOU NOW SPEAK ENGLISH WELL! AND YOU'RE A DAMN GOOD HOUSEBOY!
HELL, IF YOU WEREN'T SO DAMN UGLY, YOU'D MAKE SOMEONE A GOOD WIFE!
YOU COOK, YOU WASH LAUNDRY, YOU GARDEN AND YOU CLEAN OUR HOME...
AH GIN, IT'S GOOD TO HAVE YOU HERE
THINGS MUST HAVE BEEN PRETTY TOUGH FOR YOU TO LEAVE CHINA
TELL ME SOMETHING ABOUT YOUR HOME. TELL ME ABOUT CHINA!

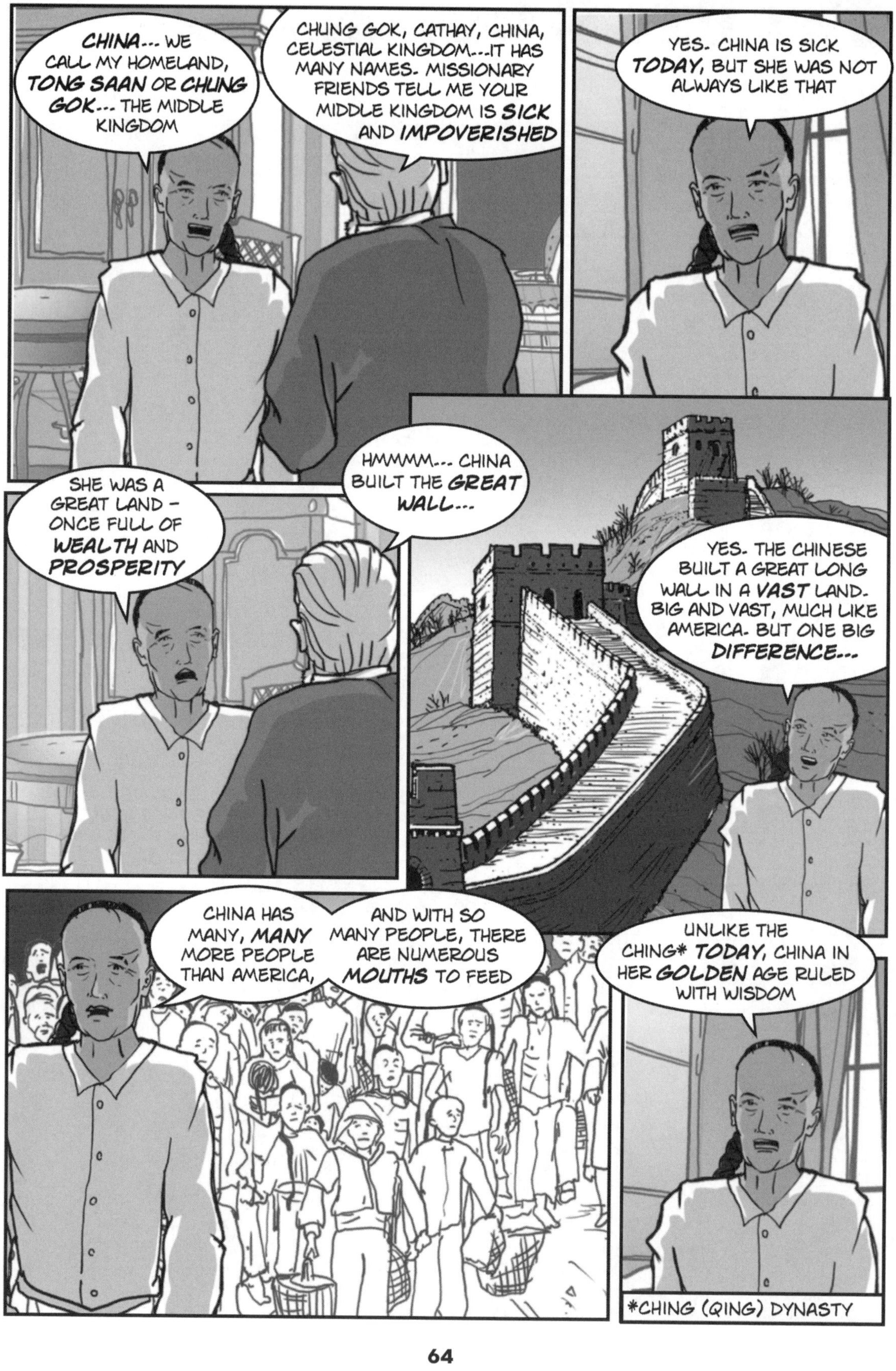
CHINA... WE CALL MY HOMELAND, TONG SAAN OR CHUNG GOK... THE MIDDLE KINGDOM
CHUNG GOK, CATHAY, CHINA, CELESTIAL KINGDOM...IT HAS MANY NAMES. MISSIONARY FRIENDS TELL ME YOUR MIDDLE KINGDOM IS SICK AND IMPOVERISHED
YES. CHINA IS SICK TODAY, BUT SHE WAS NOT ALWAYS LIKE THAT
SHE WAS A GREAT LAND – ONCE FULL OF WEALTH AND PROSPERITY
HMMMM... CHINA BUILT THE GREAT WALL...
YES. THE CHINESE BUILT A GREAT LONG WALL IN A VAST LAND. BIG AND VAST, MUCH LIKE AMERICA. BUT ONE BIG DIFFERENCE...
CHINA HAS MANY, MANY MORE PEOPLE THAN AMERICA,
AND WITH SO MANY PEOPLE, THERE ARE NUMEROUS MOUTHS TO FEED
UNLIKE THE CHING* TODAY, CHINA IN HER GOLDEN AGE RULED WITH WISDOM
*CHING (QING) DYNASTY

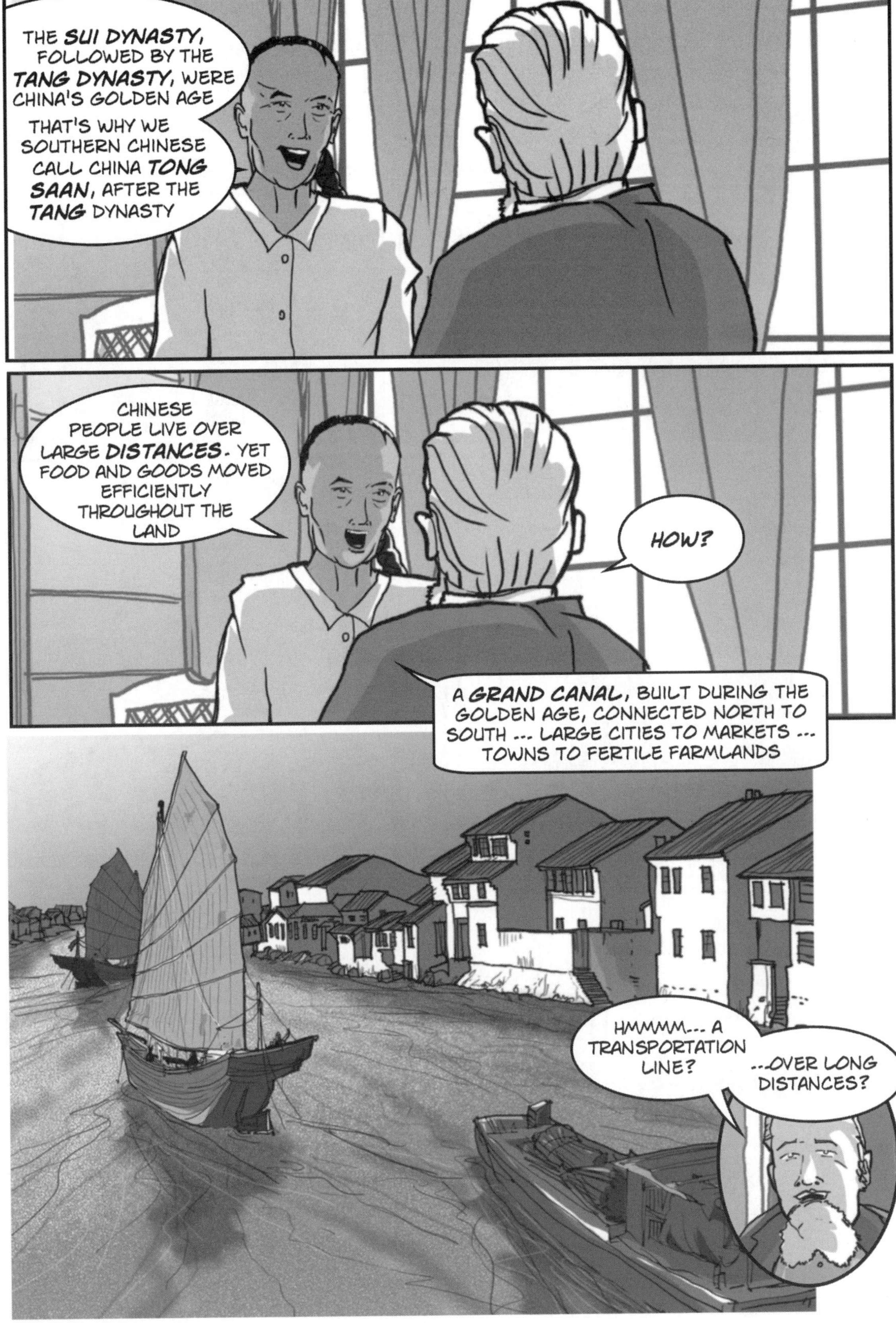
THE SUI DYNASTY, FOLLOWED BY THE TANG DYNASTY, WERE CHINA'S GOLDEN AGE
THAT'S WHY WE SOUTHERN CHINESE CALL CHINA TONG SAAN, AFTER THE TANG DYNASTY
CHINESE PEOPLE LIVE OVER LARGE DISTANCES. YET FOOD AND GOODS MOVED EFFICIENTLY THROUGHOUT THE LAND
HOW?
A GRAND CANAL, BUILT DURING THE GOLDEN AGE, CONNECTED NORTH TO SOUTH ... LARGE CITIES TO MARKETS ... TOWNS TO FERTILE FARMLANDS
HMMMM... A TRANSPORTATION LINE?
...OVER LONG DISTANCES?

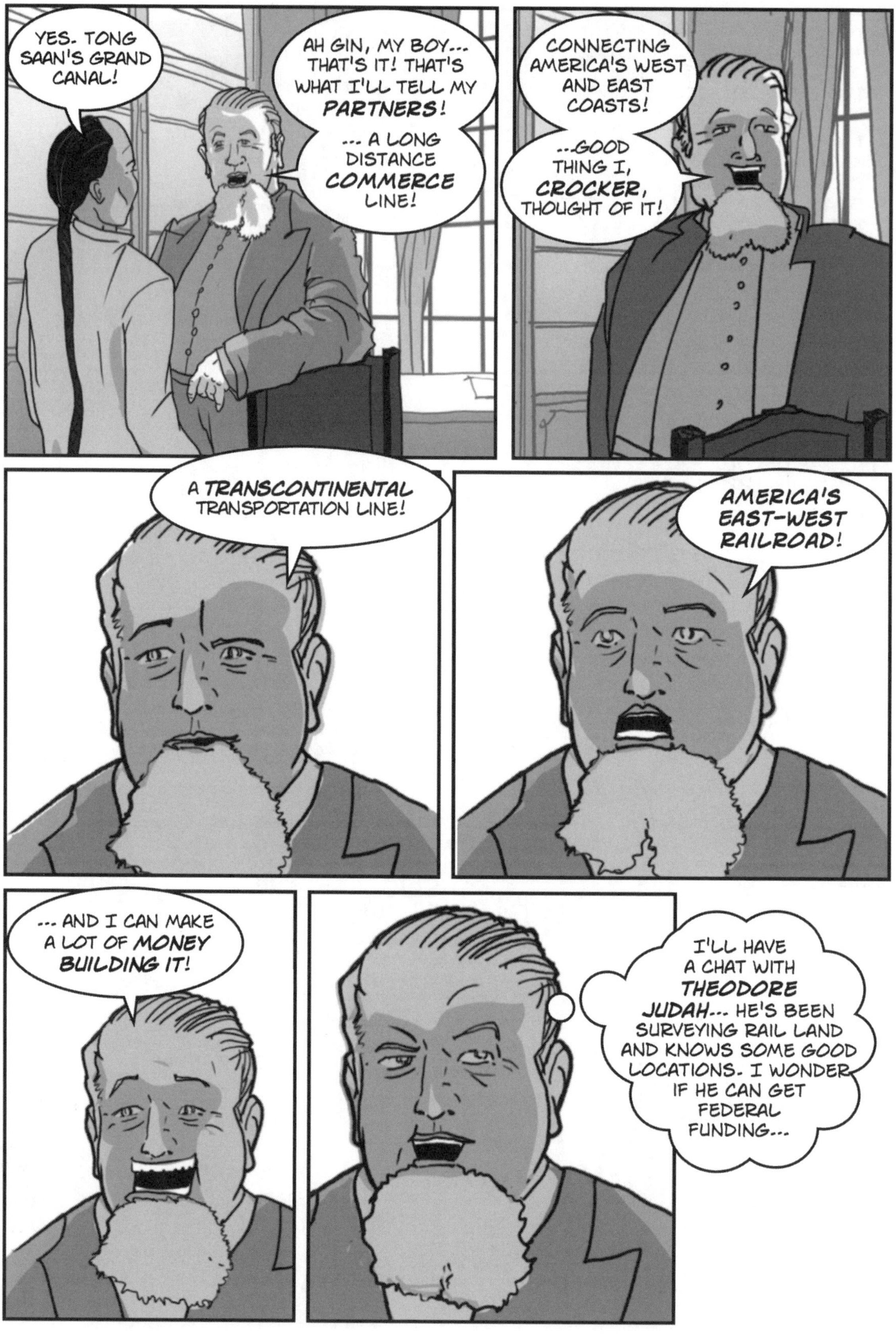
YES. TONG SAAN'S GRAND CANAL!
AH GIN, MY BOY... THAT'S IT! THAT'S WHAT I'LL TELL MY PARTNERS!
... A LONG DISTANCE COMMERCE LINE!
CONNECTING AMERICA'S WEST AND EAST COASTS!
...GOOD THING I, CROCKER, THOUGHT OF IT!
A TRANSCONTINENTAL TRANSPORTATION LINE!
AMERICA'S EAST-WEST RAILROAD!
... AND I CAN MAKE A LOT OF MONEY BUILDING IT!
I'LL HAVE A CHAT WITH THEODORE JUDAH... HE'S BEEN SURVEYING RAIL LAND AND KNOWS SOME GOOD LOCATIONS. I WONDER IF HE CAN GET FEDERAL FUNDING...

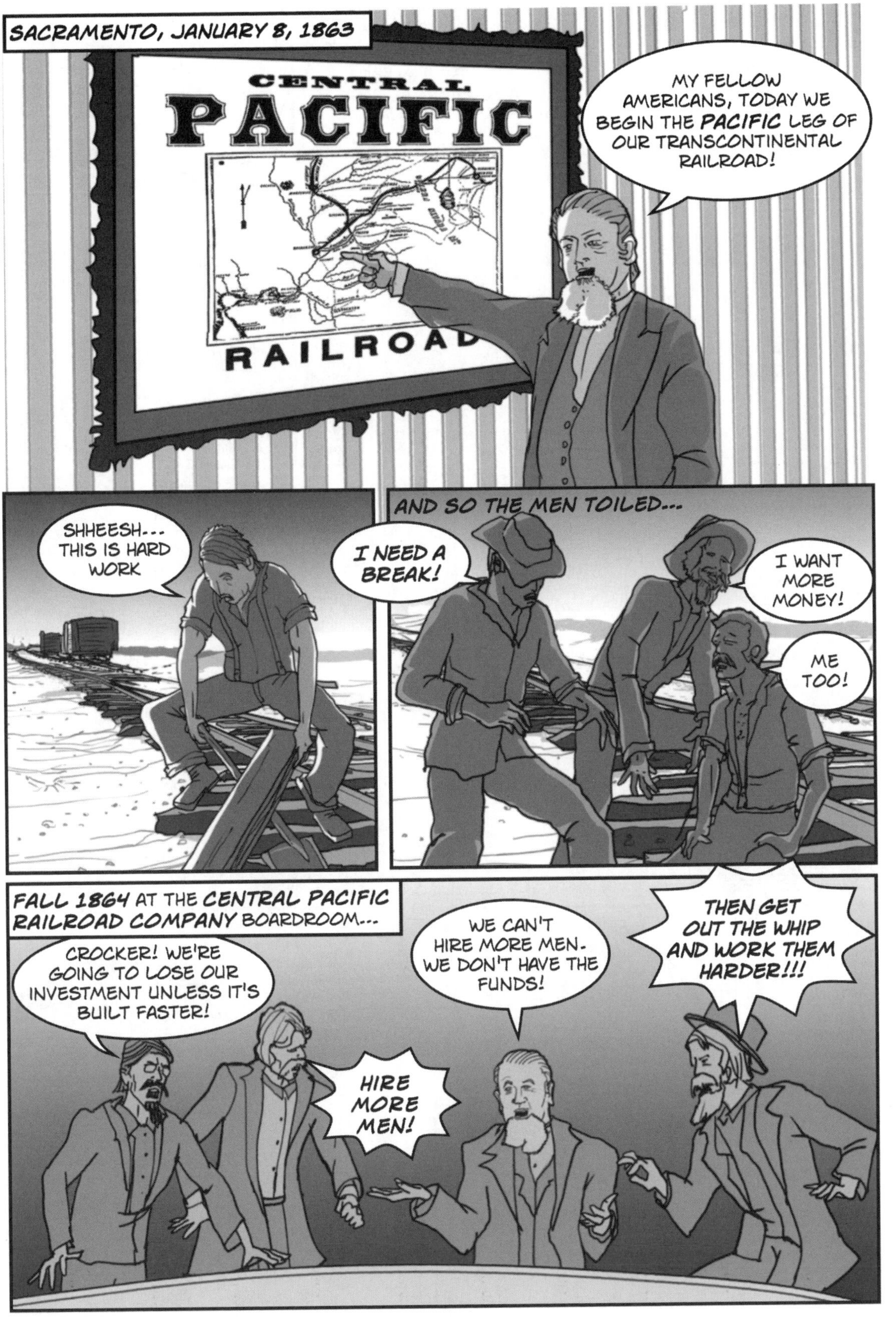
SACRAMENTO, JANUARY 8, 1863
CENTRAL PACIFIC RAILROAD
MY FELLOW AMERICANS, TODAY WE BEGIN THE PACIFIC LEG OF OUR TRANSCONTINENTAL RAILROAD!
SHHEESH... THIS IS HARD WORK
AND SO THE MEN TOILED...
I NEED A BREAK!
I WANT MORE MONEY!
ME TOO!
FALL 1864 AT THE CENTRAL PACIFIC RAILROAD COMPANY BOARDROOM...
CROCKER! WE'RE GOING TO LOSE OUR INVESTMENT UNLESS IT'S BUILT FASTER!
HIRE MORE MEN!
WE CAN'T HIRE MORE MEN. WE DON'T HAVE THE FUNDS!
THEN GET OUT THE WHIP AND WORK THEM HARDER!!!

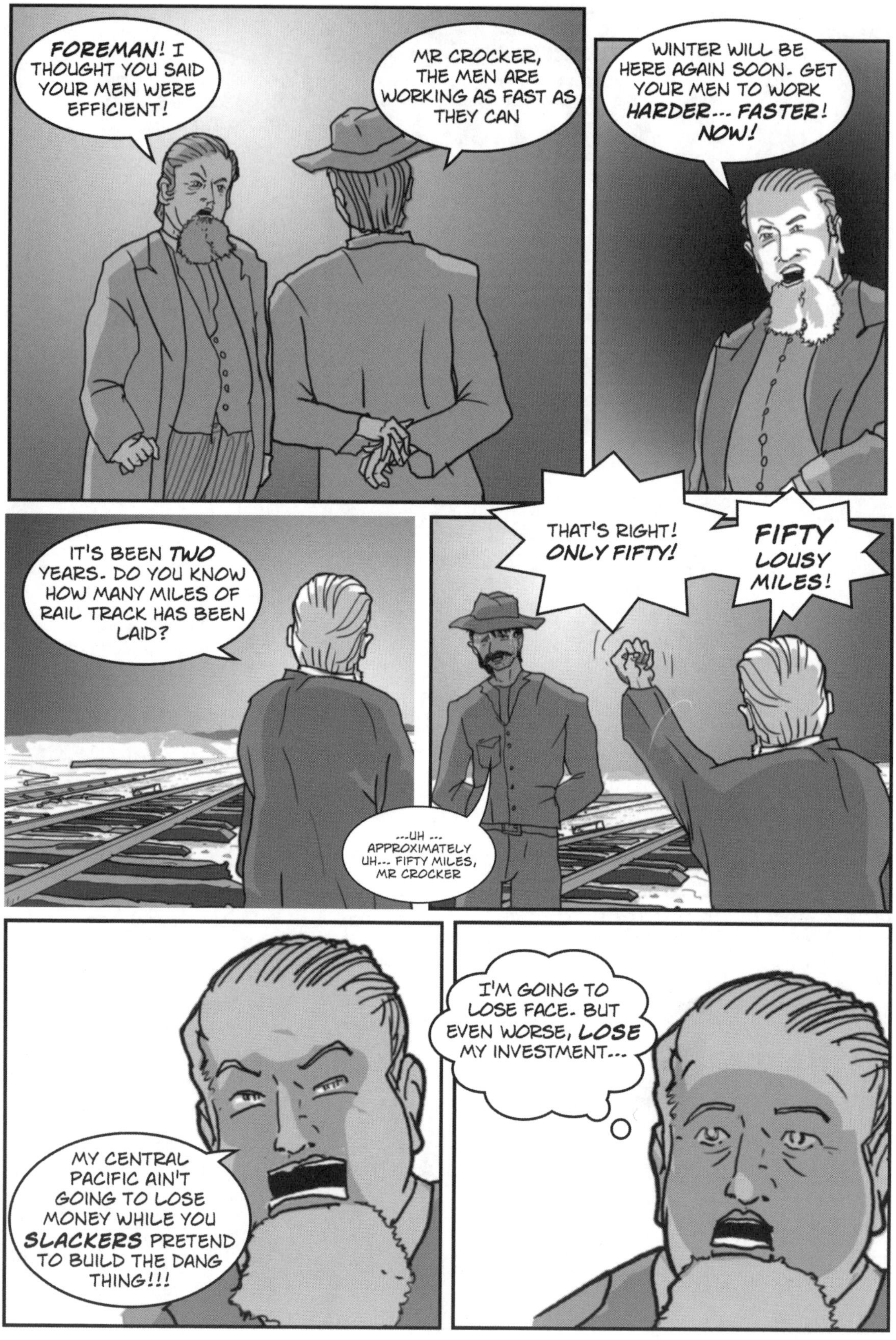
FOREMAN! I THOUGHT YOU SAID YOUR MEN WERE EFFICIENT!
MR CROCKER, THE MEN ARE WORKING AS FAST AS THEY CAN
WINTER WILL BE HERE AGAIN SOON. GET YOUR MEN TO WORK HARDER... FASTER! NOW!
IT'S BEEN TWO YEARS. DO YOU KNOW HOW MANY MILES OF RAIL TRACK HAS BEEN LAID?
...UH ... APPROXIMATELY UH... FIFTY MILES, MR CROCKER
FIFTY LOUSY MILES!
THAT'S RIGHT! ONLY FIFTY!
MY CENTRAL PACIFIC AIN'T GOING TO LOSE MONEY WHILE YOU SLACKERS PRETEND TO BUILD THE DANG THING!!!
I'M GOING TO LOSE FACE. BUT EVEN WORSE, LOSE MY INVESTMENT...

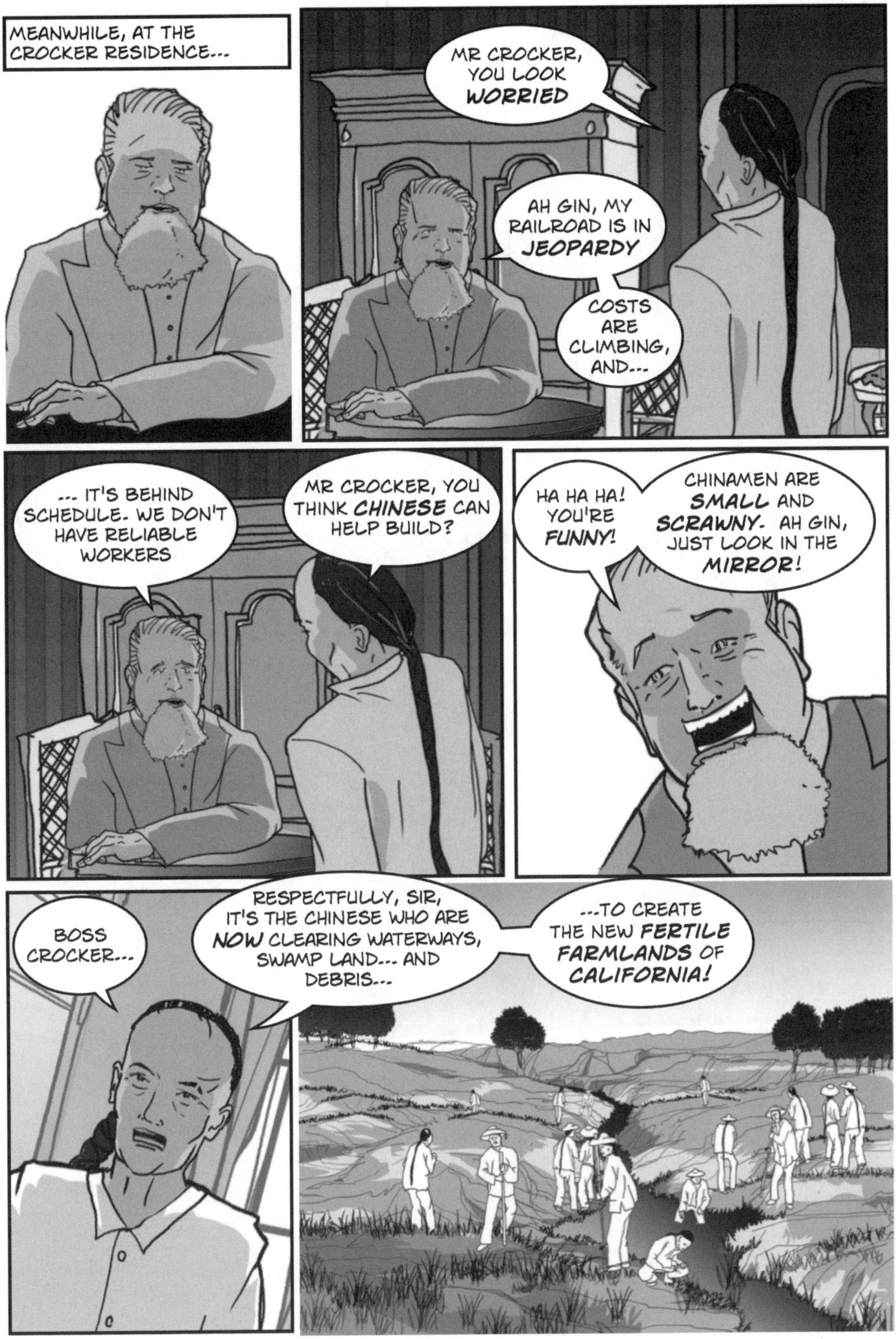
MEANWHILE, AT THE CROCKER RESIDENCE...
MR CROCKER, YOU LOOK WORRIED
AH GIN, MY RAILROAD IS IN JEOPARDY
COSTS ARE CLIMBING, AND...
... IT'S BEHIND SCHEDULE. WE DON'T HAVE RELIABLE WORKERS
MR CROCKER, YOU THINK CHINESE CAN HELP BUILD?
HA HA HA! YOU'RE FUNNY!
CHINAMEN ARE SMALL AND SCRAWNY. AH GIN, JUST LOOK IN THE MIRROR!
BOSS CROCKER...
RESPECTFULLY, SIR, IT'S THE CHINESE WHO ARE NOW CLEARING WATERWAYS, SWAMP LAND... AND DEBRIS...
...TO CREATE THE NEW FERTILE FARMLANDS OF CALIFORNIA!

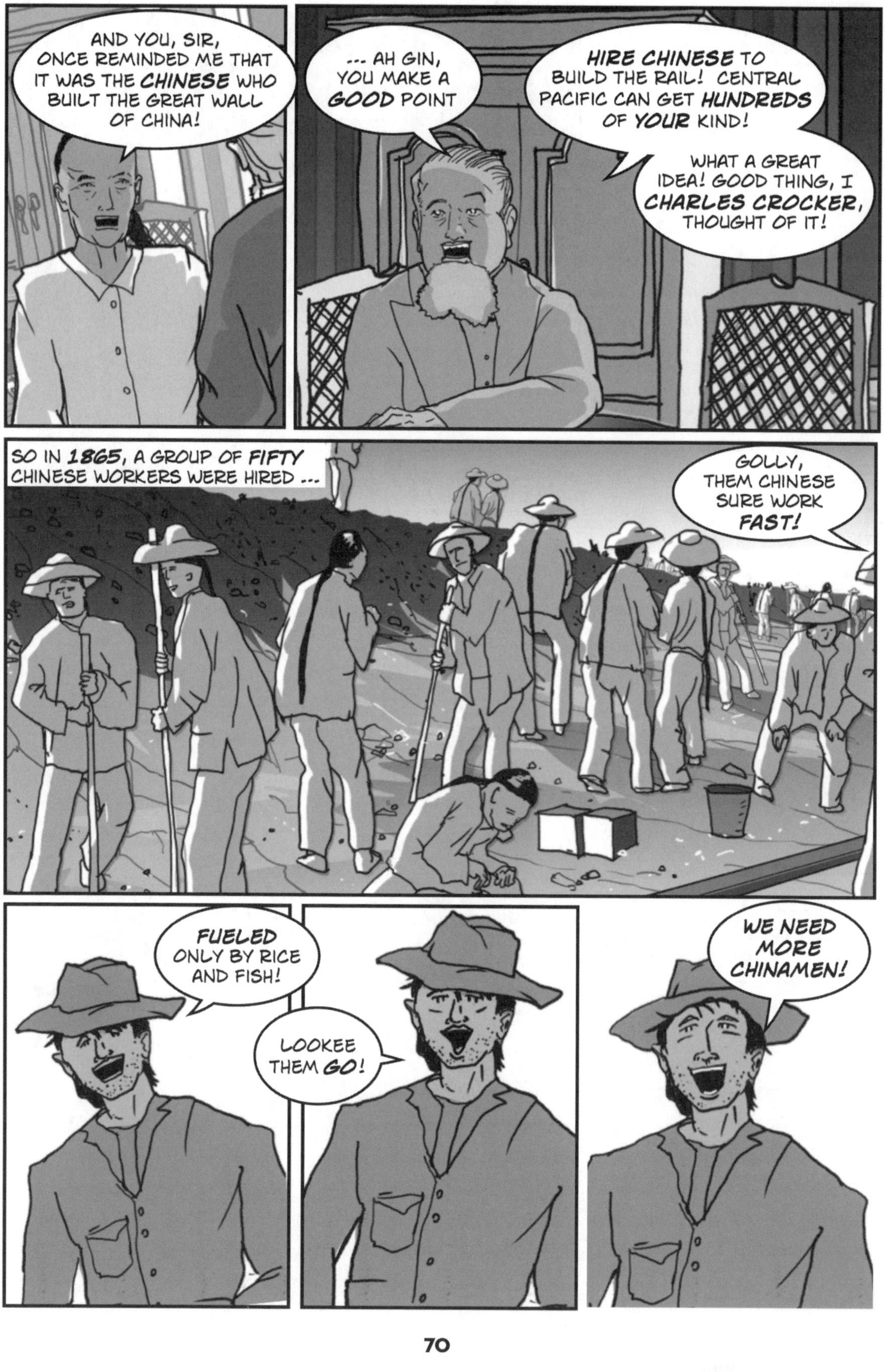
AND YOU, SIR, ONCE REMINDED ME THAT IT WAS THE CHINESE WHO BUILT THE GREAT WALL OF CHINA!
... AH GIN, YOU MAKE A GOOD POINT
HIRE CHINESE TO BUILD THE RAIL! CENTRAL PACIFIC CAN GET HUNDREDS OF YOUR KIND!
WHAT A GREAT IDEA! GOOD THING, I CHARLES CROCKER, THOUGHT OF IT!
SO IN 1865, A GROUP OF FIFTY CHINESE WORKERS WERE HIRED ...
GOLLY, THEM CHINESE SURE WORK FAST!
FUELED ONLY BY RICE AND FISH!
LOOKEE THEM GO!
WE NEED MORE CHINAMEN!

CHAPTER 5 Hello, Mei Gok (America)

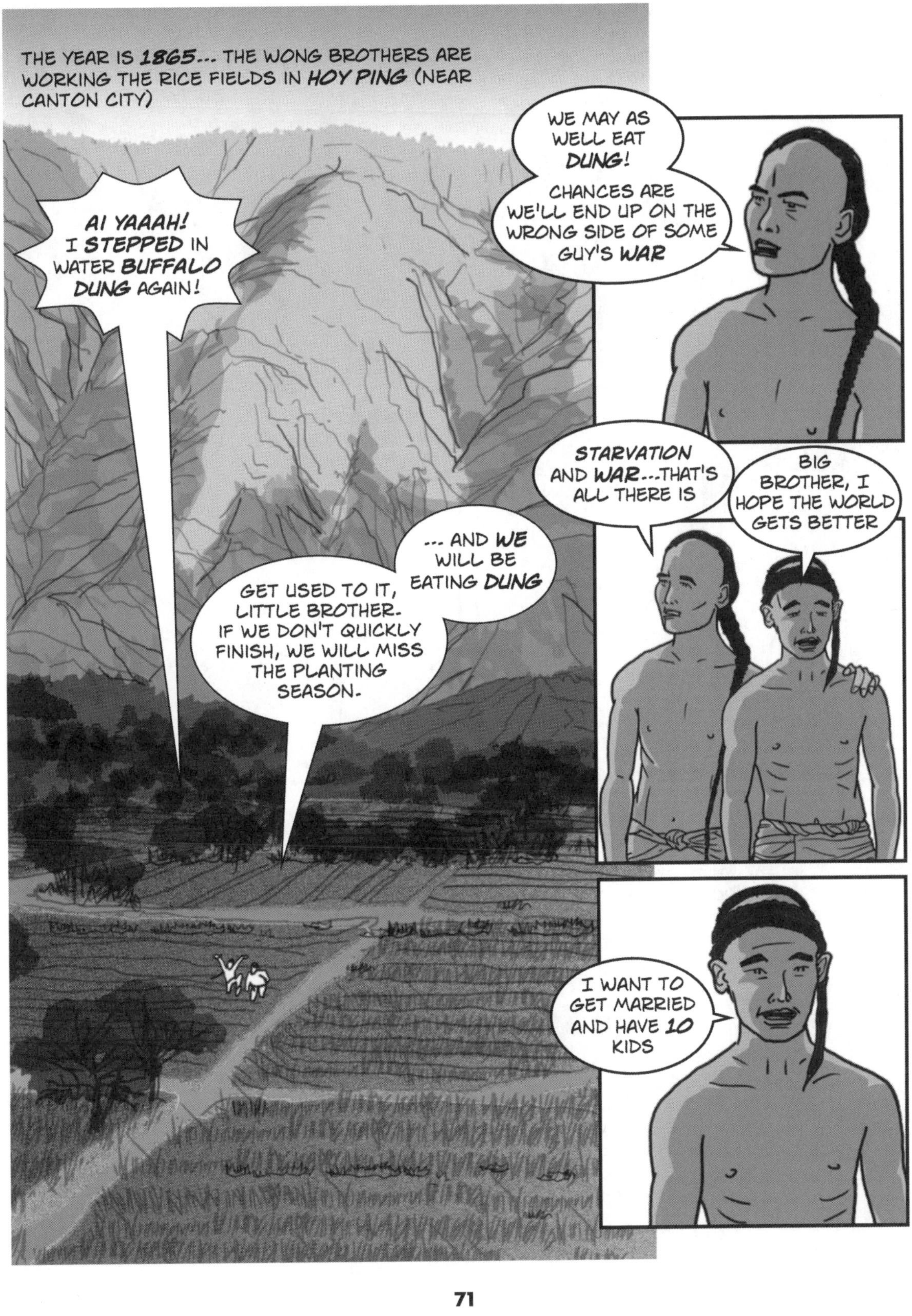
THE YEAR IS 1865... THE WONG BROTHERS ARE WORKING THE RICE FIELDS IN HOY PING (NEAR CANTON CITY)
AI YAAAH! I STEPPED IN WATER BUFFALO DUNG AGAIN!
GET USED TO IT, LITTLE BROTHER. IF WE DON'T QUICKLY FINISH, WE WILL MISS THE PLANTING SEASON.
... AND WE WILL BE EATING DUNG
WE MAY AS WELL EAT DUNG!
CHANCES ARE WE'LL END UP ON THE WRONG SIDE OF SOME GUY'S WAR
STARVATION AND WAR...THAT'S ALL THERE IS
BIG BROTHER, I HOPE THE WORLD GETS BETTER
I WANT TO GET MARRIED AND HAVE 10 KIDS

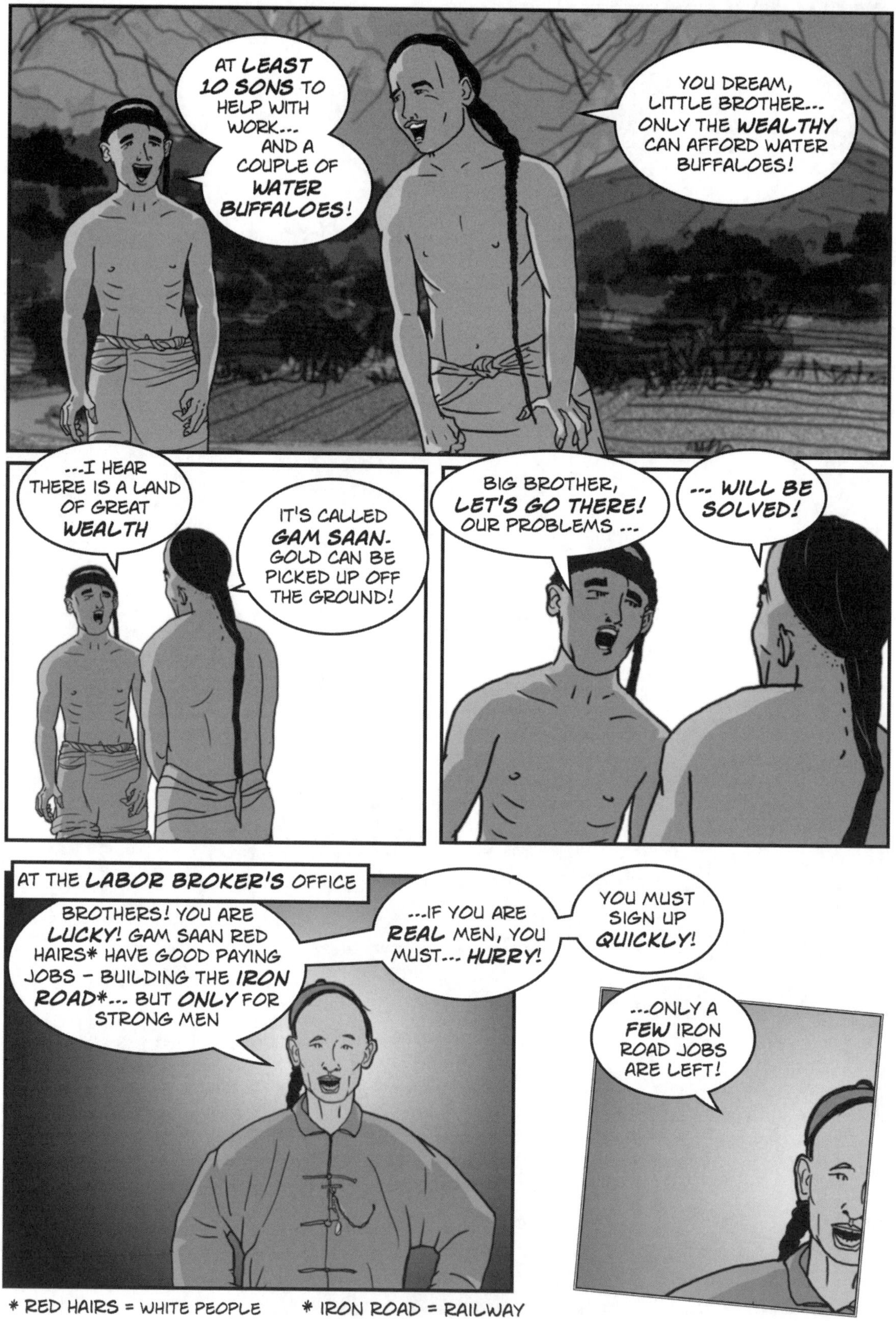
AT LEAST 10 SONS TO HELP WITH WORK... AND A COUPLE OF WATER BUFFALOES!
YOU DREAM, LITTLE BROTHER... ONLY THE WEALTHY CAN AFFORD WATER BUFFALOES!
...I HEAR THERE IS A LAND OF GREAT WEALTH
IT'S CALLED GAM SAAN. GOLD CAN BE PICKED UP OFF THE GROUND!
BIG BROTHER, LET'S GO THERE! OUR PROBLEMS ...
... WILL BE SOLVED!
AT THE LABOR BROKER'S OFFICE
BROTHERS! YOU ARE LUCKY! GAM SAAN RED HAIRS* HAVE GOOD PAYING JOBS – BUILDING THE IRON ROAD*... BUT ONLY FOR STRONG MEN
...IF YOU ARE REAL MEN, YOU MUST... HURRY!
YOU MUST SIGN UP QUICKLY!
...ONLY A FEW IRON ROAD JOBS ARE LEFT!

* RED HAIRS = WHITE PEOPLE * IRON ROAD = RAILWAY

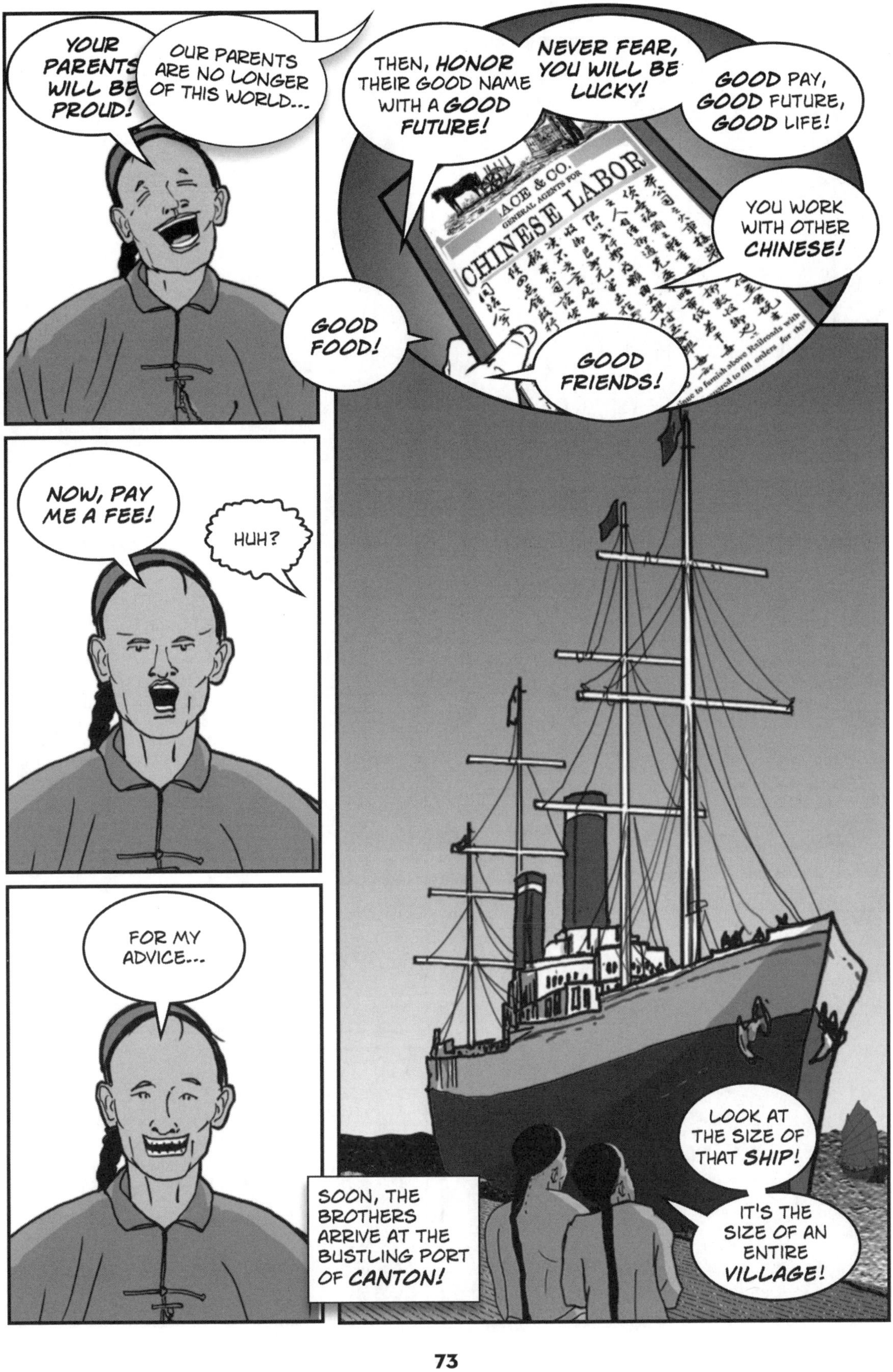
YOUR PARENTS WILL BE PROUD!
OUR PARENTS ARE NO LONGER OF THIS WORLD...
THEN, HONOR THEIR GOOD NAME WITH A GOOD FUTURE!
NEVER FEAR, YOU WILL BE LUCKY!
GOOD PAY, GOOD FUTURE, GOOD LIFE!
YOU WORK WITH OTHER CHINESE!
GOOD FOOD!
GOOD FRIENDS!
CHINESE LABOR
NOW, PAY ME A FEE!
HUH?
FOR MY ADVICE...
LOOK AT THE SIZE OF THAT SHIP!
IT'S THE SIZE OF AN ENTIRE VILLAGE!
SOON, THE BROTHERS ARRIVE AT THE BUSTLING PORT OF CANTON!

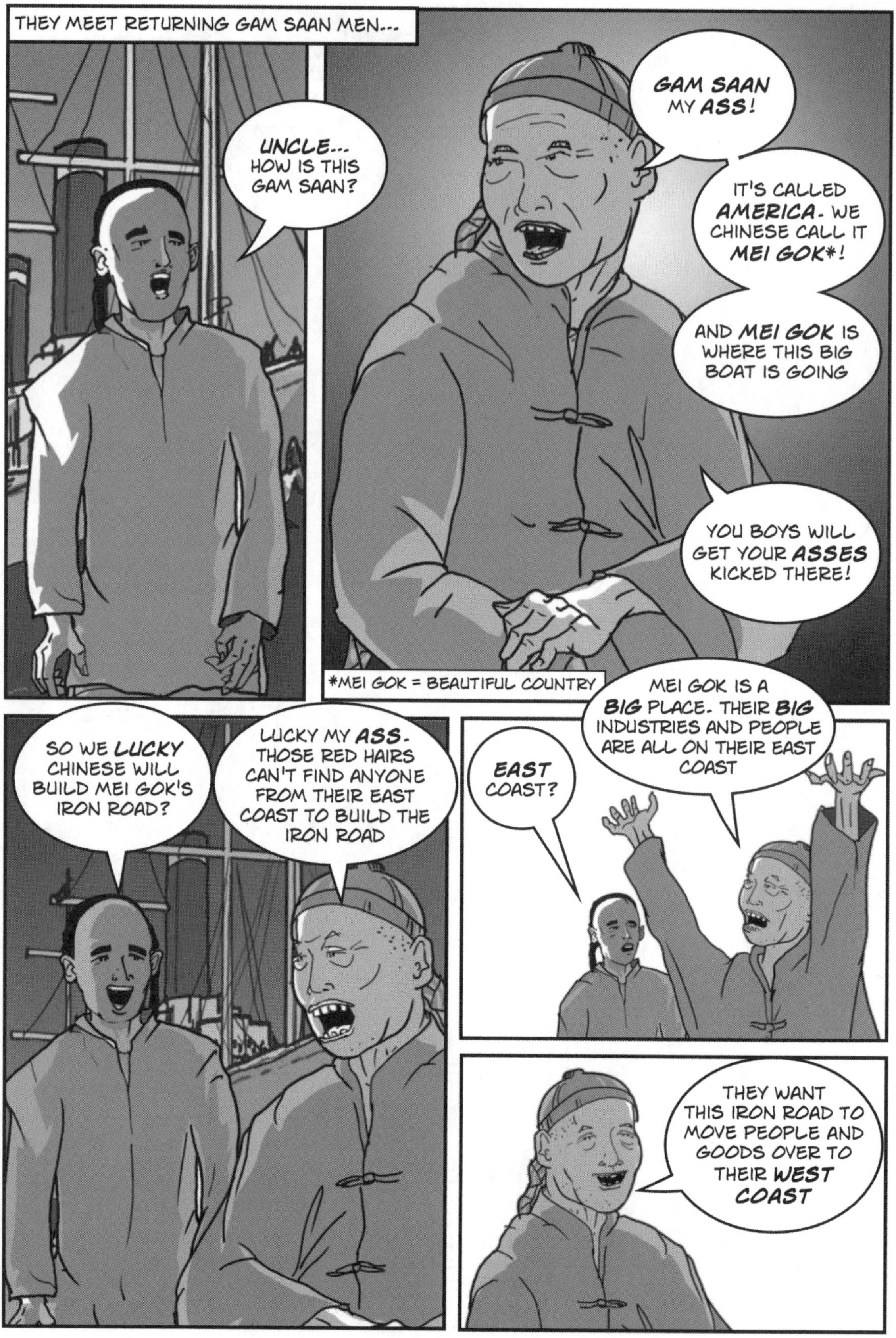
THEY MEET RETURNING GAM SAAN MEN...
UNCLE... HOW IS THIS GAM SAAN?
GAM SAAN MY ASS!
IT'S CALLED AMERICA. WE CHINESE CALL IT MEI GOK*!
AND MEI GOK IS WHERE THIS BIG BOAT IS GOING
YOU BOYS WILL GET YOUR ASSES KICKED THERE!
*MEI GOK = BEAUTIFUL COUNTRY
SO WE LUCKY CHINESE WILL BUILD MEI GOK'S IRON ROAD?
LUCKY MY ASS. THOSE RED HAIRS CAN'T FIND ANYONE FROM THEIR EAST COAST TO BUILD THE IRON ROAD
MEI GOK IS A BIG PLACE. THEIR BIG INDUSTRIES AND PEOPLE ARE ALL ON THEIR EAST COAST
EAST COAST?
THEY WANT THIS IRON ROAD TO MOVE PEOPLE AND GOODS OVER TO THEIR WEST COAST

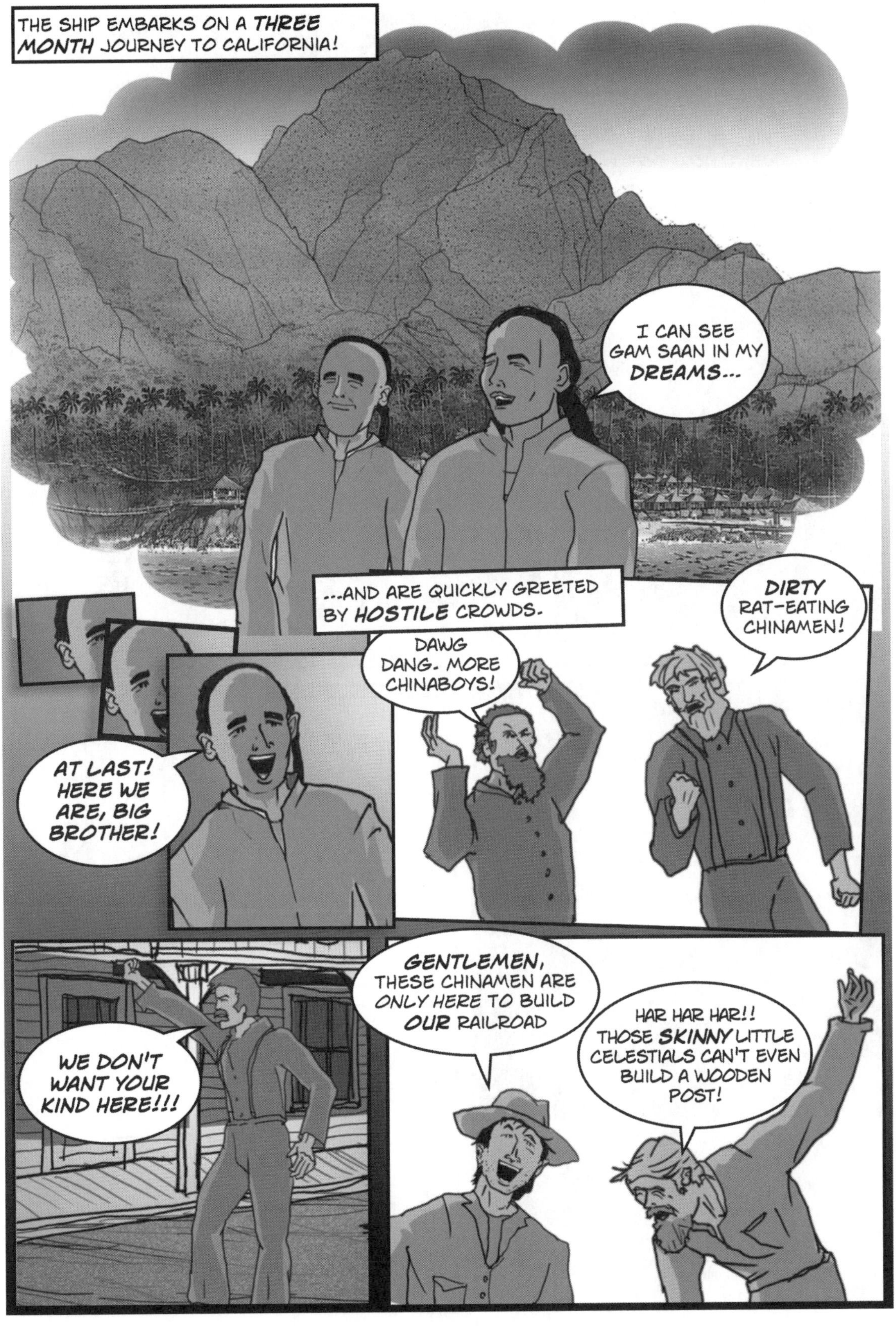
THE SHIP EMBARKS ON A THREE MONTH JOURNEY TO CALIFORNIA!
I CAN SEE GAM SAAN IN MY DREAMS...
...AND ARE QUICKLY GREETED BY HOSTILE CROWDS.
AT LAST! HERE WE ARE, BIG BROTHER!
DAWG DANG. MORE CHINABOYS!
DIRTY RAT-EATING CHINAMEN!
WE DON'T WANT YOUR KIND HERE!!!
GENTLEMEN, THESE CHINAMEN ARE ONLY HERE TO BUILD OUR RAILROAD
HAR HAR HAR!! THOSE SKINNY LITTLE CELESTIALS CAN'T EVEN BUILD A WOODEN POST!

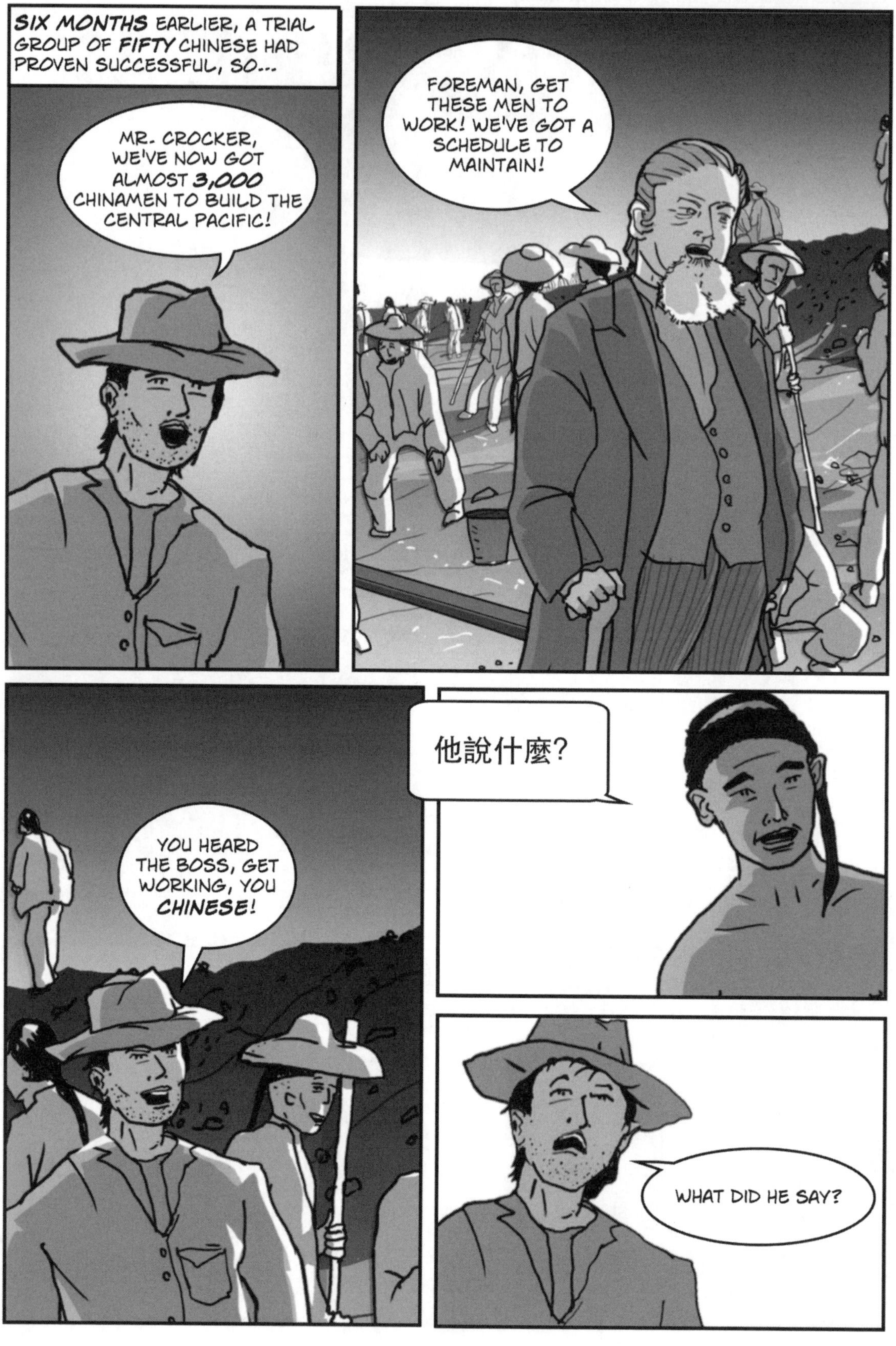
SIX MONTHS EARLIER, A TRIAL GROUP OF FIFTY CHINESE HAD PROVEN SUCCESSFUL, SO...
MR. CROCKER, WE'VE NOW GOT ALMOST 3,000 CHINAMEN TO BUILD THE CENTRAL PACIFIC!
FOREMAN, GET THESE MEN TO WORK! WE'VE GOT A SCHEDULE TO MAINTAIN!
YOU HEARD THE BOSS, GET WORKING, YOU CHINESE!
他說什麼?
WHAT DID HE SAY?

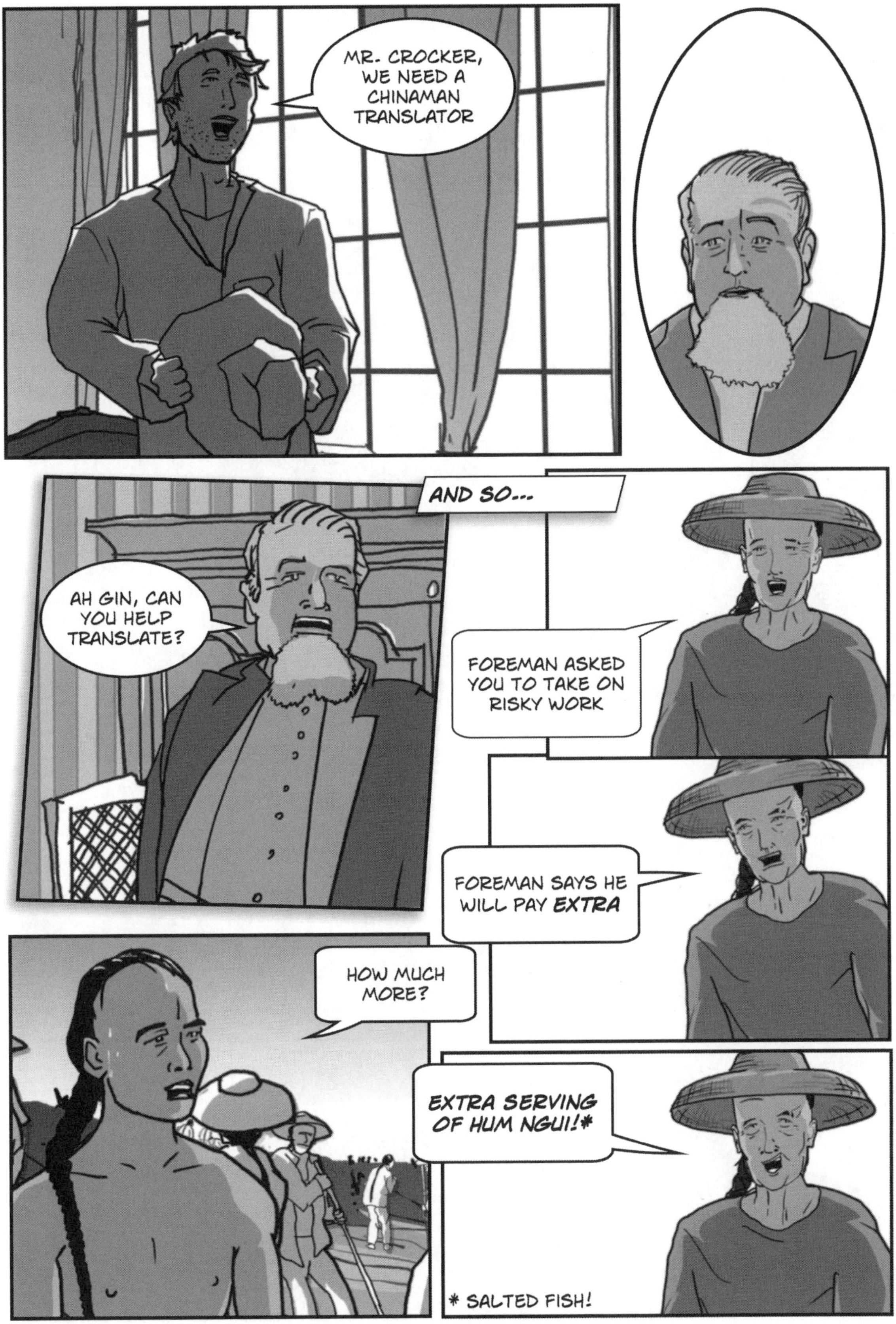
MR. CROCKER, WE NEED A CHINAMAN TRANSLATOR
AH GIN, CAN YOU HELP TRANSLATE?
AND SO...
FOREMAN ASKED YOU TO TAKE ON RISKY WORK
FOREMAN SAYS HE WILL PAY EXTRA
HOW MUCH MORE?
EXTRA SERVING OF HUM NGUI!*
* SALTED FISH!

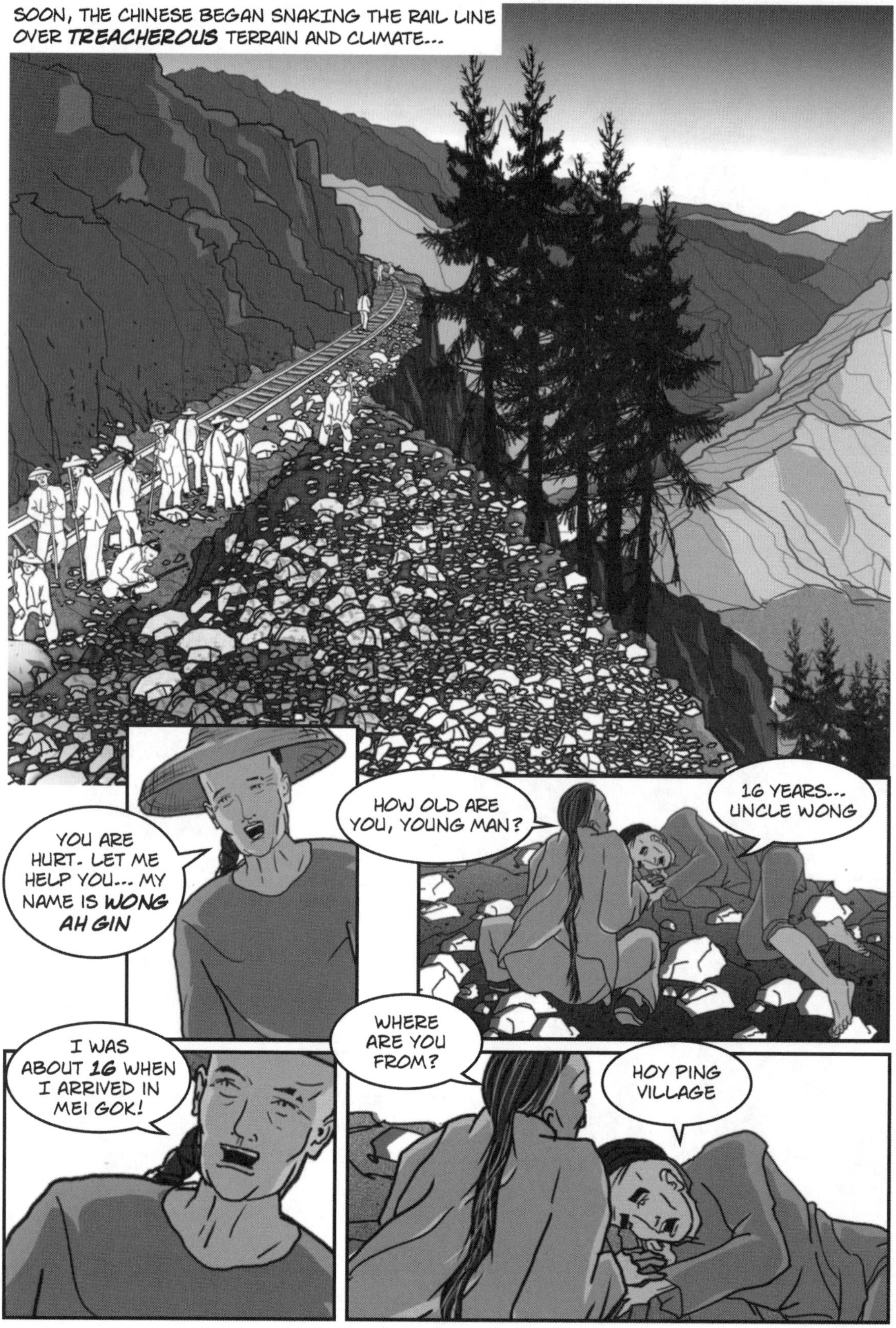
SOON, THE CHINESE BEGAN SNAKING THE RAIL LINE OVER TREACHEROUS TERRAIN AND CLIMATE...
YOU ARE HURT. LET ME HELP YOU... MY NAME IS WONG AH GIN
HOW OLD ARE YOU, YOUNG MAN?
16 YEARS... UNCLE WONG
I WAS ABOUT 16 WHEN I ARRIVED IN MEI GOK!
WHERE ARE YOU FROM?
HOY PING VILLAGE

WHY... I TOO AM FROM *HOY PING!*

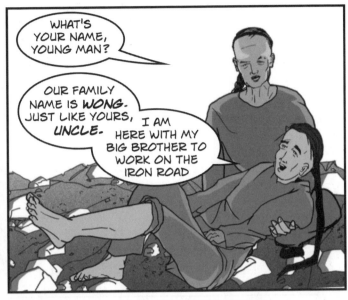

WHAT'S YOUR NAME, YOUNG MAN?

OUR FAMILY NAME IS *WONG.* JUST LIKE YOURS, *UNCLE.*

I AM HERE WITH MY BIG BROTHER TO WORK ON THE IRON ROAD

OVER THE COURSE OF THE NEXT SEVERAL MONTHS, THE CHINESE CREW OF THE *CENTRAL PACIFIC* BECOME LIKE *FAMILY,* SUPPORTING ONE ANOTHER THROUGH THE EXTREME CONDITIONS OF THE *SONORAN DESERT...*

SO DAMN *HOT* HERE DURING THE DAY!

C...C...COLD AT NIGHT. I DO NNOT HAVE MUCH C... CLOTHING ... *NO ONE* T...TOLD ME IT'S *C...COLD HERE WHEN I LEFT CH...CHINA...*

HERE, YOUNG WONG, TAKE MY BLANKET!

HERE, YOUNG WONG, HAVE MY MEAL PORTION

BUT UNCLE, YOU HAVEN'T EATEN YET

I ONLY TALK... YOU NEED NOURISHMENT FOR PHYSICAL LABOR

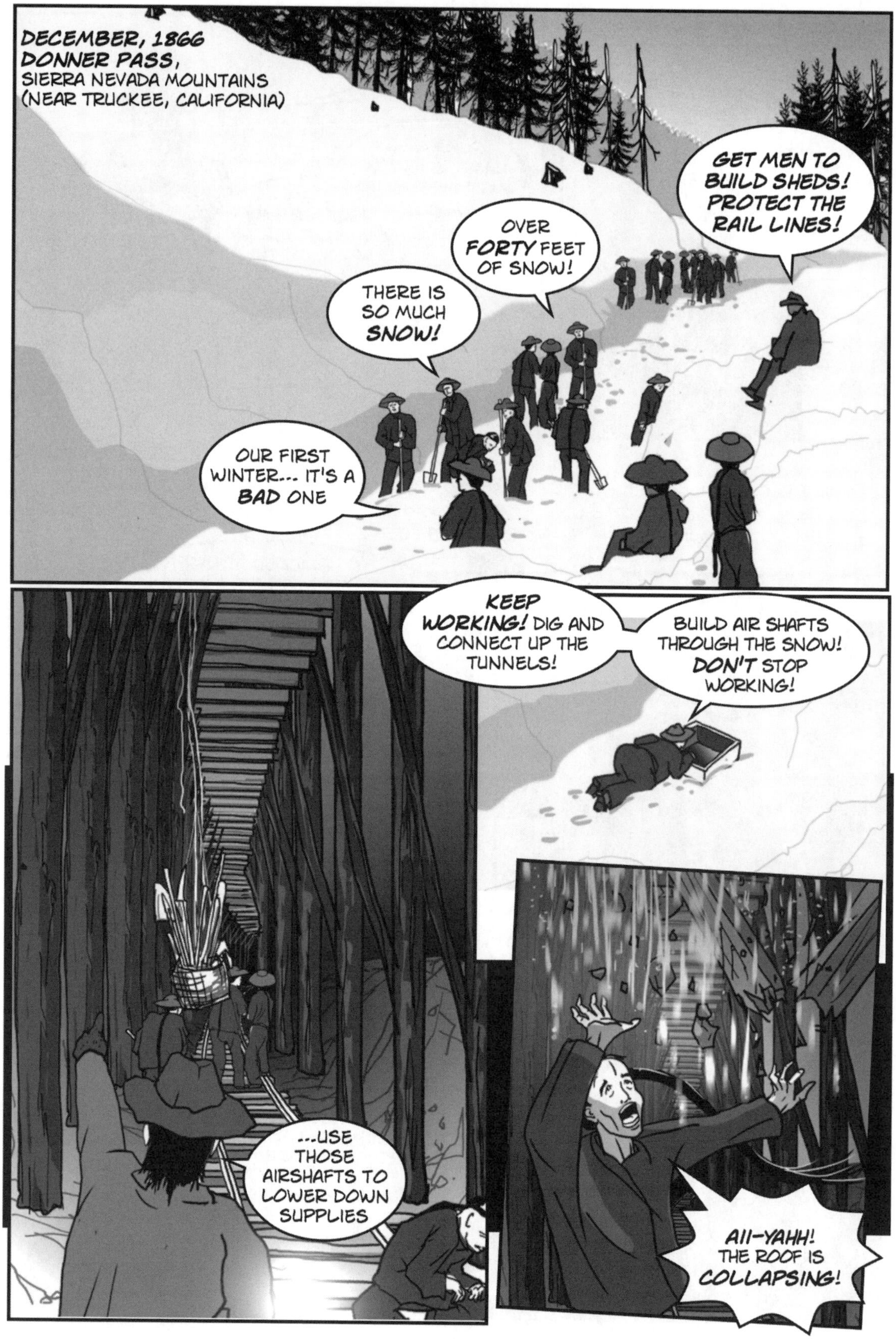
DECEMBER, 1866
DONNER PASS,
SIERRA NEVADA MOUNTAINS
(NEAR TRUCKEE, CALIFORNIA)
OUR FIRST WINTER... IT'S A BAD ONE
THERE IS SO MUCH SNOW!
OVER FORTY FEET OF SNOW!
GET MEN TO BUILD SHEDS! PROTECT THE RAIL LINES!
KEEP WORKING! DIG AND CONNECT UP THE TUNNELS!
BUILD AIR SHAFTS THROUGH THE SNOW! DON'T STOP WORKING!
...USE THOSE AIRSHAFTS TO LOWER DOWN SUPPLIES
AII-YAHH! THE ROOF IS COLLAPSING!

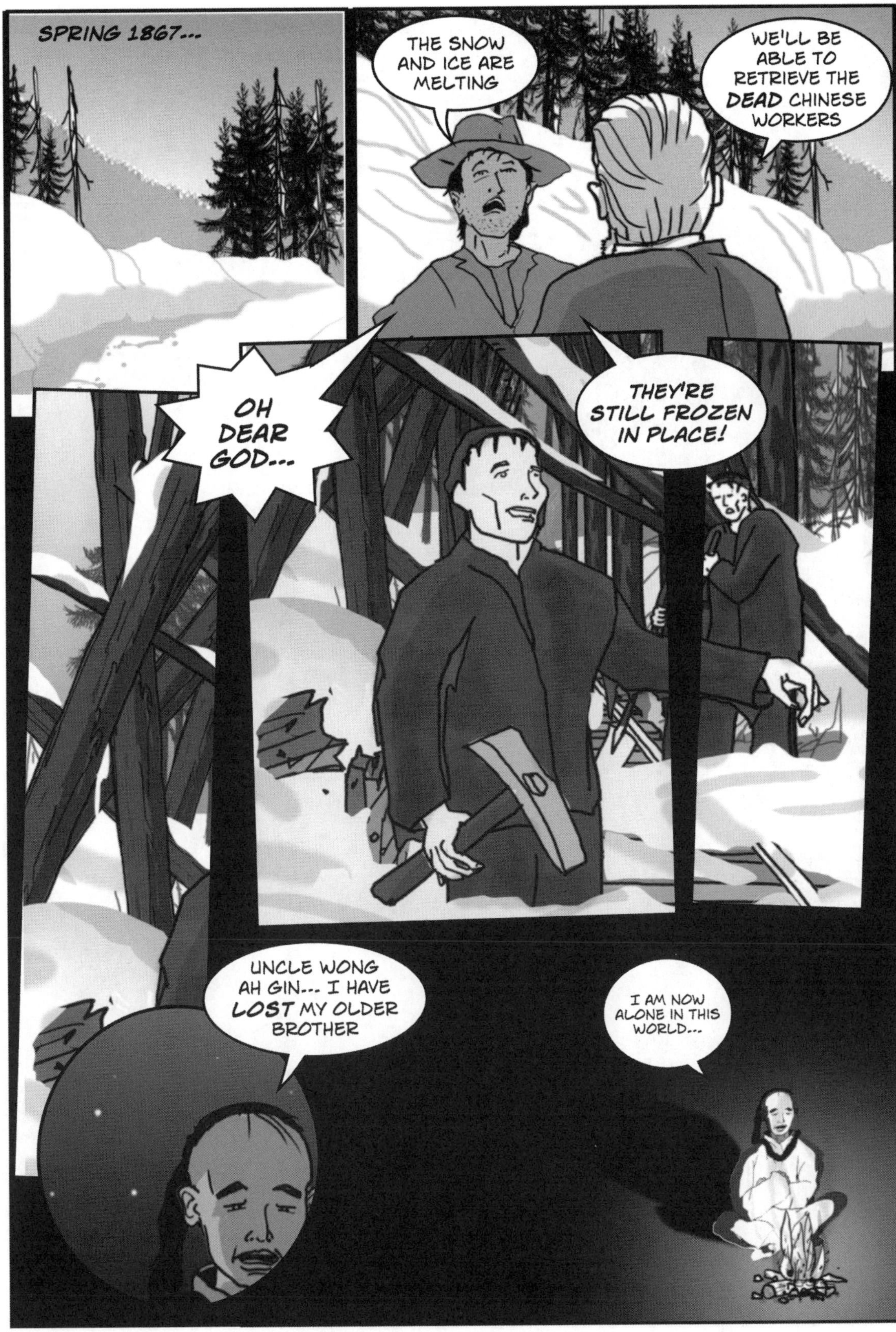
SPRING 1867...
THE SNOW AND ICE ARE MELTING
WE'LL BE ABLE TO RETRIEVE THE DEAD CHINESE WORKERS
OH DEAR GOD...
THEY'RE STILL FROZEN IN PLACE!
UNCLE WONG AH GIN... I HAVE LOST MY OLDER BROTHER
I AM NOW ALONE IN THIS WORLD...

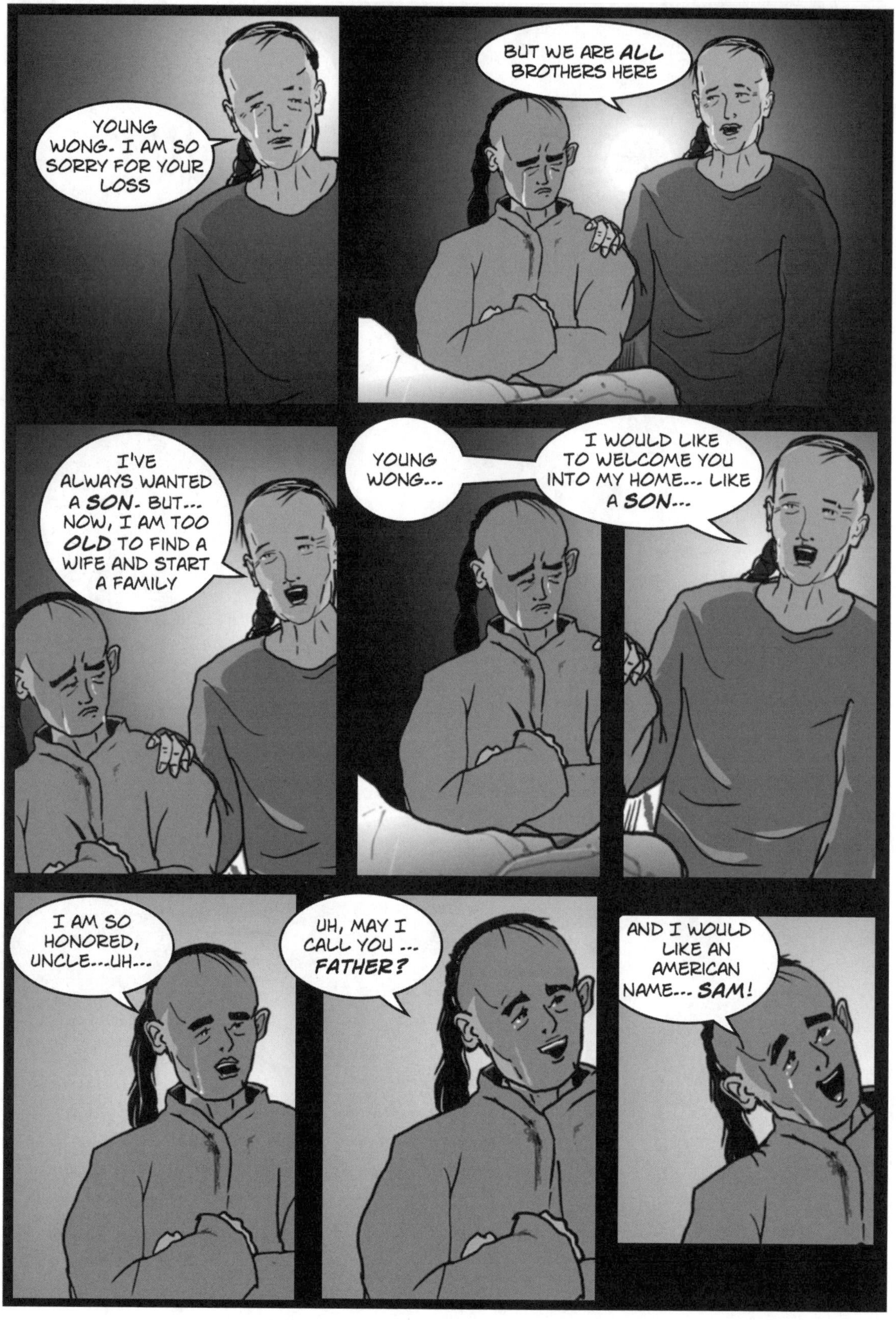
YOUNG WONG. I AM SO SORRY FOR YOUR LOSS
BUT WE ARE ALL BROTHERS HERE
I'VE ALWAYS WANTED A SON. BUT... NOW, I AM TOO OLD TO FIND A WIFE AND START A FAMILY
YOUNG WONG...
I WOULD LIKE TO WELCOME YOU INTO MY HOME... LIKE A SON...
I AM SO HONORED, UNCLE...UH...
UH, MAY I CALL YOU ... FATHER?
AND I WOULD LIKE AN AMERICAN NAME... SAM!

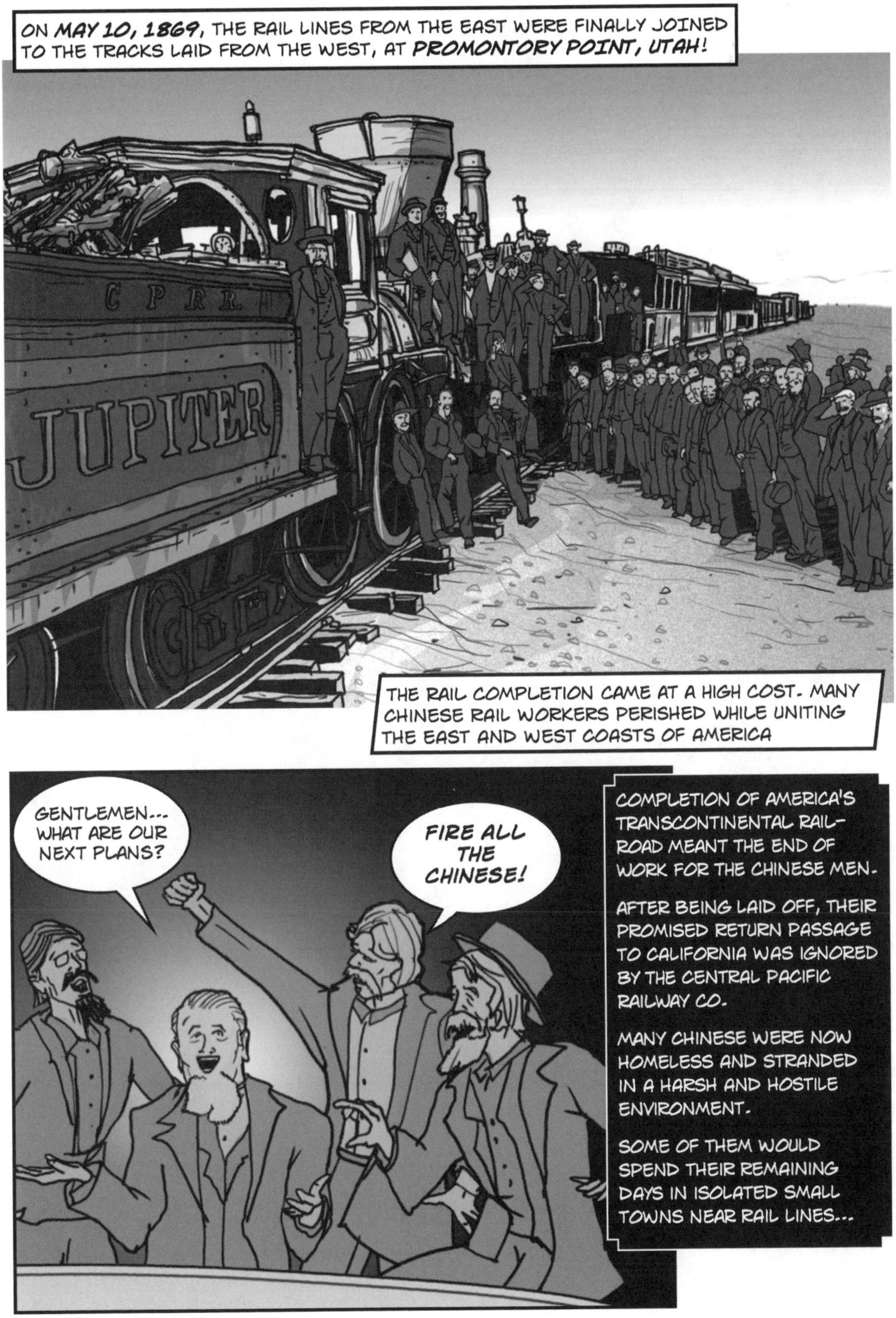
ON MAY 10, 1869, THE RAIL LINES FROM THE EAST WERE FINALLY JOINED TO THE TRACKS LAID FROM THE WEST, AT PROMONTORY POINT, UTAH!
C.P.R.R.
JUPITER
THE RAIL COMPLETION CAME AT A HIGH COST. MANY CHINESE RAIL WORKERS PERISHED WHILE UNITING THE EAST AND WEST COASTS OF AMERICA
GENTLEMEN... WHAT ARE OUR NEXT PLANS?
FIRE ALL THE CHINESE!
COMPLETION OF AMERICA'S TRANSCONTINENTAL RAILROAD MEANT THE END OF WORK FOR THE CHINESE MEN.
AFTER BEING LAID OFF, THEIR PROMISED RETURN PASSAGE TO CALIFORNIA WAS IGNORED BY THE CENTRAL PACIFIC RAILWAY CO.
MANY CHINESE WERE NOW HOMELESS AND STRANDED IN A HARSH AND HOSTILE ENVIRONMENT.
SOME OF THEM WOULD SPEND THEIR REMAINING DAYS IN ISOLATED SMALL TOWNS NEAR RAIL LINES...

CHAPTER 6 Storm Clouds of Hatred

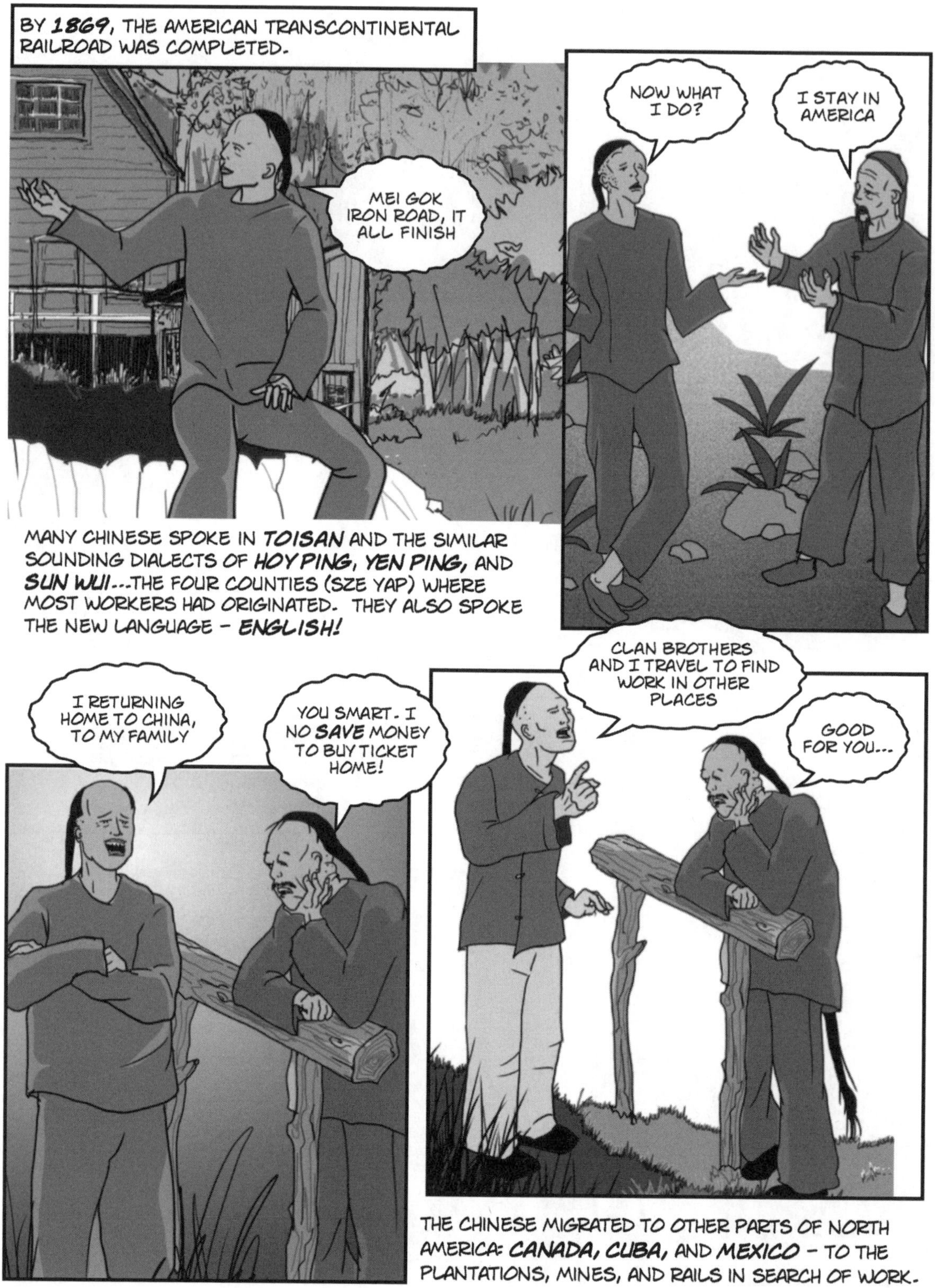
BY 1869, THE AMERICAN TRANSCONTINENTAL RAILROAD WAS COMPLETED.
MEI GOK IRON ROAD, IT ALL FINISH
MANY CHINESE SPOKE IN TOISAN AND THE SIMILAR SOUNDING DIALECTS OF HOY PING, YEN PING, AND SUN WUI...THE FOUR COUNTIES (SZE YAP) WHERE MOST WORKERS HAD ORIGINATED. THEY ALSO SPOKE THE NEW LANGUAGE - ENGLISH!
NOW WHAT I DO?
I STAY IN AMERICA
I RETURNING HOME TO CHINA, TO MY FAMILY
YOU SMART. I NO SAVE MONEY TO BUY TICKET HOME!
CLAN BROTHERS AND I TRAVEL TO FIND WORK IN OTHER PLACES
GOOD FOR YOU...
THE CHINESE MIGRATED TO OTHER PARTS OF NORTH AMERICA: CANADA, CUBA, AND MEXICO - TO THE PLANTATIONS, MINES, AND RAILS IN SEARCH OF WORK.

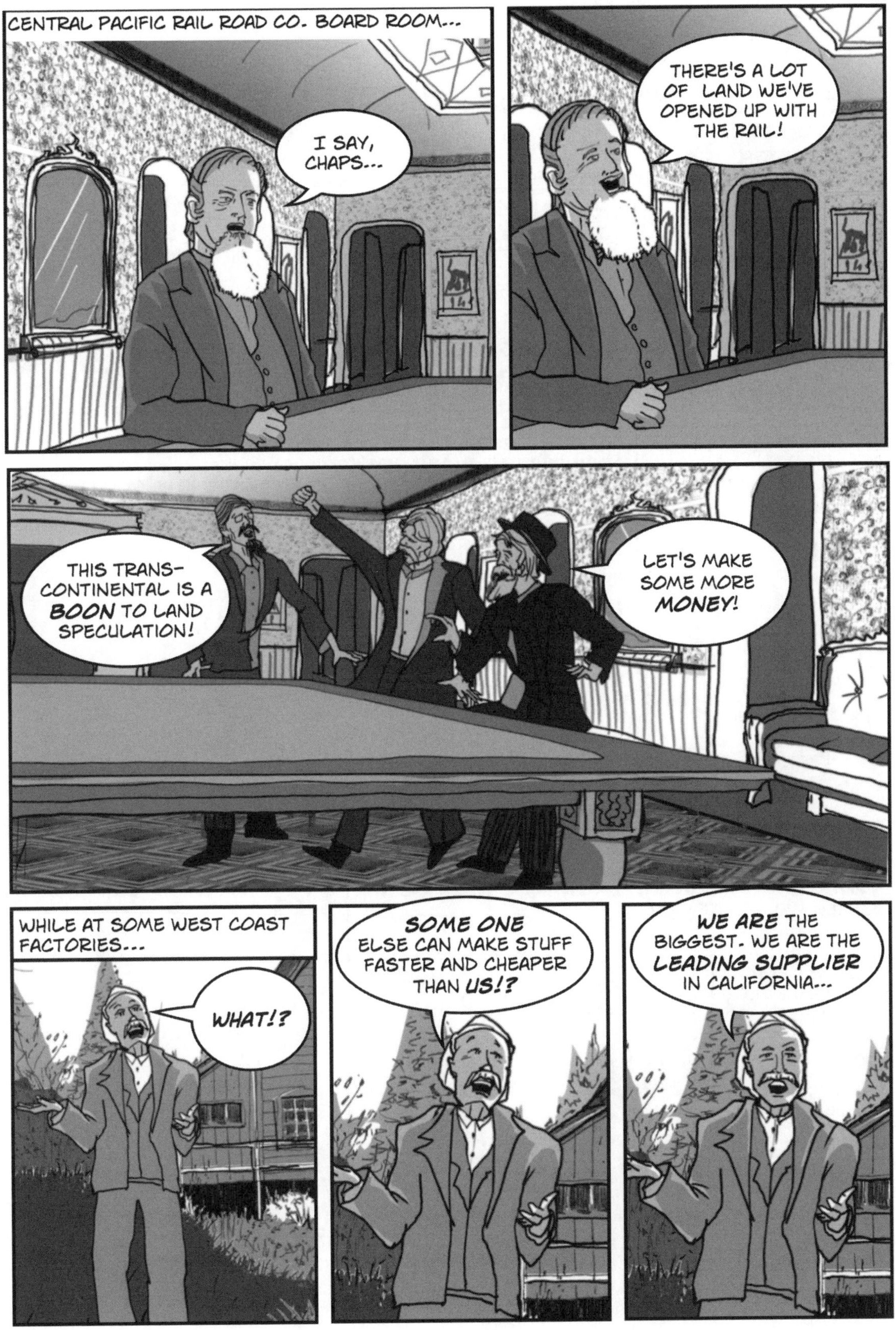
CENTRAL PACIFIC RAIL ROAD CO. BOARD ROOM...
I SAY, CHAPS...
THERE'S A LOT OF LAND WE'VE OPENED UP WITH THE RAIL!
THIS TRANS-CONTINENTAL IS A BOON TO LAND SPECULATION!
LET'S MAKE SOME MORE MONEY!
WHILE AT SOME WEST COAST FACTORIES...
WHAT!?
SOME ONE ELSE CAN MAKE STUFF FASTER AND CHEAPER THAN US!?
WE ARE THE BIGGEST. WE ARE THE LEADING SUPPLIER IN CALIFORNIA...

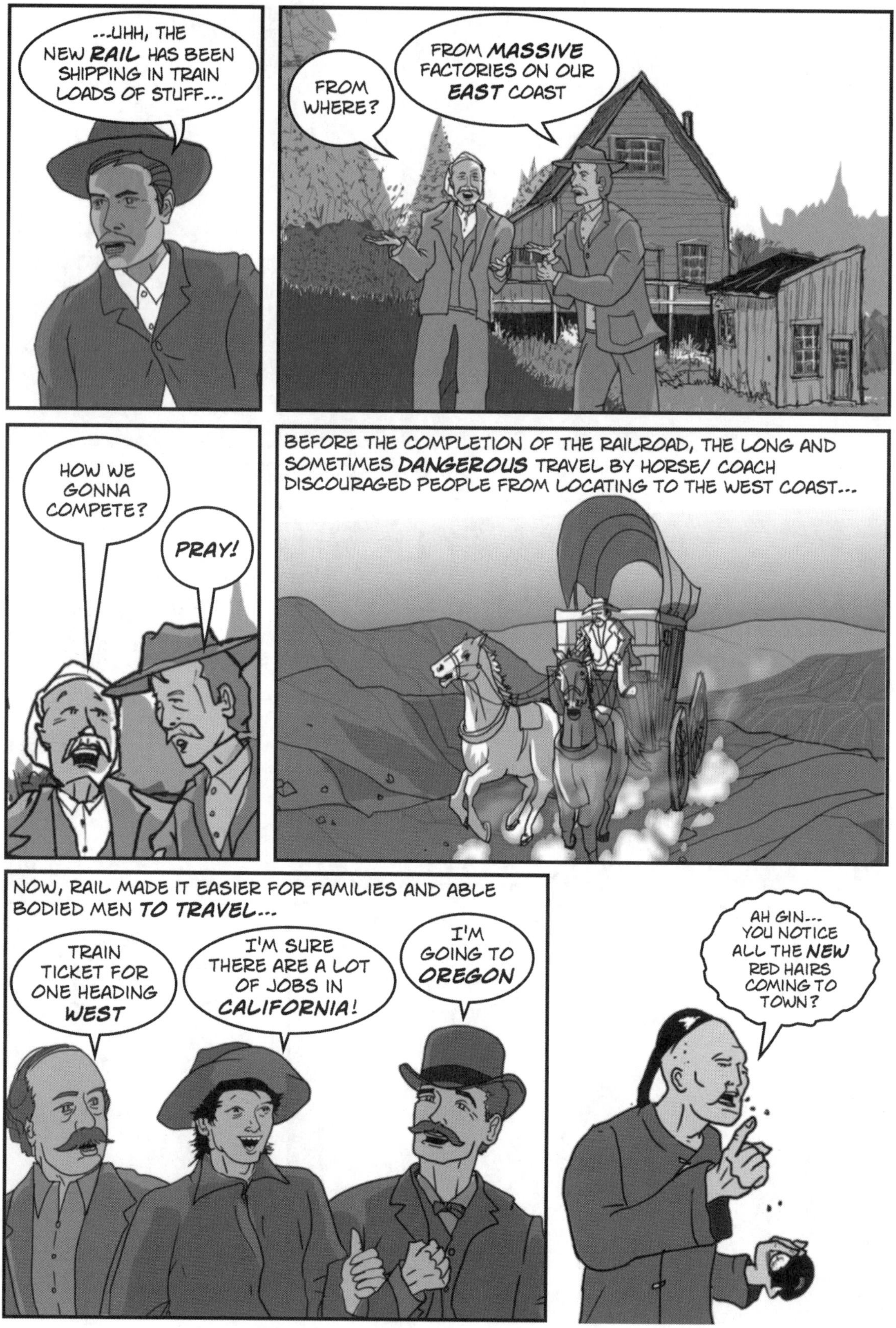
...UHH, THE NEW RAIL HAS BEEN SHIPPING IN TRAIN LOADS OF STUFF...
FROM WHERE?
FROM MASSIVE FACTORIES ON OUR EAST COAST
HOW WE GONNA COMPETE?
PRAY!
BEFORE THE COMPLETION OF THE RAILROAD, THE LONG AND SOMETIMES DANGEROUS TRAVEL BY HORSE/ COACH DISCOURAGED PEOPLE FROM LOCATING TO THE WEST COAST...
NOW, RAIL MADE IT EASIER FOR FAMILIES AND ABLE BODIED MEN TO TRAVEL...
TRAIN TICKET FOR ONE HEADING WEST
I'M SURE THERE ARE A LOT OF JOBS IN CALIFORNIA!
I'M GOING TO OREGON
AH GIN... YOU NOTICE ALL THE NEW RED HAIRS COMING TO TOWN?

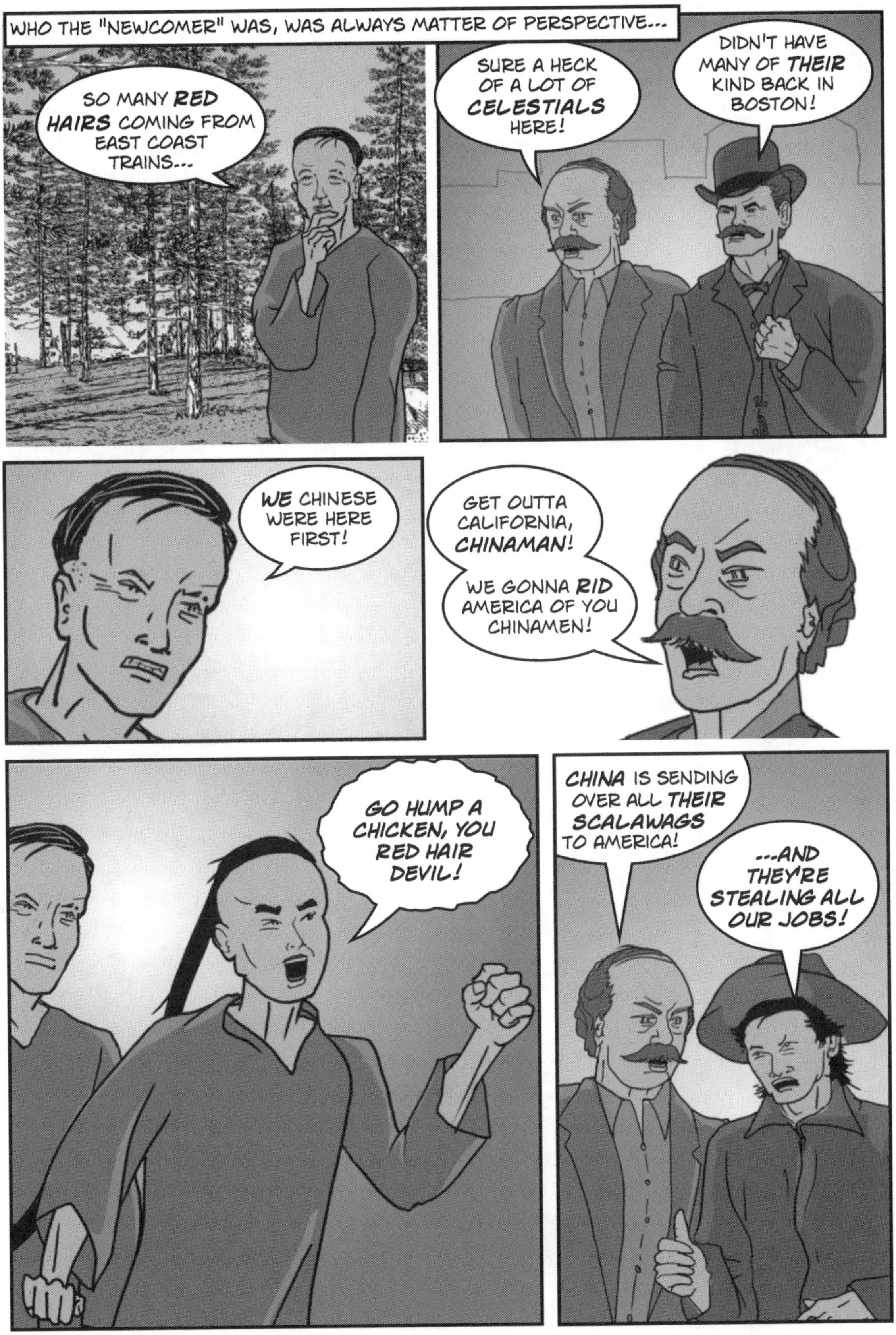
WHO THE "NEWCOMER" WAS, WAS ALWAYS MATTER OF PERSPECTIVE...
SO MANY RED HAIRS COMING FROM EAST COAST TRAINS...
SURE A HECK OF A LOT OF CELESTIALS HERE!
DIDN'T HAVE MANY OF THEIR KIND BACK IN BOSTON!
WE CHINESE WERE HERE FIRST!
GET OUTTA CALIFORNIA, CHINAMAN!
WE GONNA RID AMERICA OF YOU CHINAMEN!
GO HUMP A CHICKEN, YOU RED HAIR DEVIL!
CHINA IS SENDING OVER ALL THEIR SCALAWAGS TO AMERICA!
...AND THEY'RE STEALING ALL OUR JOBS!

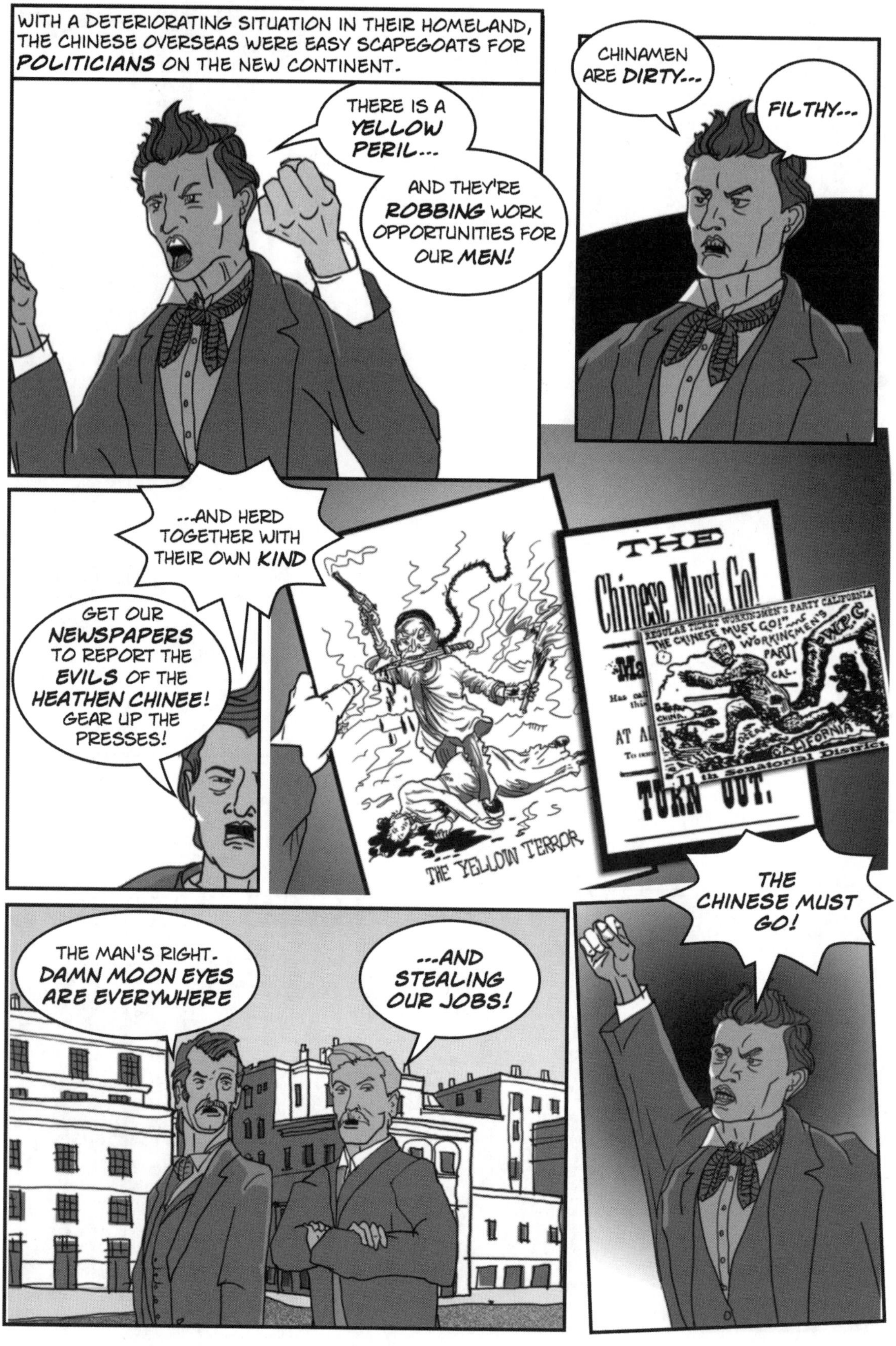

WITH A DETERIORATING SITUATION IN THEIR HOMELAND, THE CHINESE OVERSEAS WERE EASY SCAPEGOATS FOR **POLITICIANS** ON THE NEW CONTINENT.
THERE IS A **YELLOW PERIL**...
AND THEY'RE **ROBBING** WORK OPPORTUNITIES FOR OUR **MEN**!
CHINAMEN ARE **DIRTY**...
FILTHY...
...AND HERD TOGETHER WITH THEIR OWN **KIND**
GET OUR **NEWSPAPERS** TO REPORT THE **EVILS** OF THE **HEATHEN CHINEE**! GEAR UP THE PRESSES!
THE YELLOW TERROR
THE
Chinese Must Go!
TURN OUT.
THE CHINESE MUST GO!
WORKINGMEN'S
PARTY OF CAL.
CALIFORNIA
THE CHINESE MUST GO!
THE MAN'S RIGHT. **DAMN MOON EYES ARE EVERYWHERE**
...**AND STEALING OUR JOBS**!

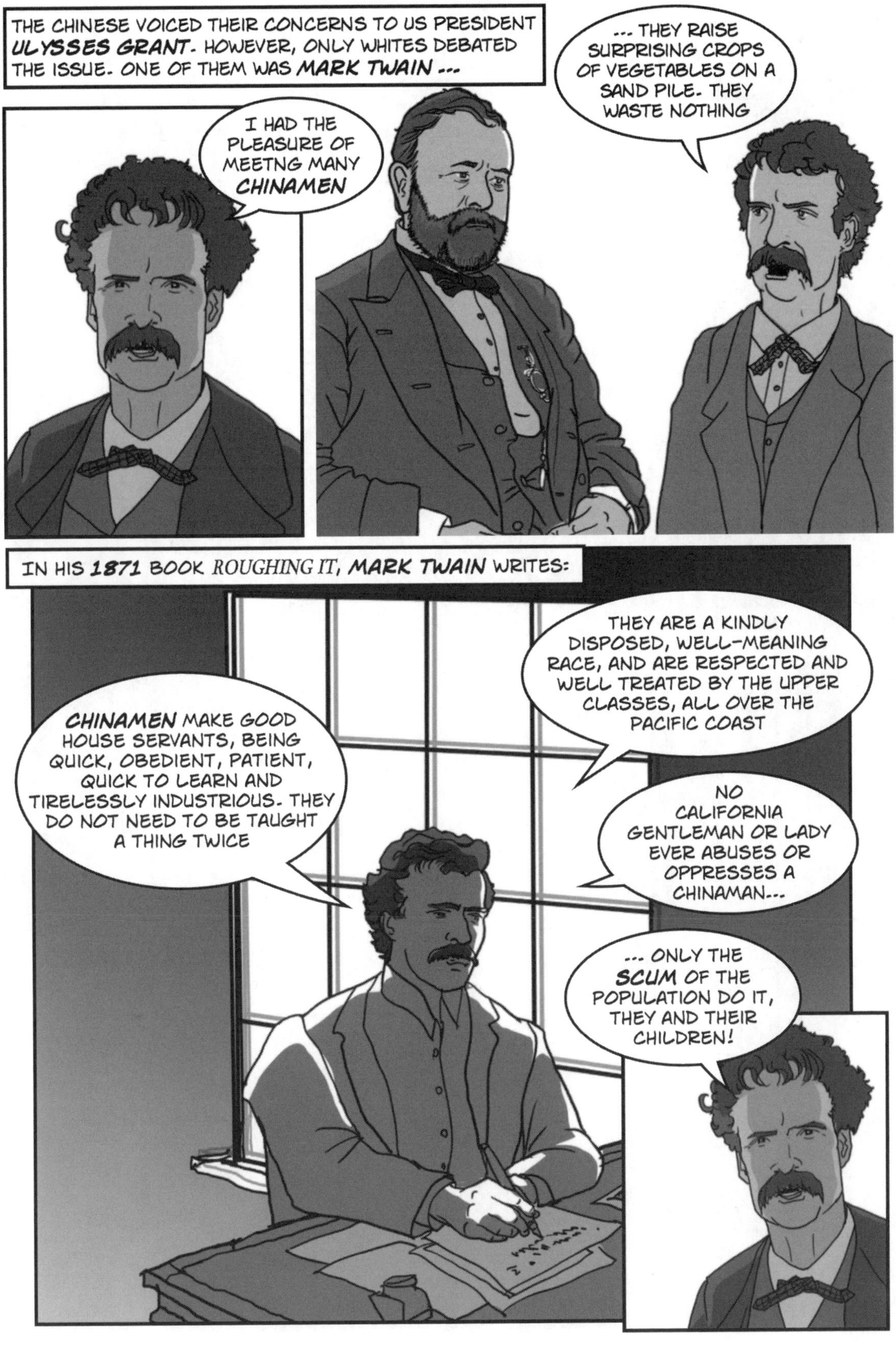
THE CHINESE VOICED THEIR CONCERNS TO US PRESIDENT ULYSSES GRANT. HOWEVER, ONLY WHITES DEBATED THE ISSUE. ONE OF THEM WAS MARK TWAIN ...
I HAD THE PLEASURE OF MEETNG MANY CHINAMEN
... THEY RAISE SURPRISING CROPS OF VEGETABLES ON A SAND PILE. THEY WASTE NOTHING
IN HIS 1871 BOOK ROUGHING IT, MARK TWAIN WRITES:
CHINAMEN MAKE GOOD HOUSE SERVANTS, BEING QUICK, OBEDIENT, PATIENT, QUICK TO LEARN AND TIRELESSLY INDUSTRIOUS. THEY DO NOT NEED TO BE TAUGHT A THING TWICE
THEY ARE A KINDLY DISPOSED, WELL-MEANING RACE, AND ARE RESPECTED AND WELL TREATED BY THE UPPER CLASSES, ALL OVER THE PACIFIC COAST
NO CALIFORNIA GENTLEMAN OR LADY EVER ABUSES OR OPPRESSES A CHINAMAN...
... ONLY THE SCUM OF THE POPULATION DO IT, THEY AND THEIR CHILDREN!

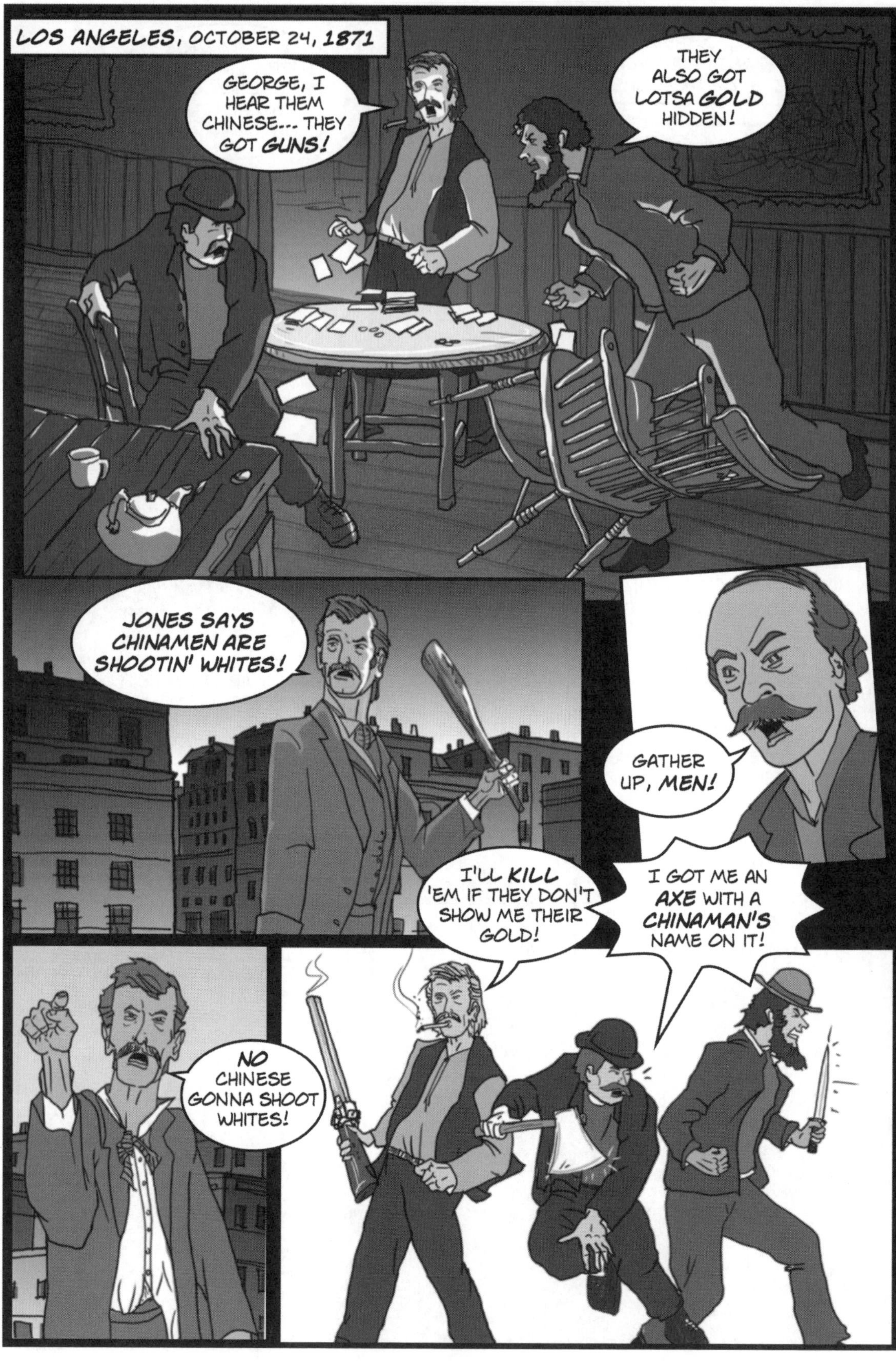
LOS ANGELES, OCTOBER 24, 1871
GEORGE, I HEAR THEM CHINESE... THEY GOT GUNS!
THEY ALSO GOT LOTSA GOLD HIDDEN!
JONES SAYS CHINAMEN ARE SHOOTIN' WHITES!
GATHER UP, MEN!
NO CHINESE GONNA SHOOT WHITES!
I'LL KILL 'EM IF THEY DON'T SHOW ME THEIR GOLD!
I GOT ME AN AXE WITH A CHINAMAN'S NAME ON IT!

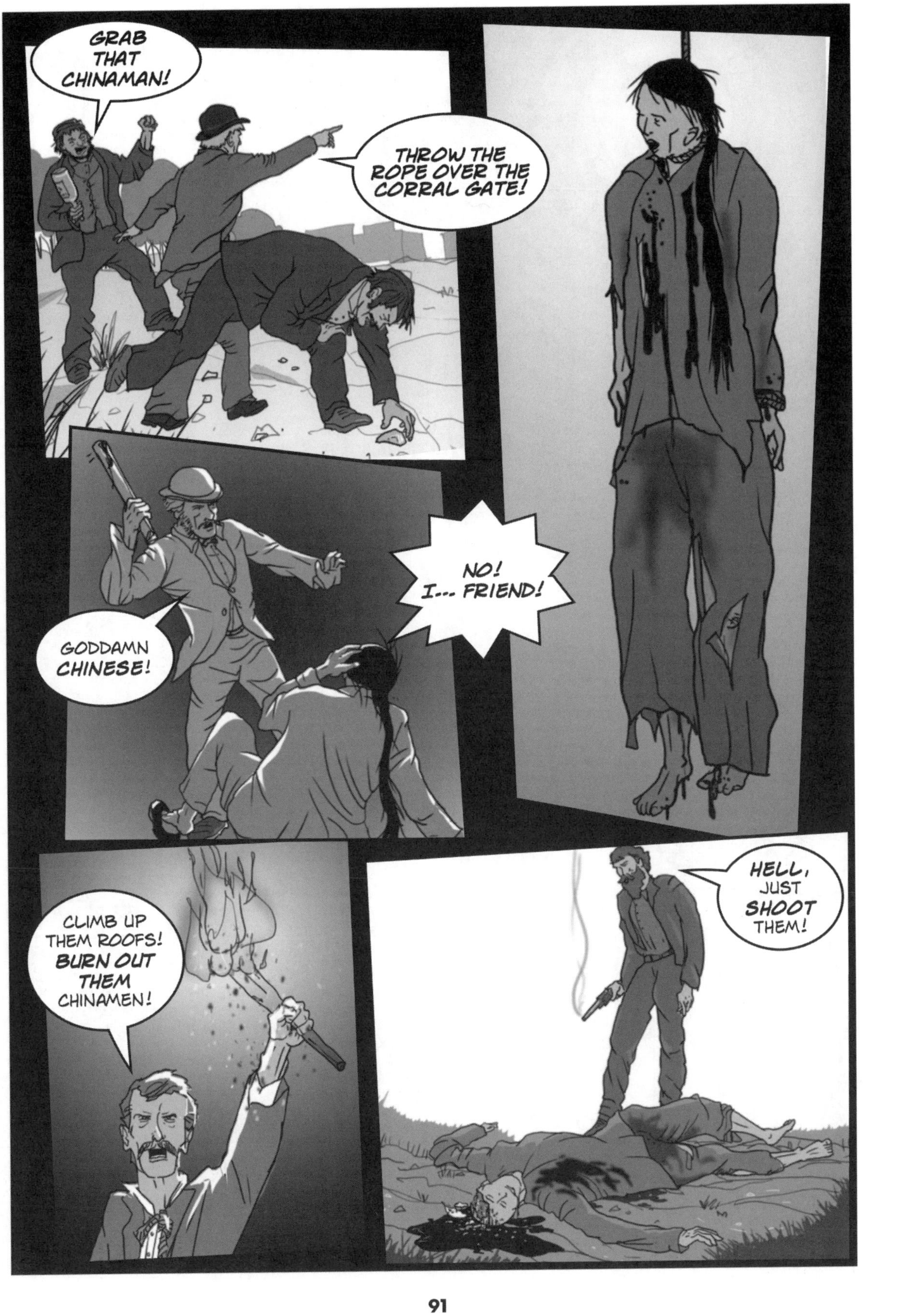
GRAB THAT CHINAMAN!
THROW THE ROPE OVER THE CORRAL GATE!
NO! I... FRIEND!
GODDAMN CHINESE!
CLIMB UP THEM ROOFS! BURN OUT THEM CHINAMEN!
HELL, JUST SHOOT THEM!

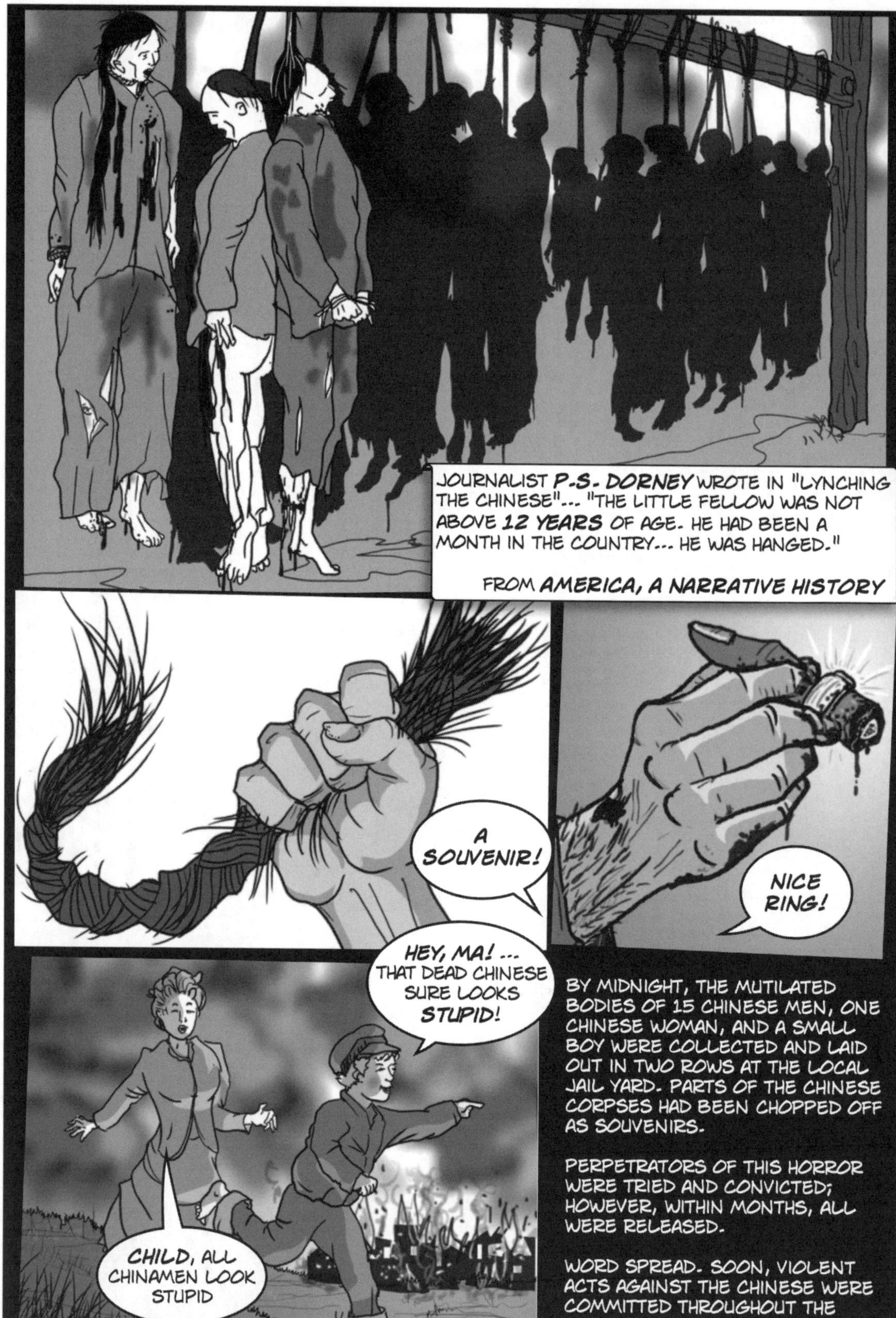
JOURNALIST P.S. DORNEY WROTE IN "LYNCHING THE CHINESE"... "THE LITTLE FELLOW WAS NOT ABOVE 12 YEARS OF AGE. HE HAD BEEN A MONTH IN THE COUNTRY... HE WAS HANGED."
FROM AMERICA, A NARRATIVE HISTORY
A SOUVENIR!
NICE RING!
HEY, MA! ... THAT DEAD CHINESE SURE LOOKS STUPID!
CHILD, ALL CHINAMEN LOOK STUPID
BY MIDNIGHT, THE MUTILATED BODIES OF 15 CHINESE MEN, ONE CHINESE WOMAN, AND A SMALL BOY WERE COLLECTED AND LAID OUT IN TWO ROWS AT THE LOCAL JAIL YARD. PARTS OF THE CHINESE CORPSES HAD BEEN CHOPPED OFF AS SOUVENIRS.
PERPETRATORS OF THIS HORROR WERE TRIED AND CONVICTED; HOWEVER, WITHIN MONTHS, ALL WERE RELEASED.
WORD SPREAD. SOON, VIOLENT ACTS AGAINST THE CHINESE WERE COMMITTED THROUGHOUT THE WEST COAST, AND IN BC, CANADA

CHAPTER 7 The Chinese Must Go!

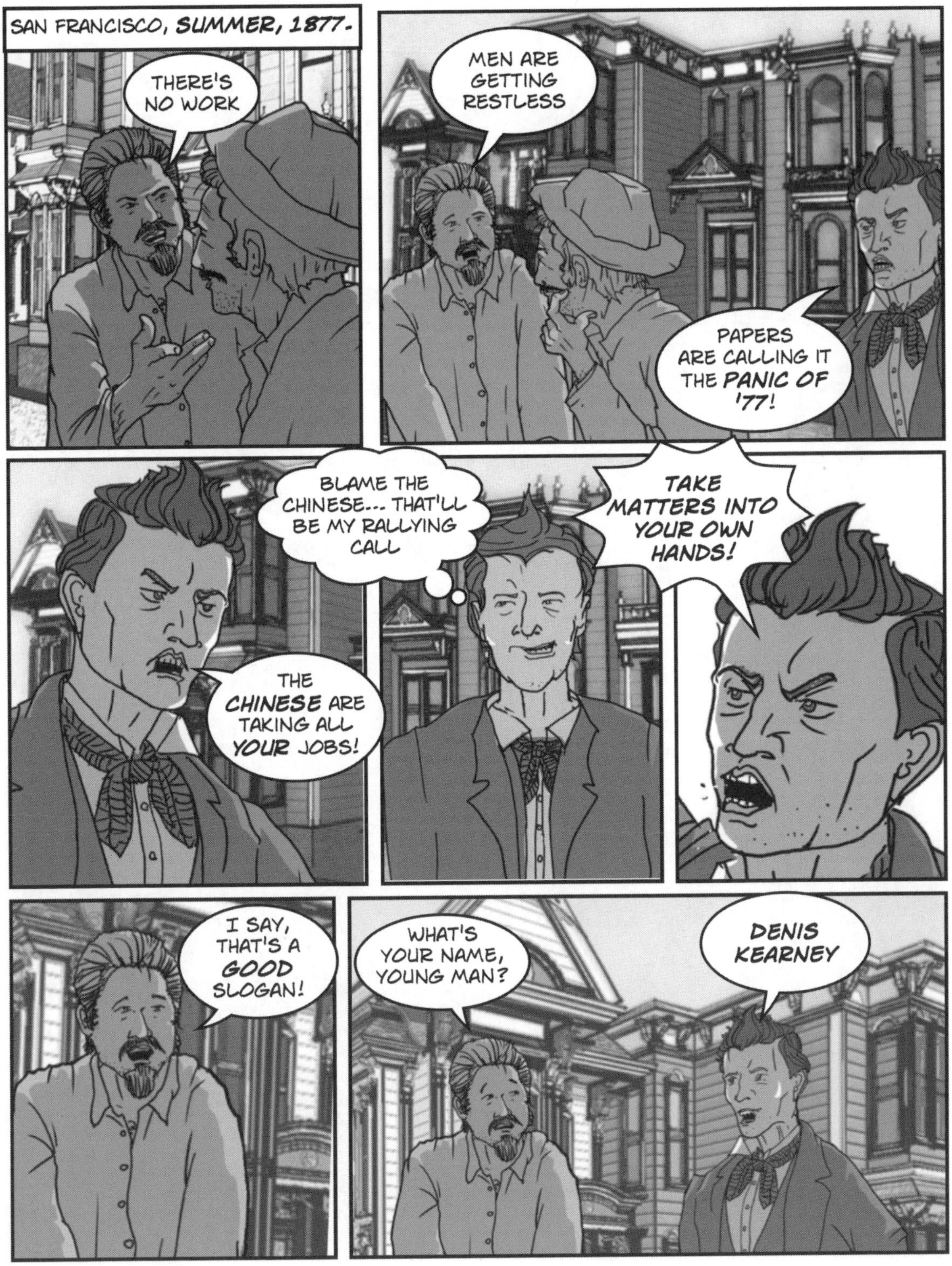

SAN FRANCISCO, SUMMER, 1877.
THERE'S NO WORK
MEN ARE GETTING RESTLESS
PAPERS ARE CALLING IT THE PANIC OF '77!
THE CHINESE ARE TAKING ALL YOUR JOBS!
BLAME THE CHINESE... THAT'LL BE MY RALLYING CALL
TAKE MATTERS INTO YOUR OWN HANDS!
I SAY, THAT'S A GOOD SLOGAN!
WHAT'S YOUR NAME, YOUNG MAN?
DENIS KEARNEY

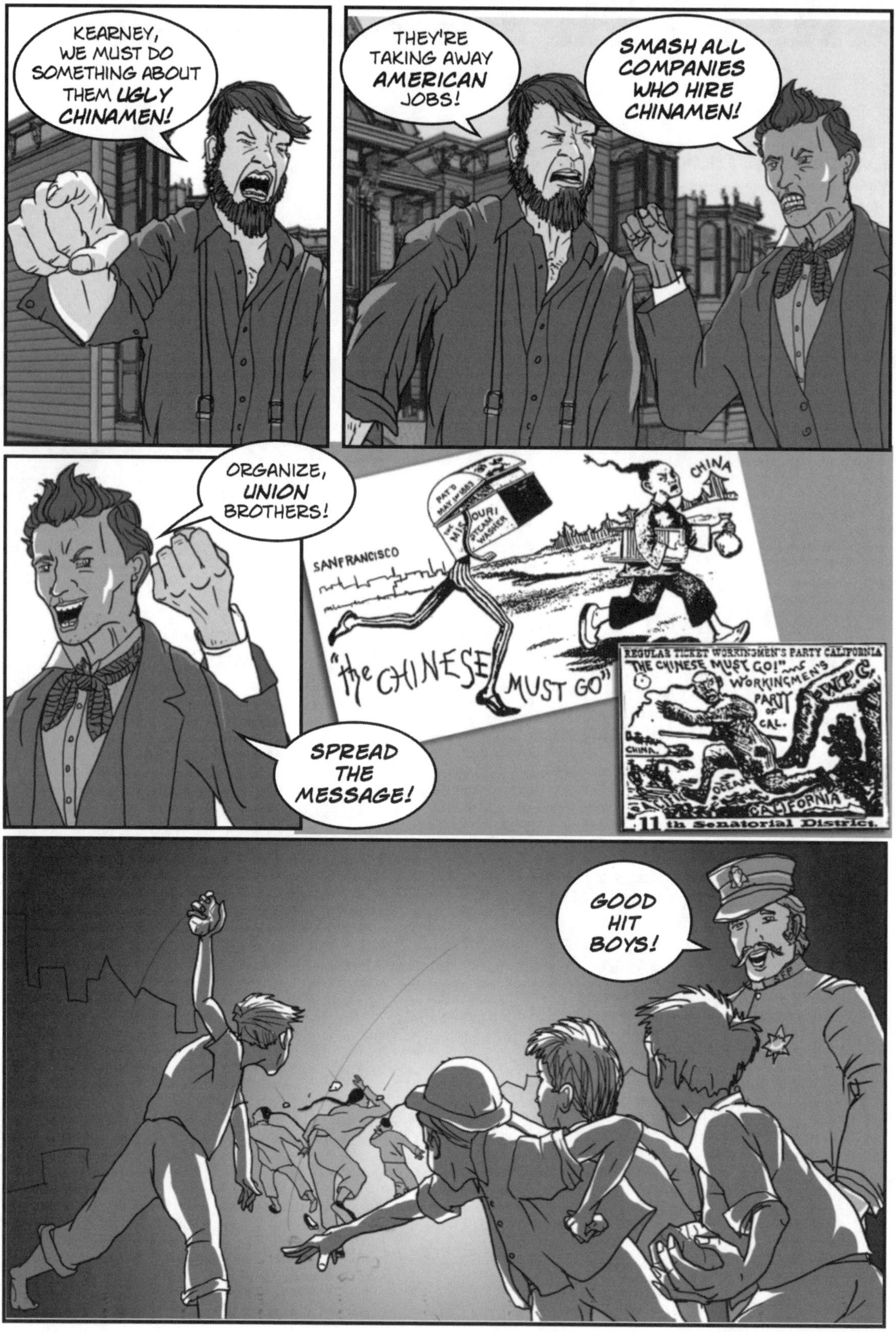
KEARNEY, WE MUST DO SOMETHING ABOUT THEM UGLY CHINAMEN!
THEY'RE TAKING AWAY AMERICAN JOBS!
SMASH ALL COMPANIES WHO HIRE CHINAMEN!
ORGANIZE, UNION BROTHERS!
SPREAD THE MESSAGE!
SAN FRANCISCO
CHINA
MISSOURI STEAM WASHER
"the CHINESE MUST GO"
REGULAR TICKET WORKINGMEN'S PARTY CALIFORNIA
"THE CHINESE MUST GO!"
WORKINGMEN'S PARTY OF CAL.
CHINA
OCEAN
CALIFORNIA
11 th Senatorial District.
GOOD HIT BOYS!

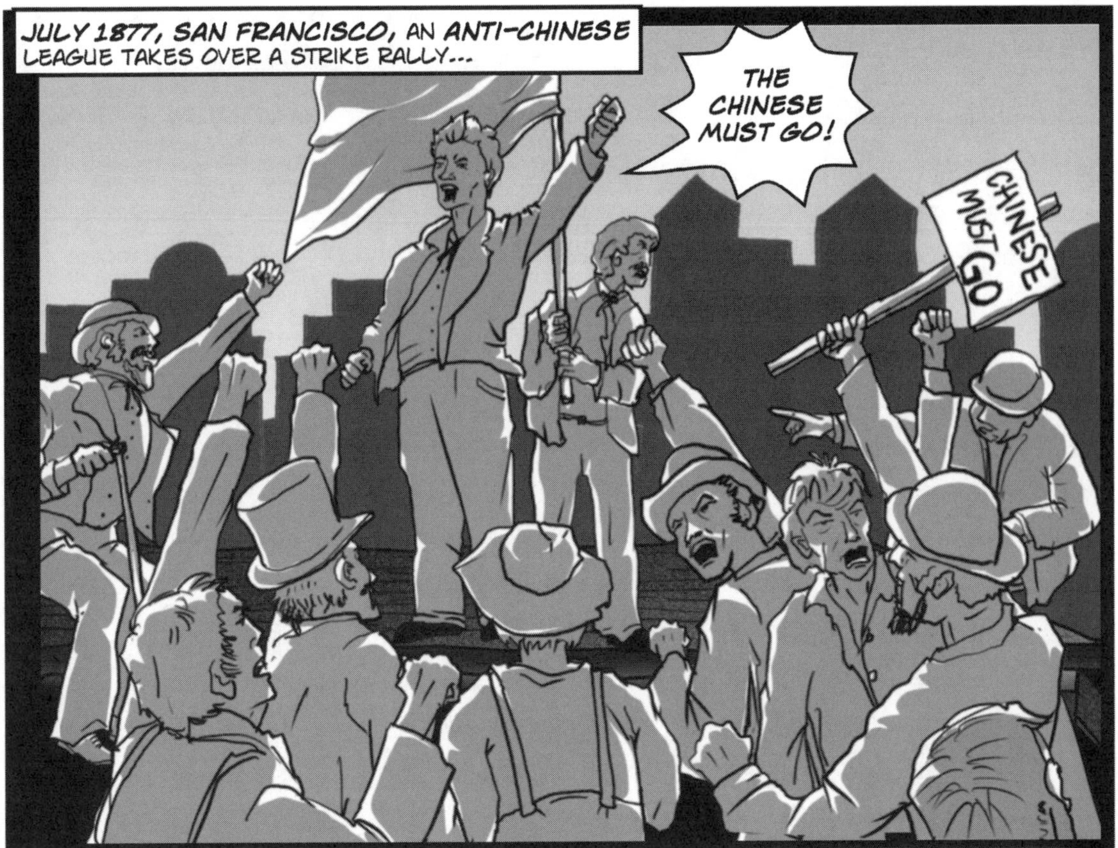
JULY 1877, SAN FRANCISCO, AN ANTI-CHINESE LEAGUE TAKES OVER A STRIKE RALLY...
THE CHINESE MUST GO!
CHINESE MUST GO

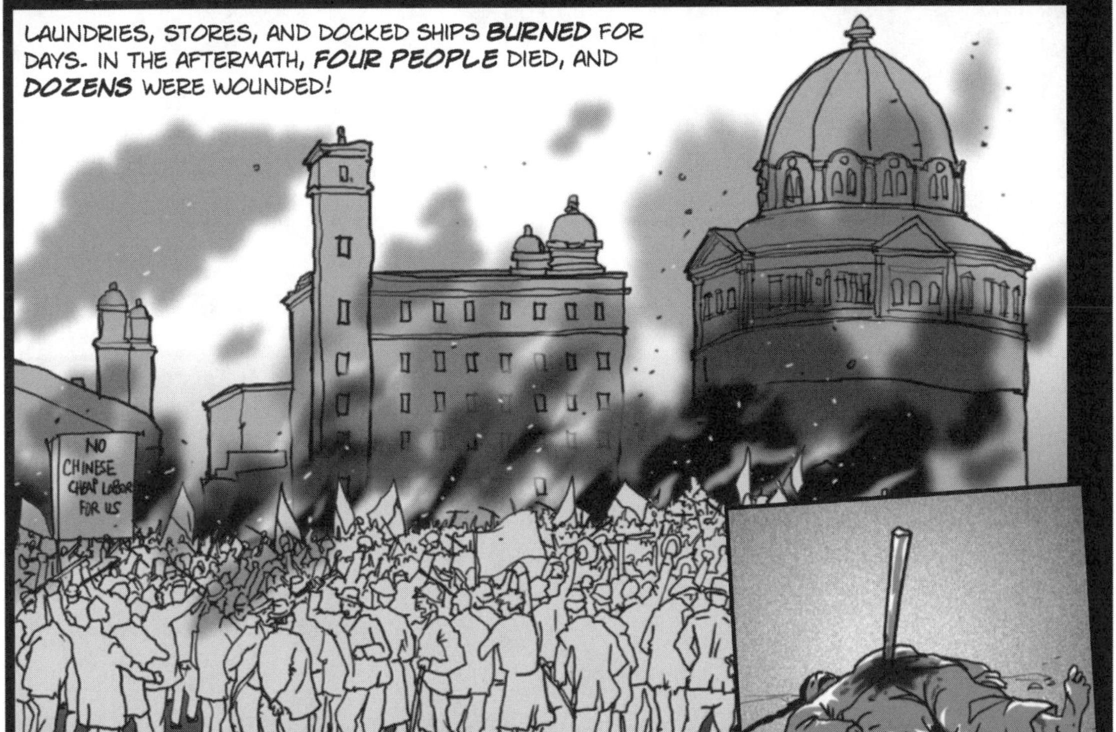
LAUNDRIES, STORES, AND DOCKED SHIPS BURNED FOR DAYS. IN THE AFTERMATH, FOUR PEOPLE DIED, AND DOZENS WERE WOUNDED!
NO CHINESE CHEAP LABOR FOR US

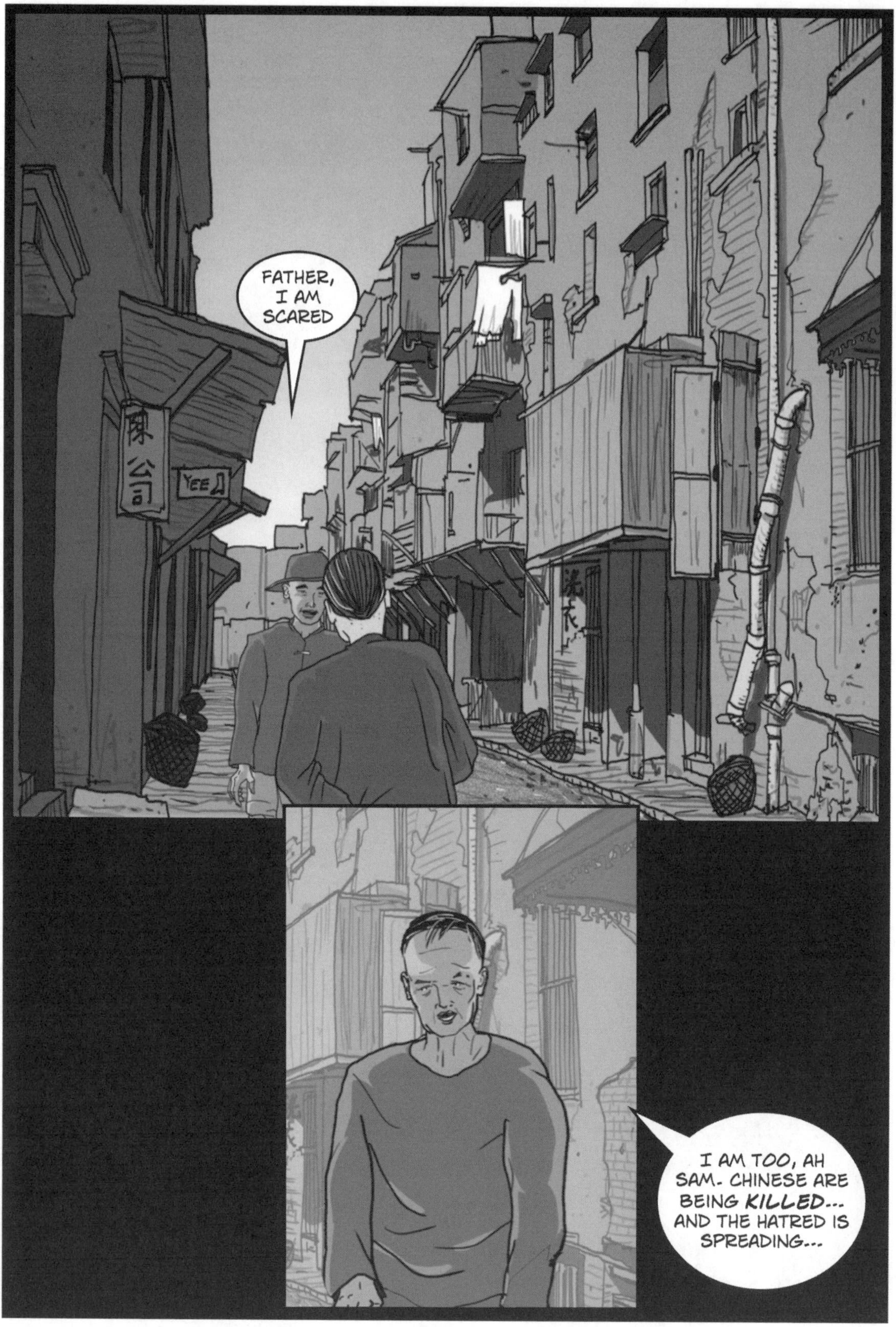
FATHER, I AM SCARED
YEE
I AM TOO, AH SAM. CHINESE ARE BEING **KILLED**... AND THE HATRED IS SPREADING...

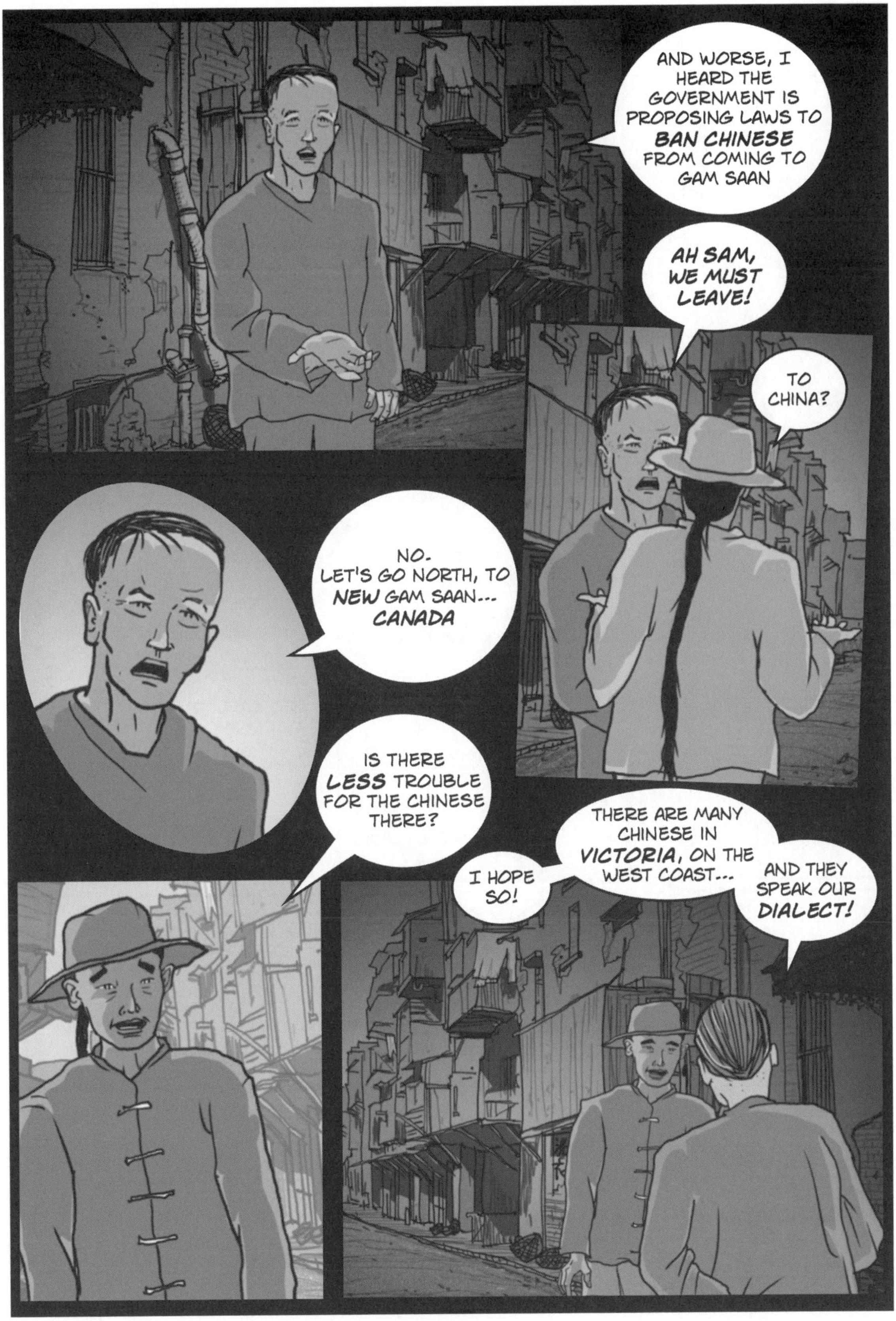
AND WORSE, I HEARD THE GOVERNMENT IS PROPOSING LAWS TO BAN CHINESE FROM COMING TO GAM SAAN
AH SAM, WE MUST LEAVE!
TO CHINA?
NO. LET'S GO NORTH, TO NEW GAM SAAN... CANADA
IS THERE LESS TROUBLE FOR THE CHINESE THERE?
I HOPE SO!
THERE ARE MANY CHINESE IN VICTORIA, ON THE WEST COAST...
AND THEY SPEAK OUR DIALECT!

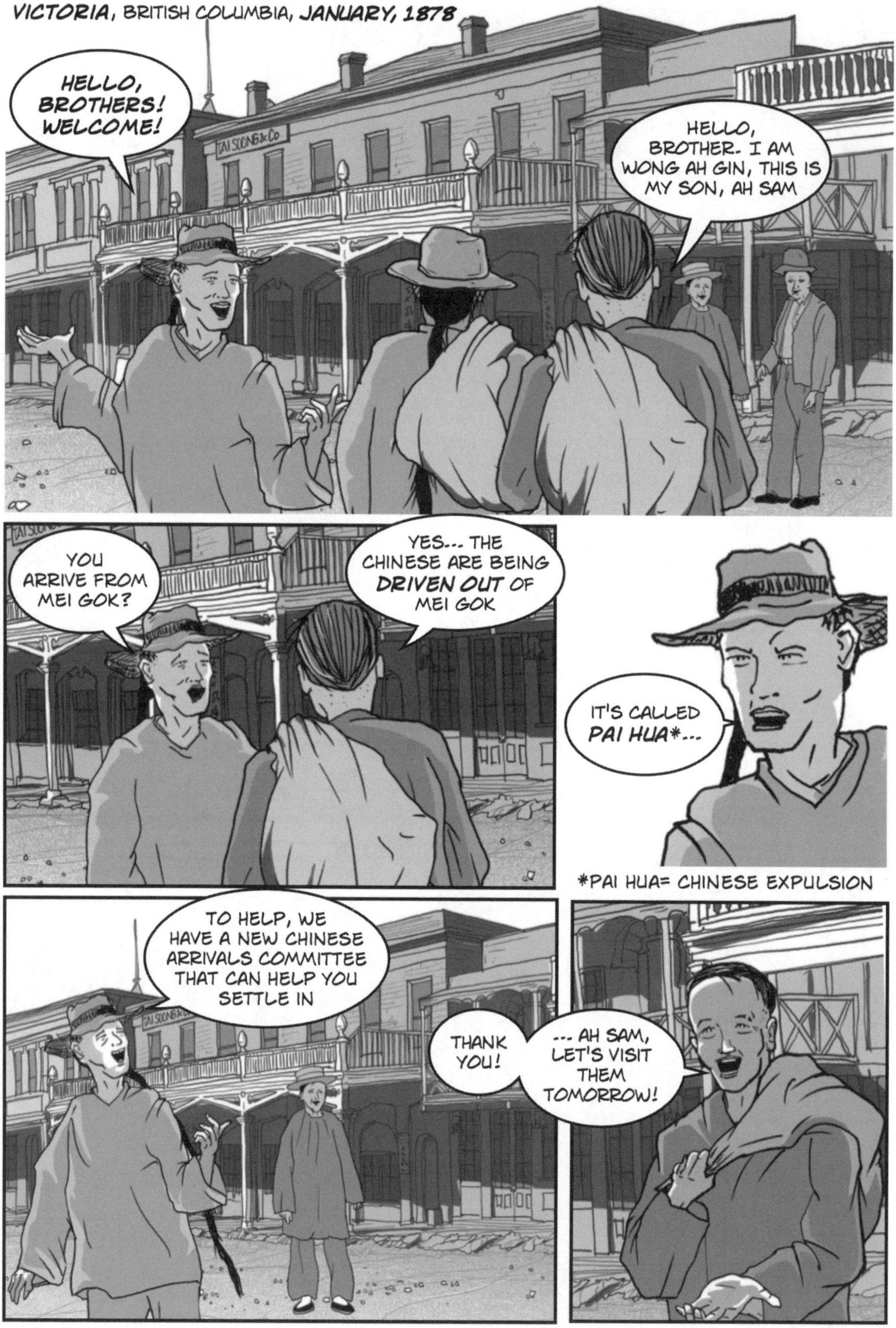
VICTORIA, BRITISH COLUMBIA, JANUARY, 1878
HELLO, BROTHERS! WELCOME!
HELLO, BROTHER. I AM WONG AH GIN, THIS IS MY SON, AH SAM
TAI SOONG & Co
YOU ARRIVE FROM MEI GOK?
YES... THE CHINESE ARE BEING DRIVEN OUT OF MEI GOK
IT'S CALLED PAI HUA*...
*PAI HUA= CHINESE EXPULSION
TO HELP, WE HAVE A NEW CHINESE ARRIVALS COMMITTEE THAT CAN HELP YOU SETTLE IN
THANK YOU!
... AH SAM, LET'S VISIT THEM TOMORROW!

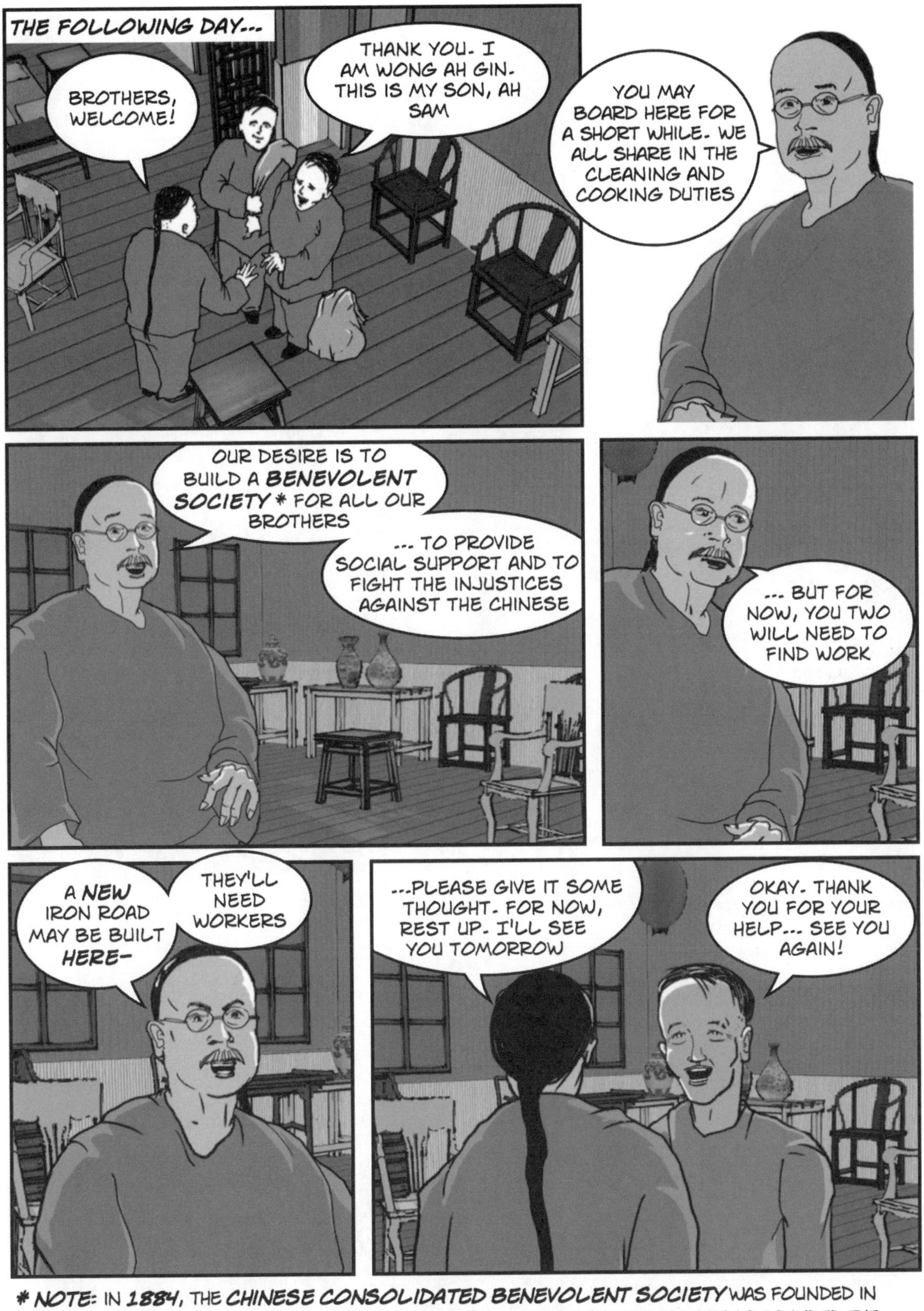
THE FOLLOWING DAY...
BROTHERS, WELCOME!
THANK YOU. I AM WONG AH GIN. THIS IS MY SON, AH SAM
YOU MAY BOARD HERE FOR A SHORT WHILE. WE ALL SHARE IN THE CLEANING AND COOKING DUTIES
OUR DESIRE IS TO BUILD A BENEVOLENT SOCIETY * FOR ALL OUR BROTHERS
... TO PROVIDE SOCIAL SUPPORT AND TO FIGHT THE INJUSTICES AGAINST THE CHINESE
... BUT FOR NOW, YOU TWO WILL NEED TO FIND WORK
A NEW IRON ROAD MAY BE BUILT HERE-
THEY'LL NEED WORKERS
...PLEASE GIVE IT SOME THOUGHT. FOR NOW, REST UP. I'LL SEE YOU TOMORROW
OKAY. THANK YOU FOR YOUR HELP... SEE YOU AGAIN!

**** NOTE:*** IN ***1884***, THE ***CHINESE CONSOLIDATED BENEVOLENT SOCIETY*** WAS FOUNDED IN VICTORIA, THE FIRST ASSOCIATION OF ITS KIND IN CANADA. IN ***1854***, SAN FRANCISCO FOUNDED THE "***SIX COMPANIES***," LATER RENAMED AS THE CHINESE CONSOLIDATED BENEVOLENT SOCIETY (***1876***).

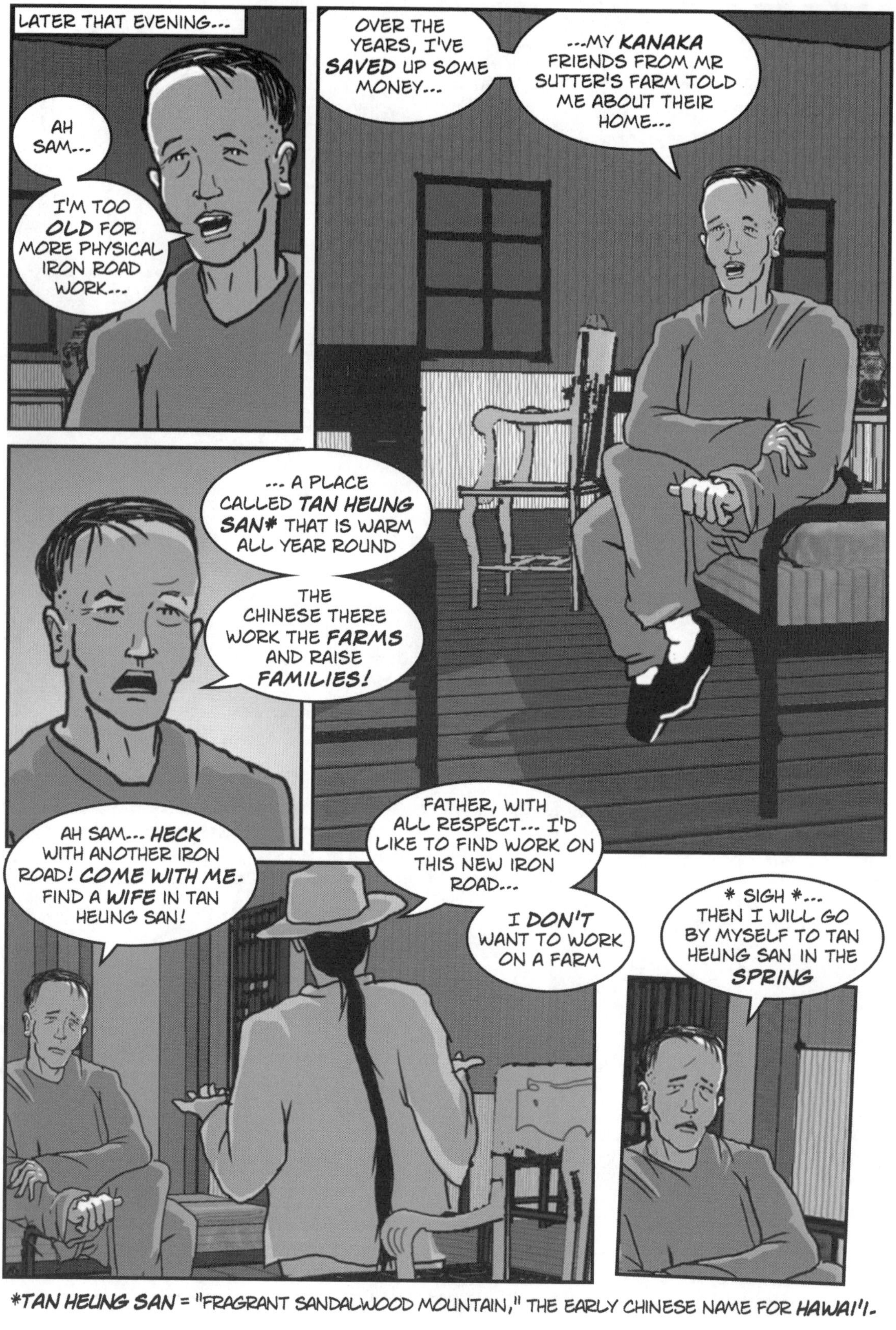
LATER THAT EVENING...
AH SAM...
I'M TOO OLD FOR MORE PHYSICAL IRON ROAD WORK...
OVER THE YEARS, I'VE SAVED UP SOME MONEY...
...MY KANAKA FRIENDS FROM MR SUTTER'S FARM TOLD ME ABOUT THEIR HOME...
... A PLACE CALLED TAN HEUNG SAN* THAT IS WARM ALL YEAR ROUND
THE CHINESE THERE WORK THE FARMS AND RAISE FAMILIES!
AH SAM... HECK WITH ANOTHER IRON ROAD! COME WITH ME. FIND A WIFE IN TAN HEUNG SAN!
FATHER, WITH ALL RESPECT... I'D LIKE TO FIND WORK ON THIS NEW IRON ROAD...
I DON'T WANT TO WORK ON A FARM
* SIGH *... THEN I WILL GO BY MYSELF TO TAN HEUNG SAN IN THE SPRING

*TAN HEUNG SAN = "FRAGRANT SANDALWOOD MOUNTAIN," THE EARLY CHINESE NAME FOR HAWAI'I.

CHAPTER 8 Kingdom of Tan Heung San

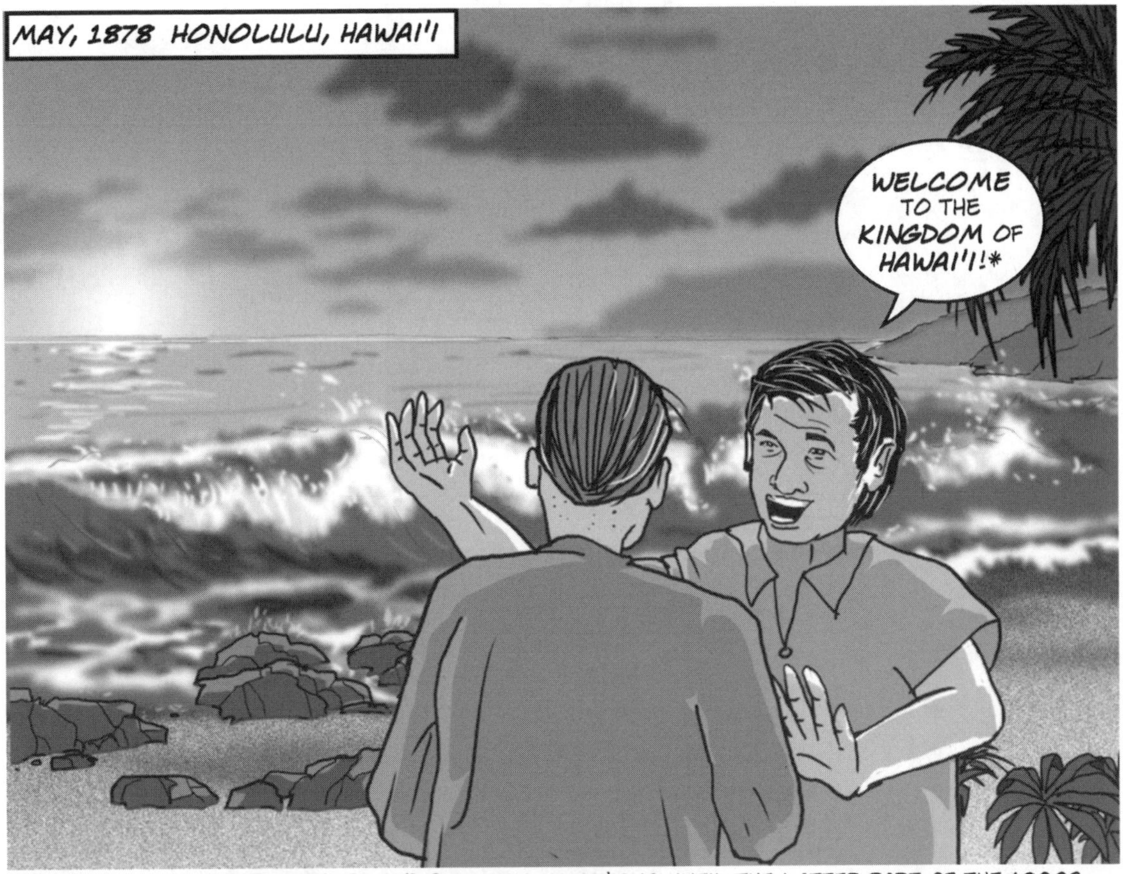
MAY, 1878 HONOLULU, HAWAI'I
WELCOME TO THE KINGDOM OF HAWAI'I!*

* KNOWN AS THE **SANDWICH ISLANDS** BY NON-HAWAI'IANS UNTIL THE LATTER PART OF THE 1800S.

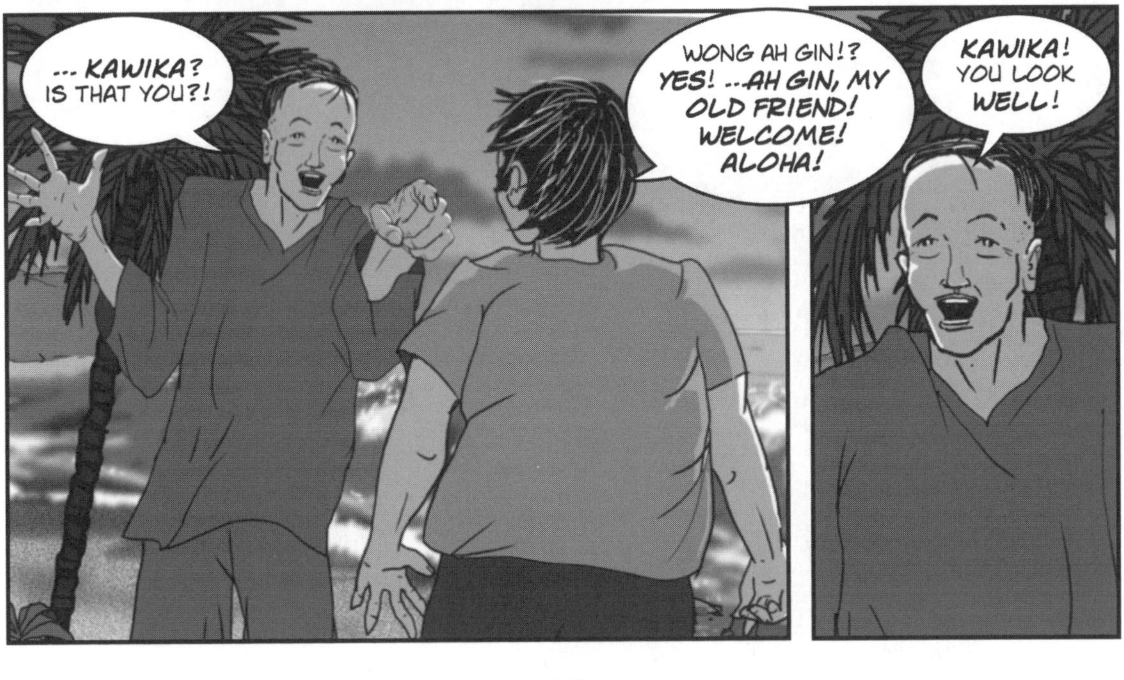
... KAWIKA? IS THAT YOU?!
WONG AH GIN!? YES! ...AH GIN, MY OLD FRIEND! WELCOME! ALOHA!
KAWIKA! YOU LOOK WELL!

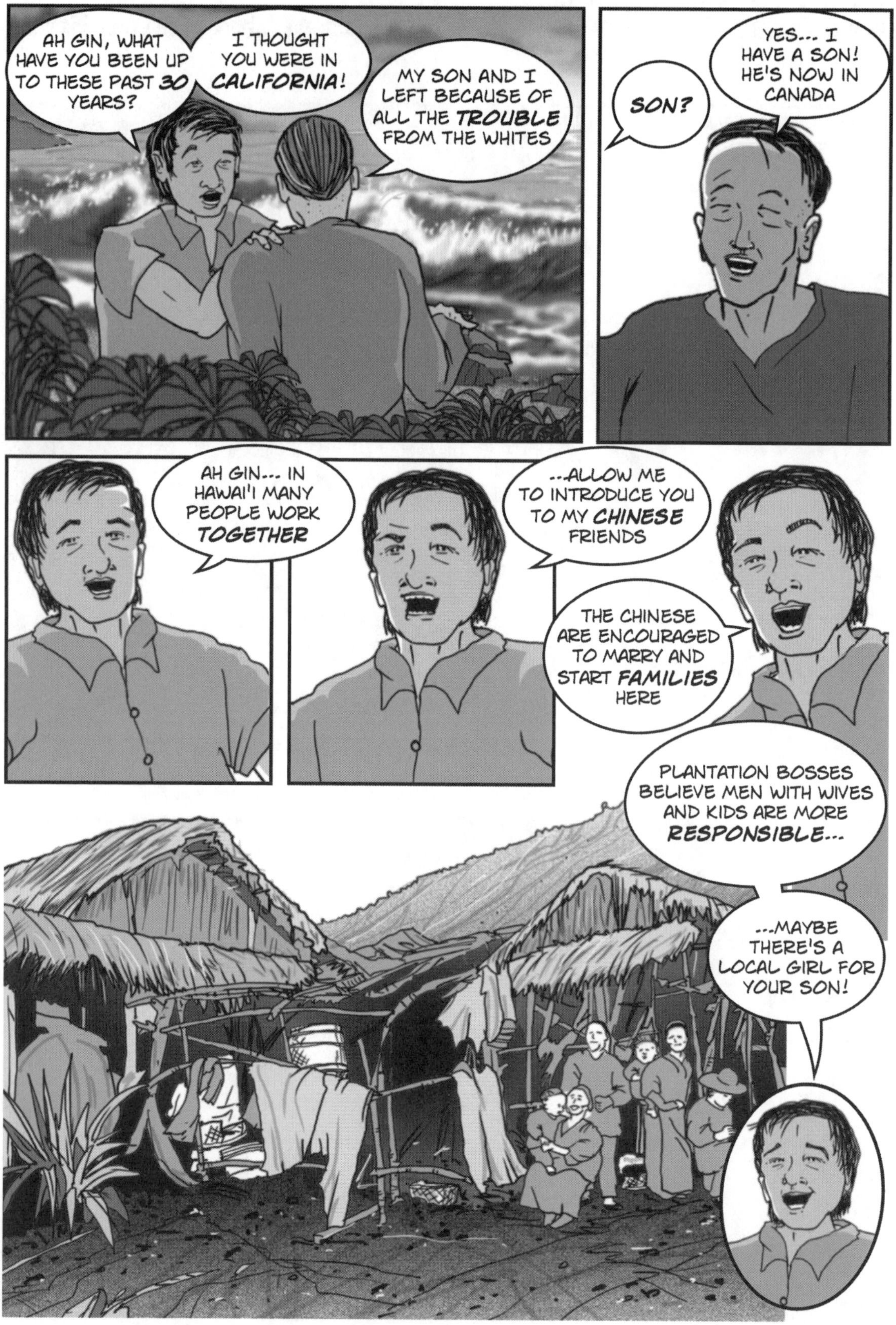
AH GIN, WHAT HAVE YOU BEEN UP TO THESE PAST 30 YEARS?
I THOUGHT YOU WERE IN CALIFORNIA!
MY SON AND I LEFT BECAUSE OF ALL THE TROUBLE FROM THE WHITES
SON?
YES... I HAVE A SON! HE'S NOW IN CANADA
AH GIN... IN HAWAI'I MANY PEOPLE WORK TOGETHER
...ALLOW ME TO INTRODUCE YOU TO MY CHINESE FRIENDS
THE CHINESE ARE ENCOURAGED TO MARRY AND START FAMILIES HERE
PLANTATION BOSSES BELIEVE MEN WITH WIVES AND KIDS ARE MORE RESPONSIBLE...
...MAYBE THERE'S A LOCAL GIRL FOR YOUR SON!

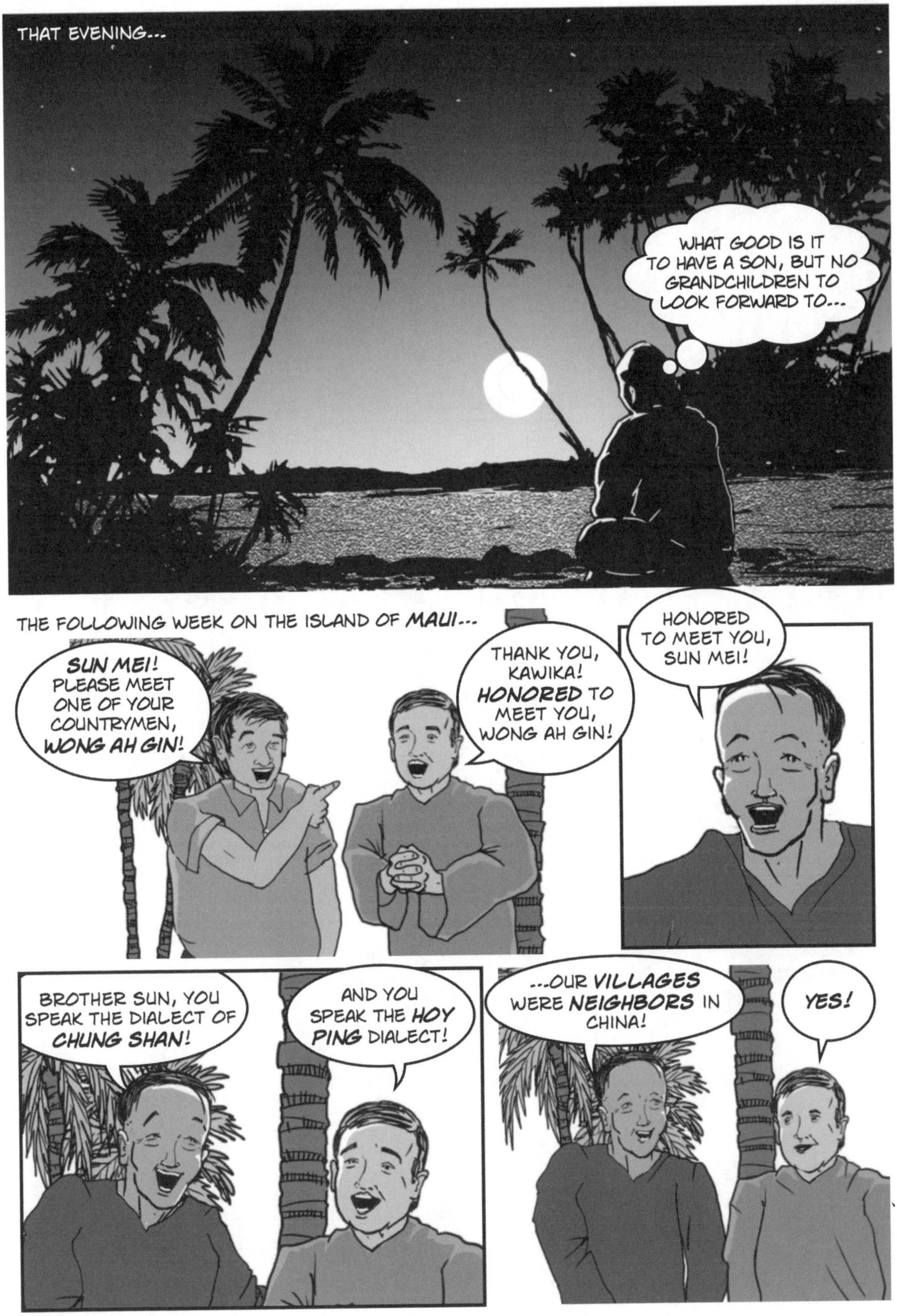
THAT EVENING...
WHAT GOOD IS IT TO HAVE A SON, BUT NO GRANDCHILDREN TO LOOK FORWARD TO...
THE FOLLOWING WEEK ON THE ISLAND OF MAUI...
SUN MEI! PLEASE MEET ONE OF YOUR COUNTRYMEN, WONG AH GIN!
THANK YOU, KAWIKA! HONORED TO MEET YOU, WONG AH GIN!
HONORED TO MEET YOU, SUN MEI!
BROTHER SUN, YOU SPEAK THE DIALECT OF CHUNG SHAN!
AND YOU SPEAK THE HOY PING DIALECT!
...OUR VILLAGES WERE NEIGHBORS IN CHINA!
YES!

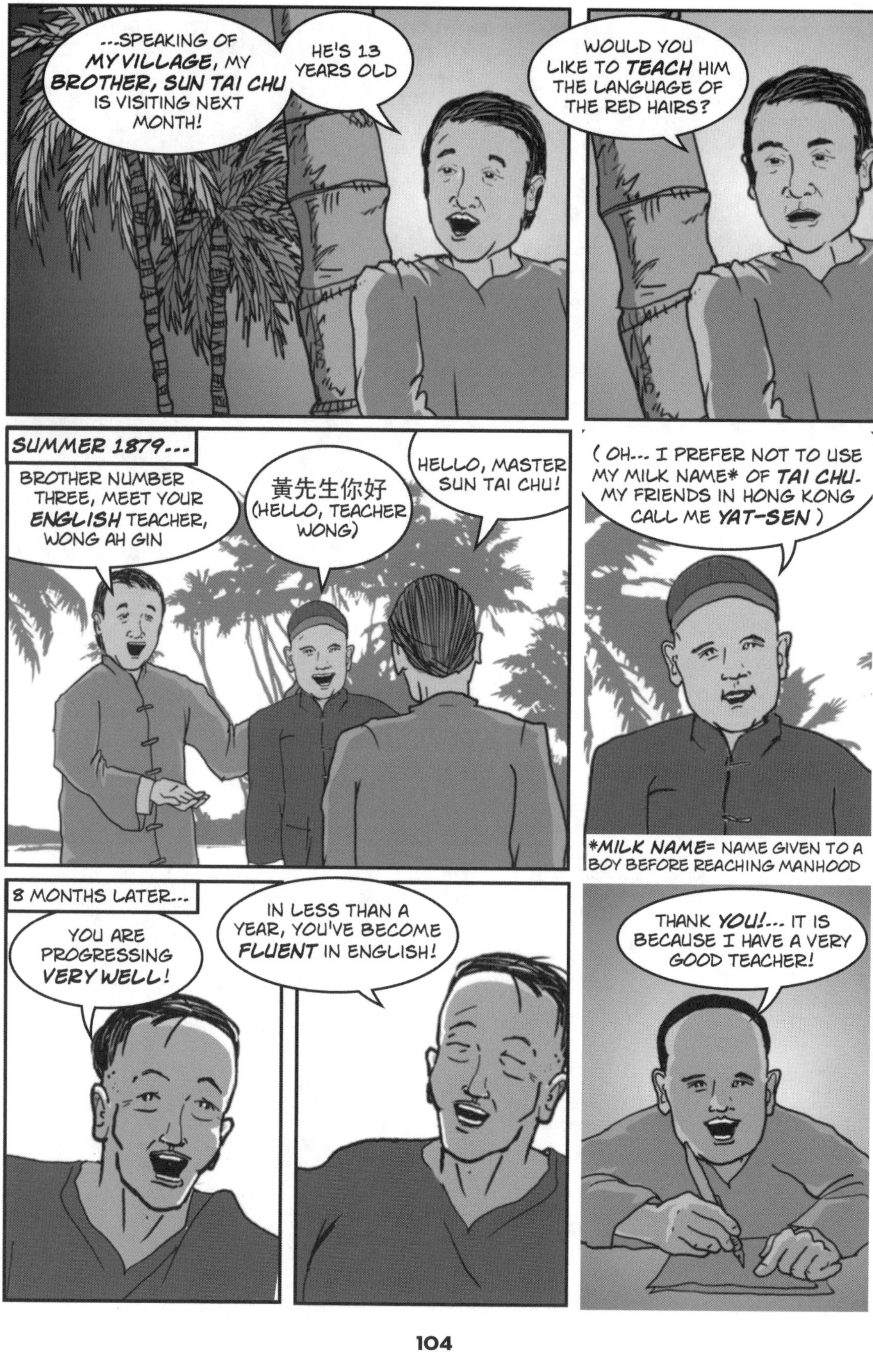
...SPEAKING OF MY VILLAGE, MY BROTHER, SUN TAI CHU IS VISITING NEXT MONTH!
HE'S 13 YEARS OLD
WOULD YOU LIKE TO TEACH HIM THE LANGUAGE OF THE RED HAIRS?
SUMMER 1879...
BROTHER NUMBER THREE, MEET YOUR ENGLISH TEACHER, WONG AH GIN
黃先生你好 (HELLO, TEACHER WONG)
HELLO, MASTER SUN TAI CHU!
(OH... I PREFER NOT TO USE MY MILK NAME* OF TAI CHU. MY FRIENDS IN HONG KONG CALL ME YAT-SEN)
*MILK NAME= NAME GIVEN TO A BOY BEFORE REACHING MANHOOD
8 MONTHS LATER...
YOU ARE PROGRESSING VERY WELL!
IN LESS THAN A YEAR, YOU'VE BECOME FLUENT IN ENGLISH!
THANK YOU!... IT IS BECAUSE I HAVE A VERY GOOD TEACHER!

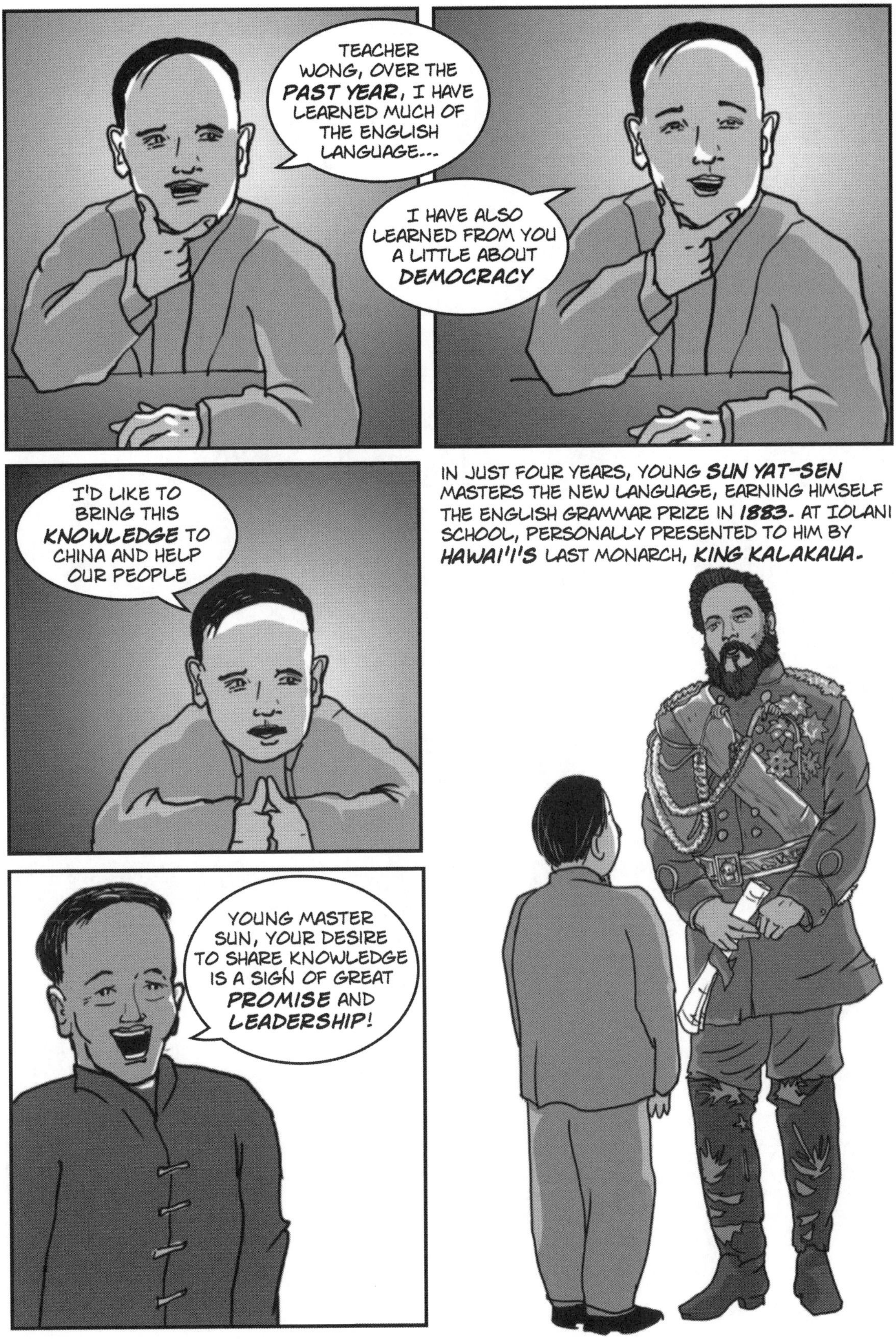
TEACHER WONG, OVER THE PAST YEAR, I HAVE LEARNED MUCH OF THE ENGLISH LANGUAGE...
I HAVE ALSO LEARNED FROM YOU A LITTLE ABOUT DEMOCRACY
I'D LIKE TO BRING THIS KNOWLEDGE TO CHINA AND HELP OUR PEOPLE
YOUNG MASTER SUN, YOUR DESIRE TO SHARE KNOWLEDGE IS A SIGN OF GREAT PROMISE AND LEADERSHIP!
IN JUST FOUR YEARS, YOUNG SUN YAT-SEN MASTERS THE NEW LANGUAGE, EARNING HIMSELF THE ENGLISH GRAMMAR PRIZE IN 1883. AT IOLANI SCHOOL, PERSONALLY PRESENTED TO HIM BY HAWAI'I'S LAST MONARCH, KING KALAKAUA.

CHAPTER 9 Nation Building

ON **FEBRUARY 16, 1881**, OTTAWA'S HOUSE OF COMMONS APPROVES THE CONSTRUCTION OF THE NATION'S TRANSCONTINENTAL RAILROAD, AND THUS GIVES BIRTH TO THE **CANADIAN PACIFIC RAILWAY** (C.P.R.) COMPANY.

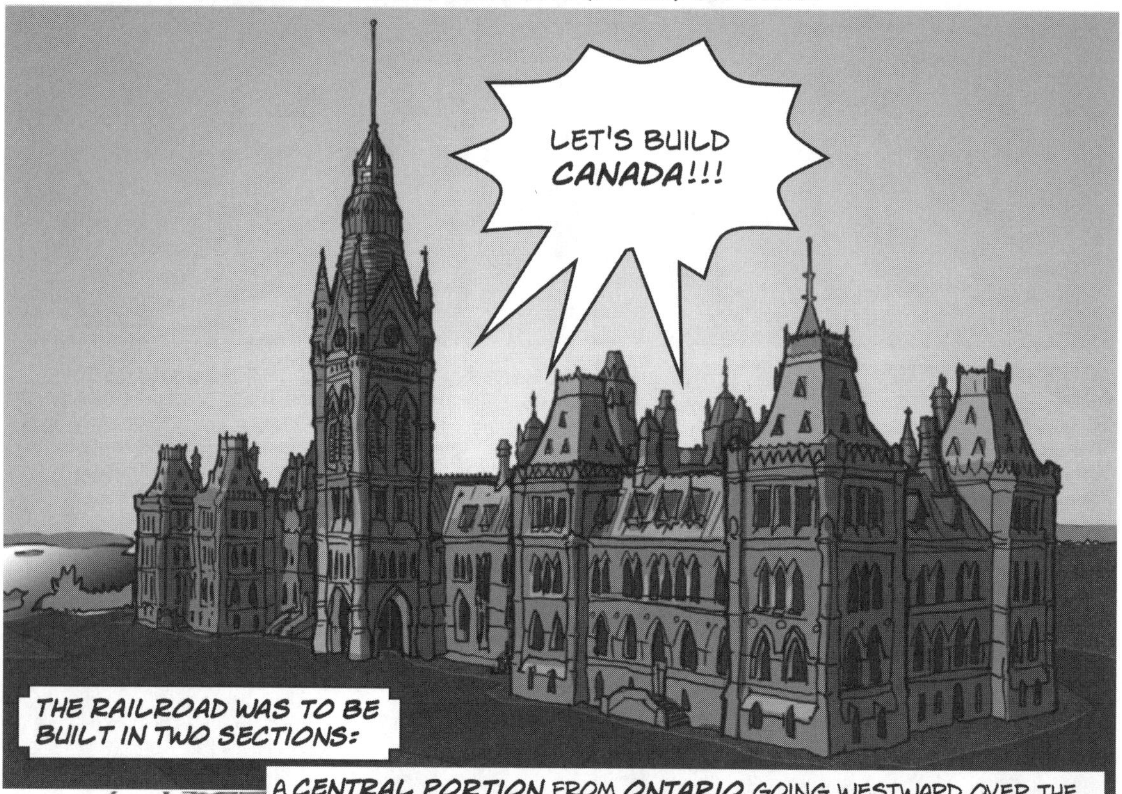
LET'S BUILD CANADA!!!
THE RAILROAD WAS TO BE BUILT IN TWO SECTIONS:

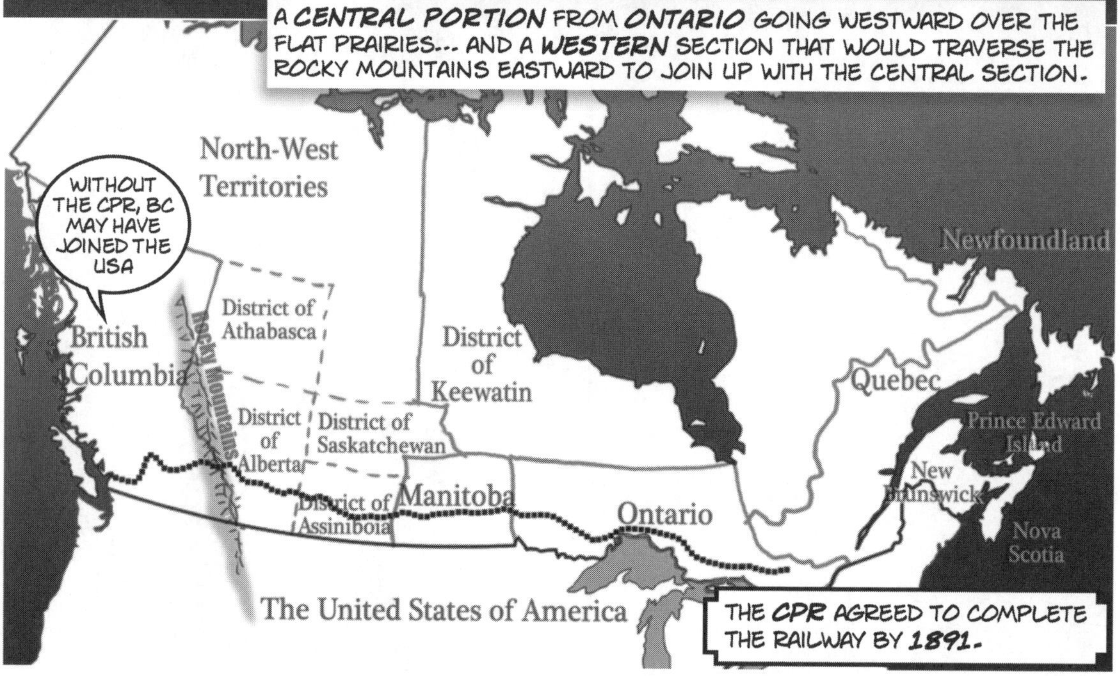
A CENTRAL PORTION FROM ONTARIO GOING WESTWARD OVER THE FLAT PRAIRIES... AND A WESTERN SECTION THAT WOULD TRAVERSE THE ROCKY MOUNTAINS EASTWARD TO JOIN UP WITH THE CENTRAL SECTION.
WITHOUT THE CPR, BC MAY HAVE JOINED THE USA
North-West Territories
Newfoundland
District of Athabasca
District of Keewatin
British Columbia
Rocky Mountains
Quebec
Prince Edward Island
District of Alberta
District of Saskatchewan
New Brunswick
District of Assiniboia
Manitoba
Ontario
Nova Scotia
The United States of America
THE CPR AGREED TO COMPLETE THE RAILWAY BY 1891.

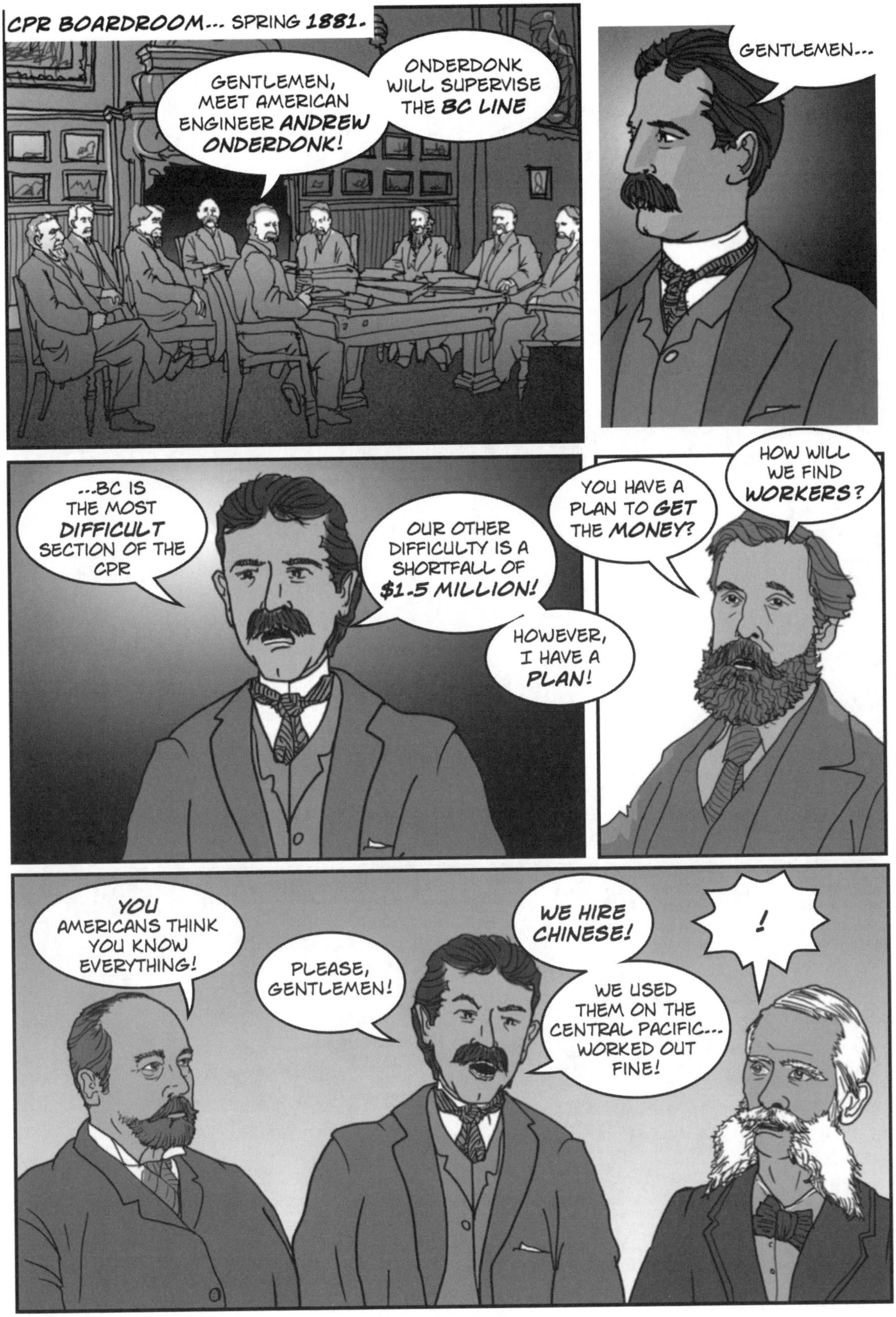
CPR BOARDROOM... SPRING 1881.
GENTLEMEN, MEET AMERICAN ENGINEER ANDREW ONDERDONK!
ONDERDONK WILL SUPERVISE THE BC LINE
GENTLEMEN...
...BC IS THE MOST DIFFICULT SECTION OF THE CPR
OUR OTHER DIFFICULTY IS A SHORTFALL OF $1.5 MILLION!
HOWEVER, I HAVE A PLAN!
YOU HAVE A PLAN TO GET THE MONEY?
HOW WILL WE FIND WORKERS?
YOU AMERICANS THINK YOU KNOW EVERYTHING!
PLEASE, GENTLEMEN!
WE HIRE CHINESE!
WE USED THEM ON THE CENTRAL PACIFIC... WORKED OUT FINE!
!

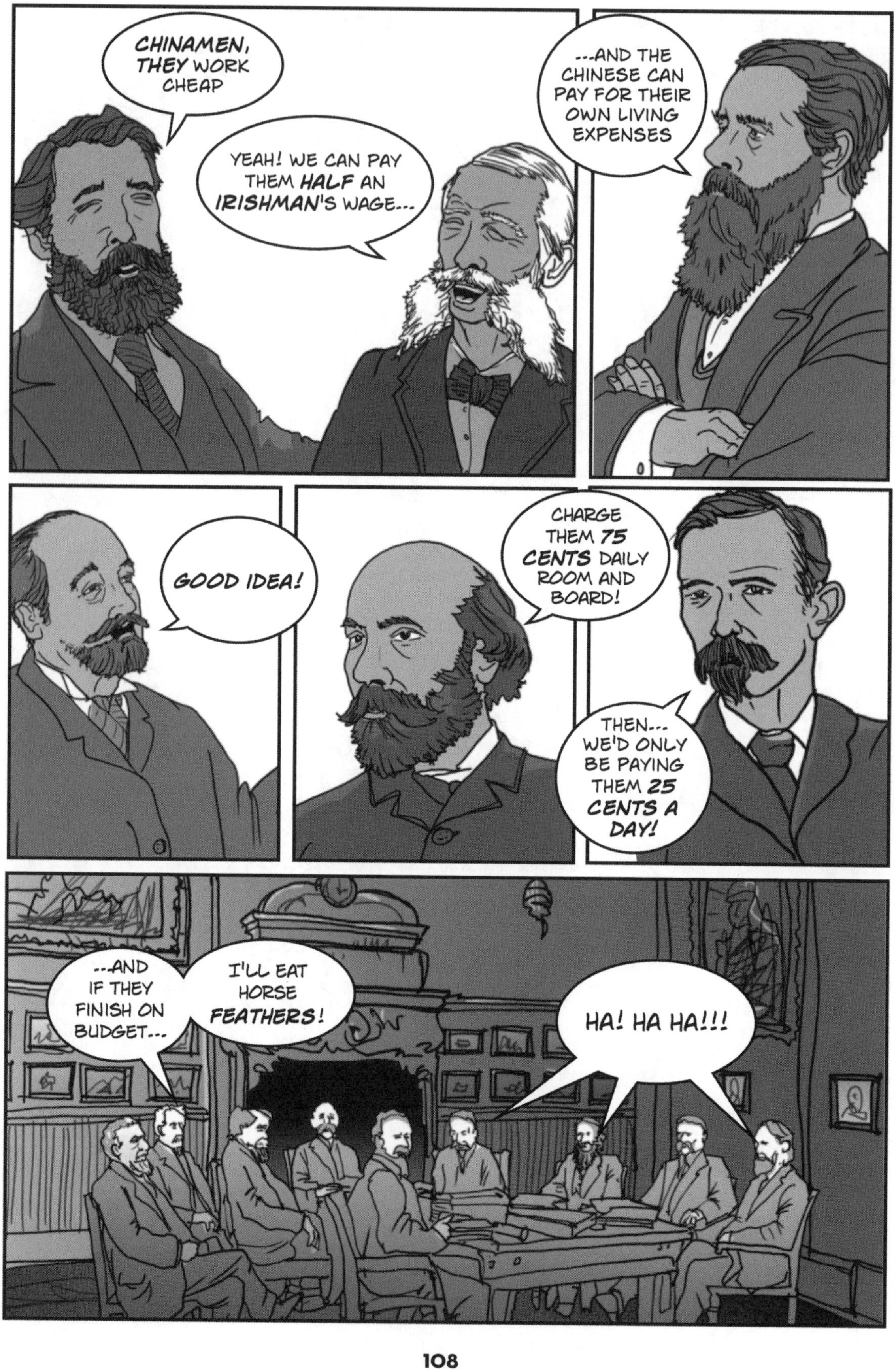
CHINAMEN, THEY WORK CHEAP
YEAH! WE CAN PAY THEM HALF AN IRISHMAN'S WAGE...
...AND THE CHINESE CAN PAY FOR THEIR OWN LIVING EXPENSES
GOOD IDEA!
CHARGE THEM 75 CENTS DAILY ROOM AND BOARD!
THEN... WE'D ONLY BE PAYING THEM 25 CENTS A DAY!
...AND IF THEY FINISH ON BUDGET...
I'LL EAT HORSE FEATHERS!
HA! HA HA!!!

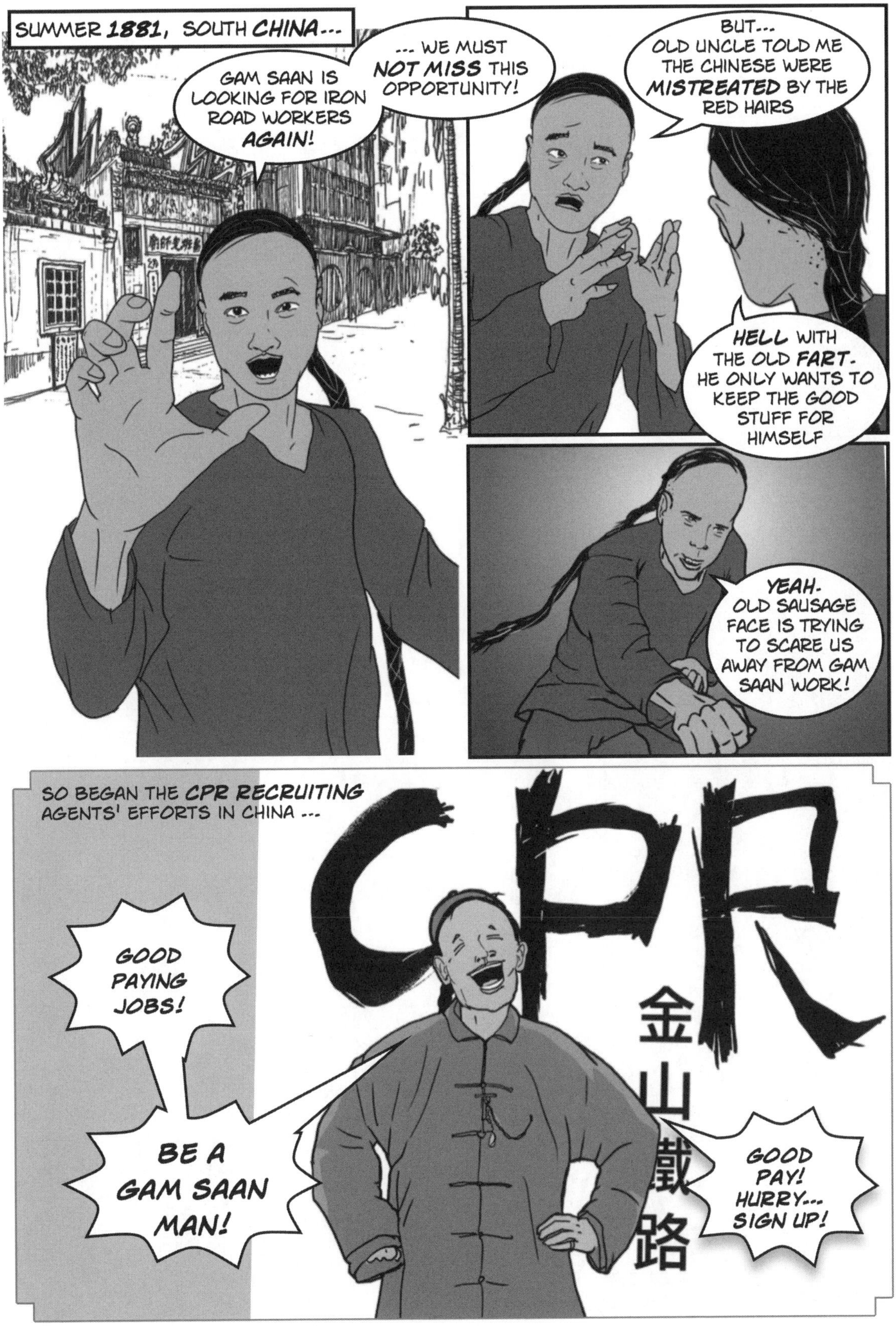
SUMMER 1881, SOUTH CHINA...
GAM SAAN IS LOOKING FOR IRON ROAD WORKERS AGAIN!
... WE MUST NOT MISS THIS OPPORTUNITY!
BUT... OLD UNCLE TOLD ME THE CHINESE WERE MISTREATED BY THE RED HAIRS
HELL WITH THE OLD FART- HE ONLY WANTS TO KEEP THE GOOD STUFF FOR HIMSELF
YEAH- OLD SAUSAGE FACE IS TRYING TO SCARE US AWAY FROM GAM SAAN WORK!
SO BEGAN THE CPR RECRUITING AGENTS' EFFORTS IN CHINA ---
CPR
金山鐵路
GOOD PAYING JOBS!
BE A GAM SAAN MAN!
GOOD PAY! HURRY... SIGN UP!

BEFORE LONG, WORK STARTED ON ***CANADA'S*** NATIONAL IRON ROAD. FOR MANY CHINESE, IT WAS LIKE NOTHING THEY HAD EVER SEEN OR EXPERIENCED. EVEN THE SEASONED AMERICAN RAIL WORKERS FELT CHALLENGED... THE RUGGED TERRAIN PRESENTED MAJOR ENGINEERING CHALLENGES- BRIDGES, TUNNELS, AND RETAINING WALLS HAD TO BE BUILT.

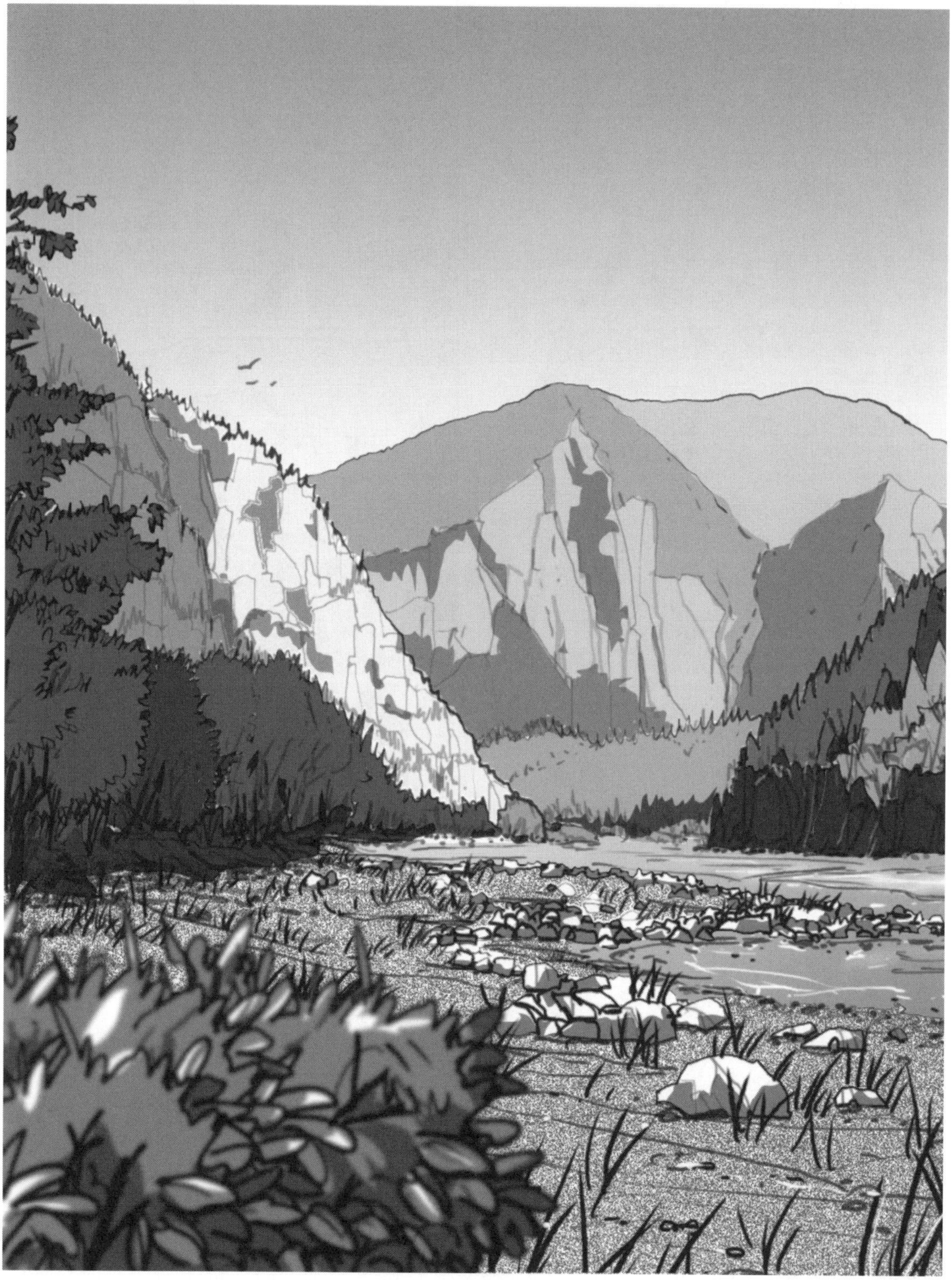

IN MAY 1880 WORK BEGAN ON THE LINE NORTH OF ***YALE***, BC, ON THE FRASER RIVER AND MOUNTAINS ON EITHER SIDE ROSE UP TO 2,438 KM (8,000 FT). THE MOUNTAINS WERE MADE OF GRANITE. IT TOOK EIGHTEEN MONTHS OF DAILY ROUND-THE-CLOCK BLASTING TO BORE FOUR MAJOR TUNNELS. MORE THAN THIRTY TUNNELS WERE CREATED IN THE FIRST 27 KM (17 MI) NORTH OF YALE, AND MORE THAN 100 TRESTLES AND BRIDGES WERE BUILT IN A 40 KM (30 MI) SECTION.

FROM "BUILDING THE CPR, THE TIES THAT BIND"

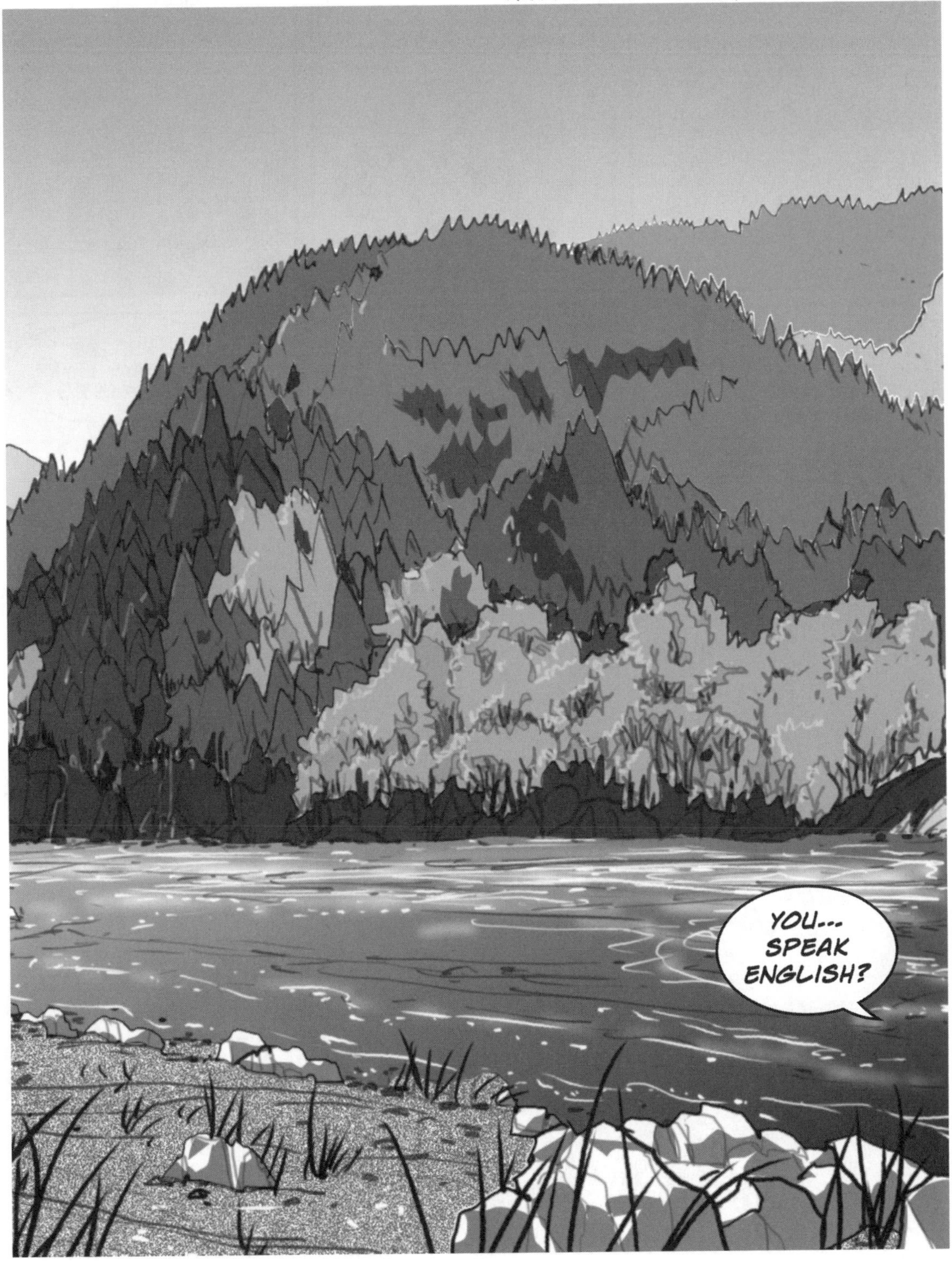
YOU... SPEAK ENGLISH?

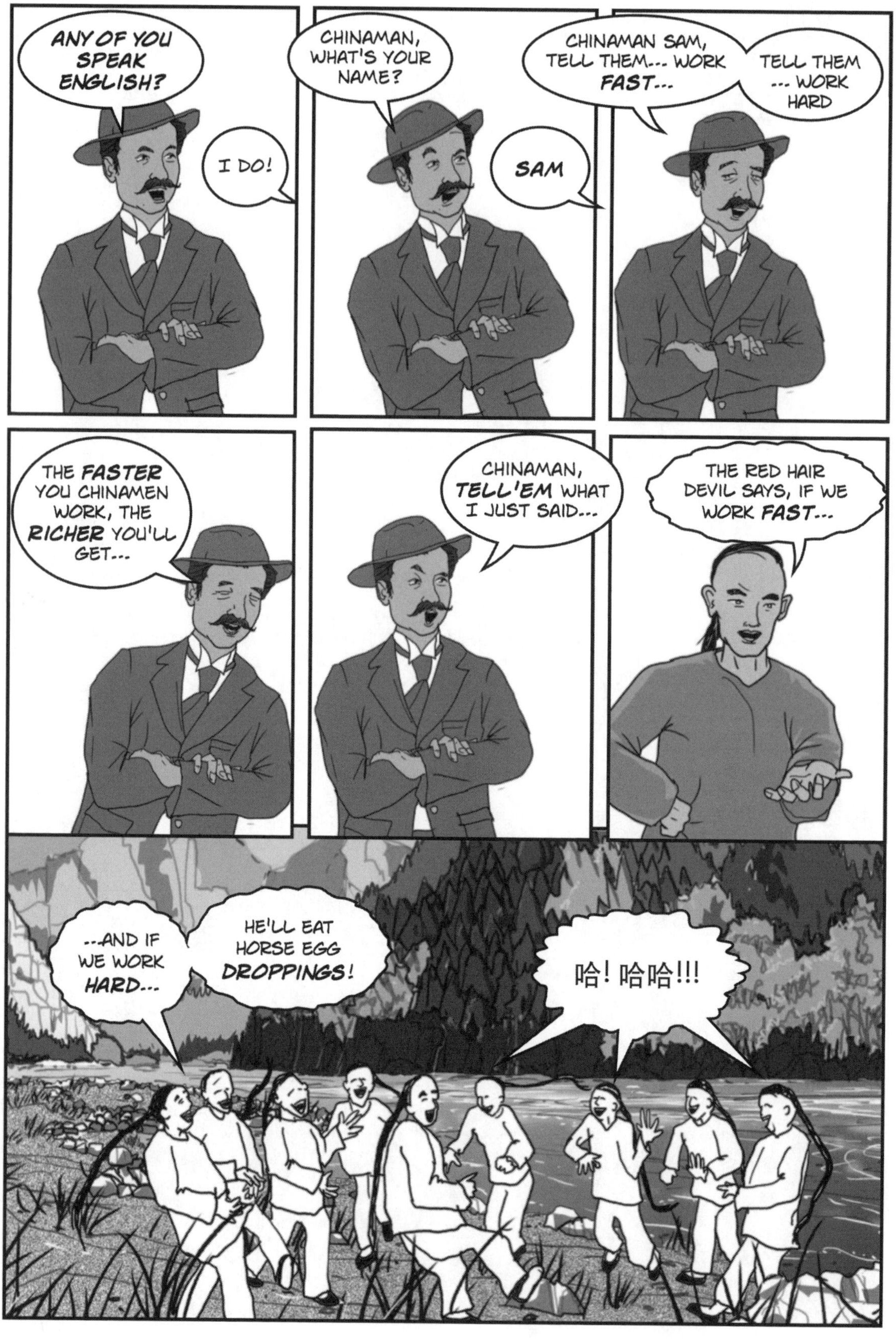
ANY OF YOU SPEAK ENGLISH?
I DO!
CHINAMAN, WHAT'S YOUR NAME?
SAM
CHINAMAN SAM, TELL THEM--- WORK FAST---
TELL THEM --- WORK HARD
THE FASTER YOU CHINAMEN WORK, THE RICHER YOU'LL GET---
CHINAMAN, TELL'EM WHAT I JUST SAID---
THE RED HAIR DEVIL SAYS, IF WE WORK FAST---
---AND IF WE WORK HARD---
HE'LL EAT HORSE EGG DROPPINGS!
哈! 哈哈!!!

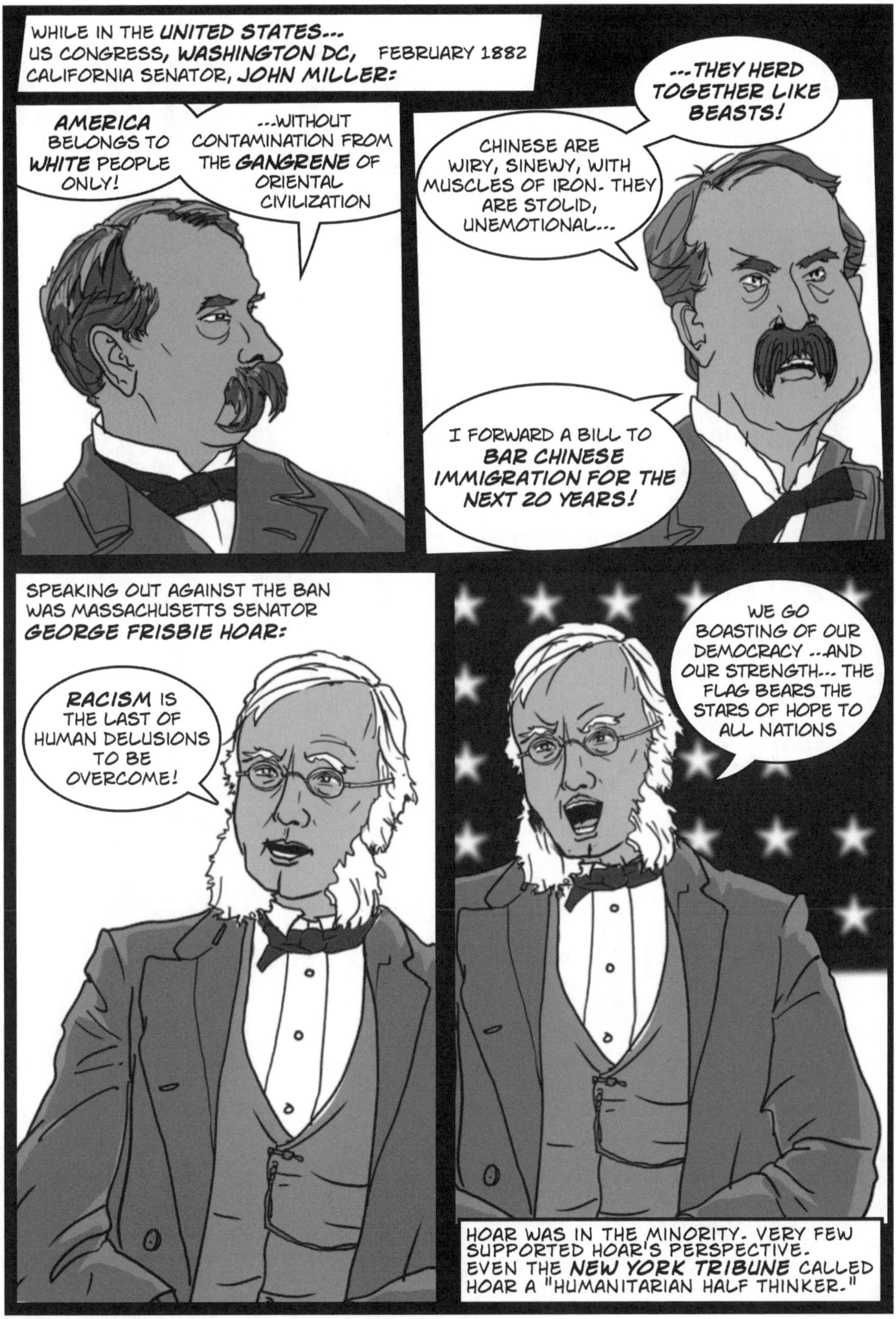
WHILE IN THE UNITED STATES... US CONGRESS, WASHINGTON DC, FEBRUARY 1882 CALIFORNIA SENATOR, JOHN MILLER:
AMERICA BELONGS TO WHITE PEOPLE ONLY!
...WITHOUT CONTAMINATION FROM THE GANGRENE OF ORIENTAL CIVILIZATION
CHINESE ARE WIRY, SINEWY, WITH MUSCLES OF IRON. THEY ARE STOLID, UNEMOTIONAL...
...THEY HERD TOGETHER LIKE BEASTS!
I FORWARD A BILL TO BAR CHINESE IMMIGRATION FOR THE NEXT 20 YEARS!
SPEAKING OUT AGAINST THE BAN WAS MASSACHUSETTS SENATOR GEORGE FRISBIE HOAR:
RACISM IS THE LAST OF HUMAN DELUSIONS TO BE OVERCOME!
WE GO BOASTING OF OUR DEMOCRACY ...AND OUR STRENGTH... THE FLAG BEARS THE STARS OF HOPE TO ALL NATIONS
HOAR WAS IN THE MINORITY. VERY FEW SUPPORTED HOAR'S PERSPECTIVE. EVEN THE NEW YORK TRIBUNE CALLED HOAR A "HUMANITARIAN HALF THINKER."

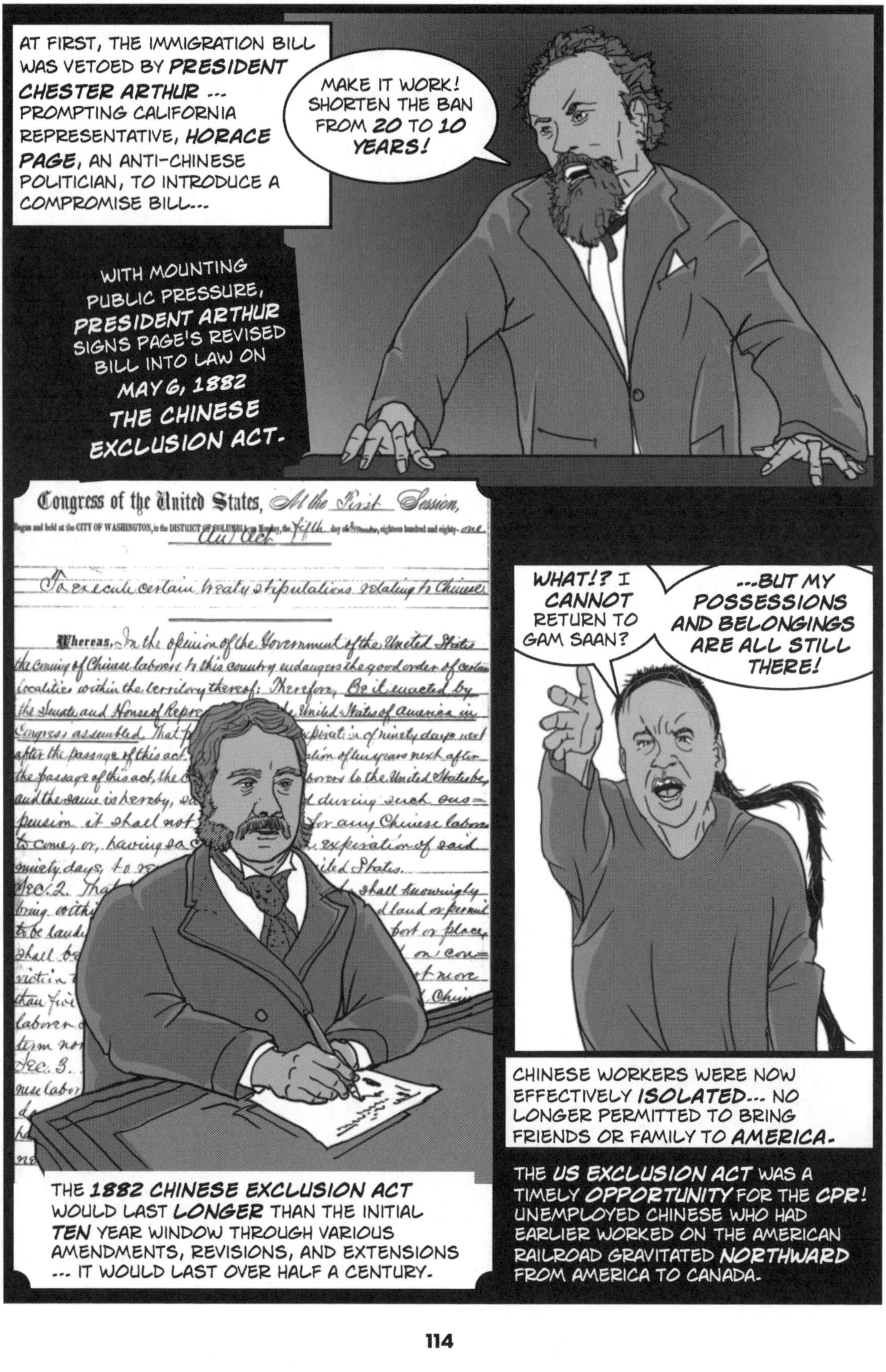
AT FIRST, THE IMMIGRATION BILL WAS VETOED BY PRESIDENT CHESTER ARTHUR ... PROMPTING CALIFORNIA REPRESENTATIVE, HORACE PAGE, AN ANTI-CHINESE POLITICIAN, TO INTRODUCE A COMPROMISE BILL...
MAKE IT WORK! SHORTEN THE BAN FROM 20 TO 10 YEARS!
WITH MOUNTING PUBLIC PRESSURE, PRESIDENT ARTHUR SIGNS PAGE'S REVISED BILL INTO LAW ON MAY 6, 1882 THE CHINESE EXCLUSION ACT.
Congress of the United States, At the First Session,
WHAT!? I CANNOT RETURN TO GAM SAAN?
...BUT MY POSSESSIONS AND BELONGINGS ARE ALL STILL THERE!
CHINESE WORKERS WERE NOW EFFECTIVELY ISOLATED... NO LONGER PERMITTED TO BRING FRIENDS OR FAMILY TO AMERICA.
THE 1882 CHINESE EXCLUSION ACT WOULD LAST LONGER THAN THE INITIAL TEN YEAR WINDOW THROUGH VARIOUS AMENDMENTS, REVISIONS, AND EXTENSIONS ... IT WOULD LAST OVER HALF A CENTURY.
THE US EXCLUSION ACT WAS A TIMELY OPPORTUNITY FOR THE CPR! UNEMPLOYED CHINESE WHO HAD EARLIER WORKED ON THE AMERICAN RAILROAD GRAVITATED NORTHWARD FROM AMERICA TO CANADA.

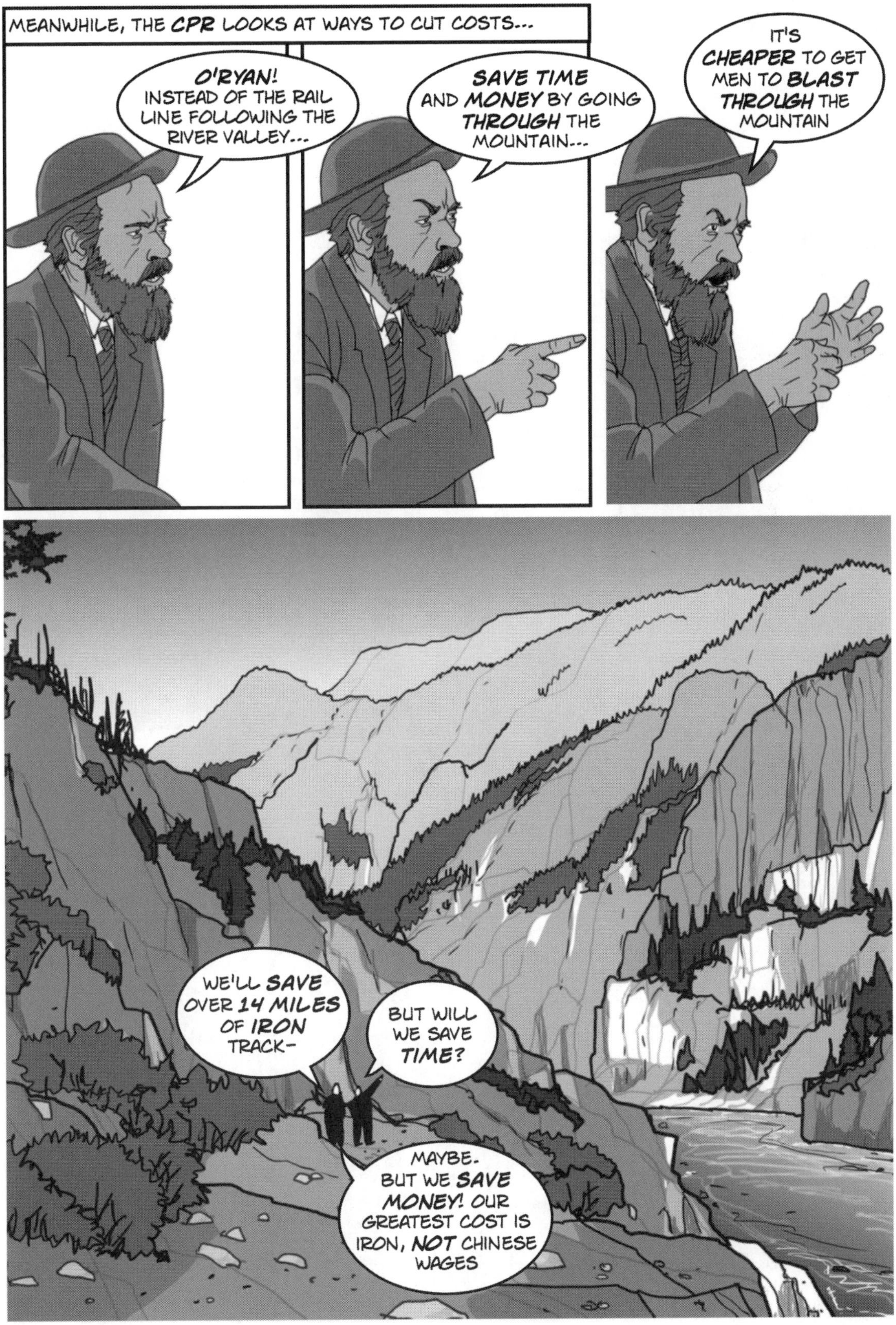
MEANWHILE, THE CPR LOOKS AT WAYS TO CUT COSTS...
O'RYAN! INSTEAD OF THE RAIL LINE FOLLOWING THE RIVER VALLEY...
SAVE TIME AND MONEY BY GOING THROUGH THE MOUNTAIN...
IT'S CHEAPER TO GET MEN TO BLAST THROUGH THE MOUNTAIN
WE'LL SAVE OVER 14 MILES OF IRON TRACK-
BUT WILL WE SAVE TIME?
MAYBE. BUT WE SAVE MONEY! OUR GREATEST COST IS IRON, NOT CHINESE WAGES

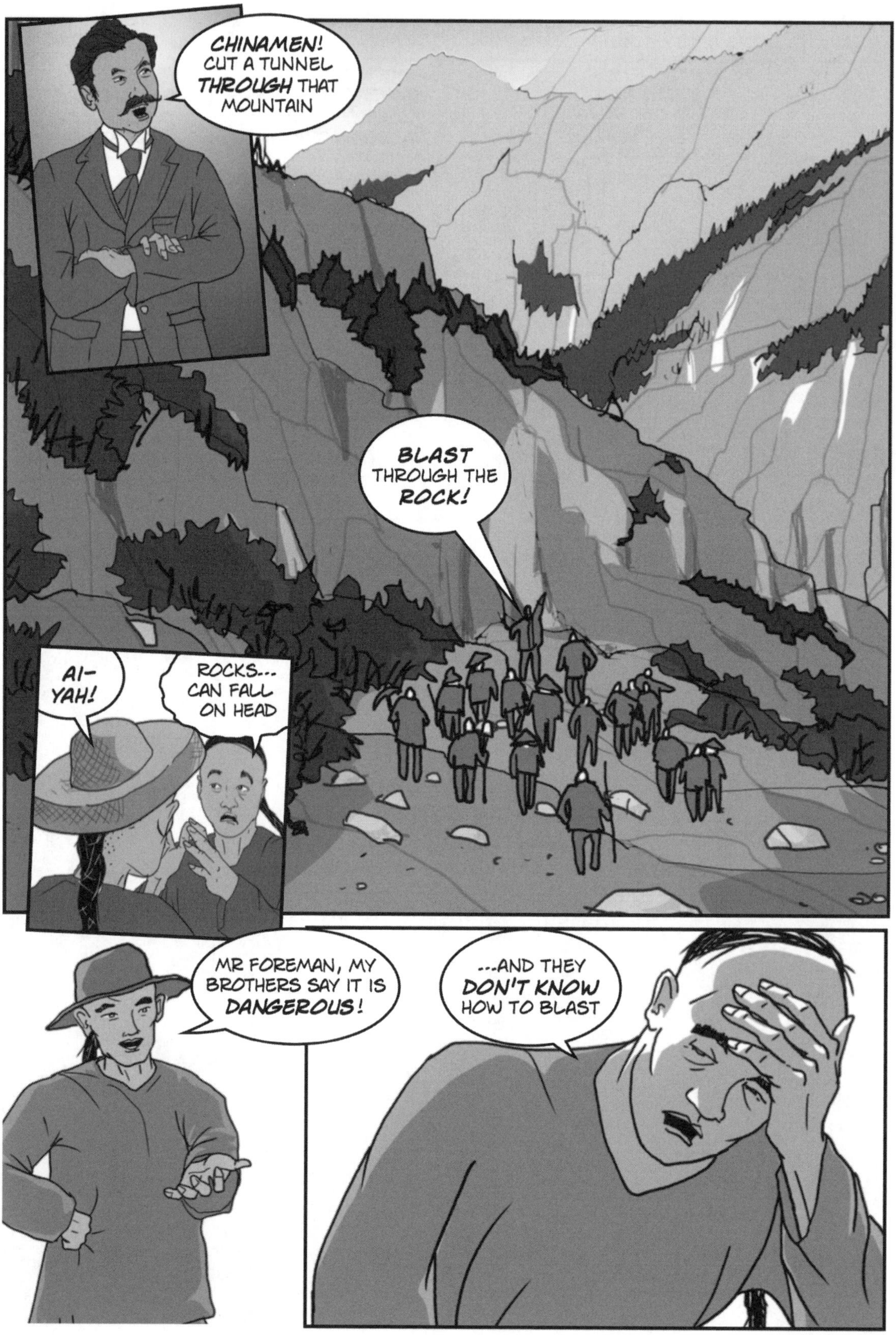
CHINAMEN! CUT A TUNNEL THROUGH THAT MOUNTAIN
BLAST THROUGH THE ROCK!
AI-YAH!
ROCKS... CAN FALL ON HEAD
MR FOREMAN, MY BROTHERS SAY IT IS DANGEROUS!
...AND THEY DON'T KNOW HOW TO BLAST

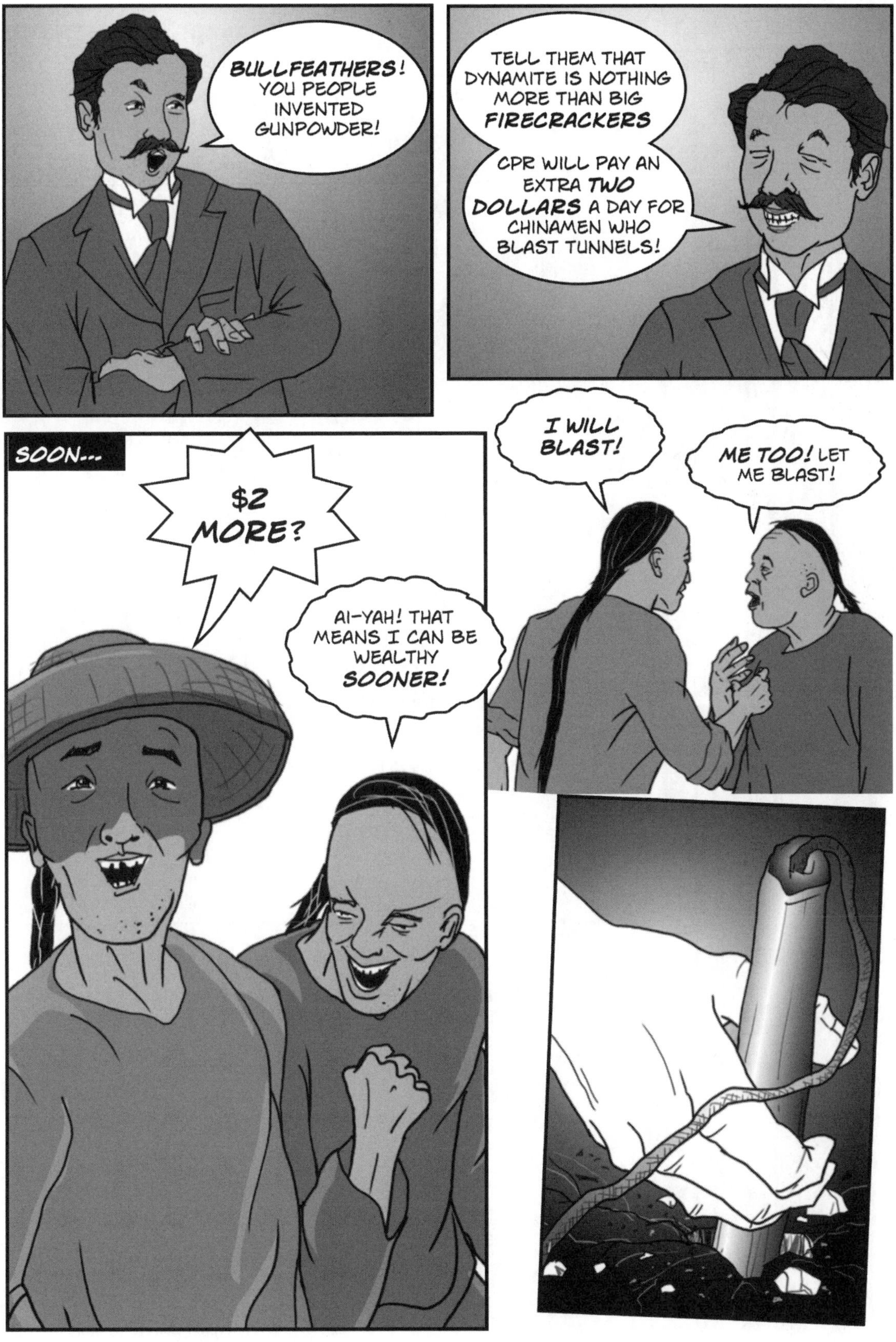
BULLFEATHERS! YOU PEOPLE INVENTED GUNPOWDER!
TELL THEM THAT DYNAMITE IS NOTHING MORE THAN BIG FIRECRACKERS
CPR WILL PAY AN EXTRA TWO DOLLARS A DAY FOR CHINAMEN WHO BLAST TUNNELS!
SOON...
$2 MORE?
AI-YAH! THAT MEANS I CAN BE WEALTHY SOONER!
I WILL BLAST!
ME TOO! LET ME BLAST!

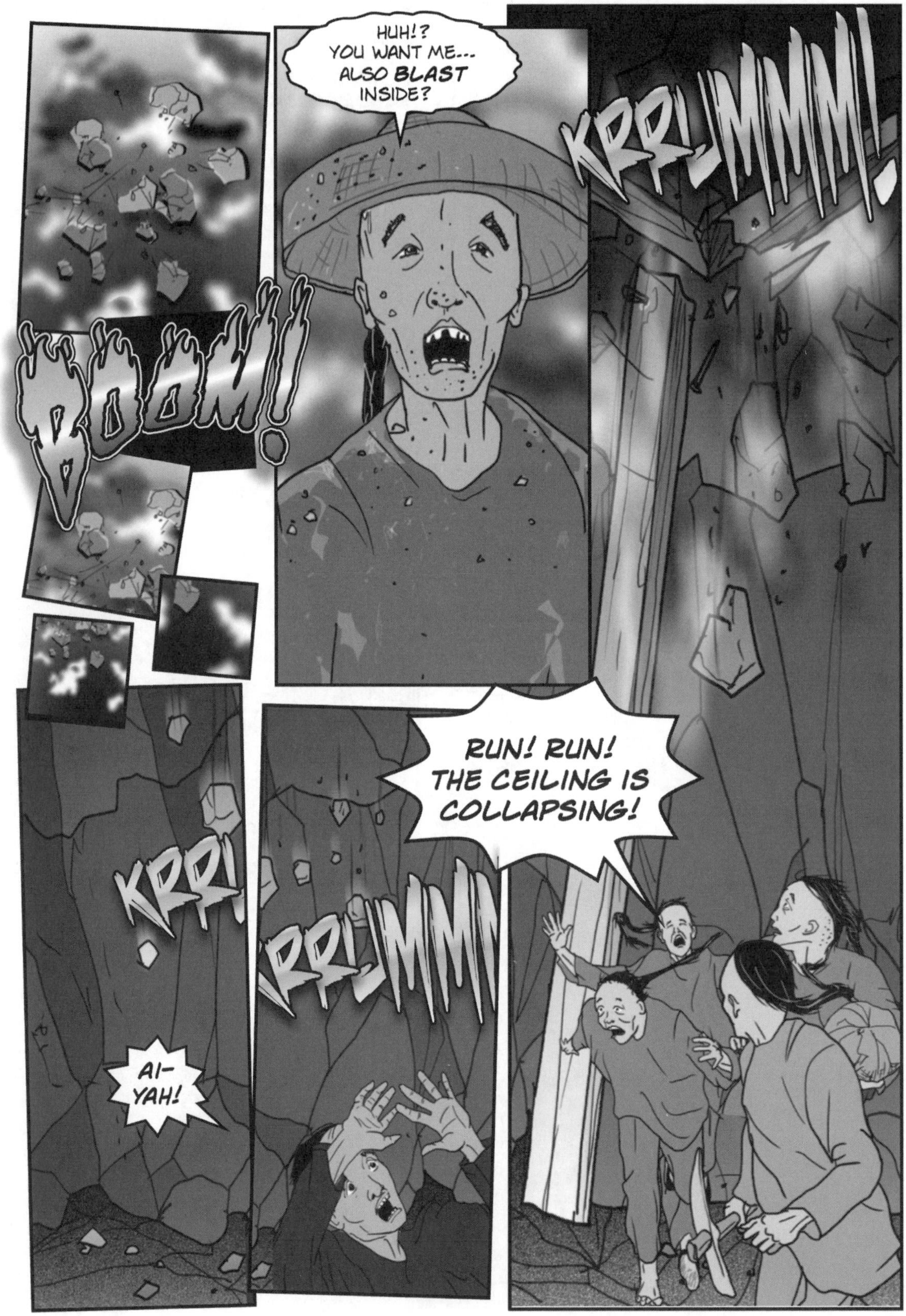
BOOM!
HUH!? YOU WANT ME... ALSO BLAST INSIDE?
KRRUMMMM!
KRRU
AI-YAH!
KRRUMMM
RUN! RUN! THE CEILING IS COLLAPSING!

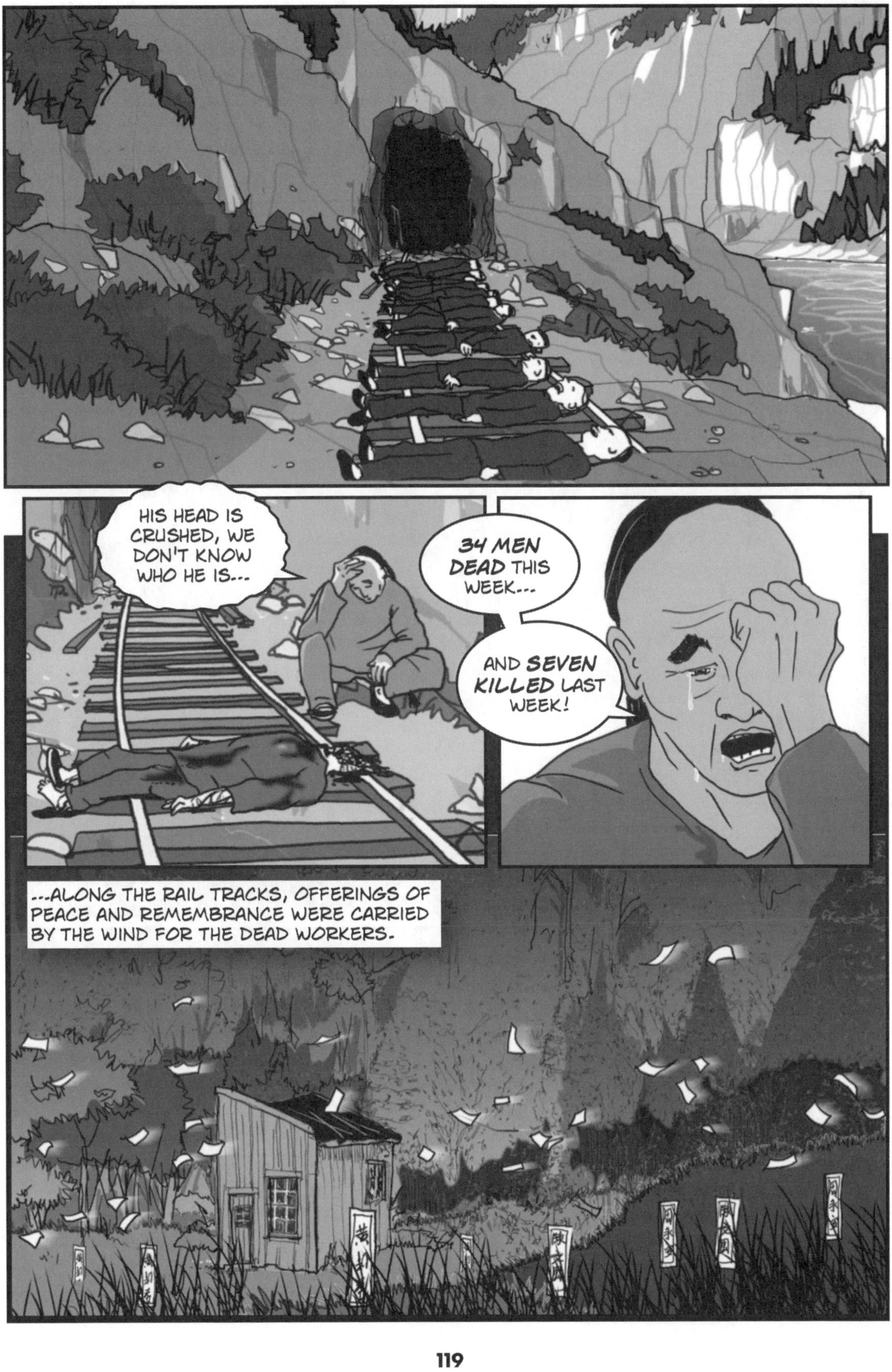
HIS HEAD IS CRUSHED, WE DON'T KNOW WHO HE IS...
34 MEN DEAD THIS WEEK...
AND SEVEN KILLED LAST WEEK!
...ALONG THE RAIL TRACKS, OFFERINGS OF PEACE AND REMEMBRANCE WERE CARRIED BY THE WIND FOR THE DEAD WORKERS.

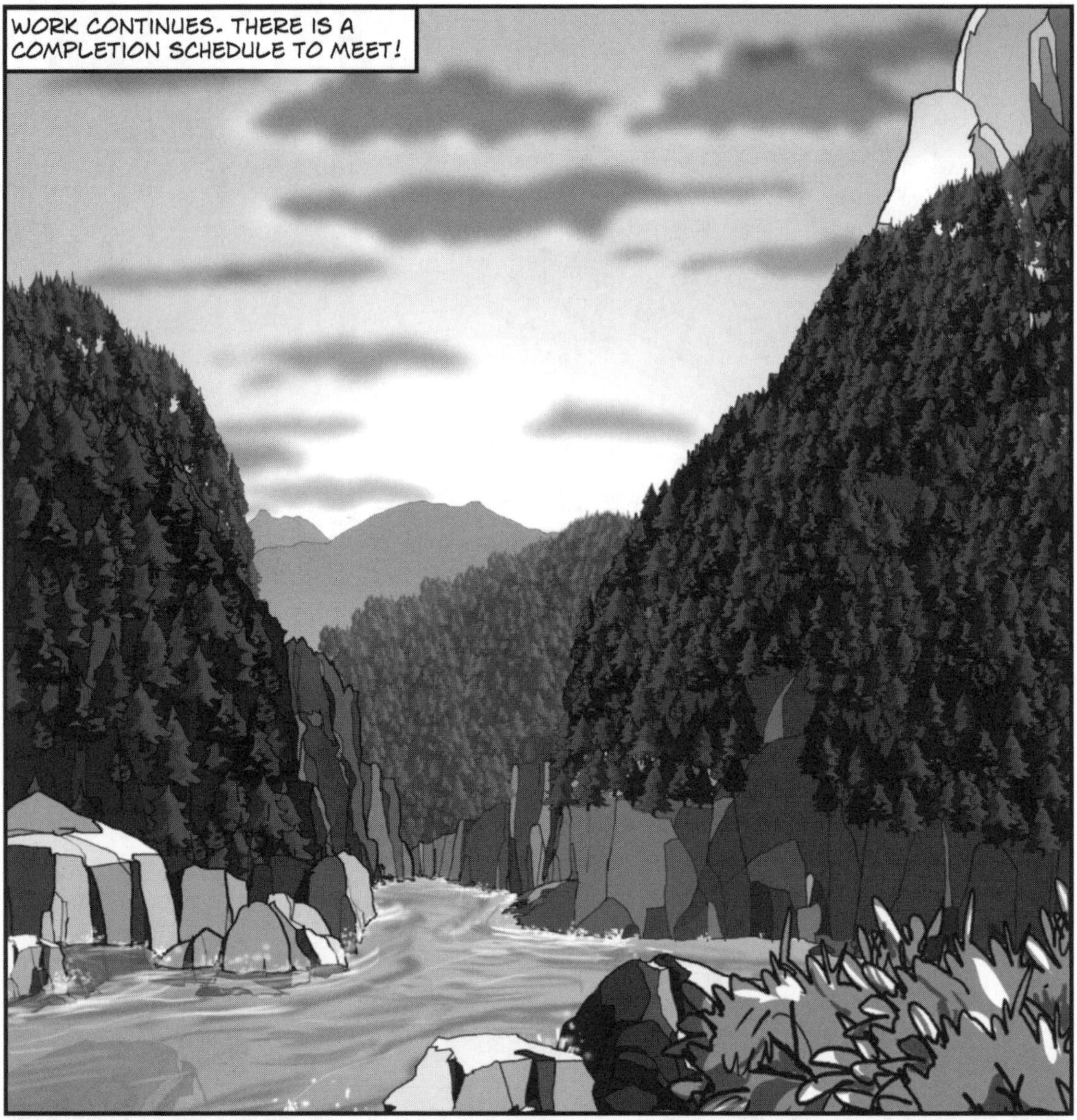
WORK CONTINUES. THERE IS A COMPLETION SCHEDULE TO MEET!

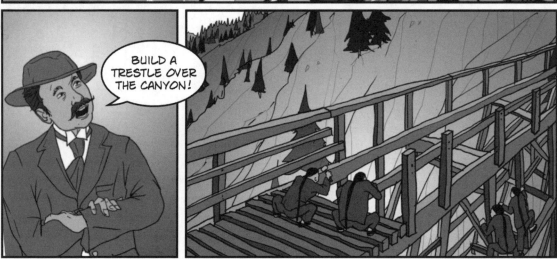

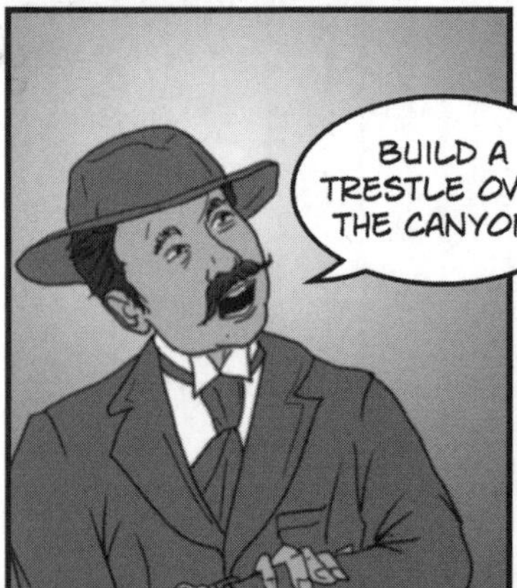
BUILD A TRESTLE OVER THE CANYON!

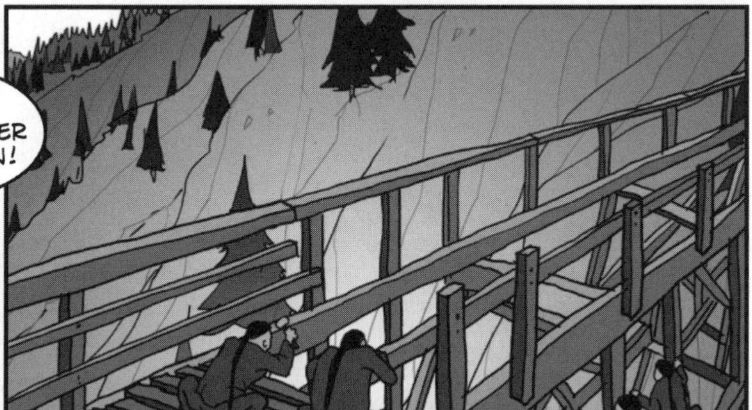

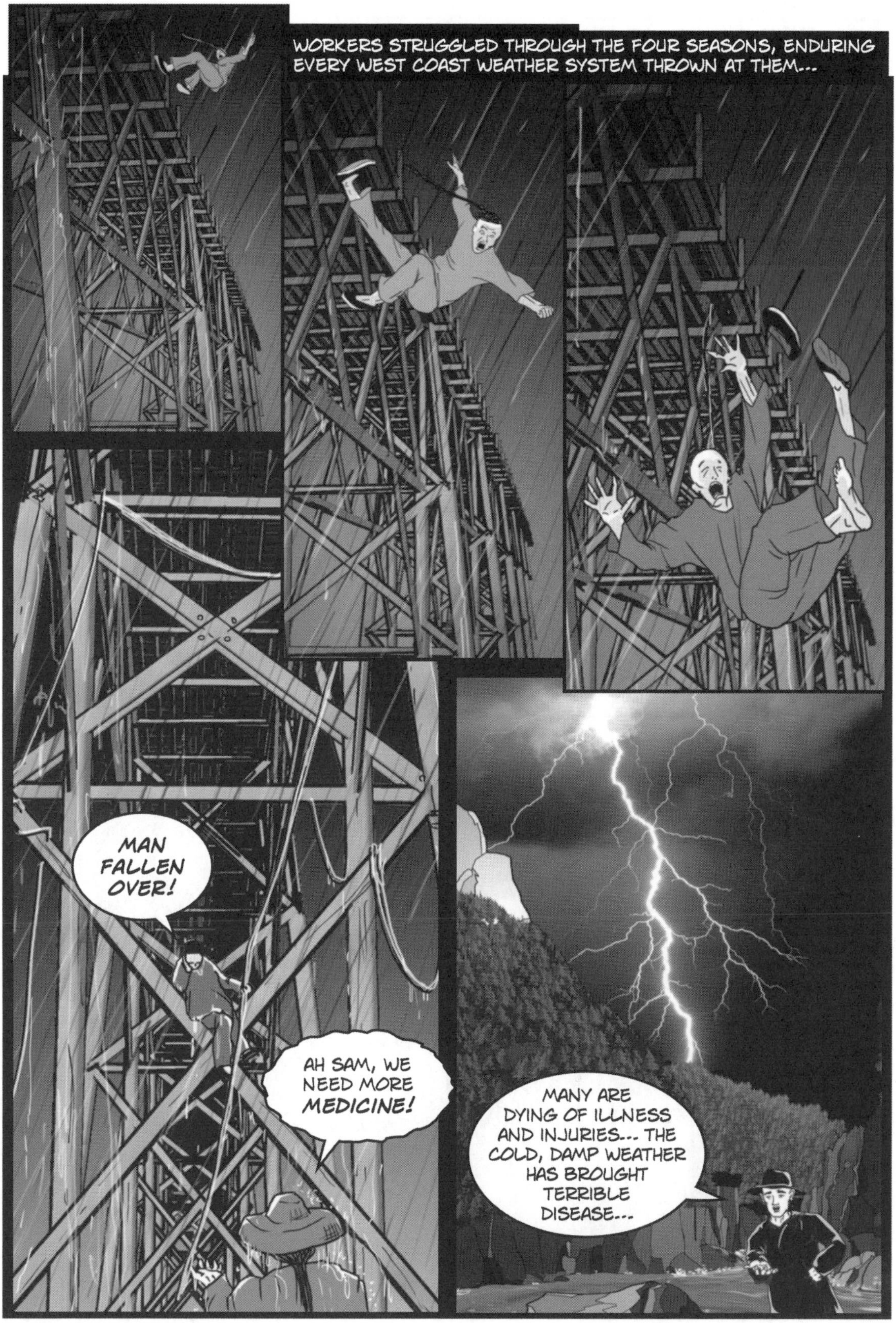
WORKERS STRUGGLED THROUGH THE FOUR SEASONS, ENDURING EVERY WEST COAST WEATHER SYSTEM THROWN AT THEM...
MAN FALLEN OVER!
AH SAM, WE NEED MORE MEDICINE!
MANY ARE DYING OF ILLNESS AND INJURIES... THE COLD, DAMP WEATHER HAS BROUGHT TERRIBLE DISEASE...

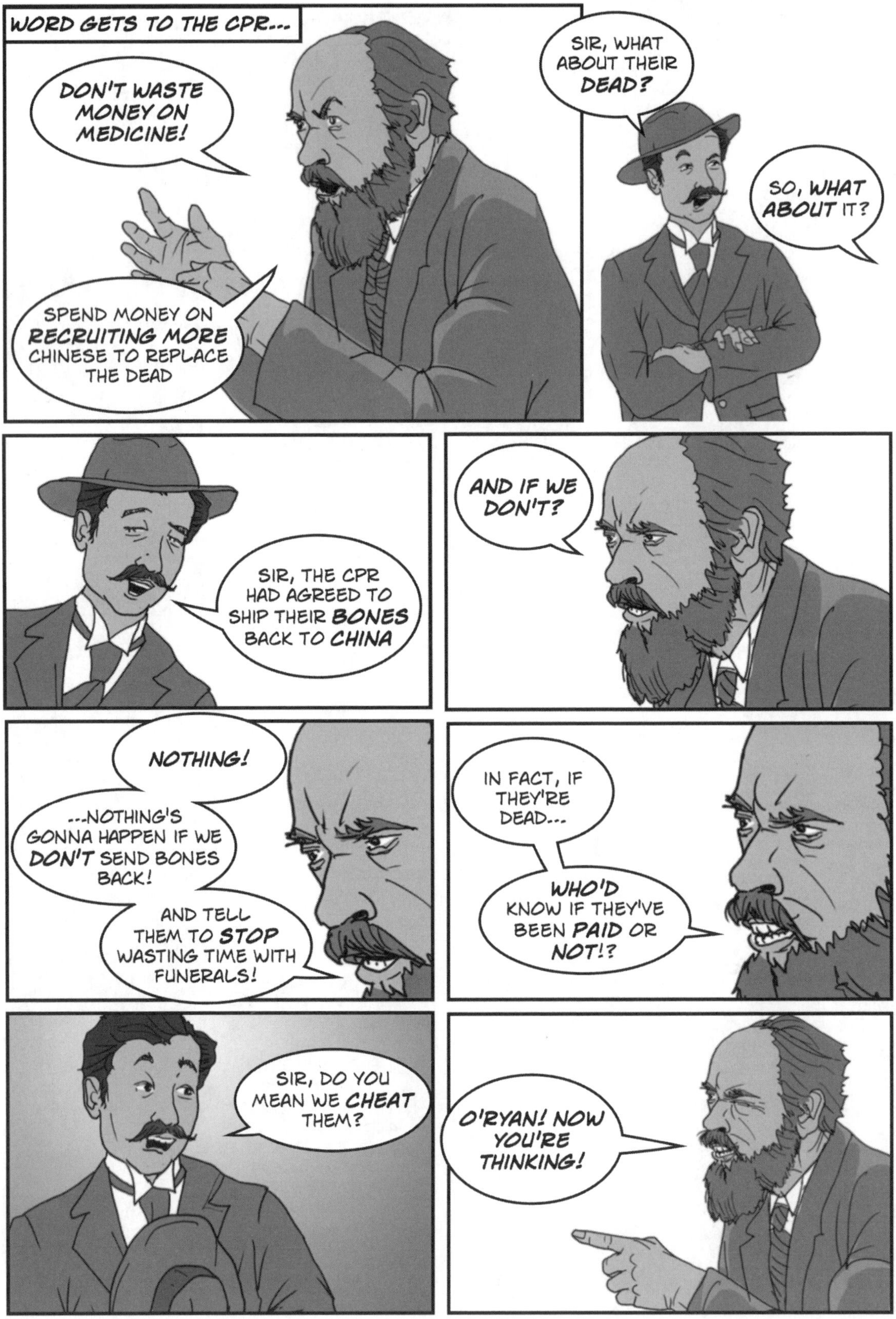
WORD GETS TO THE CPR...
DON'T WASTE MONEY ON MEDICINE!
SPEND MONEY ON RECRUITING MORE CHINESE TO REPLACE THE DEAD
SIR, WHAT ABOUT THEIR DEAD?
SO, WHAT ABOUT IT?
SIR, THE CPR HAD AGREED TO SHIP THEIR BONES BACK TO CHINA
AND IF WE DON'T?
NOTHING!
...NOTHING'S GONNA HAPPEN IF WE DON'T SEND BONES BACK!
AND TELL THEM TO STOP WASTING TIME WITH FUNERALS!
IN FACT, IF THEY'RE DEAD...
WHO'D KNOW IF THEY'VE BEEN PAID OR NOT!?
SIR, DO YOU MEAN WE CHEAT THEM?
O'RYAN! NOW YOU'RE THINKING!

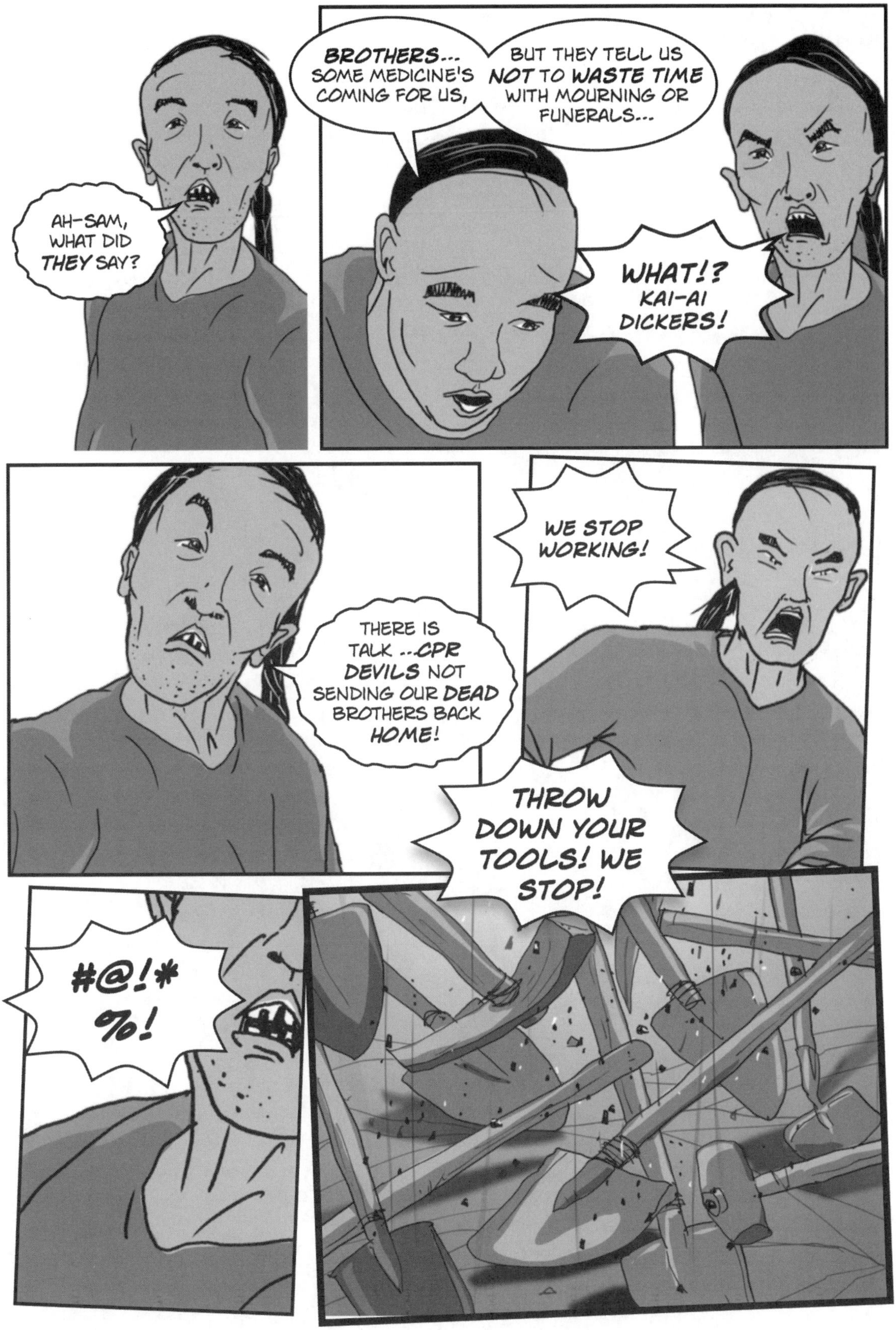
AH-SAM, WHAT DID THEY SAY?
BROTHERS... SOME MEDICINE'S COMING FOR US,
BUT THEY TELL US NOT TO WASTE TIME WITH MOURNING OR FUNERALS...
WHAT!? KAI-AI DICKERS!
THERE IS TALK ...CPR DEVILS NOT SENDING OUR DEAD BROTHERS BACK HOME!
WE STOP WORKING!
THROW DOWN YOUR TOOLS! WE STOP!
#@!* %!

CHAPTER 10 A Chinaman's Chance

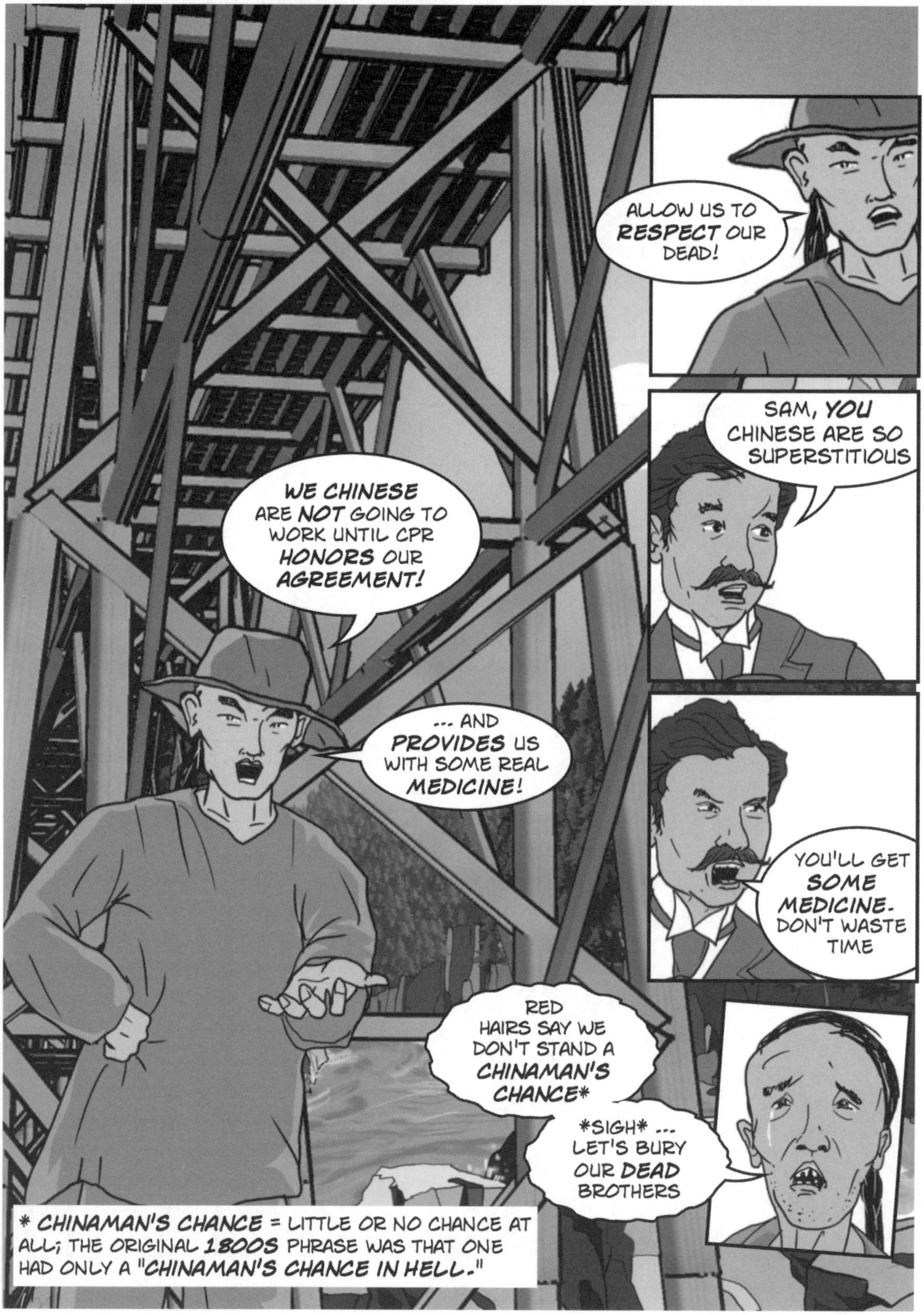

ALLOW US TO RESPECT OUR DEAD!
SAM, YOU CHINESE ARE SO SUPERSTITIOUS
WE CHINESE ARE NOT GOING TO WORK UNTIL CPR HONORS OUR AGREEMENT!
... AND PROVIDES US WITH SOME REAL MEDICINE!
YOU'LL GET SOME MEDICINE. DON'T WASTE TIME
RED HAIRS SAY WE DON'T STAND A CHINAMAN'S CHANCE*
SIGH ... LET'S BURY OUR DEAD BROTHERS

* CHINAMAN'S CHANCE = LITTLE OR NO CHANCE AT ALL; THE ORIGINAL 1800S PHRASE WAS THAT ONE HAD ONLY A "CHINAMAN'S CHANCE IN HELL."

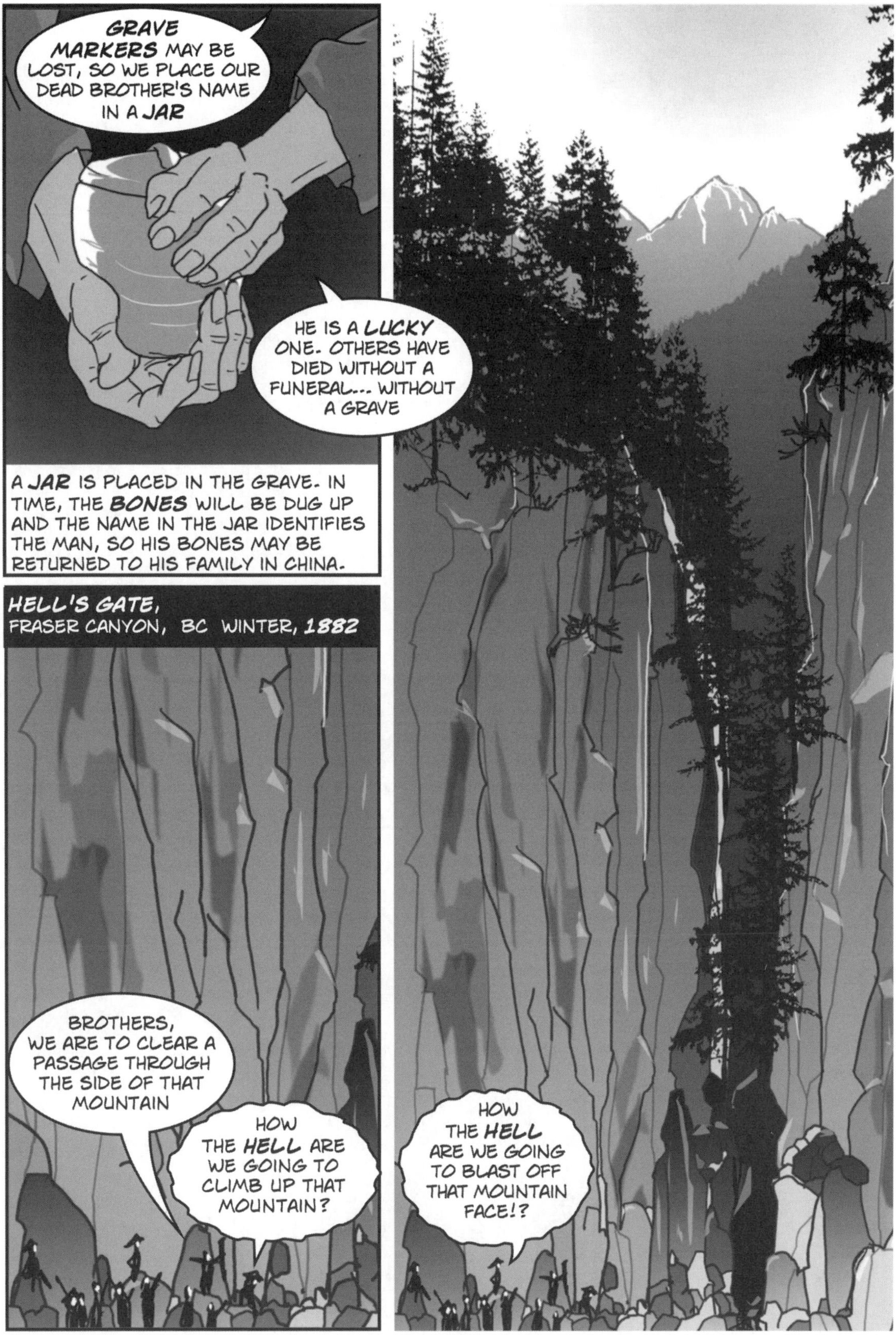
GRAVE MARKERS MAY BE LOST, SO WE PLACE OUR DEAD BROTHER'S NAME IN A JAR
HE IS A LUCKY ONE. OTHERS HAVE DIED WITHOUT A FUNERAL... WITHOUT A GRAVE
A JAR IS PLACED IN THE GRAVE. IN TIME, THE BONES WILL BE DUG UP AND THE NAME IN THE JAR IDENTIFIES THE MAN, SO HIS BONES MAY BE RETURNED TO HIS FAMILY IN CHINA.
HELL'S GATE, FRASER CANYON, BC WINTER, 1882
BROTHERS, WE ARE TO CLEAR A PASSAGE THROUGH THE SIDE OF THAT MOUNTAIN
HOW THE HELL ARE WE GOING TO CLIMB UP THAT MOUNTAIN?
HOW THE HELL ARE WE GOING TO BLAST OFF THAT MOUNTAIN FACE!?

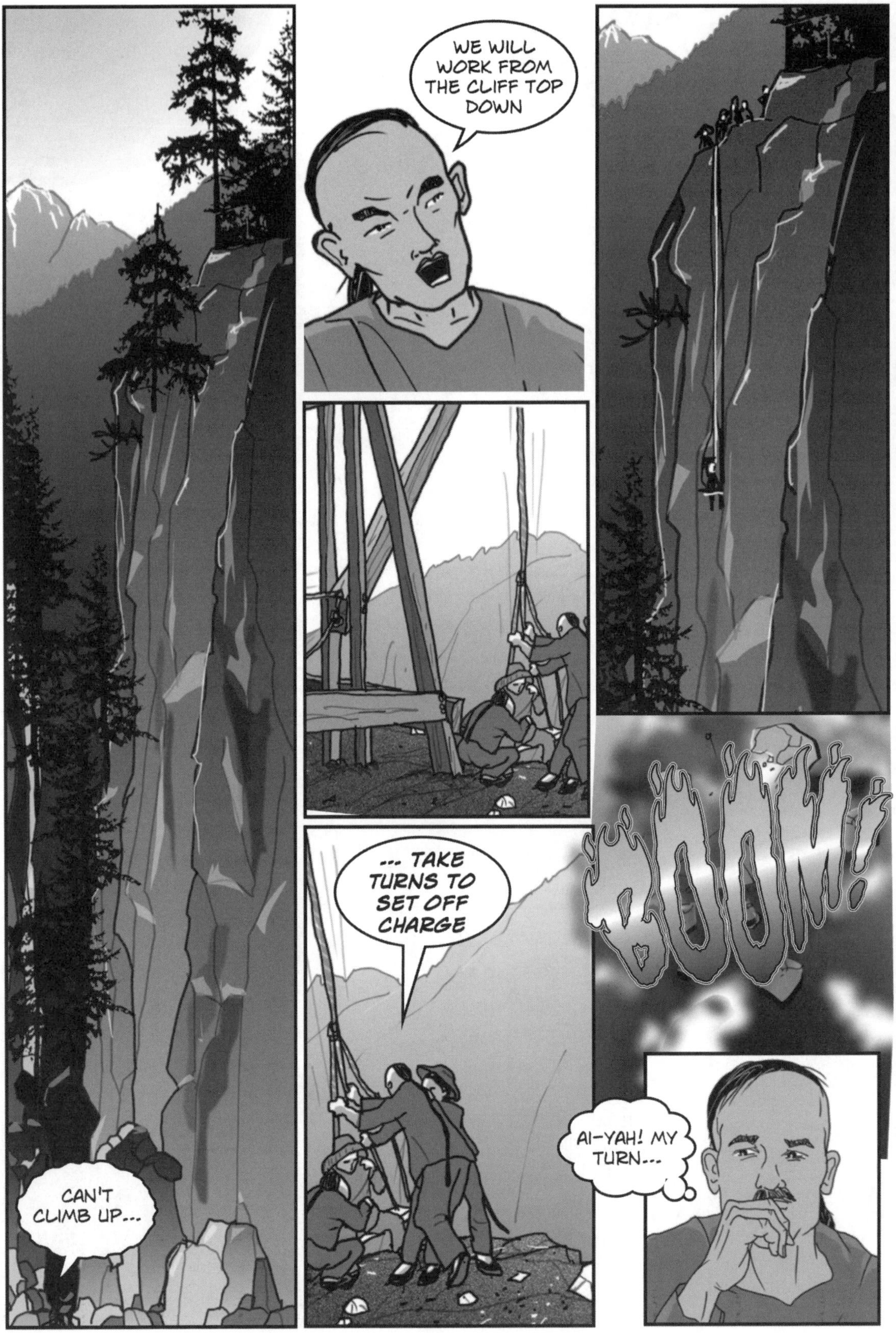
CAN'T CLIMB UP...
WE WILL WORK FROM THE CLIFF TOP DOWN
... TAKE TURNS TO SET OFF CHARGE
BOOM!
AI-YAH! MY TURN...

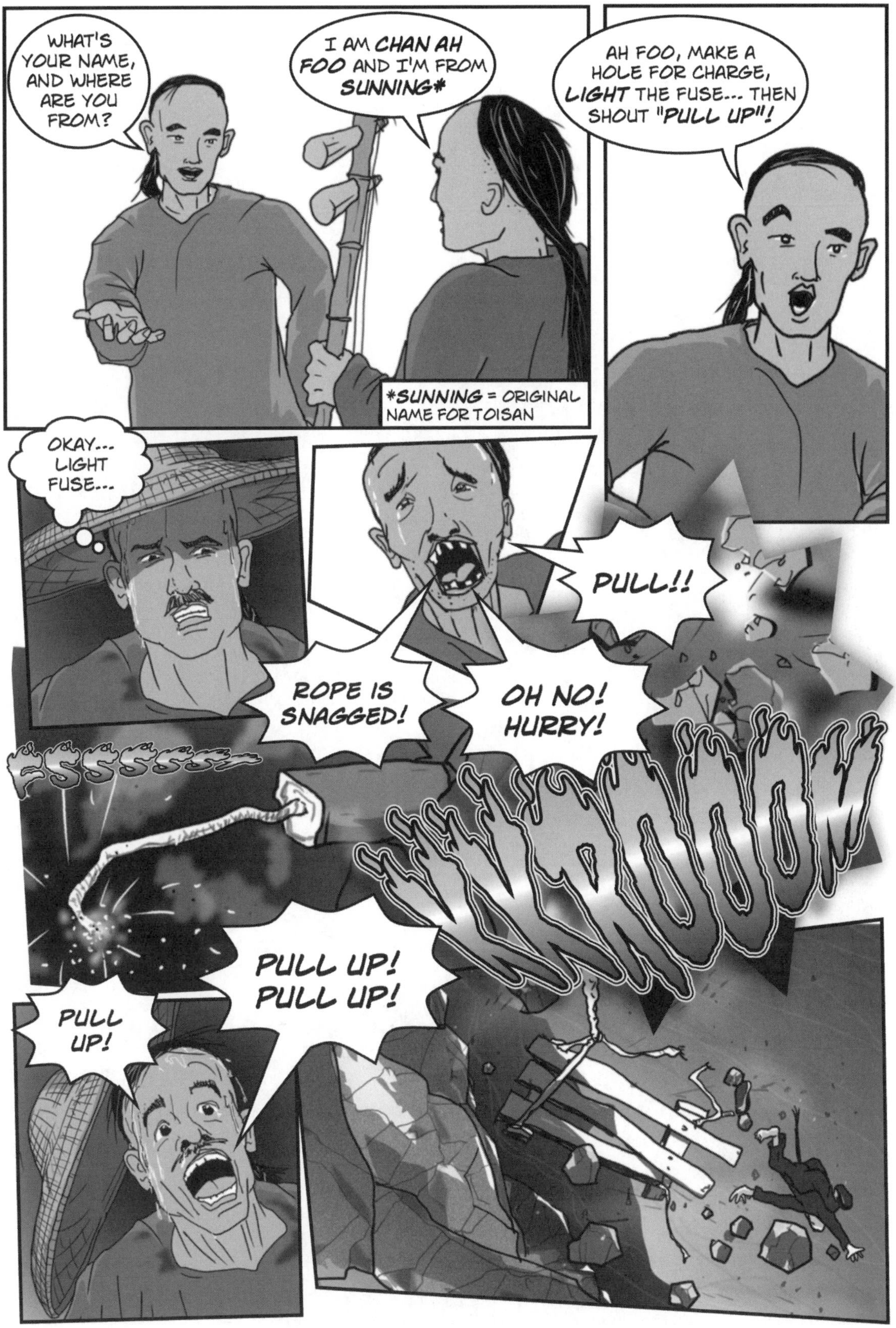
WHAT'S YOUR NAME, AND WHERE ARE YOU FROM?
I AM **CHAN AH FOO** AND I'M FROM **SUNNING***
***SUNNING** = ORIGINAL NAME FOR TOISAN
AH FOO, MAKE A HOLE FOR CHARGE, **LIGHT** THE FUSE... THEN SHOUT "**PULL UP**"!
OKAY... LIGHT FUSE...
PULL!!
ROPE IS SNAGGED!
OH NO! HURRY!
PULL UP!
PULL UP! PULL UP!

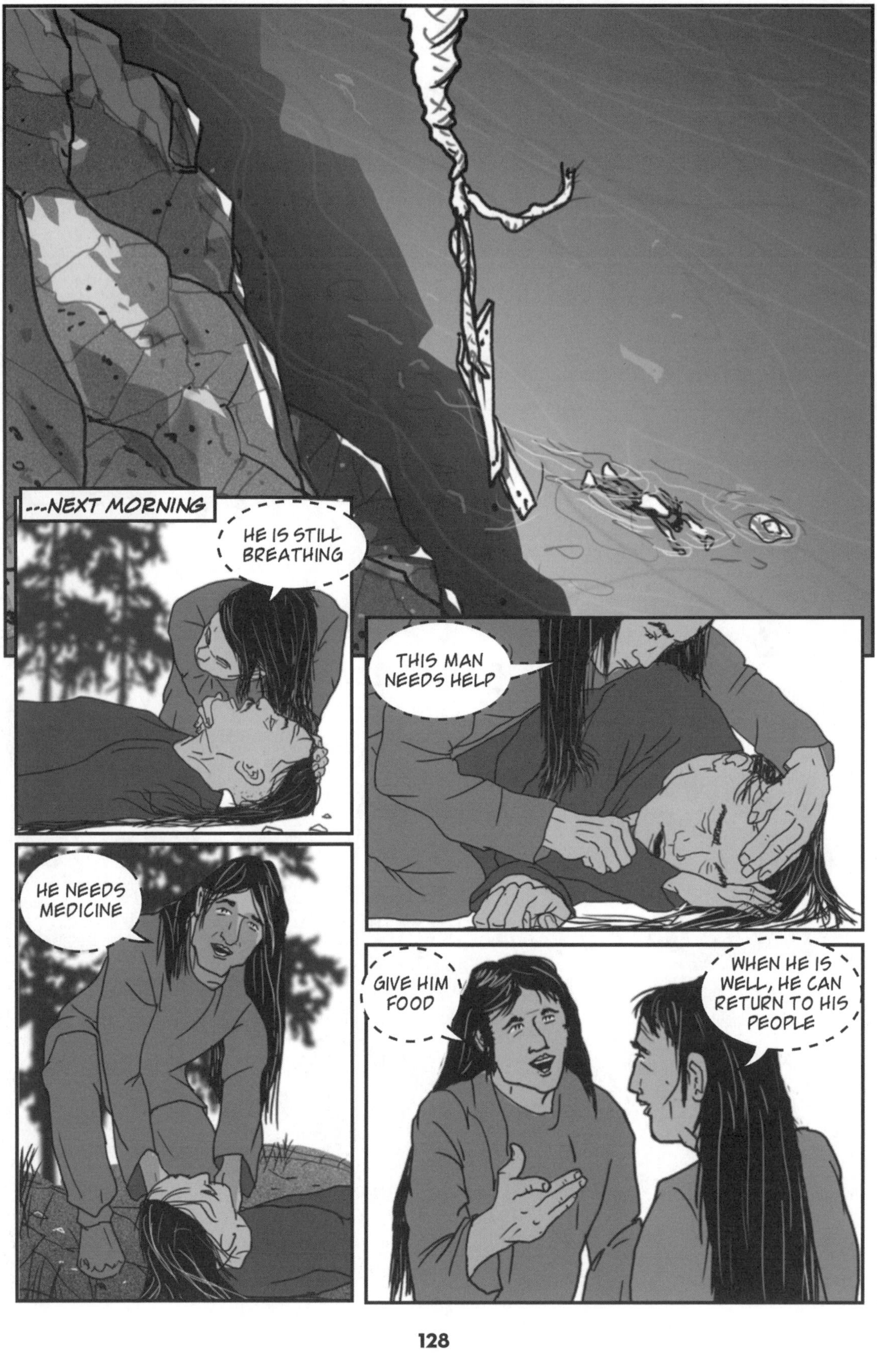

---NEXT MORNING
HE IS STILL BREATHING
THIS MAN NEEDS HELP
HE NEEDS MEDICINE
GIVE HIM FOOD
WHEN HE IS WELL, HE CAN RETURN TO HIS PEOPLE

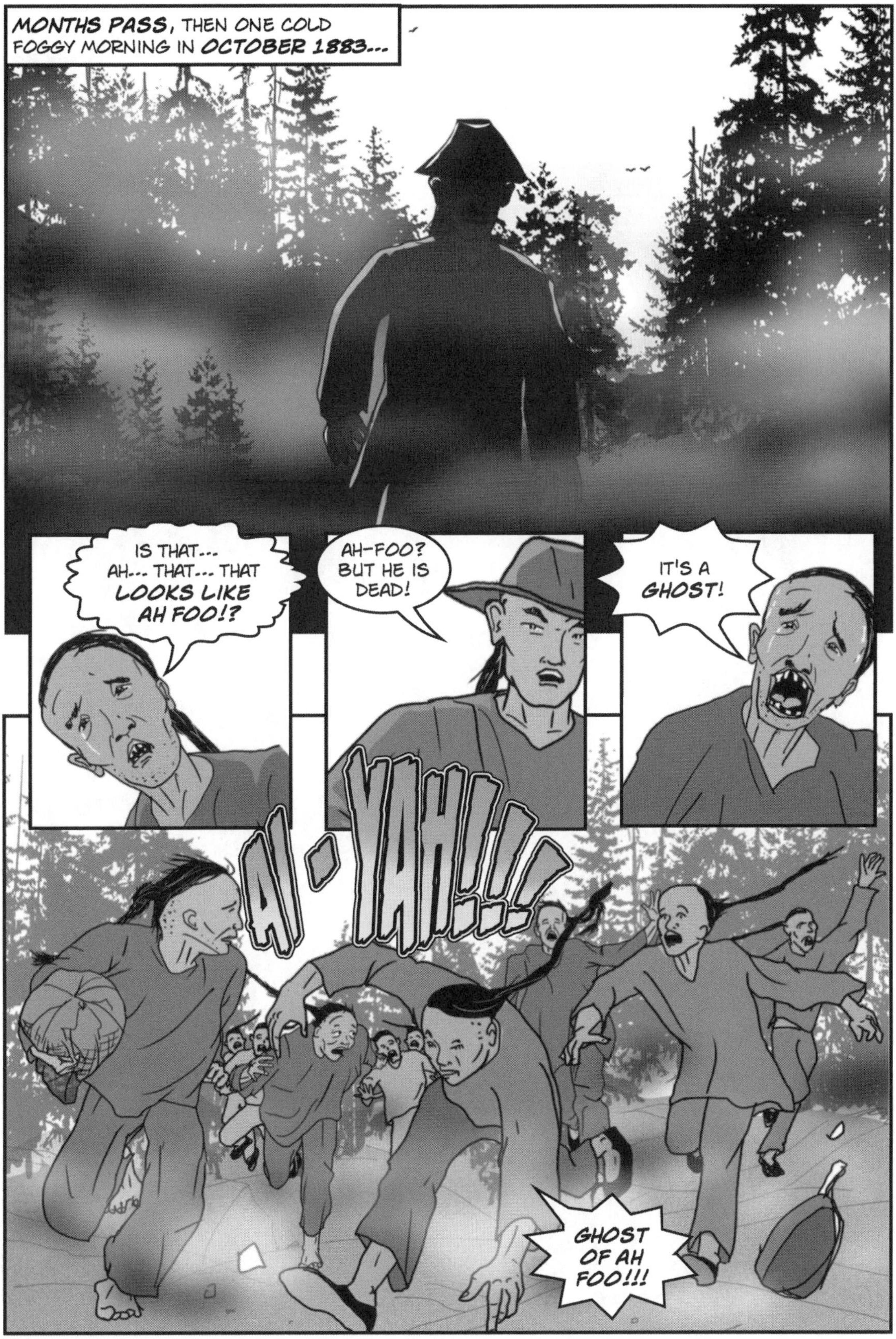
MONTHS PASS, THEN ONE COLD FOGGY MORNING IN OCTOBER 1883...
IS THAT... AH... THAT... THAT LOOKS LIKE AH FOO!?
AH-FOO? BUT HE IS DEAD!
IT'S A GHOST!
AI - YAH!!!!
GHOST OF AH FOO!!!

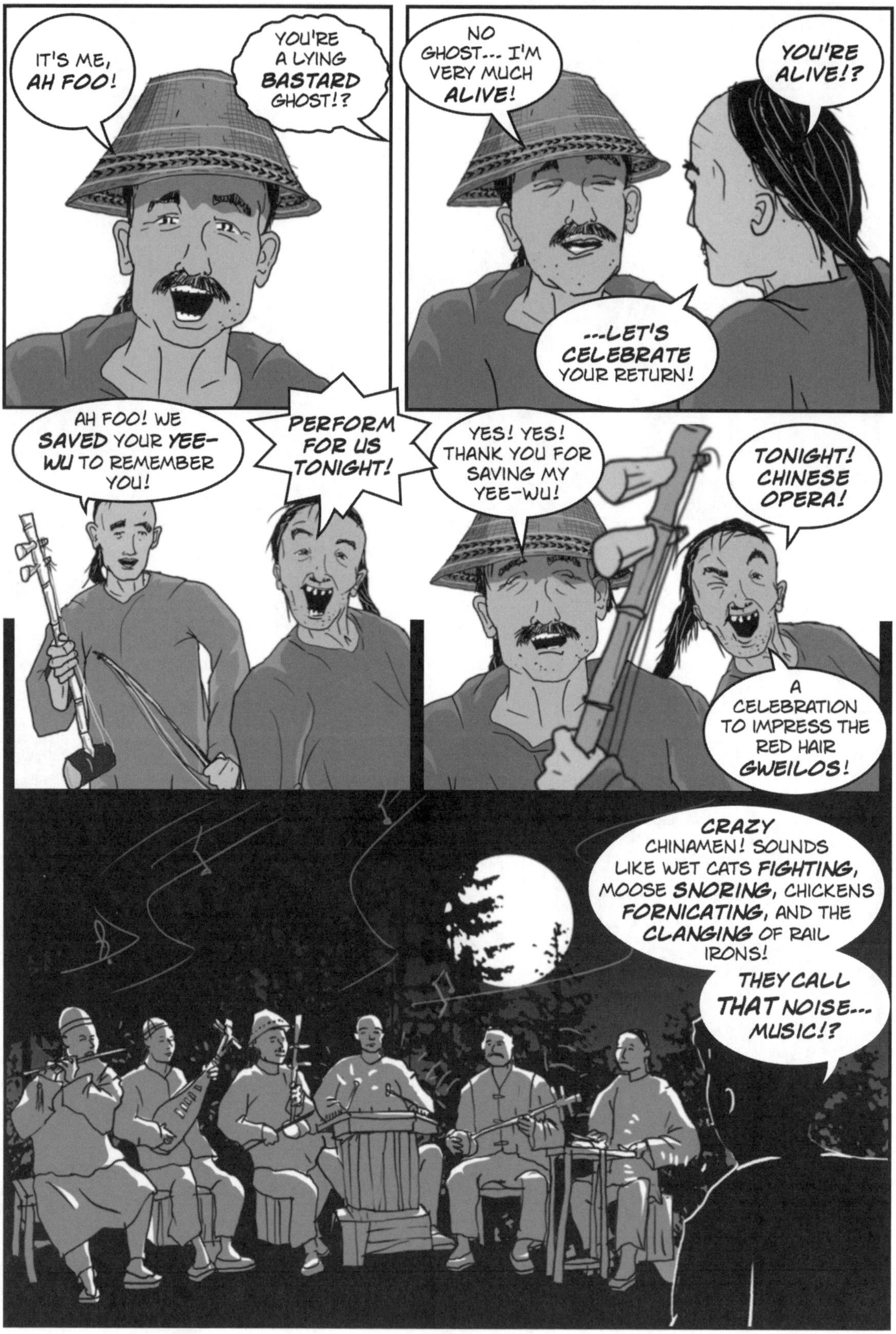
IT'S ME, AH FOO!
YOU'RE A LYING BASTARD GHOST!?
NO GHOST... I'M VERY MUCH ALIVE!
YOU'RE ALIVE!?
...LET'S CELEBRATE YOUR RETURN!
AH FOO! WE SAVED YOUR YEE-WU TO REMEMBER YOU!
PERFORM FOR US TONIGHT!
YES! YES! THANK YOU FOR SAVING MY YEE-WU!
TONIGHT! CHINESE OPERA!
A CELEBRATION TO IMPRESS THE RED HAIR GWEILOS!
CRAZY CHINAMEN! SOUNDS LIKE WET CATS FIGHTING, MOOSE SNORING, CHICKENS FORNICATING, AND THE CLANGING OF RAIL IRONS!
THEY CALL THAT NOISE... MUSIC!?

CHAPTER 11 Profiting from Racism

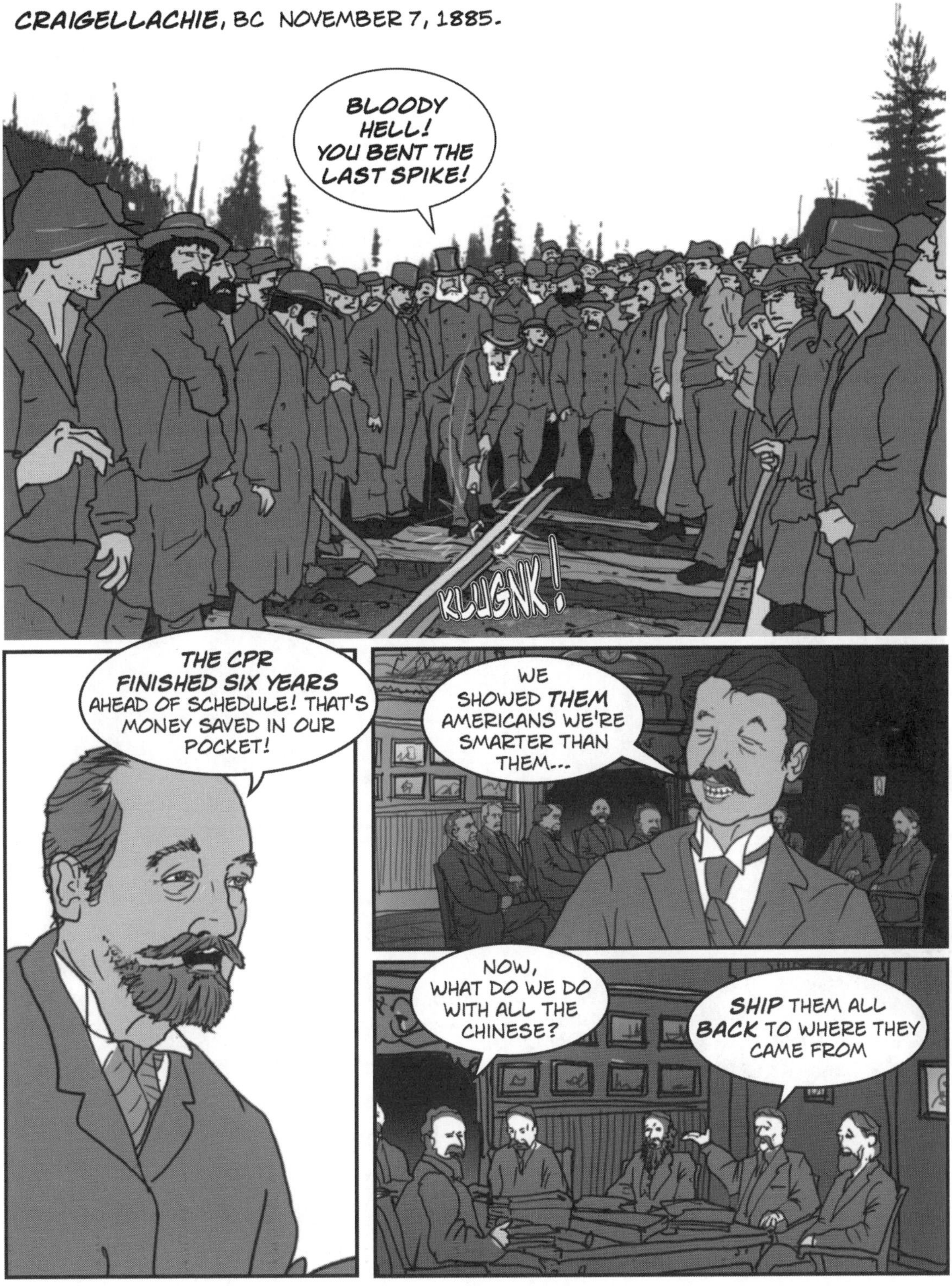
CRAIGELLACHIE, BC NOVEMBER 7, 1885.
BLOODY HELL! YOU BENT THE LAST SPIKE!
KLUGNK!
THE CPR FINISHED SIX YEARS AHEAD OF SCHEDULE! THAT'S MONEY SAVED IN OUR POCKET!
WE SHOWED THEM AMERICANS WE'RE SMARTER THAN THEM...
NOW, WHAT DO WE DO WITH ALL THE CHINESE?
SHIP THEM ALL BACK TO WHERE THEY CAME FROM

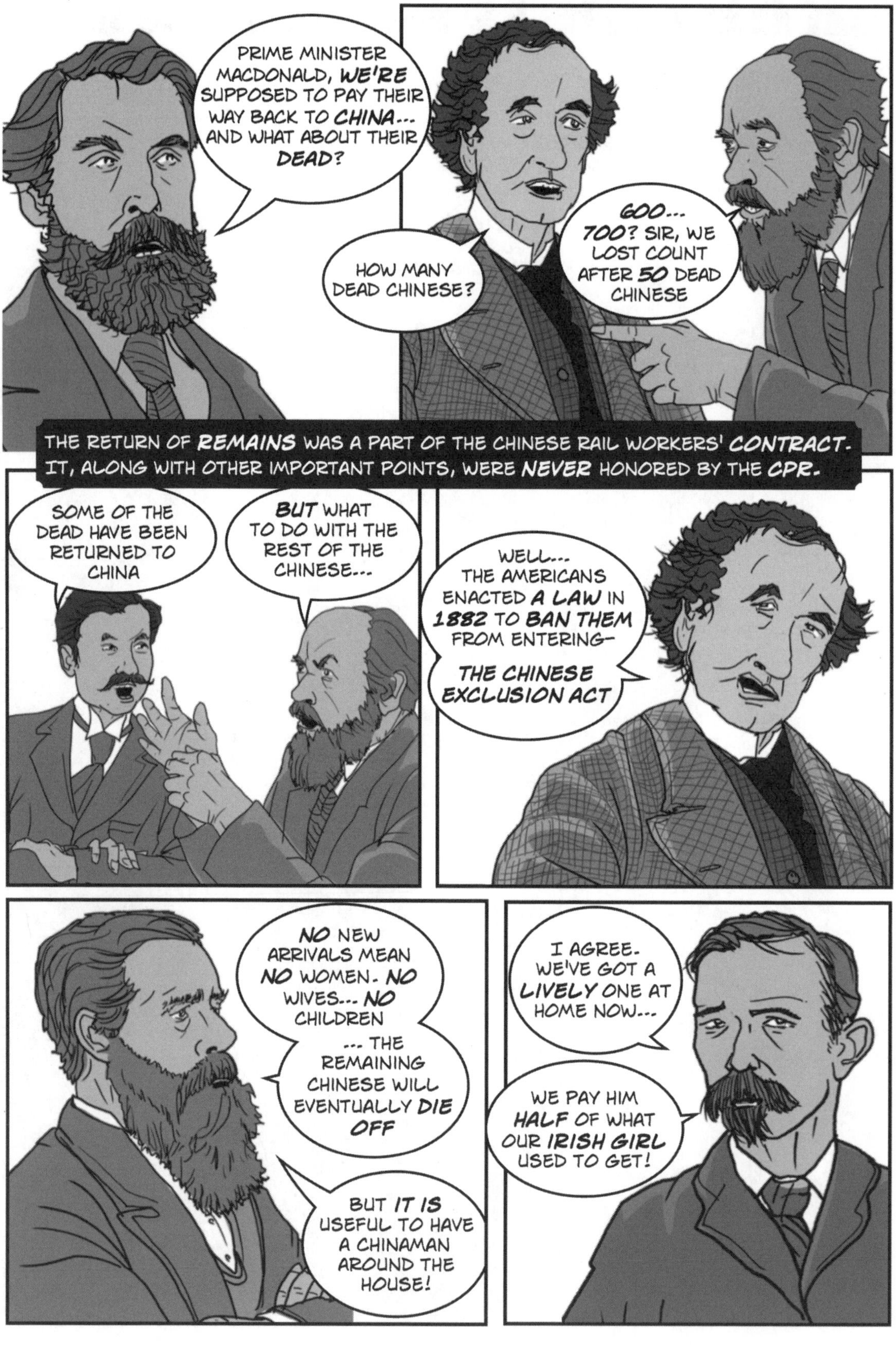
PRIME MINISTER MACDONALD, WE'RE SUPPOSED TO PAY THEIR WAY BACK TO CHINA... AND WHAT ABOUT THEIR DEAD?
HOW MANY DEAD CHINESE?
600... 700? SIR, WE LOST COUNT AFTER 50 DEAD CHINESE
THE RETURN OF REMAINS WAS A PART OF THE CHINESE RAIL WORKERS' CONTRACT. IT, ALONG WITH OTHER IMPORTANT POINTS, WERE NEVER HONORED BY THE CPR.
SOME OF THE DEAD HAVE BEEN RETURNED TO CHINA
BUT WHAT TO DO WITH THE REST OF THE CHINESE...
WELL... THE AMERICANS ENACTED A LAW IN 1882 TO BAN THEM FROM ENTERING—
THE CHINESE EXCLUSION ACT
NO NEW ARRIVALS MEAN NO WOMEN. NO WIVES... NO CHILDREN
... THE REMAINING CHINESE WILL EVENTUALLY DIE OFF
BUT IT IS USEFUL TO HAVE A CHINAMAN AROUND THE HOUSE!
I AGREE. WE'VE GOT A LIVELY ONE AT HOME NOW...
WE PAY HIM HALF OF WHAT OUR IRISH GIRL USED TO GET!

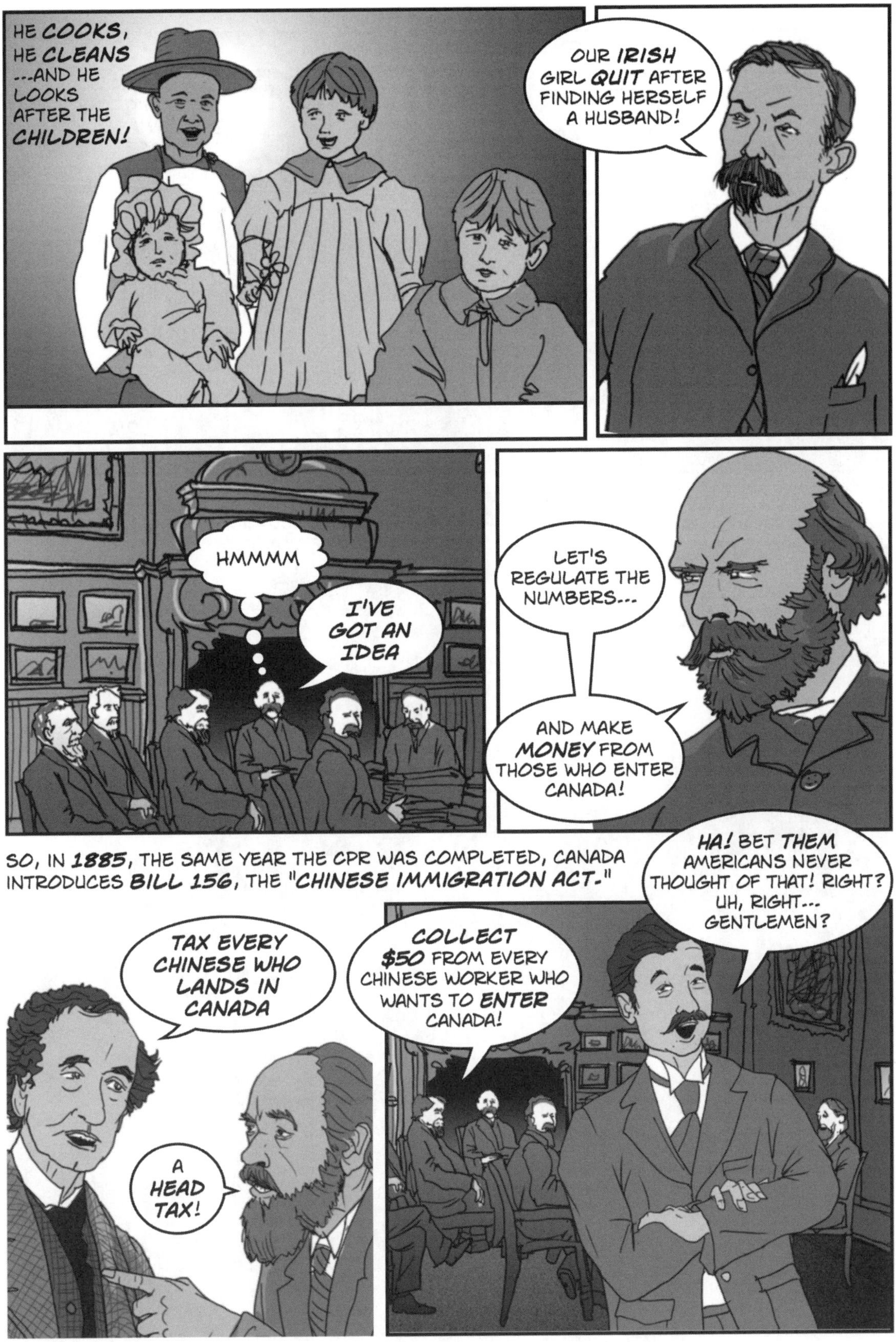
HE COOKS, HE CLEANS ...AND HE LOOKS AFTER THE CHILDREN!
OUR IRISH GIRL QUIT AFTER FINDING HERSELF A HUSBAND!
HMMMM
I'VE GOT AN IDEA
LET'S REGULATE THE NUMBERS...
AND MAKE MONEY FROM THOSE WHO ENTER CANADA!
SO, IN 1885, THE SAME YEAR THE CPR WAS COMPLETED, CANADA INTRODUCES BILL 156, THE "CHINESE IMMIGRATION ACT."
TAX EVERY CHINESE WHO LANDS IN CANADA
A HEAD TAX!
COLLECT $50 FROM EVERY CHINESE WORKER WHO WANTS TO ENTER CANADA!
HA! BET THEM AMERICANS NEVER THOUGHT OF THAT! RIGHT? UH, RIGHT... GENTLEMEN?

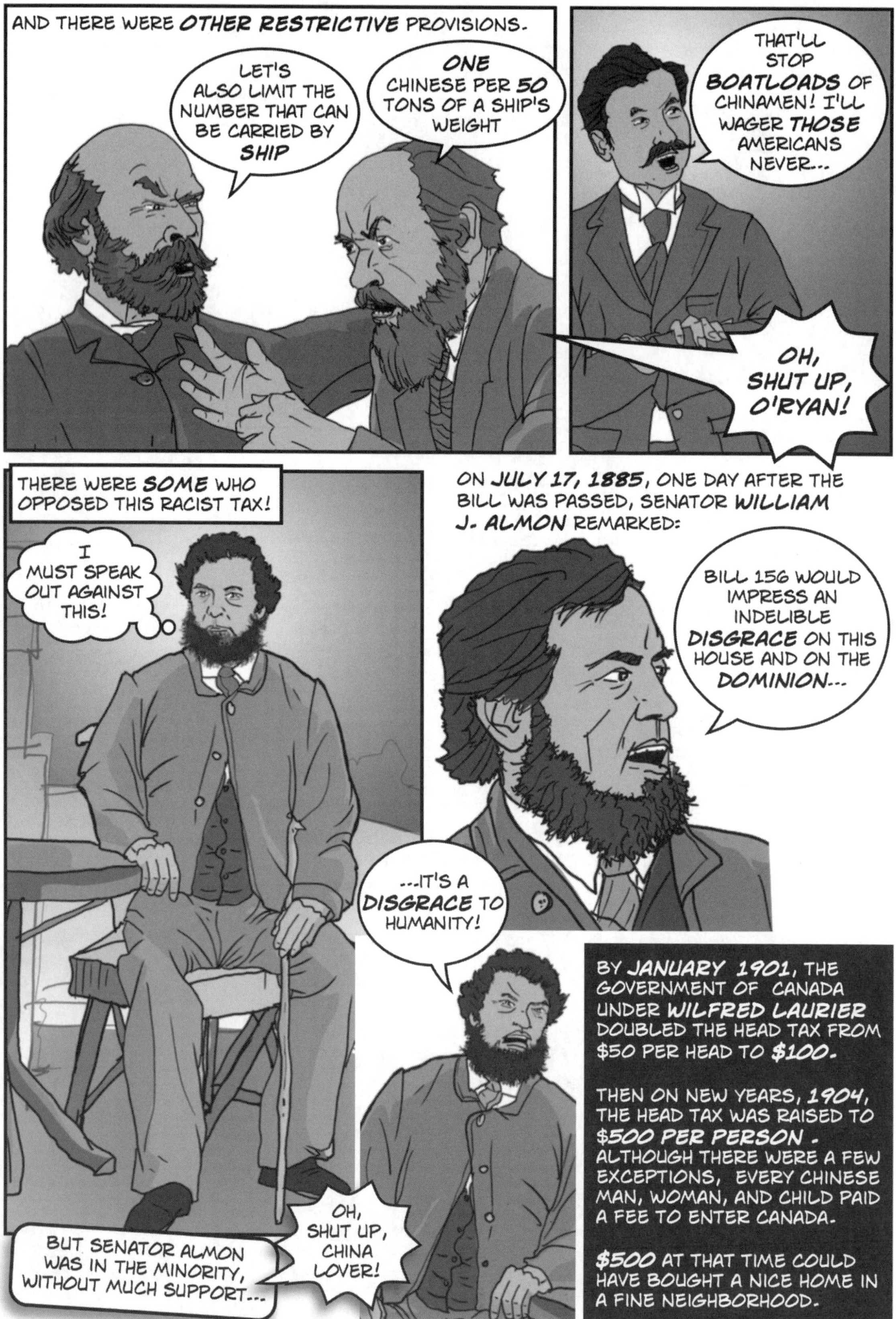
AND THERE WERE OTHER RESTRICTIVE PROVISIONS.
LET'S ALSO LIMIT THE NUMBER THAT CAN BE CARRIED BY SHIP
ONE CHINESE PER 50 TONS OF A SHIP'S WEIGHT
THAT'LL STOP BOATLOADS OF CHINAMEN! I'LL WAGER THOSE AMERICANS NEVER...
OH, SHUT UP, O'RYAN!
THERE WERE SOME WHO OPPOSED THIS RACIST TAX!
I MUST SPEAK OUT AGAINST THIS!
ON JULY 17, 1885, ONE DAY AFTER THE BILL WAS PASSED, SENATOR WILLIAM J. ALMON REMARKED:
BILL 156 WOULD IMPRESS AN INDELIBLE DISGRACE ON THIS HOUSE AND ON THE DOMINION...
...IT'S A DISGRACE TO HUMANITY!
BUT SENATOR ALMON WAS IN THE MINORITY, WITHOUT MUCH SUPPORT...
OH, SHUT UP, CHINA LOVER!
BY JANUARY 1901, THE GOVERNMENT OF CANADA UNDER WILFRED LAURIER DOUBLED THE HEAD TAX FROM $50 PER HEAD TO $100.
THEN ON NEW YEARS, 1904, THE HEAD TAX WAS RAISED TO $500 PER PERSON - ALTHOUGH THERE WERE A FEW EXCEPTIONS, EVERY CHINESE MAN, WOMAN, AND CHILD PAID A FEE TO ENTER CANADA.
$500 AT THAT TIME COULD HAVE BOUGHT A NICE HOME IN A FINE NEIGHBORHOOD.

CANADA'S **HEAD TAX** WAS VERY **PROFITABLE!** IT WAS A BIG SOURCE OF REVENUE... BEFORE INCOME TAXES WERE IMPOSED.**

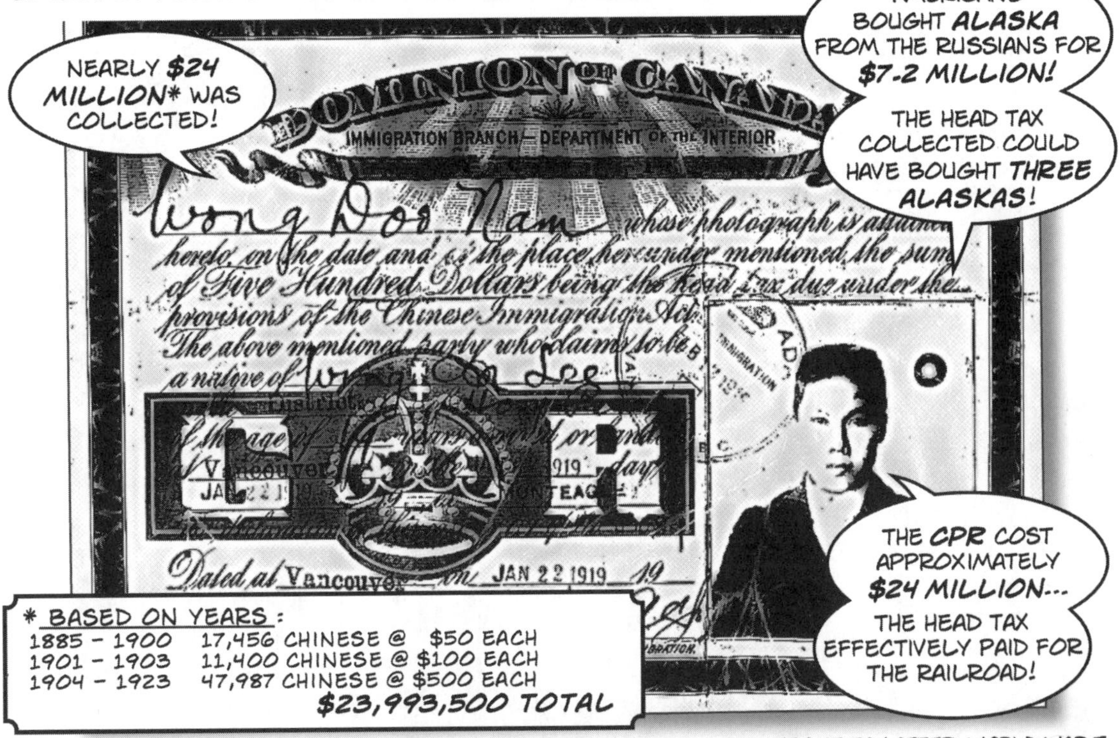
NEARLY **$24 MILLION*** WAS COLLECTED!
AMERICANS BOUGHT **ALASKA** FROM THE RUSSIANS FOR **$7.2 MILLION!**
THE HEAD TAX COLLECTED COULD HAVE BOUGHT **THREE ALASKAS!**
DOMINION OF CANADA
IMMIGRATION BRANCH — DEPARTMENT OF THE INTERIOR
Wong Dos Nam whose photograph is attached
hereto, on the date and at the place hereunder mentioned the sum
of Five Hundred Dollars being the head tax due under the
provisions of the Chinese Immigration Act.
The above mentioned party who claims to be
a native of
Vancouver
JAN 22 1919
Dated at Vancouver on JAN 22 1919 19
THE **CPR** COST APPROXIMATELY **$24 MILLION...**
THE HEAD TAX EFFECTIVELY PAID FOR THE RAILROAD!
* BASED ON YEARS:
1885 – 1900 17,456 CHINESE @ $50 EACH
1901 – 1903 11,400 CHINESE @ $100 EACH
1904 – 1923 47,987 CHINESE @ $500 EACH
$23,993,500 TOTAL

** CANADA ONLY BEGAN TO COLLECT INCOME TAX AFTER WORLD WAR I.

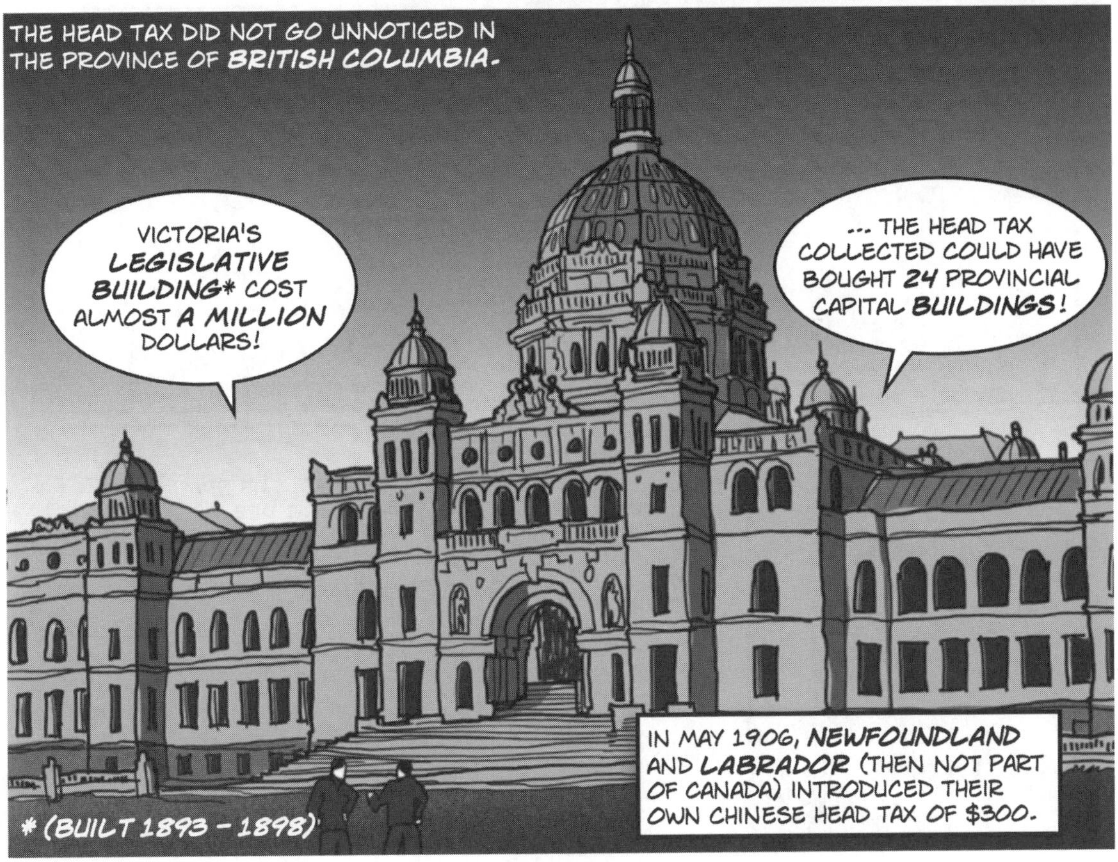
THE HEAD TAX DID NOT GO UNNOTICED IN THE PROVINCE OF **BRITISH COLUMBIA.**
VICTORIA'S **LEGISLATIVE BUILDING*** COST ALMOST **A MILLION** DOLLARS!
... THE HEAD TAX COLLECTED COULD HAVE BOUGHT **24** PROVINCIAL CAPITAL **BUILDINGS!**
IN MAY 1906, **NEWFOUNDLAND** AND **LABRADOR** (THEN NOT PART OF CANADA) INTRODUCED THEIR OWN CHINESE HEAD TAX OF $300.
* (BUILT 1893 – 1898)

CHAPTER 12 Pai Hua (Expelling the Chinese)

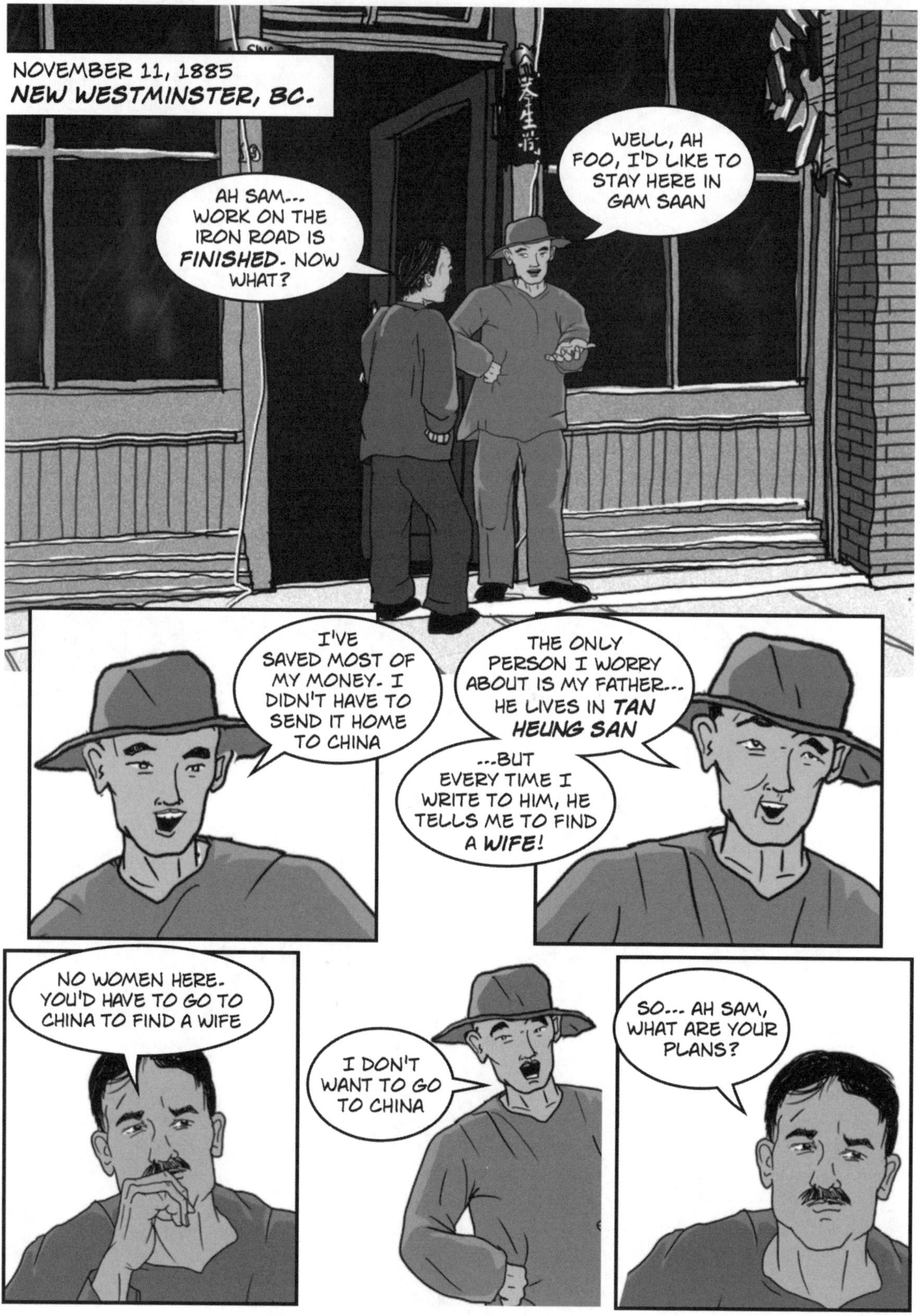
NOVEMBER 11, 1885
NEW WESTMINSTER, BC.
AH SAM... WORK ON THE IRON ROAD IS FINISHED. NOW WHAT?
WELL, AH FOO, I'D LIKE TO STAY HERE IN GAM SAAN
I'VE SAVED MOST OF MY MONEY. I DIDN'T HAVE TO SEND IT HOME TO CHINA
THE ONLY PERSON I WORRY ABOUT IS MY FATHER... HE LIVES IN TAN HEUNG SAN
...BUT EVERY TIME I WRITE TO HIM, HE TELLS ME TO FIND A WIFE!
NO WOMEN HERE. YOU'D HAVE TO GO TO CHINA TO FIND A WIFE
I DON'T WANT TO GO TO CHINA
SO... AH SAM, WHAT ARE YOUR PLANS?

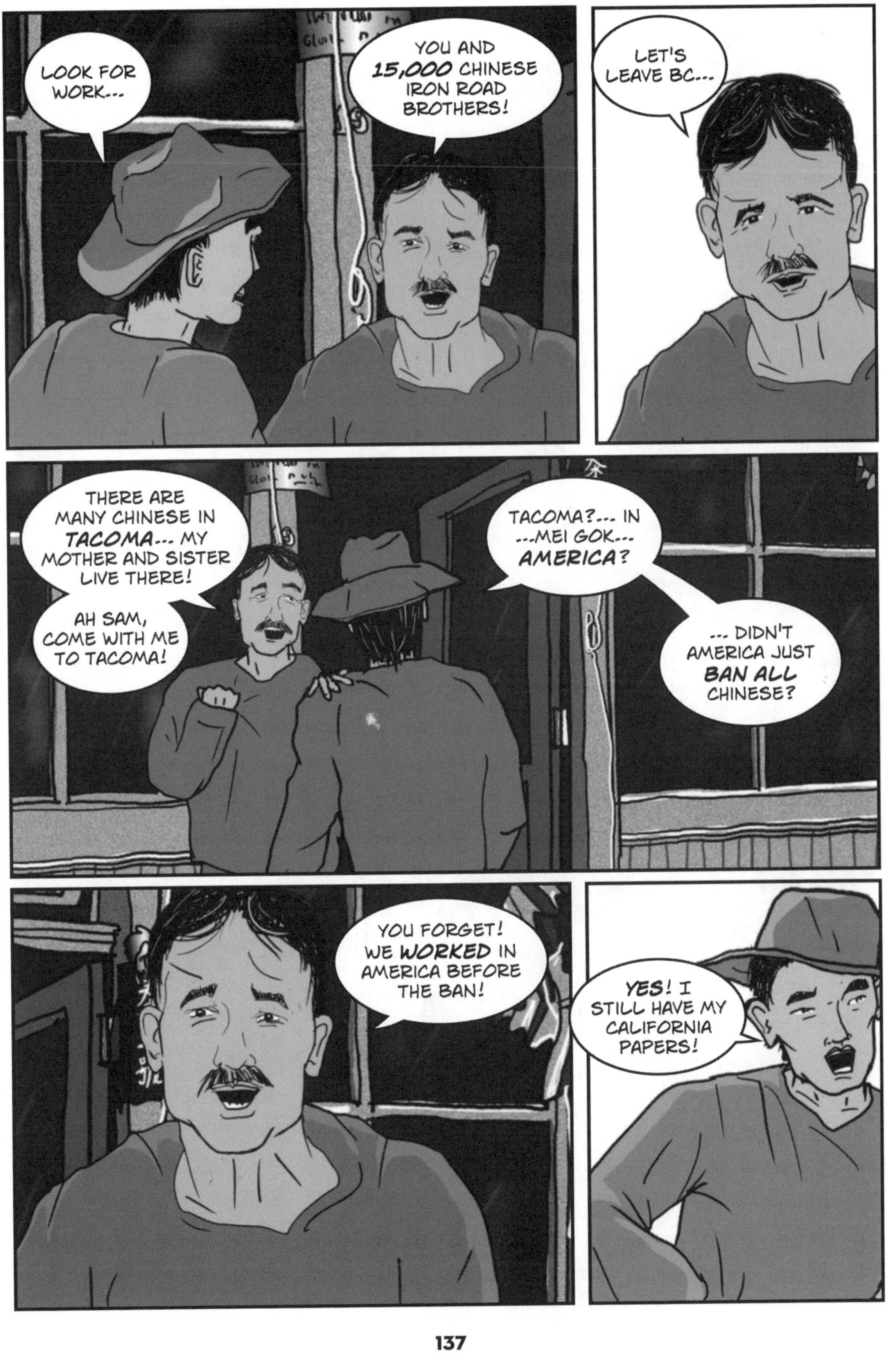
LOOK FOR WORK...
YOU AND 15,000 CHINESE IRON ROAD BROTHERS!
LET'S LEAVE BC...
THERE ARE MANY CHINESE IN TACOMA... MY MOTHER AND SISTER LIVE THERE!
AH SAM, COME WITH ME TO TACOMA!
TACOMA?... IN ...MEI GOK... AMERICA?
... DIDN'T AMERICA JUST BAN ALL CHINESE?
YOU FORGET! WE WORKED IN AMERICA BEFORE THE BAN!
YES! I STILL HAVE MY CALIFORNIA PAPERS!

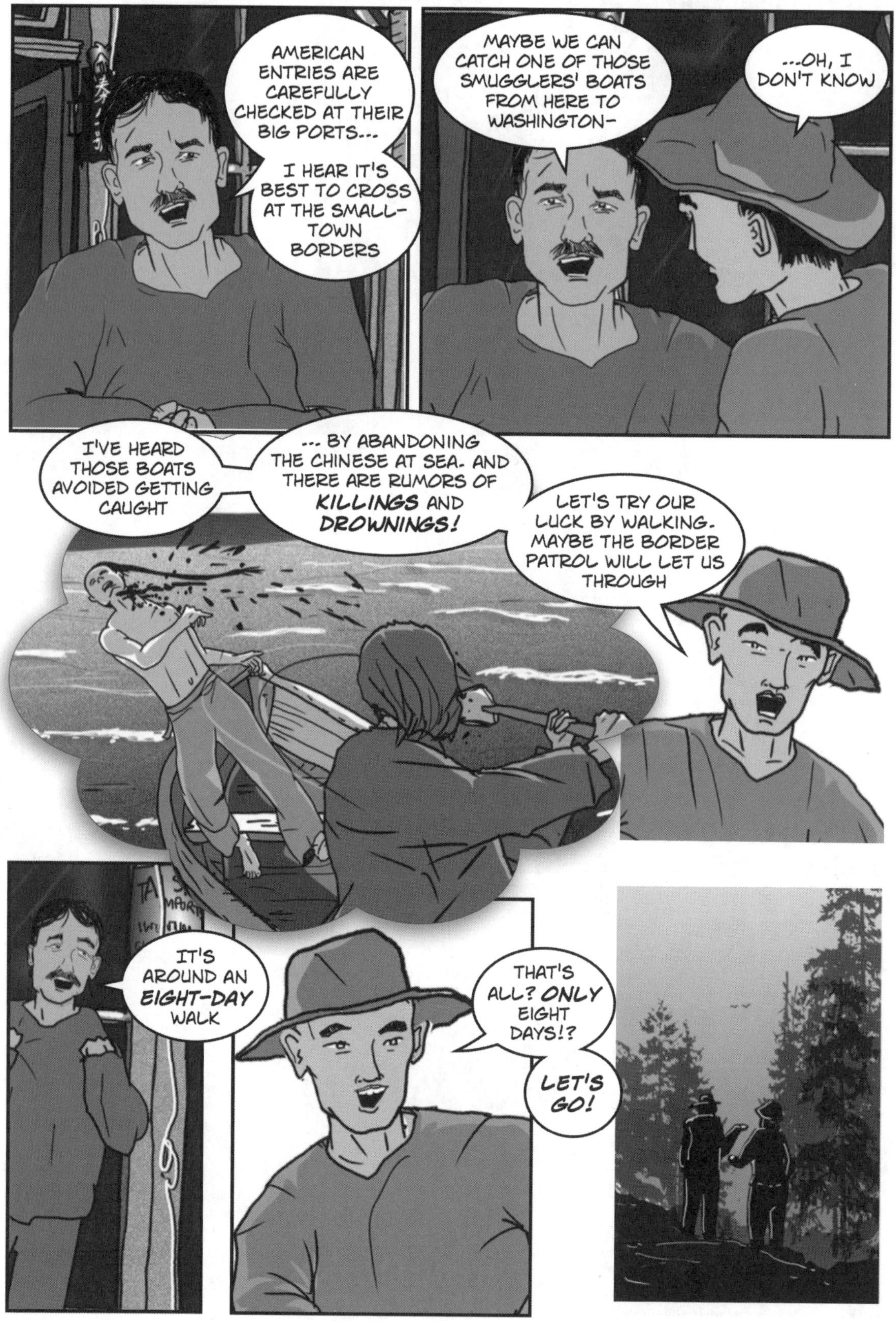
AMERICAN ENTRIES ARE CAREFULLY CHECKED AT THEIR BIG PORTS...
I HEAR IT'S BEST TO CROSS AT THE SMALL-TOWN BORDERS
MAYBE WE CAN CATCH ONE OF THOSE SMUGGLERS' BOATS FROM HERE TO WASHINGTON-
...OH, I DON'T KNOW
I'VE HEARD THOSE BOATS AVOIDED GETTING CAUGHT
... BY ABANDONING THE CHINESE AT SEA. AND THERE ARE RUMORS OF KILLINGS AND DROWNINGS!
LET'S TRY OUR LUCK BY WALKING. MAYBE THE BORDER PATROL WILL LET US THROUGH
IT'S AROUND AN EIGHT-DAY WALK
THAT'S ALL? ONLY EIGHT DAYS!?
LET'S GO!

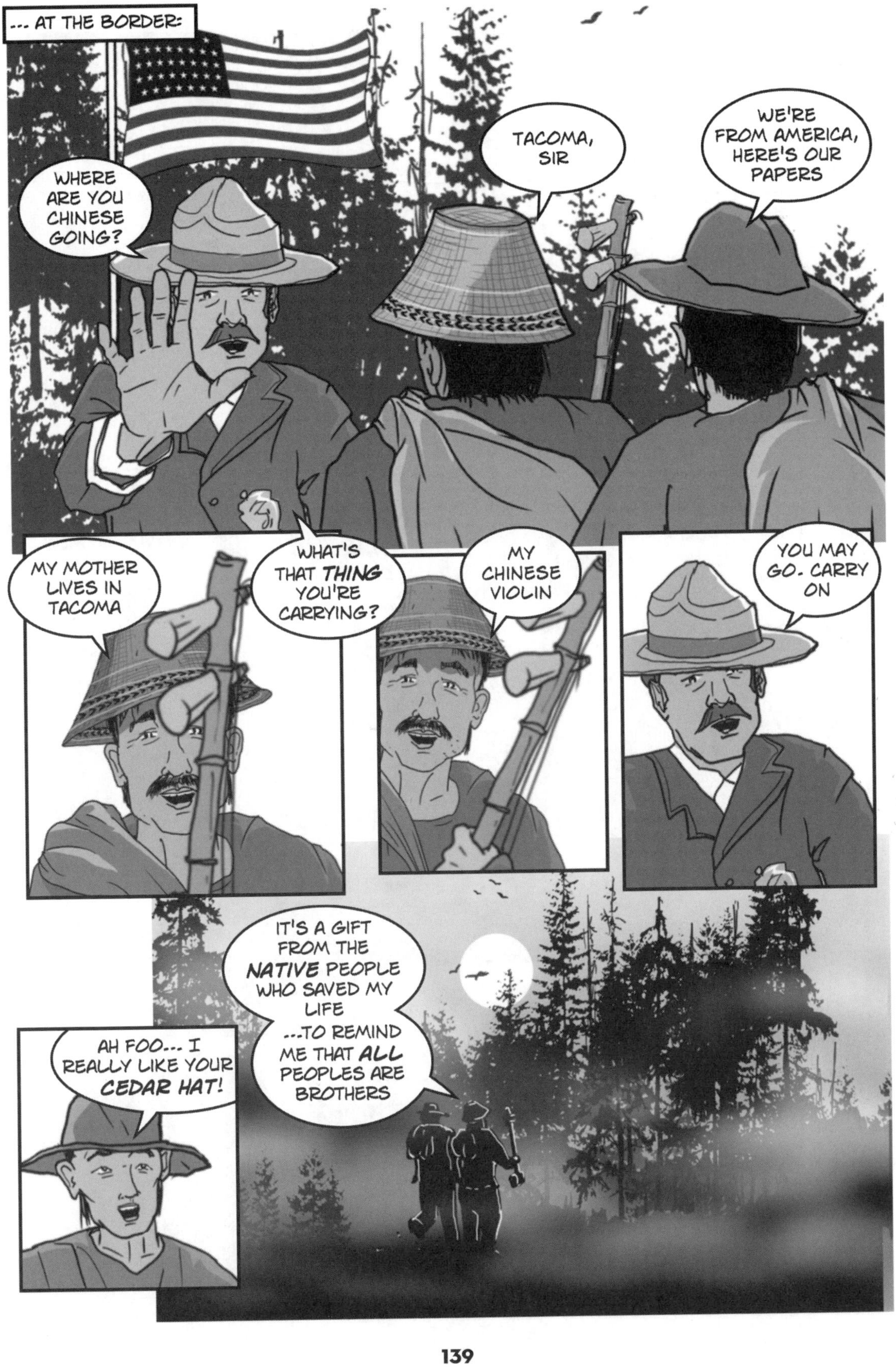
... AT THE BORDER:
WHERE ARE YOU CHINESE GOING?
TACOMA, SIR
WE'RE FROM AMERICA, HERE'S OUR PAPERS
MY MOTHER LIVES IN TACOMA
WHAT'S THAT THING YOU'RE CARRYING?
MY CHINESE VIOLIN
YOU MAY GO. CARRY ON
AH FOO... I REALLY LIKE YOUR CEDAR HAT!
IT'S A GIFT FROM THE NATIVE PEOPLE WHO SAVED MY LIFE
...TO REMIND ME THAT ALL PEOPLES ARE BROTHERS

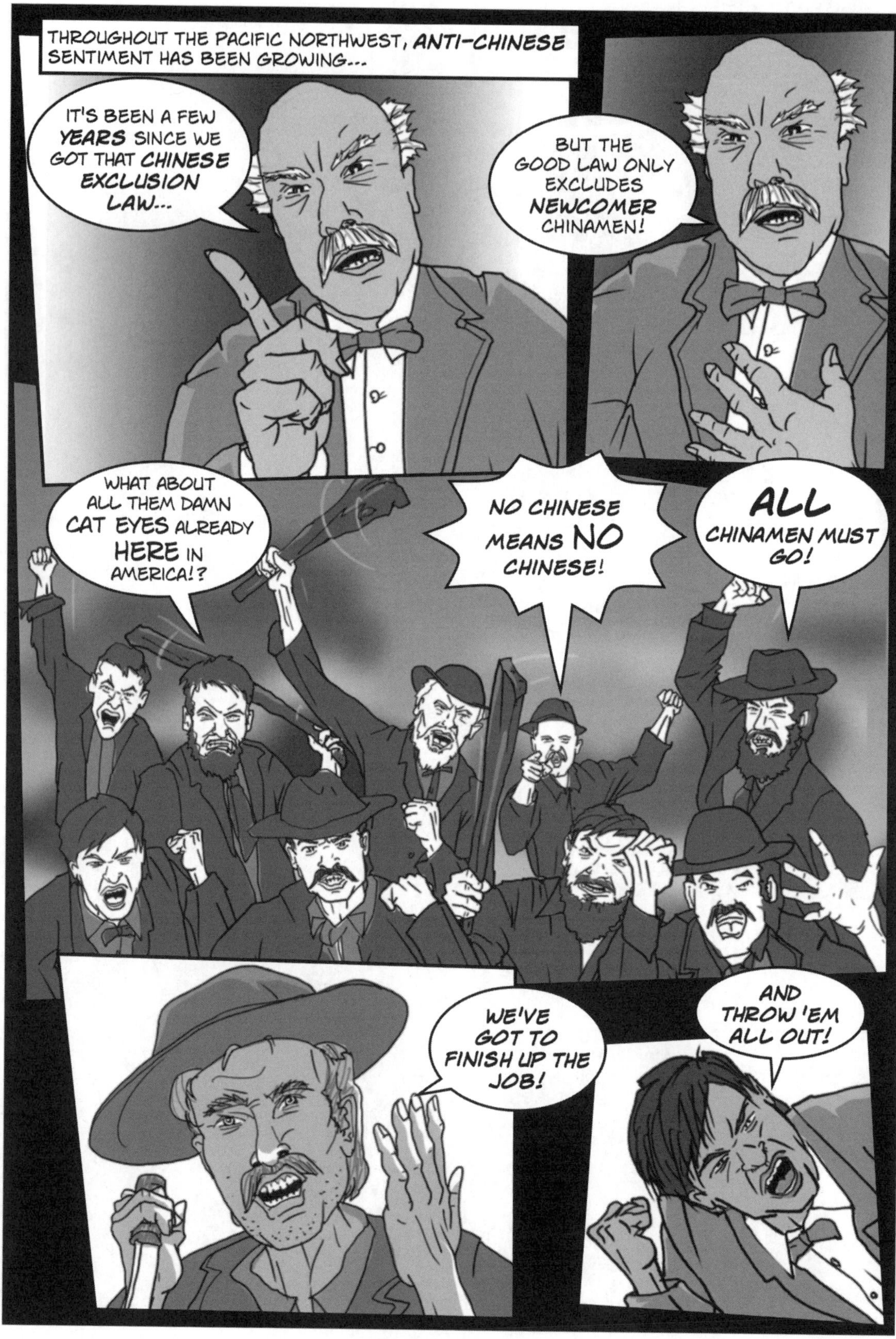
THROUGHOUT THE PACIFIC NORTHWEST, ANTI-CHINESE SENTIMENT HAS BEEN GROWING...
IT'S BEEN A FEW YEARS SINCE WE GOT THAT CHINESE EXCLUSION LAW...
BUT THE GOOD LAW ONLY EXCLUDES NEWCOMER CHINAMEN!
WHAT ABOUT ALL THEM DAMN CAT EYES ALREADY HERE IN AMERICA!?
NO CHINESE MEANS NO CHINESE!
ALL CHINAMEN MUST GO!
WE'VE GOT TO FINISH UP THE JOB!
AND THROW 'EM ALL OUT!

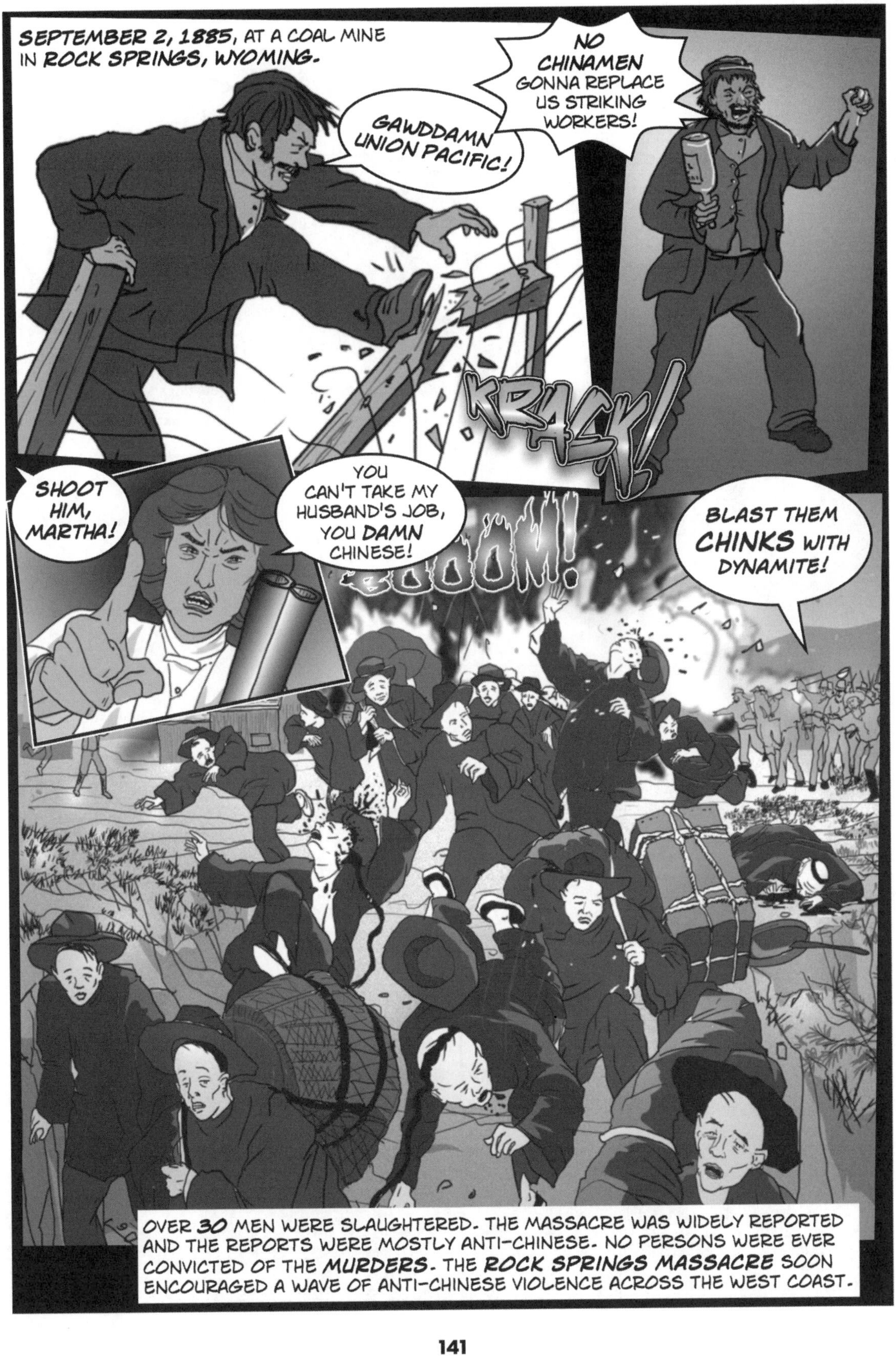
SEPTEMBER 2, 1885, AT A COAL MINE IN ROCK SPRINGS, WYOMING.
GAWDDAMN UNION PACIFIC!
NO CHINAMEN GONNA REPLACE US STRIKING WORKERS!
KRACK!
SHOOT HIM, MARTHA!
YOU CAN'T TAKE MY HUSBAND'S JOB, YOU DAMN CHINESE!
BLAST THEM CHINKS WITH DYNAMITE!
OVER 30 MEN WERE SLAUGHTERED. THE MASSACRE WAS WIDELY REPORTED AND THE REPORTS WERE MOSTLY ANTI-CHINESE. NO PERSONS WERE EVER CONVICTED OF THE MURDERS. THE ROCK SPRINGS MASSACRE SOON ENCOURAGED A WAVE OF ANTI-CHINESE VIOLENCE ACROSS THE WEST COAST.

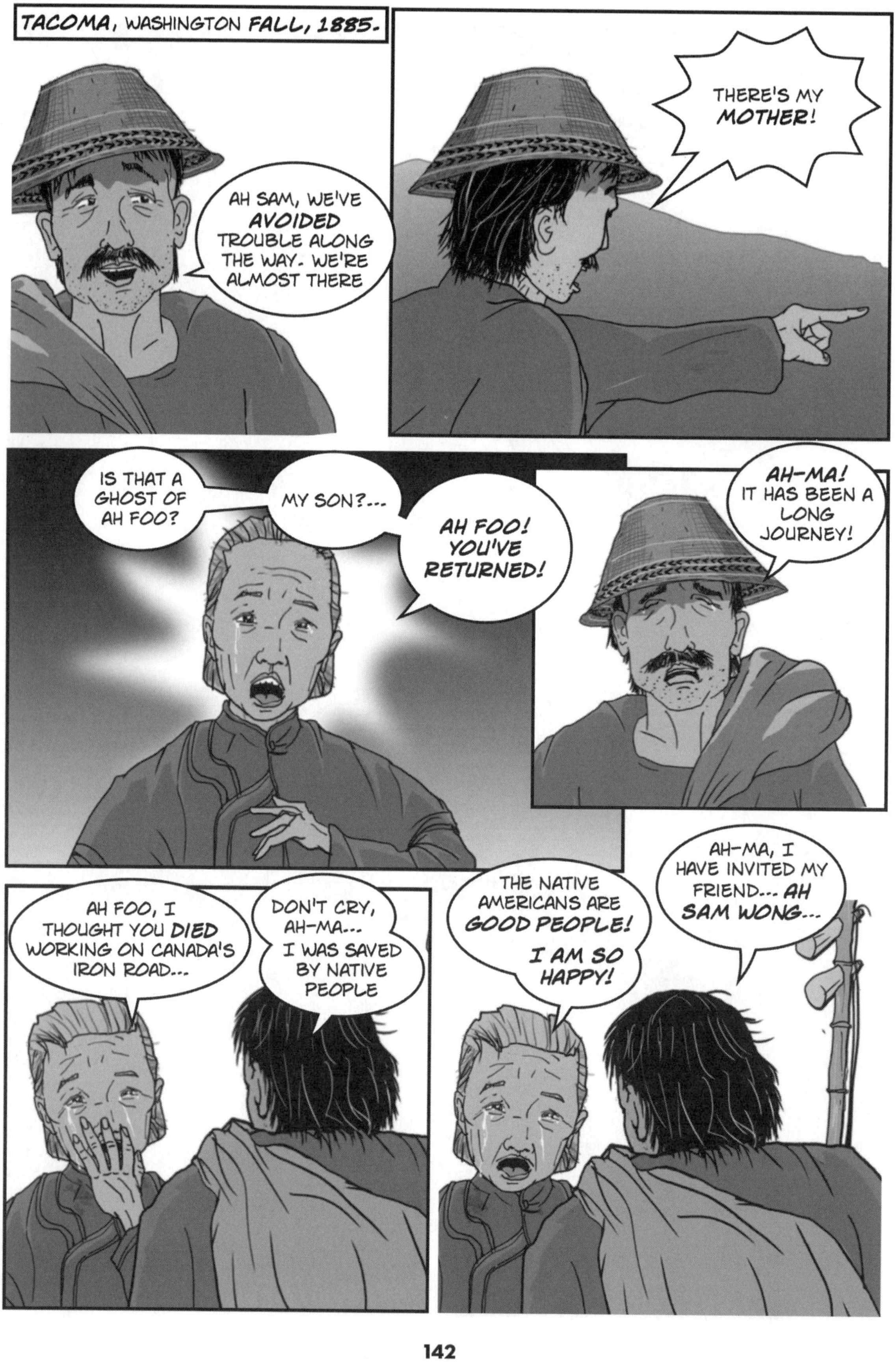
TACOMA, WASHINGTON FALL, 1885.
AH SAM, WE'VE AVOIDED TROUBLE ALONG THE WAY. WE'RE ALMOST THERE
THERE'S MY MOTHER!
IS THAT A GHOST OF AH FOO?
MY SON?...
AH FOO! YOU'VE RETURNED!
AH-MA! IT HAS BEEN A LONG JOURNEY!
AH FOO, I THOUGHT YOU DIED WORKING ON CANADA'S IRON ROAD...
DON'T CRY, AH-MA... I WAS SAVED BY NATIVE PEOPLE
THE NATIVE AMERICANS ARE GOOD PEOPLE!
I AM SO HAPPY!
AH-MA, I HAVE INVITED MY FRIEND... AH SAM WONG...

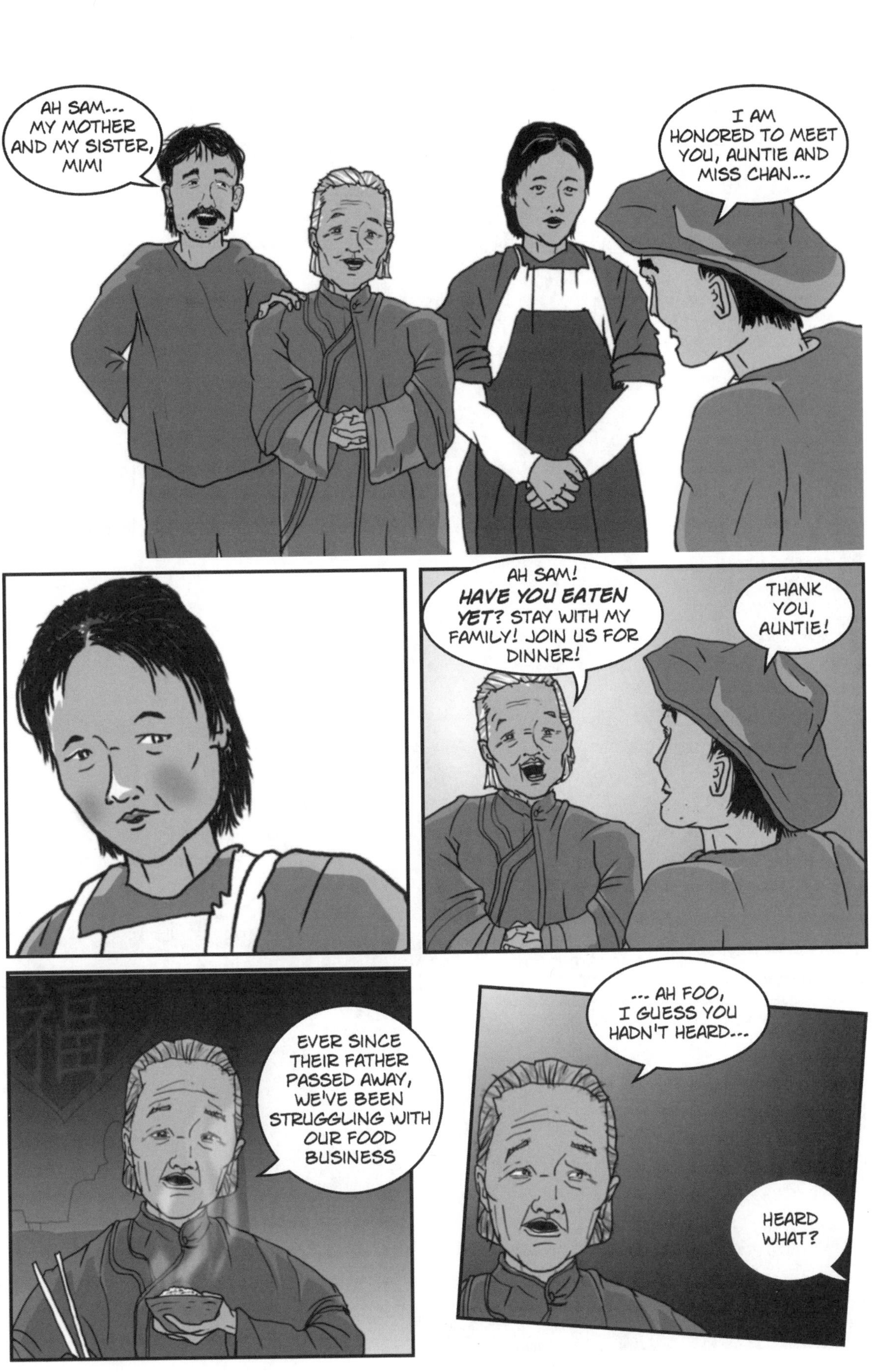
AH SAM... MY MOTHER AND MY SISTER, MIMI
I AM HONORED TO MEET YOU, AUNTIE AND MISS CHAN...
AH SAM! **HAVE YOU EATEN YET?** STAY WITH MY FAMILY! JOIN US FOR DINNER!
THANK YOU, AUNTIE!
EVER SINCE THEIR FATHER PASSED AWAY, WE'VE BEEN STRUGGLING WITH OUR FOOD BUSINESS
... AH FOO, I GUESS YOU HADN'T HEARD...
HEARD WHAT?

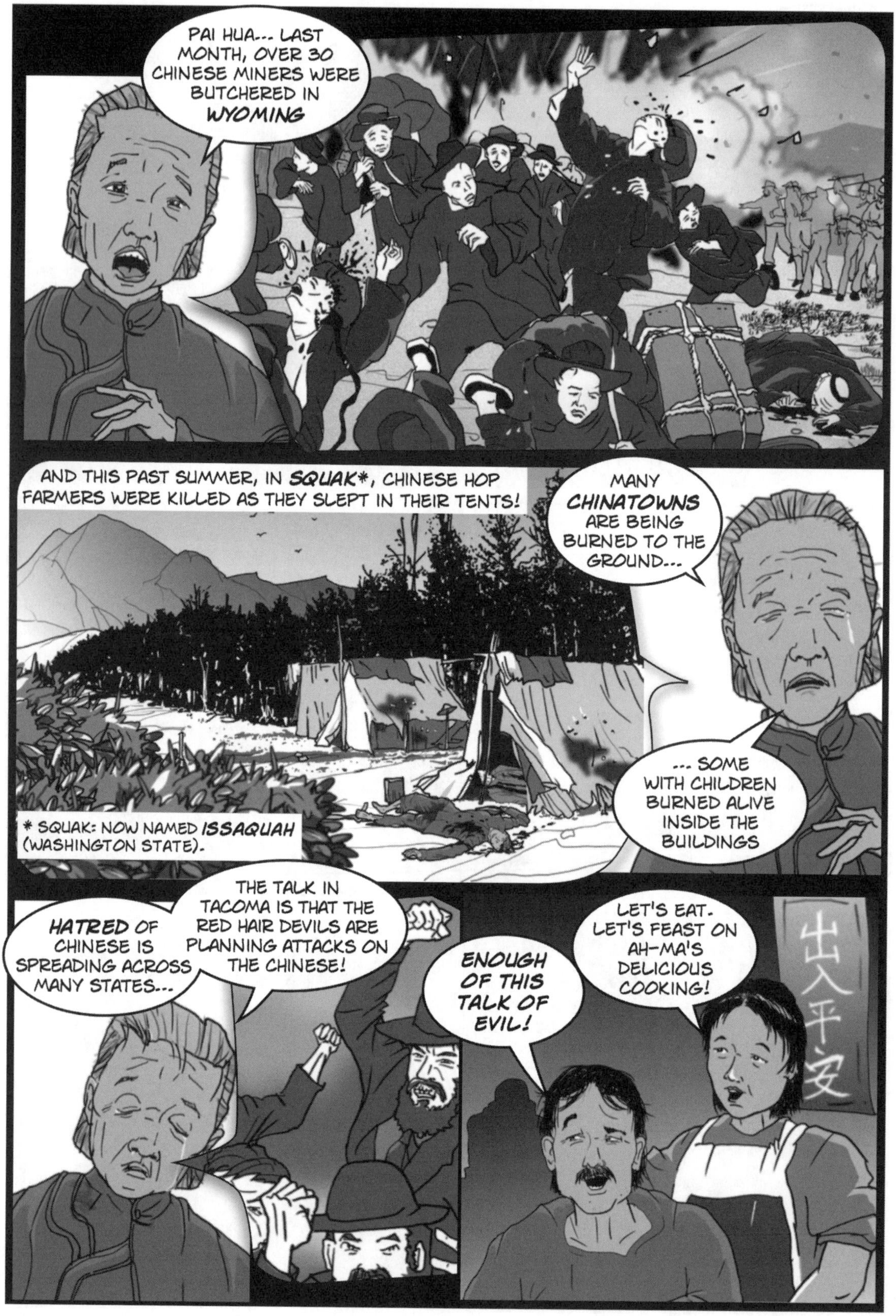
PAI HUA... LAST MONTH, OVER 30 CHINESE MINERS WERE BUTCHERED IN WYOMING
AND THIS PAST SUMMER, IN SQUAK*, CHINESE HOP FARMERS WERE KILLED AS THEY SLEPT IN THEIR TENTS!
MANY CHINATOWNS ARE BEING BURNED TO THE GROUND...
... SOME WITH CHILDREN BURNED ALIVE INSIDE THE BUILDINGS
* SQUAK: NOW NAMED ISSAQUAH (WASHINGTON STATE).
HATRED OF CHINESE IS SPREADING ACROSS MANY STATES...
THE TALK IN TACOMA IS THAT THE RED HAIR DEVILS ARE PLANNING ATTACKS ON THE CHINESE!
ENOUGH OF THIS TALK OF EVIL!
LET'S EAT. LET'S FEAST ON AH-MA'S DELICIOUS COOKING!
出入平安

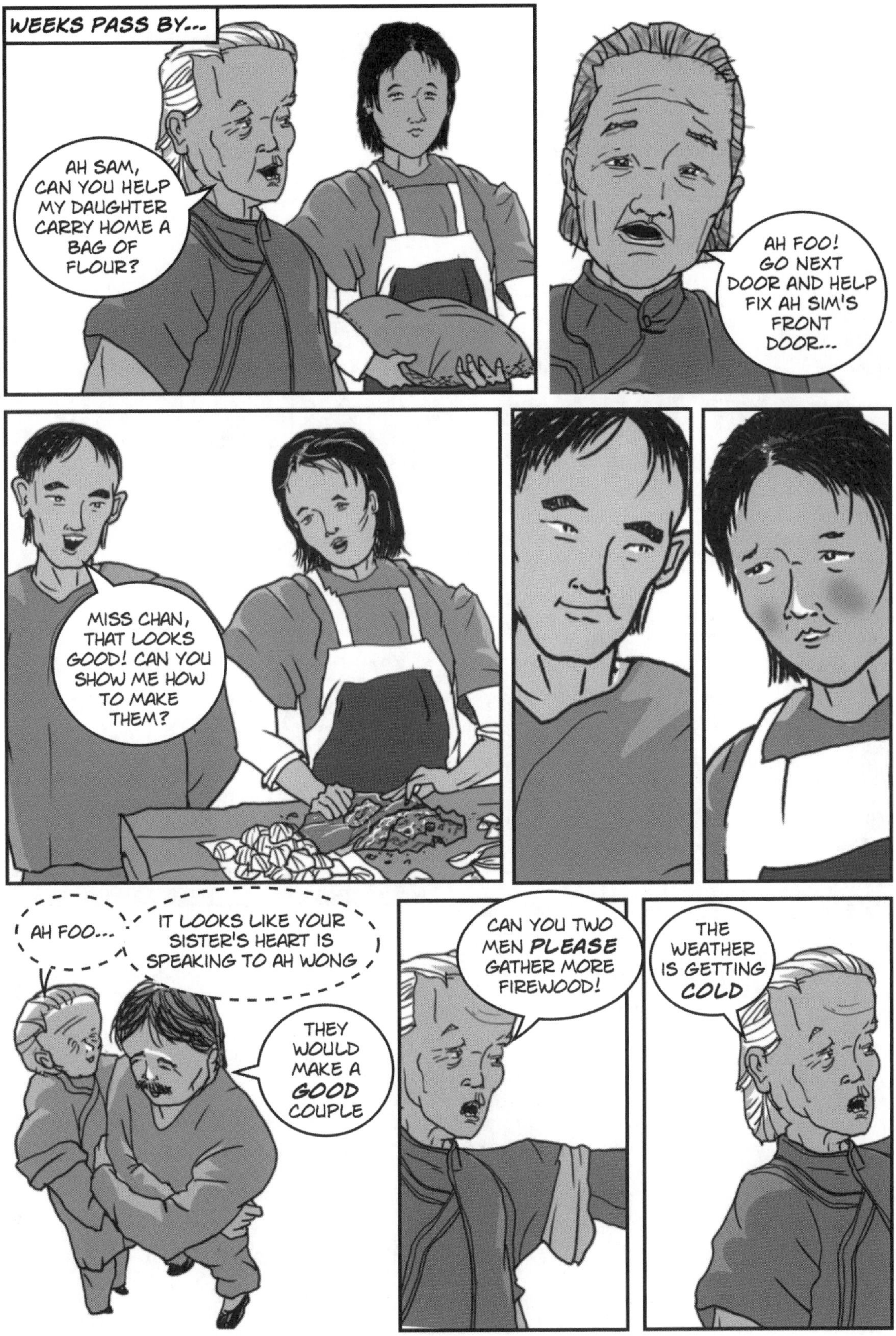
WEEKS PASS BY...
AH SAM, CAN YOU HELP MY DAUGHTER CARRY HOME A BAG OF FLOUR?
AH FOO! GO NEXT DOOR AND HELP FIX AH SIM'S FRONT DOOR...
MISS CHAN, THAT LOOKS GOOD! CAN YOU SHOW ME HOW TO MAKE THEM?
AH FOO...
IT LOOKS LIKE YOUR SISTER'S HEART IS SPEAKING TO AH WONG
THEY WOULD MAKE A GOOD COUPLE
CAN YOU TWO MEN PLEASE GATHER MORE FIREWOOD!
THE WEATHER IS GETTING COLD

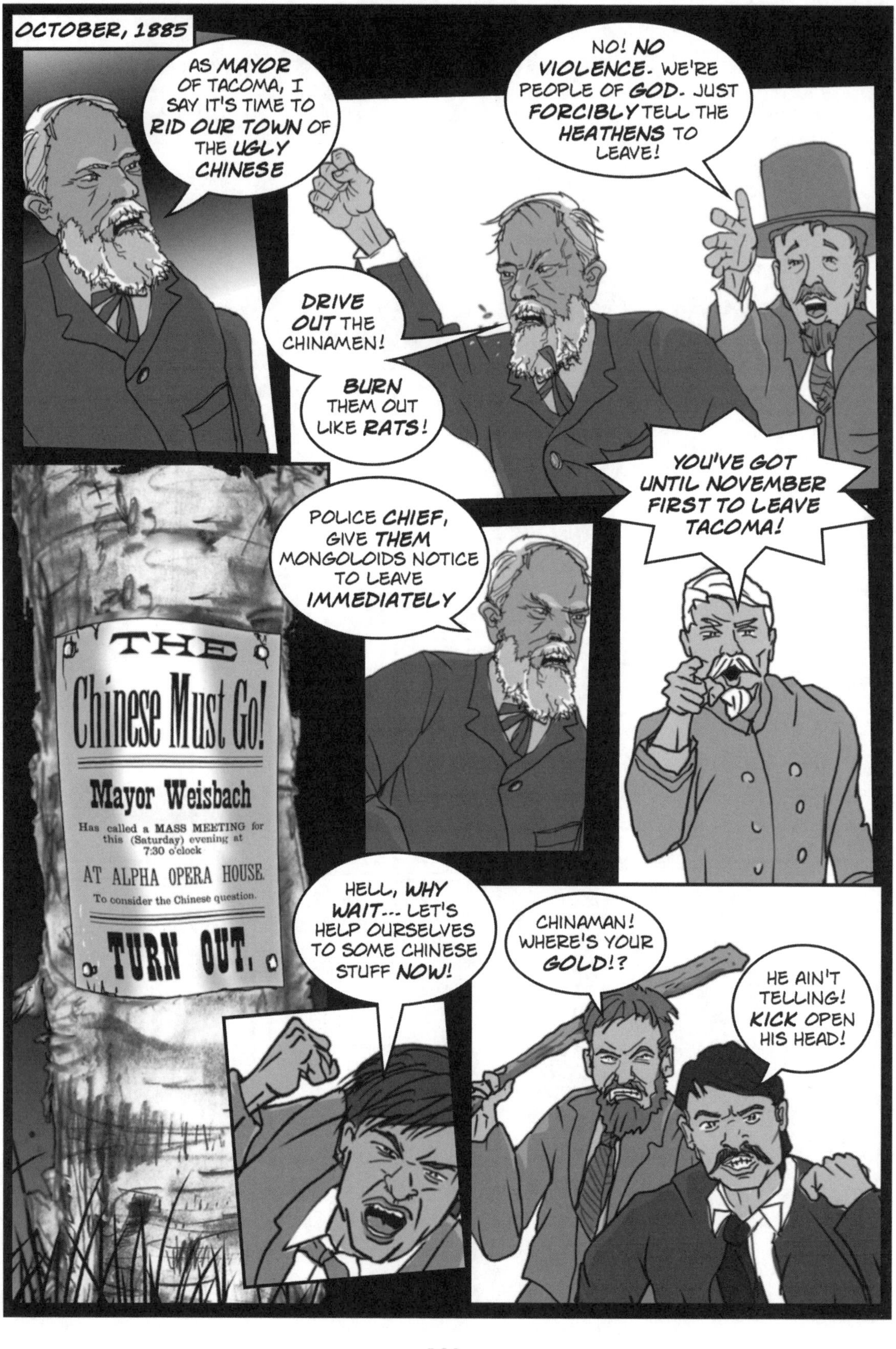
OCTOBER, 1885
AS MAYOR OF TACOMA, I SAY IT'S TIME TO RID OUR TOWN OF THE UGLY CHINESE
NO! NO VIOLENCE. WE'RE PEOPLE OF GOD. JUST FORCIBLY TELL THE HEATHENS TO LEAVE!
DRIVE OUT THE CHINAMEN!
BURN THEM OUT LIKE RATS!
POLICE CHIEF, GIVE THEM MONGOLOIDS NOTICE TO LEAVE IMMEDIATELY
YOU'VE GOT UNTIL NOVEMBER FIRST TO LEAVE TACOMA!
THE
Chinese Must Go!
Mayor Weisbach
Has called a MASS MEETING for this (Saturday) evening at 7:30 o'clock
AT ALPHA OPERA HOUSE.
To consider the Chinese question.
TURN OUT.
HELL, WHY WAIT... LET'S HELP OURSELVES TO SOME CHINESE STUFF NOW!
CHINAMAN! WHERE'S YOUR GOLD!?
HE AIN'T TELLING! KICK OPEN HIS HEAD!

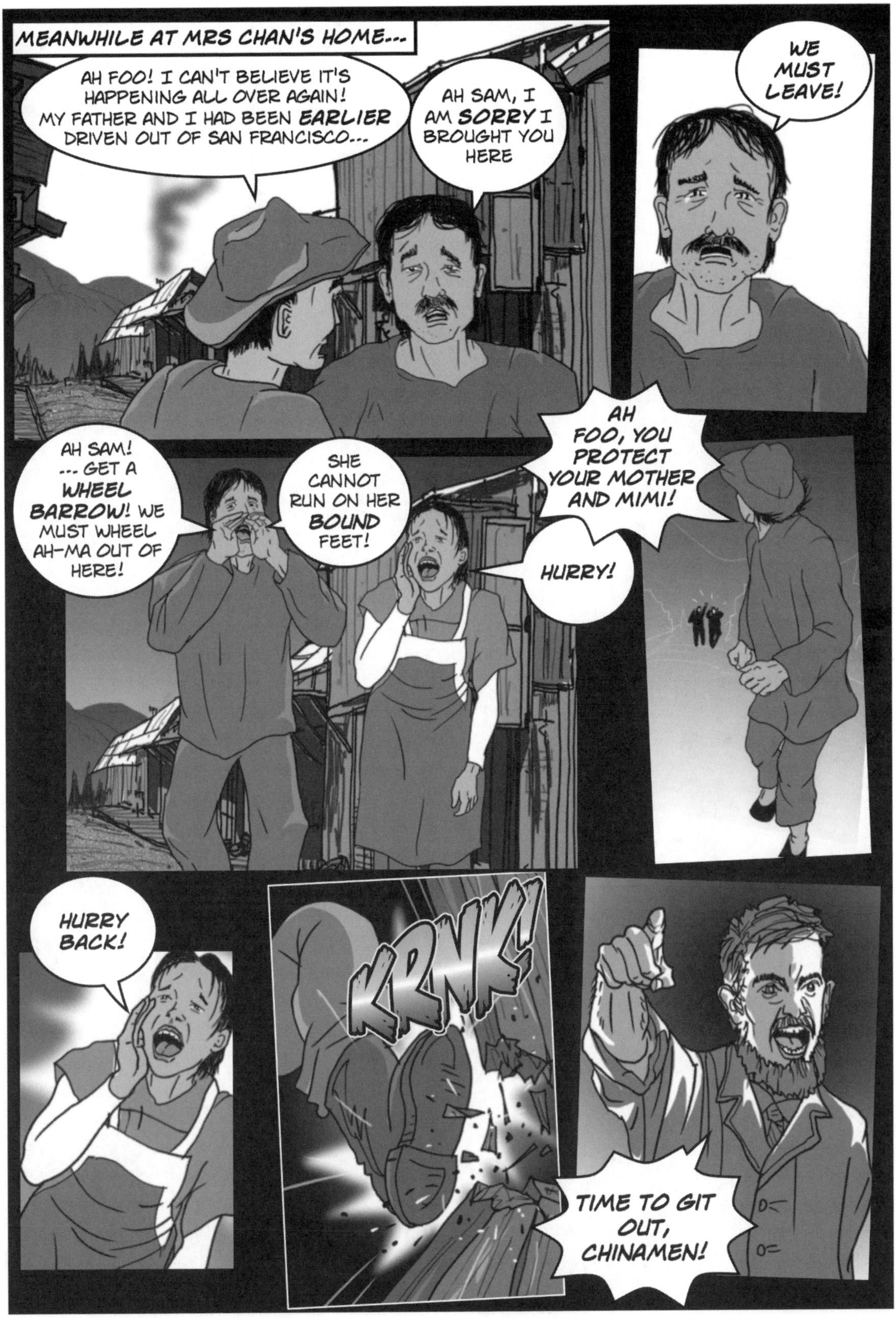
MEANWHILE AT MRS CHAN'S HOME...
AH FOO! I CAN'T BELIEVE IT'S HAPPENING ALL OVER AGAIN! MY FATHER AND I HAD BEEN EARLIER DRIVEN OUT OF SAN FRANCISCO...
AH SAM, I AM SORRY I BROUGHT YOU HERE
WE MUST LEAVE!
AH SAM! ... GET A WHEEL BARROW! WE MUST WHEEL AH-MA OUT OF HERE!
SHE CANNOT RUN ON HER BOUND FEET!
AH FOO, YOU PROTECT YOUR MOTHER AND MIMI!
HURRY!
HURRY BACK!
KRNK!
TIME TO GIT OUT, CHINAMEN!

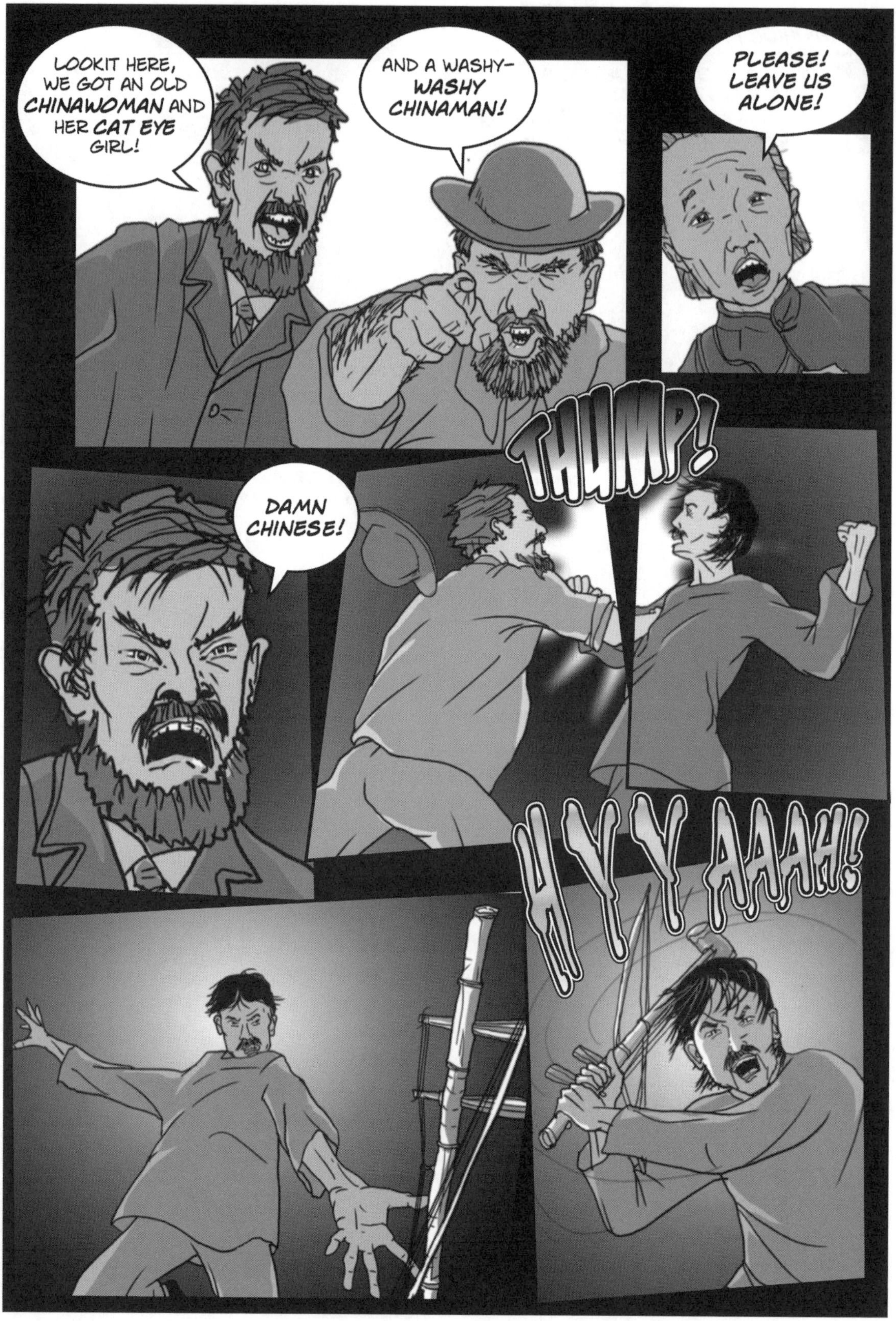
LOOKIT HERE, WE GOT AN OLD CHINAWOMAN AND HER CAT EYE GIRL!
AND A WASHY-WASHY CHINAMAN!
PLEASE! LEAVE US ALONE!
THUMP!
DAMN CHINESE!
HYYAAAH!

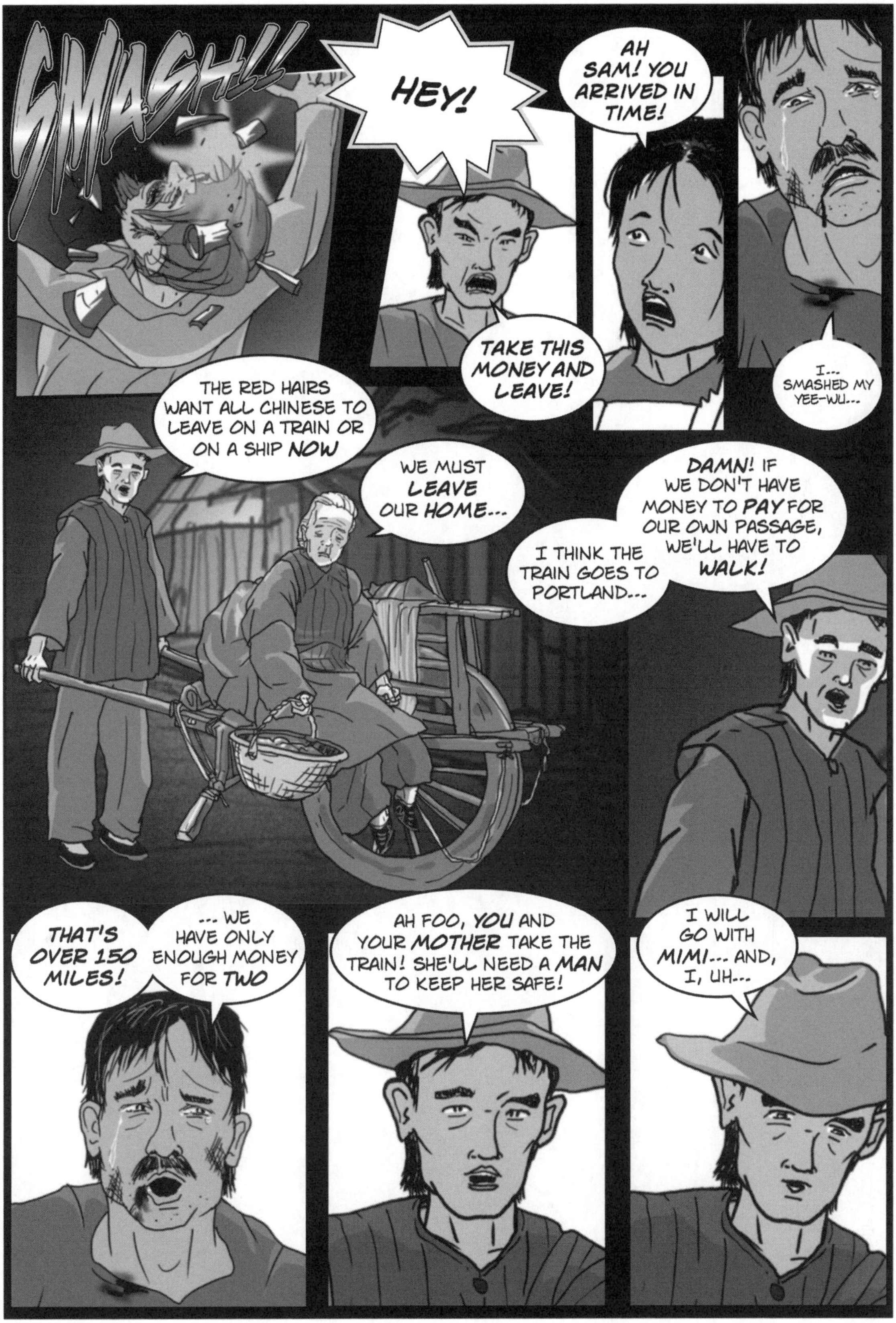
SMASH!!
HEY!
AH SAM! YOU ARRIVED IN TIME!
TAKE THIS MONEY AND LEAVE!
I... SMASHED MY YEE-WU...
THE RED HAIRS WANT ALL CHINESE TO LEAVE ON A TRAIN OR ON A SHIP NOW
WE MUST LEAVE OUR HOME...
I THINK THE TRAIN GOES TO PORTLAND...
DAMN! IF WE DON'T HAVE MONEY TO PAY FOR OUR OWN PASSAGE, WE'LL HAVE TO WALK!
THAT'S OVER 150 MILES!
... WE HAVE ONLY ENOUGH MONEY FOR TWO
AH FOO, YOU AND YOUR MOTHER TAKE THE TRAIN! SHE'LL NEED A MAN TO KEEP HER SAFE!
I WILL GO WITH MIMI... AND, I, UH...

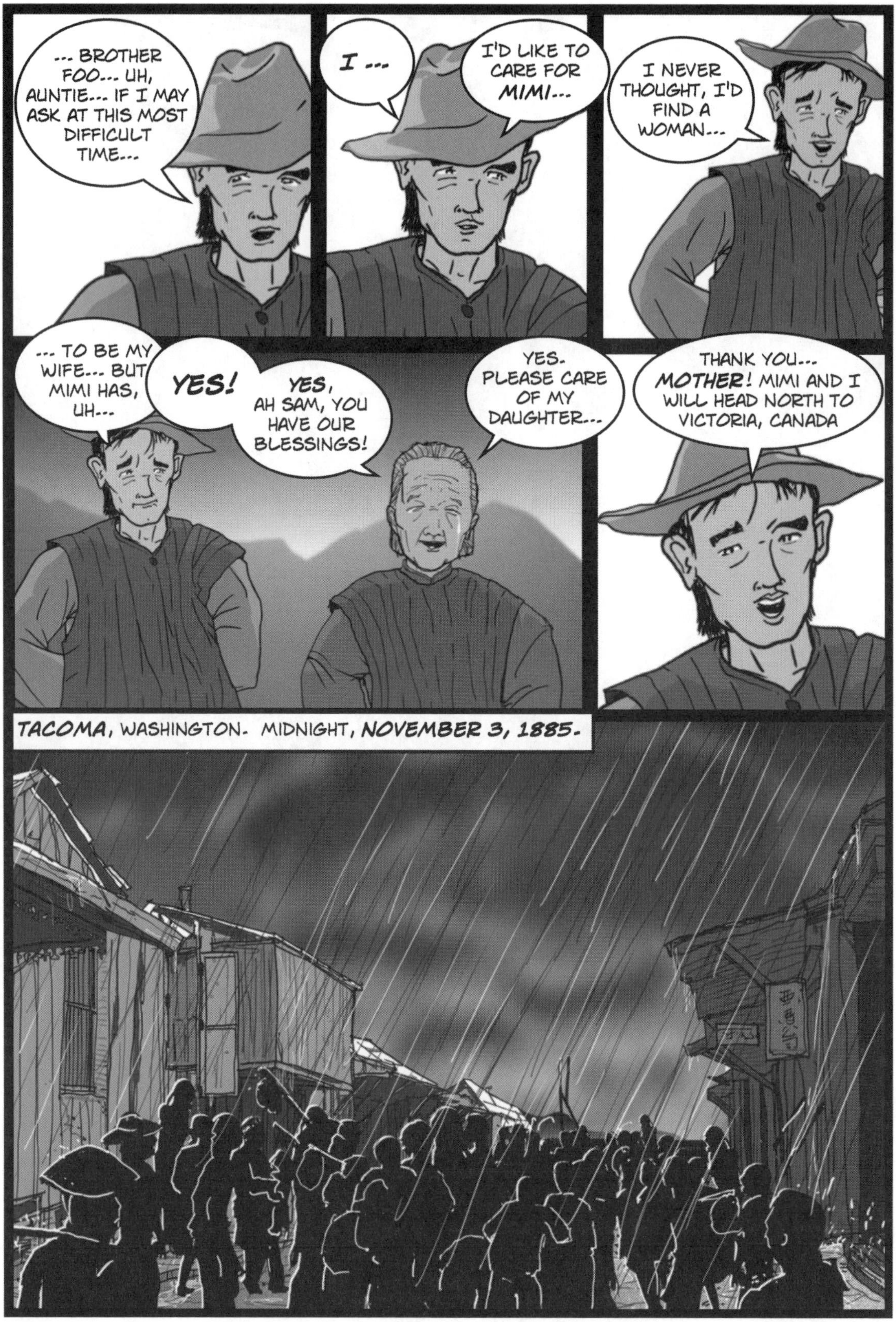
... BROTHER FOO... UH, AUNTIE... IF I MAY ASK AT THIS MOST DIFFICULT TIME...
I ...
I'D LIKE TO CARE FOR MIMI...
I NEVER THOUGHT, I'D FIND A WOMAN...
... TO BE MY WIFE... BUT MIMI HAS, UH...
YES!
YES, AH SAM, YOU HAVE OUR BLESSINGS!
YES. PLEASE CARE OF MY DAUGHTER...
THANK YOU... MOTHER! MIMI AND I WILL HEAD NORTH TO VICTORIA, CANADA
TACOMA, WASHINGTON. MIDNIGHT, NOVEMBER 3, 1885.

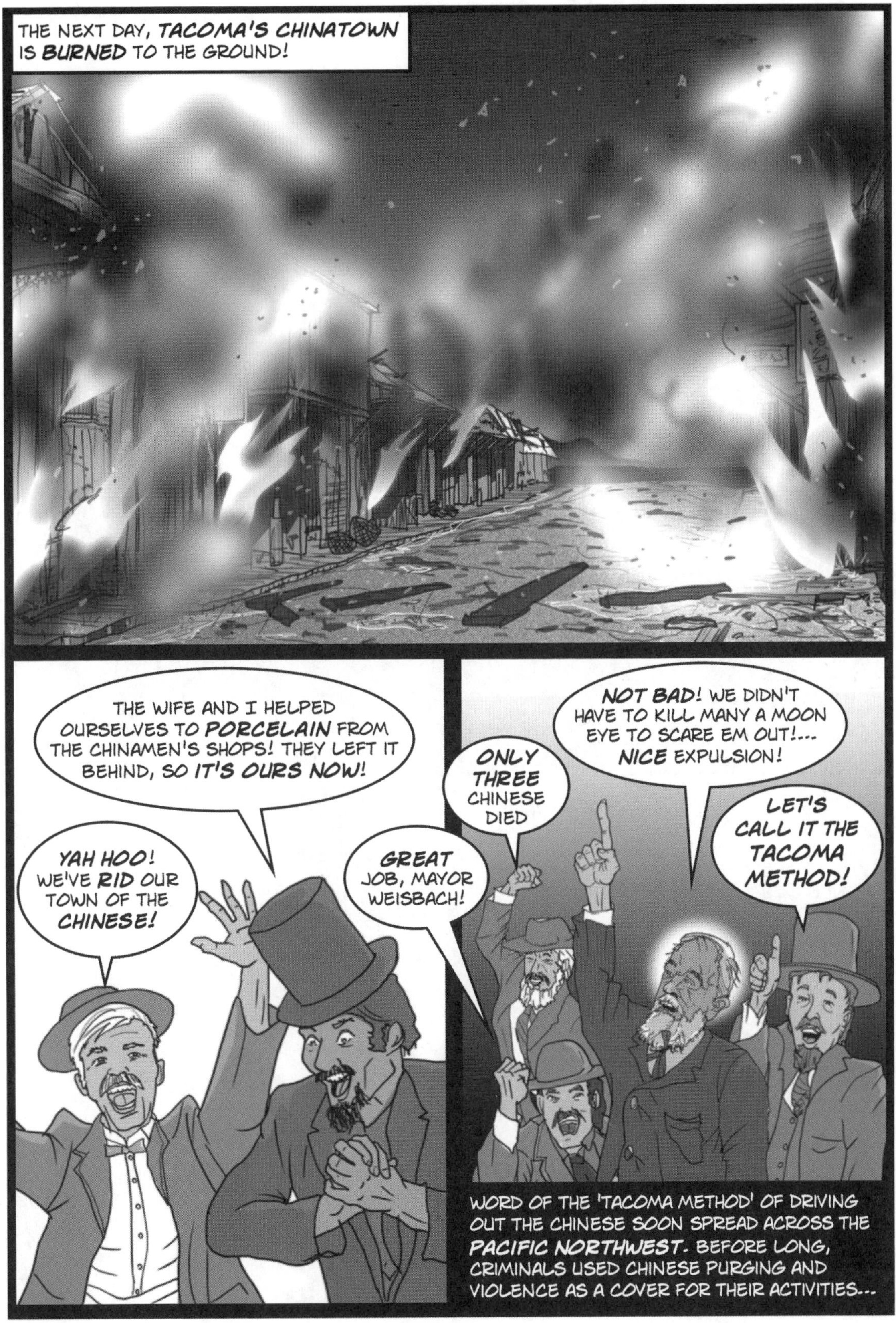
THE NEXT DAY, TACOMA'S CHINATOWN IS BURNED TO THE GROUND!
THE WIFE AND I HELPED OURSELVES TO PORCELAIN FROM THE CHINAMEN'S SHOPS! THEY LEFT IT BEHIND, SO IT'S OURS NOW!
YAH HOO! WE'VE RID OUR TOWN OF THE CHINESE!
GREAT JOB, MAYOR WEISBACH!
NOT BAD! WE DIDN'T HAVE TO KILL MANY A MOON EYE TO SCARE EM OUT!... NICE EXPULSION!
ONLY THREE CHINESE DIED
LET'S CALL IT THE TACOMA METHOD!
WORD OF THE 'TACOMA METHOD' OF DRIVING OUT THE CHINESE SOON SPREAD ACROSS THE PACIFIC NORTHWEST. BEFORE LONG, CRIMINALS USED CHINESE PURGING AND VIOLENCE AS A COVER FOR THEIR ACTIVITIES...

CHAPTER 13 Cooks & Revolutionaries

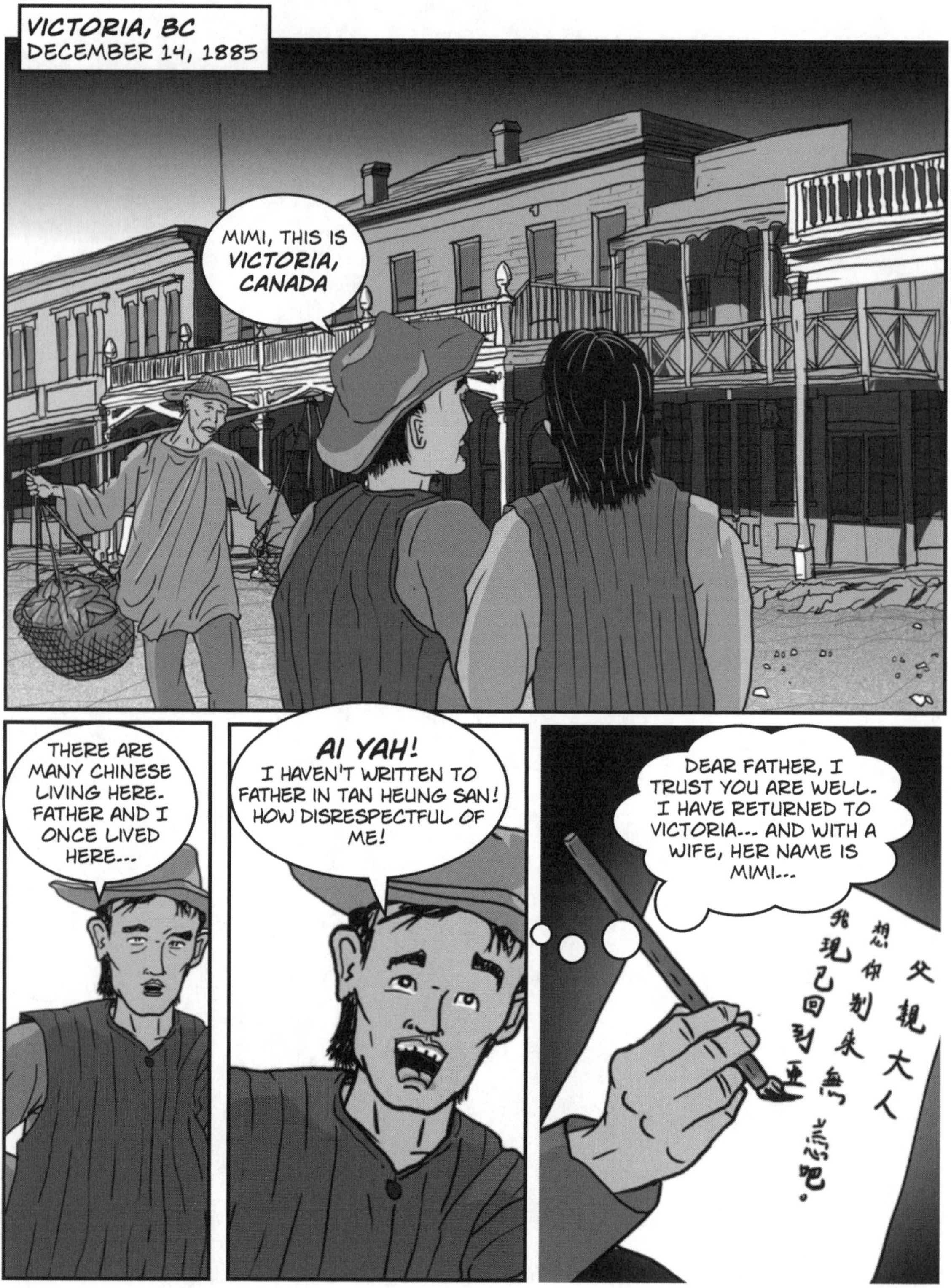

VICTORIA, BC
DECEMBER 14, 1885
MIMI, THIS IS VICTORIA, CANADA
THERE ARE MANY CHINESE LIVING HERE. FATHER AND I ONCE LIVED HERE...
AI YAH! I HAVEN'T WRITTEN TO FATHER IN TAN HEUNG SAN! HOW DISRESPECTFUL OF ME!
DEAR FATHER, I TRUST YOU ARE WELL. I HAVE RETURNED TO VICTORIA... AND WITH A WIFE, HER NAME IS MIMI...
父親大人

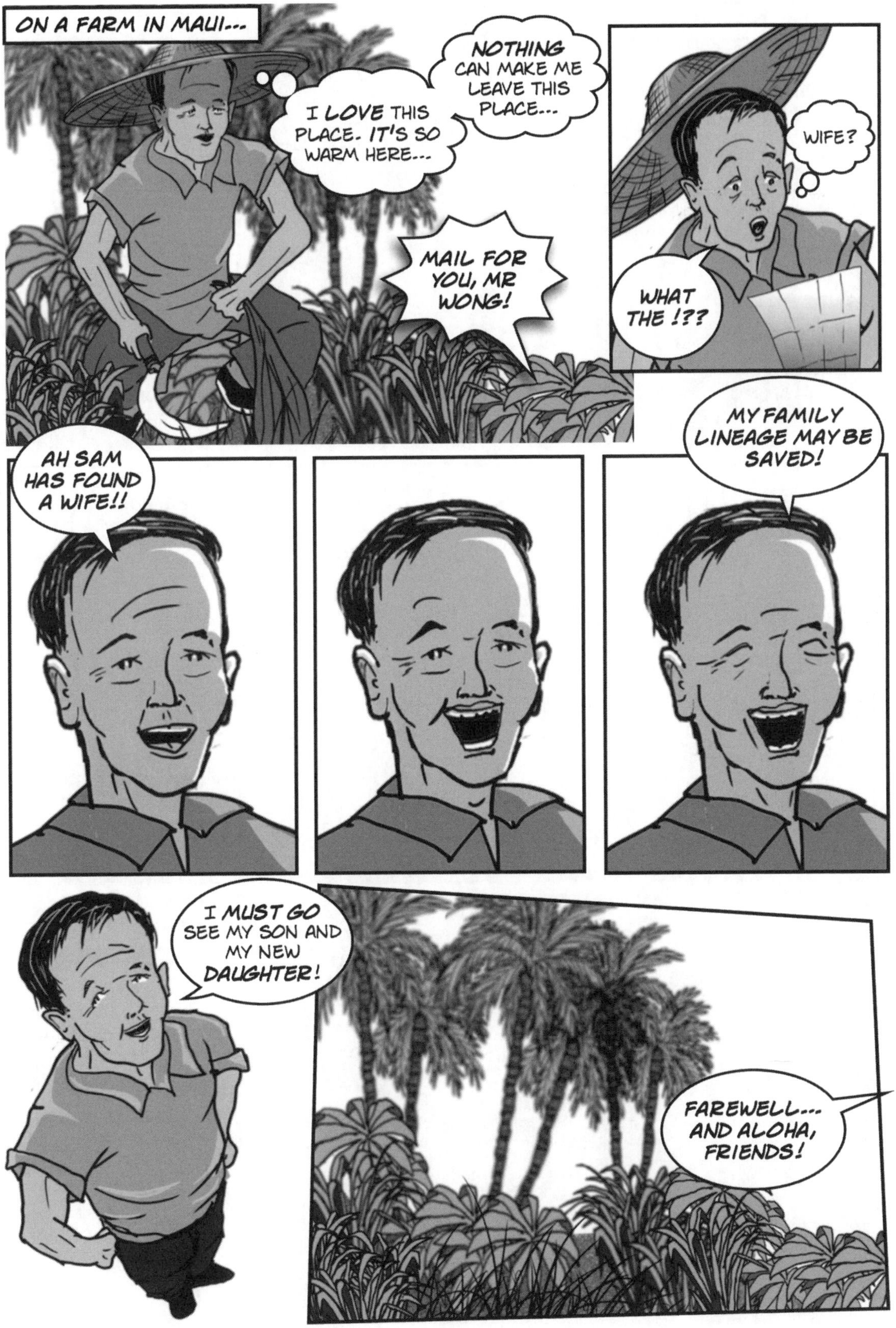
ON A FARM IN MAUI...
I LOVE THIS PLACE. IT'S SO WARM HERE...
NOTHING CAN MAKE ME LEAVE THIS PLACE...
MAIL FOR YOU, MR WONG!
WIFE?
WHAT THE !??
AH SAM HAS FOUND A WIFE!!
MY FAMILY LINEAGE MAY BE SAVED!
I MUST GO SEE MY SON AND MY NEW DAUGHTER!
FAREWELL... AND ALOHA, FRIENDS!

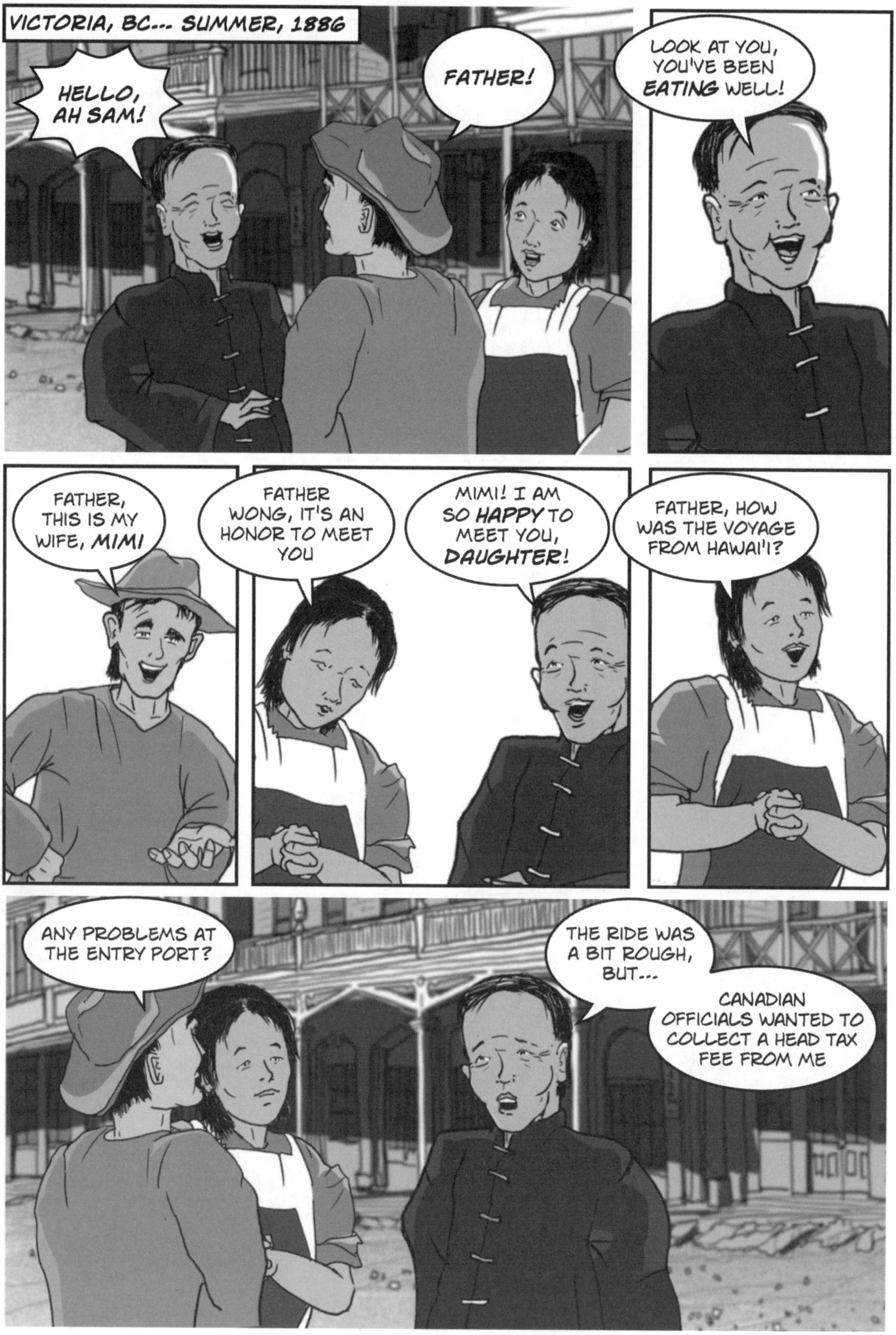
VICTORIA, BC... SUMMER, 1886
HELLO, AH SAM!
FATHER!
LOOK AT YOU, YOU'VE BEEN EATING WELL!
FATHER, THIS IS MY WIFE, MIMI
FATHER WONG, IT'S AN HONOR TO MEET YOU
MIMI! I AM SO HAPPY TO MEET YOU, DAUGHTER!
FATHER, HOW WAS THE VOYAGE FROM HAWAI'I?
ANY PROBLEMS AT THE ENTRY PORT?
THE RIDE WAS A BIT ROUGH, BUT...
CANADIAN OFFICIALS WANTED TO COLLECT A HEAD TAX FEE FROM ME

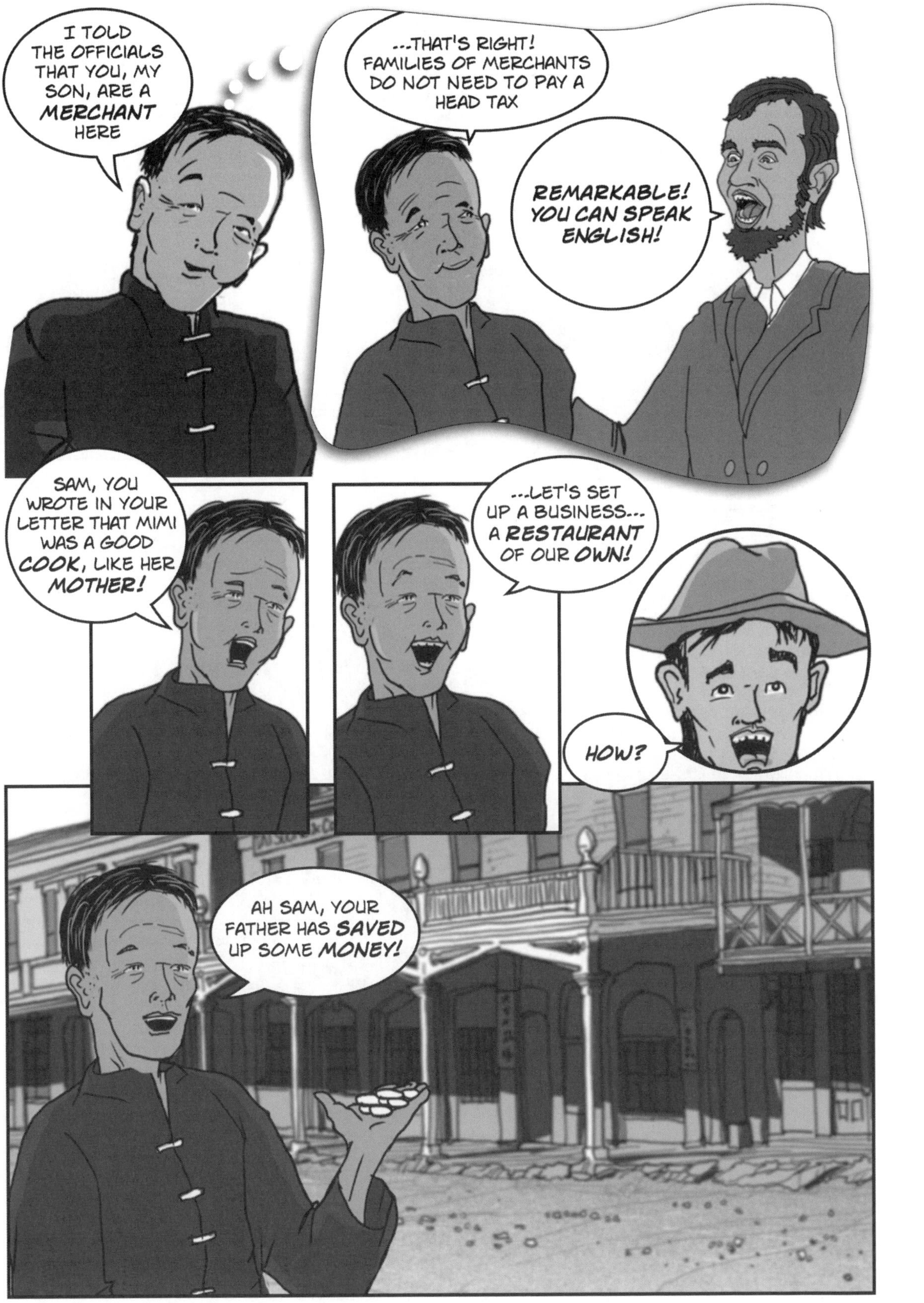
I TOLD THE OFFICIALS THAT YOU, MY SON, ARE A MERCHANT HERE
...THAT'S RIGHT! FAMILIES OF MERCHANTS DO NOT NEED TO PAY A HEAD TAX
REMARKABLE! YOU CAN SPEAK ENGLISH!
SAM, YOU WROTE IN YOUR LETTER THAT MIMI WAS A GOOD COOK, LIKE HER MOTHER!
...LET'S SET UP A BUSINESS... A RESTAURANT OF OUR OWN!
HOW?
AH SAM, YOUR FATHER HAS SAVED UP SOME MONEY!

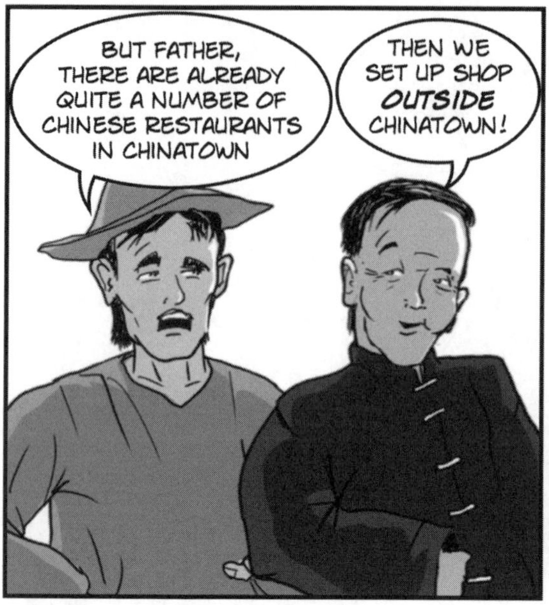
BUT FATHER, THERE ARE ALREADY QUITE A NUMBER OF CHINESE RESTAURANTS IN CHINATOWN
THEN WE SET UP SHOP OUTSIDE CHINATOWN!

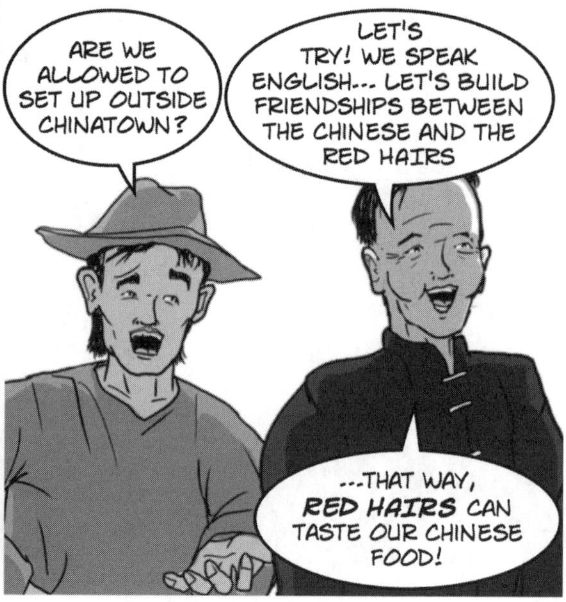
ARE WE ALLOWED TO SET UP OUTSIDE CHINATOWN?
LET'S TRY! WE SPEAK ENGLISH... LET'S BUILD FRIENDSHIPS BETWEEN THE CHINESE AND THE RED HAIRS
...THAT WAY, RED HAIRS CAN TASTE OUR CHINESE FOOD!

SEVERAL MONTHS LATER...

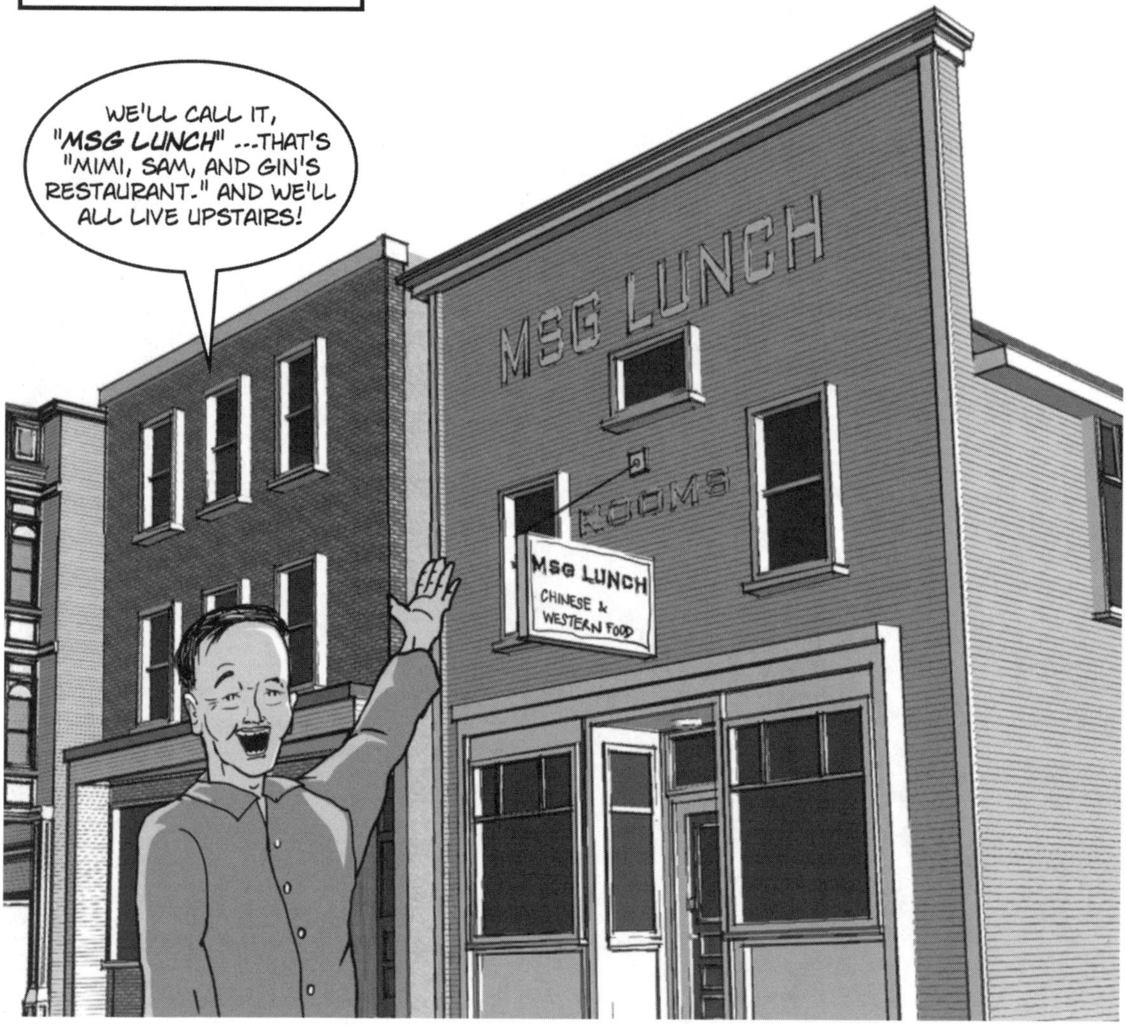
WE'LL CALL IT, "MSG LUNCH" ...THAT'S "MIMI, SAM, AND GIN'S RESTAURANT." AND WE'LL ALL LIVE UPSTAIRS!
MSG LUNCH
ROOMS
MSG LUNCH
CHINESE & WESTERN FOOD

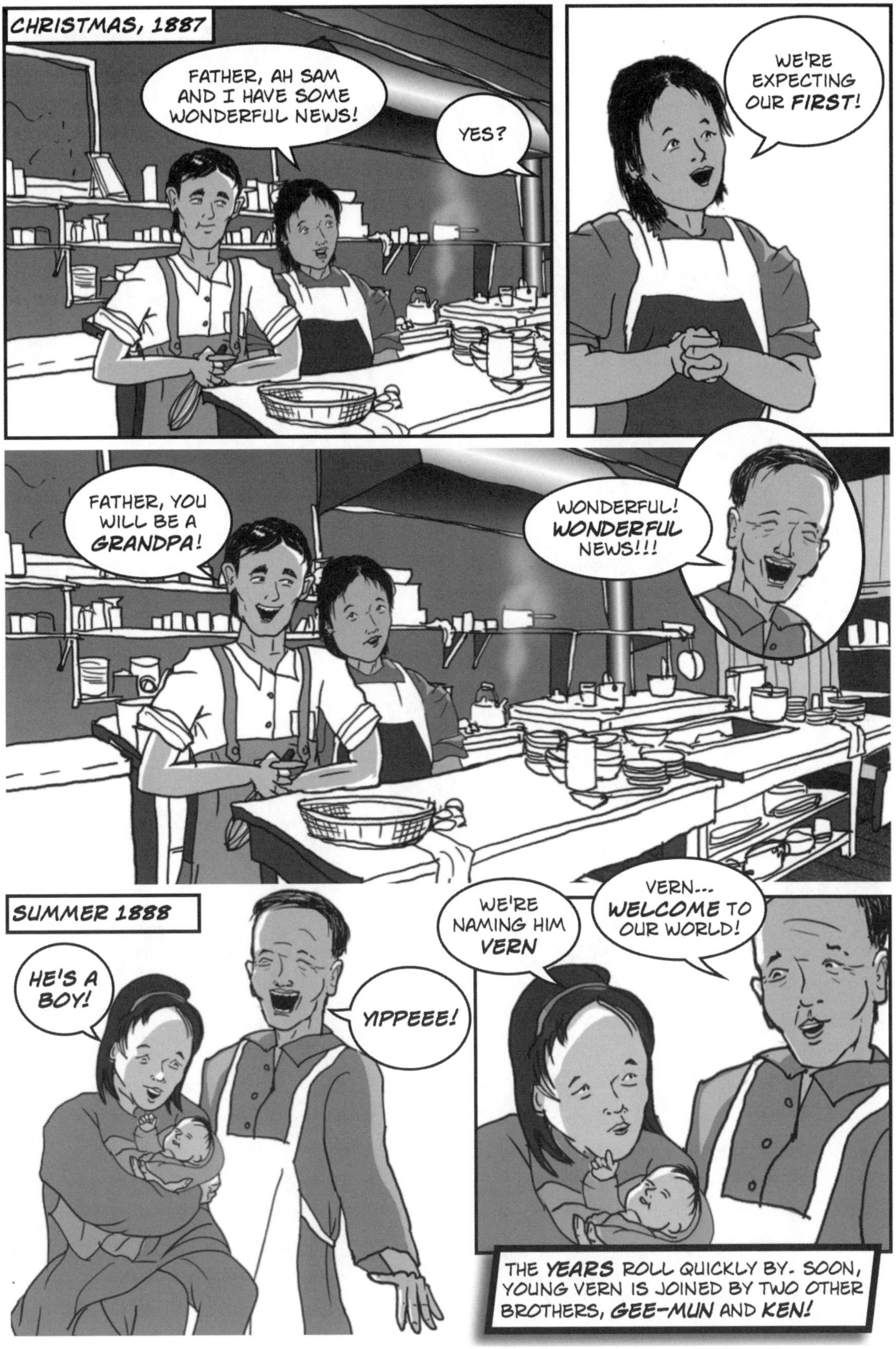
CHRISTMAS, 1887
FATHER, AH SAM AND I HAVE SOME WONDERFUL NEWS!
YES?
WE'RE EXPECTING OUR FIRST!
FATHER, YOU WILL BE A GRANDPA!
WONDERFUL! WONDERFUL NEWS!!!
SUMMER 1888
HE'S A BOY!
YIPPEEE!
WE'RE NAMING HIM VERN
VERN... WELCOME TO OUR WORLD!
THE YEARS ROLL QUICKLY BY. SOON, YOUNG VERN IS JOINED BY TWO OTHER BROTHERS, GEE-MUN AND KEN!

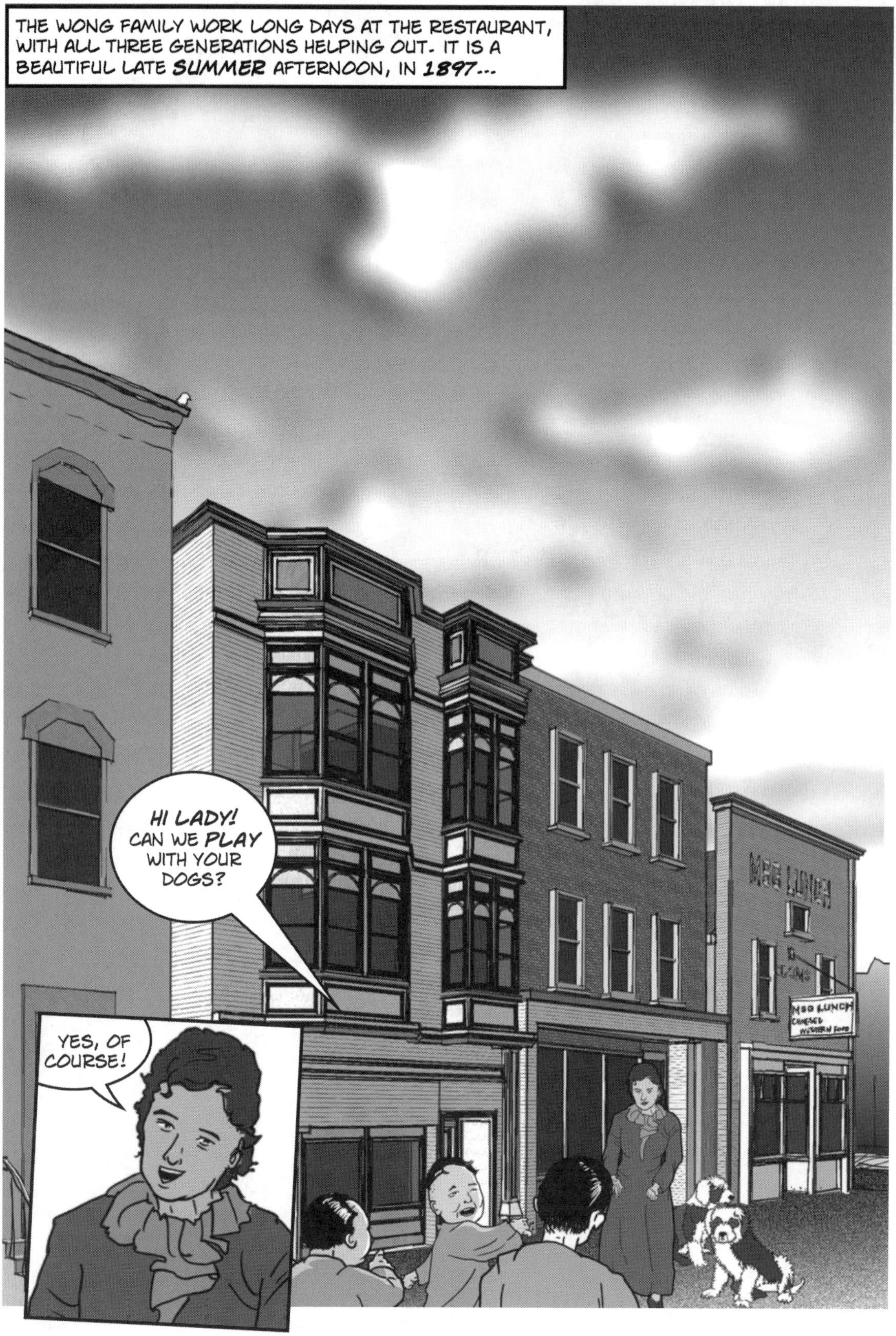
THE WONG FAMILY WORK LONG DAYS AT THE RESTAURANT, WITH ALL THREE GENERATIONS HELPING OUT. IT IS A BEAUTIFUL LATE SUMMER AFTERNOON, IN 1897...
HI LADY! CAN WE PLAY WITH YOUR DOGS?
YES, OF COURSE!

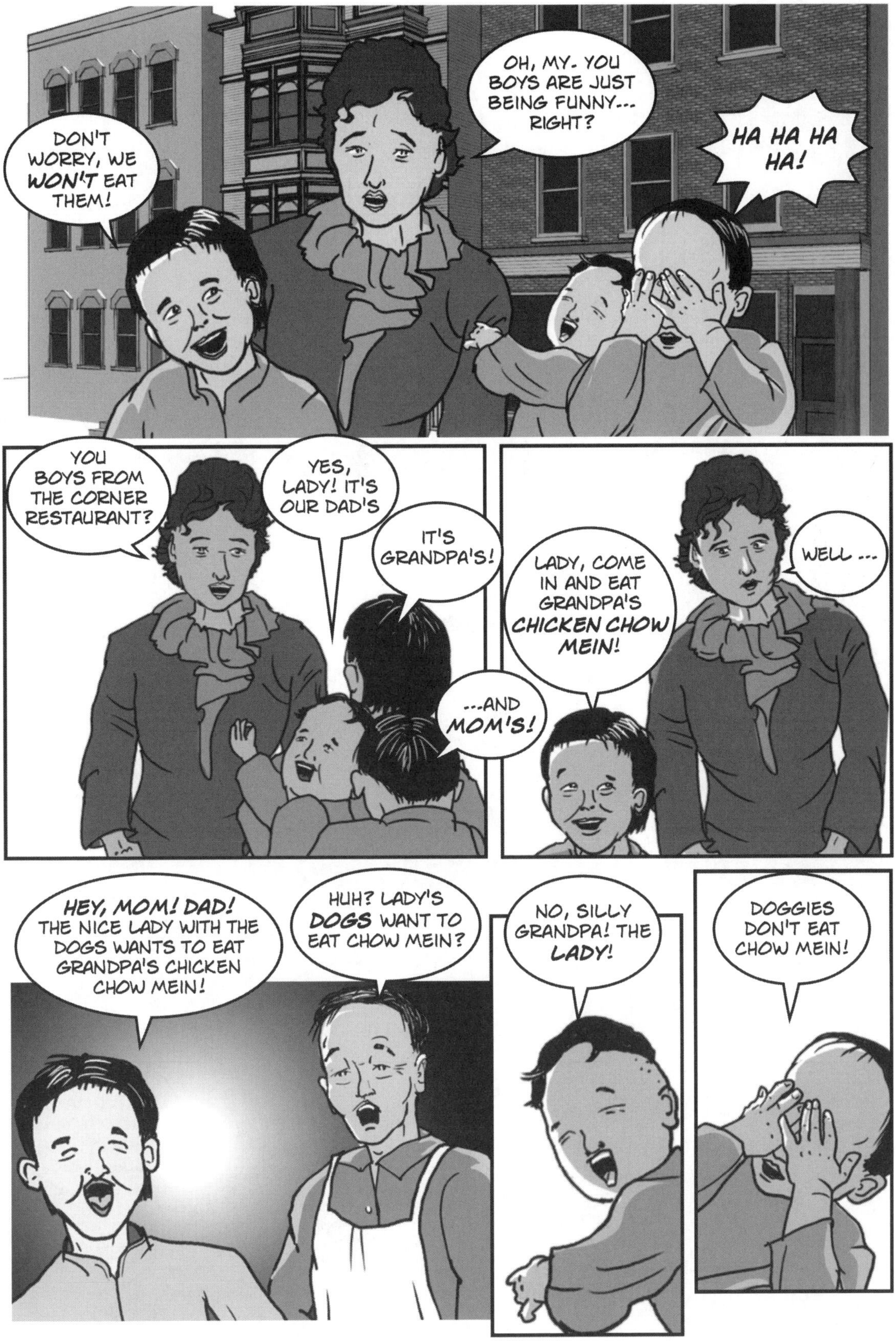

DON'T WORRY, WE WON'T EAT THEM!
OH, MY- YOU BOYS ARE JUST BEING FUNNY... RIGHT?
HA HA HA HA!
YOU BOYS FROM THE CORNER RESTAURANT?
YES, LADY! IT'S OUR DAD'S
IT'S GRANDPA'S!
...AND MOM'S!
LADY, COME IN AND EAT GRANDPA'S CHICKEN CHOW MEIN!
WELL ...
HEY, MOM! DAD! THE NICE LADY WITH THE DOGS WANTS TO EAT GRANDPA'S CHICKEN CHOW MEIN!
HUH? LADY'S DOGS WANT TO EAT CHOW MEIN?
NO, SILLY GRANDPA! THE LADY!
DOGGIES DON'T EAT CHOW MEIN!

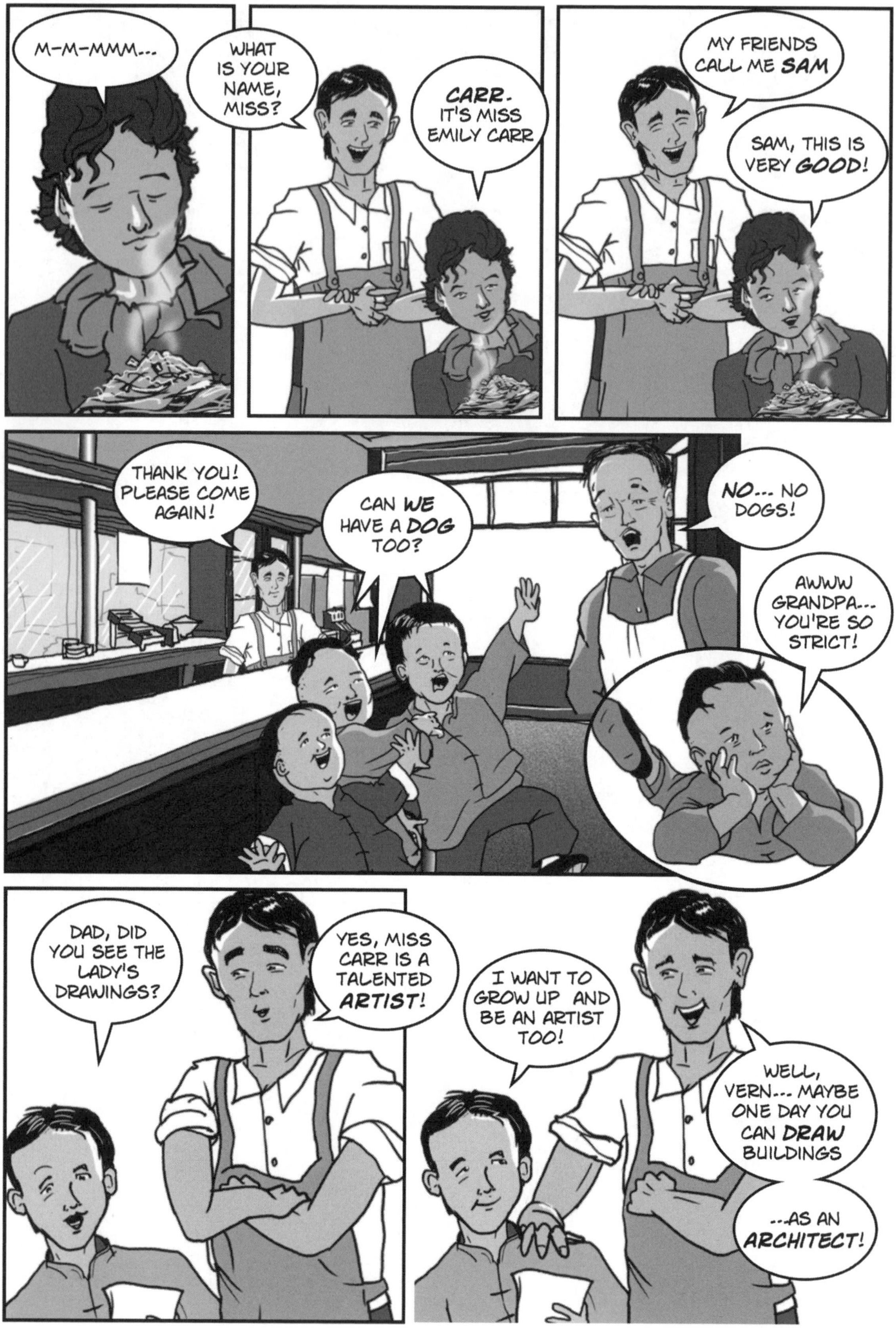

M-M-MMM...
WHAT IS YOUR NAME, MISS?
CARR. IT'S MISS EMILY CARR
MY FRIENDS CALL ME SAM
SAM, THIS IS VERY GOOD!
THANK YOU! PLEASE COME AGAIN!
CAN WE HAVE A DOG TOO?
NO... NO DOGS!
AWWW GRANDPA... YOU'RE SO STRICT!
DAD, DID YOU SEE THE LADY'S DRAWINGS?
YES, MISS CARR IS A TALENTED ARTIST!
I WANT TO GROW UP AND BE AN ARTIST TOO!
WELL, VERN... MAYBE ONE DAY YOU CAN DRAW BUILDINGS
...AS AN ARCHITECT!

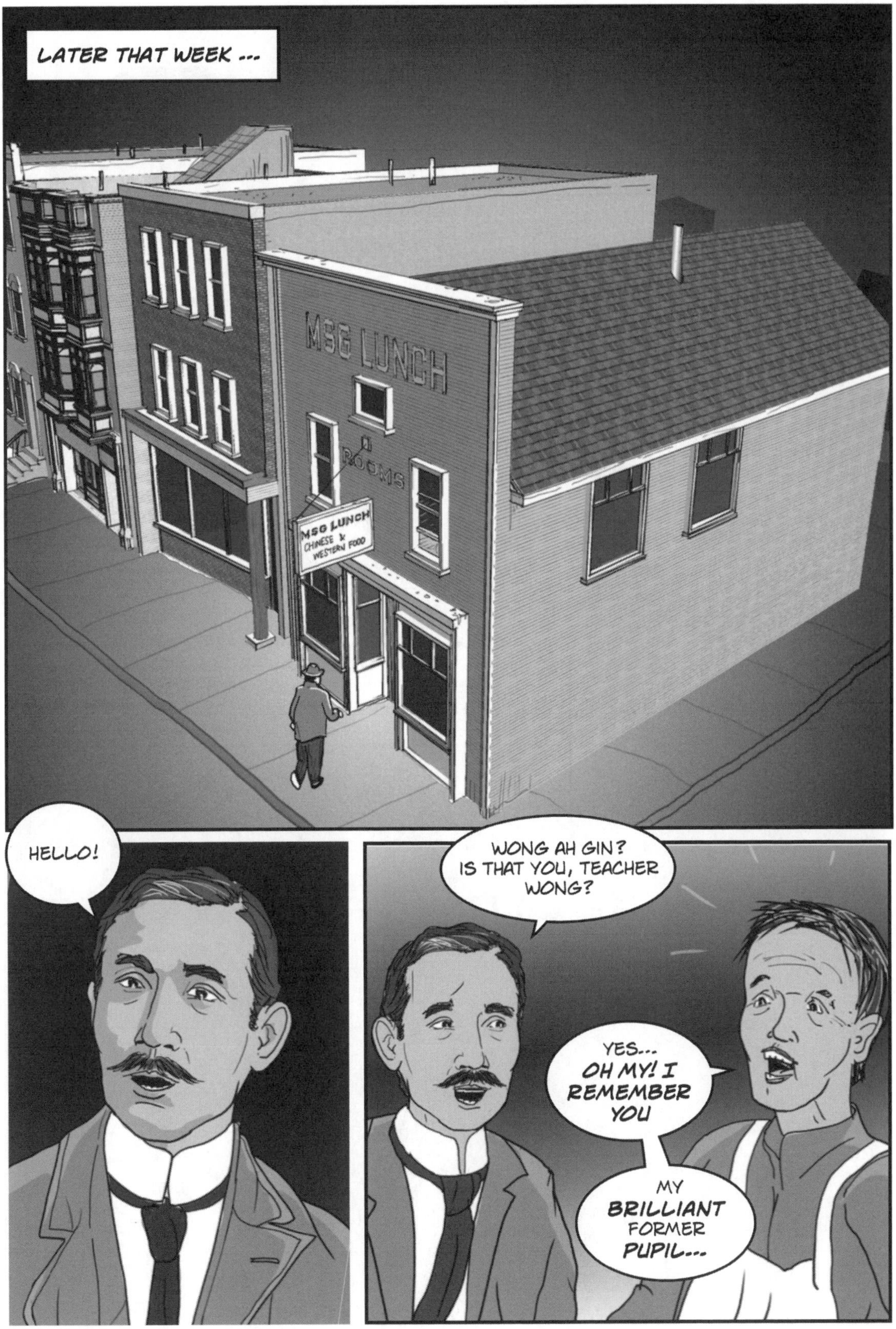
LATER THAT WEEK ...
MSG LUNCH
ROOMS
MSG LUNCH
CHINESE & WESTERN FOOD
HELLO!
WONG AH GIN? IS THAT YOU, TEACHER WONG?
YES... OH MY! I REMEMBER YOU
MY BRILLIANT FORMER PUPIL...

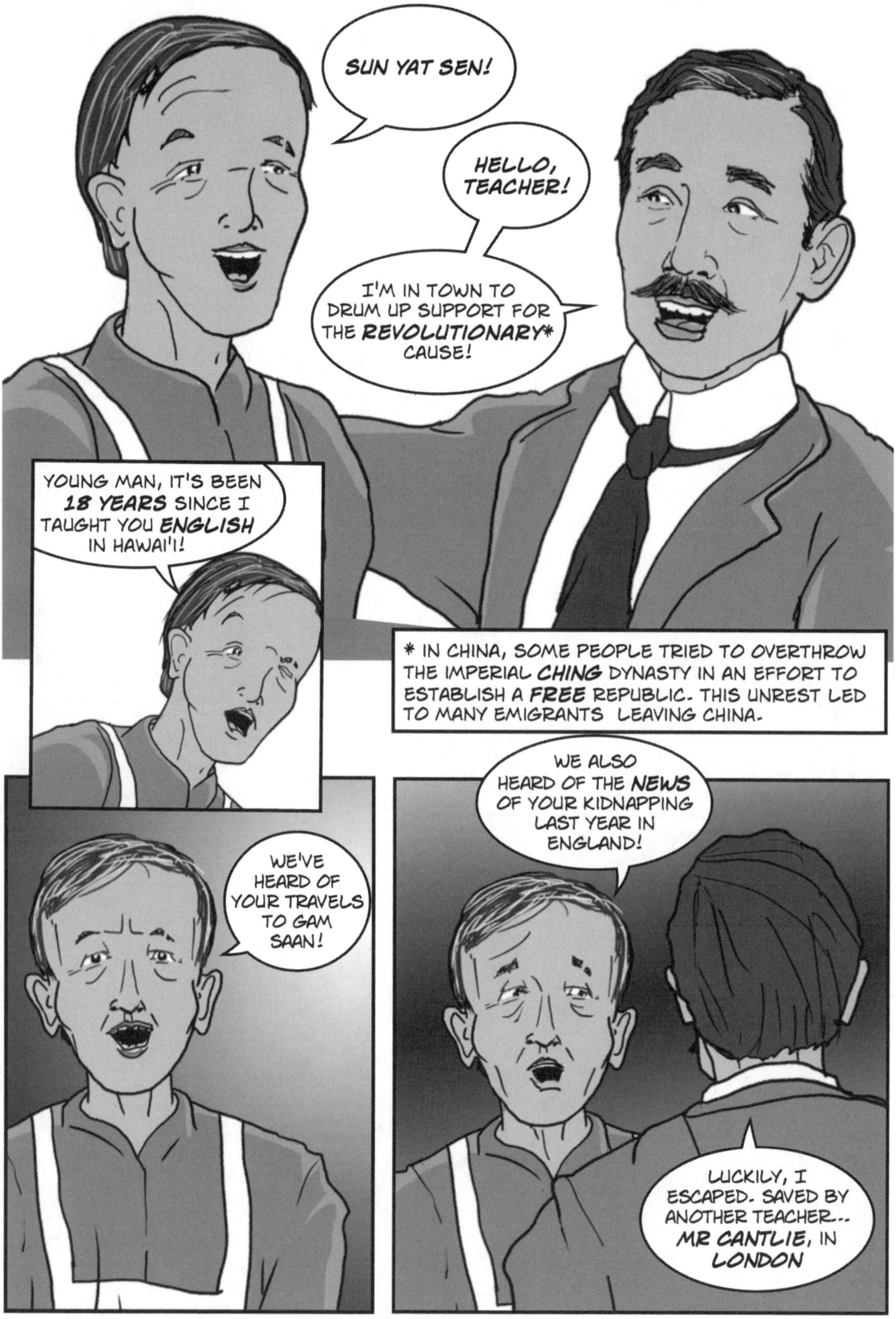
SUN YAT SEN!
HELLO, TEACHER!
I'M IN TOWN TO DRUM UP SUPPORT FOR THE REVOLUTIONARY* CAUSE!
YOUNG MAN, IT'S BEEN 18 YEARS SINCE I TAUGHT YOU ENGLISH IN HAWAI'I!
* IN CHINA, SOME PEOPLE TRIED TO OVERTHROW THE IMPERIAL CHING DYNASTY IN AN EFFORT TO ESTABLISH A FREE REPUBLIC. THIS UNREST LED TO MANY EMIGRANTS LEAVING CHINA.
WE'VE HEARD OF YOUR TRAVELS TO GAM SAAN!
WE ALSO HEARD OF THE NEWS OF YOUR KIDNAPPING LAST YEAR IN ENGLAND!
LUCKILY, I ESCAPED. SAVED BY ANOTHER TEACHER... MR CANTLIE, IN LONDON

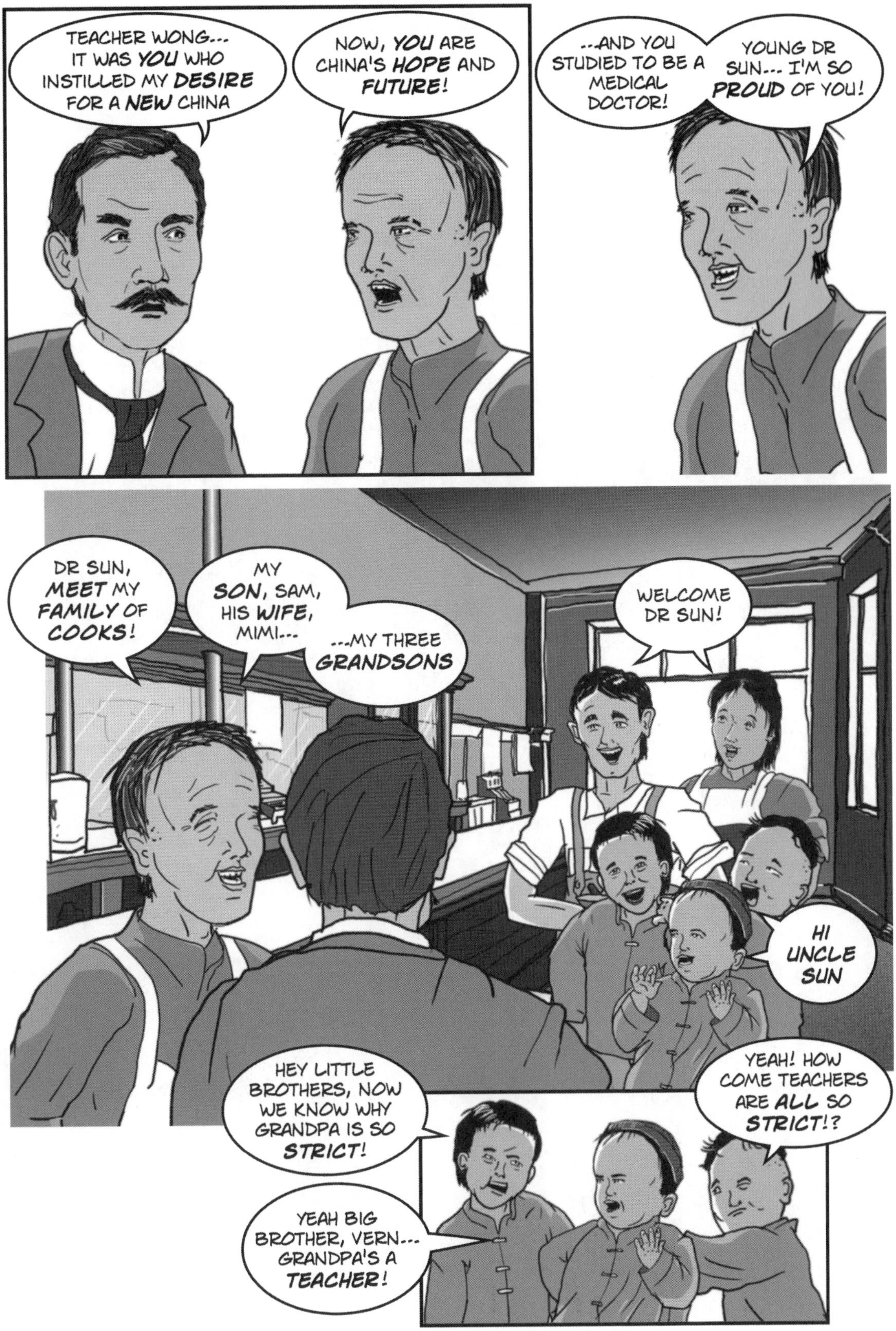
TEACHER WONG... IT WAS YOU WHO INSTILLED MY DESIRE FOR A NEW CHINA
NOW, YOU ARE CHINA'S HOPE AND FUTURE!
...AND YOU STUDIED TO BE A MEDICAL DOCTOR!
YOUNG DR SUN... I'M SO PROUD OF YOU!
DR SUN, MEET MY FAMILY OF COOKS!
MY SON, SAM, HIS WIFE, MIMI...
...MY THREE GRANDSONS
WELCOME DR SUN!
HI UNCLE SUN
HEY LITTLE BROTHERS, NOW WE KNOW WHY GRANDPA IS SO STRICT!
YEAH! HOW COME TEACHERS ARE ALL SO STRICT!?
YEAH BIG BROTHER, VERN... GRANDPA'S A TEACHER!

CHAPTER 14 Birthing Paper Sons

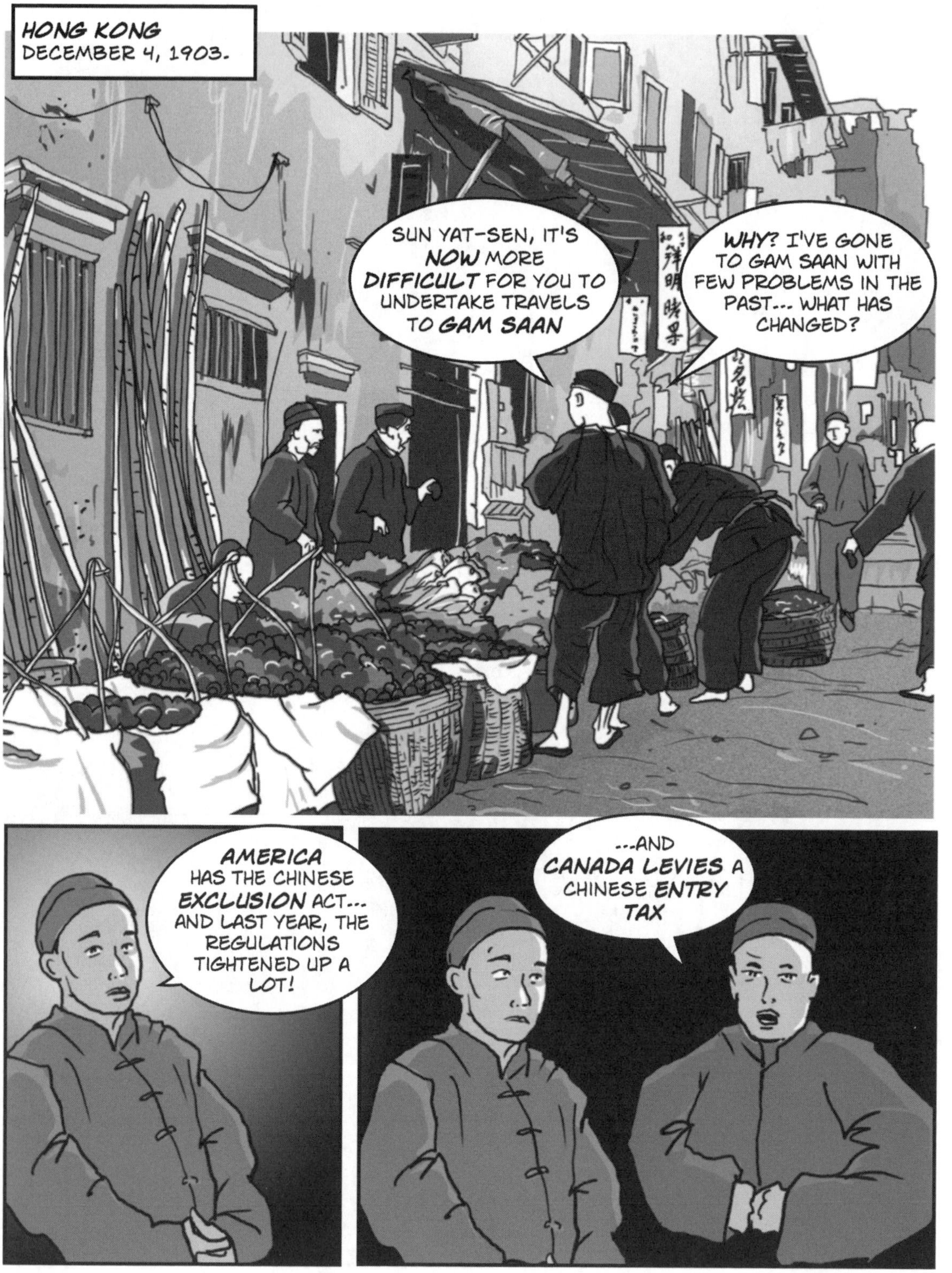
HONG KONG
DECEMBER 4, 1903.
SUN YAT-SEN, IT'S NOW MORE DIFFICULT FOR YOU TO UNDERTAKE TRAVELS TO GAM SAAN
WHY? I'VE GONE TO GAM SAAN WITH FEW PROBLEMS IN THE PAST... WHAT HAS CHANGED?
AMERICA HAS THE CHINESE EXCLUSION ACT... AND LAST YEAR, THE REGULATIONS TIGHTENED UP A LOT!
...AND CANADA LEVIES A CHINESE ENTRY TAX

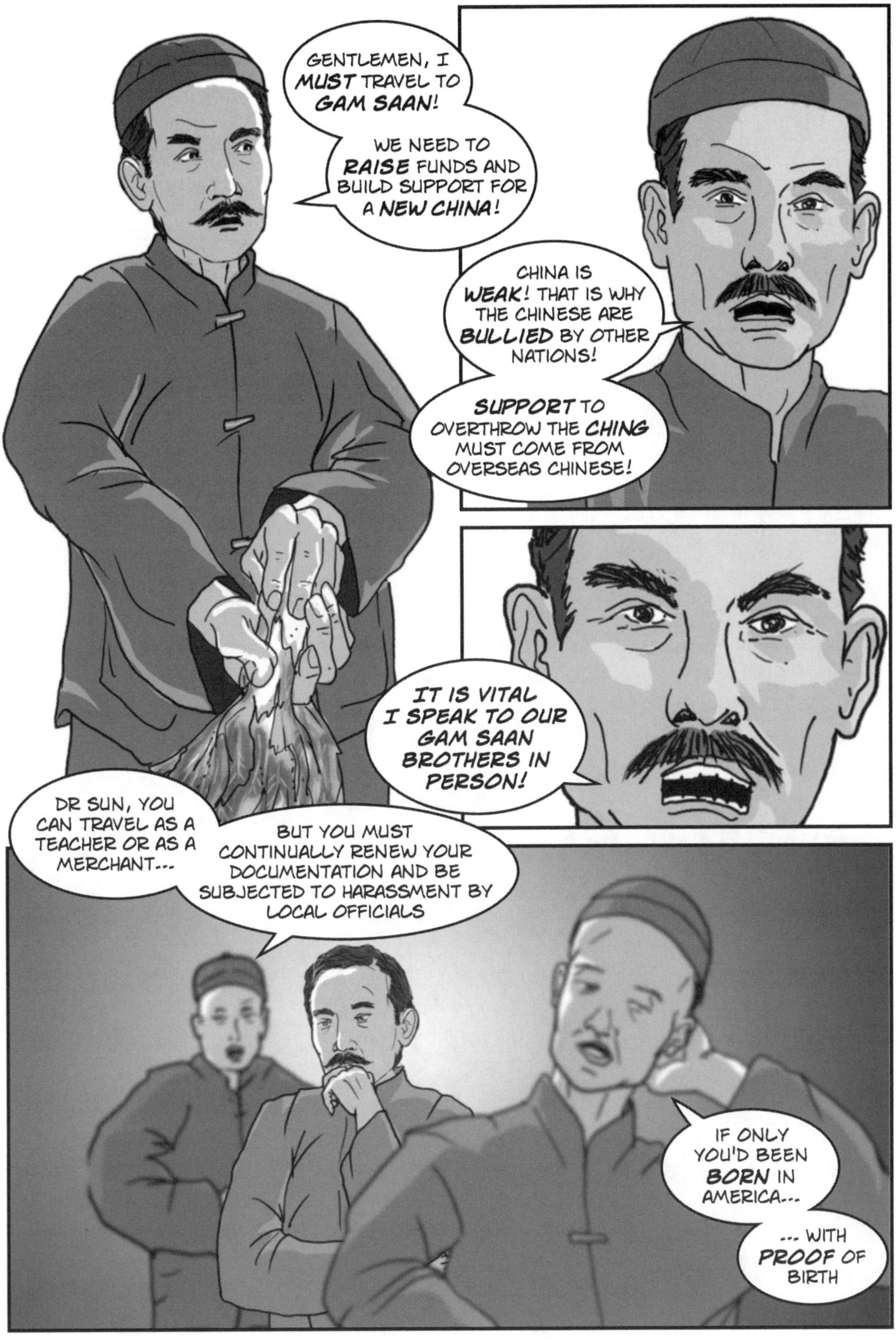
GENTLEMEN, I MUST TRAVEL TO GAM SAAN!
WE NEED TO RAISE FUNDS AND BUILD SUPPORT FOR A NEW CHINA!
CHINA IS WEAK! THAT IS WHY THE CHINESE ARE BULLIED BY OTHER NATIONS!
SUPPORT TO OVERTHROW THE CHING MUST COME FROM OVERSEAS CHINESE!
IT IS VITAL I SPEAK TO OUR GAM SAAN BROTHERS IN PERSON!
DR SUN, YOU CAN TRAVEL AS A TEACHER OR AS A MERCHANT...
BUT YOU MUST CONTINUALLY RENEW YOUR DOCUMENTATION AND BE SUBJECTED TO HARASSMENT BY LOCAL OFFICIALS
IF ONLY YOU'D BEEN BORN IN AMERICA...
... WITH PROOF OF BIRTH

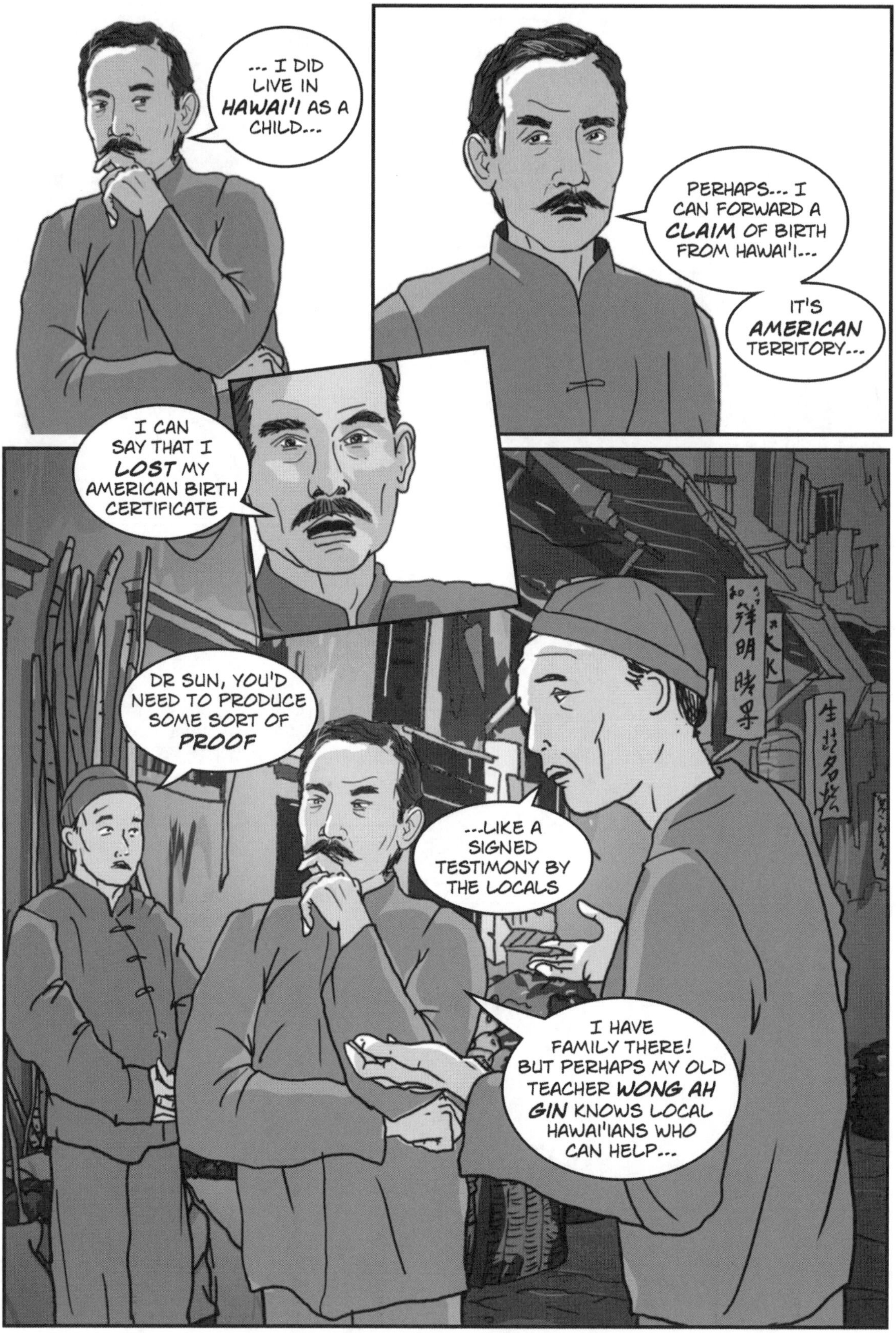

... I DID LIVE IN HAWAI'I AS A CHILD...
PERHAPS... I CAN FORWARD A CLAIM OF BIRTH FROM HAWAI'I...
IT'S AMERICAN TERRITORY...
I CAN SAY THAT I LOST MY AMERICAN BIRTH CERTIFICATE
DR SUN, YOU'D NEED TO PRODUCE SOME SORT OF PROOF
...LIKE A SIGNED TESTIMONY BY THE LOCALS
I HAVE FAMILY THERE! BUT PERHAPS MY OLD TEACHER WONG AH GIN KNOWS LOCAL HAWAI'IANS WHO CAN HELP...

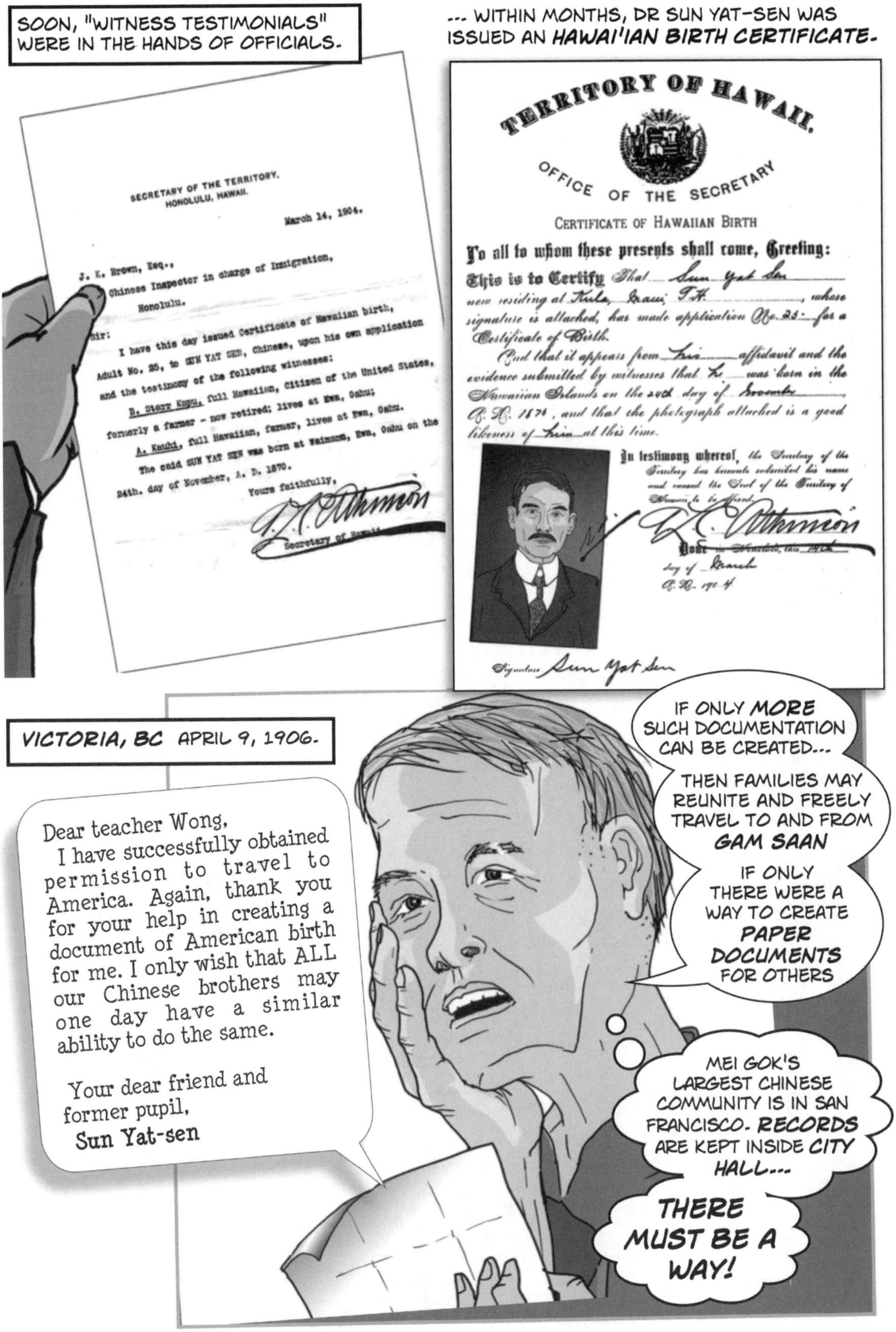
SOON, "WITNESS TESTIMONIALS" WERE IN THE HANDS OF OFFICIALS.
SECRETARY OF THE TERRITORY.
HONOLULU, HAWAII.
March 14, 1904.
J. K. Brown, Esq.,
Chinese Inspector in charge of Immigration,
Honolulu.
Sir:
I have this day issued Certificate of Hawaiian birth, Adult No. 25, to SUN YAT SEN, Chinese, upon his own application and the testimony of the following witnesses:
D. Starr Kapu, full Hawaiian, citizen of the United States, formerly a farmer - now retired; lives at Ewa, Oahu;
A. Kauhi, full Hawaiian, farmer, lives at Ewa, Oahu.
The said SUN YAT SEN was born at Waimanu, Ewa, Oahu on the 24th. day of November, A. D. 1870.
Yours faithfully,
Secretary of Hawaii
... WITHIN MONTHS, DR SUN YAT-SEN WAS ISSUED AN HAWAI'IAN BIRTH CERTIFICATE.
TERRITORY OF HAWAII.
OFFICE OF THE SECRETARY
CERTIFICATE OF HAWAIIAN BIRTH
To all to whom these presents shall come, Greeting:
This is to Certify That Sun Yat Sen now residing at Kula, Maui, T.H., whose signature is attached, has made application No. 25 for a Certificate of Birth.
And that it appears from his affidavit and the evidence submitted by witnesses that he was born in the Hawaiian Islands on the 24th day of November, and that the photograph attached is a good likeness of him at this time.
In testimony whereof, the Secretary of the Territory has hereunto subscribed his name and caused the Seal of the Territory of Hawaii to be affixed.
Done in Honolulu, this 14th day of March A.D. 1904
Signature Sun Yat Sen
VICTORIA, BC APRIL 9, 1906.
Dear teacher Wong, I have successfully obtained permission to travel to America. Again, thank you for your help in creating a document of American birth for me. I only wish that ALL our Chinese brothers may one day have a similar ability to do the same. Your dear friend and former pupil, Sun Yat-sen
IF ONLY MORE SUCH DOCUMENTATION CAN BE CREATED...
THEN FAMILIES MAY REUNITE AND FREELY TRAVEL TO AND FROM GAM SAAN
IF ONLY THERE WERE A WAY TO CREATE PAPER DOCUMENTS FOR OTHERS
MEI GOK'S LARGEST CHINESE COMMUNITY IS IN SAN FRANCISCO. RECORDS ARE KEPT INSIDE CITY HALL...
THERE MUST BE A WAY!

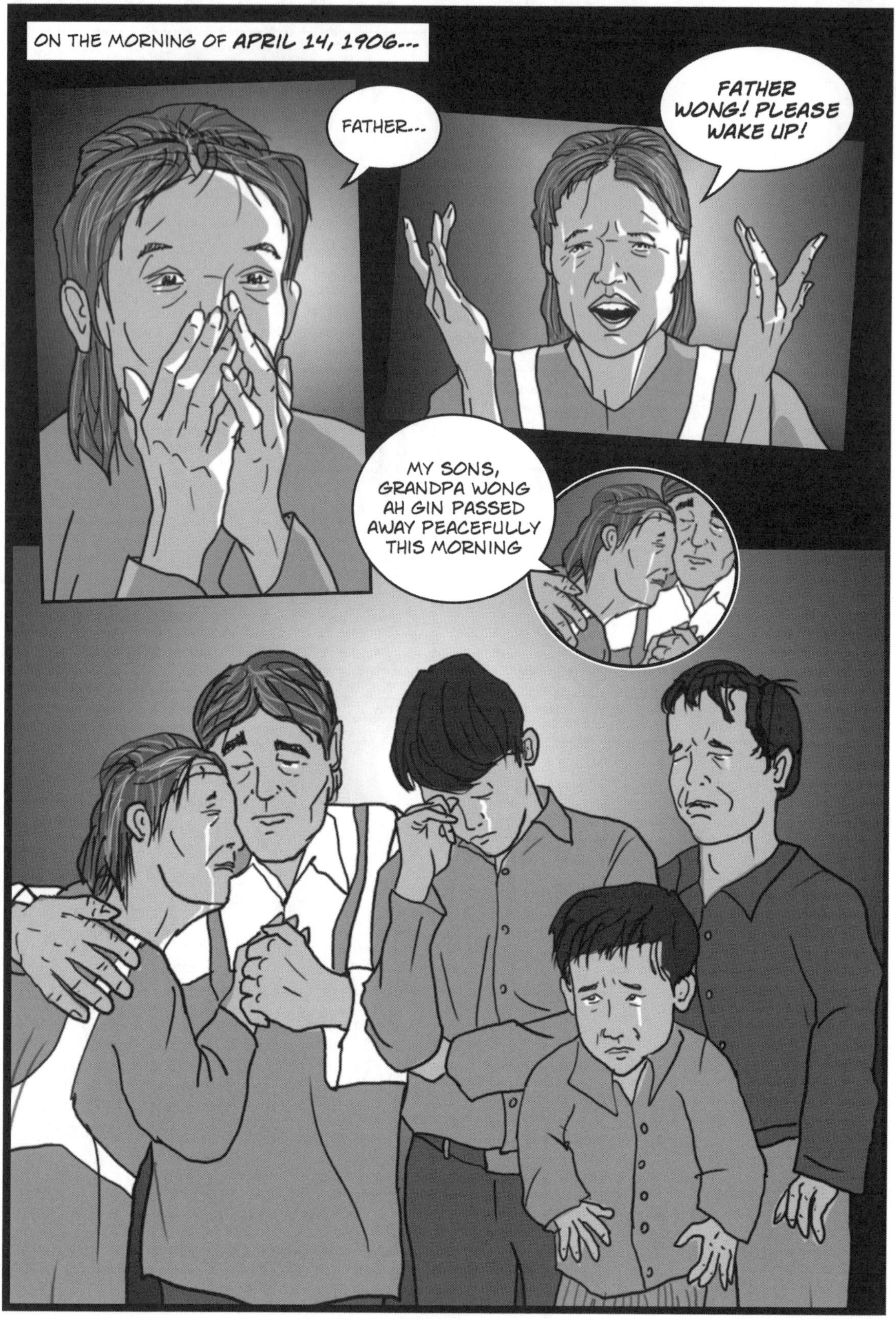
ON THE MORNING OF APRIL 14, 1906...
FATHER...
FATHER WONG! PLEASE WAKE UP!
MY SONS, GRANDPA WONG AH GIN PASSED AWAY PEACEFULLY THIS MORNING

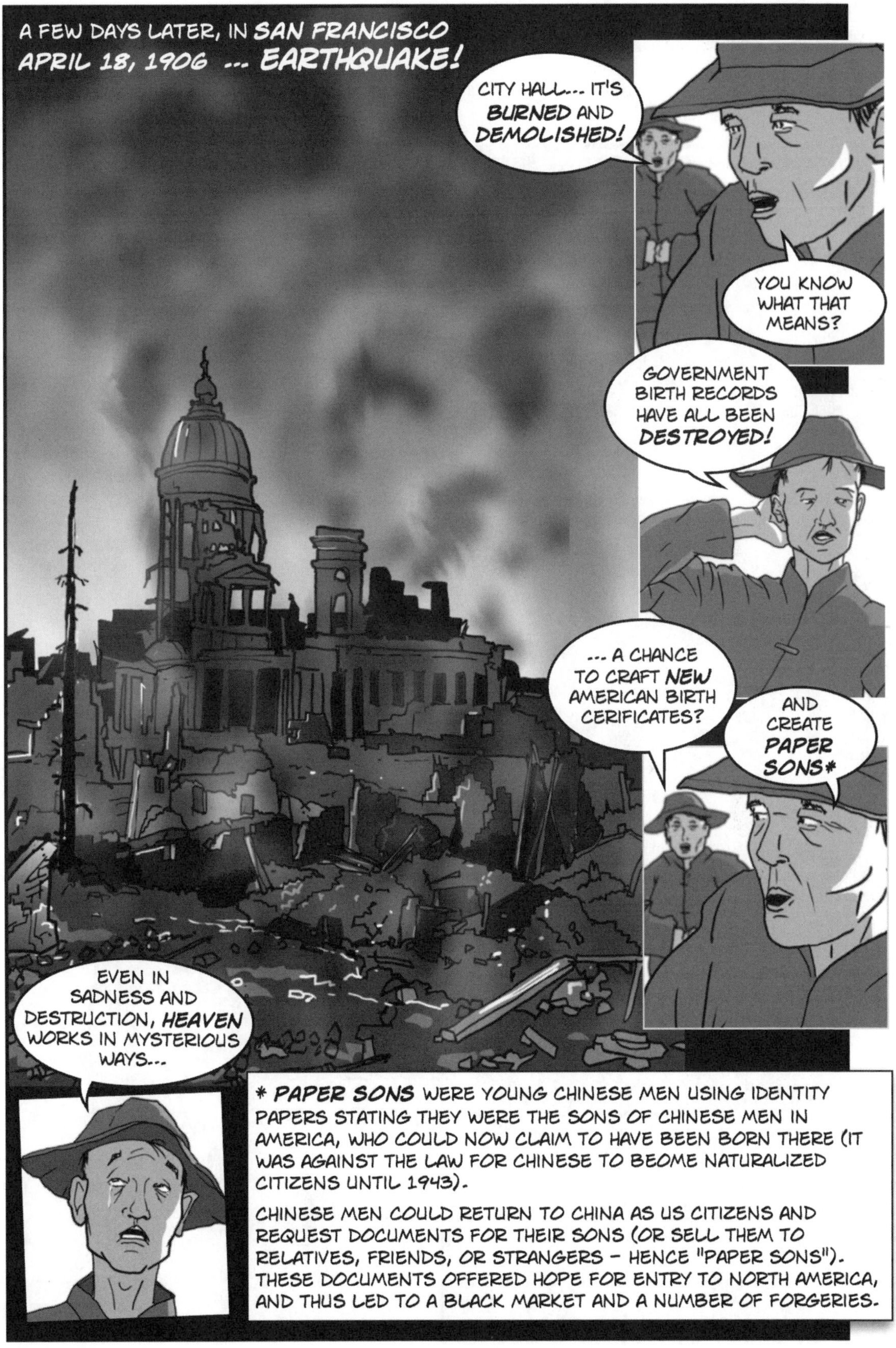
A FEW DAYS LATER, IN SAN FRANCISCO
APRIL 18, 1906 ... EARTHQUAKE!
CITY HALL... IT'S BURNED AND DEMOLISHED!
YOU KNOW WHAT THAT MEANS?
GOVERNMENT BIRTH RECORDS HAVE ALL BEEN DESTROYED!
... A CHANCE TO CRAFT NEW AMERICAN BIRTH CERIFICATES?
AND CREATE PAPER SONS*
EVEN IN SADNESS AND DESTRUCTION, HEAVEN WORKS IN MYSTERIOUS WAYS...
* PAPER SONS WERE YOUNG CHINESE MEN USING IDENTITY PAPERS STATING THEY WERE THE SONS OF CHINESE MEN IN AMERICA, WHO COULD NOW CLAIM TO HAVE BEEN BORN THERE (IT WAS AGAINST THE LAW FOR CHINESE TO BEOME NATURALIZED CITIZENS UNTIL 1943).
CHINESE MEN COULD RETURN TO CHINA AS US CITIZENS AND REQUEST DOCUMENTS FOR THEIR SONS (OR SELL THEM TO RELATIVES, FRIENDS, OR STRANGERS - HENCE "PAPER SONS"). THESE DOCUMENTS OFFERED HOPE FOR ENTRY TO NORTH AMERICA, AND THUS LED TO A BLACK MARKET AND A NUMBER OF FORGERIES.

CHAPTER 15 The Next GenerAsian

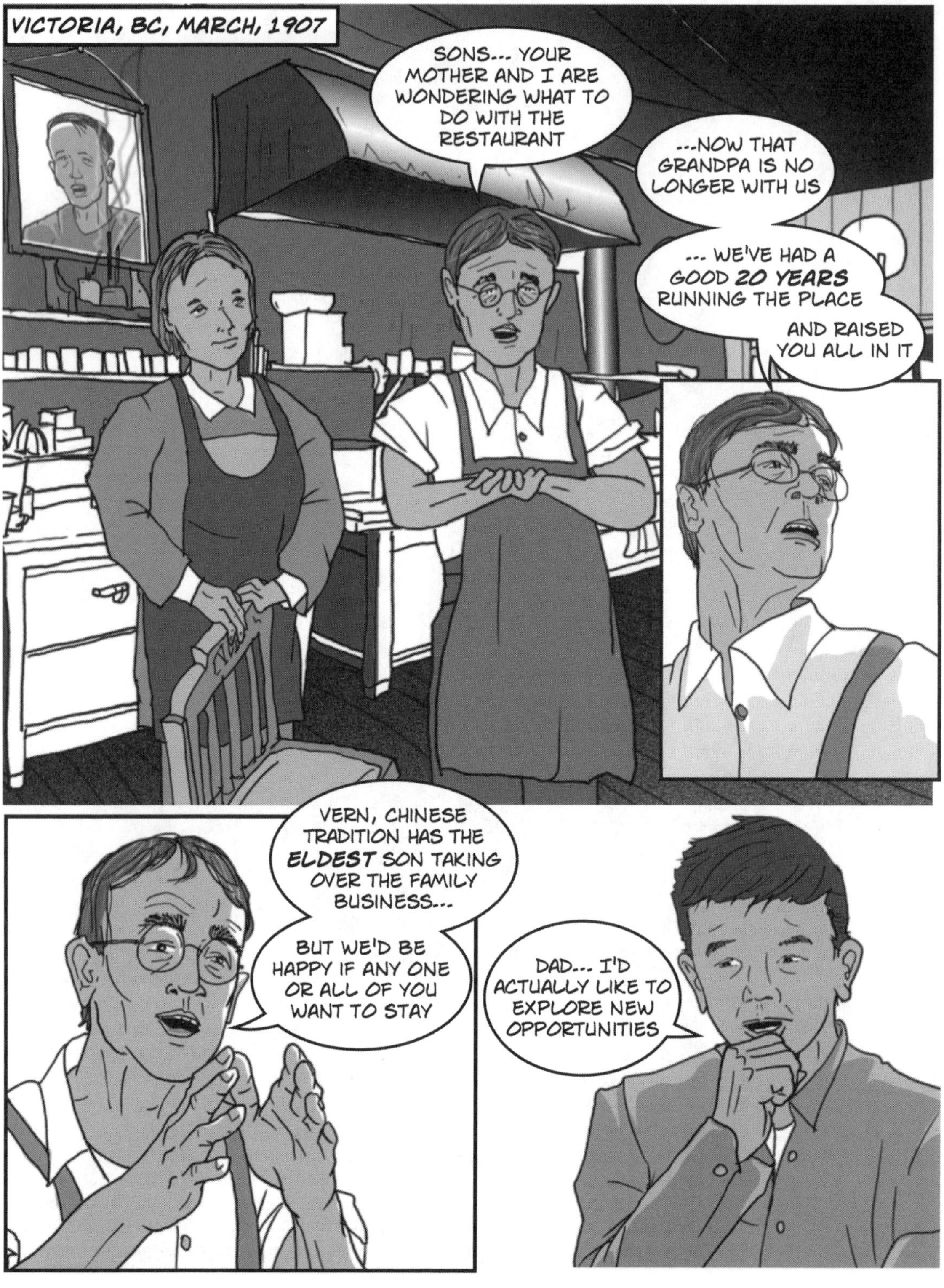
VICTORIA, BC, MARCH, 1907
SONS... YOUR MOTHER AND I ARE WONDERING WHAT TO DO WITH THE RESTAURANT
...NOW THAT GRANDPA IS NO LONGER WITH US
... WE'VE HAD A GOOD **20 YEARS** RUNNING THE PLACE
AND RAISED YOU ALL IN IT
VERN, CHINESE TRADITION HAS THE ***ELDEST*** SON TAKING OVER THE FAMILY BUSINESS...
BUT WE'D BE HAPPY IF ANY ONE OR ALL OF YOU WANT TO STAY
DAD... I'D ACTUALLY LIKE TO EXPLORE NEW OPPORTUNITIES

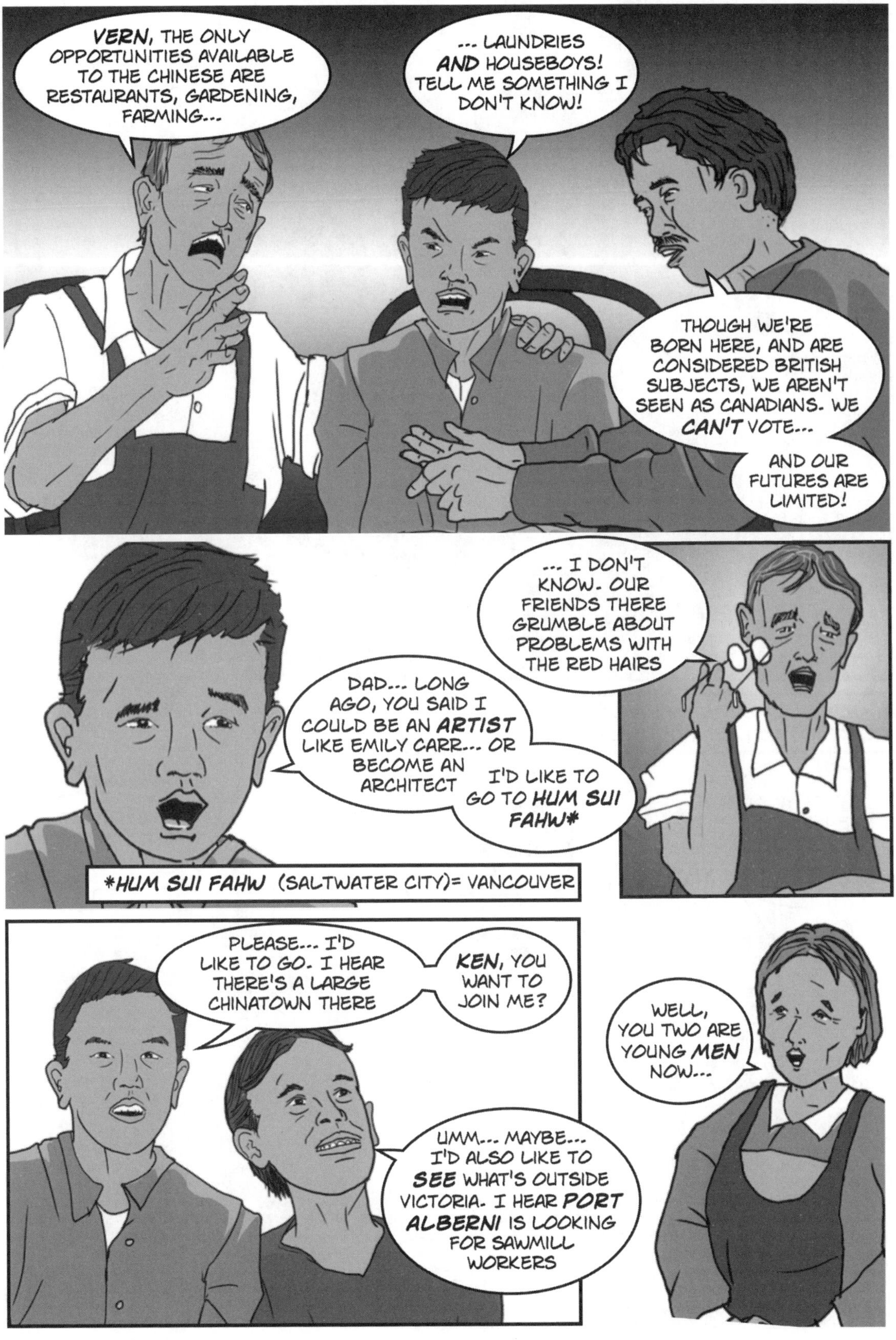
VERN, THE ONLY OPPORTUNITIES AVAILABLE TO THE CHINESE ARE RESTAURANTS, GARDENING, FARMING...
... LAUNDRIES AND HOUSEBOYS! TELL ME SOMETHING I DON'T KNOW!
THOUGH WE'RE BORN HERE, AND ARE CONSIDERED BRITISH SUBJECTS, WE AREN'T SEEN AS CANADIANS. WE CAN'T VOTE...
AND OUR FUTURES ARE LIMITED!
DAD... LONG AGO, YOU SAID I COULD BE AN ARTIST LIKE EMILY CARR... OR BECOME AN ARCHITECT
I'D LIKE TO GO TO HUM SUI FAHW*
... I DON'T KNOW. OUR FRIENDS THERE GRUMBLE ABOUT PROBLEMS WITH THE RED HAIRS
*HUM SUI FAHW (SALTWATER CITY)= VANCOUVER
PLEASE... I'D LIKE TO GO. I HEAR THERE'S A LARGE CHINATOWN THERE
KEN, YOU WANT TO JOIN ME?
UMM... MAYBE... I'D ALSO LIKE TO SEE WHAT'S OUTSIDE VICTORIA. I HEAR PORT ALBERNI IS LOOKING FOR SAWMILL WORKERS
WELL, YOU TWO ARE YOUNG MEN NOW...

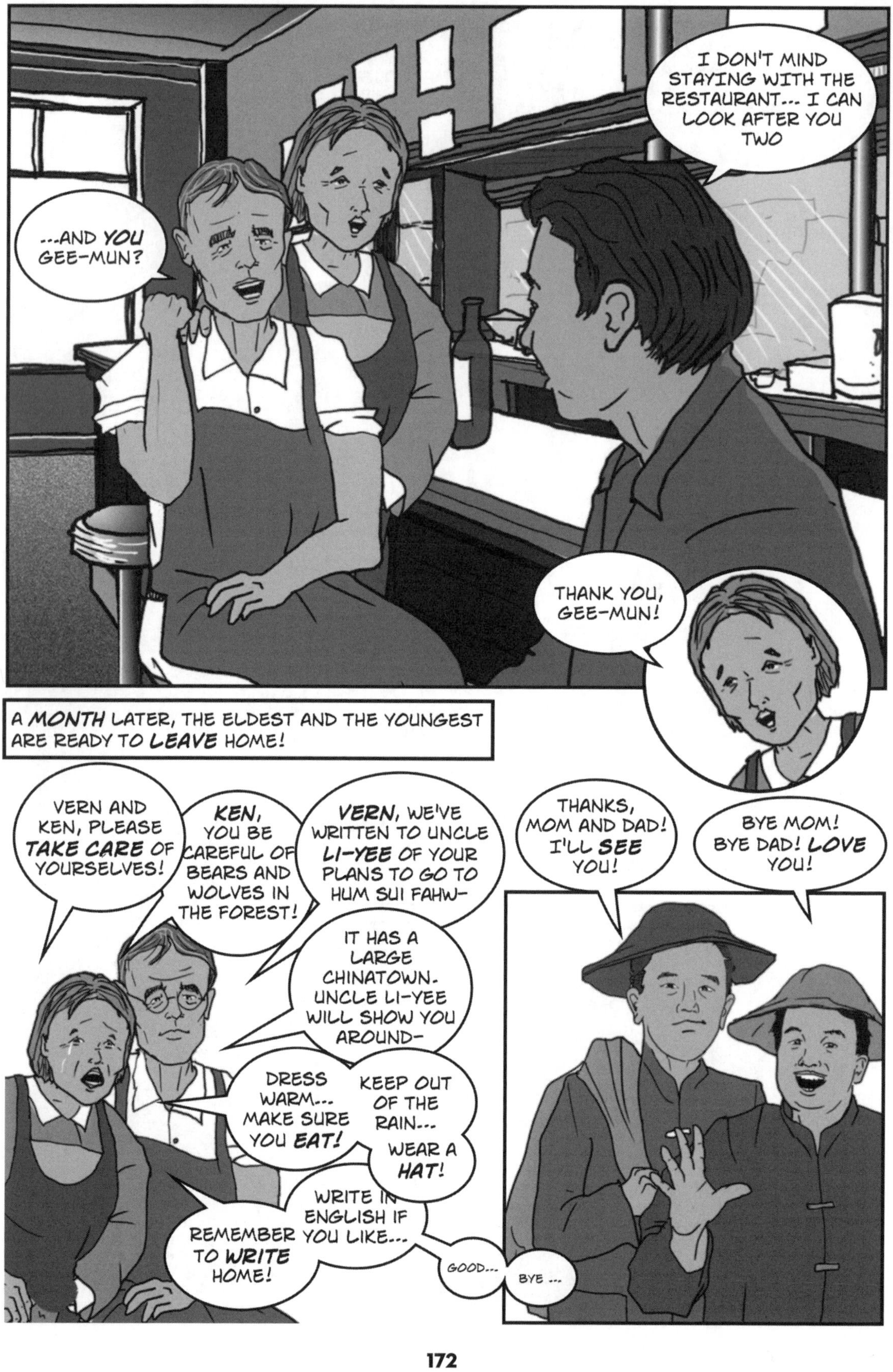
I DON'T MIND STAYING WITH THE RESTAURANT--- I CAN LOOK AFTER YOU TWO
---AND YOU GEE-MUN?
THANK YOU, GEE-MUN!
A MONTH LATER, THE ELDEST AND THE YOUNGEST ARE READY TO LEAVE HOME!
VERN AND KEN, PLEASE TAKE CARE OF YOURSELVES!
KEN, YOU BE CAREFUL OF BEARS AND WOLVES IN THE FOREST!
VERN, WE'VE WRITTEN TO UNCLE LI-YEE OF YOUR PLANS TO GO TO HUM SUI FAHW-
IT HAS A LARGE CHINATOWN. UNCLE LI-YEE WILL SHOW YOU AROUND-
DRESS WARM--- MAKE SURE YOU EAT!
KEEP OUT OF THE RAIN---
WEAR A HAT!
WRITE IN ENGLISH IF YOU LIKE---
REMEMBER TO WRITE HOME!
THANKS, MOM AND DAD! I'LL SEE YOU!
BYE MOM! BYE DAD! LOVE YOU!
GOOD---
BYE ---

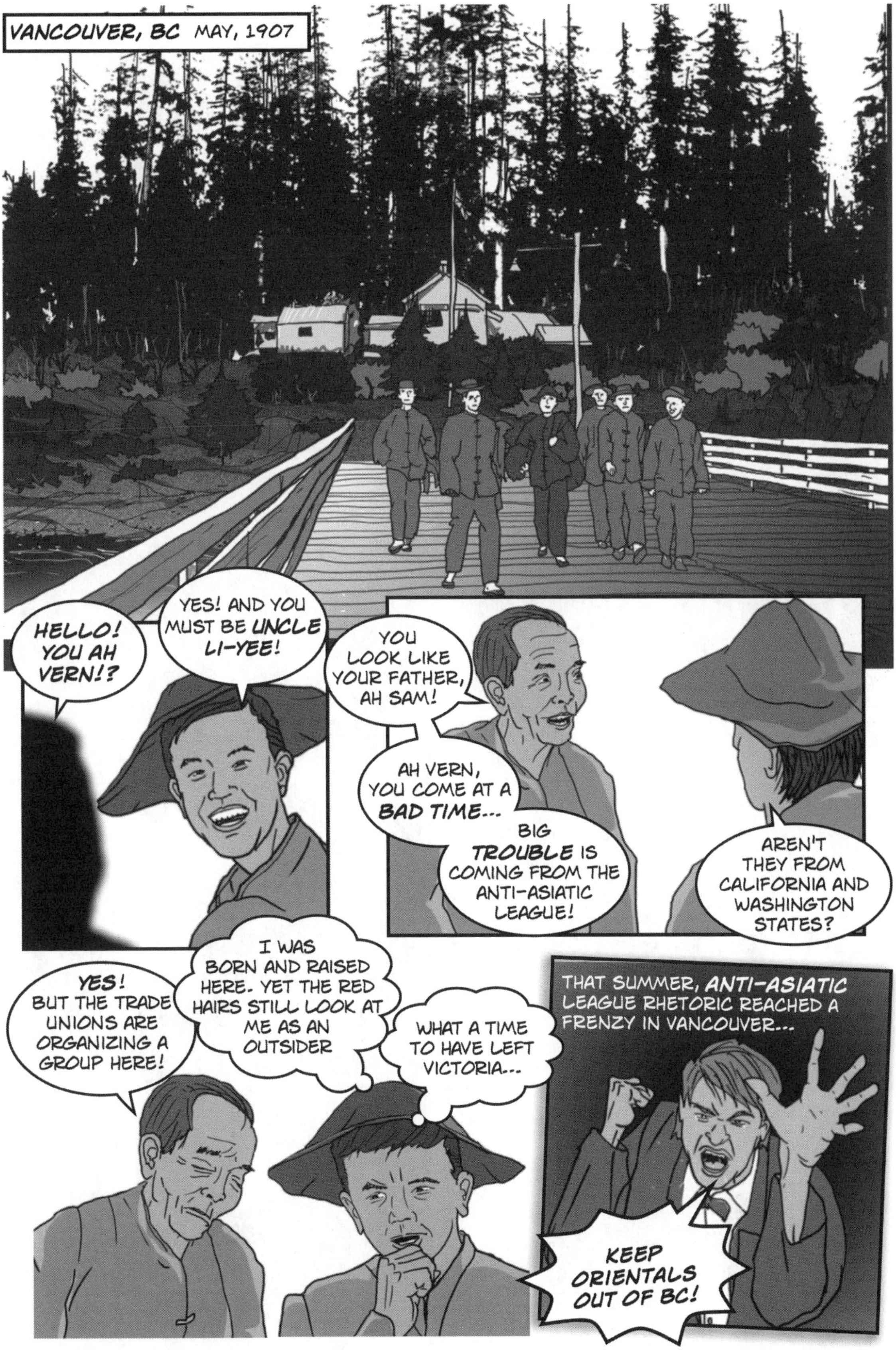
VANCOUVER, BC MAY, 1907
HELLO! YOU AH VERN!?
YES! AND YOU MUST BE UNCLE LI-YEE!
YOU LOOK LIKE YOUR FATHER, AH SAM!
AH VERN, YOU COME AT A BAD TIME...
BIG TROUBLE IS COMING FROM THE ANTI-ASIATIC LEAGUE!
AREN'T THEY FROM CALIFORNIA AND WASHINGTON STATES?
YES! BUT THE TRADE UNIONS ARE ORGANIZING A GROUP HERE!
I WAS BORN AND RAISED HERE. YET THE RED HAIRS STILL LOOK AT ME AS AN OUTSIDER
WHAT A TIME TO HAVE LEFT VICTORIA...
THAT SUMMER, ANTI-ASIATIC LEAGUE RHETORIC REACHED A FRENZY IN VANCOUVER...
KEEP ORIENTALS OUT OF BC!

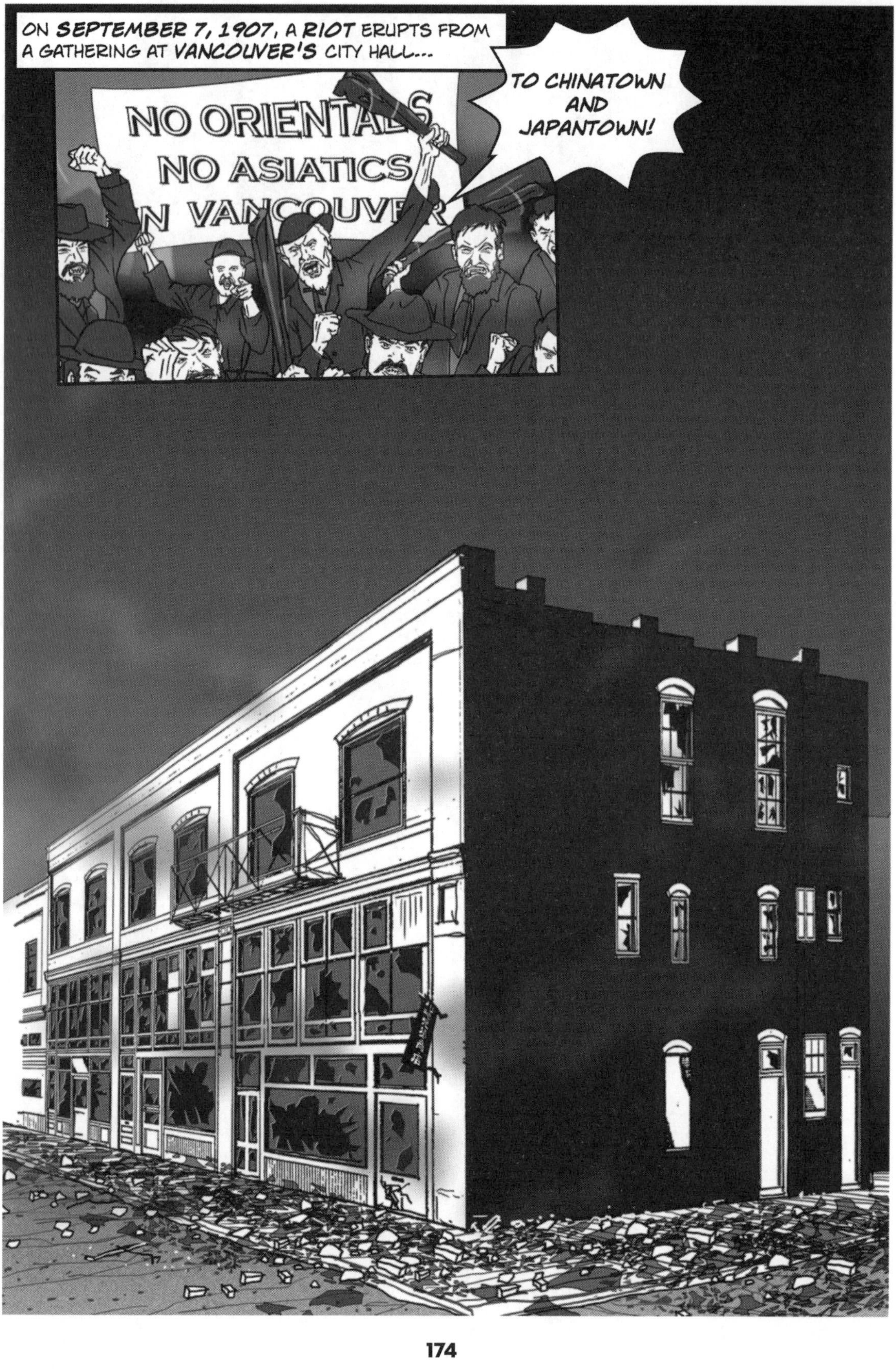
ON SEPTEMBER 7, 1907, A RIOT ERUPTS FROM A GATHERING AT VANCOUVER'S CITY HALL...
NO ORIENTALS NO ASIATICS IN VANCOUVER
TO CHINATOWN AND JAPANTOWN!

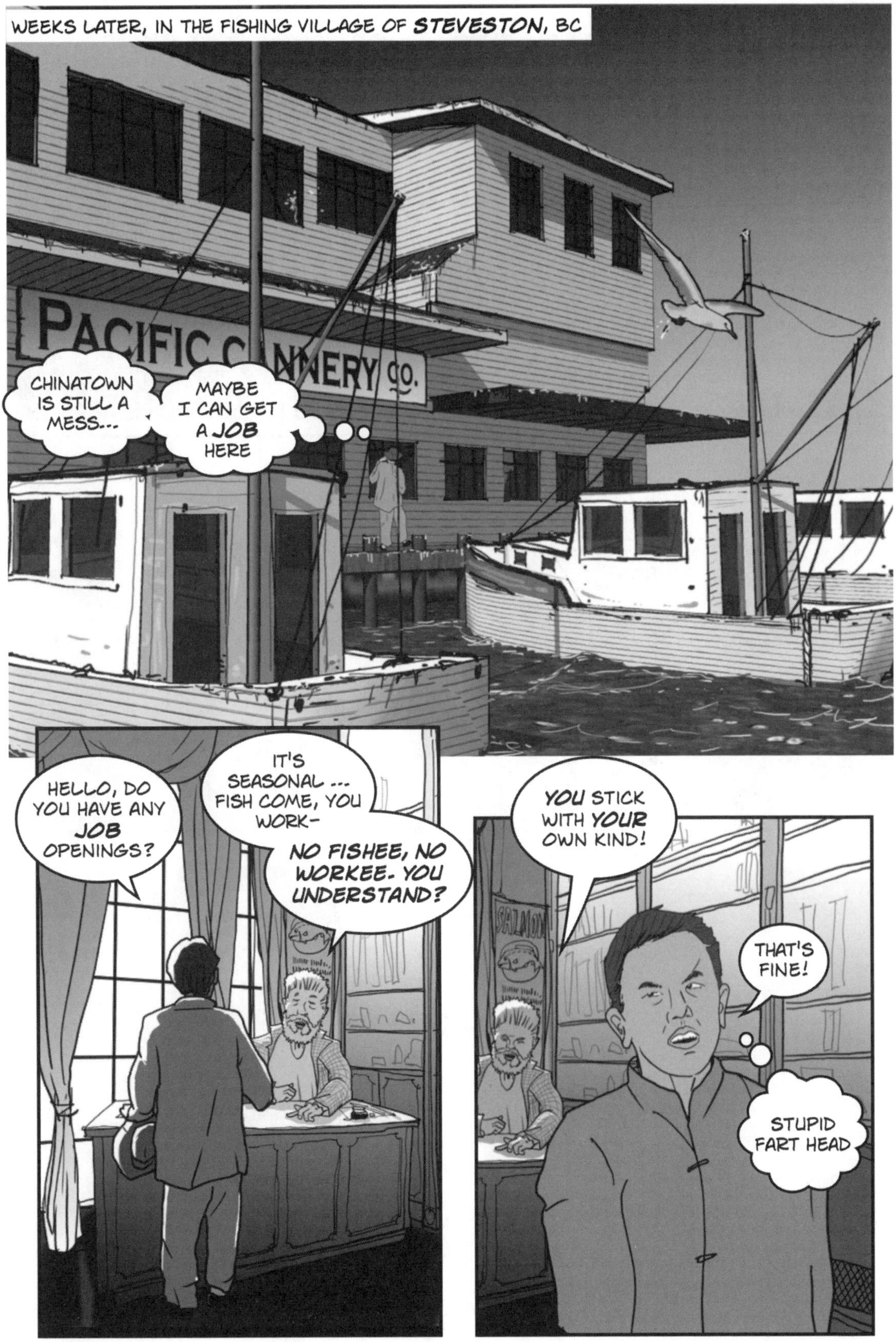
WEEKS LATER, IN THE FISHING VILLAGE OF STEVESTON, BC
PACIFIC CANNERY CO.
CHINATOWN IS STILL A MESS...
MAYBE I CAN GET A JOB HERE
HELLO, DO YOU HAVE ANY JOB OPENINGS?
IT'S SEASONAL ... FISH COME, YOU WORK-
NO FISHEE, NO WORKEE. YOU UNDERSTAND?
YOU STICK WITH YOUR OWN KIND!
THAT'S FINE!
STUPID FART HEAD

THE FOLLOWING WEEK...

HELLO MISS. MY NAME IS *VERN* WONG!

... HELLO

HOW'S THE WORK HERE?

YOU'RE EXPECTED TO WORK FAST, BUT ... CAREFUL YOU DON'T CUT YOUR HANDS—

ESPECIALLY DURING COLD WEATHER... YOU CAN'T FEEL ANYTHING!

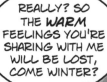

REALLY? SO THE *WARM* FEELINGS YOU'RE SHARING WITH ME WILL BE LOST, COME WINTER?

!

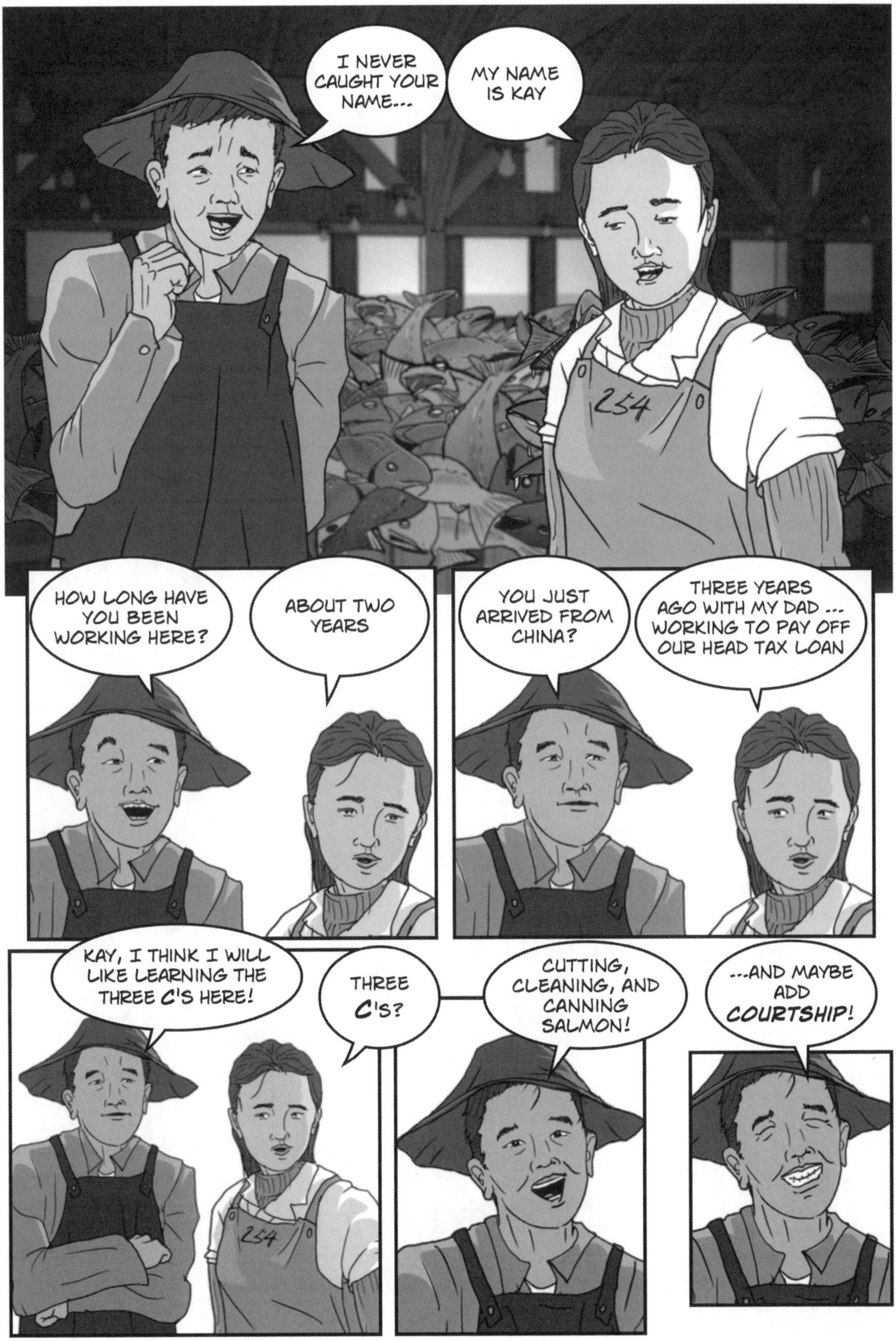
I NEVER CAUGHT YOUR NAME...
MY NAME IS KAY
HOW LONG HAVE YOU BEEN WORKING HERE?
ABOUT TWO YEARS
YOU JUST ARRIVED FROM CHINA?
THREE YEARS AGO WITH MY DAD ... WORKING TO PAY OFF OUR HEAD TAX LOAN
KAY, I THINK I WILL LIKE LEARNING THE THREE C'S HERE!
THREE C'S?
CUTTING, CLEANING, AND CANNING SALMON!
...AND MAYBE ADD COURTSHIP!

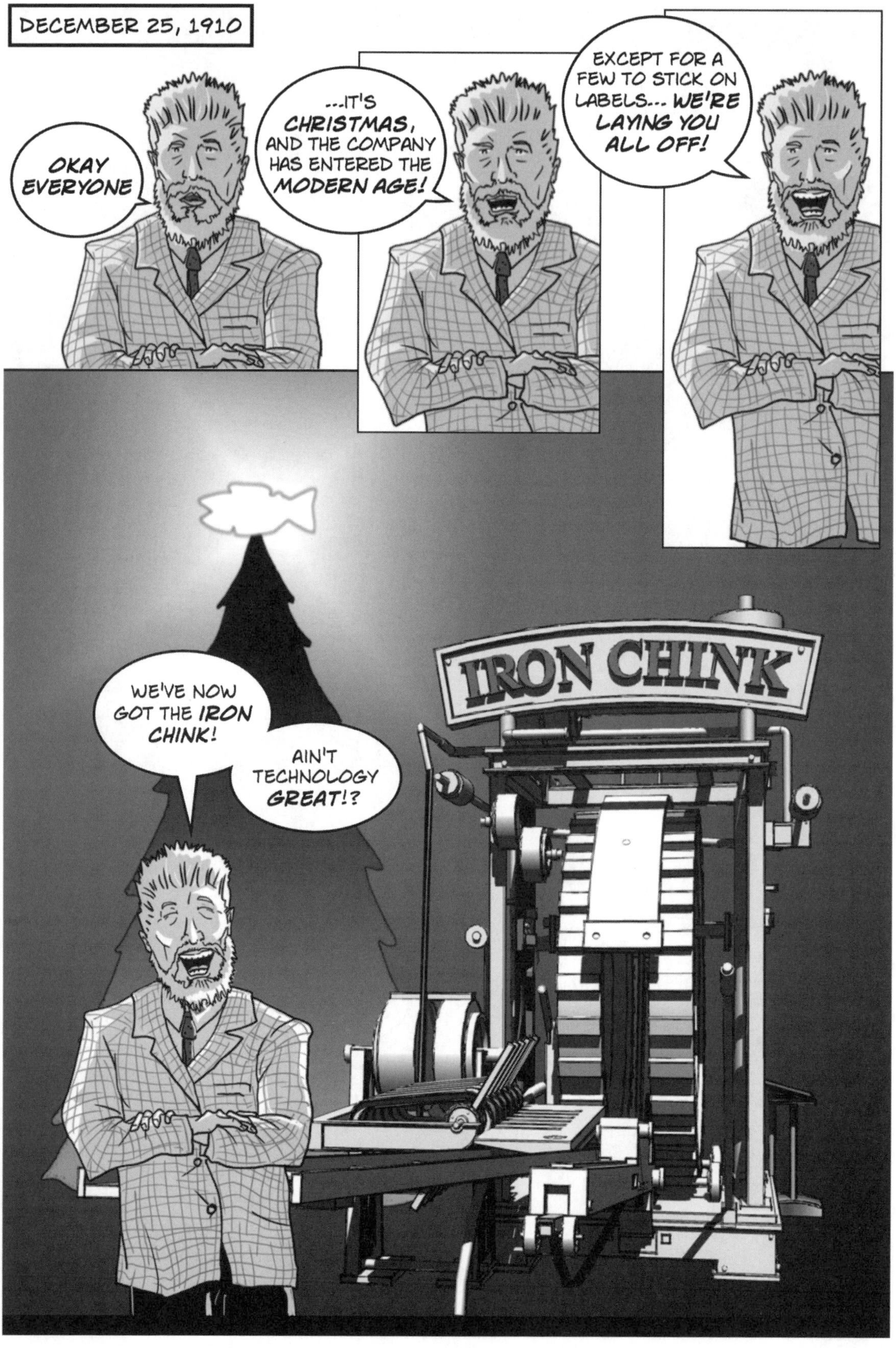
DECEMBER 25, 1910
OKAY EVERYONE
...IT'S CHRISTMAS, AND THE COMPANY HAS ENTERED THE MODERN AGE!
EXCEPT FOR A FEW TO STICK ON LABELS... WE'RE LAYING YOU ALL OFF!
IRON CHINK
WE'VE NOW GOT THE IRON CHINK!
AIN'T TECHNOLOGY GREAT!?

CHAPTER 16 Saving for the Head Tax

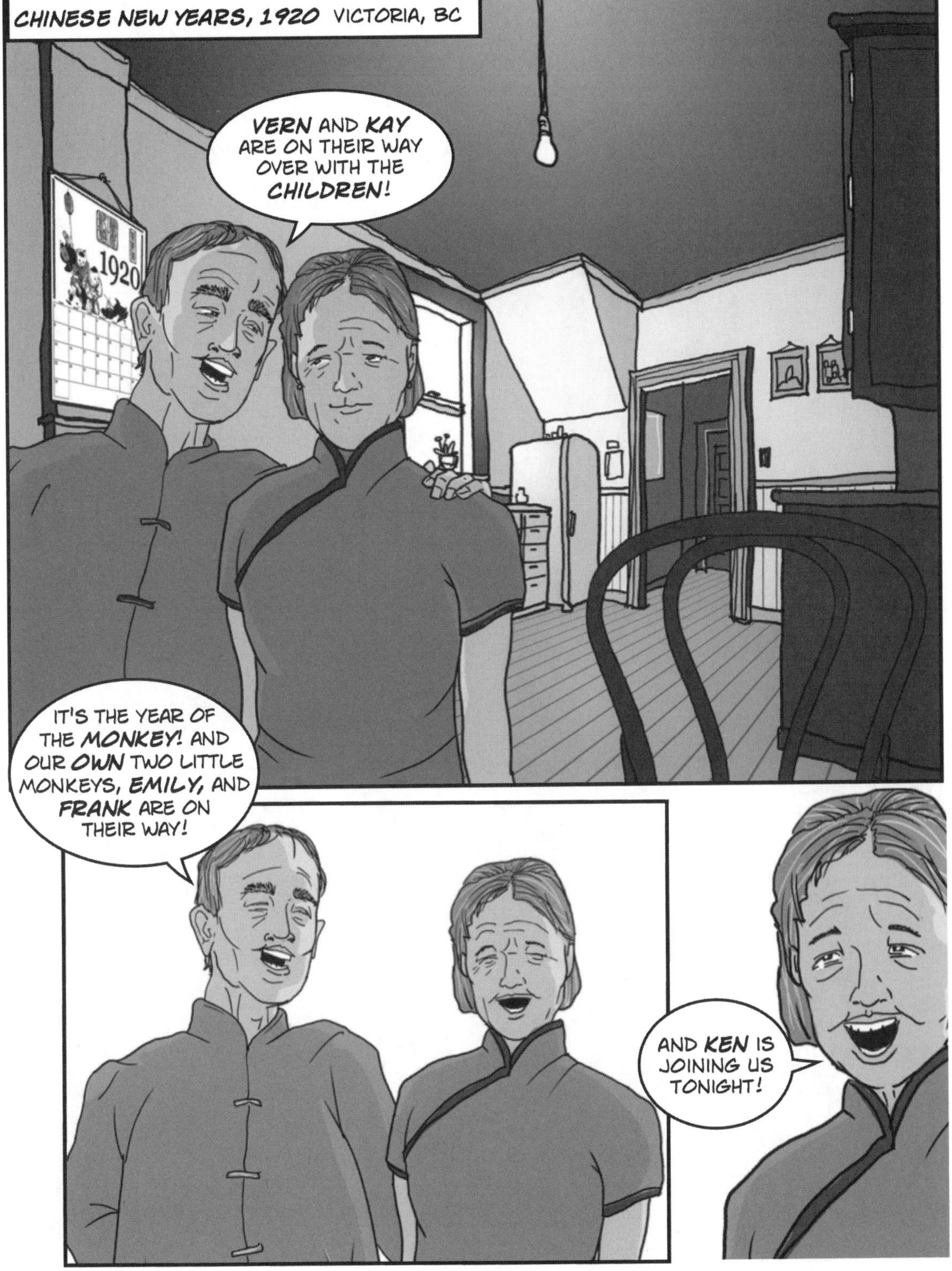
CHINESE NEW YEARS, 1920 VICTORIA, BC
1920
VERN AND KAY ARE ON THEIR WAY OVER WITH THE CHILDREN!
IT'S THE YEAR OF THE MONKEY! AND OUR OWN TWO LITTLE MONKEYS, EMILY, AND FRANK ARE ON THEIR WAY!
AND KEN IS JOINING US TONIGHT!

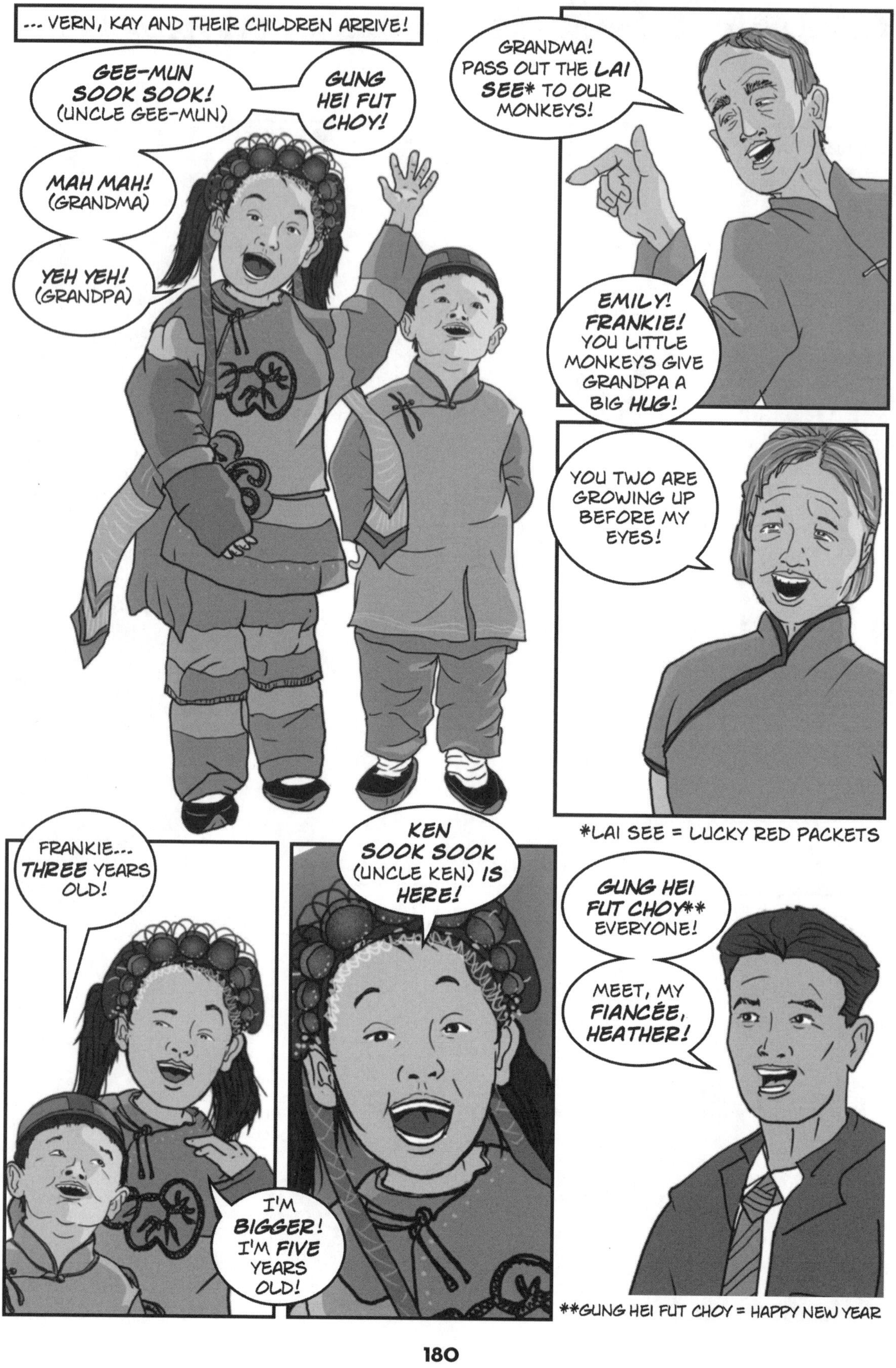
... VERN, KAY AND THEIR CHILDREN ARRIVE!
GEE-MUN SOOK SOOK! (UNCLE GEE-MUN)
GUNG HEI FUT CHOY!
MAH MAH! (GRANDMA)
YEH YEH! (GRANDPA)
GRANDMA! PASS OUT THE LAI SEE* TO OUR MONKEYS!
EMILY! FRANKIE! YOU LITTLE MONKEYS GIVE GRANDPA A BIG HUG!
YOU TWO ARE GROWING UP BEFORE MY EYES!
FRANKIE... THREE YEARS OLD!
I'M BIGGER! I'M FIVE YEARS OLD!
KEN SOOK SOOK (UNCLE KEN) IS HERE!
GUNG HEI FUT CHOY** EVERYONE!
MEET, MY FIANCÉE, HEATHER!

*LAI SEE = LUCKY RED PACKETS

**GUNG HEI FUT CHOY = HAPPY NEW YEAR

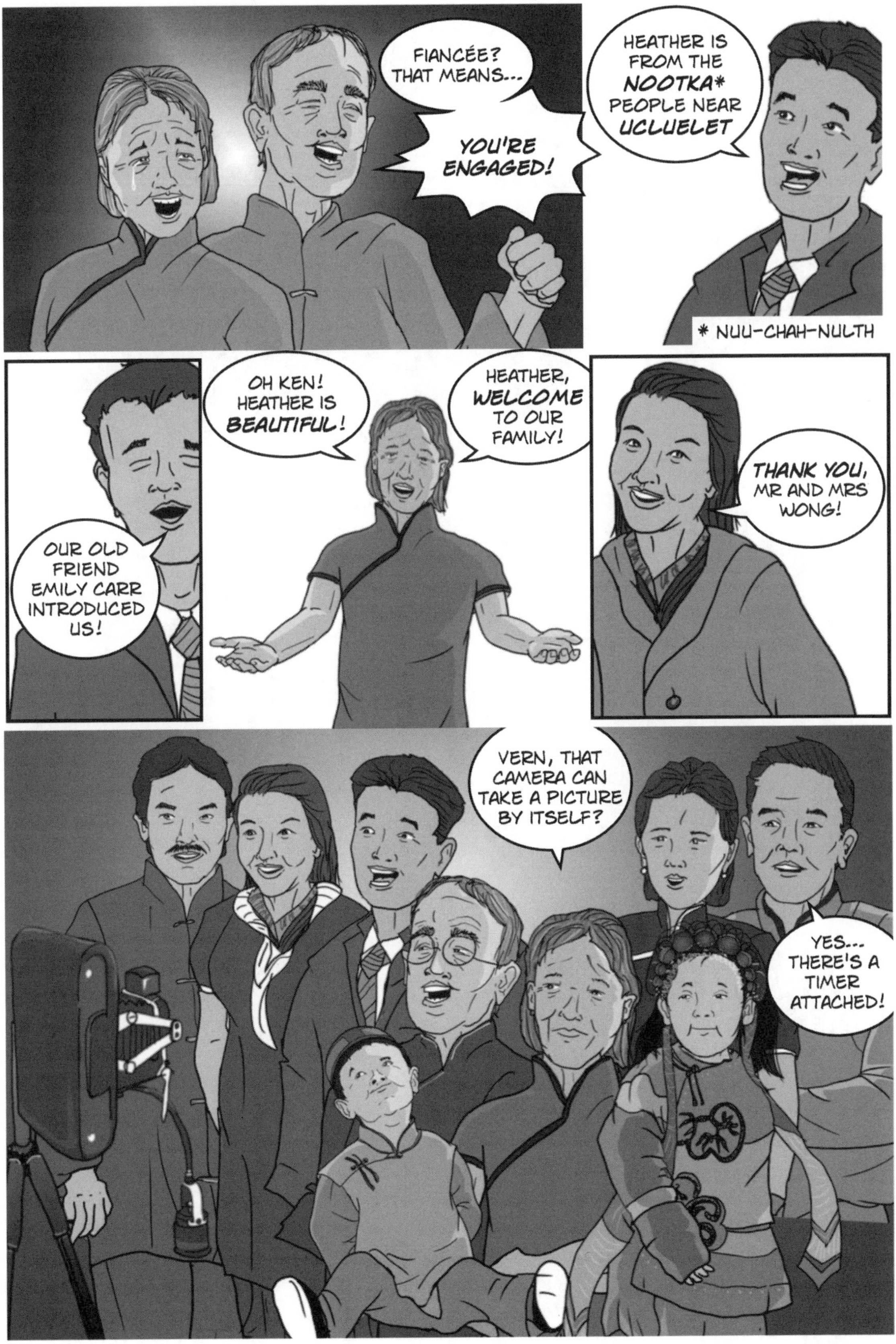
FIANCÉE? THAT MEANS...
YOU'RE ENGAGED!
HEATHER IS FROM THE NOOTKA* PEOPLE NEAR UCLUELET
* NUU-CHAH-NULTH
OUR OLD FRIEND EMILY CARR INTRODUCED US!
OH KEN! HEATHER IS BEAUTIFUL!
HEATHER, WELCOME TO OUR FAMILY!
THANK YOU, MR AND MRS WONG!
VERN, THAT CAMERA CAN TAKE A PICTURE BY ITSELF?
YES... THERE'S A TIMER ATTACHED!

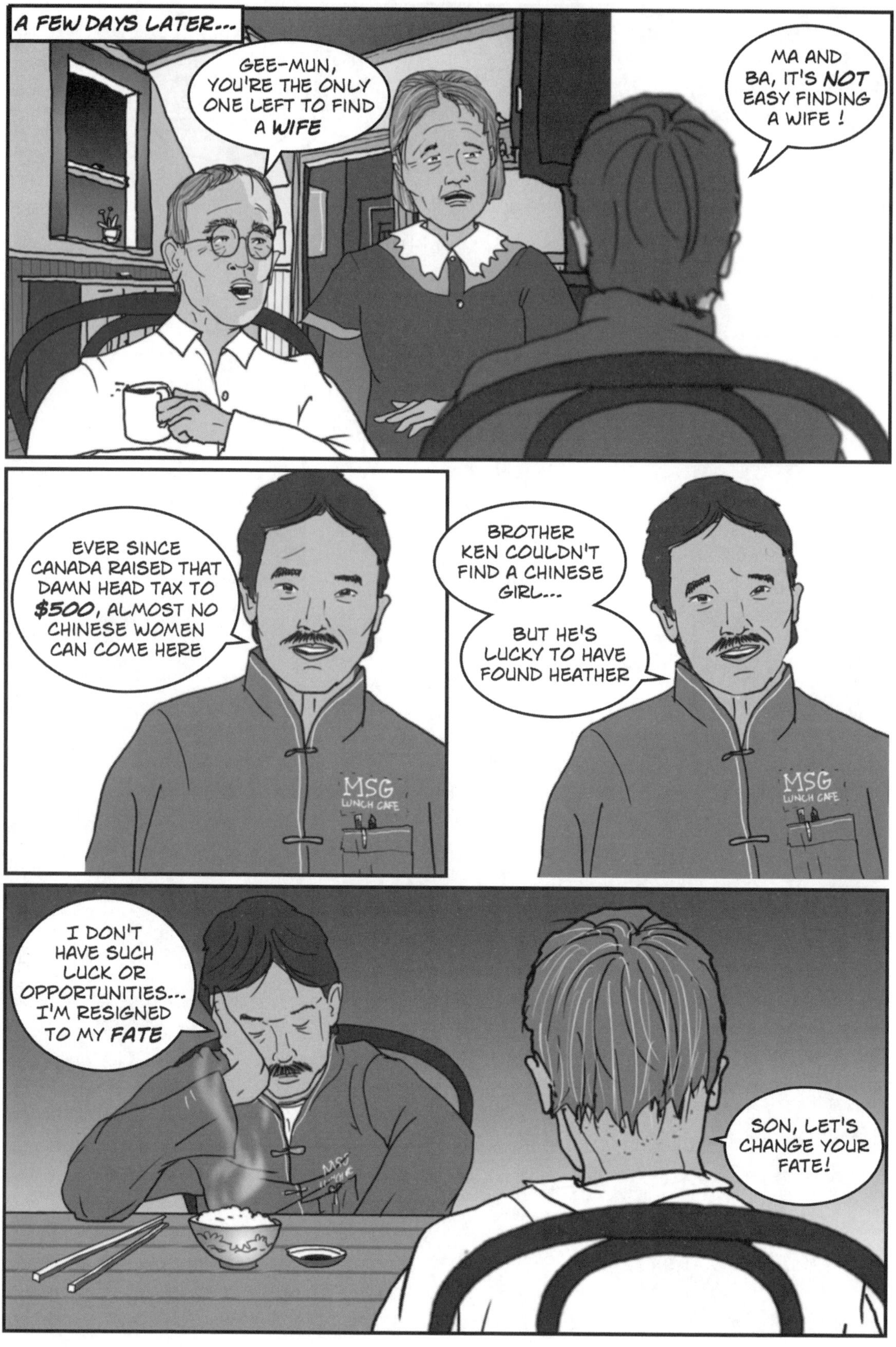
A FEW DAYS LATER...
GEE-MUN, YOU'RE THE ONLY ONE LEFT TO FIND A **WIFE**
MA AND BA, IT'S **NOT** EASY FINDING A WIFE !
EVER SINCE CANADA RAISED THAT DAMN HEAD TAX TO **$500**, ALMOST NO CHINESE WOMEN CAN COME HERE
MSG LUNCH CAFE
BROTHER KEN COULDN'T FIND A CHINESE GIRL...
BUT HE'S LUCKY TO HAVE FOUND HEATHER
MSG LUNCH CAFE
I DON'T HAVE SUCH LUCK OR OPPORTUNITIES... I'M RESIGNED TO MY **FATE**
SON, LET'S CHANGE YOUR FATE!

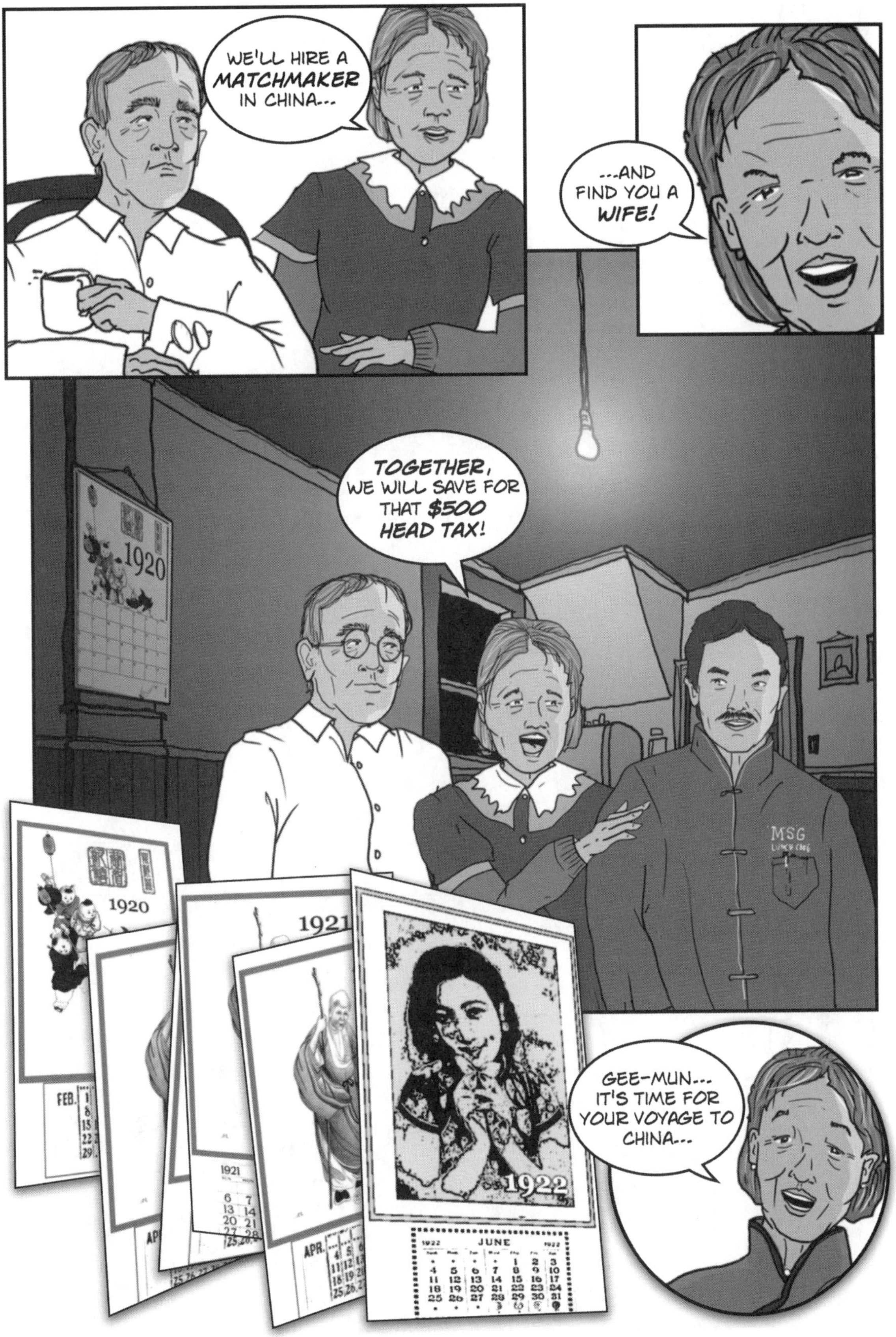
WE'LL HIRE A MATCHMAKER IN CHINA...
...AND FIND YOU A WIFE!
TOGETHER, WE WILL SAVE FOR THAT $500 HEAD TAX!
MSG
1920
1921
1922
JUNE
GEE-MUN... IT'S TIME FOR YOUR VOYAGE TO CHINA...

CHAPTER 17 An Arranged Marriage

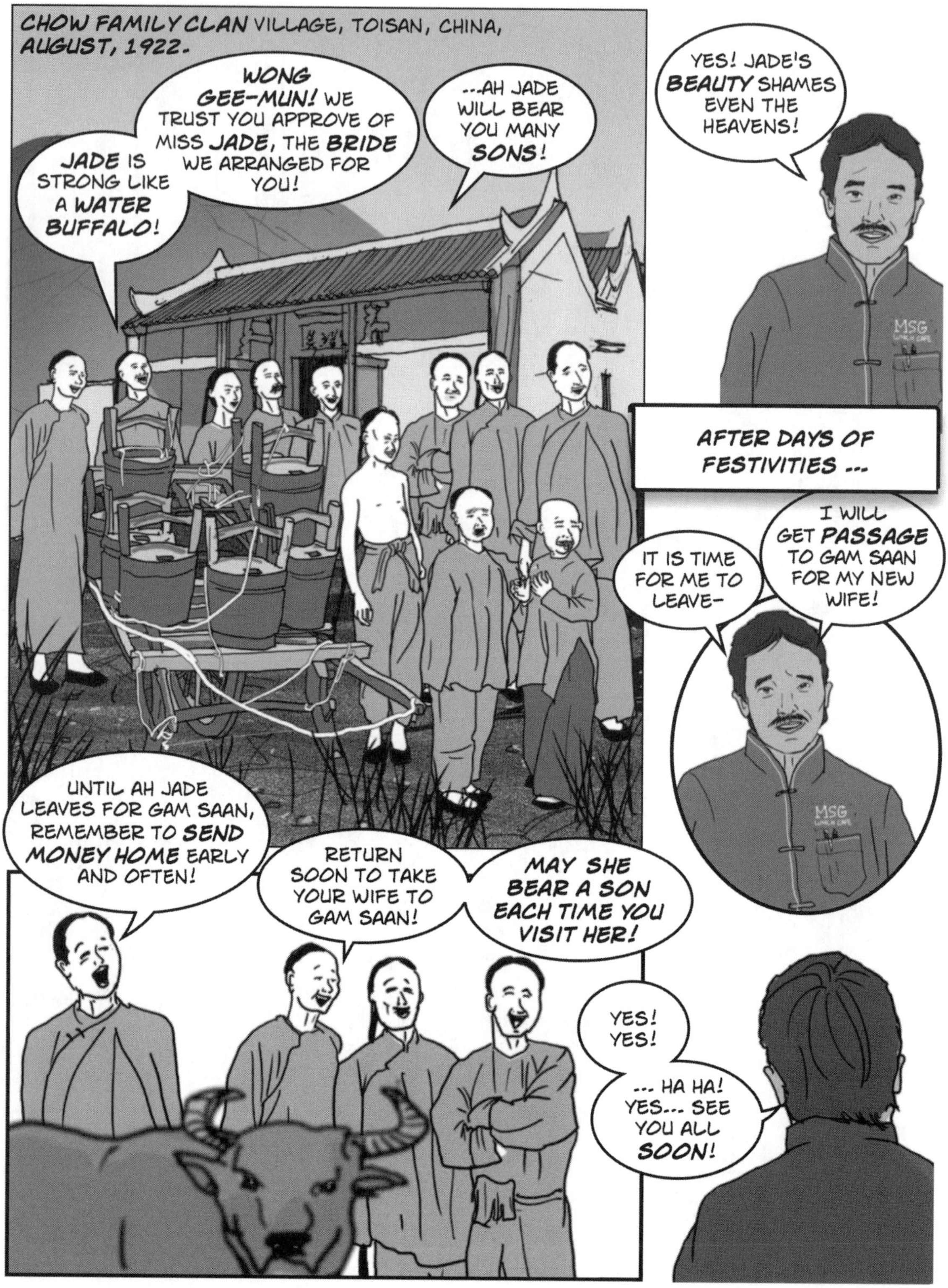
CHOW FAMILY CLAN VILLAGE, TOISAN, CHINA, AUGUST, 1922.
WONG GEE-MUN! WE TRUST YOU APPROVE OF MISS JADE, THE BRIDE WE ARRANGED FOR YOU!
JADE IS STRONG LIKE A WATER BUFFALO!
--AH JADE WILL BEAR YOU MANY SONS!
YES! JADE'S BEAUTY SHAMES EVEN THE HEAVENS!
AFTER DAYS OF FESTIVITIES ---
IT IS TIME FOR ME TO LEAVE-
I WILL GET PASSAGE TO GAM SAAN FOR MY NEW WIFE!
UNTIL AH JADE LEAVES FOR GAM SAAN, REMEMBER TO SEND MONEY HOME EARLY AND OFTEN!
RETURN SOON TO TAKE YOUR WIFE TO GAM SAAN!
MAY SHE BEAR A SON EACH TIME YOU VISIT HER!
YES! YES!
--- HA HA! YES--- SEE YOU ALL SOON!

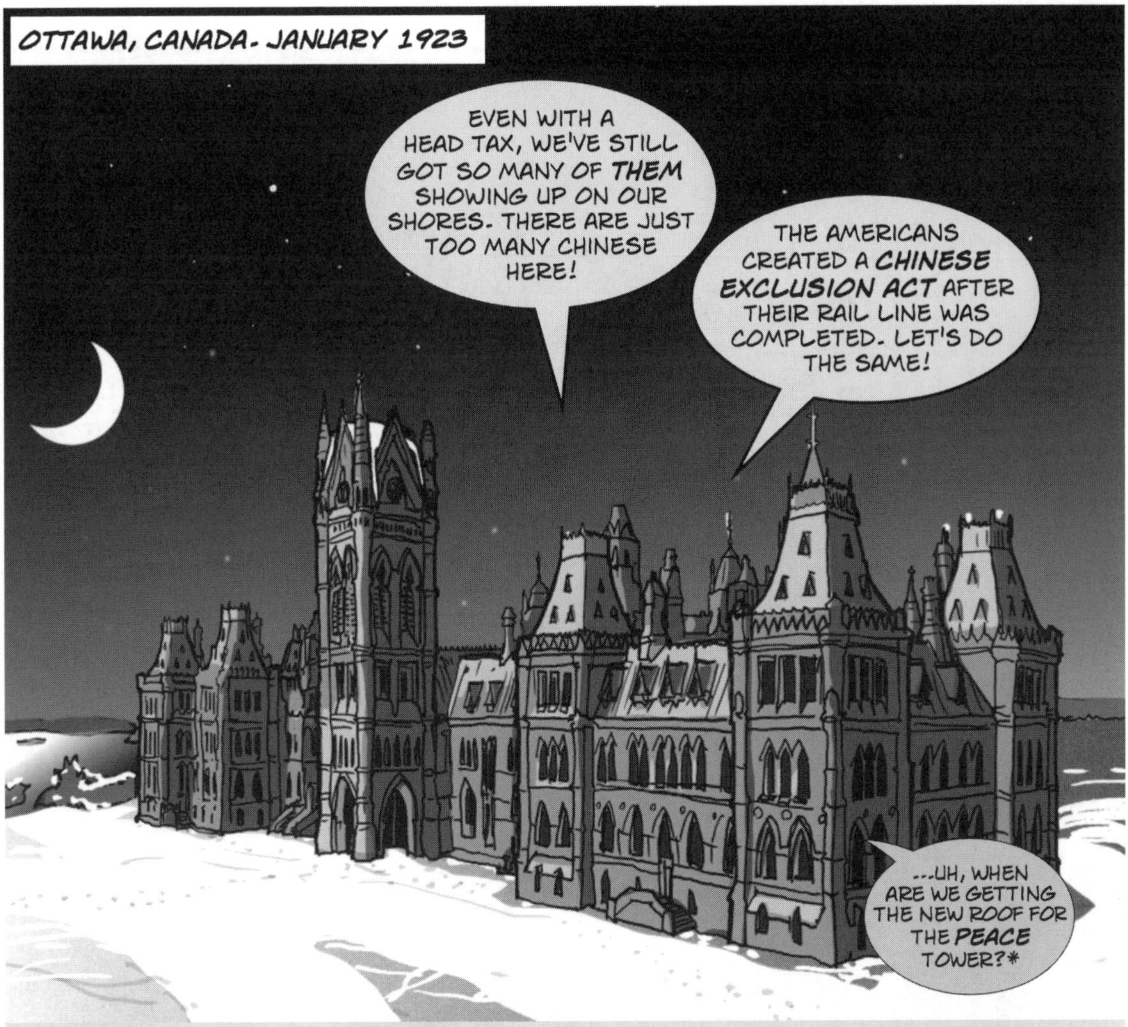
OTTAWA, CANADA. JANUARY 1923
EVEN WITH A HEAD TAX, WE'VE STILL GOT SO MANY OF *THEM* SHOWING UP ON OUR SHORES. THERE ARE JUST TOO MANY CHINESE HERE!
THE AMERICANS CREATED A **CHINESE EXCLUSION ACT** AFTER THEIR RAIL LINE WAS COMPLETED. LET'S DO THE SAME!
...UH, WHEN ARE WE GETTING THE NEW ROOF FOR THE *PEACE* TOWER?*

* CANADA'S PARLIAMENT BUILDING HAD CAUGHT FIRE IN 1916, DESTROYING THE CENTER BLOCK. THE NEW BUILDING WAS COMPLETED BY 1922, BUT THE TOWER WAS FINISHED LATER IN 1927.

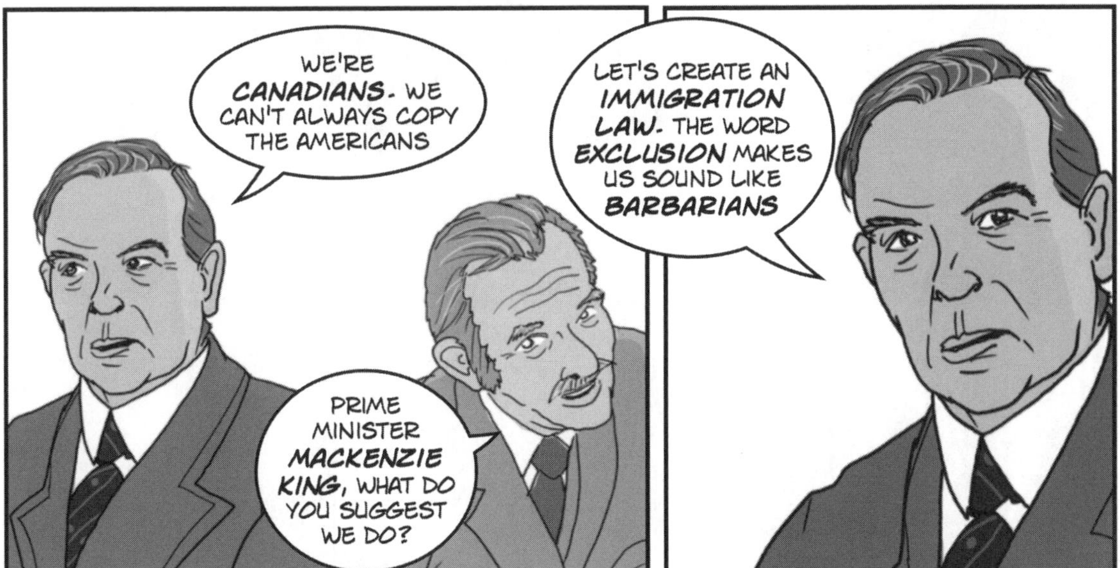
WE'RE **CANADIANS**. WE CAN'T ALWAYS COPY THE AMERICANS
PRIME MINISTER **MACKENZIE KING**, WHAT DO YOU SUGGEST WE DO?
LET'S CREATE AN **IMMIGRATION LAW**. THE WORD **EXCLUSION** MAKES US SOUND LIKE **BARBARIANS**

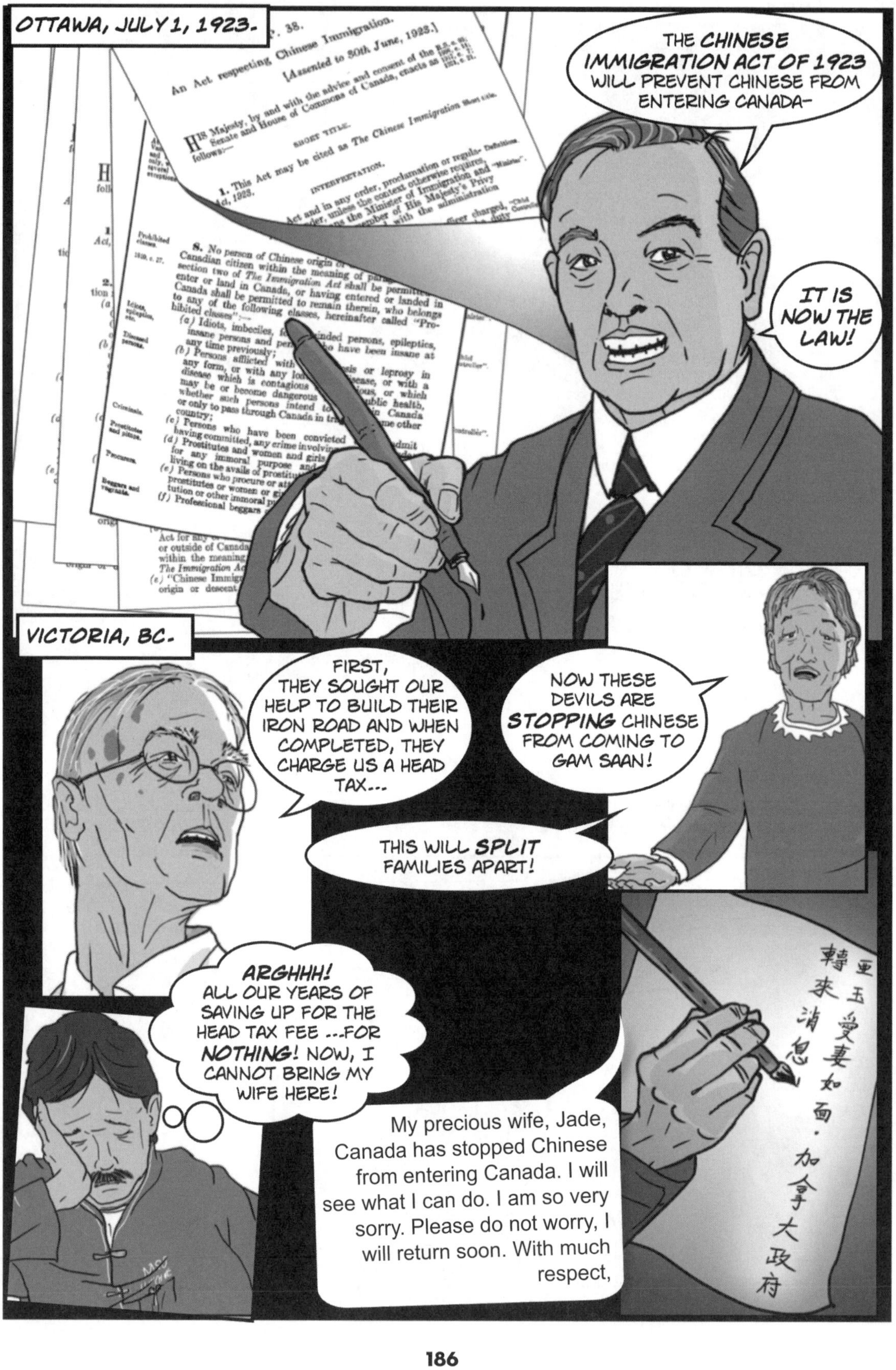
OTTAWA, JULY 1, 1923.
An Act respecting Chinese Immigration.
THE CHINESE IMMIGRATION ACT OF 1923 WILL PREVENT CHINESE FROM ENTERING CANADA–
IT IS NOW THE LAW!
VICTORIA, BC.
FIRST, THEY SOUGHT OUR HELP TO BUILD THEIR IRON ROAD AND WHEN COMPLETED, THEY CHARGE US A HEAD TAX...
NOW THESE DEVILS ARE STOPPING CHINESE FROM COMING TO GAM SAAN!
THIS WILL SPLIT FAMILIES APART!
ARGHHH! ALL OUR YEARS OF SAVING UP FOR THE HEAD TAX FEE ...FOR NOTHING! NOW, I CANNOT BRING MY WIFE HERE!
My precious wife, Jade, Canada has stopped Chinese from entering Canada. I will see what I can do. I am so very sorry. Please do not worry, I will return soon. With much respect,
亞玉 愛妻如面·加拿大政府
轉来消息

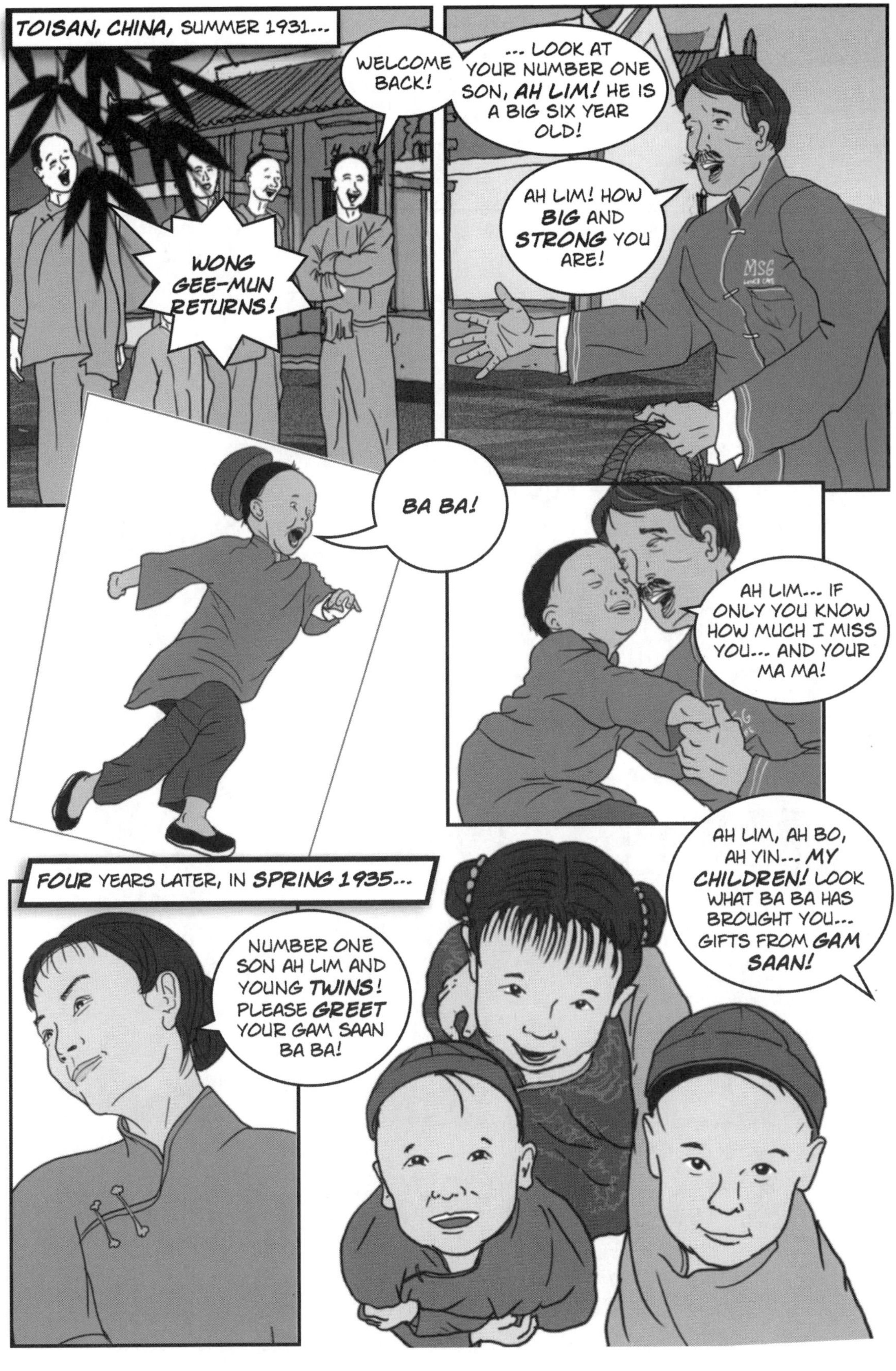
TOISAN, CHINA, SUMMER 1931...
WELCOME BACK!
... LOOK AT YOUR NUMBER ONE SON, AH LIM! HE IS A BIG SIX YEAR OLD!
WONG GEE-MUN RETURNS!
AH LIM! HOW BIG AND STRONG YOU ARE!
BA BA!
AH LIM... IF ONLY YOU KNOW HOW MUCH I MISS YOU... AND YOUR MA MA!
FOUR YEARS LATER, IN SPRING 1935...
NUMBER ONE SON AH LIM AND YOUNG TWINS! PLEASE GREET YOUR GAM SAAN BA BA!
AH LIM, AH BO, AH YIN... MY CHILDREN! LOOK WHAT BA BA HAS BROUGHT YOU... GIFTS FROM GAM SAAN!

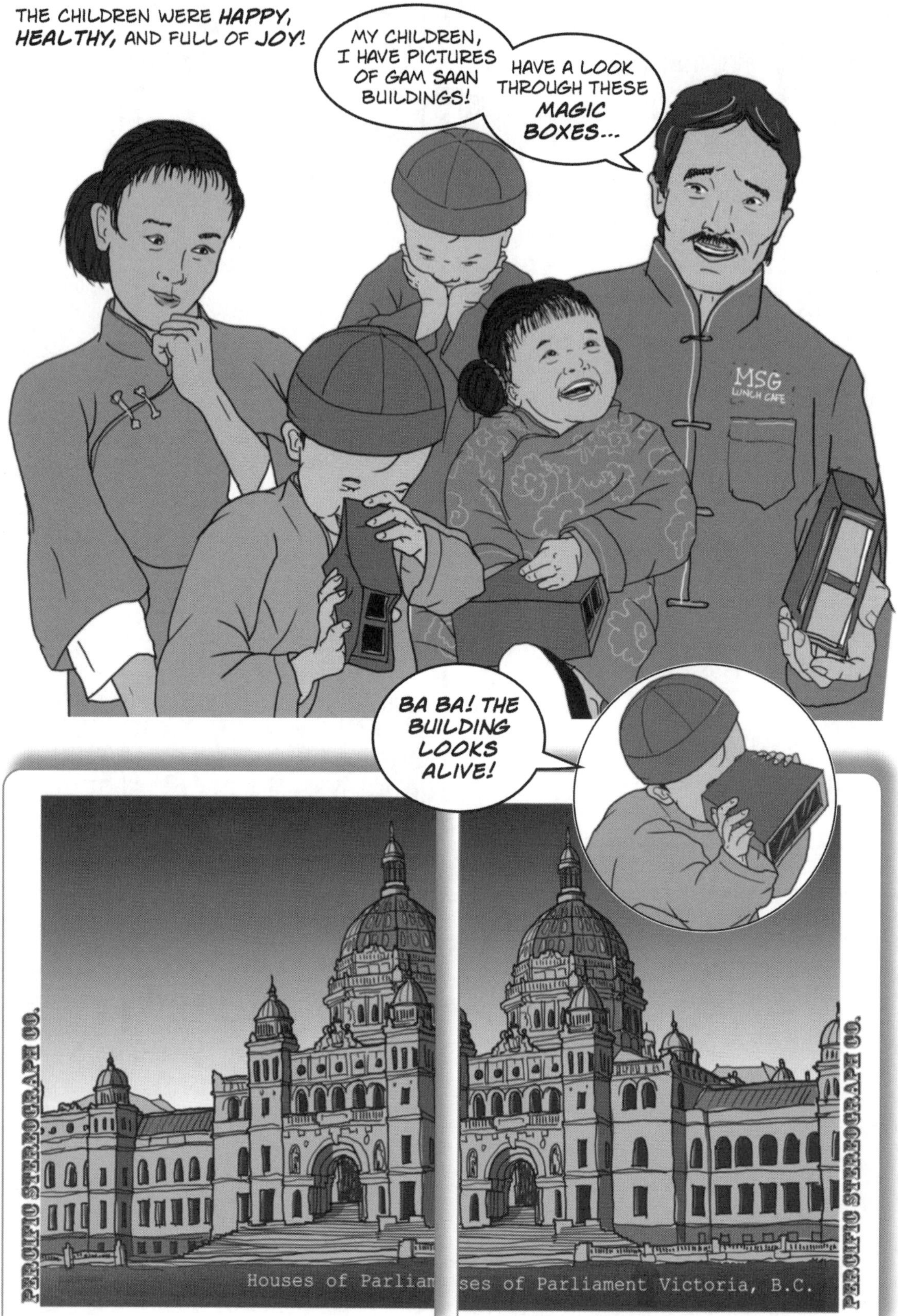
THE CHILDREN WERE HAPPY, HEALTHY, AND FULL OF JOY!
MY CHILDREN, I HAVE PICTURES OF GAM SAAN BUILDINGS!
HAVE A LOOK THROUGH THESE MAGIC BOXES...
MSG LUNCH CAFE
BA BA! THE BUILDING LOOKS ALIVE!
PACIFIC STEREOGRAPH CO.
Houses of Parliam ses of Parliament Victoria, B.C.
PACIFIC STEREOGRAPH CO.

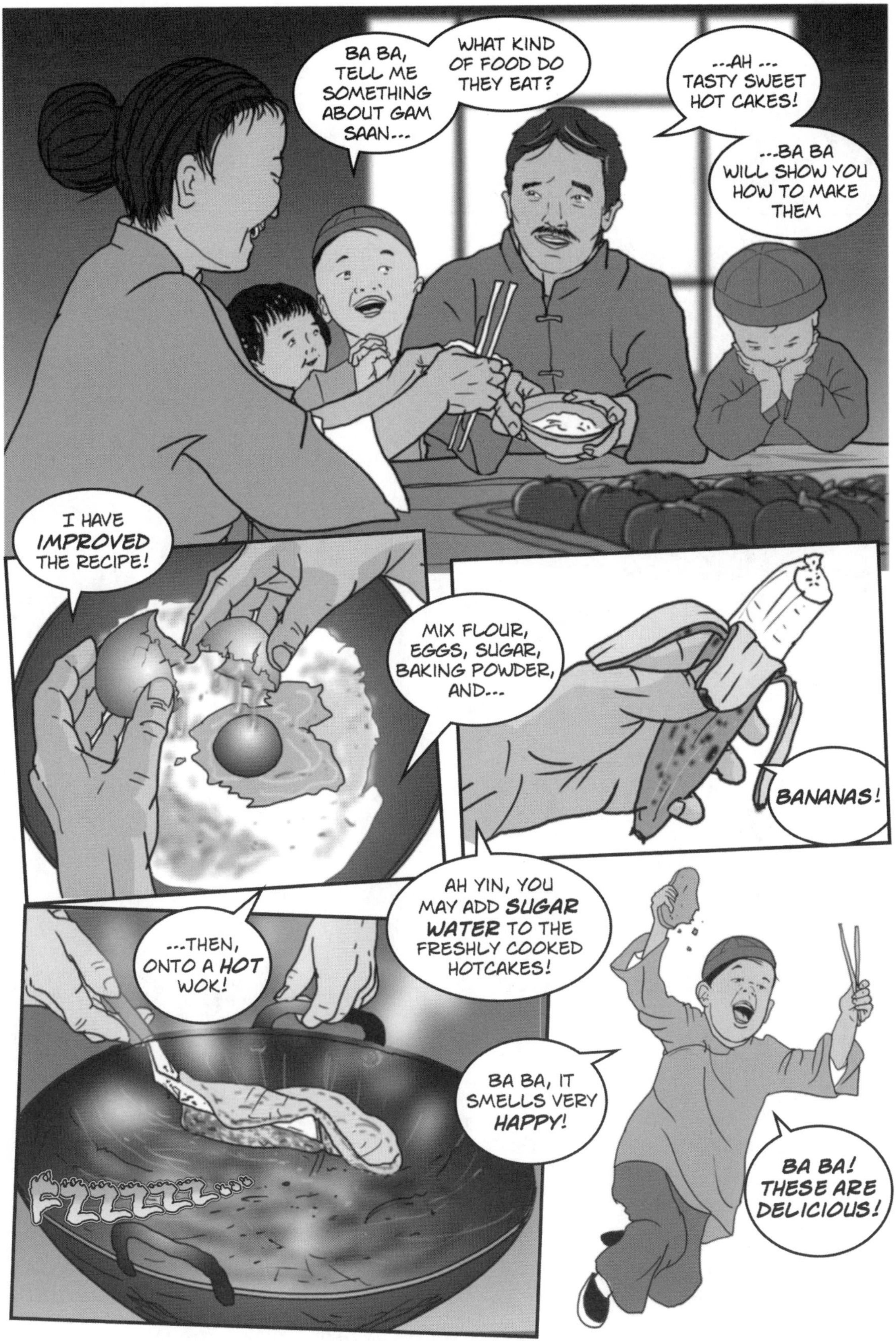
BA BA, TELL ME SOMETHING ABOUT GAM SAAN...
WHAT KIND OF FOOD DO THEY EAT?
...AH ... TASTY SWEET HOT CAKES!
...BA BA WILL SHOW YOU HOW TO MAKE THEM
I HAVE IMPROVED THE RECIPE!
MIX FLOUR, EGGS, SUGAR, BAKING POWDER, AND...
BANANAS!
...THEN, ONTO A HOT WOK!
AH YIN, YOU MAY ADD SUGAR WATER TO THE FRESHLY COOKED HOTCAKES!
FZZZZZ...
BA BA, IT SMELLS VERY HAPPY!
BA BA! THESE ARE DELICIOUS!

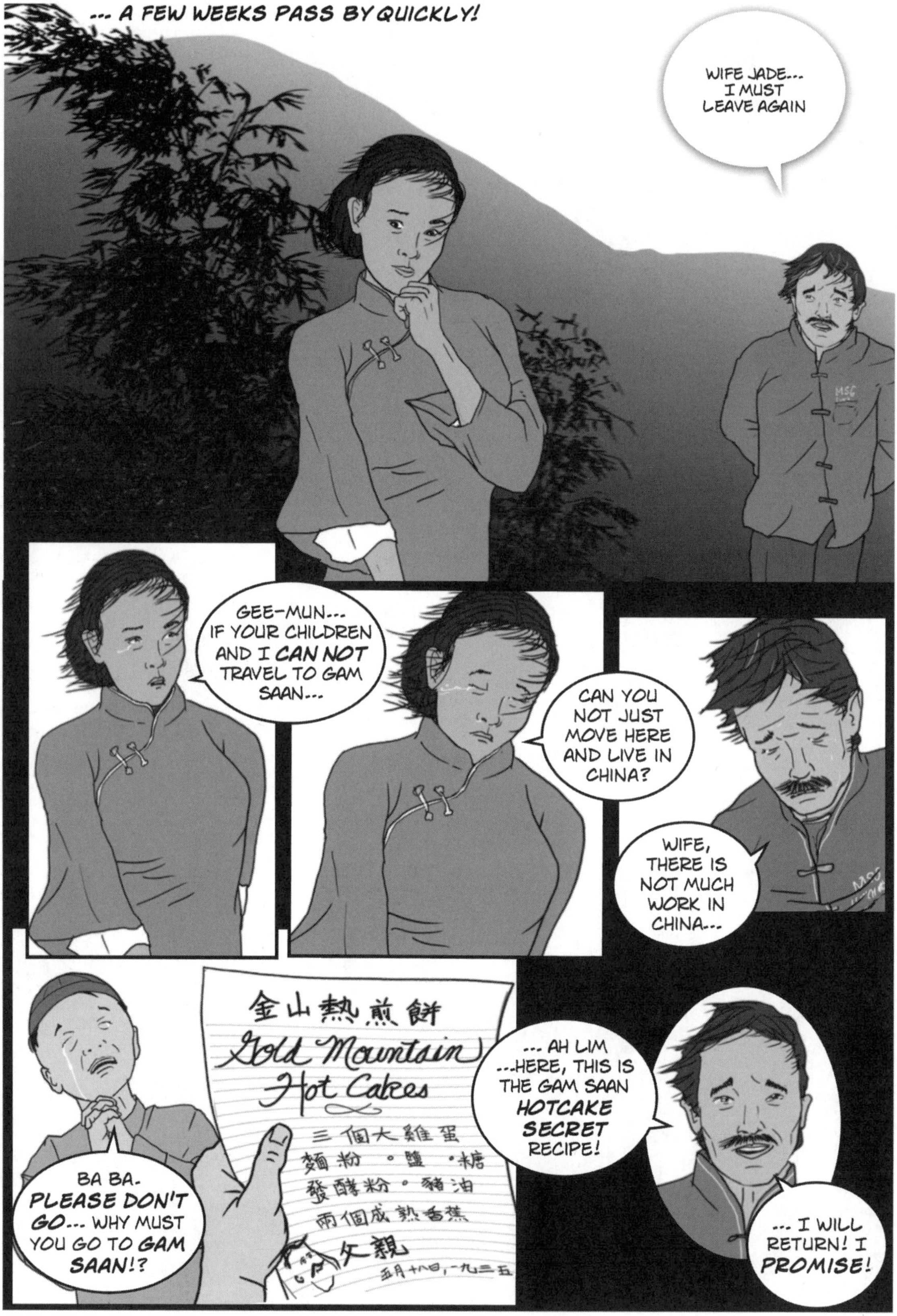
... A FEW WEEKS PASS BY QUICKLY!
WIFE JADE... I MUST LEAVE AGAIN
GEE-MUN... IF YOUR CHILDREN AND I **CAN NOT** TRAVEL TO GAM SAAN...
CAN YOU NOT JUST MOVE HERE AND LIVE IN CHINA?
WIFE, THERE IS NOT MUCH WORK IN CHINA...
BA BA. **PLEASE DON'T GO**... WHY MUST YOU GO TO **GAM SAAN**!?
金山熱煎餅
Gold Mountain Hot Cakes
三個大雞蛋
麵粉 ・鹽 ・糖
發酵粉・豬油
兩個成熟香蕉
父親
五月十八日,一九三五
... AH LIM ...HERE, THIS IS THE GAM SAAN **HOTCAKE SECRET** RECIPE!
... I WILL RETURN! I **PROMISE**!

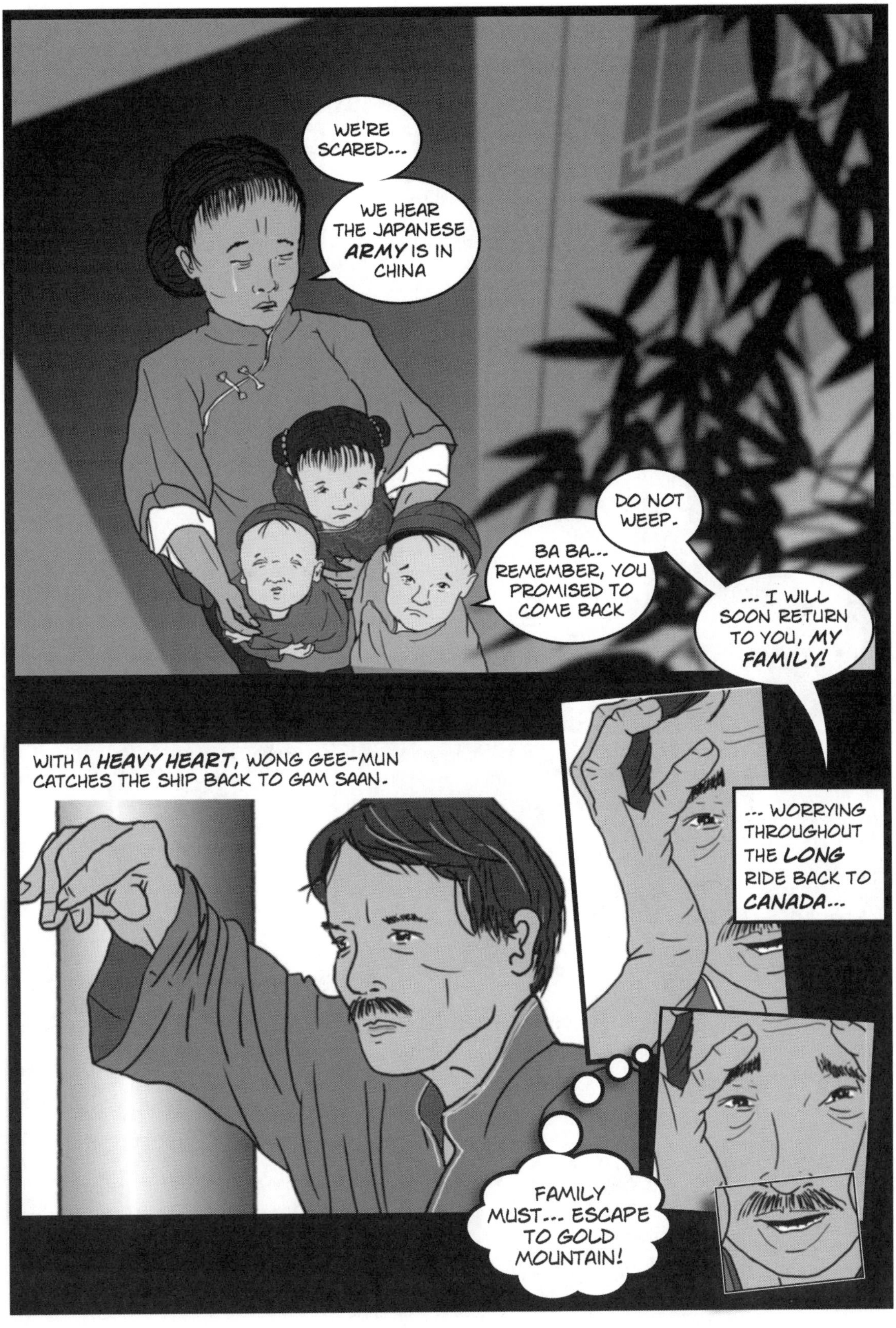
WE'RE SCARED...
WE HEAR THE JAPANESE ARMY IS IN CHINA
BA BA... REMEMBER, YOU PROMISED TO COME BACK
DO NOT WEEP.
... I WILL SOON RETURN TO YOU, MY FAMILY!
WITH A HEAVY HEART, WONG GEE-MUN CATCHES THE SHIP BACK TO GAM SAAN.
... WORRYING THROUGHOUT THE LONG RIDE BACK TO CANADA...
FAMILY MUST... ESCAPE TO GOLD MOUNTAIN!

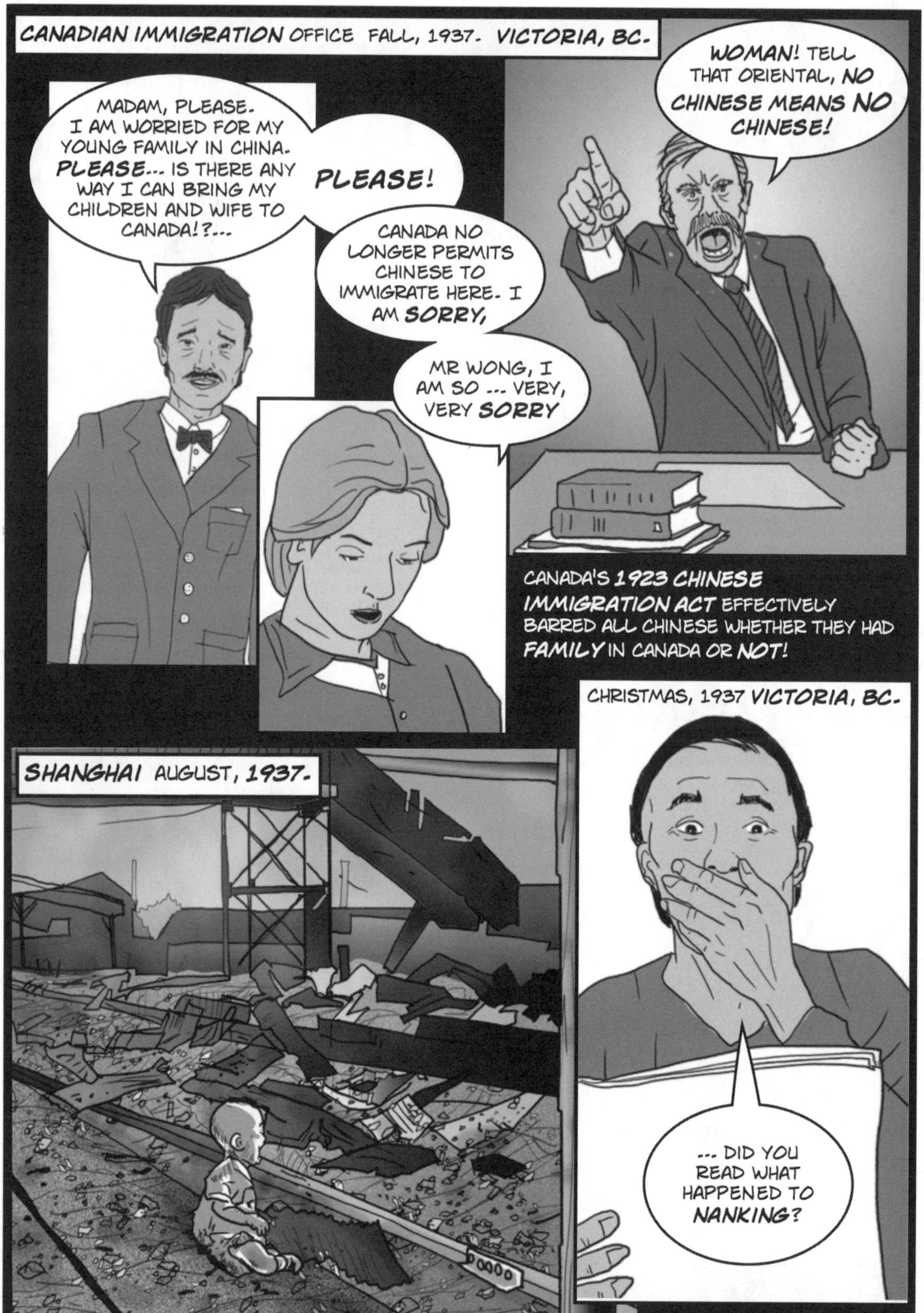
CANADIAN IMMIGRATION OFFICE FALL, 1937. VICTORIA, BC.
MADAM, PLEASE. I AM WORRIED FOR MY YOUNG FAMILY IN CHINA. PLEASE... IS THERE ANY WAY I CAN BRING MY CHILDREN AND WIFE TO CANADA!?...
PLEASE!
CANADA NO LONGER PERMITS CHINESE TO IMMIGRATE HERE. I AM SORRY,
MR WONG, I AM SO ... VERY, VERY SORRY
WOMAN! TELL THAT ORIENTAL, NO CHINESE MEANS NO CHINESE!
CANADA'S 1923 CHINESE IMMIGRATION ACT EFFECTIVELY BARRED ALL CHINESE WHETHER THEY HAD FAMILY IN CANADA OR NOT!
SHANGHAI AUGUST, 1937.
CHRISTMAS, 1937 VICTORIA, BC.
... DID YOU READ WHAT HAPPENED TO NANKING?

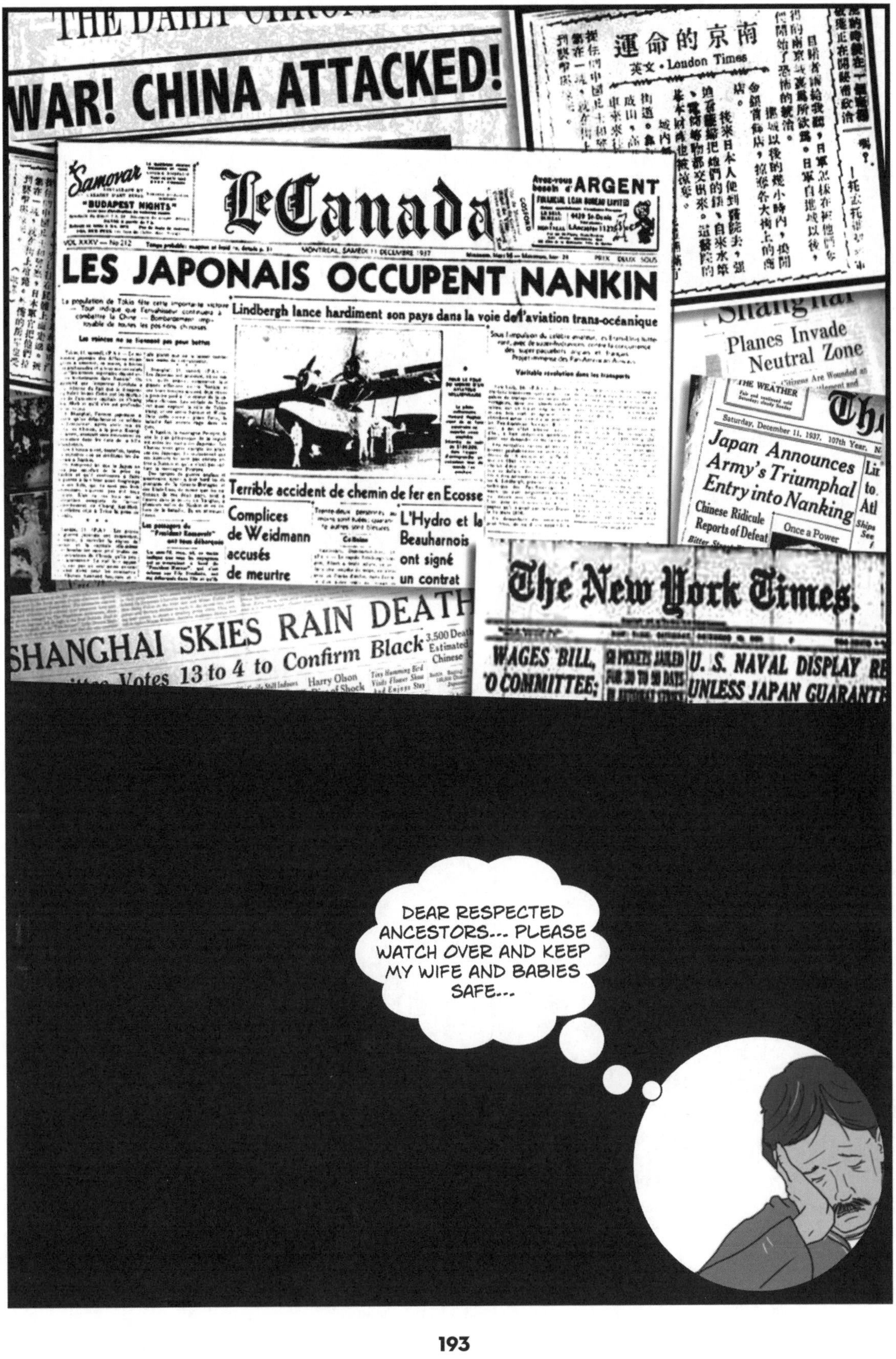
WAR! CHINA ATTACKED!
南京的命運
英文 • London Times
Samovar
"BUDAPEST NIGHTS"
Le Canada
ARGENT
LES JAPONAIS OCCUPENT NANKIN
Lindbergh lance hardiment son pays dans la voie de l'aviation trans-océanique
Terrible accident de chemin de fer en Ecosse
Complices de Weidmann accusés de meurtre
L'Hydro et la Beauharnois ont signé un contrat
Planes Invade Neutral Zone
THE WEATHER
Saturday, December 11, 1937. 107th Year.
Japan Announces Army's Triumphal Entry into Nanking
Chinese Ridicule Reports of Defeat
Once a Power
SHANGHAI SKIES RAIN DEATH
13 to 4 to Confirm Black
The New York Times
WAGES BILL
U. S. NAVAL DISPLAY
DEAR RESPECTED ANCESTORS... PLEASE WATCH OVER AND KEEP MY WIFE AND BABIES SAFE...

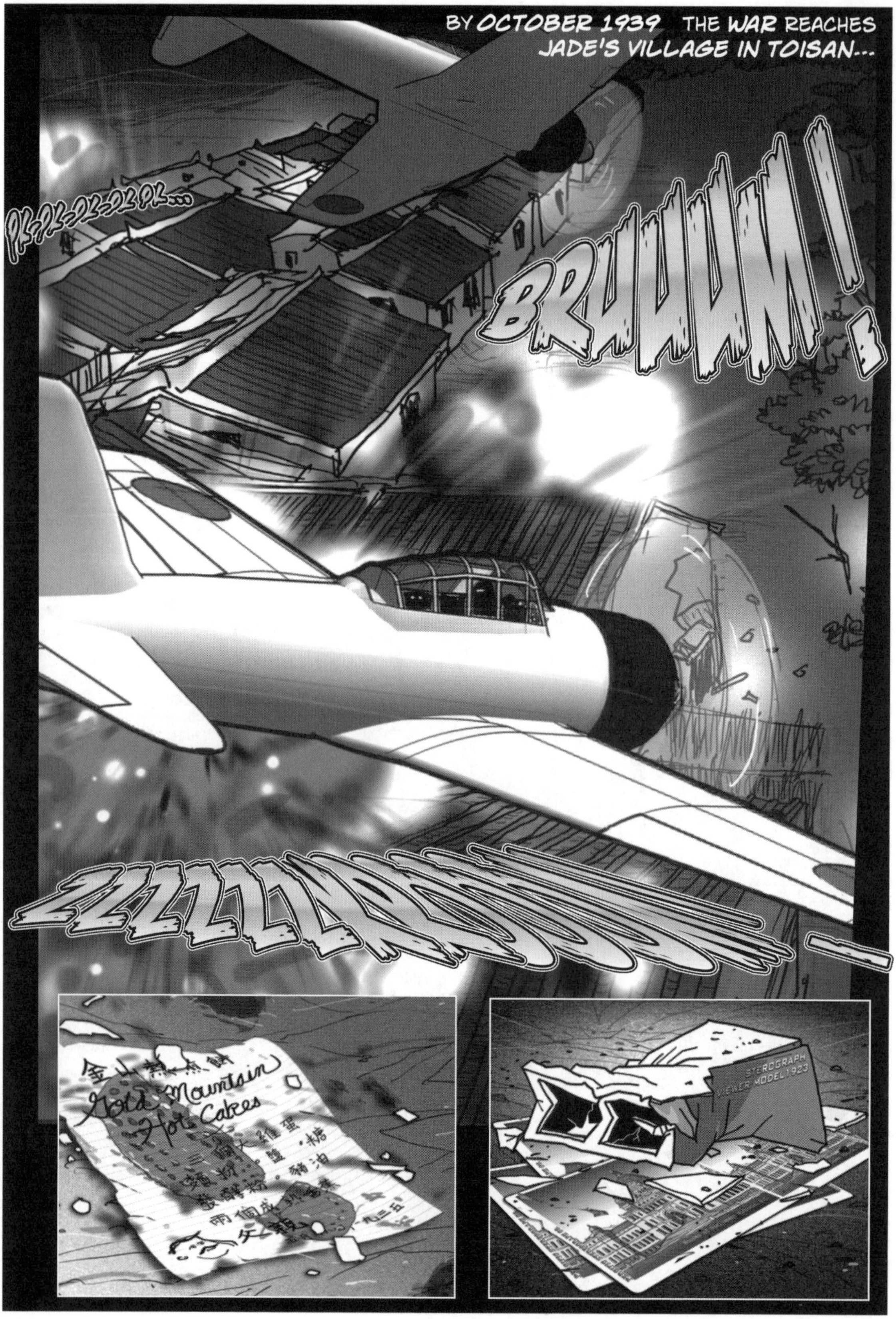
BY OCTOBER 1939 THE WAR REACHES JADE'S VILLAGE IN TOISAN...
BRUUUM!
Gold Mountain Hot Cakes
STEROGRAPH VIEWER MODEL 1923

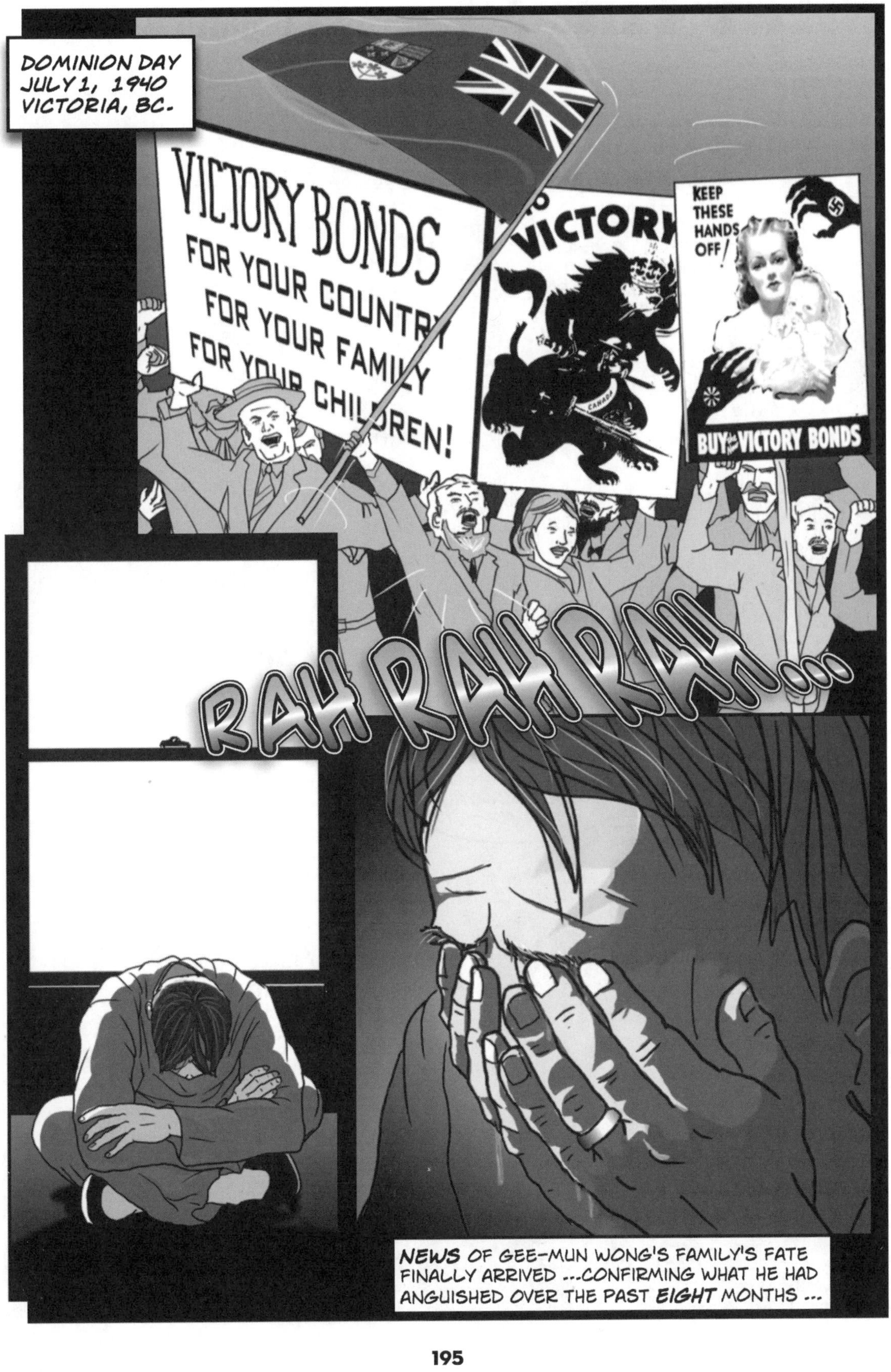
DOMINION DAY
JULY 1, 1940
VICTORIA, BC.
VICTORY BONDS
FOR YOUR COUNTRY
FOR YOUR FAMILY
FOR YOUR CHILDREN!
VICTORY
KEEP THESE HANDS OFF!
BUY VICTORY BONDS
RAH RAH RAH...
NEWS OF GEE-MUN WONG'S FAMILY'S FATE FINALLY ARRIVED ...CONFIRMING WHAT HE HAD ANGUISHED OVER THE PAST EIGHT MONTHS ...

CHAPTER 18 Earning Dignity & Respect

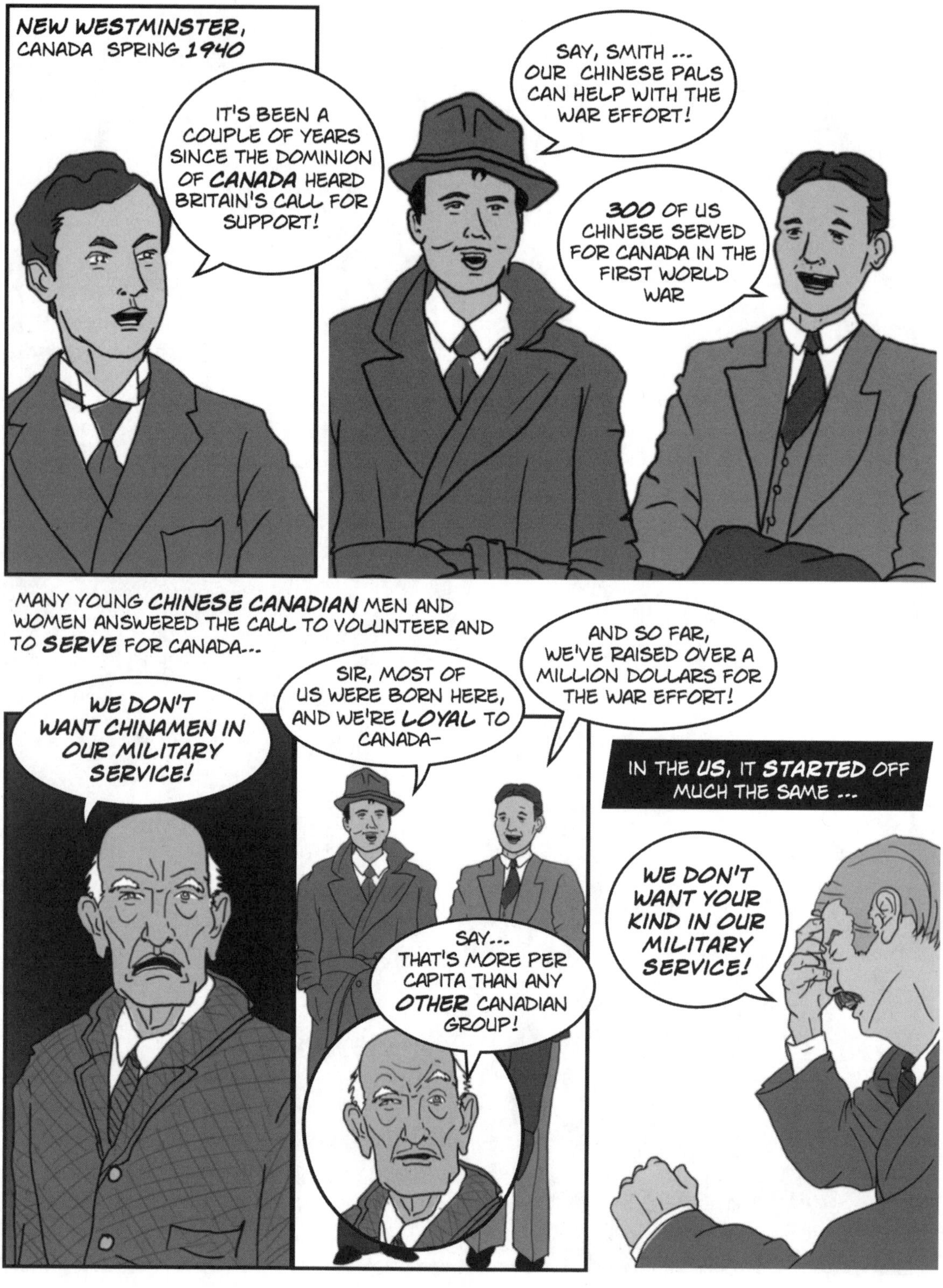
NEW WESTMINSTER, CANADA SPRING 1940
IT'S BEEN A COUPLE OF YEARS SINCE THE DOMINION OF CANADA HEARD BRITAIN'S CALL FOR SUPPORT!
SAY, SMITH ... OUR CHINESE PALS CAN HELP WITH THE WAR EFFORT!
300 OF US CHINESE SERVED FOR CANADA IN THE FIRST WORLD WAR
MANY YOUNG CHINESE CANADIAN MEN AND WOMEN ANSWERED THE CALL TO VOLUNTEER AND TO SERVE FOR CANADA...
WE DON'T WANT CHINAMEN IN OUR MILITARY SERVICE!
SIR, MOST OF US WERE BORN HERE, AND WE'RE LOYAL TO CANADA-
AND SO FAR, WE'VE RAISED OVER A MILLION DOLLARS FOR THE WAR EFFORT!
SAY... THAT'S MORE PER CAPITA THAN ANY OTHER CANADIAN GROUP!
IN THE US, IT STARTED OFF MUCH THE SAME ...
WE DON'T WANT YOUR KIND IN OUR MILITARY SERVICE!

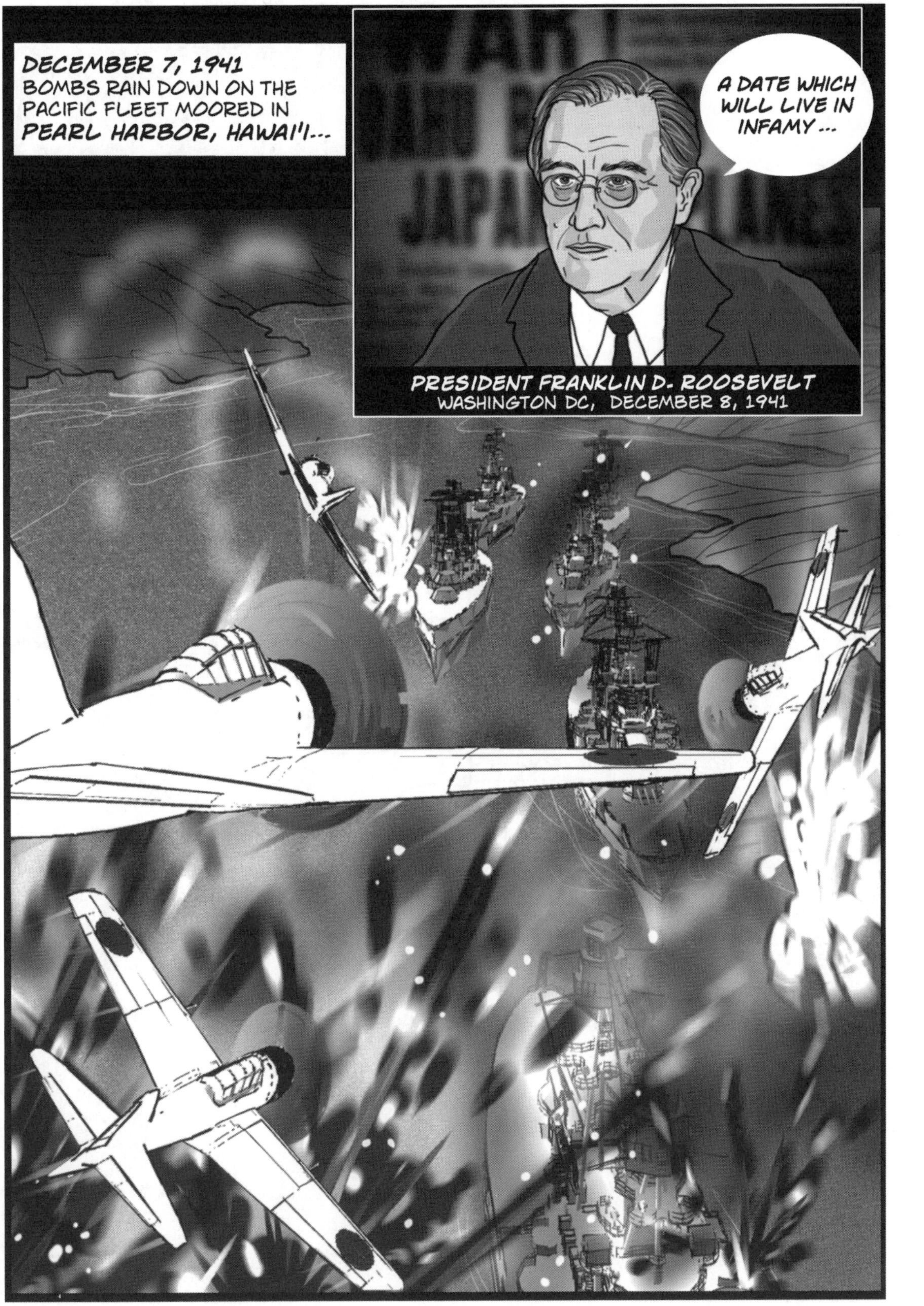
DECEMBER 7, 1941
BOMBS RAIN DOWN ON THE PACIFIC FLEET MOORED IN PEARL HARBOR, HAWAI'I...
A DATE WHICH WILL LIVE IN INFAMY ...
PRESIDENT FRANKLIN D. ROOSEVELT
WASHINGTON DC, DECEMBER 8, 1941

ALMOST A CENTURY OF INSULT AND VIOLENCE TARGETING THE **HEATHEN CHINESE** GAVE WAY TO A NEW SHARED GOAL AT HOME AND ABROAD —TO FIGHT THE JAPANESE IMPERIAL ARMY.

SIR, MOST OF THE **CHINESE** IN AMERICA ARE WITHOUT DEPENDENTS

---THEY'RE THE RIGHT AGE AND CATEGORY FOR COMBAT

GOOD. ENLIST THEM, OR DRAFT THEM!

NEARLY ONE IN FOUR CHINESE HAVE JOINED*

HELP CHINA!

CHINA IS HELPING US UNITED CHINA RELIEF

* 13,499 OR 22% OF ALL CHINESE MALES IN AMERICA JOINED THE US ARMED FORCES.

BUT IN CANADA---

MUST **CANADIANS** ALWAYS COPY WHAT THE AMERICANS DO?

IN SPRING 1942, VERN'S SON, **FRANK WONG,** WANTED TO SERVE FOR CANADA.

WHAT!? I **FAILED** MY MEDICAL?

WHAT'D YOU EXPECT? YOU'RE **CHINESE!**

--- WE GOT **REJECTED** TOO!

GARY LEE GOT **REJECTED** ... SO HE SIGNED UP FOR **BRITAIN**

LOST YEARS

198

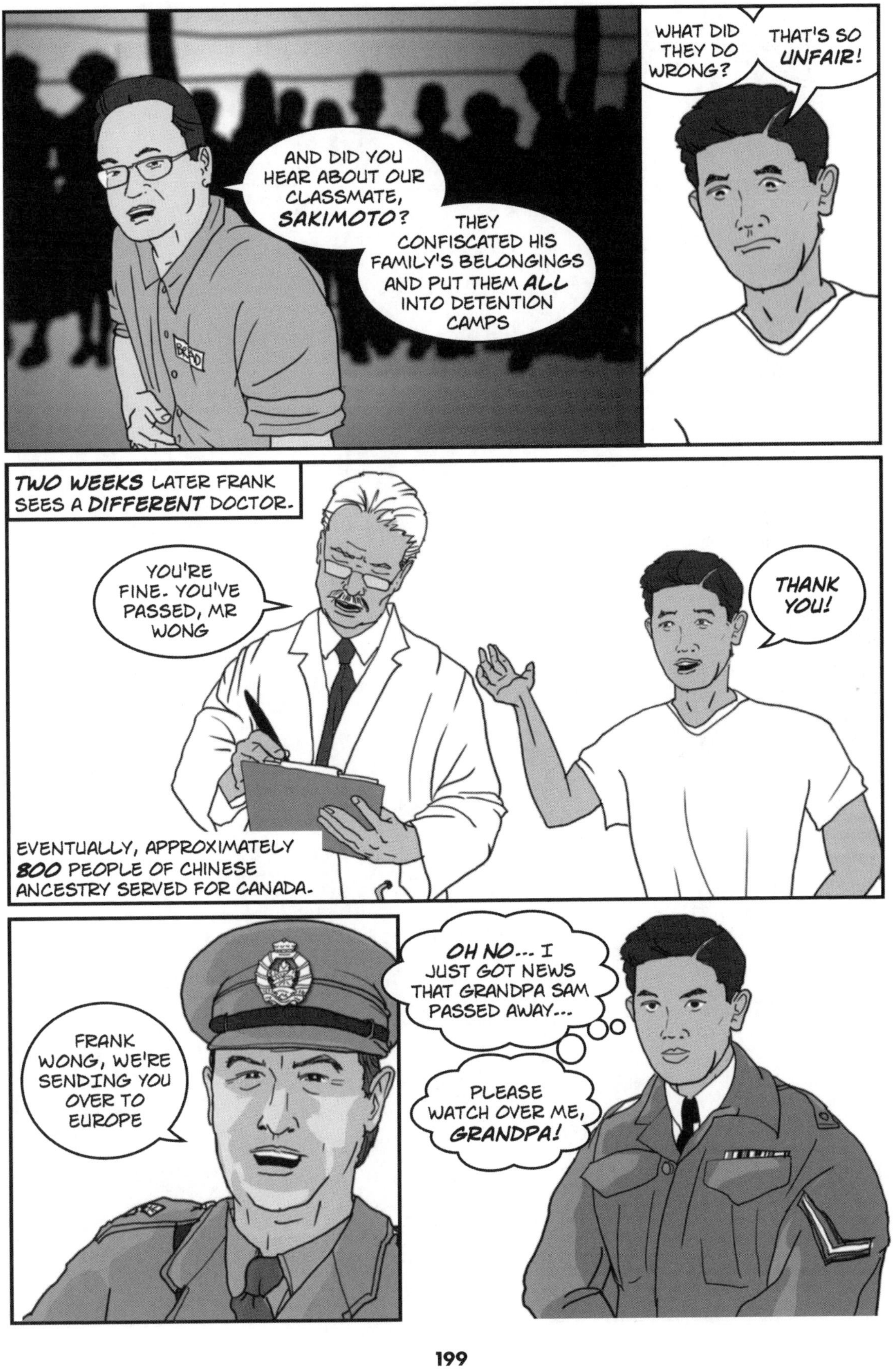
AND DID YOU HEAR ABOUT OUR CLASSMATE, **SAKIMOTO**?
THEY CONFISCATED HIS FAMILY'S BELONGINGS AND PUT THEM **ALL** INTO DETENTION CAMPS
BRAD
WHAT DID THEY DO WRONG?
THAT'S SO **UNFAIR!**
TWO WEEKS LATER FRANK SEES A **DIFFERENT** DOCTOR.
YOU'RE FINE. YOU'VE PASSED, MR WONG
THANK YOU!
EVENTUALLY, APPROXIMATELY **800** PEOPLE OF CHINESE ANCESTRY SERVED FOR CANADA.
FRANK WONG, WE'RE SENDING YOU OVER TO EUROPE
OH NO... I JUST GOT NEWS THAT GRANDPA SAM PASSED AWAY...
PLEASE WATCH OVER ME, **GRANDPA!**

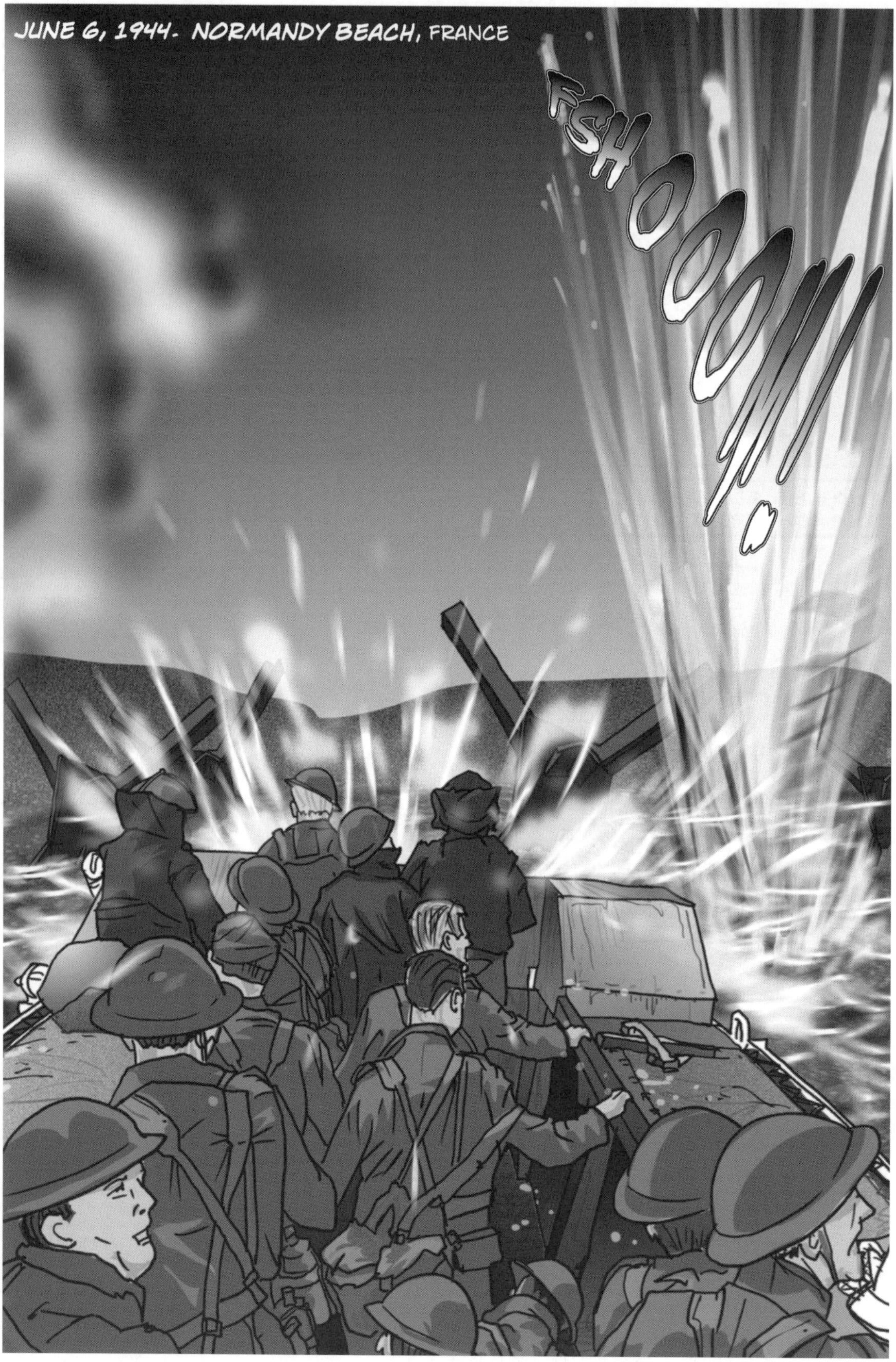
JUNE 6, 1944. NORMANDY BEACH, FRANCE
FSHOOOM!!

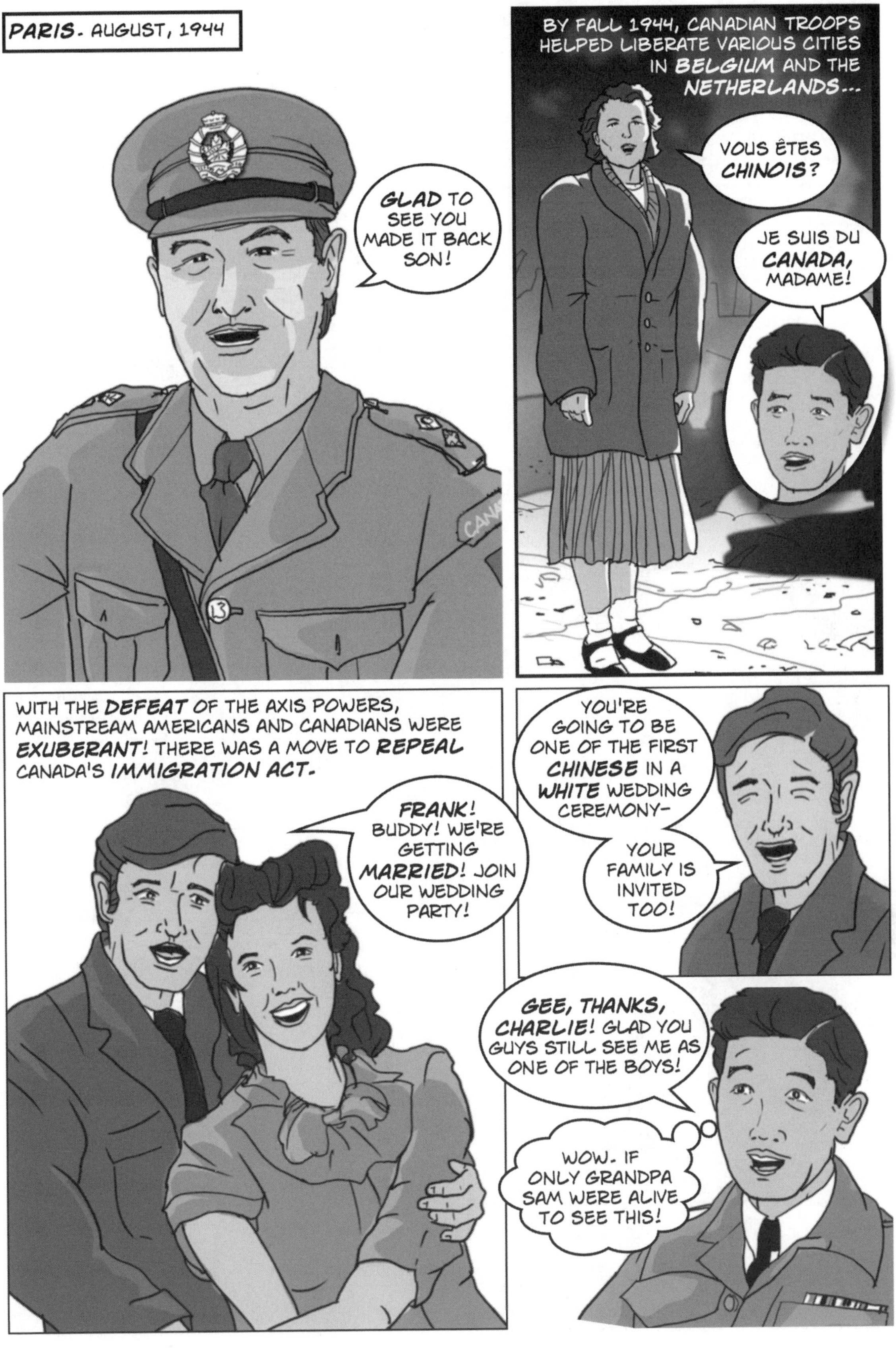
PARIS- AUGUST, 1944
GLAD TO SEE YOU MADE IT BACK SON!
BY FALL 1944, CANADIAN TROOPS HELPED LIBERATE VARIOUS CITIES IN BELGIUM AND THE NETHERLANDS...
VOUS ÊTES CHINOIS?
JE SUIS DU CANADA, MADAME!
WITH THE DEFEAT OF THE AXIS POWERS, MAINSTREAM AMERICANS AND CANADIANS WERE EXUBERANT! THERE WAS A MOVE TO REPEAL CANADA'S IMMIGRATION ACT.
FRANK! BUDDY! WE'RE GETTING MARRIED! JOIN OUR WEDDING PARTY!
YOU'RE GOING TO BE ONE OF THE FIRST CHINESE IN A WHITE WEDDING CEREMONY-
YOUR FAMILY IS INVITED TOO!
GEE, THANKS, CHARLIE! GLAD YOU GUYS STILL SEE ME AS ONE OF THE BOYS!
WOW. IF ONLY GRANDPA SAM WERE ALIVE TO SEE THIS!

CHAPTER 19 Blossoming Influence

AS AMERICA'S AND CANADA'S CHINESE MEN SERVE THEIR RESPECTIVE COUNTRIES, THE ***WOMEN*** OF GAM SAAN WERE ADVANCING THEIR ROLE IN SOCIETY!

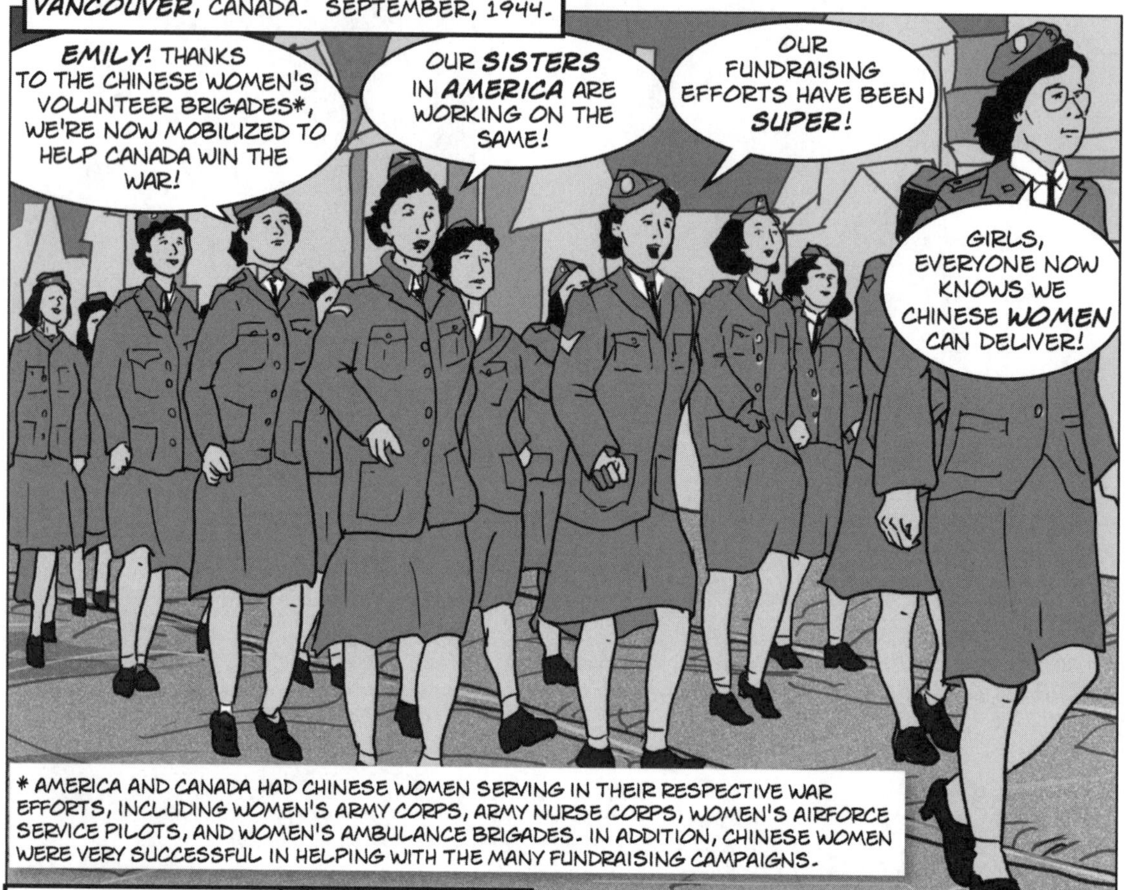
VANCOUVER, CANADA. SEPTEMBER, 1944.
EMILY! THANKS TO THE CHINESE WOMEN'S VOLUNTEER BRIGADES*, WE'RE NOW MOBILIZED TO HELP CANADA WIN THE WAR!
OUR SISTERS IN AMERICA ARE WORKING ON THE SAME!
OUR FUNDRAISING EFFORTS HAVE BEEN SUPER!
GIRLS, EVERYONE NOW KNOWS WE CHINESE WOMEN CAN DELIVER!
* AMERICA AND CANADA HAD CHINESE WOMEN SERVING IN THEIR RESPECTIVE WAR EFFORTS, INCLUDING WOMEN'S ARMY CORPS, ARMY NURSE CORPS, WOMEN'S AIRFORCE SERVICE PILOTS, AND WOMEN'S AMBULANCE BRIGADES. IN ADDITION, CHINESE WOMEN WERE VERY SUCCESSFUL IN HELPING WITH THE MANY FUNDRAISING CAMPAIGNS.

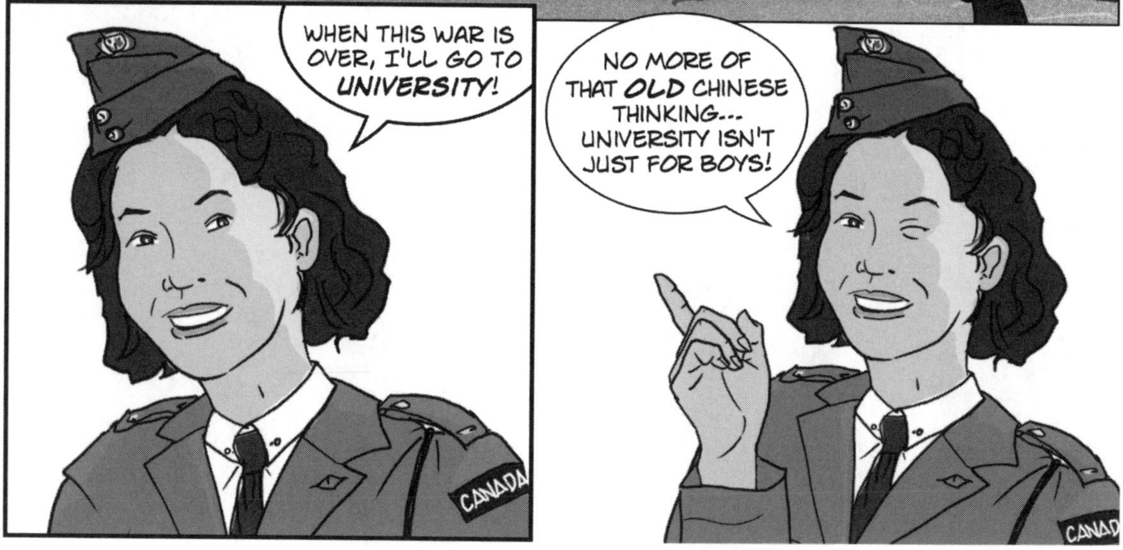
WHEN THIS WAR IS OVER, I'LL GO TO UNIVERSITY!
CANADA
NO MORE OF THAT OLD CHINESE THINKING... UNIVERSITY ISN'T JUST FOR BOYS!

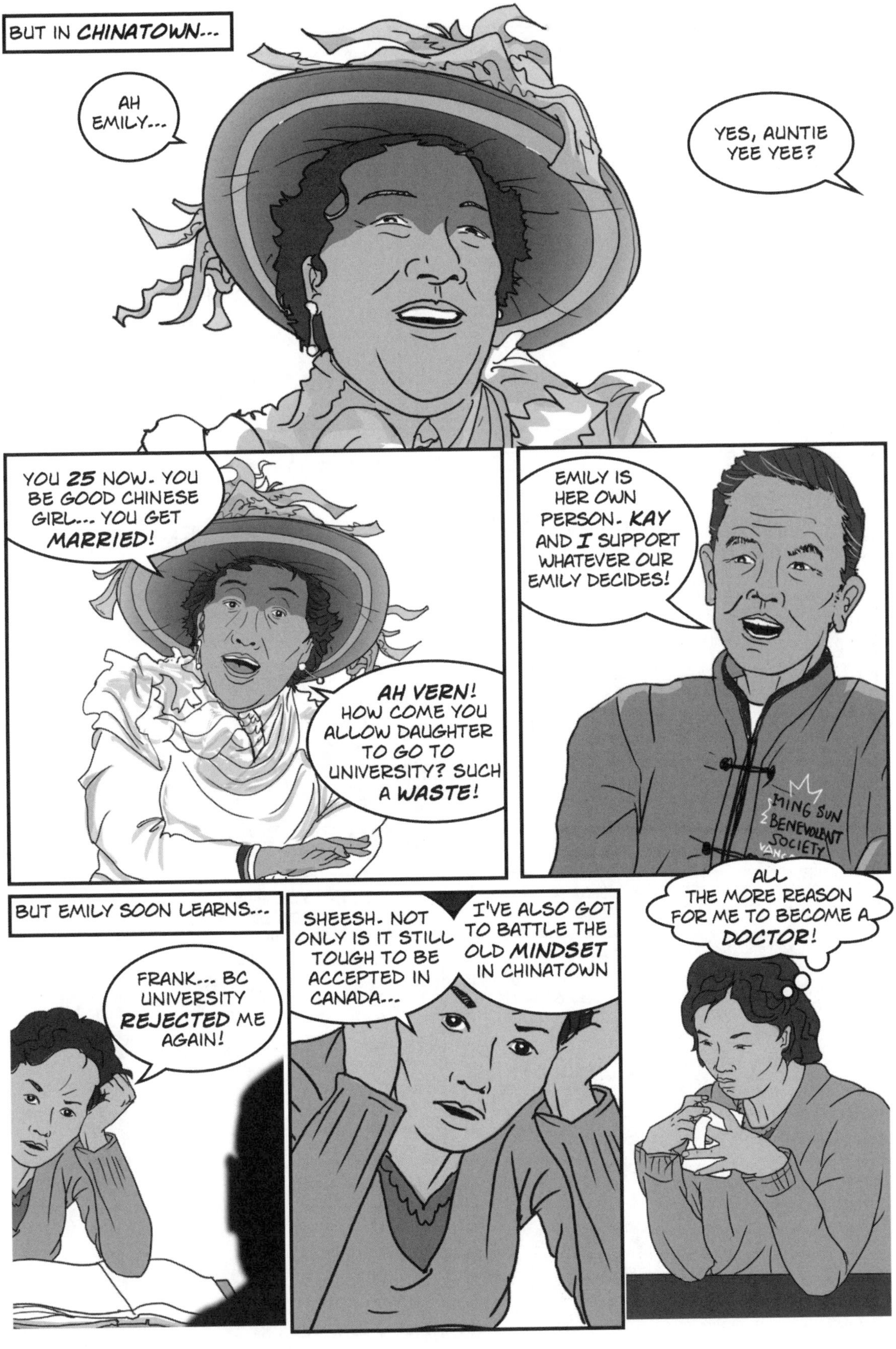
BUT IN CHINATOWN...
AH EMILY...
YES, AUNTIE YEE YEE?
YOU 25 NOW. YOU BE GOOD CHINESE GIRL... YOU GET MARRIED!
AH VERN! HOW COME YOU ALLOW DAUGHTER TO GO TO UNIVERSITY? SUCH A WASTE!
EMILY IS HER OWN PERSON. KAY AND I SUPPORT WHATEVER OUR EMILY DECIDES!
MING SUN BENEVOLENT SOCIETY
BUT EMILY SOON LEARNS...
FRANK... BC UNIVERSITY REJECTED ME AGAIN!
SHEESH. NOT ONLY IS IT STILL TOUGH TO BE ACCEPTED IN CANADA...
I'VE ALSO GOT TO BATTLE THE OLD MINDSET IN CHINATOWN
ALL THE MORE REASON FOR ME TO BECOME A DOCTOR!

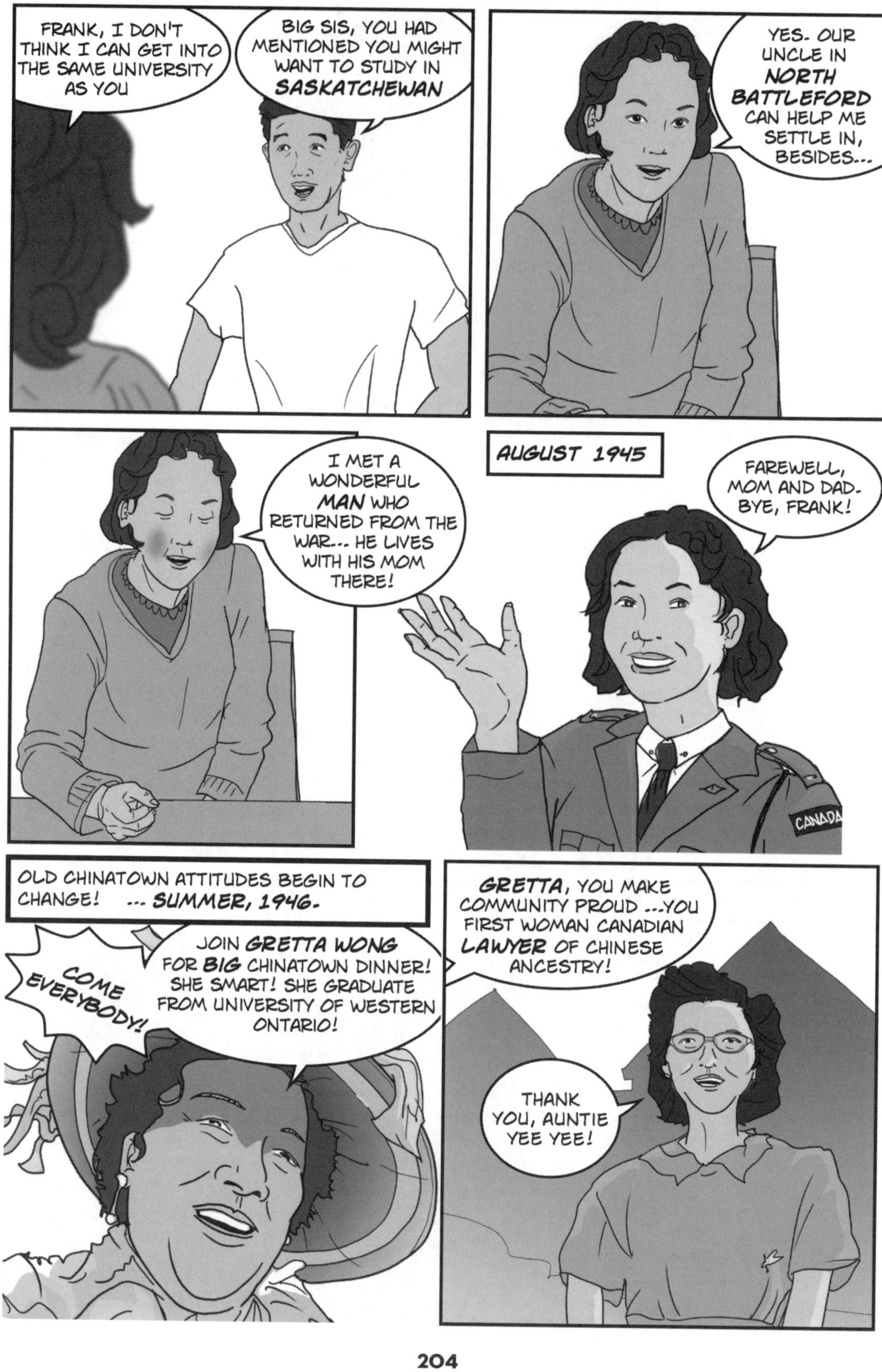
FRANK, I DON'T THINK I CAN GET INTO THE SAME UNIVERSITY AS YOU
BIG SIS, YOU HAD MENTIONED YOU MIGHT WANT TO STUDY IN SASKATCHEWAN
YES. OUR UNCLE IN NORTH BATTLEFORD CAN HELP ME SETTLE IN, BESIDES...
I MET A WONDERFUL MAN WHO RETURNED FROM THE WAR... HE LIVES WITH HIS MOM THERE!
AUGUST 1945
FAREWELL, MOM AND DAD. BYE, FRANK!
CANADA
OLD CHINATOWN ATTITUDES BEGIN TO CHANGE! ... SUMMER, 1946.
COME EVERYBODY!
JOIN GRETTA WONG FOR BIG CHINATOWN DINNER! SHE SMART! SHE GRADUATE FROM UNIVERSITY OF WESTERN ONTARIO!
GRETTA, YOU MAKE COMMUNITY PROUD ...YOU FIRST WOMAN CANADIAN LAWYER OF CHINESE ANCESTRY!
THANK YOU, AUNTIE YEE YEE!

AMERICA'S CHINESE EXCLUSION ACT WAS FINALLY REPEALED WITH THE ***MAGNUSON ACT*** IN ***1943***. BUT IT TOOK ANOTHER FOUR YEARS BEFORE CANADA'S CHINESE IMMIGRATION ACT WAS ALSO REPEALED IN ***1947***. SO, AFTER A ***QUARTER OF A CENTURY***, THE ***BAN*** ON CHINESE IMMIGRATION WOULD COME TO AN END (WELL, ALMOST)...

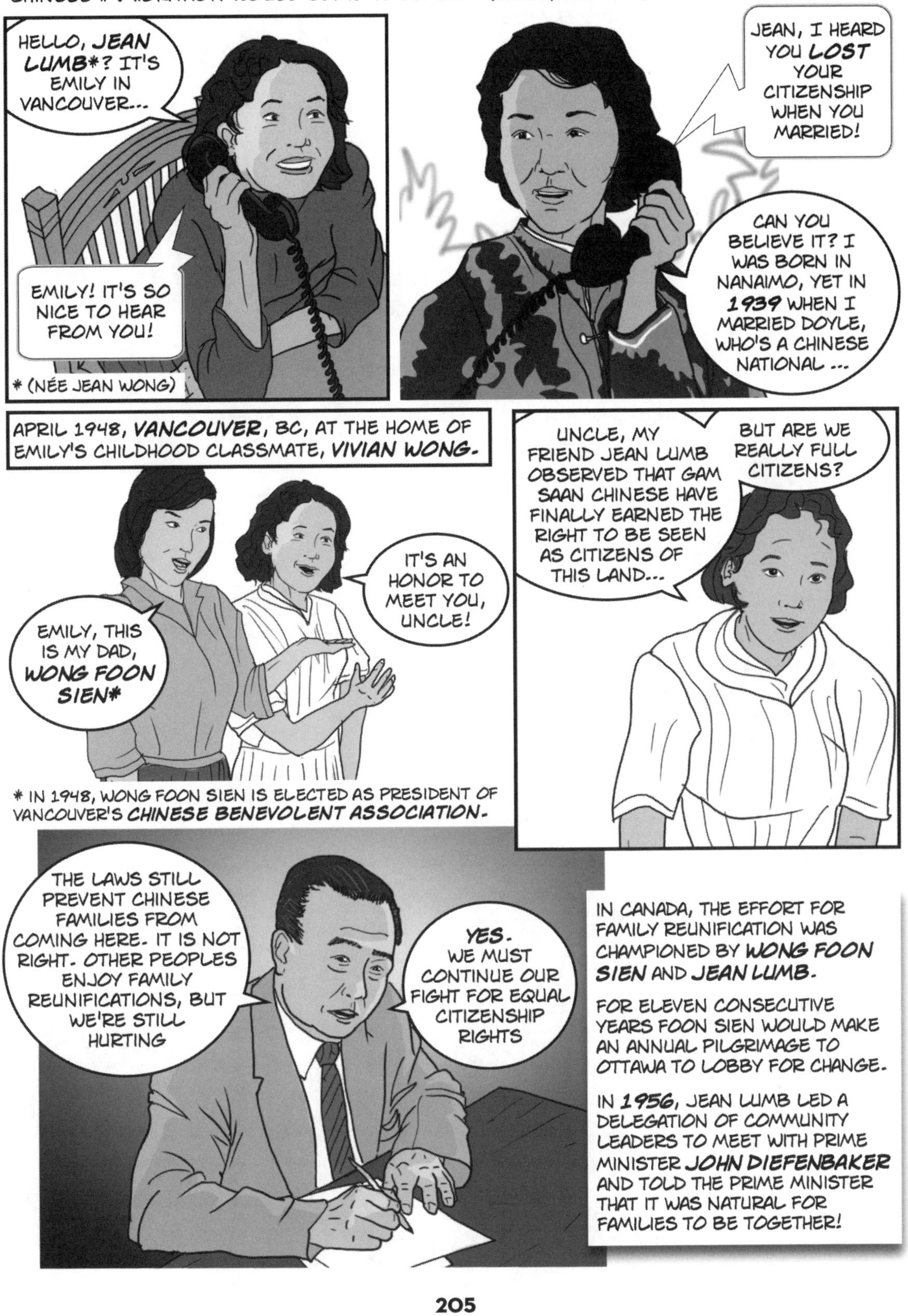
HELLO, JEAN LUMB*? IT'S EMILY IN VANCOUVER...
EMILY! IT'S SO NICE TO HEAR FROM YOU!
* (NÉE JEAN WONG)
JEAN, I HEARD YOU LOST YOUR CITIZENSHIP WHEN YOU MARRIED!
CAN YOU BELIEVE IT? I WAS BORN IN NANAIMO, YET IN 1939 WHEN I MARRIED DOYLE, WHO'S A CHINESE NATIONAL ...
APRIL 1948, VANCOUVER, BC, AT THE HOME OF EMILY'S CHILDHOOD CLASSMATE, VIVIAN WONG.
EMILY, THIS IS MY DAD, WONG FOON SIEN*
IT'S AN HONOR TO MEET YOU, UNCLE!
* IN 1948, WONG FOON SIEN IS ELECTED AS PRESIDENT OF VANCOUVER'S CHINESE BENEVOLENT ASSOCIATION.
UNCLE, MY FRIEND JEAN LUMB OBSERVED THAT GAM SAAN CHINESE HAVE FINALLY EARNED THE RIGHT TO BE SEEN AS CITIZENS OF THIS LAND...
BUT ARE WE REALLY FULL CITIZENS?
THE LAWS STILL PREVENT CHINESE FAMILIES FROM COMING HERE. IT IS NOT RIGHT. OTHER PEOPLES ENJOY FAMILY REUNIFICATIONS, BUT WE'RE STILL HURTING
YES. WE MUST CONTINUE OUR FIGHT FOR EQUAL CITIZENSHIP RIGHTS
IN CANADA, THE EFFORT FOR FAMILY REUNIFICATION WAS CHAMPIONED BY WONG FOON SIEN AND JEAN LUMB.
FOR ELEVEN CONSECUTIVE YEARS FOON SIEN WOULD MAKE AN ANNUAL PILGRIMAGE TO OTTAWA TO LOBBY FOR CHANGE.
IN 1956, JEAN LUMB LED A DELEGATION OF COMMUNITY LEADERS TO MEET WITH PRIME MINISTER JOHN DIEFENBAKER AND TOLD THE PRIME MINISTER THAT IT WAS NATURAL FOR FAMILIES TO BE TOGETHER!

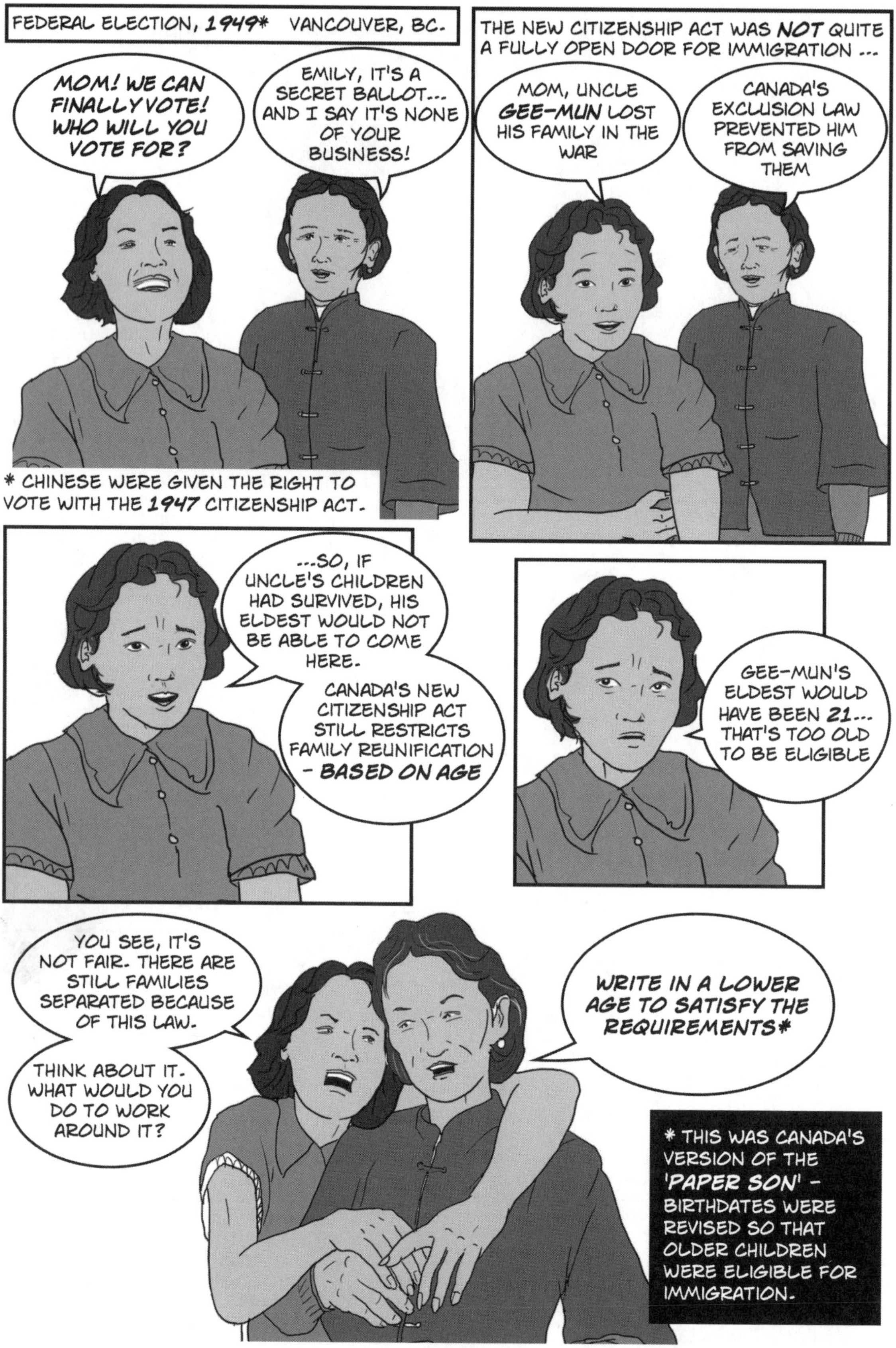
FEDERAL ELECTION, 1949* VANCOUVER, BC.
MOM! WE CAN FINALLY VOTE! WHO WILL YOU VOTE FOR?
EMILY, IT'S A SECRET BALLOT... AND I SAY IT'S NONE OF YOUR BUSINESS!
* CHINESE WERE GIVEN THE RIGHT TO VOTE WITH THE 1947 CITIZENSHIP ACT.
THE NEW CITIZENSHIP ACT WAS NOT QUITE A FULLY OPEN DOOR FOR IMMIGRATION ...
MOM, UNCLE GEE-MUN LOST HIS FAMILY IN THE WAR
CANADA'S EXCLUSION LAW PREVENTED HIM FROM SAVING THEM
...SO, IF UNCLE'S CHILDREN HAD SURVIVED, HIS ELDEST WOULD NOT BE ABLE TO COME HERE.
CANADA'S NEW CITIZENSHIP ACT STILL RESTRICTS FAMILY REUNIFICATION - BASED ON AGE
GEE-MUN'S ELDEST WOULD HAVE BEEN 21... THAT'S TOO OLD TO BE ELIGIBLE
YOU SEE, IT'S NOT FAIR. THERE ARE STILL FAMILIES SEPARATED BECAUSE OF THIS LAW.
THINK ABOUT IT. WHAT WOULD YOU DO TO WORK AROUND IT?
WRITE IN A LOWER AGE TO SATISFY THE REQUIREMENTS*
* THIS WAS CANADA'S VERSION OF THE 'PAPER SON' - BIRTHDATES WERE REVISED SO THAT OLDER CHILDREN WERE ELIGIBLE FOR IMMIGRATION.

THE FOLLOWING YEARS SAW A RISE IN AWARENESS OF PROGRESSIVE SOCIAL ISSUES. TOGETHER WITH PEOPLE INVOLVED IN THE CIVIL RIGHTS MOVEMENTS, A GENERATION OF ***ASIAN NORTH AMERICAN*** ACTIVISTS, MANY OF WHOM WERE SONS AND DAUGHTERS OF PIONEER GOLD FIELD AND RAILROAD GAM SAAN MEN, BECAME PIONEERS IN THEIR OWN RIGHT!

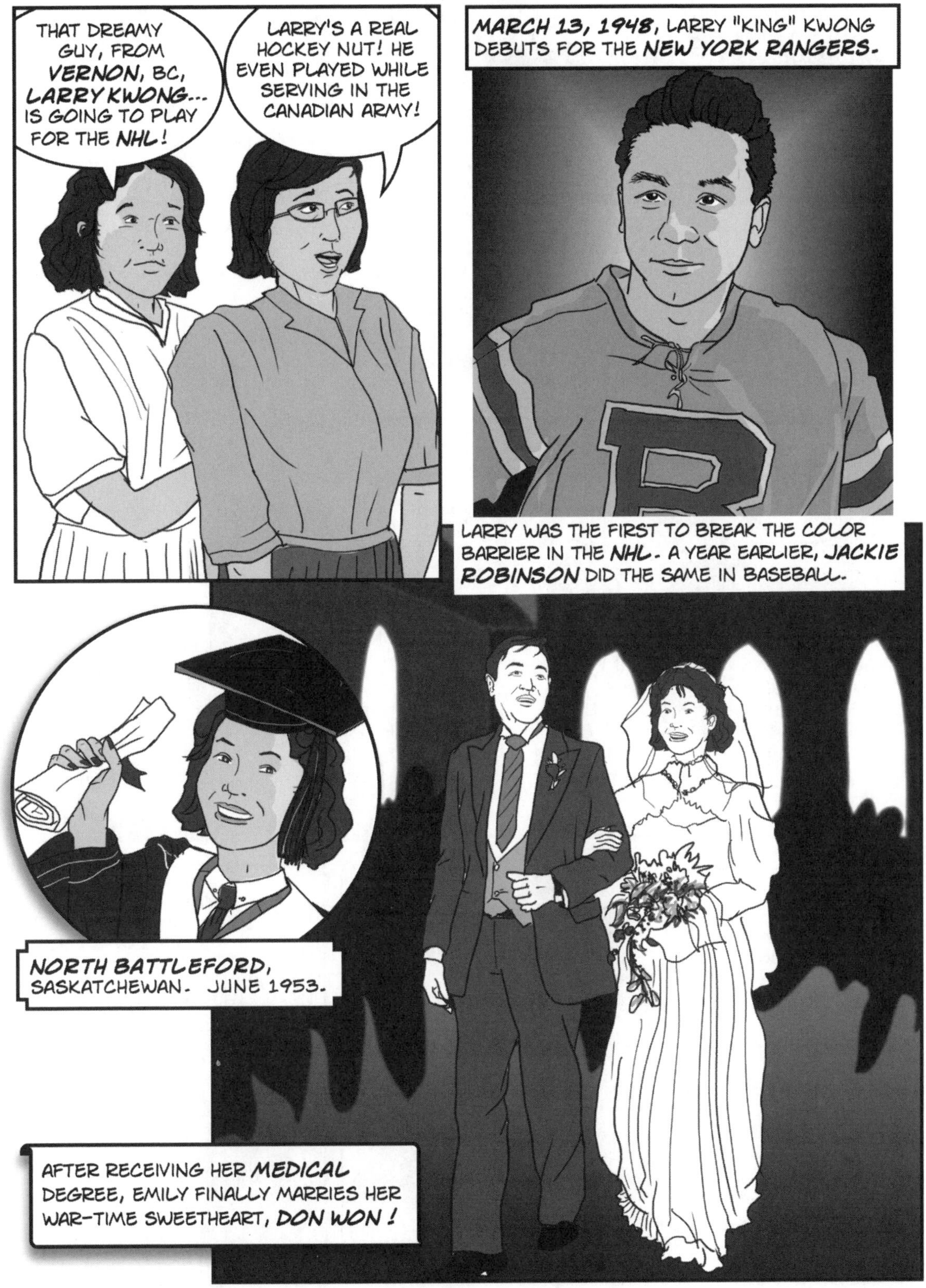
THAT DREAMY GUY, FROM VERNON, BC, LARRY KWONG... IS GOING TO PLAY FOR THE NHL!
LARRY'S A REAL HOCKEY NUT! HE EVEN PLAYED WHILE SERVING IN THE CANADIAN ARMY!
MARCH 13, 1948, LARRY "KING" KWONG DEBUTS FOR THE NEW YORK RANGERS.
LARRY WAS THE FIRST TO BREAK THE COLOR BARRIER IN THE NHL. A YEAR EARLIER, JACKIE ROBINSON DID THE SAME IN BASEBALL.
NORTH BATTLEFORD, SASKATCHEWAN. JUNE 1953.
AFTER RECEIVING HER MEDICAL DEGREE, EMILY FINALLY MARRIES HER WAR-TIME SWEETHEART, DON WON!

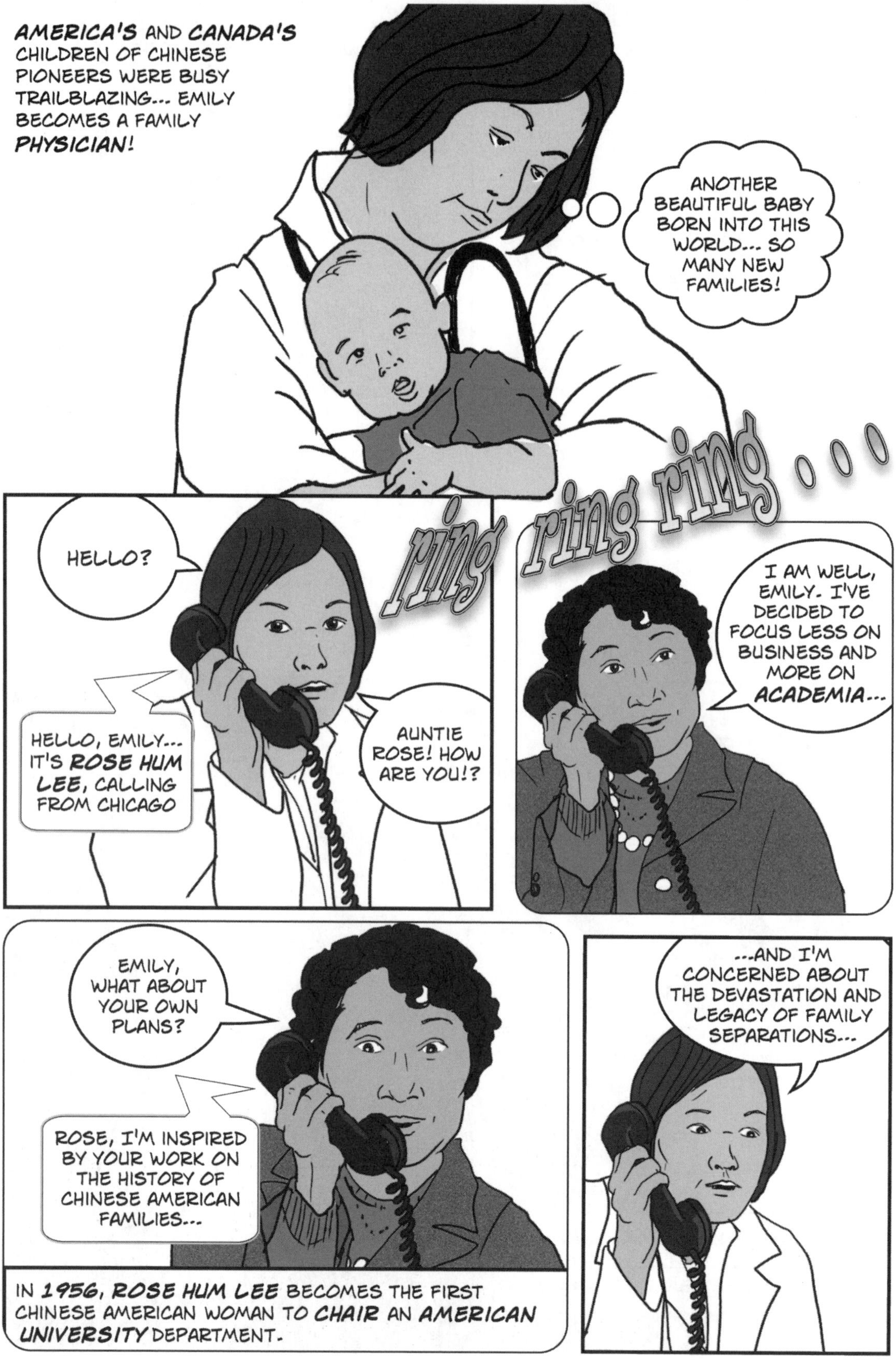

AMERICA'S AND CANADA'S CHILDREN OF CHINESE PIONEERS WERE BUSY TRAILBLAZING... EMILY BECOMES A FAMILY PHYSICIAN!
ANOTHER BEAUTIFUL BABY BORN INTO THIS WORLD... SO MANY NEW FAMILIES!
ring ring ring . . .
HELLO?
HELLO, EMILY... IT'S ROSE HUM LEE, CALLING FROM CHICAGO
AUNTIE ROSE! HOW ARE YOU!?
I AM WELL, EMILY. I'VE DECIDED TO FOCUS LESS ON BUSINESS AND MORE ON ACADEMIA...
EMILY, WHAT ABOUT YOUR OWN PLANS?
ROSE, I'M INSPIRED BY YOUR WORK ON THE HISTORY OF CHINESE AMERICAN FAMILIES...
IN 1956, ROSE HUM LEE BECOMES THE FIRST CHINESE AMERICAN WOMAN TO CHAIR AN AMERICAN UNIVERSITY DEPARTMENT.
...AND I'M CONCERNED ABOUT THE DEVASTATION AND LEGACY OF FAMILY SEPARATIONS...

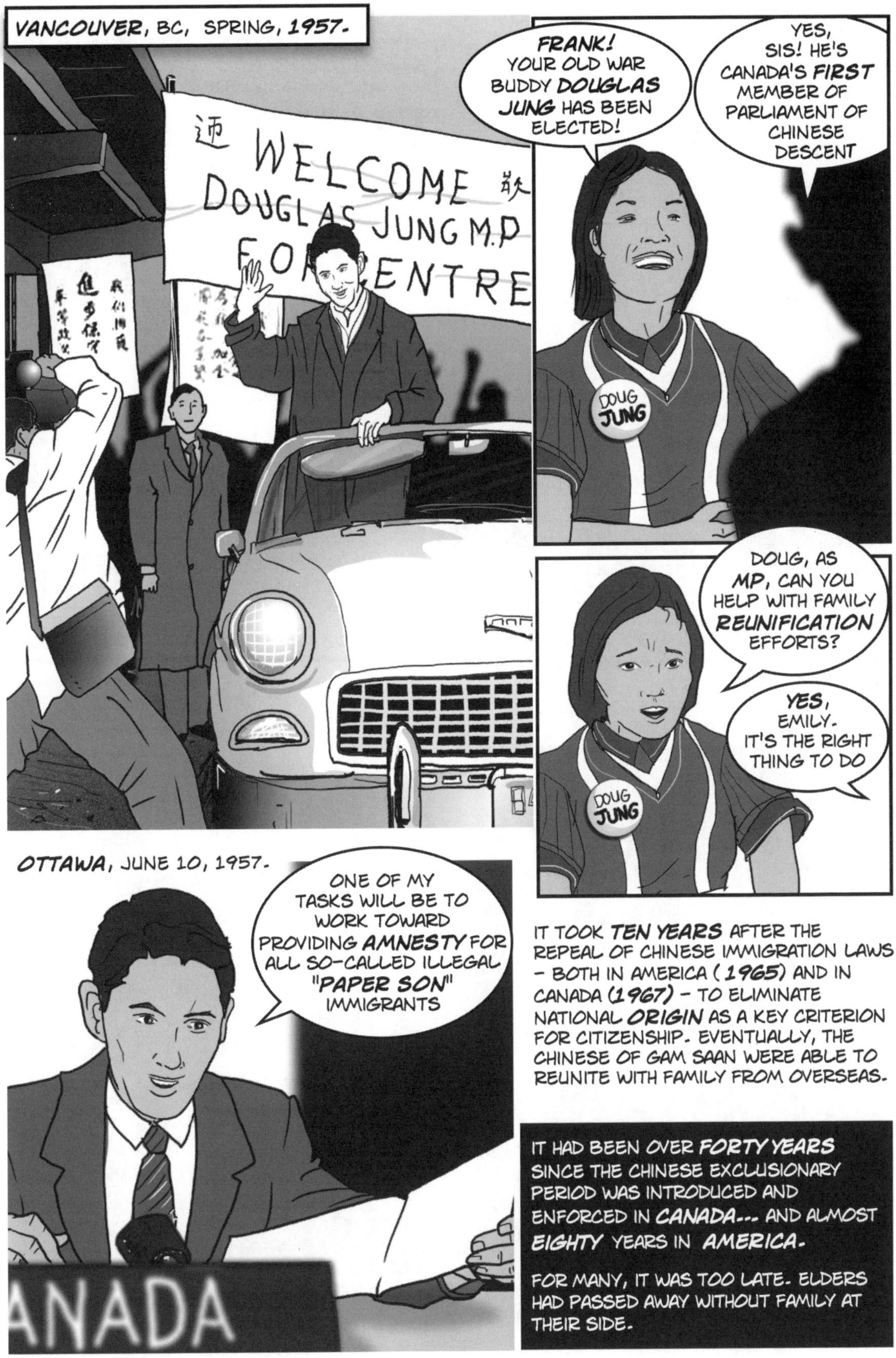
VANCOUVER, BC, SPRING, 1957.
WELCOME
DOUGLAS JUNG M.P
FRANK! YOUR OLD WAR BUDDY DOUGLAS JUNG HAS BEEN ELECTED!
YES, SIS! HE'S CANADA'S FIRST MEMBER OF PARLIAMENT OF CHINESE DESCENT
DOUG JUNG
DOUG, AS MP, CAN YOU HELP WITH FAMILY REUNIFICATION EFFORTS?
YES, EMILY. IT'S THE RIGHT THING TO DO
DOUG JUNG
OTTAWA, JUNE 10, 1957.
ONE OF MY TASKS WILL BE TO WORK TOWARD PROVIDING AMNESTY FOR ALL SO-CALLED ILLEGAL "PAPER SON" IMMIGRANTS
ANADA
IT TOOK TEN YEARS AFTER THE REPEAL OF CHINESE IMMIGRATION LAWS - BOTH IN AMERICA (1965) AND IN CANADA (1967) - TO ELIMINATE NATIONAL ORIGIN AS A KEY CRITERION FOR CITIZENSHIP. EVENTUALLY, THE CHINESE OF GAM SAAN WERE ABLE TO REUNITE WITH FAMILY FROM OVERSEAS.
IT HAD BEEN OVER FORTY YEARS SINCE THE CHINESE EXCLUSIONARY PERIOD WAS INTRODUCED AND ENFORCED IN CANADA... AND ALMOST EIGHTY YEARS IN AMERICA.
FOR MANY, IT WAS TOO LATE. ELDERS HAD PASSED AWAY WITHOUT FAMILY AT THEIR SIDE.

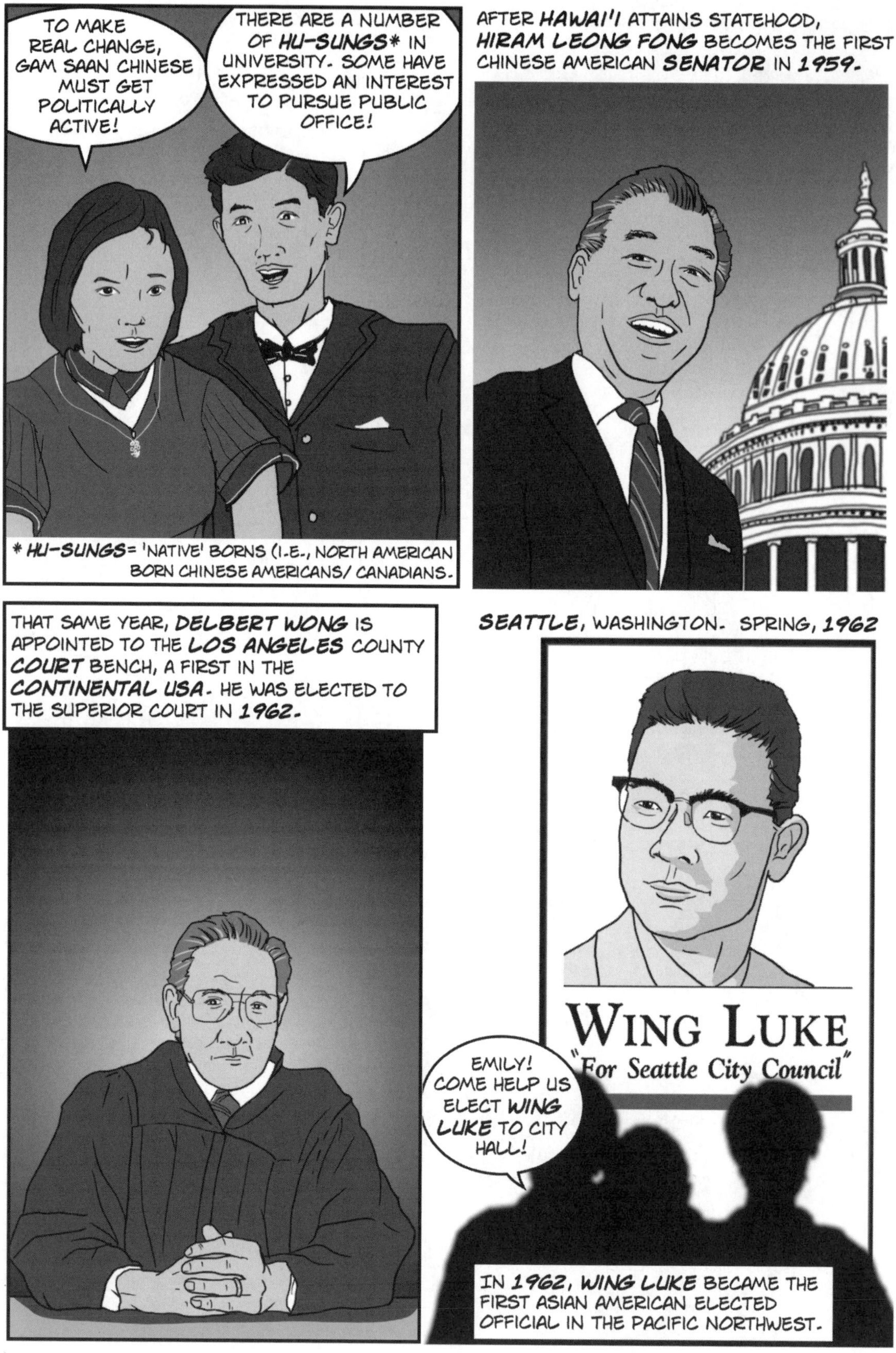

TO MAKE REAL CHANGE, GAM SAAN CHINESE MUST GET POLITICALLY ACTIVE!
THERE ARE A NUMBER OF HU-SUNGS* IN UNIVERSITY. SOME HAVE EXPRESSED AN INTEREST TO PURSUE PUBLIC OFFICE!
* HU-SUNGS= 'NATIVE' BORNS (I.E., NORTH AMERICAN BORN CHINESE AMERICANS/ CANADIANS.
AFTER HAWAI'I ATTAINS STATEHOOD, HIRAM LEONG FONG BECOMES THE FIRST CHINESE AMERICAN SENATOR IN 1959.
THAT SAME YEAR, DELBERT WONG IS APPOINTED TO THE LOS ANGELES COUNTY COURT BENCH, A FIRST IN THE CONTINENTAL USA. HE WAS ELECTED TO THE SUPERIOR COURT IN 1962.
SEATTLE, WASHINGTON. SPRING, 1962
WING LUKE
"For Seattle City Council"
EMILY! COME HELP US ELECT WING LUKE TO CITY HALL!
IN 1962, WING LUKE BECAME THE FIRST ASIAN AMERICAN ELECTED OFFICIAL IN THE PACIFIC NORTHWEST.

THE ***1960S*** CONTINUED TO SEE MANY MORE ***FIRSTS*** IN GAM SAAN CHINESE COMMUNITIES:

NORTH AMERICA'S FIRST CHINESE ***MAYOR (1966) PETER WING.***

CALIFORNIA'S FIRST CHINESE ***ASSEMBLYWOMAN (1966) MARCH FONG EU.***

CANADA'S FIRST CHINESE ***CROWN COUNSEL (1967) RANDALL WONG.***

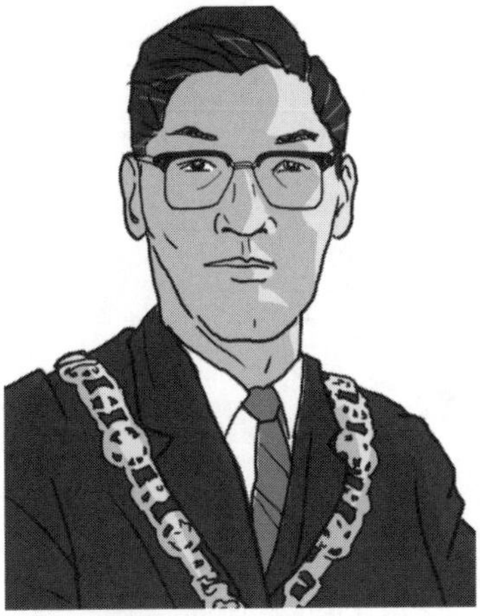

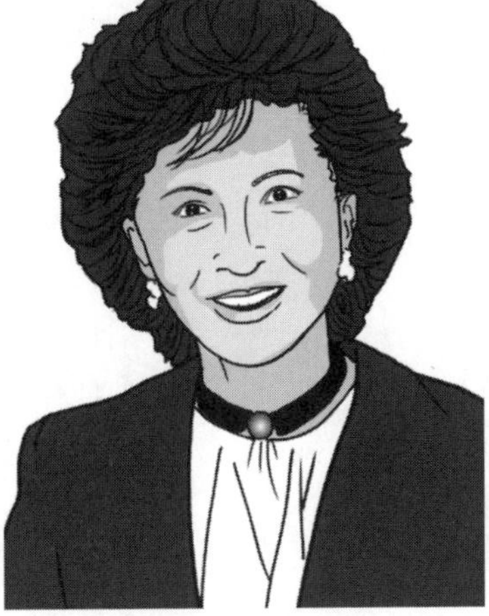

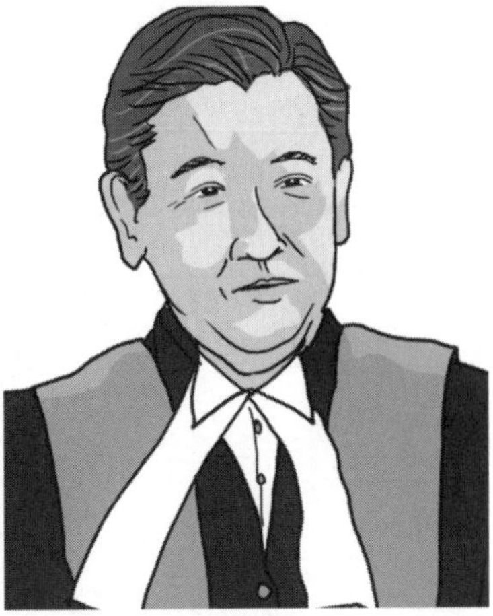

KAMLOOPS, BC. EARLIER ELECTED AS ALDERMAN IN ***1960.***

SHE LATER BECAME SECRETARY OF STATE IN ***1974.***

IN ***1981*** HE BECAME THE FIRST CHINESE CANADIAN FEDERALLY APPOINTED PROVINCIAL JUDGE.

VANCOUVER CHINATOWN, DECEMBER 1972.

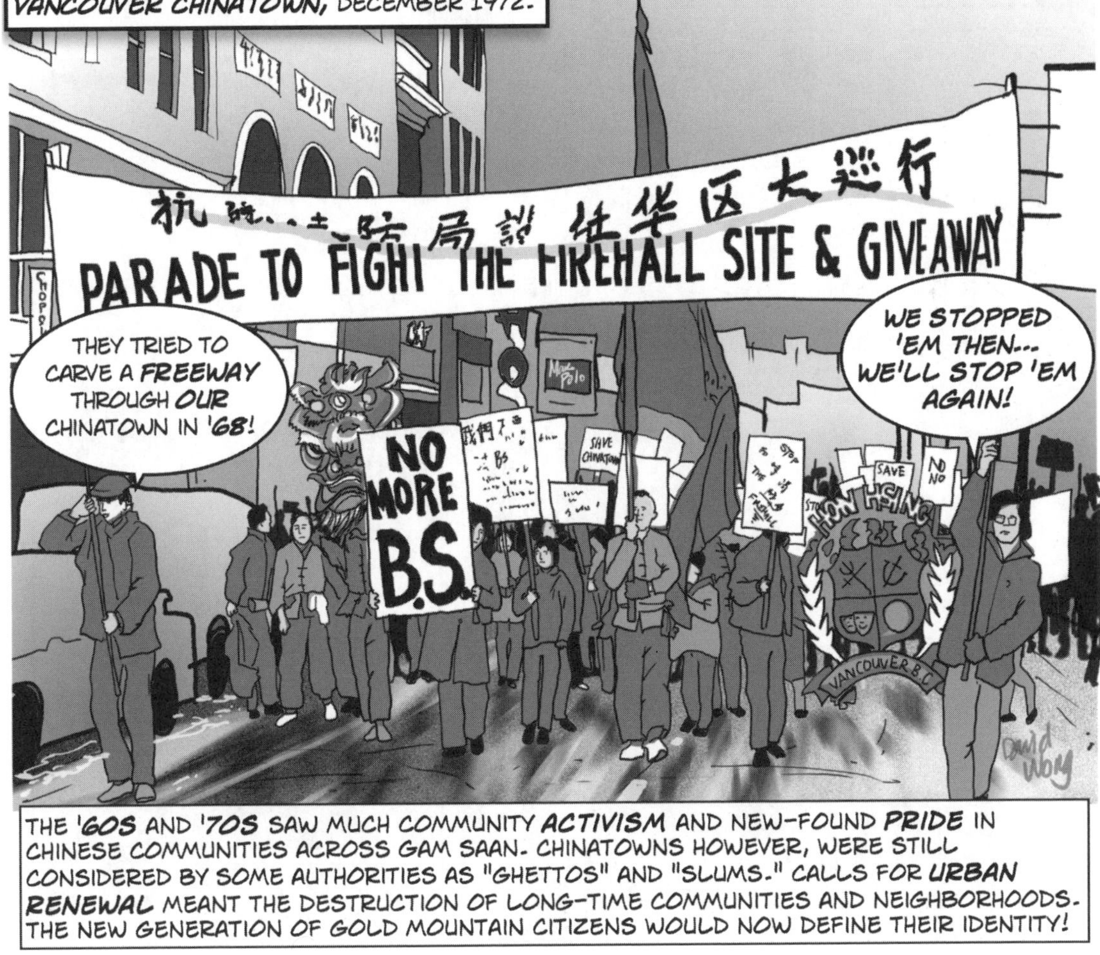
PARADE TO FIGHT THE FIREHALL SITE & GIVEAWAY
THEY TRIED TO CARVE A FREEWAY THROUGH OUR CHINATOWN IN '68!
WE STOPPED 'EM THEN... WE'LL STOP 'EM AGAIN!
NO MORE B.S.
SAVE CHINATOWN
VANCOUVER B.C.

THE ***'60S*** AND ***'70S*** SAW MUCH COMMUNITY ***ACTIVISM*** AND NEW-FOUND ***PRIDE*** IN CHINESE COMMUNITIES ACROSS GAM SAAN. CHINATOWNS HOWEVER, WERE STILL CONSIDERED BY SOME AUTHORITIES AS "GHETTOS" AND "SLUMS." CALLS FOR ***URBAN RENEWAL*** MEANT THE DESTRUCTION OF LONG-TIME COMMUNITIES AND NEIGHBORHOODS. THE NEW GENERATION OF GOLD MOUNTAIN CITIZENS WOULD NOW DEFINE THEIR IDENTITY!

CHAPTER 20 Angels Watching Over

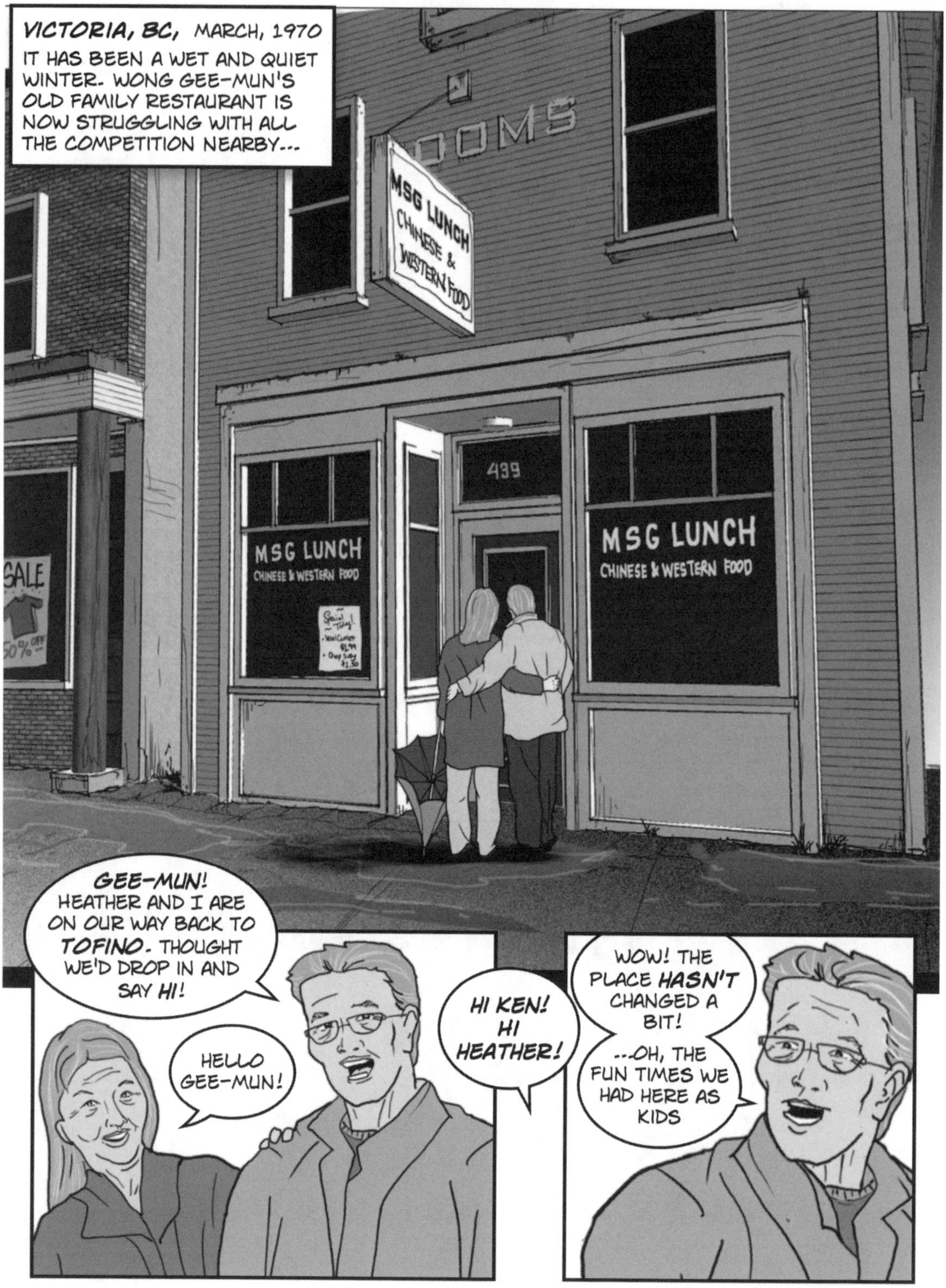

VICTORIA, BC, MARCH, 1970
IT HAS BEEN A WET AND QUIET WINTER. WONG GEE-MUN'S OLD FAMILY RESTAURANT IS NOW STRUGGLING WITH ALL THE COMPETITION NEARBY...
OOMS
MSG LUNCH CHINESE & WESTERN FOOD
439
MSG LUNCH CHINESE & WESTERN FOOD
MSG LUNCH CHINESE & WESTERN FOOD
SALE
GEE-MUN! HEATHER AND I ARE ON OUR WAY BACK TO TOFINO. THOUGHT WE'D DROP IN AND SAY HI!
HELLO GEE-MUN!
HI KEN! HI HEATHER!
WOW! THE PLACE HASN'T CHANGED A BIT!
...OH, THE FUN TIMES WE HAD HERE AS KIDS

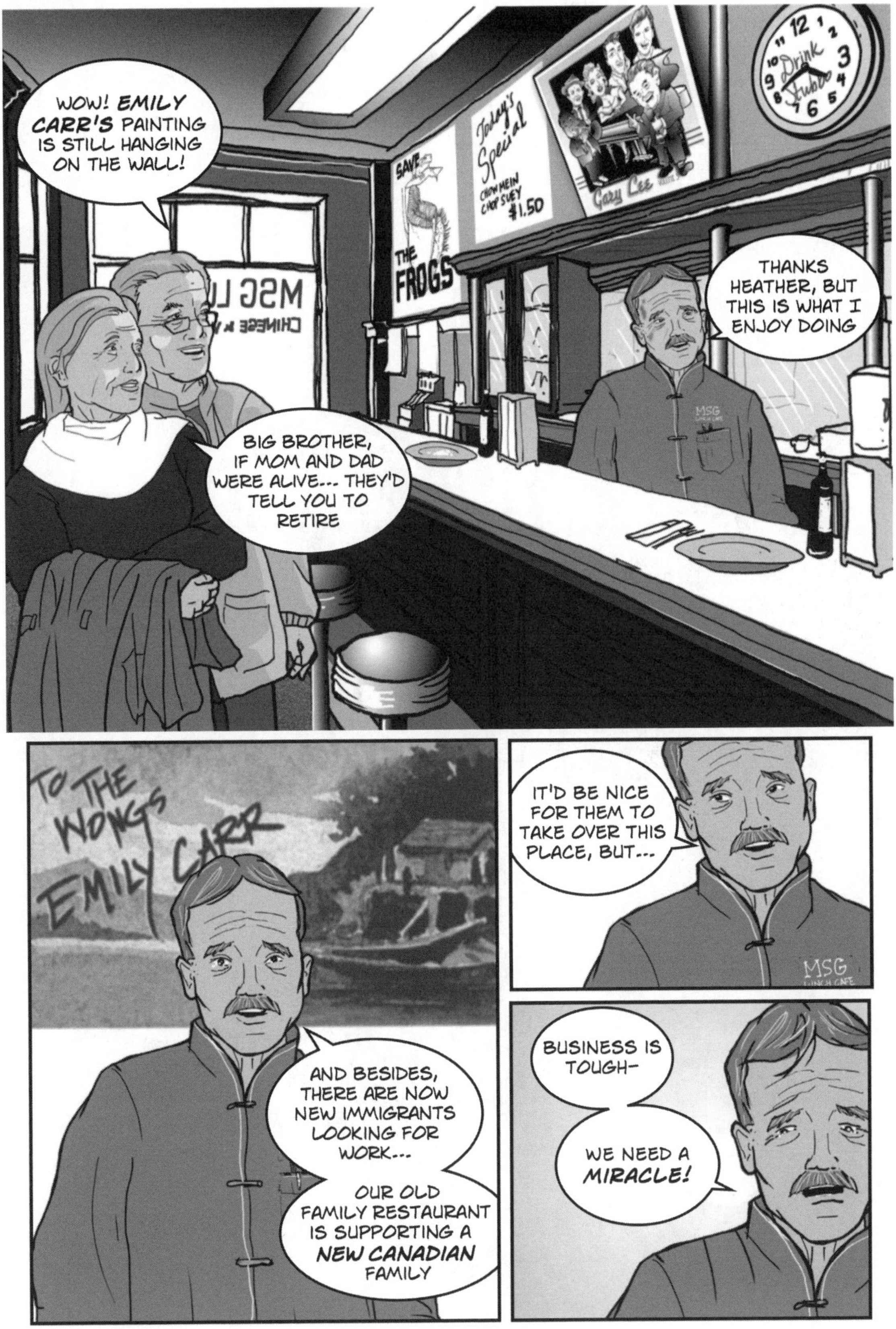
WOW! **EMILY CARR'S** PAINTING IS STILL HANGING ON THE WALL!
SAVE THE FROGS
Today's Special CHOW MEIN CHOP SUEY $1.50
Gary Lee
THANKS HEATHER, BUT THIS IS WHAT I ENJOY DOING
BIG BROTHER, IF MOM AND DAD WERE ALIVE... THEY'D TELL YOU TO RETIRE
TO THE WONGS EMILY CARR
IT'D BE NICE FOR THEM TO TAKE OVER THIS PLACE, BUT...
AND BESIDES, THERE ARE NOW NEW IMMIGRANTS LOOKING FOR WORK...
OUR OLD FAMILY RESTAURANT IS SUPPORTING A ***NEW CANADIAN*** FAMILY
BUSINESS IS TOUGH-
WE NEED A ***MIRACLE!***

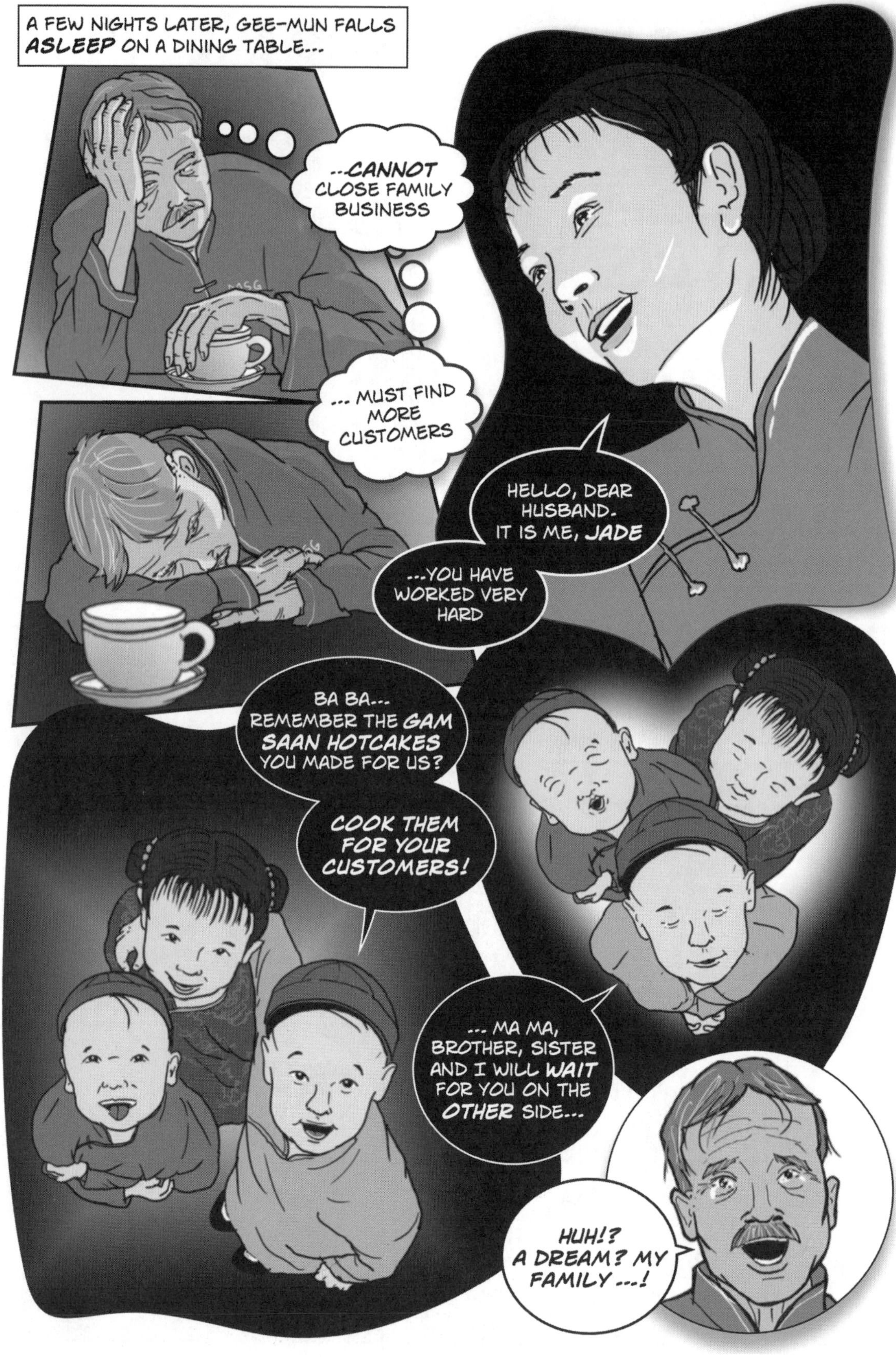
A FEW NIGHTS LATER, GEE-MUN FALLS ASLEEP ON A DINING TABLE...
...CANNOT CLOSE FAMILY BUSINESS
... MUST FIND MORE CUSTOMERS
HELLO, DEAR HUSBAND. IT IS ME, JADE
...YOU HAVE WORKED VERY HARD
BA BA... REMEMBER THE GAM SAAN HOTCAKES YOU MADE FOR US?
COOK THEM FOR YOUR CUSTOMERS!
... MA MA, BROTHER, SISTER AND I WILL WAIT FOR YOU ON THE OTHER SIDE...
HUH!? A DREAM? MY FAMILY ...!

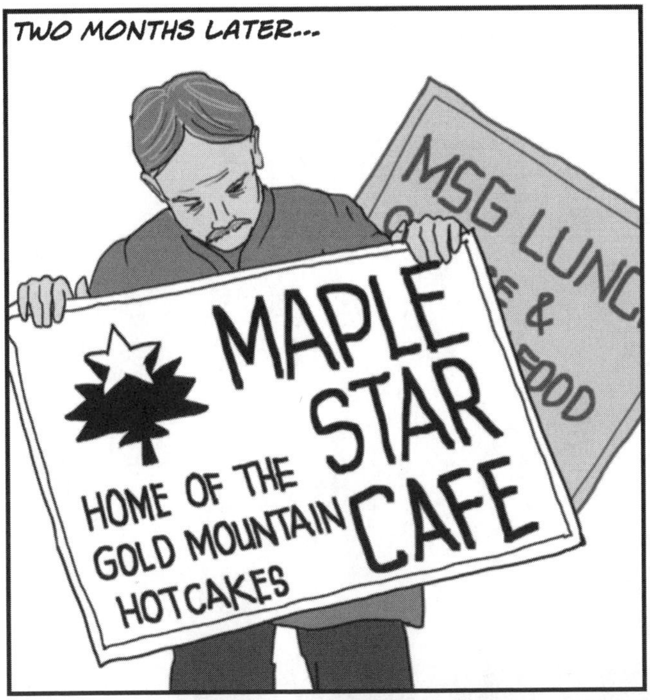
TWO MONTHS LATER...
MSG LUNCH
MAPLE STAR CAFE
HOME OF THE GOLD MOUNTAIN HOTCAKES

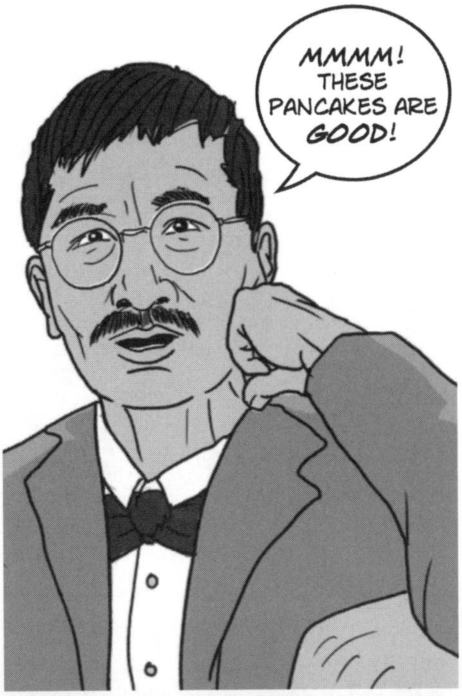
MMMM! THESE PANCAKES ARE GOOD!

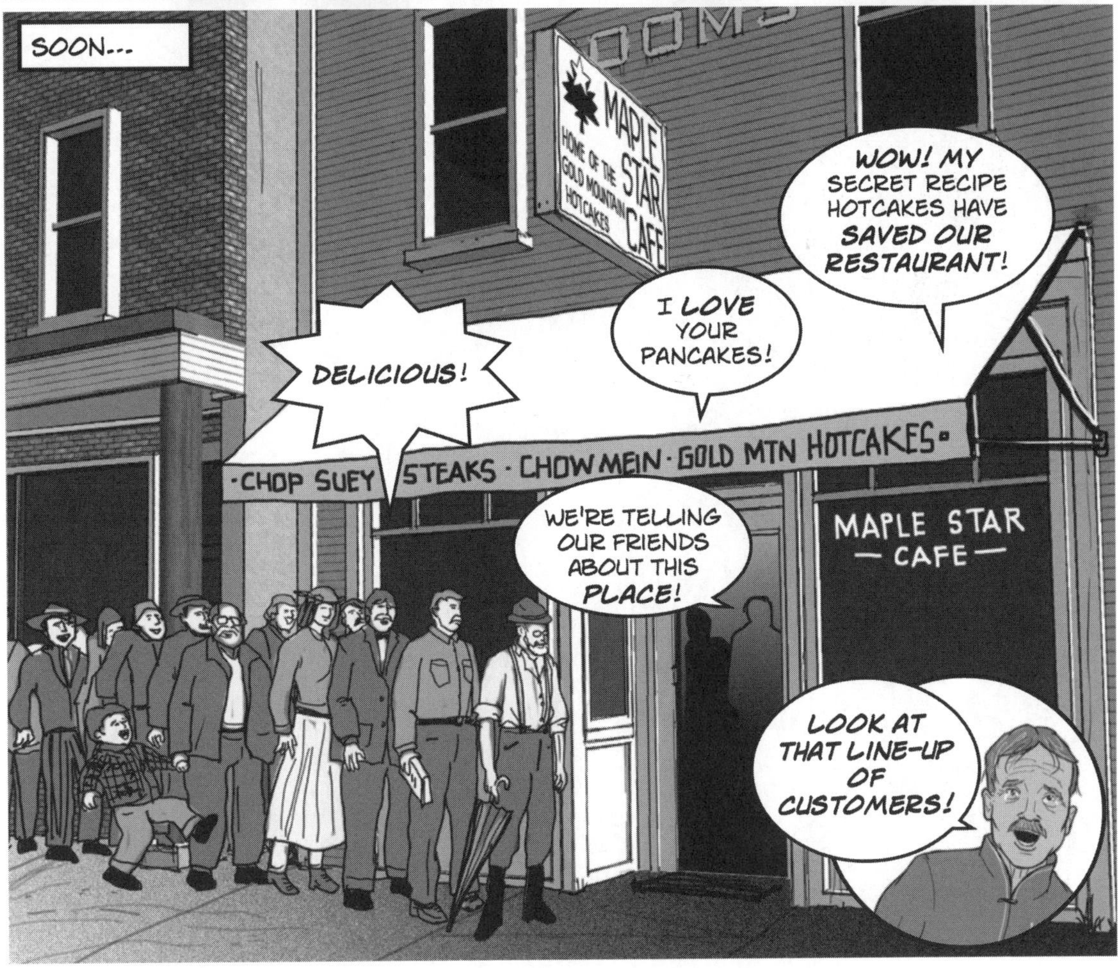
SOON...
MAPLE STAR CAFE
HOME OF THE GOLD MOUNTAIN HOTCAKES
WOW! MY SECRET RECIPE HOTCAKES HAVE SAVED OUR RESTAURANT!
I LOVE YOUR PANCAKES!
DELICIOUS!
·CHOP SUEY STEAKS · CHOW MEIN · GOLD MTN HOTCAKES·
WE'RE TELLING OUR FRIENDS ABOUT THIS PLACE!
MAPLE STAR
— CAFE —
LOOK AT THAT LINE-UP OF CUSTOMERS!

CHAPTER 21 Old Foes, New Relations

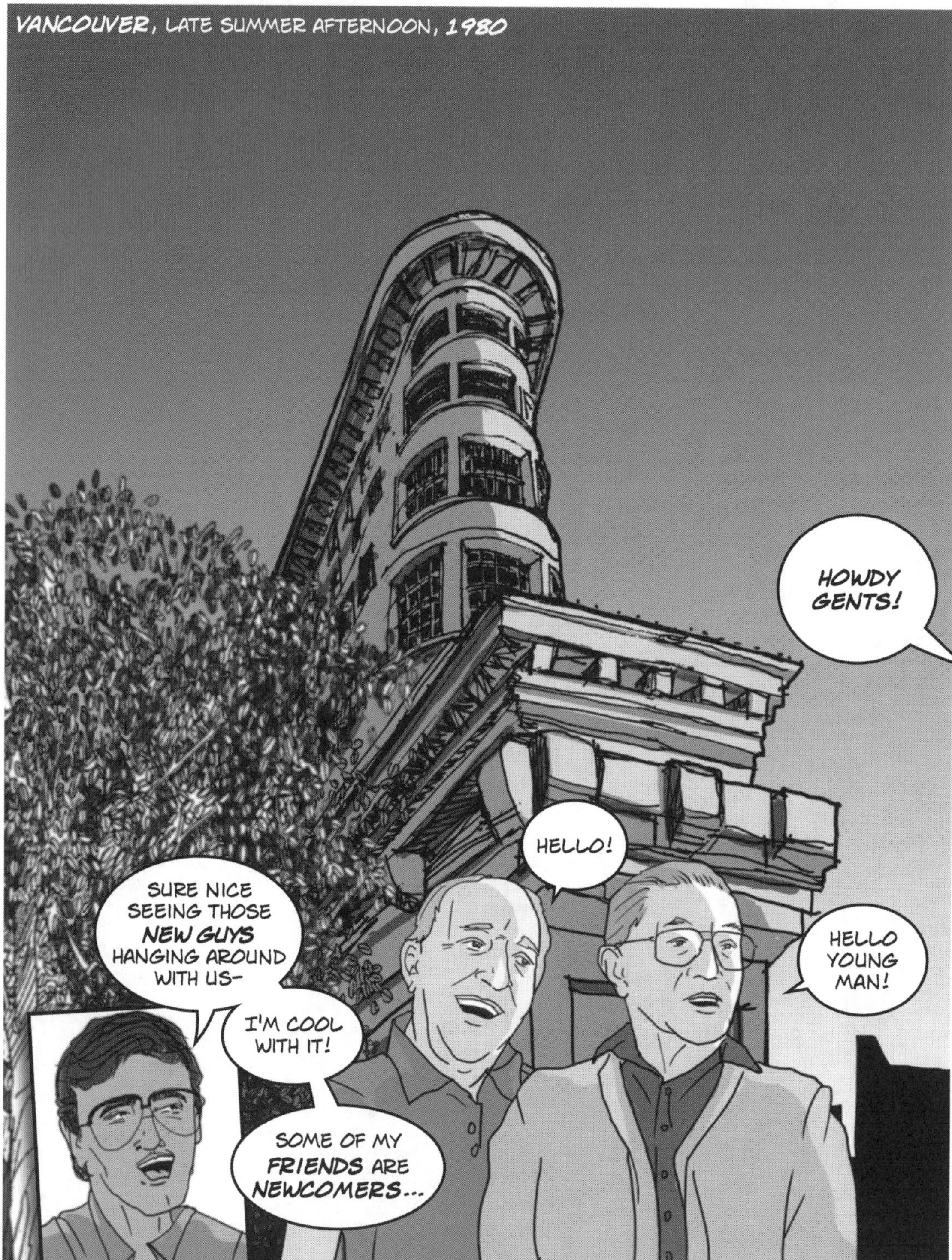
VANCOUVER, LATE SUMMER AFTERNOON, 1980
HOWDY GENTS!
HELLO!
HELLO YOUNG MAN!
SURE NICE SEEING THOSE NEW GUYS HANGING AROUND WITH US-
I'M COOL WITH IT!
SOME OF MY FRIENDS ARE NEWCOMERS...

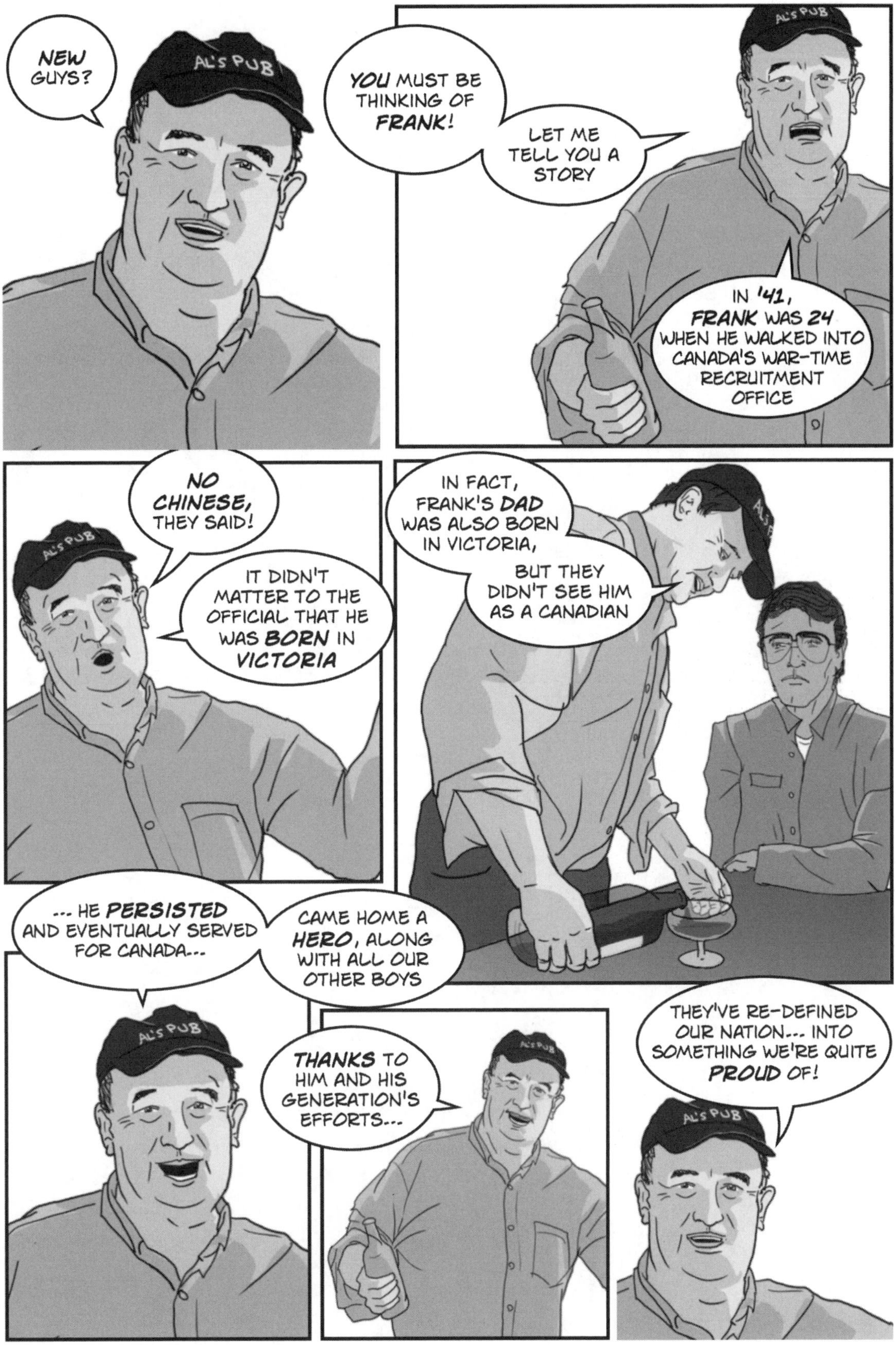
NEW GUYS?
AL'S PUB
YOU MUST BE THINKING OF FRANK!
LET ME TELL YOU A STORY
IN '41, FRANK WAS 24 WHEN HE WALKED INTO CANADA'S WAR-TIME RECRUITMENT OFFICE
NO CHINESE, THEY SAID!
IT DIDN'T MATTER TO THE OFFICIAL THAT HE WAS BORN IN VICTORIA
IN FACT, FRANK'S DAD WAS ALSO BORN IN VICTORIA,
BUT THEY DIDN'T SEE HIM AS A CANADIAN
--- HE PERSISTED AND EVENTUALLY SERVED FOR CANADA---
CAME HOME A HERO, ALONG WITH ALL OUR OTHER BOYS
THANKS TO HIM AND HIS GENERATION'S EFFORTS---
THEY'VE RE-DEFINED OUR NATION--- INTO SOMETHING WE'RE QUITE PROUD OF!

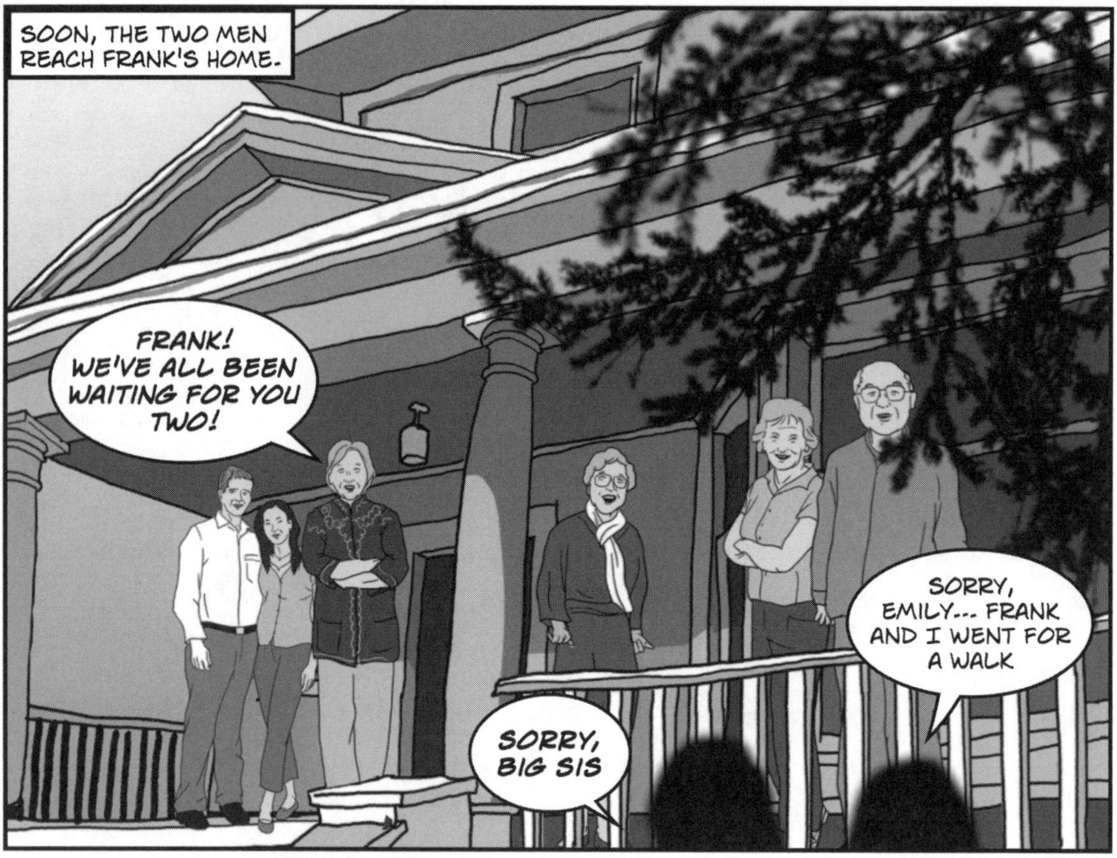
SOON, THE TWO MEN REACH FRANK'S HOME.
FRANK! WE'VE ALL BEEN WAITING FOR YOU TWO!
SORRY, EMILY... FRANK AND I WENT FOR A WALK
SORRY, BIG SIS

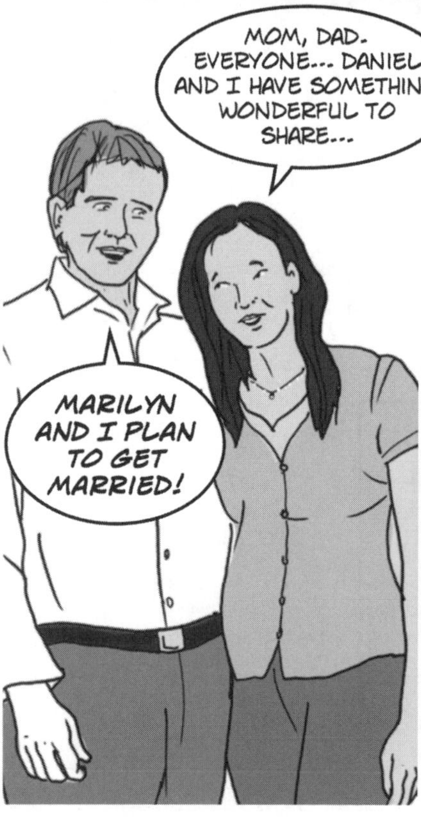
MOM, DAD. EVERYONE... DANIEL AND I HAVE SOMETHING WONDERFUL TO SHARE...
MARILYN AND I PLAN TO GET MARRIED!

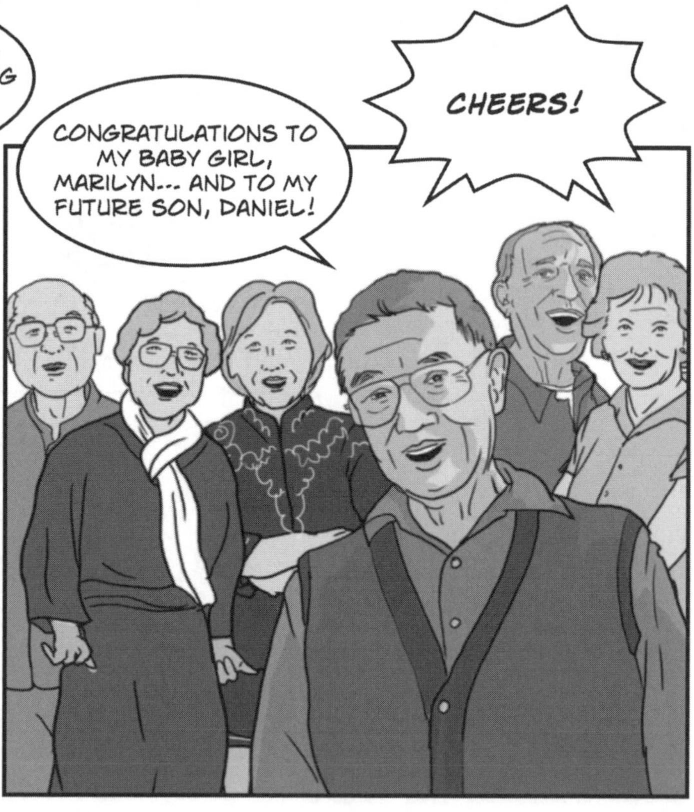
CONGRATULATIONS TO MY BABY GIRL, MARILYN... AND TO MY FUTURE SON, DANIEL!
CHEERS!

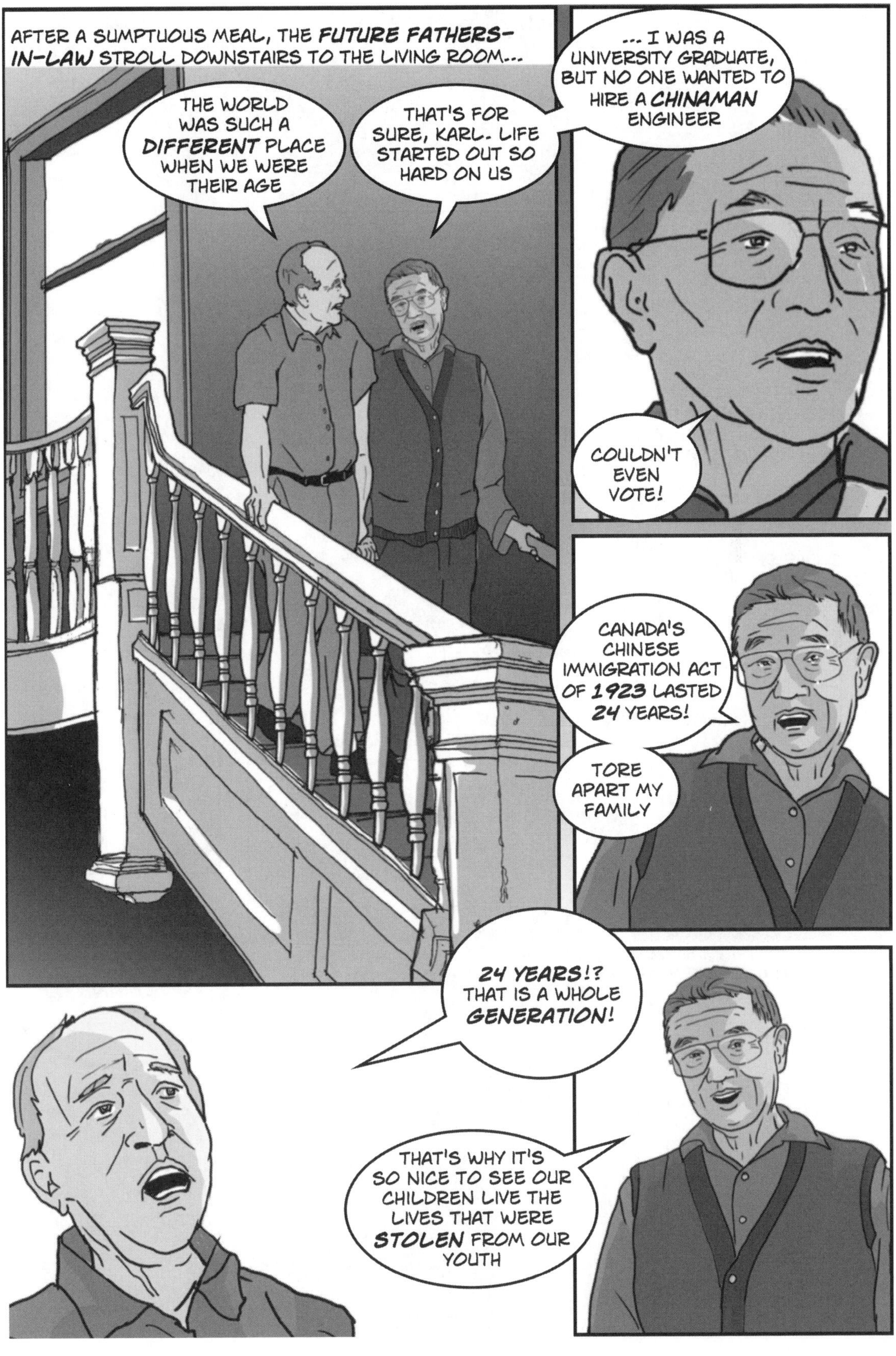
AFTER A SUMPTUOUS MEAL, THE FUTURE FATHERS-IN-LAW STROLL DOWNSTAIRS TO THE LIVING ROOM...
THE WORLD WAS SUCH A DIFFERENT PLACE WHEN WE WERE THEIR AGE
THAT'S FOR SURE, KARL. LIFE STARTED OUT SO HARD ON US
... I WAS A UNIVERSITY GRADUATE, BUT NO ONE WANTED TO HIRE A CHINAMAN ENGINEER
COULDN'T EVEN VOTE!
CANADA'S CHINESE IMMIGRATION ACT OF 1923 LASTED 24 YEARS!
TORE APART MY FAMILY
24 YEARS!? THAT IS A WHOLE GENERATION!
THAT'S WHY IT'S SO NICE TO SEE OUR CHILDREN LIVE THE LIVES THAT WERE STOLEN FROM OUR YOUTH

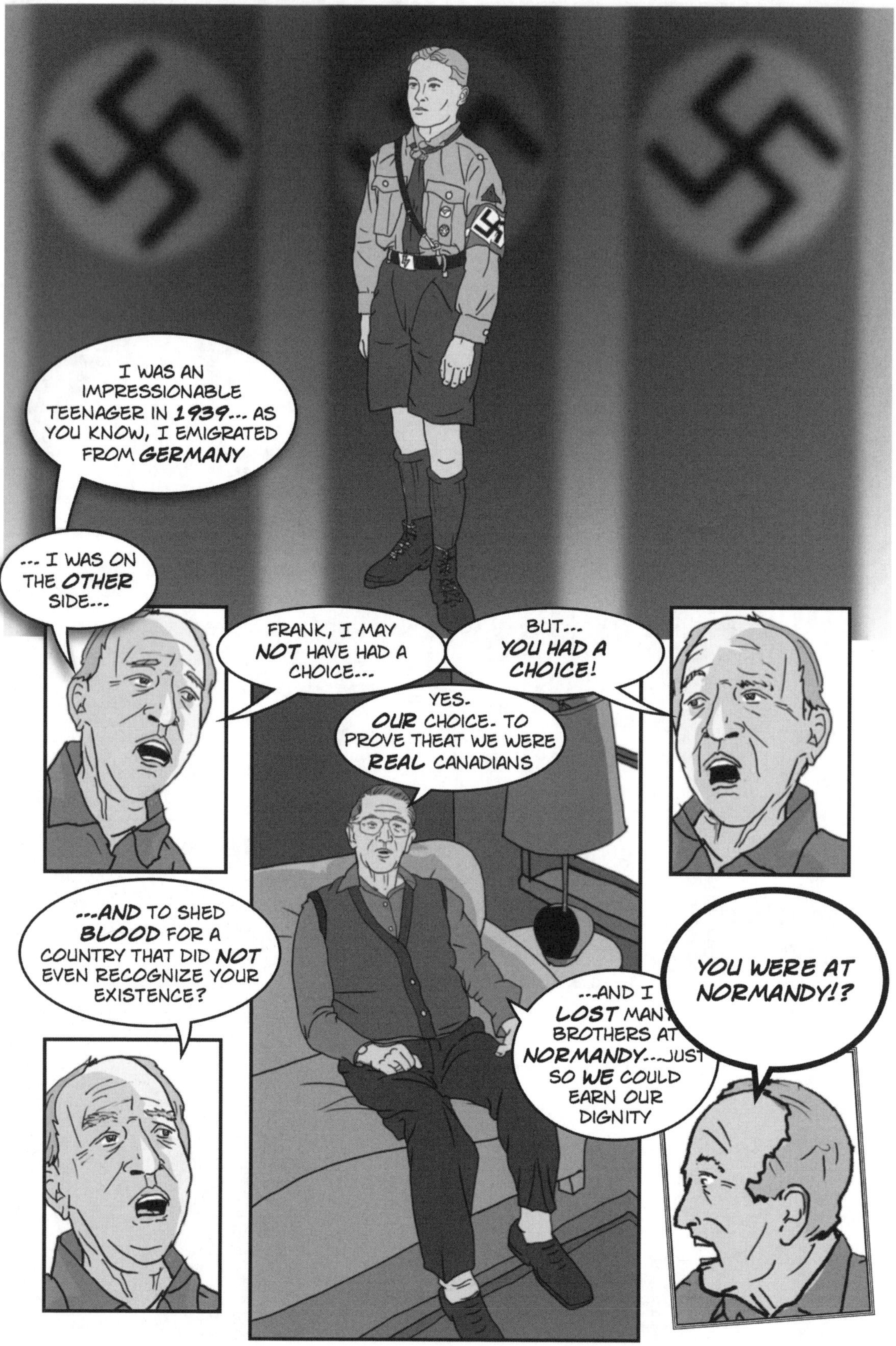
I WAS AN IMPRESSIONABLE TEENAGER IN 1939... AS YOU KNOW, I EMIGRATED FROM GERMANY
... I WAS ON THE OTHER SIDE...
FRANK, I MAY NOT HAVE HAD A CHOICE...
BUT... YOU HAD A CHOICE!
YES. OUR CHOICE. TO PROVE THEAT WE WERE REAL CANADIANS
...AND TO SHED BLOOD FOR A COUNTRY THAT DID NOT EVEN RECOGNIZE YOUR EXISTENCE?
...AND I LOST MANY BROTHERS AT NORMANDY...JUST SO WE COULD EARN OUR DIGNITY
YOU WERE AT NORMANDY!?

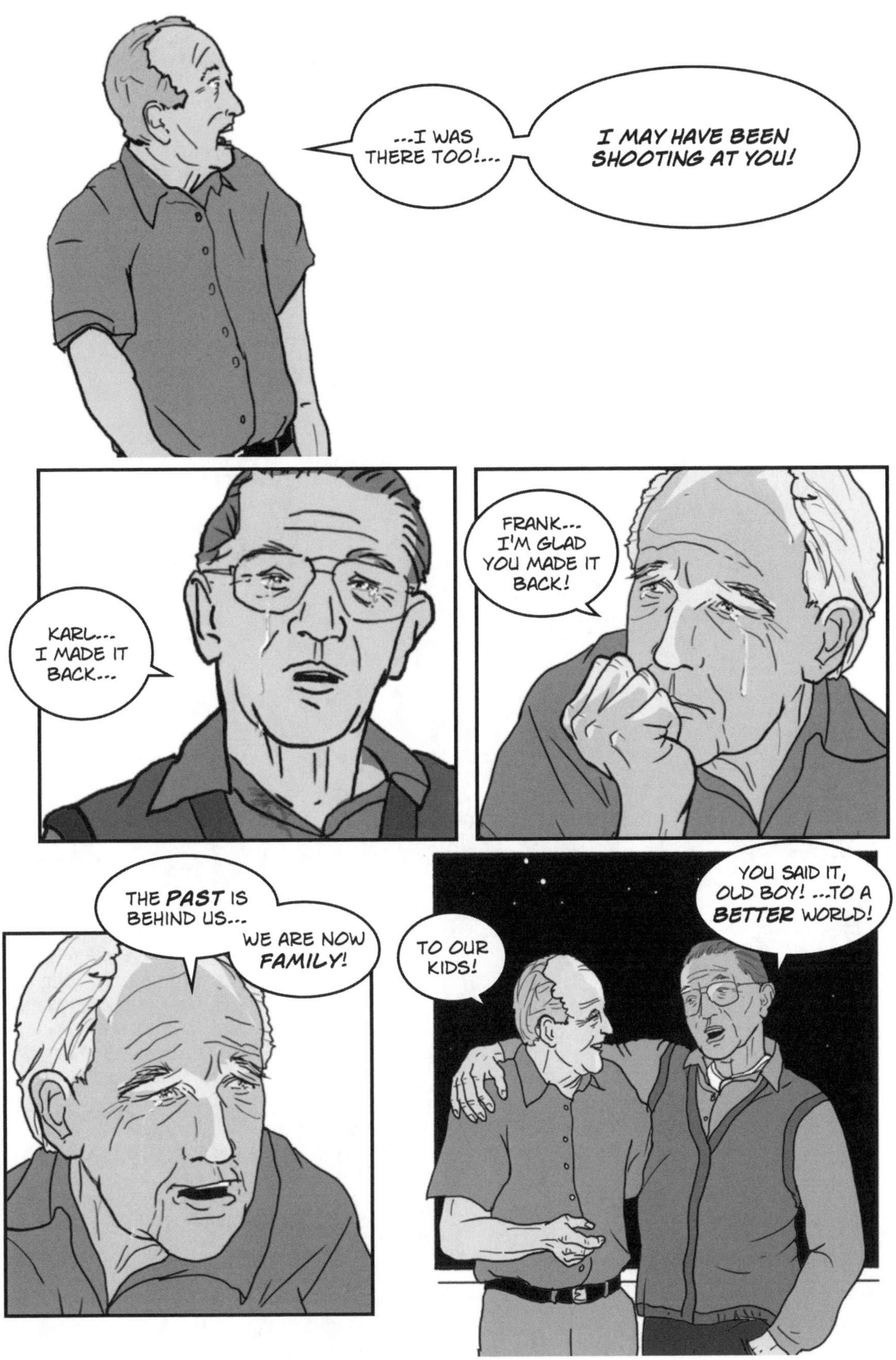
...I WAS THERE TOO!...
I MAY HAVE BEEN SHOOTING AT YOU!
KARL... I MADE IT BACK...
FRANK... I'M GLAD YOU MADE IT BACK!
THE PAST IS BEHIND US...
WE ARE NOW FAMILY!
TO OUR KIDS!
YOU SAID IT, OLD BOY! ...TO A BETTER WORLD!

CHAPTER 22 Doe Heem (Apology)

THERE ARE MANY STORIES FROM THE *IMMIGRANTS* WHO HAVE MADE *GAM SAAN* THEIR *NEW HOME.* THIS HAS BEEN THE STORY OF ONE FAMILY, THE WONGS.

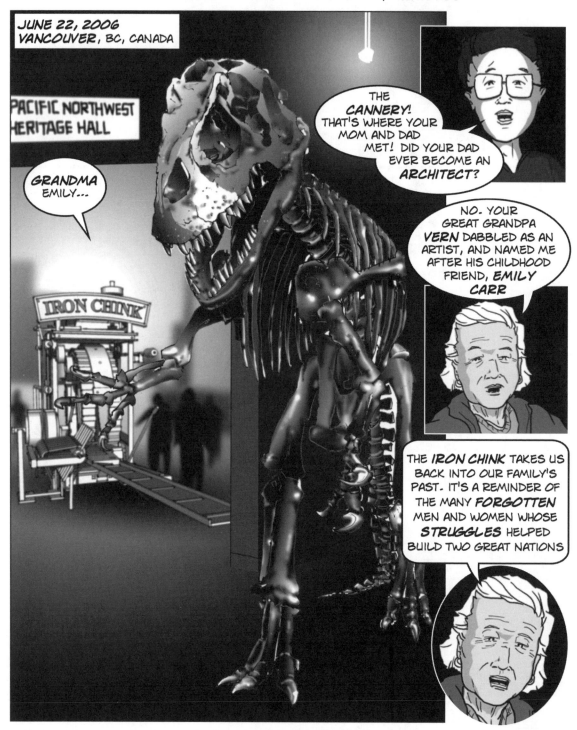

JUNE 22, 2006
VANCOUVER, BC, CANADA

PACIFIC NORTHWEST
HERITAGE HALL

GRANDMA
EMILY...

IRON CHINK

THE *CANNERY!* THAT'S WHERE YOUR MOM AND DAD MET! DID YOUR DAD EVER BECOME AN *ARCHITECT?*

NO. YOUR GREAT GRANDPA *VERN* DABBLED AS AN ARTIST, AND NAMED ME AFTER HIS CHILDHOOD FRIEND, *EMILY CARR*

THE *IRON CHINK* TAKES US BACK INTO OUR FAMILY'S PAST. IT'S A REMINDER OF THE MANY *FORGOTTEN* MEN AND WOMEN WHOSE *STRUGGLES* HELPED BUILD TWO GREAT NATIONS

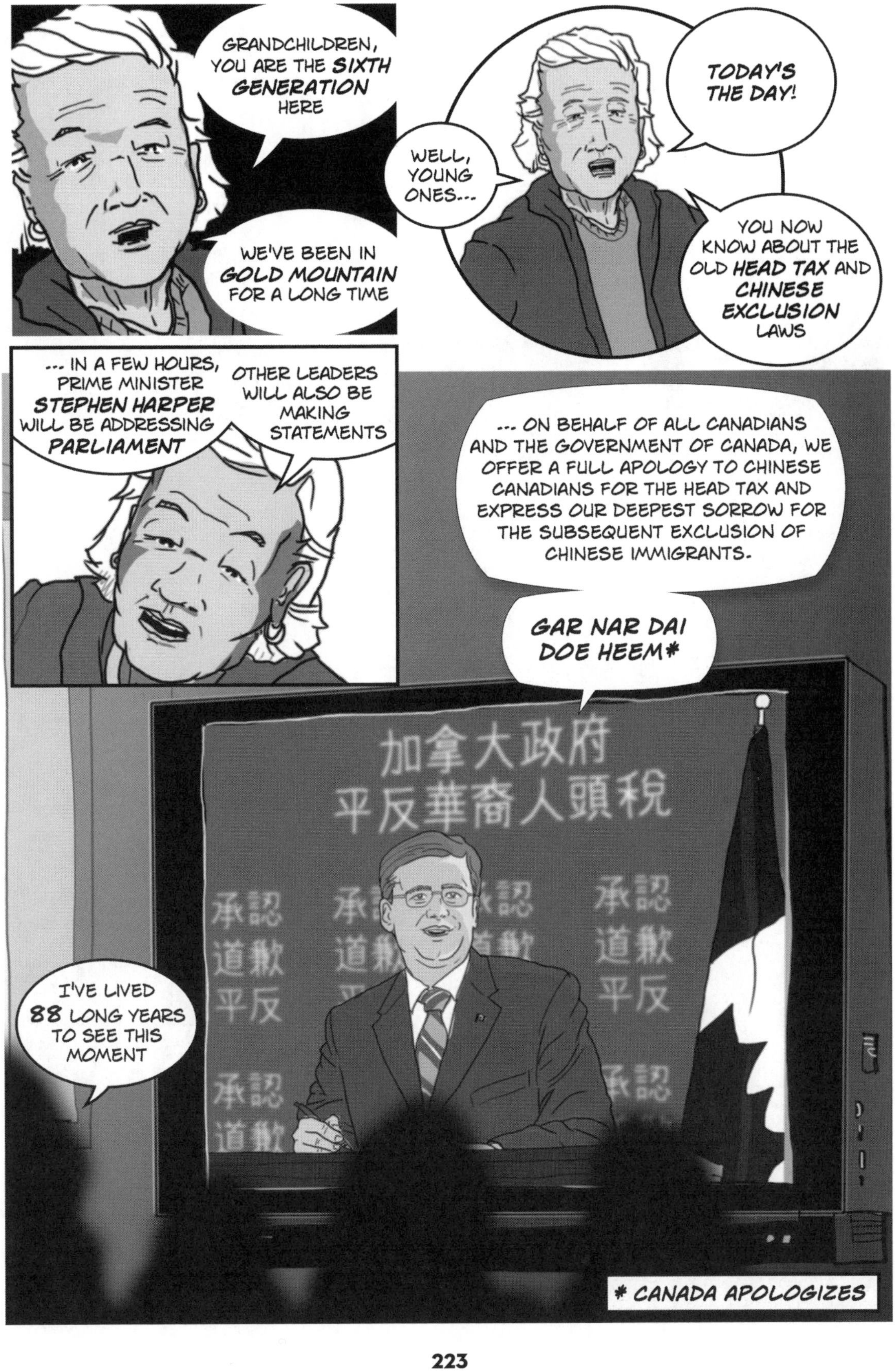
GRANDCHILDREN, YOU ARE THE SIXTH GENERATION HERE
WE'VE BEEN IN GOLD MOUNTAIN FOR A LONG TIME
WELL, YOUNG ONES...
TODAY'S THE DAY!
YOU NOW KNOW ABOUT THE OLD HEAD TAX AND CHINESE EXCLUSION LAWS
... IN A FEW HOURS, PRIME MINISTER STEPHEN HARPER WILL BE ADDRESSING PARLIAMENT
OTHER LEADERS WILL ALSO BE MAKING STATEMENTS
... ON BEHALF OF ALL CANADIANS AND THE GOVERNMENT OF CANADA, WE OFFER A FULL APOLOGY TO CHINESE CANADIANS FOR THE HEAD TAX AND EXPRESS OUR DEEPEST SORROW FOR THE SUBSEQUENT EXCLUSION OF CHINESE IMMIGRANTS.
GAR NAR DAI DOE HEEM*
加拿大政府
平反華裔人頭稅
承認
道歉
平反
I'VE LIVED 88 LONG YEARS TO SEE THIS MOMENT
* CANADA APOLOGIZES

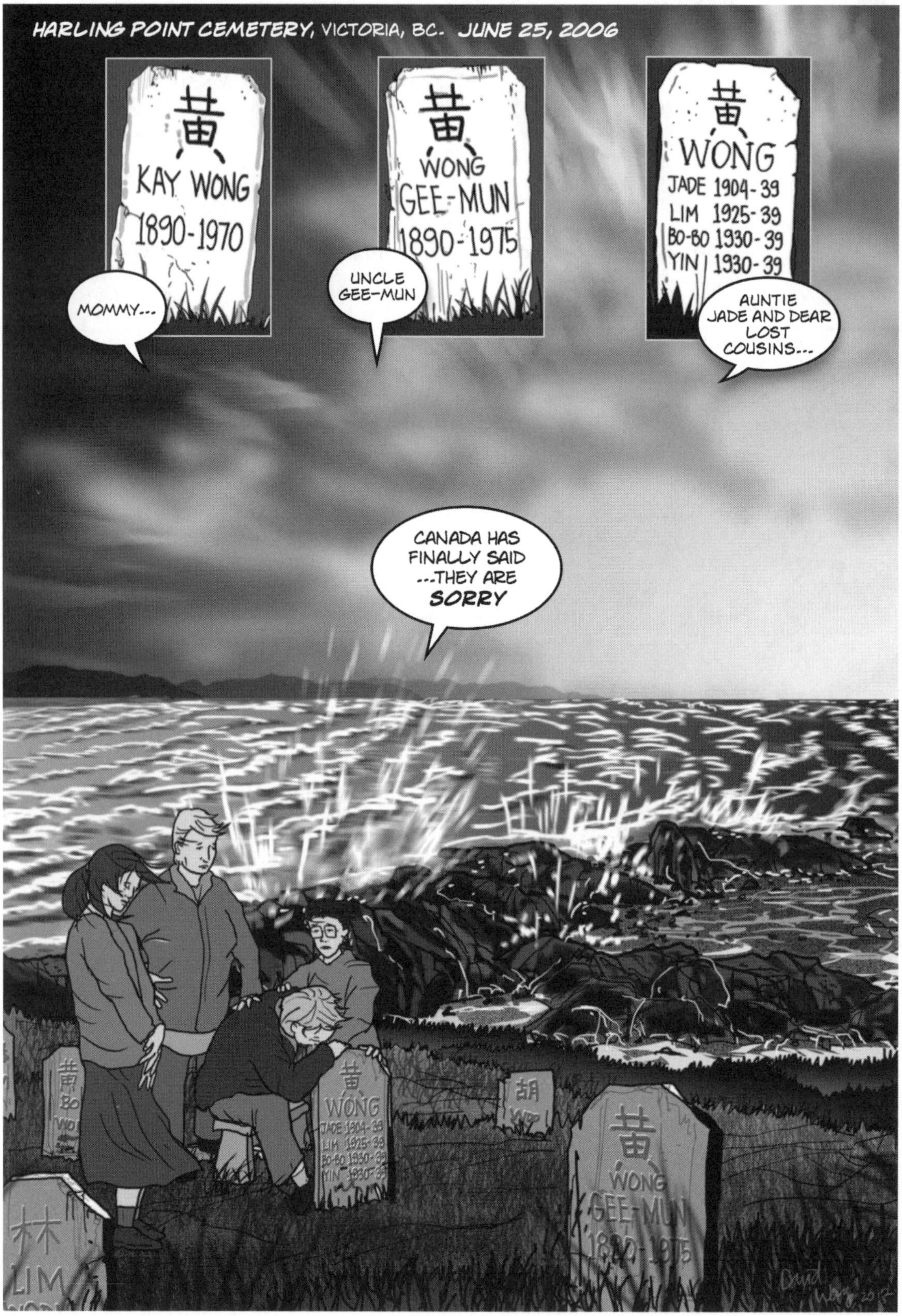
HARLING POINT CEMETERY, VICTORIA, BC. JUNE 25, 2006
黃
KAY WONG
1890-1970
MOMMY...
黃
WONG
GEE-MUN
1890-1975
UNCLE GEE-MUN
黃
WONG
JADE 1904-39
LIM 1925-39
BO-BO 1930-39
YIN 1930-39
AUNTIE JADE AND DEAR LOST COUSINS...
CANADA HAS FINALLY SAID ...THEY ARE **SORRY**

AFTERWORD

Three and a half years. That's how long this book has taken me to finish. Throughout the effort, the world kept running ahead ... as you will read in the last paragraph of this afterword.

As my characters grew old and eventually passed away, I often felt sad and missed them. I felt mortal watching my characters age. And as the story got revised, I sometimes wondered if the historic racist rhetoric and violence should be toned down. The book's original title, **The Iron Chink**, was changed, because though it is a historically accurate name of a real artifact, people today will not accept these sorts of racist terms.

I did not want to aggravate readers over historic injustices and ignite fresh diatribes based on a person's skin color. That is why, the penultimate chapter, "Old Foes, New Relations," is so important to me: it shows that old grudges need not be continued by future generations and that people from different cultures share a common desire—joy

for successive generations. In fact, that entire chapter is based on a real WWII veteran, Frank Wong. His daughter married a Canadian whose father served for the Nazi regime. My friends and I are, as of this writing, working to have Frank Wong recognized with a Queen's Diamond Jubilee medal. It will be well deserved!

What else is real in **Escape to Gold Mountain**? When I was a child, I heard stories of Native Americans (First Nations) who helped Chinese railway workers. So it was a

poignant moment, while researching this book, to meet elders from Native communities in the Fraser Canyon who had similar stories. To hear the same stories, after so many years, from the two communities was truly inspiring.

My characters' meetings with Dr. Sun Yat-sen, Charles Crocker, and Emily Carr may be a bit of artistic license, but I wanted to inspire interest in these historic figures. If you do a little research, you'll be amazed at their lives and their connection to the Gam Saan Chinese. The Carr family, for example, employed a Chinese houseboy named "Bong." I also wanted to show Emily Carr, who I've always admired, when she was a beautiful young woman.

Dr Sun Yat-sen's Hawai'ian connection shows the creative efforts he and others employed during the Chinese Exclusion era.

Charles Crocker ... I would have had enjoyed meeting this enterprising man who seemed to always want things done his way.

America and Canada are nations built by people from diverse cultures all over our world. We all have our own stories, and I hope that this graphic novel will inspire others to write illustrated histories of their own communities' experiences.

There was a lot of violence directed at the early Gam Saan Chinese, most of it a result of fear of the unknown, strangers who appeared different, communications in an unknown language, and mannerisms that were unfamiliar. The Chinese thus became easy scapegoats. Let's share knowledge and learn about each other's history and culture so our children may enjoy the enlightened future we all desire.

As I was completing this graphic novel, an important historic event occurred, one that was 130 years in the making. I'll let the following illustrated panels explain:

WASHINGTON, DC, MAY 26, 2011 GAM SAAN PIONEER DESCENDANT AND CALIFORNIA REPRESENTATIVE, *JUDY CHU*:

I RISE TODAY TO ANNOUNCE AN ACTION TO ADDRESS AN INJUSTICE CARRIED OUT ON THIS VERY FLOOR THAT *CONGRESS* HAS NEVER ATONED FOR, *THE CHINESE EXCLUSION ACT OF 1882*

...THE CHINESE WERE CALLED RACIAL SLURS, WERE SPAT UPON IN THE STREETS, AND EVEN BRUTALLY MURDERED

... ALL PEOPLE, NO MATTER THE COLOR OF THEIR SKIN OR NATION OF ORIGIN, ARE THE EQUALS OF EVERY OTHER MAN OR WOMAN

ON *OCTOBER 6, 2011* THE US *SENATE* UNANIMOUSLY PASSED THE RESOLUTION AND EXPRESSED REGRET FOR THE CHINESE EXCLUSION LAWS.

... FOLLOWED BY THE UNANIMOUS PASSING OF RESOLUTION OF REGRET BY THE *US HOUSE OF REPRESENTATIVES* ON *JUNE 18, 2012!*

NOTES & REFERENCES

Notes

Sketch (top left) of author's ancestral village, Wong family Chee Tong (Wong family Ancestral Hall 祠堂), with Tianlu diaolou (碉樓) tower behind it (built in 1925). Village and surrounding diaolous were designated as a UNESCO World Heritage site in 2007.

TRAVEL MAP
Duration of trans-Pacific voyage varied depending on time of year, season, and weather.

Toishan was originally named Sunning (Xinning in Mandarin). In 1914 it was re-named to avoid confusion with the Sunnings of Hunan and Sichuan provinces.

PROLOGUE
The name Fusang has purportedly been identified in documents dating back to the third century CE. Cartographers de l'Isle and Zatta mapped Fusang based on a popular essay written by the French historian Joseph de Guignes in his 1761 article, "Le Fou-Sang des Chinois est-il l'Amérique?"

The term "old Gold mountain" (舊金山) is generally associated with San Francisco, California.

The vessel sketched on p. 23 is a fifteenth-century Chinese sailing vessel that belonged to Admiral Zheng He of the Ming Dynasty.

John O'Donnell, captain of the ship Pallas, named three Chinese seamen. See, in References, Wong-Chu and Tzang,

Image of John O'Donnell referenced from "A Swashbuckling Merchant," in the Historical Marker Database, **www.hmdb.org**.

Captain John Meares arrived at Nootka Sound with fifty to seventy Chinese. This is in the 1790 edition of Meares' **Voyages Made in the Years 1788 and 1789, from China to the N. W. Coast of America**.

CHAPTER 1: THE IRON CHINK
An information page on the Iron Chink is located at the end of this Notes section.

Reference to various nationalities working at cannery (indigenous, Chinese, and Japanese) source: personal communications with past cannery workers and their families, including the Tabata family.

Pacific Coast Cannery was built in 1893 in Steveston, BC, and operated until 1917, then was used as a herring saltery. By 1930, the structure became a storage shed for seine nets. The building was demolished in 1997.

CHAPTER 2: CHINA, THE SICK MAN OF ASIA
The Taiping Rebellion (Heavenly Kingdom Rebellion) 1851–64 was led by a delusional Christian convert named Hong Xiuquan, who claimed he was the younger brother of Jesus Christ, against the Qing Dynasty. About twenty million people died.

Opium clipper ships were built for speed to rush the perishable opium to market.

Children sold by family members to pay for opium referenced in a number of sources, including Iris Chang's **The Chinese in America**.

Indemnities for the First Opium War (a.k.a First Anglo-Chinese War) were outlined in the Treaty of Nanking (August 29, 1842). China ceded the island of Hong Kong to Great Britain, opened five Treaty ports (Canton, Amoy, Foochow, Shanghai, and Ningbo) to Western trade and residence, granted Britain most-favored nation status for trade, and paid $21 million dollars in reparations (**Cambridge Encyclopedia of China**).

Indemnities for the Second Opium or "Arrow" War (named after a ship) were laid out in the Treaty of Tientsin (June 1858), China had to open eleven more major ports. In the Convention of Peking October 18, 1860, the ports of Hankou, Chinkiang, Kiukiang, Tamsui, Tainan, Swatow,

Chefoo, Kiungchow, Nanking, and Tientsin were ceded in addition to 10 million taels each to France and Britain, and another 2 million taels to British merchants (**Cambridge Encyclopedia of China**).

James Bruce (Lord Elgin), former governor of the province of Canada (1847–54), oversaw the destruction of the Old Summer Palace (Yuan Ming Yuan) in 1860. This is considered to be one of history's greatest acts of criminal vandalism.

CHAPTER 3: ESCAPE TO GOLD MOUNTAIN
Yerba Buena named San Francisco (January 30, 1847).

Gold found at John Sutter's mill (January 24, 1848). Background image of Sutter's mill structure referenced from a photograph taken in 1850.

Kanaka was the term used in the nineteenth and early twentieth centuries for Pacific Island workers, but was originally used to describe native Hawai'ians.

Mayor John White Geary welcomed the Chinese, referenced in **The Chinese in America** and Virtual Museum of the City of San Francisco, Gold Rush Chronology, **sfmuseum.org/hist/chron2.html**; at a parade on July 4, 1852, from Choy, **The Architecture of San Francisco Chinatown**.

American flag of 1852 shows thirty-one stars (1851–58).

New Helvetia means "New Switzerland"(named by Swiss pioneer John Sutter in 1840). It was originally called, in Spanish, **Nueva Helvetia**. The site is a few miles east of where Sutter's son, John Sutter, Jr, would later establish Sacramento.

John Sutter's image referenced from various Wikimedia sources.

Map of gold-rush towns referenced from various Wikipedia sources.

CHAPTER 4: CROCKER'S IRON ROAD
Charles Crocker's image based on photos dating from the time of Central Pacific Railroad (CPRR) construction.

Crocker's reference to Great Wall of China: Evans, **They Made America**.

Start of Pacific line (January 8, 1863): California History Collection website, **memory.loc.gov/ammem/cbhtml/cbrush.html**.

Chinese clearing swamp lands: Chang, **The Chinese in America**.

First fifty Chinese on CPRR in 1865: "Asian Americans Who Have Made a Difference" Scholastic, **www.teacher.scholastic.com/activities/asian-american/notables.htm**.

CHAPTER 5: HELLO, MEI GOK (AMERICA)
Chinese hiring circular: Chang, **The Chinese in America**.

Frozen corpses at Donner Pass from Takaki, **Strangers from a Different Shore**; See, **On Gold Mountain**.

Promontory Point image based on photograph at Wikimedia Commons.

Death toll for Chinese railroad workers has ranged between 130 to more than 1,000. The actual number of workers who were killed in accidents or died from illness has been a topic of ongoing debate. Chang, in **The Chinese in America**, places the number at 1,000. Chang also writes: "The rest of the Chinese former railway workers were now homeless as well as jobless, in a harsh and hostile environment. Left to fend for themselves, some straggled by foot through the hinterlands of America, looking for work that would allow them to survive, a journey that would disperse them throughout the nation" (64).

CHAPTER 6: STORM CLOUDS OF HATRED
Land speculation reference: Land-grant maps, which were published for many years, "were frequently used by land speculators to advertise railroad lands for sale to the public. As early as 1868 most western railroads established profitable land departments and bureaus of immigration, with offices in Europe, to sell land and promote foreign settlement in the western United States." Source: **memory.loc.gov/ammem/gmdhtml/rrhtml/rrintro.html**.

Image for Denis Kearney referenced from various Wikimedia Commons images.

Mark Twain, **Roughing It**, originally published in 1871.

The Los Angeles Chinatown riot occurred in a place called "Calles de los Negros" on October 24, 1871 (fifteen men, one woman, and one child were killed): Jean Pfaelzer, **Driven Out**.

Dorney quote from David Colbert, ed., **Eyewitness to the American West**.

CHAPTER 7: THE CHINESE MUST GO!
Panic of 1877: See, "Unrest in California" by John D. Hicks in **The American Nation: A History of the United States from 1865 to the Present**, www.sfmuseum.org/hist6/kearneyism.html.

Denis Kearney's, "Take matters into your own hands" (Working Men's Party of California) handbills and posters redrawn from historic records. (Wikimedia Commons; New York State Archives, **www.iarchives.nysed.gov/gallery/gallery.jsp?id=141**.

July 1877 Sandlot rally illustration based on image published in Frank Leslie's **Illustrated Newspaper**, March 20, 1880.

"Several" Chinese were killed: Jerome A. Hart, **In Our Second Century: From an Editor's Note-book**.

Pai Hua, 排華 term used by the Chinese for driving out the Chinese.

Hawai'i was known as Tan Heung San 檀香山.

CHAPTER 8: KINGDOM OF TAN HEUNG SAN
Chung shan and Hoy ping communities. Source: conversations with Henry Yu, Department of History, University of British Columbia; Oo Syak Gee Lu Society, Hawai'i website, **www.oosyakgeelu.com/history.html**.

Sun family in Maui: personal conversations with Dr Lily Sun (1981) and from Sun, Dr Lily Sui-fong, ed., **A Great Man and Epoch-Maker: An Album in Memory of Dr. Sun Yat-sen**.

Sun Yat-sen made six visits to Hawai'i, his first from June 1878 to July 1883.

Sun's milk name, Sun Tai Chu, mentioned in various documents, including a Punahou School ledger dated June 30, 1883, **www.sunyatsenhawaii.org/en/hawaii-roots/his-six-visits-to-hawaii/89-first-visit-june1878-july-1883**.

1883 King Kalaukua award to Sun Yat-sen mentioned in various sources, including **Kalamalama: Hawaii Pacific University Newspaper**, www.hpulamalama.com/chinatown_exhibit.php.

CHAPTER 9: NATION BUILDING
Canada's House of Parliament image based on 1878 government of Canada photograph. Note original central tower design, which was rebuilt and completed in 1922 (after a fire).

Work on the western line of the CPR had already begun at Yale, BC in spring 1880, a year prior to the formation of the Canadian Pacific Railway Co. **mhso.ca/tiesthatbind/BuildingCPR.php**.

Although Andrew Onderdonk is shown with a beard in many photos during the construction of the CPR, it appears that he did not have a beard during the early contract negotiations. Onderdonk's image referenced from Wikimedia Commons.

Cast of characters on page following Onderdonk:
  Richard B. Angus (1831–1922) co-founder and VP of CPR
  William C. Van Horne (1843–1915) VP of CPR
  Albert B. Rogers (1829–89) American Surveyor for CPR
  George Stephen (1829–1921) first President of CPR
  James Hill (1838–1916) Railway builder
  Thomas G. Shaughnessy (1853–1923) President of CPR

Chinese workers charged for room and board, in Ma, Chinese Pioneers.

"The Chinese are inhabitants of another planet. Machine like. They are automatic engines of flesh and blood. Why not discriminate? Why aid in the increase and distribution over our domain of a degraded and inferior race, and the progenitors of an inferior sort of men. We ask you to secure us American Anglo-Saxon civilization without contamination or adulteration. Let us keep pure the blood, which circulates through our political system. And preserve our life from the gangrene of oriental civilization." John Miller's 1881 speech in US Senate (Gyory, 224).

George Frisbie Hoar (1826–1904) speech and reference to **New York Tribune** calling Senator Hoar a "Humanitarian Half Thinker" cited in Chang, **The Chinese in America and Daniels, Coming to America**.

Chinese Exclusion Act, see **www.1882project.org/history**.

Tunnel collapses and worker deaths. Personal conversations with Chinese-Canadian and Native American (First Nations) elders from the Cheam Nation (Fraser Canyon) at an abandoned CPR tunnel. Author visited an abandoned rail tunnel in 2011 with community activist Bill Chu, who told him: "The tunnel construction was abandoned part way due to the high number of Chinese fatalities." See also **The Ties that Bind, mhso.ca/tiesthatbind/WorkingConditions.php**.

Disease and illness toll, Ma, **Chinese Pioneers**.

Chinese burial customs, see: **www.cinarc.org/Death-2.html#anchor_14**.

CHAPTER 10: A CHINAMAN'S CHANCE
Image of Hells Gate passage in the Fraser Canyon based on a compilation of personal photographs.

CPR construction of the Hells Gate segment during winter 1882 based on maps and documents of Andrew Onderdonk presented by the Kamloops Art Gallery, on Onderdonk's Way, **www.kag.bc.ca/Exhibitions/AllAboard/allaboard.html?RD=1**.

Native Americans saving character Ah Foo based on stories the author heard while growing up and a story told to the author by people from the Salish Nation near Lillooet, BC, in 2011.

Chinese opera and music was an integral part of daily life at the railroad work camps; referenced in Ma, **Chinese Pioneers**.

The **yee-wu** (二胡) more popularly known as the **erhu** in Mandarin, is a two-stringed bowed musical instrument, known also as the Chinese violin.

Ah Foo's hat is woven from cedar in the Coast Salish Nation style.

CHAPTER 11: PROFITING FROM RACISM
Last spike image based on photograph from Library and Archives Canada.

There were at least three "last spikes." The first spike was bent by Donald Smith; the second was removed and placed in a Montreal museum; the existing spike is now in place at Cragellachie, BC. Approximately 300 other "last spikes" were given out to dignitaries at the event as souvenirs. (From personal communications with journalist and Chinese-Canadian historian Brad Lee.) and **theglobeandmail.com/news/national/legendary-railway-spike-thought-lost-to-history-until-now/article4365698/**.

CPR did not ship bones back, see Ma, **Chinese Pioneers**.

1885 Royal Commission on Chinese Immigration: Early Canadiana Online, **eco.canadiana.ca/view/oocihm.14563/3?r=0&s=1**.

Scan of Bill 156, the 1885 Chinese Immigration Act: Early Canadiana Online, **eco.canadiana.ca/view/oocihm.9_02345/19?r=0&s=1**.

O'Ryan's tongue-in-cheek comments about Americans reflect the ongoing Canadian obsession with "made in Canada" culture.

Head tax valuation and comparison figures: Ma, **Chinese Pioneers**.

William J. Almon's (1816–1901) fight against the 1885 Chinese Immigration Act may be seen in dissertation by Christopher G. Anderson, "The Senate and the Fight Against the 1885 Chinese Immigration Act", **revparl.ca/english/issue.asp?art=1241&param=181**.

Cost of building the CPR: The Ties That Bind, "Building the CPR," **mhso.ca/tiesthatbind/BuildingCPR.php**.

British Columbia Legislature building (constructed 1893–98) was built for $967, 298.98: Geoscience Canada, **journals.hil.unb.ca/index.php/gc/article/view/11087/11746**.

Newfoundland was not part of Canada until 1949. On August 8, 1906, Newfoundland enacted its own Chinese

Head tax of $300 on each Chinese immigrant. **www.heritage.nf.ca/society/headtax.html**.

CHAPTER 12: PAI HUA (EXPELLING THE CHINESE)
Drawing of old Victoria Chinatown based on various photographs dating from that era in Wright, **In A Strange Land**; **www.bcarchives.gov.bc.ca/exhibits/timemach/galler02/frames/chinatown2.htm**.

Smuggling Chinese across the border, see Griffith "Border Crossings: Race, Class, and Smuggling in Pacific Coast Chinese Immigrant Society" **Western Historical Quarterly**, 5(4)(2008): 473–92; **www.historylink.org/index.cfm?DisplayPage=output.cfm&file_id=5485; and cinarc.org/History.html#anchor_201**.

American Flag of 1885 shows thirty-eight stars (1877–90).

See "Massacre of the Chinese at Rock Springs, Wyoming," **Harper's Weekly** 29 (September 26, 1885): 637. The number of Chinese murdered has ranged, in different accounts, from twenty-eight to thirty-two.

Locations of the Pai hua: see Chinese in Northwest American Research Committee **cinarc.org/Violence.html**.

Background Chinese characters: 福 (**fook**) = luck; 出入平安 (**chut yap ping on**) = leave and enter in peace and safety.

"Tacoma Method," see Pfaezler, **Driven Out**.

Tacoma residents stealing porcelain after expulsion of Chinese, see Hunt, **Tacoma: Its History and its Builders**.

Tacoma's Chinatown is still small; see Chinese in Northwest American Research Committee **www.cinarc.org/Violence-2.html#anchor_86**.

Criminals used purging as a cover for their activities: Chang, **The Chinese in America; Snake River Massacre**, oregonencyclopedia.org/entry/view/chinese_massacre_at_deep_creek/; Nokes, **Massacred For Gold: The Chinese in Hells Canyon**.

CHAPTER 13: COOKS & REVOLUTIONARIES
Merchants, government officials, and students

exempt from head tax, see **eco.canadiana.ca/view/oocihm.9_02345/19? r=0&s=1**.

Emily Carr (1871–1945) drawings based on photographs from **collectionscanada.gc.ca; web.uvic.ca**; and **emilycarr.com/gallery**.

Dr Sun Yat-sen made three visits to Canada. His first was to Victoria and Vancouver in 1897. He subsequently visited other parts of Canada. See **generasian.ca/CHA-eng1/66.165.42.33/cv/html/en/panel_05.html**.

Dr Sun Yat-sen trained at the Canton Hospital (also known as the Guangzhou Boji Hospital), then earned a license to practice as a medical doctor from the Hong Kong College of Medicine for Chinese (precursor of the University of Hong Kong) in 1892.

Drawing of the MSG Lunch building pays homage to Vancouver's Ming Sun Benevolent Society building and is based, in part, on a photograph of a 1911 "Chinese-Western food" restaurant in Olds, Alberta: **mhso.ca/tiesthatbind/content/UNIT1_Photo_Set2_with_captions.pdf**.

CHAPTER 14: BIRTHING PAPER SONS
Street scene in Hong Kong based on a 1903 photograph taken of Dr Sun Yat-sen's clandestine storefront that held revolutionary planning meetings. The photograph of D'Aguilar Street is exhibited at the Dr Sun Yat-sen museum in Hong Kong. See also: Hong Kong University **100.hku.hk/sunyatsen/links.html**.

Local testimonials and copies of certificates from A. A. Smyser, "Sun Yat-sen's strong links to Hawaii, Hawaii's World" **Honolulu Bulletin** March 16, 2000, **archives.starbulletin.com/2000/03/16/editorial/smyser.html**.

1906 San Francisco earthquake, see The Virtual Museum of the City of San Francisco **sfmuseum.net/press/clip.html**.

Destruction of Chinese birth records and paper sons, see Chang, **Chinese in America**; Cao and Novas, **Everything You Need To Know About Asian-American History**.

CHAPTER 15: THE NEXT GENERASIAN
The Asiatic Exclusion League was formed in the early twentieth century to prevent immigration of Asians to Canada and the US.

Vancouver Chinatown riot: Ng, **The Chinese in Vancouver**; Ma, **Chinese Pioneers**; Yee, **Saltwater City**; Lee, **Portraits of a Challenge**; Wickberg, **From China to Canada**.

Image of post-riot building based on photographs and descriptions collected by the author.

Number written on character Kay's apron: numbers were used to identify workers. Source: BC Provincial Museum Exhibit; BC Packers website: **intheirwords.ca/english/people.html**.

CHAPTER 16: SAVING FOR THE HEAD TAX
Children's formal wear source: **alamedainfo.com/San_francisco_Chinese.htm**.

Ken says his fiancée is a member of the Nootka (Nuu-chah-nulth) Nation from Ucluelet, BC, and attributes their introduction to Emily Carr. Carr visited and made sketches of a number of Native villages, including the villages in Ucluelet, in 1899. See **ecotrust.ca/clayoquot/governance**.

Image of 1922 No.1-A Autographic Kodak Jr. camera sourced from Wikimedia Commons.

CHAPTER 17: AN ARRANGED MARRIAGE
Pages from July 1, 1923 Chinese Immigration Act used as a background. Section 8 of the Act, Prohibited classes, reads: "Idiots, imbeciles, feeble-minded persons, epileptics, insane persons and persons who have been insane at any time previously."

Drawing of stereograph showing BC Legislative building description based on an actual stereograph in a Chinese language book titled 小资开平杨大洲 (**Westernized Hoy Ping**) by Yang, Taizhou (杨大洲) ([n.l.]: China Tourism Press, 2006) . The book describes the UNESCO Heritage diaolou and overseas Chinese families who once lived in Hoy Ping (Kaiping) and contains many old photographs of turn-of-the-century artifacts sent by Gam Saan Chinese to families back in Hoy Ping.

Crying Shanghai baby photo was taken by H. S. Wong of **Hearst Metrotone News** on August 28, 1937. The photograph (disputed by some) was published in the October 4, 1937 issue of **LIFE** magazine.

Canadian flag of 1940 shows red ensign and Royal Arms of Canada (the de facto Canadian flag from 1922–65). The present flag was introduced in 1965.

CHAPTER 18: EARNING DIGNITY & RESPECT
Number of Chinese Canadians enlisted from Canada, Department of National Defence, **Fighting for Canada**.

Number of Chinese Americans (13,499) who enlisted from Cao and Novas.

Reference to Britain accepting Chinese-Canadians from personal conversations with Chinese-Canadian war vets and with Larry Wong, past President of the Chinese Canadian Military Museum Society (Vancouver).

Americans and Canadians of Japanese descent were interred during World War II, beginning in December 1941. About 22,000 Japanese-Canadians (14,000 of whom were born in Canada) were placed in various detention camps including those in Slocan, British Columbia, and Taber, Alberta.

In the United States, approximately 110, 000 Japanese Americans were placed in internment camps throughout the western states, including "relocation centers" in Arkansas, California, Idaho, and Utah.

CHAPTER 19: BLOSSOMING INFLUENCE
Drawing of parading service women based on photograph taken of the Women Ambulance Corps at Main and Georgia Streets, Vancouver, 1944. Source: **ccmms.ca/chinese-canadian-history/gallery/**.

Gretta J. Wong Grant, born in London, Ontario, in 1921. She was called to the bar in autumn 1946. See **Road to Justice, roadtojustice.ca/first-lawyers/gretta-wong-grant**.

Larry Kwong, born in Vernon, BC, in 1923, played professional hockey from 1941–59. He played for the Trail [BC] Smoke Eaters, then signed on with the New York Rangers, making his NHL debut against the Montreal Canadiens in the Montreal Forum on March 13, 1948. **mhso.ca/tiesthatbind/LarryKwong.php**.

Rose Hum Lee (1904–64) information from Yu, **Thinking Orientals and the Mai Wah Society maiwah.org/rhlee.shtml**.

The Magnuson Act (Chinese Exclusion Repeal Act of 1943) was proposed by US Representative Warren G. Magnuson of Washington and signed into law on December 17, 1943. **library.uwb.edu/guides/USimmigration/57%20stat%20600.pdf**.

Canadian Parliament repealed the Chinese Immigration Act of 1923 on May 14, 1947 (following the proclamation of the 1946 Canadian Citizenship Act). However, independent Chinese immigration to Canada came only after the liberalization of Canadian immigration policy in 1967. **mhso.ca/chinesecanadianwomen/en/timeline.php?e=15 and cic.gc.ca/english/multiculturalism/asian/60act.asp**.

Jean Lumb, née Wong (1919–2002), born in Nanaimo, BC, was the first Chinese-Canadian woman to receive the Order of Canada. In 1939, she married Doyle J. Lumb, a Chinese national, causing her to lose her citizenship.

Wong Foon Sien's eleven annual pilgrimages to Ottawa, from personal conversations with his brother-in-law, Larry Wong.

About 11,000 Chinese came to Canada illegally as "paper sons." In 1960, the Chinese Adjustment Statement Program was established to provide an amnesty to all the paper sons. Douglas Jung, the first Chinese Canadian Member of Parliament, played a role in pushing for the amnesty.

Douglas Jung (1924–2002), born in Victoria, BC, was a Progressive Conservative Member of Parliament who won his seat in the riding of Vancouver Centre under the John Diefenbaker government on June 10, 1957.

Hiram Leong Fong (1906–2001), born in Honolulu, was elected into office before Hawai'i achieved statehood. After the Admission Act of 1959, Hawaii became a US state and saw Hiram L. Fong become the first Asian-American Senator. He was also the first Asian American to actively seek the Presidential nomination for the Republican Party in 1964 and 1968. **senatorfong.com/**.

Delbert Wong (1920–2006) was born in Hanford, California. In 1949 he became the first Chinese-American graduate of Stanford Law school. **chssc.org/honorees/2005/Wong.htm**.

Wing Luke (1925–65) was born in a village near Canton, China. His family moved to the US when he was five years old. Wing Luke became a Seattle City Councilor and was sworn into office on March 13, 1962. **wingluke.org/about.htm**.

Peter Wing (1014–2007) was born in Kamloops, BC. He was first elected as an Alderman in 1960. He later served as Kamloops' mayor for three terms starting in 1966. **orderofbc.gov.bc.ca/members/obc-1990/1990-peter-wing/**.

March Fong Eu was born in 1922 in Oakdale, California. She was first elected to the California State Assembly in 1966, then was elected Secretary of State of California in 1974, becoming the first Asian-American woman in a state constitutional office. **democrats.assembly.ca.gov/apileg-caucus/history_haacl.htm**.

Randall S. K. Wong was born in Vancouver in 1941. He became the first Chinese-Canadian provincial crown counsel in Canada in 1967, and a BC provincial court judge in 1974. In 1981, he was the first federally appointed Chinese-Canadian judge. **roadtojustice.ca/first-lawyers/randall-sun-kue-wong**.

Drawing of Chinatown protest parade based on a photograph taken in December 1972 (photographer: Jim Wong-Chu). The largest civil demonstration by the Vancouver Chinese community (over 1,000 strong) protested the building of a proposed firehall. See Ng, **The Chinese in Vancouver**.

CHAPTER 20: ANGELS WATCHING OVER
Emily Carr artwork in background shows 1890's-period work.

Conversation regarding New Canadian immigrant family reflects the liberalization of Canadian immigration policy in 1967 that allowed independent Chinese immigration to Canada. See **Forging Our Legacy** at **cic.gc.ca/english/resources/publications/legacy/index.asp**.

Hotcakes was the term used by Chinese pioneers, the Loh Wah Kiu (老華橋), to describe pancakes.

CHAPTER 21: OLD FOES, NEW RELATIONS
Inspired by a personal interview with World War II veteran Frank Wong, who was born in Vancouver in

1919 and volunteered for overseas draft with the Royal Canadian Ordinance Corps. He landed on Juno Beach in Normandy in 1943. **ccmms.ca/veteran-stories/army/frank-wong/**.

CHAPTER **22:** DOE HEEM (APOLOGY)
Transcript of Canadian Prime Minister Stephen Harper's apology (June 22, 2006) may be seen at **pm.gc.ca/eng/media.asp?id=1221**.

Harling Point Chinese Cemetery in Victoria, BC, was designated as a National Historic Site of Canada in 1995. The site was acquired by the Chinese Consolidated Benevolent Association in 1903 and served the local community until 1950. According to the Parks Canada website: "The Cemetery's geographical characteristics and the orientation of the graves and altar clearly demonstrate the application of feng shui (literally: wind and water) and its centrality to Chinese religious beliefs. These principles of feng shui include the orientation (open views of the Strait of Juan de Fuca and the Olympic Mountains, sloping gently to the southwest, protected by Gonzales Hill to the north, a rocky outcropping to the east and Clover Point to the west), the absence of trees and shrubbery and the modesty of the grave markers." **pc.gc.ca/culture/ppa-ahp/itm1-/page02_e.asp**.

AFTERWORD
California Representative Judy Chu was born in Los Angeles in 1953. She was first elected into office in 1985 as a school district board member. Over the course of the next two decades, she served in various civic offices including city councilor and mayor of Monterey Park. She became the first Chinese-American woman elected to the US Congress in 2009.

Transcript of the 112th Congress for House Resolution 683, Expression of Regret for the 1882 Chinese Exclusion Act may be accessed online at **thomas.loc.gov/cgi-bin/query/z?c112:H.RES.683.IH:/**.

References

Amasol, Alyssa. "Chinatown exhibit honors revolutionary leader," **Kalamalama: Hawaii Pacific University Newspaper** [n.d.]. http://hpulamalama.com/chinatown_exhibit.php.

Anderson, Christopher G. "The Senate and the Fight Against the 1885 Chinese Immigration Act," **Canadian Parliamentary Review** 2007, 30(2). http://www.revparl.ca/english/issue.asp?art=1241&param=181.

Archbold, Rick. **I Stand For Canada: The Story of the Maple Leaf Flag**. Toronto: MacFarlane Walter & Ross, 2002.

Canada. **The Early Chinese Canadians: 1858-1947**. Ottawa: Library and Archives, 2009. http://www.lac-bac.gc.ca/chinese-canadians/021022-1000-e.html.

Canada. "Chinese Cemetery at Harling Point National Historic Site," **Asian Heritage Portal**. Ottawa: Parks Canada, 2010. http://www.pc.gc.ca/culture/ppa-ahp/itm1-/page02_e.asp.

Canada. **First Nations in Canada**. Ottawa: Northern Development, 1997. http://www.aadnc-aandc.gc.ca/eng/1307460755710.

Canada. **An Act Respecting Chinese Immigration, 1923**. 13-14 George V, Chapter 38: 301-315. Ottawa, ON: F.A. Acland. http://eco.canadiana.ca/view/oocihm.9_08043/2?r=0&s=1.

Canada. **Forging Our Legacy: Canadian Citizenship and Immigration, 1900–1977**. Ottawa: Citizen and Immigration Canada, 2006. http://www.cic.gc.ca/english/resources/publications/legacy/preface.asp.

Canada. Report of the Royal Commission on Chinese Immigration: **Report and Evidence. Ottawa: Printed by order of the Commission, 1885**. http://www.eco.canadiana.ca/view/oocihm.14563/2?r=0&s=1

Cao, Lan, and Novas, Himilce. **Everything You Need To Know About Asian-American History**. New York: Plume, 1996.

Chang, Iris. **The Chinese in America: A Narrative History**. New York: Penguin Books, 2003.

Chinese Canadian National Council. Women's Book Committee. **Jin Guo: Voices of Chinese Canadian Women**. Toronto, ON: Women's Press, 1992.

Choy, Philip P. **The Architecture of San Francisco Chinatown**. San Francisco: Chinese Historical Society of America, 2008.

Colbert, David, ed. **Eyewitness to the American West: 500 Years of Firsthand History**. New York: Penguin Books, 1999.

Crean, Susan, ed. **Opposite Contraries: The Unknown Journals of Emily Carr and Other Writings**. Vancouver: Douglas & McIntyre, 2003.

Daniels, Roger. **Coming to America: A History of Immigration and Ethnicity in American Life**. New York: Perennial, 2002.

Evans, Harold. **They Made America: From the Steam Engine to the Search Engine: Two Centuries of Innovators**. New York: Hachette Book Group, 2004.

Griffith, Sarah M., "Border Crossings: Race, Class, and Smuggling in Pacific Coast Chinese Immigrant Society," **Western Historical Quarterly** 2004, 35(4): 473–492.

Gyory, Andrew. **Closing the Gate: Race, Politics, and the Chinese Exclusion Act**. Chapel Hill, NC: University of North Carolina Press, 1998.

Hart, Jerome A. **In Our Second Century: From an Editor's Note-book**. San Francisco: The Pioneer Press, 1931.

Hicks, John D. "Unrest in California," in **The American Nation; A History of the United States from 1865 to the Present**. New York: Houghton Mifflin Company, 1937. Available online at http://www.sfmuseum.org/hist6/kearneyism.html.

Hong Kong Going and Gone: Western Victoria. Hong Kong: Royal Asiatic Society, 1980.

Hook, Brian, et al. **The Cambridge Encyclopedia of China**. New York: Cambridge University Press, 1982.

Hunt, Herbert. **Tacoma: Its History and its Builders; A Half Century of Activity, Vol. 1**. Chicago: S.J. Clarke Publishing Company, 1916.

Jean Lumb Foundation. **The Story of Jean Lumb: A Pioneer Chinese Canadian Woman**. http://www.jean-lumbfoundation.ca/story.html.

Lai, David Chuenyan. **A Brief Chronology of Chinese Canadian History: From Segregation to Integration**. Vancouver: Simon Fraser University. David Lam Centre, 2011. http://www.sfu.ca/chinese-canadian-history/chart_en.html.

Lim, Christine Suchen. **Hua Song: Stories of the Chinese Diaspora**. San Francisco: Long River Press, 2005.

Ma, Ching. **Chinese Pioneers: Materials Concerning the Immigration of Chinese to Canada and Sino-Canadian Relations**. Vancouver: Versatile, 1979.

"Massacre of the Chinese at Rock Springs, Wyoming" **Harper's Weekly** 29 (September 26, 1885): 637.

McLaughlin, Dennis and Leslie. **Fighting for Canada: Chinese and Japanese Canadians in Military Service**. Ottawa: Department of National Defense Canada, 2003.

Meares, John. **Voyages Made in the Years 1788 and 1789, from China to the N. W. Coast of America**. London: Logographic Press. 1790. Available online at http://archive.org/details/cihm_37636.

Modelski, Andrew M. **Railroad Maps of the United States: A Selective Annotated Bibliography of Original 19th-century Maps in the Geography and Map Division of the Library of Congress**. Washington, DC: The Library, 1975.

Nokes, Gregory R. **Massacred for Gold: The Chinese in Hells Canyon**. Oregon State University Press, 2009.

Ng, Wing Chung. **The Chinese in Vancouver, 1945–80: The Pursuit of Identity and Power**. Vancouver: University of British Columbia Press, 1999.

Pfaelzer, Jean. **Driven Out: The Forgotten War Against Chinese Americans**. Los Angeles: University of California Press, 2007.

Roy, Patricia E. **A White Man's Province: British Columbia Politicians and Chinese and Japanese Immigrants, 1858–1914**. Vancouver: University of British Columbia Press, 1989.

Scott, Jo B. "Smith's Iron Chink: One Hundred Years of the Mechanical Fish Butcher," **British Columbia History**, 2005, 38(2): 21–24.

See, Lisa. **On Gold Mountain: The One-Hundred-Year Odyssey of My Chinese-American Family**. New York: St. Martin's Press, 1995.

Steiner, Stan. **Fusang, The Chinese Who Built America**. New York: Harper & Row Publishers, 1979.

Sun, Dr Lily Sui-fong, ed. **A Great Man and Epoch-Maker: An Album in Memory of Dr. Sun Yat-sen**. Hong Kong: Chow Hoi Cultural Enterprise, 2000.

Smyser, A. A. "Sun Yat-sen's strong links to Hawaii," **Honolulu Star-Bulletin**, March 16, 2000. http://www.archives.starbulletin.com/2000/03/16/editorial/smyser.html.

Twain, Mark (Samuel Langhorne Clemens). **Roughing It**. Hartford, CT: American Publishing Company, 1872. Available online at: http://www.gutenberg.org/files/3177/3177-h/3177-h.htm.

Takaki, Ronald. **Strangers from a Different Shore: A History of Asian Americans**. New York: Little, Brown and Company, 1989.

Wai-man, Lee. **Portraits of a Challenge: An Illustrated History of the Chinese Canadians**. Toronto: Council of Chinese Canadians in Ontario, 1984.

Ward, W. Peter. **White Canada Forever: Popular Attitudes and Public Policy Towards Orientals in British Columbia**. Montréal: McGill-Queen's University Press, 1978.

Wickberg, Edgar. **From China to Canada: A History of the Chinese Communities in Canada**. Toronto: McClelland and Stewart, 1982.

Wong, H.S. "Bloody Saturday," **LIFE** (October 4, 1937) 3(14): 102.

Wong, Jade Snow. **Fifth Chinese Daughter**. Seattle, WA: University of Washington Press, 1989.

Wong-chu, Jim, and Tzang, Linda K. **A Brief History of Asian North America**. Vancouver: Asian Heritage Month Society, 2001.

Wright, Thomas Richard. **In a Strange Land, A Pictorial Record of the Chinese in Canada 1788–1923**. Saskatoon: Western Producer Prairie Books, 1988.

Yamashita, Michael. **Zheng He: Tracing the Epic Voyage of China's Greatest Explorer**. Vercelli, Italy: White Star Publishers, 2006.

Yee, Paul. **Saltwater City: An Illustrated History of the Chinese in Vancouver**. Vancouver: Douglas & McIntyre, 1988.

Yee, Paul. **Chinatown: An Illustrated History of the Chinese Communities of Victoria, Vancouver, Calgary, Winnipeg, Toronto, Ottawa, Montreal and Halifax**. Toronto, ON: James Lorimer & Co., 2005.

Yu, Henry. **Thinking Orientals: Migration, Contact, and Exoticism in Modern America**. New York: Oxford University Press, 2001.

Websites

1882 Project
www.1882project.org

California Historical Society
californiahistoricalsociety.org/

California History Collection
memory.loc.gov/ammem/cbhtml

Canadian Wong Family Genealogy (author's website)
generasian.ca

Chinese Canadian Historical Society of British Columbia
cchsbc.ca/

Chinese Canadian Military Museum Society
ccmms.ca/

Chinese Canadian Women: 1923–1967
mhso.ca/chinesecanadianwomen/en/index.php

Chinese Historical Society of America
chsa.org

Chinese in Northwest America Research Committee
cinarc.org

Early Canadiana Online
eco.canadiana.ca

Historical Marker Database
hmdb.org

Kamloops Art Gallery, "Onderdonk's Way"
kag.bc.ca/Exhibitions/AllAboard/allaboard.html

Mai Wah Society, Montana
maiwah.org/

Museum of the City of San Francisco
sfmuseum.org/

Museum of Chinese in the Americas
mocanyc.org

Oo Syak Gee Lu Society, Hawai'i
oosyakgeelu.com

Road to Justice
roadtojustice.ca

Sun Yat-sen Hawaii Foundation
sunyatsenhawaii.org

The Ties That Bind
mhso.ca/tiesthatbind

University of British Columbia Chinese Canadian Stories
chinesecanadian.ubc.ca

Vancouver Public Library: Chinese-Canadian Geneaology
vpl.ca/ccg/

Wing Luke Museum
wingluke.org

THE IRON CHINK

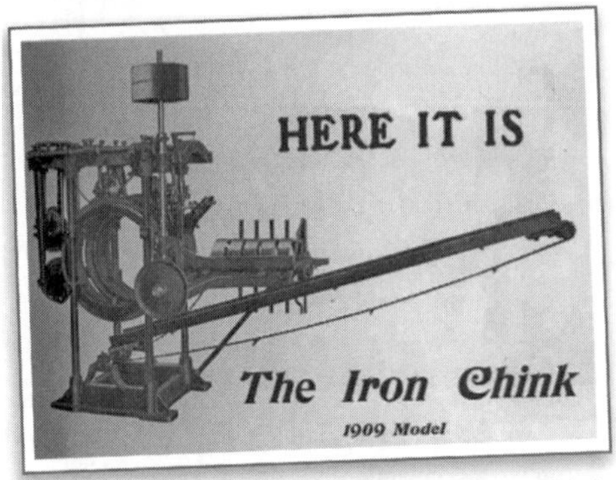
HERE IT IS
The Iron Chink
1909 Model

Copy of ad for the 1909 Iron Chink

Canned salmon from the Pacific Northwest had, by the 1860s, found markets as far away as England.

Canneries along the west coast of North America employed a diverse labor force of Chinese, Japanese, and Native American people. They were segregated along ethnic lines, both at work and in their cannery living quarters. Chinese contractors hired, fed, housed, and paid laborers for cannery companies, but workers were subjected to low wages, substandard housing, and poor food.

Working conditions were grueling. Through open floorboards the ocean could be seen below, and the temperature in the cannery was either very cold or very hot, depending on weather conditions. The building always stank of fish. Initially, the work was undertaken by men, but soon women worked alongside them, often with their babies strapped to their backs.

There were so many salmon that piers would sag with the load of freshly caught fish. During busy times, workers would often succumb to fatigue to keep up with the large bounty, and this led to many accidents. At other times, and unpredictably, smaller catches meant a smaller workforce was required; the seasonal and variable nature of the resource affected efficiency, and thus cannery profitability.

At the turn of the century, everything changed with the arrival of the first mechanized fish-gutting machine. The machine was designed in 1903 by Ontario-born inventor Edmund A. Smith. It could behead, split, gut, and clean salmon in one continuous operation.

Replacing skilled Chinese workers and reflecting racist anti-Asian attitudes of the time, Smith registered his invention as the "Iron Chink" on his first US patent. He later changed the patented name to "Smith Butcher Machine," but the name "Iron Chink" literally stuck, as this designation was affixed to the manufacturer's plates on the machines for many years afterward.

The automated machine could accomplish the work of forty people, increasing cannery profits, but forcing thousands of employees out of work. Smith improved on his original design, producing newer models, and by 1908 one piece of equipment was able to handle up to three salmon canning lines.

SOURCES:

Scott, Jo B. "Smith's Iron Chink: One Hundred Years of the Mechanical Fish Butcher," **British Columbia History** 38 (2) (2005) 21-24.

Oregon History Project. "Nature in the Cannery." www.ohs.org/the-oregon-history-project/narratives/canneries-on-the-columbia/nature-of-salmon-canneries/nature-of-cannery.cfm

Washington State Historical Society, Washington Stories. http://stories.washingtonhistory.org

TODAY, THE IRON CHINK MAY BE VIEWED AT THE FOLLOWING LOCATIONS:

George Inlet Cannery, Ketchikan, Alaska, USA (no website)
Icy Strait Point Cannery, Hoonah, Alaska, USA **www.icystraitpoint.com**
Columbia River Maritime Museum, Astoria, Oregon, USA **www.crmm.org**
Museum of History and Industry, Seattle, Washington, USA **www.seattlehistory.org**
Gulf of Georgia Cannery, Steveston (Vancouver), BC Canada **www.gulfofgeorgiacannery.com**
North Pacific Cannery Village, Port Edward (Prince Rupert) BC Canada **www.memorybc.ca**
Royal BC Museum, Victoria, BC Canada **www.royalbcmuseum.bc.ca**

ACKNOWLEDGMENTS

THANK YOU:
Vancouver's **Ming Sun Benevolent Society**, a proud historic Vancouver institution.

Canada's **Community Historic Recognition Program** (CHRP).

Arsenal Pulp Press for supporting an architect's dream to draw cartoons; especially my eagle-eyed editor, Susan Safyan.

My patient and wonderful spouse, Susanna, and my boys, Cameron and Colten, who are the sixth generation in Gam Saan.

MY ADVISORY TEAM:
Jean Barman, Jim Wong-Chu, Susan Crean, Kenda Gee, Brad Lee, Colleen McGuinness, Suzanne Tabata, Hayne Wai, Micaela Wong, and Dr. Henry Yu.

The following persons and organizations have been very supportive of this effort. I am most grateful for their kind support, their sharing of stories, resources, assistance, and encouragement.

Robert Ballantyne
Bill Chu
Claudia Corlett
Senator Lillian Dyck
Cynara Geissler
Jack Gin
Jim Halliday
George Ing
Kelly Ip
Maggie Ip
Tammy Knowlan-Manley
Brian Lam
Gary Lee
Howe Lee
Ray Charles Lee
Dr. Imogene Lim
Wesley Lowe
Ruth Lowther
Bettie Luke
Fred Mah
Gerilee McBride
Wing Chun Quan
Bev Nann
Therese Rochefort
Shyla Seller
Dr. Connie So
Sid Chow Tan
Ying Wang
Bev Wong
Bing Wong
Daniel Wong
Frank Wong
Larry Wong
Marilyn Muldoon Wong
Arthur Yap
Paul Yee
Donald Yen
Dina Youldassis

Army, Navy and Air Force Veterans in Canada, Pacific Unit 280
Chinese Canadian Historical Society of BC, Vancouver
Chinese Canadian Military Museum, Vancouver
Chinese Historical Society of America Museum, San Francisco
Chinese in Northwest America Research Committee, Seattle
Wing Luke Museum, Seattle

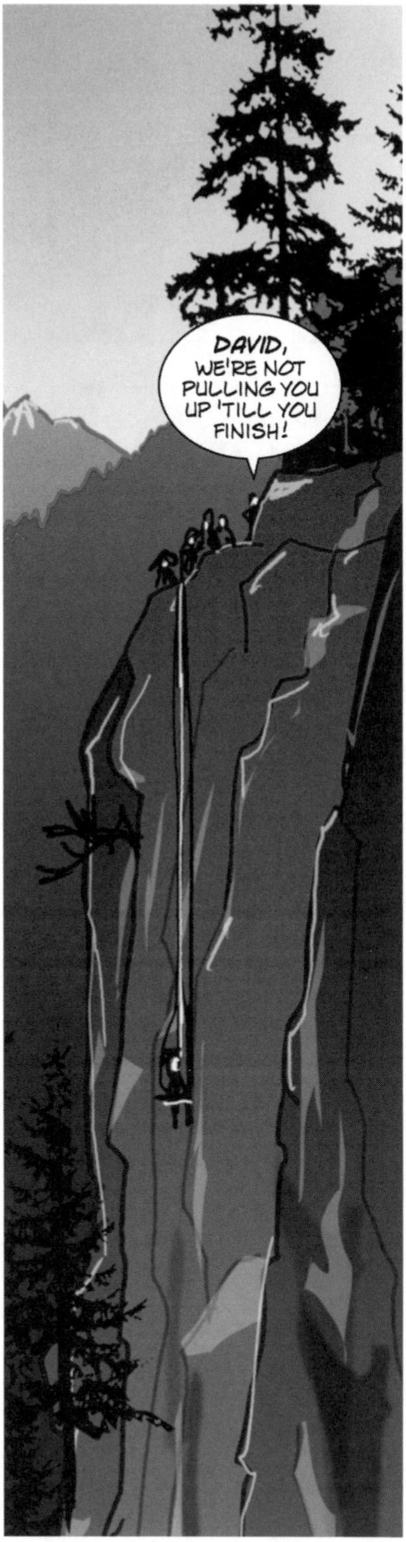
DAVID, WE'RE NOT PULLING YOU UP 'TILL YOU FINISH!

David H.T. Wong was born and raised in Vancouver. He is a respected Asian Canadian community activist whose family first came to Canada from China 130 years ago. He is also an accomplished architect and urban ecologist, and helped found one of Singapore's largest design firms. He also runs the websites **generasian.ca** and **UglyChineseCanadian.com**.

Escape to Gold Mountain, a graphic novel about how the Chinese came to North America, is his first book.